The Norsunder War, Book IV

A Chain of Braided Silver

SARTORIAS-DELES BOOKS

HISTORICAL ARC

"Lily and Crown"
Inda
The Fox
King's Shield
Treason's Shore
Time of Daughters (two volumes)
Banner of the Damned

The Young Allies as Kids Series

The CJ Notebooks
Senrid
Spy Princess
Sartor
Fleeing Peace

A Stranger to Command
Crown Duel
The Trouble with Kings

The Rise of the Alliance Series

A Sword Named Truth
The Blood Mage Texts
The Hunters and the Hunted
Nightside of the Sun
Sasharia En Garde
The Wicked Skill
Ship Without Sails
Marend of Marloven Hess
Seek to Hold the Wind
All Things Betray

The Norsunder War IV

A Chain of Braided Silver

SHERWOOD SMITH

BOOK VIEW CAFE

BOOK VIEW CAFE

Dedicated to my daily readers at Patreon.
I'm so grateful. Your cogent comments and
enthusiasm mean the world to me.

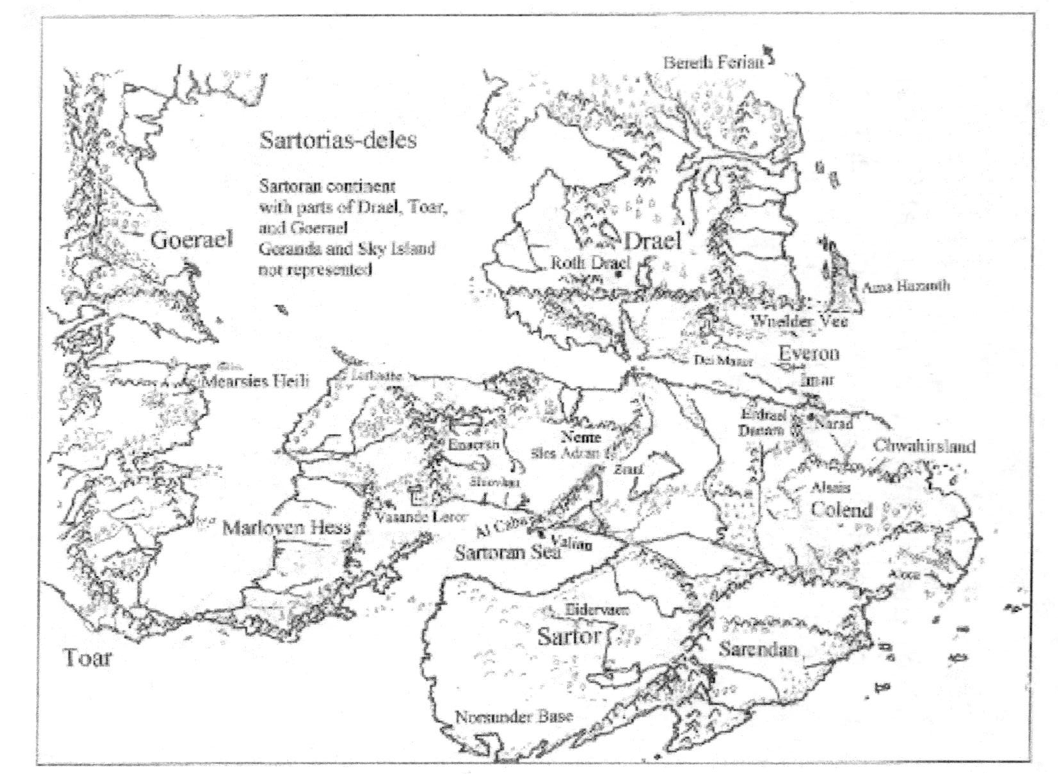

Sartorias-deles
Sartoran continent with parts of Drael, Toar, and Goerael
Geranda and Sky Island not represented
Goerael
Bereth Ferian
Drael
Roth Drael
Ama Hazanth
Wnelder Vee
Everon
Imar
Dei Maar
Eidrael Danara
Narad
Chwahirsland
Neme
Sles Adran
Znat
Alsais
Colend
Emaerin
Shereban
Mearsies Heili
Lirfadhe
Vasande Leror
Al Cab
Valian
Marloven Hess
Sartoran Sea
Eidervaen
Sartor
Sarendan
Toar
Norsunder Base

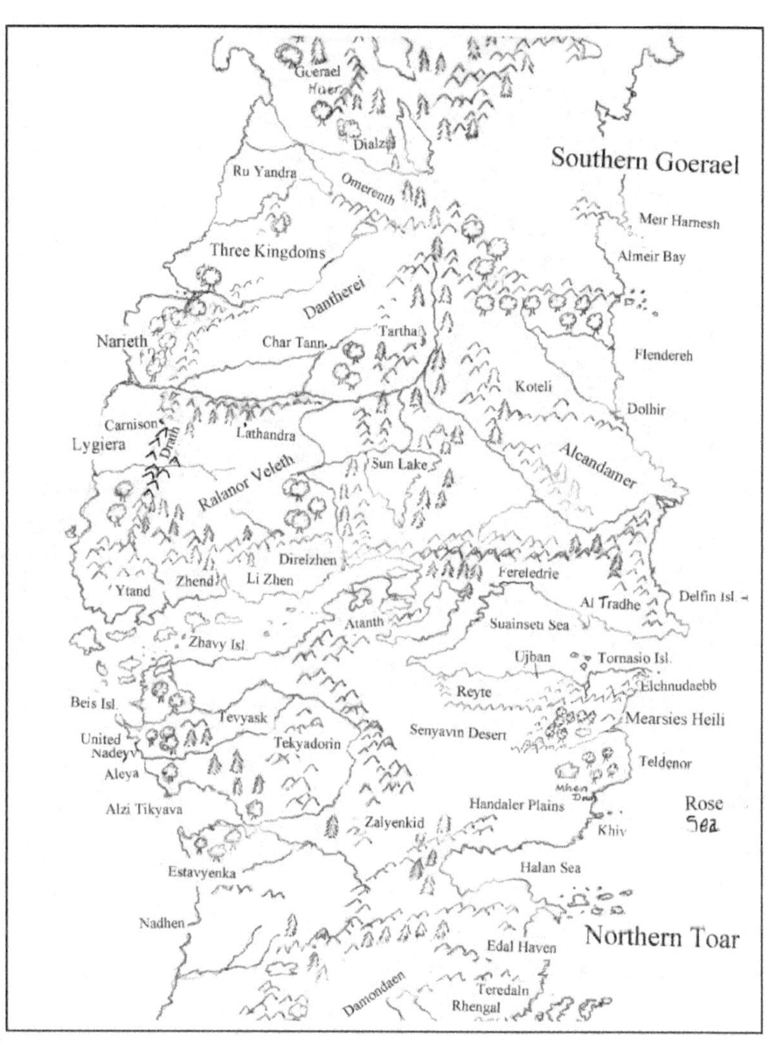

Goerael Huer
Dialzel
Ru Yandra
Omerenth
Southern Goerael
Three Kingdoms
Meir Harnesh
Almeir Bay
Dantherei
Narieth
Char Tann
Tartha
Koteli
Flendereh
Dolhir
Carnison
Drath
Lathandra
Lygiera
Ralanor Veleth
Sun Lake
Alcandamer
Direlzhen
Zhend
Li Zhen
Fereledrie
Al Tradhe
Delfin Isl
Ytand
Atanth
Suainseu Sea
Zhavy Isl.
Ujban
Tornasio Isl.
Reyte
Elchnudaebb
Beis Isl.
Tevyask
Mearsies Heili
Senyavin Desert
United Nadeyv
Tekyadorin
Teldenor
Aleya
Mhen Drau
Alzi Tikyava
Handaler Plains
Rose Sea
Zalyenkid
Khiv
Estavyenka
Halan Sea
Nadhen
Northern Toar
Edal Haven
Damondaen
Teredaln
Rhengal

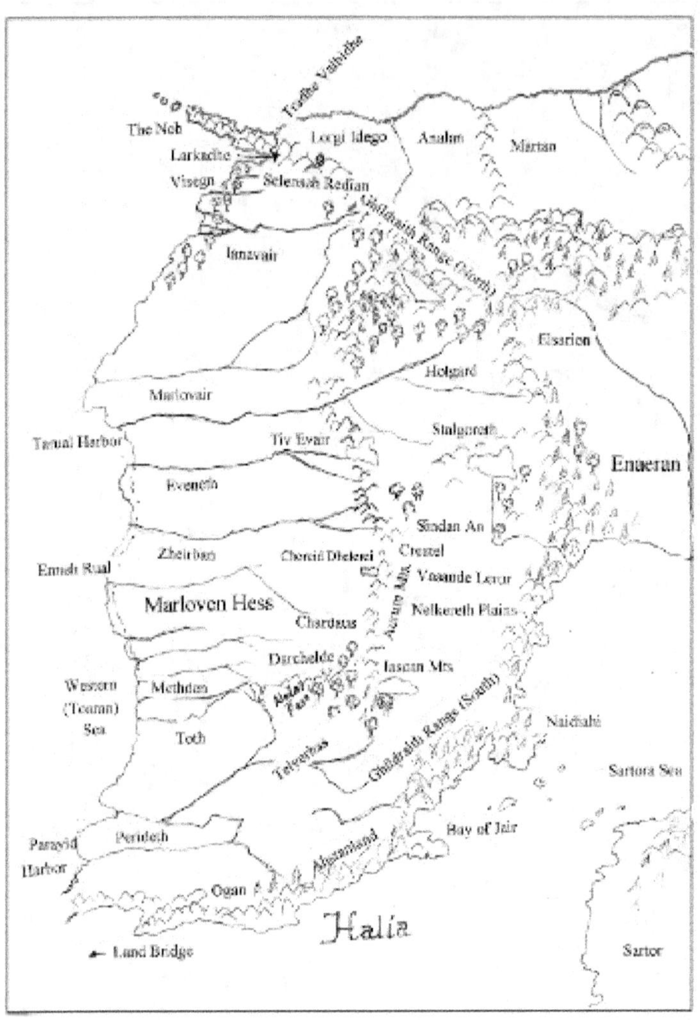

The Nob
Larkadhe
Visegn
Inmavair
Lorgi Idego
Selenseh Redian
Analin
Martan
Vdhaveth Range (North)
Elsarion
Holgard
Marlovair
Stalgoreth
Tamal Harbor
Tiv Evair
Enneran
Eveneth
Sindan An
Zheirban
Choreid Dhelerei
Crestel
Emeth Rual
Vasande Leror
Marloven Hess
Nelkereth Plains
Chardaas
Darchelde
Jasan Mts
Andal Pass
Western
(Toaran)
Sea
Methden
Naichahi
Toth
Telgarthas
Ghael-rahi Range (South)
Sartora Sea
Bay of Jair
Parayid
Harbor
Perideth
Abramtand
Ogan
Halia
Sartor
Land Bridge

DRAMATIS PERSONAE

NOTE: Norsundrians, Ex-Norsundrians, and Detlev's boys at the end.

Name most frequently used comes first, so sometimes first name, sometimes last, sometimes nickname.

LIGHT MAGIC MAGES AIDING THE ALLIANCE

Erai-Yanya Vithyavadnais: One of a long line of mages dwelling in the ruined city of Roth Drael. Trained partly by the northern Mage School at Bereth Ferian, and partly by Tsauderei, she works independently, her specialty magical wards. She has one son, ARTHUR (see BERETH FERIAN). Erai-Yanya's student mage is the Marloven exile Hibern Askan.

Evend: [deceased] One-time colleague of Tsauderei, King of Bereth Ferian (a courtesy title only) and head of the mage school there, he surrendered his life to bind rift magic from being used in Sartorias-deles by Norsunder. His place as titular king was taken by ARTHUR.

Igkai: Hermit mage living on the peninsula on the Sartoran Sea. An oddball all his life, he is a friend to birds and animals — and tolerates humans who do well by animals.

Lilith the Guardian: A lower ranking mage and what might be called an officer of rites and rituals in Ancient Sartor, which was as close to a government as they got. She had one daughter, Erdrael, who was killed along with most of the rest of the population when Norsunder tried to wrest control of the world, for reasons explored in a volume to come. Her name is a modern adaptation, and she found herself trying to combat Norsunder on this and other worlds around the sun Erhal; she comes out of hiding beyond time whenever she finds evidence that Detlev has been in the world, acting for Norsunder's Host of Lords.

Mondros "Rosey": Big, bluff, and bearded, he began life as an exiled son of the disgraced Glenereth family, warlords of Ralanor Veleth. He studied magic, aided by Gwasan Sonscarna, Princess of the Chwahir, whom he married and had a son, REL (see SARTOR). When Mondros made it his life's goal to defeat Wan-Edhe of Chwahirsland, he stashed Rel with a trusted friend, where Rel grew up a part of the family, until the urge to travel caused him to take to the road. Father and son found one another relatively recently.

Murial of Mearsies Heili: Recluse mage, living hidden in the western wilds of Mearsies Heili. Born a princess, she supported the transfer of the throne to her niece CLAIR (see MEARSIES HEILI) on the death of her sister. Protecting the kingdom from a distance, she has seen to it that Clair got magical training.

Oalthoreh: [deceased] Head of the northern mage school in Bereth Ferian

Randon Amdrelya: Originally from Vandary, Randon is an accomplished mage who did the Child Spell when around thirteen, to avoid limiting expectations of his culture. Travels around looking for kids to rescue.

Tarael of Drael: A morvende mage of a Drael geliath, captured by the Host.

Tsauderei: Oldest of the senior mages, independent of the two leading mage schools, living in a historic mage retreat located in the mountains bordering Sarendan and Sartor in the Valley of Delfina.

FROM OFF-WORLD

Caris-Merian Rhoderan of Geth-deles: "Rhoderan" is a name adopted by her father, the disinherited and disgraced Harold Dei, who tried to take the throne of Everon a couple of times before he was booted off-world. He had three children, the middle one being Caris-Merian. She came to Sartorias-deles's northern mage school to study magic right before the invasion. An accomplished singer and a scholar, when she is not seeking revenge for her brother's death.

Les (Leskander) Rhoderan of Geth-deles: [deceased] elder brother to Caris-Merian, and a problematical figure in his home archipelago. He discovered vagabond magic, and tried to weaponize it, (he said) in order to win freedom for the underaged and poor. Very charismatic.

Mildred of Geth-deles: a martial artist.

Zairna Raadi from Sri Fortnu: A worldgate traveler and beginning mage, born a prince in a very problematic kingdom; a dragonflower inked into his neck and curling up over one ear testifies to serious rituals. Ditto the diamond earrings he never removes. Ended up at the Northern School of Magic.

June from Earth: From a parallel of Earth in even worse shape, who got caught in someone else's conflict. Has been traveling through Worldgates since, and become a sort of magical lightning rod without knowing. No matter how far or fast she goes, she cannot outrun her own shadow.

The Young Allies and Others,
Listed by Kingdom

Alcandaamera

Charlana, Queen of Alcandamer: A mage of sorts, possessor of the double crown, which distinguishes between lies and truth.

Ama Hazanth

Crow (Prince Marseth Ghandorjien): Crown prince, keeper of the Fire Ruby (which wards storms from the island)

BARBAN

Dara, Leela, Yovres, Honey-blossom: vagabonds, present day

Ancient Tower that once had a window to the past, and to residents from the world Elesh Orom-alsh, guardians of the Fifth Protection of Alsheya (the cup Ethe)

BERETH FERIAN

Arthur (Yrtur) Vithyavadnais: He adopted the nickname Arthur after his rescue by young world-gate crossing friends. Son of mage Erai-Yanya, he early showed great ability in learning and magic, but he was unhappy living in isolation. He was adopted as heir by Evend, the former head mage of the Bereth Ferian Mage School, and presiding King of the loose federation headquartered at Bereth Ferian. After Evend's death, Arthur shared this courtesy title with Liere Fer Eider in her persona as Sartora, the Girl Who Saved the World.

Evend: (see Light Mages)

Liere Fer Eider: Also known as the Girl Who Saved the World, she was the first of her generation to be born with *Dena Yeresbeth*. At ten years old she left her small town to escape being captured by Siamis, who had extended an enchantment over the world, which Liere later broke. The enchantment is generally known as The Lost Year, as most lived in a dream world while it lasted. She was lauded by all, and given the courtesy title of Queen in Bereth Ferian, a title with no powers or responsibilities whatsoever—but which still chafed her unbearably. Liere was the poster child for Imposter Syndrome until she went to Geth-deles for five years to study magic, and re-turned recently.

CHWAHIRSLAND (AKA LAND OF THE CHWAHIR)

Dassler Anjit, Company Scribe, Crimson Army of Chwahirsland: One of the "Sunrise Generation"—so named after Jilo removed enough of Wan-Edhe's toxic magic for awareness to return. A leader of the resistance to Wan-Edhe.

Dirk Sonscarna: Son of the problematical Kessler (see below), on the verge of teenhood. Has Dena Yeresbeth and considerable martial arts as well as magical knowledge.

Crimson General Furo: Chwahir general on Jilo's side. Worked a silent truce of sorts with Shontande Lirendi, without Norsunder realizing.

Gwasan Sonscarna: [deceased] Princess and mage, married a disinherited swordsman from Ralanor Veleth who later became the mage Mondros (SEE Mages). Their son is Rel the Traveler (SEE Sartor)

Kirech, Gold Army General: Utterly loyal to Chwahirsland, which for most of his life was embodied in Wan-Edhe. So loyal that to call his work into question—his loyalty—was a blow worse than mere sword wounds.

Jilo: Son of a lowly one-syllable sergeant, heir to elderly *Prince Kwenz Sonscarna,* he finds himself acting king of Chwahirsland, after Norsunder's removal of the previous king, who had ruled for more than a century. What that means is, he is slowly poisoning himself trying to remove the toxic accretion of dark magic enchantments over Chwahirsland, and especially its capital.

Prince Kessler Sonscarna: (SEE also Ex-Norsundrians) The single living descendant of the ruling Sonscarnas, who were systematically killed off by Wan-Edhe, blood relations notwithstanding. Prince Kessler escaped at a young age, made his way to a martial arts group where he mastered military arts. He allied with a Norsundrian mage, Dejain, and began to assemble followers for his plan to remove all hereditary rulers of the world and replace them with his followers, chosen solely on merit. When defeated, he was forced into Norsunder by Dejain, who betrayed him.

Gold Admiral Opun: current naval commander, after several

purges of his predecessors for mad reasons, or no reason at all. Like Furo, a two-syllable Chwahir, meaning not the lowest background, but low enough—no Nanijo, or warlord background—that Wan-Edhe did not think it necessary to hold his entire family hostage, or slaughter them outright in case any of them thought of conspiracy.

Wan-Edhe (born Shnit Sonscarna), King of the Chwahir: Descendant of the ruling Sonscarna family, has ruled for close to a century. A powerful dark magic mage, he has managed to create a powerful citadel in the heart of his kingdom where time itself is distorted in his effort to ensure that he will live and rule forever. He killed off his family and descendants, including his brilliant heir, Princess Gwasan; only his grandson Kessler escaped, but years of abuse told on Kessler's emotional landscape.

Colend

"Bee" (Aural) Keperi: Chief scribe to Shontande Lirendi. Being blind, he does all his work by memorization.

King Carlael Lirendi: [deceased] Regarded generally as Mad King Carlael before he was assassinated by Efael of Norsunder. He was as beautiful as he was strange. He mostly existed in a world of dreams imposed by magic, from which he emerged now and then, very alert and very aware. There was a regency council made up of the chief nobles who oversaw the kingdom when he was unable to respond to the world around him, and they ruled until very recently, refusing to relinquish power, though Carlael's son Shontande had come of age.

Prince Shontande Lirendi: Son of Carlael, King of Colend, and new king.

Karhin Keperi: [deceased] She was a teenage scribe student in a small town in the west of Colend, who volunteered to function as the center of the young allies' communication network. An indefatigable letter writer, she first met Puddlenose of the Mearsieans, and gradually got drawn into the Alliance; she was murdered by one of Detlev's boys, and she is still missed.

Lisbet Keperi: Younger sister of Thad and Karhin.

Thad Keperi: Red-haired brother of Karhin, also a scribe student, but much less passionate about the scribe life. Very social, and friend to all the Alliance; he and his brother Bee are very close to Shontande Lirendi.

ENAERAN

Adon Marsael: Distantly related to the royal Elsarion family, tried to take throne. Allied with Norsunder in order to keep the throne.

Andri Malcolin Elsarion: Inherited his throne very recently, after years of civil war.

Gared Inmael: Close friend and adoptive brother of Andri Elsarion: Gared's father, the Elsarion Master of Horse, took in Andri when he was disinherited. The boys grew up together.

Marten (Martande) Eldias: Lifelong friend to Andri Elsarion.

Baras Parael Otobris: [deceased] The new king's Commander of the King's Guard.

Thadara Otobris, Duchas of Merith: The new king's Chief Minister and treasurer, who has her eye on marrying Andri and sharing his throne.

Trevor Macael Elsarion: cousin to Andri, from what had been the main branch of the family. Holds the rank of duchas in Elsarion, a very old province.

EVERON

King Berthold and Queen Mersedes Carinna Delieth: [deceased] Former king and queen, survivors of rough earlier years. Mersedes, daughter of a con man, became one of the Knights of Dei, dedicated to protecting the kingdom. They were both killed (at different times) by Henerek of Norsunder, who had come from Everon, and had been booted out of the elite Knights of Dei for countless crimes.

Prince Glenn Delieth: [deceased] Heir to the throne of Everon, and convinced that a strong army solves all questions, especially the threat of Norsunder attacking; he died in a duel with David, one of Detlev's boys, after forcing the fight on him.

Hatahra Delieth (Tahra), Queen of Everon: Younger sister of Glenn, passionate about numbers, and in her unrelenting hatred of Detlev and his boys. When the war begins, has two children, Jessan and "Carl" (Berthold Jessan, and Mersedes Carinna), and three infants: Madelon, and twins Sedron and Glenn.

Roderic Dei: Commander of the Knights of Dei, once defenders and protectors of the realm. The Knights were decimated in the war Henerek brought, and Kessler Sonscarna finished. Roderic Dei survived to serve as regent for Tahra Delieth until she reached the age of majority.

IMAR

Fer Eider family: Liere's mother, Elen; one of Liere's brothers, who owns a pastry shop. Has two sons and a daughter: Lesim, Milnat, and Marga.

Marga Fer Eider: cousin to Lyren-Sartora, niece to Liere Fer Eider

Tolia: baker, Marga Fer Eider's best friend. ERAS, harbor-worker, Marga's male best friend. Both regarded Marga as their beloveds.

KHANERENTH

Jehan Merindar Zhavalieshin: Adopted into the ruling family on his marriage to Sasharia. Became king not long before the war began. Attended the Marlovan academy as a teen, and spent many years afterward at sea, fighting pirates and dodging his father's forces until the former king, Math, was restored.

Sasha (Sasharia) Zhavalieshin: Daughter of former king Math, married Jehan Merindar, who adopted into her family. She and Jehan became co-rulers when her father retired from the throne, not long before the war began. Sasha studied some magic before she and her mother, Sun, lived for a number of years on Earth as fugitives.

Marloven Hess

Crystal Ingrid Montredaun-An: [deceased] Daughter and heir to Senrid, the king. Five years old. Her chief passion is dogs.

Daltan: Cobbler, middle aged. She is a resistance leader.

Forthan, Retren: [deceased] A young man from a farm background, Forthan is the best of the leaders to come out of the military academy. He became Harskiald, a resurrected title that means trusted commander in chief of Marloven Hess's standing army; before then, commanders in chief were appointed per mission. Struck his banner at Aladas Pass before the defeat of Marloven Hess.

Fox, Elgar the Fox, born Savarend Montredavan-An of Darchelde: due to political treachery, his family was ousted from the newly formed Marlovan kingship and confined to their own land at Darchelde for ten generations. Fox went to sea, and when his ship was hijacked by pirates, became a pirate until Inda Elgar led a mutiny, after which Fox became Inda's second in command as pirate fighters. Fox sailed the seas fighting pirates, and the Venn, until shortly after Inda died. He was offered an ancient Venn king's drakan, by the mysterious figure Ramis, and he and his crew sailed out of time until recently.

Hibern Askan: Light magic student, tutored by Erai-Yanya of Roth Drael, who learned in the northern mage school. Hibern was disinherited by her family.

Indevan-Harvaldar Montredaun-An, previous king of Marloven Hess: [deceased] Second son of Kethadrend, and raised to be a scholar. Indevan was, like his elder brother, skilled in martial arts, but he was never competitive. His leadership was entirely through a likable, easy-going nature and intelligence. He traveled to the neighboring lands, where he conducted himself so well and so knowledgeably that he did a great deal to lessen the negative Marloven reputation. Married the King of Telyerhas's daughter, Lesra. Had one son, SENRID, [see below] before he was killed by his younger brother Tdanerend, who was appalled at his ideas about limiting royal power and disbanding the army in favor of a militia defense.

Ivandred Montredaun-An: King of Marloven Hesea four centuries ago, at the height of Marloven military expertise. Married the famous, beautiful Lasva of Colend, and had a son, before his ancestral castle at Darchelde nearly became a rift to Norsunder, and has been blasted land ever since. He and his elite cavalry First Lancers rode into a Norsunder rift, after which the Fox Banner was discredited, and Ivandred became a cautionary tale.

Mordan Nauldra: formerly the royal desk jockey for the Jarl of Methden **Kendred Montredaun-An, Prince of Marloven Hess**: [deceased] Eldest son of Kethadrend, son of the grim Senrid who caused the various treaties to be made limiting Marloven Hess. Trained in martial arts at a very young age, sent to the academy too young. He had too much of his grandfather's angry drive, and when his father failed in various forays against those treaties, Kendred tried to rally the young Marloven heirs around him to take the throne. He ended up escaping over the border at a gallop with a company hot on his heels. Had two sons, both of whom he sold after unsuccessful plots. Changed his name, became a pirate before joining Norsunder, dead by age thirty.

Keriam, Janec: Career military man, Commander of the Marloven military academy, also titular head of the Palace Guard. Acted as guardian and foster-father to Senrid, protecting him from the regent as much as possible.

Mordan Nauldra: formerly the royal desk jockey for the Jarl of Methden.

Senelac, Fenis: Wife to Retren Forthan, and head of horse training for the military academy, equal rank to the Master of Horse in the city guard.

Senelac, Jan: Cavalry Captain in the army, now chief of Senrid's coverts.

Senrid Montredaun-An: Young king of Marloven Hess, a mage studying both dark and light magic. First friend to Liere Fer Eider, and second to make his unity in *Dena Yeresbeth*. The Marloven army is one of the most formidable in the world.

Stad, Indevan (Van): Second in command, Marloven army

Tdanerend Montredaun-An, Prince of Marloven Hess: [deceased] Third son of Kethadrend, raised to be "shield arm" to his brother Indevan. Tdanerend was short-tempered as well as short-sighted, and uncoordinated. He tried to learn magic, but where that came easy to Indevan, as well as everything else, he had trouble learning and eventually surrounded himself by toadies and traditionalists who were uneasy at the changes Indevan contemplated. He married Caras, the second princess of Telyerhas, and there, too, he was unfortunate: she was ambitious, despising him as much as he came to despise her after she tried to scorn the Marlovens into setting up a court. He killed her before he took out Indevan and Lesra. His daughter, Ndand, was Senrid's chief companion. Tdanerend tried control spells on her meant for Senrid, which motivated Senrid to master magic at a young age so he could fix his cousin. Tdanerend went over to Norsunder before losing the kingdom, and then his life.

NDAND left the kingdom to become a musician.

MEARSIES HEILI

Aurora of Mearsies Heili: Clair's small daughter, already showing signs of being a wanderer, like her Uncle Puddlenose.

Clair of Mearsies Heili: Young queen of Mearsies Heili, a small agrarian polity on the northeast corner of the continent Toar. Niece of the hermit-mage *Murial*, and cousin to the wandering boy known only as *Puddlenose*, she has adopted a group of girls, most of them runaways. Her right-hand and designated 'heir' is *C.J.*

C.J. (Cherenneh Jenet): Found by Clair, who traveled through the World-gate, C.J. is from Earth, adopted into Clair's gang of runaways and rejects. She learns magic fitfully, and is generally regarded as the leader of Clair's gang of girls.

CJ's Gang of Girls: Falinneh and Dhana currently wear human form but are not actually human; Seshe has a mysterious past, suspected of being a runaway princess (which is actually correct); Irenne thought the world was a stage and she was the heroine of the play, which got her killed by accident by one of Detlev's boys, but she is still very much a presence among the girls; Diana is a martial artist and forester; Sherry and Gwen are followers. They are a very tight found family.

Mearsieanne: [deceased] Once Queen of Mearsies Heili, on her return to the present time she stepped in and in the nicest way possible shouldered aside Clair, her great-granddaughter, in order to show her how ruling ought to be done. After the invasion she bound Mearsies Heili in a protective lattice-ward that was tied to herself, then she walked into a Selenseh Redian and surrendered her life, binding the enchantment onto her. The key is Clair.

Murial: *(see Light Mages)*

Puddlenose of Mearsies Heili: Bereft of family at a very young age, thus no one knows what his actual name was. He was abducted and used by The King of the Chwahir in his complicated plots; rescued several times by Rosey (Mondros, see LIGHT MAGES). He wanders the world, determined to have fun. His chief companion is a world-gate wanderer from Earth named Christoph, but sometimes he's joined by Rel (see SARTOR). Gradually he traveled on land less and on the sea more, until he was made second in command by Captain Heraford of the *Tzasilia*, former privateer.

REMALNA

Bran (Branaric) Astiar, Count of Tlanth: brother to Meliara, wife NEE

Meliara Astiar, Queen of Remalna: children Alaraec and Elestra

Nadav Savona: Vidanric's oldest friend and chief aid, son Nadav

Vidanric Renselaeus, King of Remalna: children Alaraec and Elestra

RALANOR VELETH

Flian Elandersi, Queen of Ralanor Veleth: was a princess from Lygiera, distant cousin to Garian Herlester of Drath.

Jaim Szinzar: Brother to the king, and nominal leader of the army, though Jason commands in action.

Jaimas Szinzar: Younger child of king and queen

Jason Szinzar, King of Ralanor Veleth: [deceased] military background, inherited the throne, and the care of his siblings, at a young age. His chief rival is PRINCE GARIAN HERLESTER OF DRATH

Jewel Szinzar: married to the King of Lygiera, MAXL ELANDERSI, has several children

Liara Viana Szinzar: Eldest child of king and queen

Markham Glenereth: disinherited, technically denied the Glenereth name, though the king intended that to be temporary. Liege to the king, a martial artist of superlative skill.

Lexan Glenereth: son of Markham Glenereth

SARENDAN

Darian Irad: [deceased] After his defeat in a vicious civil war, Darian Irad stepped down from the throne and ended up as a military consultant on the sister-world Geth-deles. On his nephew Peitar's assassination, Darian Irad insisted that he was a regent for Peitar's son Darian, and not a king: he had gone to Geth, where he married and had a family.

Darian Selenna: son of Peitar Selenna, and heir to the throne. Has Dena Yeresbeth.

Derek Diamagan: [deceased] Charismatic leader of the revolution, a commoner who wished to overthrow all the nobles, and institute common rule. He was a far better speech maker than he was an organizer; his revolution was a disaster. Close friend of Peitar Selenna until his assassination by Siamis, at that time nominally of Norsunder.

Lilah Selenna, Princess of Sarendan: [deceased] Younger Sister to Peitar. She, with friends *Bren* (artist), *Innon* (a noble-born accountant at heart) and *Deon* were deeply involved in the revolution.

Peitar Selenna, King of Sarendan: [deceased] Reluctant king who would rather study magic, he came to the throne after an especially vicious civil war. He, nephew to the former king, Darian Irad, was one of the leaders of the revolution, but advocated non-violent means. His accession was a compromise between the commoners, who adore him, and the nobles, who recognized that at least he is nominally one of their own; on his assassination, he was, at his own order, replaced by his uncle.

SARTOR

Atan, (Queen Yustnesveas Landis V): New young queen of Sartor, after the oldest kingdom in the world was removed from time by nearly a century. She was found as an infant on the border by Tsauderei the mage, and raised by him before the enchantment was broken. She began her queenship as a mage student with little training in statecraft, but well-read in history.

Gehlei: Former guard in the days before Sartor was enchanted for a century, escaped with the infant Atan. Raised Atan to age fifteen along with Tsauderei the mage.

Hinder and Sinder: Morvende (cave dwellers), friends of Atan.

Julian Landis: born Julian Dei, she is Atan's cousin who wore the Child Spell for a considerable time. She relinquished it on Atan's promise that she would not be considered an heir, nor a princess. She is a wanderer by nature, and was happiest when staying with Dtheldevor of Wnelder Vee's gang.

Mistress Veltos Jhaer: [deceased] Former chief of the prestigeous Sartoran mage guild, until the enchantment the foremost mage school in the world. Now a century behind. She was further burdened by guilt for having lost the kingdom to enchantment, she left the guild woefully behind as they struggled to recover their old prestige. Assassinated by Efael of Norsunder, she was replaced for a time by Tsauderei the mage.

Old Helas: One of Rel's city guards, left from before Sartor's 100-year enchantment. Along with BEAK, a young guard.

Rel: Known as Rel the shepherd's son and more widely as Rel the Traveler, he was happily raised by a guardian in Tser Mearsies until wanderlust caused him to leave home. Met Puddle-nose of the Mearsieans and consequently became tangled in some of the Mearsieans' adventures. Friends with Atan, and one of the Rescuers. He was the only outsider ever invited to join the Knights of Dei in Everon; in the previous volume he discovered his parentage (SEE Mondros the mage), which he is still trying to process.

Rescuers: The name given to a band of children who had lived in a magic-protected forest during the enchantment. They sheltered Atan before the enchantment was broken. Ostensibly highly regarded as heroes by the Sartorans, there are the aristocratic Rescuers, and the non-aristocratic, Rel among them.

SLES ADRAN

Bartal na Shagal, King of Sles Adran: Allied with Adon Marsael of Enaeran, and Norsunder.

Chantala Shagal: Niece and heir to Bartal, daughter of Chantal, Bartal's sister. Cared for by her elderly nanny MARIANA, who was Chantal's devoted nanny.

Haries: Last name of the pair of artists who shelter Chantala na Shagal during the war.

Kinarde, Arandos: Sarendan-born Norsundrian placed as watch-dog and then commander over Bartal by Norsunder

Navor Mandracar: army commander, close friend of the king.

Master Orthal: runs an art school along the river. Other artists in training: LEMETH, LISI.

TELYERHAS

Havlan Casarod, King: Family the most direct descendant of the Cassadas, who were regarded as visionaries (or mad). Son of a queen known for her lack of skill at ruling but her genius for music, he had two sisters, LESRA and CARAS, who married Marloven princes and ended up dead. A scholar, he has a consort, who is also a scholar but he handles a lot of minor ruling issues. Has a son and a daughter.

VASANDE LEROR

Kyale Marlonen: Adoptive sister to Leander, relishes being a princess, and is jealous of Leander's attention.

Leander Tlennen-Hess: Like Senrid, a young king, though of a tiny polity that historically belonged to the Marlovens, then broke away four centuries previous. Leander prefers scholarship, and before the second year of the war began, formally ceded Vasande Leror back to Senrid.

Llhei: [deceased] Sarendan-trained nanny (sister to Lizana, nurse to the royal children of *Sarendan*), governess to Kyale, remained after evil Queen Mara Jinia defeated.

Alaxandar: Captain of royal guard, quit under evil queen Mara Jinia, protected Leander.

LAND OF THE VENN

Erenlara Sofar: Barely into her teens, princess of the Venn until her brother's death in the invasion. Has Dena Yeresbeth.

Kerendal Sofar: [deceased] Was king of the Venn, until the invasion. He committed suicide rather than submit to a blood-binding forcing him to act according to Norsunder's will. Met Rel the Traveler [see SARTOR] the one time he was able to escape Venn and his duties, as a young boy.

WNELDER VEE

Dtheldevor: Daughter of a privateer (some say pirate) who was killed when Dtheldevor was small, but not before she was taught martial arts. She became the champion for the young prince Murgeh Troiad, sailing against pirates infesting the shores, and helping to fight off an enterprising Norsundrian.

She has a hideout called Dthel Rendm, on one of the hundreds of islands off Wnelder Vee's coast. She did the Child Spell decades ago; in lived time she is in her late seventies. She accepts kids on the Wander on her ship and her island, but her most loyal shipmates are: Sarmonwilda, born a dawnsinger; Sharly, a centaur from the northern reaches, and Sidres, another centaur; Gloriel and Peridot Warren (twins, from Earth, born with mundane names) and Joey and Ellen Warren.

Her most frequent visitor who doesn't live with the privateers is Julian Dei Landis of Sartor.

Troy, King Murgeh Troiad: was regarded as king in Wnelder Vee. Though kingship was little more than a title—the guilds do what little governing is required in small, very rural Wnelder Vee—he resisted even that much, preferring to wander the world and master music, and kept the Child Spell in order to avoid royal duties. Was considerably skilled as a bard.

NORSUNDER

Aldon: Military leader with a thirst for warfare, the bloodier the better. Wants to command the invasion in order to foster eternal war.

Alsaes: First came to notice as Kessler Sonscarna's companion in Kessler's plan to take over the world. Given a mortal wound, surrendered self in exchange for bloodknife spell to preserve his life. Extremely vain. Dyes hair blond to hide Chwahir origins.

Benin: [deceased] Ambitious mage, his specialty the soul-bound (those caught at the point of death, their wills bound to the command of whoever holds the soul-bound magic). Tends to not wait until potential soul-bound are dead in order to experiment.

Bergan: one of Imry Llyenthur's staff, along with COLLERON, and Duin [see below] These are all typical flunkies, though Bergan sells info to whoever will buy it, most of all to Aldon.

Bostian: [deceased] Ambitious Norsundrian military captain, obsessed with making himself king of Sartor.

Connanre of the Host of Lords: [deceased] A charismatic musician. It's still unknown if he was turned or born without a vestige of conscience. He was the one who precipitated the Fall of Old Sartor by turning one of the rituals into a bloodbath, it is said to win the attention of Yeres. He is the Host's master spy.

Dejain: [deceased] Mage specializing in dark magic, one of a succession of Norsunder Base commanders, who tended to be summarily replaced by violence. Now deceased

Duin, Fassler: (Duin his chosen name) Imry Llyenthur's chief aide-de-camp. Born in Chwahirsland.

Efael: Considers himself one of the Host of Lords, the authors of Norsunder. Has a penchant for cruelty. He is the Host of Lords' chief assassin, bloodhound, interrogator, and errand boy; he and his sister Yeres consider Detlev their rival for a seat among the Host of Lords.

Elzhier: One of Connanre of the Host's best spies. She joined Norsunder as a young, angry teen.

Henerek: [deceased] Ambitious low-ranking young Norsunder military captain, originated in Everon. Wanted to be one of the Knights of Dei, but was cashiered due to excess cruelty, drunkenness, and inability to follow orders. Led a brutal war in Everon, now deceased.

Host of Lords: Authors of Norsunder, existing beyond time, readying for a second try at taking the world. Or worlds. Why, and who, they are will become clearer in succeeding volumes.

Hyath: Young, ambitious, and cruel mage, studies under Yeres.

Ilerian of the Host of Lords: Currently wears the shape of a beautiful and promising morvende, though morvende did not come out of their caves until a couple thousand years after the Fall of Old Sartor. The story put around is that his turning was Detlev's first act on emerging from Norsunder-Beyond. Ilerian is the architect of Norsunder he founded Norsunder-Beyond using the life of the architect, Sfenaraec.

Imry Llyenthur: Shares field command of invasion with Efael of the Host. A mage and a martial artist, he has Dena Yeresbeth. He's essentially a strategist.

Lesca: Apparently lazy steward in charge of Norsunder Base. Overlook her at your peril.

Svirle Treloar of the Host of Lords: He was heir to Yssel and still uses that title though Yssel is long gone. His underlings address him as "Lord Svir", the word 'lord' being an ancient title. He was the organizer of the Fall of Old Sartor, recruiting and forming plans. He is the ultimate in assumed privilege: nothing he does could be wrong because he deserves the world. It was he who lured Ilerian to the world, then discovered that he could not control this fascinating entity, so he exerts himself to function as go-between between Ilerian and everyone else.

Theronezhe of the Host of Lords: Their military chief.

Yeres: She and Efael, her brother, were born off-world and so thoroughly and spectacularly corrupted that they caught the attention of Svirle of Yssel, one of the authors of Norsunder. Yeres is a powerful mage. She and Efael gladly execute the errands that the Host of Lords, steeped in evil, consider too distasteful.

EX-NORSUNDRIANS

Detlev Reverael ne Hindraeldrei: Chief visible mage and sometime military leader, answerable to Norsunder's Host of Lords. Born four thousand years ago, has lived in and outside time ever since. Like his nephew Siamis, has Dena Yeresbeth. Left Norsunder in 4753: much speculation on both sides as to why.

Kessler Sonscarna: Renegade Chwahir prince with considerable military abilities, forced into Norsunder as result of treachery by the mage Dejain. Hates Norsunder. (See *Chwahirsland* below)

Siamis Reverael: Nephew to Detlev. Formidable mage, and like Detlev, has Dena Yeresbeth. Left Norsunder previous to Detlev, after furnishing the means to free the Venn from an eight-century-old binding of their magic. Adopted Yanli, the last descendant of someone Siamis was close to on his first visit to Sartorias-deles. He has reason to believe that the woman, Isa Cassadas, was pregnant with his child before he was forced to return to Norsunder. They were both teenagers.

Sveneric Reverael Hindraeldrei: Detlev's son, trained with the boys.

Detlev's Boys

Adam: Artist, formidable talents in Dena Yeresbeth, artist until his hands were ruined by Efael

Alaki (Ferret): Acutely observant, aware of overlapping worlds, spy

Curtas: [deceased] Strongly responsive to line and harmony, especially in building

David: Captain of the group, best in most areas

Erol: Chwahir born, plucked off a battlefield. Excellent at stealth

Edde (Noser): [deceased] Taken from another world, at best a mascot

Laban: Volatile and longing for what he cannot have, a Dei descendant

Leefan*:* Quiet, strong martial artist, cousin to Rolfin

Mal Venn (MV): Martial artist, studying magic, excellent sailor

Rolfin*:* Cousin to Leefan, superlative martial artist

Roy*:* Strong Dena Yeresbeth, mage and scholar

Silvanas*:* Martial artist and horse master

FOR MORE INFORMATION

Visit the Sartorias-deles wiki at http://reqfd.net/s-d/

PART ONE

One

WE ALL KNOW THAT wind and weather exist completely independent of human emotions, if not of human meddling, and yet songs, poems and stories have for centuries been filled with weeping skies over scenes of mourning, and balmy spring days gracing celebrations.

The day a sole fishing boat headed eastward into the sea off the coast of Khanerenth, more than one person aboard sensed tension in a world entirely gray, from sky to sea. Tension to varying degrees had become a part of life, as Norsunder's invasion advanced into its second year. On this particular day, it felt as if all the world held its breath.

The fishing boat had sunk the land well behind it when the command passed back to loosen sail and let the way come off the boat. Though the season was too early for winter, snow began to fall, at first the occasional flake but very soon the world closed in around the fishing boat, white stippling the thousand shades of gray.

Two coated figures stood at the prow, the crew remaining well back. The taller of the two watched as the other hurled a glimmering sphere high into the air. It vanished into the sea, and then, with a surge of water, a great Venn drakan ship appeared, of a like not seen for a thousand years. Even the present-day Venn no longer built those great curved prows meant to suggest a dragon rising from the waters; this ancient drakan even had its dragon head affixed, which had meant in the long-ago days when the Venn ruled the seas that the ship was going to war.

The fisher's small crew—trained in stealth and martial skills all—had been warned what to expect, but the reality was so much greater that they stared upward in a mixture of awe and trepidation as ship and boat rocked on the choppy waters.

A tall, lean man sauntered to the drakan's rail, his black clothing blending with the pure black of the slackened mainsail. Everyone aboard the fisher gazed up at his bony face and his silver-touched dark red hair, smoldering dots of fiery red at either ear: rubies.

He gazed back down, taking in the two at the prow, one tall, blond, young, the other perhaps mid-thirties, brown of hair. Both, in spite of the blur of snow and the bulky winter clothes, betraying in a hundred indefinable ways the stances of skilled warriors.

"Eh, Ramis," he called lazily across the water. "It seems I'm back."

He spoke in a version of Marloven that was nearly unintelligible to David, standing beside Detlev. David knew the real history behind the various legends of Elgar the Fox; he'd had to learn it, along with the version of Marloven spoken at the time, in order to be ready for what Detlev had called the Norsunder-Beyond treasure hunt. But hearing it spoken aloud was jolting.

Detlev said, "Savarend. Permission to come aboard?" He also spoke in that old-fashioned version of Marloven, or rather Marlovan.

David stared. This truly was Savarend Montredavan-An, his own ancestor—known in those days as Fox. David peered upward through the snow at the foresail, barely making out an eight-hundred-year-old version of the infamous fox banner that had belonged to his family. Savarend and Inda Algara-Vayir had made it famous four centuries before Ivandred and the First Lancers rode it into Norsunder and infamy. Or so the world believed.

"Could I stop you?" Fox waved a lazy hand, the gesture ironic.

Detlev and David were not going to risk drawing any Norsundrian attention by even so small a spell as a transfer to get them from the fisher to the drakan, so they had to let down the fisher's rowboat, fight their way over the heaving gray seas, and then hook the boat to the beautifully straked hull of the

Treason in order to climb aboard.

When they reached the deck, Fox had already gone inside the cabin. The silent crew—who all looked like old-fashioned drawings of pirates, to the earrings with rubies affixed to them— tracked them as the two walked aft. David heard a whisper that sounded very like, "…and where are Ramis's burn scars?"

There had to be a story behind the name Ramis, but Detlev was maddeningly reticent about his past. His rare references were almost always what he'd observed, rarely what he'd done, and never what he felt.

They'd have to pry that story out of Siamis; then David forgot the matter when he got a look inside the cabin. His jaw dropped. It wasn't just the artistry, though he'd expected sumptuousness when he'd vaulted over the rail worked with gold leaf. It was as if he had slipped unknowing through a World Gate into another sort of existence entirely.

David had been on ships on two worlds, but on neither had he seen bulkheads carved in gilt fretwork forming interlocking circles. Between this framework a stylized marquetry tree wound upward, ending in leaves of gold. This, he knew, represented the ancient Tree of Ydrasal, which was replicated a candelabra with nine branches ending in candle holders. Over the captain's table hung a chandelier of intertwined branches, into which twenty-seven candles would fit. All were of gold.

The cabin was fit for a king.

"Where are we?" Fox asked as he snapped open a chart. "And who is this?" He flicked a glance at David.

"His name is David," Detlev said.

"Marlovan pronunciation," Fox observed.

Detlev did not respond to the implied question. "We are very near your old training grounds—here." He reached to tap the ocean off Khanerenth's southeastern corner.

"That answers where," Fox said. "Now we come to what." He leaned back in the curule chair, arms crossed. "When we first met, you beat the shit out of me. Not saying it was undeserved. I *was* a shit. Then you turned around and promised me this ship if I did certain things. I met those conditions."

"Agreed," Detlev said.

"Then we met up once more after you took us through the rift into Nightland."

"That meeting was roughly eight centuries later, as time is measured on this world," Detlev said. "But make your point."

"You gave me a choice: you'd push us through what you called a world-gate to some other world, where we could start new lives. More truthfully, finish out our old age, as strangers. Or you would call upon us to fight Norsunder here. We chose to remain in the world we know. And here we are. I'm gathering that fight is now."

"Correct."

"Now to my question. When we first met, you were part of Norsunder. You hurled us to Norsunder by their magic. What I want to know is, is this fight some rivalry between Norsunder commanders, like, ah, say, Gannan Marshig up against the likes of Boruin and Majarian for control of the strait? Is Marshig alive? Am I expected to fight him for some Norsundrian shit's entertainment?"

"To address your last question first, Marshig was released a year or so ago, and didn't survive a turn of the glass. His crew obeys the commands of Norsunder."

"And yet you took him, just as you took me. For the same purpose?"

"No, he was told he would fight for Norsunder when released."

Fox lifted his eyebrows. "During my day, I remember that you took a lot of vicious souleaters like Marshig. For what purpose? To pit us against each other?"

David stirred; famous ancestor or not, Fox Montredavan-An's derisive tone infuriated him. At least he was having less of a problem understanding.

Detlev flattened his hand briefly. "It's a fair question." He turned to Fox. "You will probably face some of those pirates, but not for my entertainment. I am unlikely to be there to see it."

"Oh?"

"The rift magic you remember was extremely dangerous. Powerful. Wasteful. I had to make myself the master of it, so that I controlled it, which meant entertaining those who created it, as they disliked coming forth to use it themselves. They needed to see a sufficient spectacle, which I gave them. I knew that Sharl the Brainsmasher and Marshig and their like would be far more trouble than aid. Further, every sixth or seventh rift, I was able to push through someone like you — after establishing a suitable reputation. But you and these select others were kept elsewhere, out of Norsunder's reach. They think they had them all."

"Ah." Fox sat back.

"And so, to answer your first question, I am fighting against Norsunder. I want to destroy them."

"You're a traitor?" Fox's eyes narrowed.

"I am."

Fox's grin even at the age of seventy was a masterpiece of insolence. "I like traitors against those I hate." He swept his hand to include the entire ship—which he'd renamed *Treason.* "Who are these select others?"

"You shall meet them today. You have maybe a week to make a fleet out of them. Less than a week, if you can manage it."

Fox looked down, then up. He wiped his hand over his face, then blinked, as though it was strange to be feeling real wind and weather again. "You do remember that I was never the strategist. That was always Inda. And Jeje after the battle at the strait."

"You trained Inda's fleet."

"I did. But a week, to prepare for a war?"

"You will not be leading them in the world's defense. Not yet. As the situation stands now, imagine four, five times the Venn fleet you faced in the strait that year, against maybe of third of what you and Inda had. Even if we possessed twelve Indas, the enemy would still overwhelm you."

Fox's expression tightened.

Detlev went on, "Events have progressed rapidly. Too rapidly in some regards. Not rapidly enough in others. This latest turn in this war could make a difference, but to deflect the enemy's attention as long as possible, we need a subterfuge."

Fox let out a bark of laughter. "A ruse?"

"This ruse is vital," Detlev said. "It has to be sufficiently large to…" Detlev lifted his head as though listening to something.

Fox heard nothing but chatter from his crew, and the wash-splash of the sea against the hull. Used to being in command, uneasiness tightened the back of his neck.

Detlev slid his hand inside his jacket, pulled out a rather crumpled rectangular paper, and glanced at it. "David will explain more," he said, on a lighter note—and vanished.

Fox expelled a breath. "The only man to ever scare me. Scares me still," he commented. "So. What type of ruse?"

"Draw Norsunder's attention to this ocean," David said. "And keep it here."

Two

Mearsies Heili

APPROXIMATELY THE SAME moment Detlev and David climbed aboard the *Treason*, Sveneric Reverael ne-Hindraeldrei appeared via magic transfer in the Mearsies Heili Selenseh Redian. Desperate, he had dared to use Siamis, his cousin, as a Destination, which was always risky.

The contrast between the warm, arid, still air of the Host's manor in Imar and the cold, pure air of the cave, even after a night, was more than a physical shock. It was a shock to the spirit.

Sveneric stood taut with tension as he looked around wildly, taking in the makeshift bookcase, the lap desk, the quires of paper already written on next to those waiting for writing, the bedroll waiting to be laid out, and last, he turned to Siamis, who smiled a welcome.

Sveneric fell to his knees, a single sob escaping him.

"Bad, eh?" Siamis asked.

"Squalid," Sveneric whispered.

"Squalid," Siamis repeated, on a note of confirmation.

"It's the only word for how my mind felt after every conversation. There were not a lot of them—I think Svir found me disappointing. It was just as you told me once, how much he relished describing the things they made Detlev do, and how funny it was that they were never going to let you go and Detlev was too stupid to realize it…"

Siamis waved a hand. "I heard much the same. What did you tell them?"

Sveneric's gaze lifted. "Norsunder Base," he said, and Siamis understood that Sveneric had given Svir and Ilerian the Detlev of the Norsunder days. "Ilerian wouldn't let me see what he's doing, but I could feel how terrible it is. No life within a day's travel, probably more."

"Did you learn anything?"

"I think I did, though it might be the, the, what MV calls the shit sandwich, that is, the lie wrapped in truth. The way I gave them the Norsunder Base Detlev. Oh, Svir seems to think that Detlev wants Norsunder-Beyond, that he left them to set up as an emperor, and I let myself be shocked, and blabbered a lot about emperors in history, how much I admire them."

Siamis waited patiently through this cascade of words, for he sensed that Sveneric was barely holding himself together.

A quick frown, and Sveneric said, "So, the truth. Or lie-in-truth. Svir kept coming back to Songre Silde."

"Ah, the most magically powerful of the worlds circling Erhal, and they never succeeded there," Siamis said calmly, in an effort to bring Sveneric's freefalling emotions down.

"He acted amused, but I could tell he hated that Songre Silde had helped the fifth world hide all life, all those centuries ago, leaving to Norsunder that barren world. Except for the guardians under the mountains. Because that was *their* failure, the Host's, I mean. But Svir seems to think Detlev was fooled, too, when the enchantment was released and there was all the hidden life, but Norsunder was warded from it all. Svir thinks Detlev is angry that he missed his chance to take that world, and that's why he left, to set up an empire here … Siamis, I know I was stupid. I thought, talking to Imry would *fix* things, would … I can't find Detlev. I know I shouldn't try, but … Where is he?"

So that was the fear Siamis sensed. Not a residue of the boy's recent experiences as a prisoner of the Host.

"I believe he's somewhere on the ocean east of Khane-renth," Siamis answered, his tone calm. "Don't risk the mental plane again. I have some of my magic-papers left. You are welcome to write to him. You left yours behind, I trust, before you embarked on your expedition?"

"Left it in Marloven Hess." Sveneric could sometimes seem

years—centuries—past his age, but right now he was very much a thirteen-year old, his bruised face anxious. He had lost either the ability or the desire to hide his distress.

Siamis gestured toward the desk, where a long, rectangular, beige-colored paper lay. To anyone who could perceive it, the paper scintillated with magic. It had taken Siamis several years of hard work to construct the inlaid spells.

Sveneric grabbed up the pen, dipped it, and wrote rapidly. He laid the pen down and crouched over the paper, staring intently—unbreathing. Five, ten heartbeats passed—long ones—and Sveneric exhaled, his head dropping back and his eyes closing for a heartbeat or two in deep-felt relief.

Then he looked up, and Siamis did not comment on Sveneric's struggle to recover himself as he glanced at the battered notebook on the desk. "What is that? It's not your writing."

"CJ's records. Aurora thought I ought to read them, and CJ gave permission from up north."

Sveneric's smile was quick. "CJ would never let me read them. I translated that to mean she was pretty fluent about Detlev and the rest of us. Why you?"

"I wrote to ask."

"I asked, too. Dirk said they're so biased that he thought them funny."

"Perhaps she consented because Aurora also asked. Or perhaps because she is far enough away that she won't see my reaction, whatever she imagines it might be. She did add that I deserved what I'd read. She also said I could share them with anyone idiot enough to crack their eyes on them."

Sveneric's lips twitched in an almost-smile. "That sounds exactly like her. She's gone, you said?"

"To the Venn. She said it was you who sent her there."

"A suggestion only. I thought CJ was adamant about remaining here as watchdog over Clair."

"Erenlara, apparently, was—"

Detlev appeared in the room. As the transfer-magic dissipated and displaced air ruffled past the others' faces he sat on the edge of the table. Sveneric ran into Detlev's arms, which closed tightly around him, their thoughts melding faster than light.

Then, over Sveneric's head, Detlev met Siamis's gaze: *David is releasing the last capture-spheres. Is Jilo recovered enough to speak?*

Siamis responded: *Upstairs arguing with Arthur, who is trying to stop him for all the wrong reasons. Jilo's in terrible shape. I fear he won't last out the month.*

Detlev released Sveneric and stood up. "What about those four?" he asked his son—a reference, Siamis found out later, to the Norsundrians Sveneric killed with his bare hands when he invaded Imry Llyenthur's headquarters in Larkadhe.

"Soulbound. All of them desired release. Of course I read them first."

Desired release echoed in Siamis's memory, producing a brief, vivid image of Derek Diamagan's face as Siamis raised the bow.

Sveneric added, "I could have taken another half-dozen." Siamis knew Sveneric spoke the truth, but he was amused by the thirteen-year-old bravado in his tone.

Detlev cast a look of comical dismay at his son, then Sveneric laughed and said quickly, "It's wonderful how heroic one can be when they're hampered by orders to disarm-and-secure."

Siamis said, "If I have to wait another moment to find out how you managed to get free, I'll be forced to go ask Ilerian myself."

"I caught Yeres by surprise. I couldn't bring myself to kill her," Sveneric said, his anxious gaze a question. "The way I couldn't kill any but the soulbound, who are really already dead."

Detlev answered the real question: "We can contrive to find ways that do not necessitate you becoming an assassin at age thirteen. Carry on."

Reassured, Sveneric said, "I made her transfer me to the border here. Where I passed out. I holed up on the beach and slept, and when I woke I did the transfer to the cave. But listen, though I didn't kill her, I did a mind-raid. And I found out that Connanre did indeed discover the treasure hunt, and dangled it as a lure to Yeres. Though she knew none of the details. I don't think they'd told Svir or Ilerian, or I'd have been questioned about it," Sveneric added, looking troubled. "But I wouldn't trust that they don't know now."

Detlev looked a question at Siamis, whose answer came on the mental plane: *They know. For a heartbeat both were wide open. Worse, they believe you planted Hibern there.*

An expletive escaped Detlev, testament to how tired he

was. But Svir and Ilerian would have accelerated their attempts to break Kessler's ward, whatever the cost, even if they hadn't leaped to that assumption about Hibern.

That said, the timing could not be worse.

Detlev turned to Sveneric. "Ilerian was certain to do a mind-raid on Yeres himself, to see what you learned from her. What you said to her. That will explain the recent acceleration of their efforts."

Sveneric closed his eyes. "My fault."

"Connanre catching on was the risk, and you had nothing to do with that. I gambled on him wanting to keep it secret until he could figure a way to use it. The revelation was inevitable. It's the timing that is regrettable."

Siamis capped his ink, and sat back. "At least they can't get to Norsunder-Beyond to do anything about it, whether they know or not."

"They're trying," Sveneric said. "It's terrible. Oh. And Yeres pushed Efael to attack Imry with a poison knife."

"We know," Detlev said. "David found Imry, then lost him—most likely while you were asleep on the beach. Imry seems to have removed himself from immediate danger, but he'll be recovering for a while."

"Then Efael will get command at last," Siamis said. "At this stage, is that going to be a worse blow for them or for us?"

Detlev's expression lightened briefly in a semblance of a smile. "Both. Like most assassins he's worthless at command, but that won't stop him from doing it anyway, then slaughtering the nearest helpless individuals to assuage his temper."

Siamis said, "My news is that Laban's reached Marloven Hess. Or did you know that?" He turned to Detlev.

Sveneric exclaimed, "Are they practicing the circle? Then I must—"

Detlev said, "Stay here."

"But they'll need me—"

"Perhaps," Detlev said gently, "you desire to be free of cooperative obligation?"

Sveneric was silenced.

Detlev said to Siamis, "Release him when you are satisfied that he has fully recovered." And he vanished.

Sveneric rubbed his eyes. "I had to do it," he said. "I thought I could reach Imry by telling him about the healing, and that was the only way." He added, his eyes and mind distant,

"He looked terrible."

Siamis knew that the second *he* referred not to Imry Llyenthur, but to Detlev, who indeed looked as if he had gone without rest for far too long.

Siamis said comfortingly, "Your father knows his limits; I've seen him worse." *Though not often.* "Let's get some untainted food into you, and some fresh air, and I'll bring you up to date on all the rest of the bad news that you've missed while you were enjoying the Host's hospitality."

Sveneric said, "Jessan and Carl first."

Siamis sighed, looking up as he considered his wording. "Jessan managed to keep Carl from finding out what you'd done until a few days ago," he said finally, opting for bluntness.

Sveneric flinched. Though Jessan and Carl Delieth were twins, Carl was so much smaller and frailer than Jessan, as though she had put all her strength into Dena Yeresbeth reach instead of growing. She was so very sensitive to the others in their tight little circle of youngsters, that ever since they found one another, they'd fallen into the habit of protecting her.

Siamis said, "Tahra Delieth has not rescinded her command to Atan that her children be denied proximity to you and your father."

"Physical proximity," Sveneric said quickly, not quite a question.

Instead of answering, Siamis gestured outward. "I'll bring some food for you."

Of course he knew that Sveneric would go into immediate rapport with the Delieth twins. It was something they had done when they were small, and Sveneric was still living at Norsunder Base with the boys. It had been Siamis's task to create a safe space within the mental realm for them to find one another, and practice contact, while Detlev was losing the struggle to postpone the invasion.

When Siamis returned with a tray, Sveneric sat with his knees pulled up and his head resting on his crossed arms. What strength Sveneric had left he used to reassure Jessan that he was back, and unharmed in essentials.

He ate what Siamis brought him, and left soon after.

The Mearsiean white palace was filled with fine furnished rooms, all clean and swept and dust free, but Sveneric did not even look at any of them. He had just escaped an equally fine palace, if utterly different in atmosphere. His instincts homed for a certain kind of comfort, and so he transferred from the light, air-swept serenity of Clair's mountaintop palace to the underground hideout that she had made for her friends many years before.

The main room was circular, tree roots dangling overhead. The room was empty, but someone had been here, and recently; the brightly-colored throw rug on the beaten soil of the ground was covered with closely written sheets of paper, and a grubby book. Sveneric bent to look. The tiny, close lettering was Chwahir.

Ordinarily he would be curious, but he was exhausted, ached in every bone and muscle, and emotionally he was drained.

He looked around, sniffing the air as he scanned on the mental plane. No one around.

Sveneric enjoyed this place. Its atmosphere of laughter and excitement, of the tight bond of friendship, lingered somehow in the rough curves of dirt and tree roots, the homey, age-battered furnishings. He walked past the papers on the rug without disturbing their order, and found an empty room. When he snapped a zaplight, he discovered that this was CJ's room. A candle sat on the old dresser. He lit it and the shadows sprang back.

He dropped onto the green bedspread, which smelled faintly of dust and of mildew. The books on the shelf under the old paintings leaned. A knife belt lay draped over a chair back, the limpness of each end indicating an uninterrupted stay of several months. The wardrobe was partly open, and a fold of midnight-blue velvet protruded. The green rag-rug on the hard-packed dirt floor was pleasantly dusted with long-dried muddy footprints.

He breathed deeply. The air was a little dusty, and smelled of pine and wet soil. The last of the decorative, icy poison of Svirle Treloar of Yssel's stolen palace leached from his mind and body.

He liked this room. It was comfortable.

He thought, I made my decision alone. I acted on it alone, and now I must consider the consequences on my own.

There was a rightness to this process that partially eased the desolation echoing emptily in his thoughts. It was a hint at the inevitability of a permanent separation. It hurt.

A month ago he'd been impatient with the restraints

imposed by time. And now he wished time would stop, and let him relish each moment to the fullest before releasing it. He was so *tired*. He lay on top of the bed, and snuffed the candleflame with a wave. As he settled from recent habit into a straight, flat position, his healing ribs twinged dully. A week or two more and they'd only hurt if he coughed or did something strenuous. But that was not "fully recovered."

He knew what Detlev meant. It wasn't just his cuts and bruises that required time.

Closing his eyes, he fell into exhausted sleep.

Three

WHILE SVENERIC HAD BEEN in rapport with the Delieths, Detlev transferred straight to the white palace. He entered the library, which had become a sort of command center. His gaze swept the maps, then he spotted Arthur and Jilo in an alcove, Arthur surrounded by a moat of books, and Jilo slouched on a stool, thin hands dangling between his knees. His complexion was shockingly gray.

"Detlev," Arthur exclaimed. "Tell him not to try sneaking onto those Chwahir ships out there in the water."

"Why would anyone wish to?" Detlev asked.

And though he knew the answer—having had Siamis monitor Jilo among his many other tasks—he waited patiently as Jilo muttered, "The blood poison spell. Wan-Edhe puts on his commanders. To control them. I figured out how to despell it. I'm going to go despell them all. Before Wan-Edhe releases the dormant part of the spell and kills more of them, for some whim or other. He's taken to doing it for no reason, to, to keep them obedient." His voice husked toward the end, as if talking this much had exhausted him, but he was determined to defend his decision.

Somewhat to his surprise, Detlev offered no argument. "Did you use that book Kessler gave you?"

"Yes."

"How much of the work had he done?"

Jilo drew a hissing, shaky breath. "He only put the … the … the fundamentals. What he adapted from the blood mage texts. I don't think he was interested in pursuing it farther. But I did it." Jilo looked down at his hands, frowning as he tried unsuccessfully to control the tremble. "I don't know what Kessler is doing. I think," he added, and looked up, his face far too bony for his age.

"You think?" Detlev repeated.

"I think he abandoned all these other pursuits. No idea why. At least there was enough. For me to go on," Jilo murmured.

A shake of the head, as Jilo's overlong, lank black hair brushed the sharp bone of his cheek and swung back. "What I have here pertains to mirror wards. Lattices in specific. The underpinnings of Wan-Edhe's structure in Narad. There is only as much of the blood mage text … as relates to mirror wards. Using the lattice structure. Wan-Edhe was too hasty in making it." He slumped more, worn out from this long speech, and brushed a hand over the book.

Detlev opened it.

For certain definitions of hasty, he was thinking as he glanced down the closely written pages. "I see the general outline," he said. "And I agree with your intent. But not immediately."

Jilo flung back his head. "Every day the Chwahir captains have to labor under that threat, while Wan-Edhe gets more insane—"

Detlev raised a hand. "I'm not suggesting you leave this matter for some unnamed future. I am with you in believing the sooner the better." From very long practice, he kept his tone even, without revealing the almost overwhelming desire to thrust Jilo into the field at this moment—or to explain how desperately they needed a possible change in the balance of power, which right now favored Norsunder. But Jilo would not survive a week, from the looks of him.

Detlev said, easily, "I mean a matter of days. First, I believe we ought to test it."

Arthur burst in, "He tried to test it on himself! It knocked him flat. If it hadn't been for Retren Ndarga, who found him unconscious, bleeding from the nose, he might have died."

"Exactly," Detlev said, without telling them that Siamis had been right behind Retren. "And I see the damage, Jilo. You have to be feeling it."

Jilo looked away, then back. He reminded Detlev of a comet speeding like a streak of white fire across the firmament before dwindling to ash. Such geniuses were driven to their own destruction if not checked.

Jilo was wavering, even now.

"You will not make it past two spells," Detlev said bluntly. That got Jilo's attention. "Whereas, if you go to the Selenseh Redian, and spend a few days recovering, you will be able to rid yourself of the residual poison of your experiments."

"Days? I could rest a couple days," Jilo muttered. *I am so very tired.*

"Excellent. Then permit me to take this."

"The writing. At the back. Is mine. I can give you a better paper. I copied it out."

"I want to see what Kessler has written, in case there is a necessity for alteration of the basics."

"Test how?" Jilo asked, his brow puckering with faint hope. "*Not* on you."

"No. I salute your bravery and determination in trying the dormant phase of the blood poison spell on yourself then removing it, but as you no doubt are feeling, the effect is still cumulative. I'll approach one of Wan-Edhe's victims directly, once I study your work. Then I will return and report to you. Agreed?"

Arthur looked from one to the other, acutely aware that he was utterly out of his depth here; once again he wished Roy was with him, but he was still undercover in Fhleria.

Jilo said, "A week." His eyes closed.

Detlev vanished and returned to the Selenseh Redian. He said to Siamis, "Jilo ought to turn up at any moment. He is beyond both of our skills, but you still have the Ethe cup, yes?"

Siamis said, "I do. I made a false one for June, in case Ilerian gets to Clair. You said the real cup should not be used."

"Emphatically not, unless a miracle occurs and the other four turn up. Which I doubt. I'm fairly certain that Svir got to them at the outset, and only this one escaped his search, due to the Guardian's having shoved it into other-space with that time window. But the cost was diminishment of its potency over that time. Every use thins it, and eventually it will burn itself out. It must be held back for the greatest need—with this one exception."

"Jilo?"

"Yes. He's lived under the threat of Wan-Edhe for so long he regards himself as walking dead. The Ethe artifact is the only antidote to the residual poison that his body has not been able to throw off."

"What do I do? I know nothing about the silver cup's magic."

"No more do I, except this much: we can't do anything overt. Only someone born off-world, for that is the enchantment the Guardian laid on it. However, it will act passively if you keep it near Jilo when he sleeps, and let him drink out of it. As I recall, the Guardian admitted having sipped from it when she felt ill, and it restored her strength. Jilo is so poisoned that it'll take far more than a sip. More like three or four days. Make it five, to be sure, then give it back to June, and tell her to wrap it up and store it at the bottom of a trunk."

"Very well."

"Also, do try to convince Jilo that he is not in fact one of the walking dead."

Siamis laughed. "I'm not the one to do that, but I know who is."

"Oh?"

"One of the Mearsieans, whose main motivation is kindness. The only times Jilo took a break from his efforts were to supervise Retren's studies, and to talk to Seshe, who looked after them both."

"That is far better than I'd hoped," Detlev said. "He needs connection with people. The more the better. Ah. When Sveneric turns up, he can keep Jilo company. It would be good for them both."

"Agreed."

Four

Eastern Sea

ON BOARD THE *TREASON*, Fox pinched his fingers between his brows, wishing that his head would not pang so hard, and that he wasn't so thirsty. He fixed his gaze on the young man with the blond hair and the Marlovan name. "Who is it we're drawing attention away from?"

"A good part of the Chwahir fleet."

Fox thumbed his temples, and David said, "Will you take my advice? I've spent only a few years in the Beyond, not centuries, but I know what it feels like to come back to time's flow again. The best thing you and your crew can do is to drink water, or steep, and sleep the night through."

"While you do what?"

"I'm going to sow dragon's teeth," David said, hand out toward the sea. "Once all the promised ships are back in the world, I'll go among them and tell them an all-captains meeting will be held here in the morning. How's that?"

"Tell me first what sort of a fleet I'm getting, if you can."

David said, "This is what I've been told: like you, all are from other times. All are unmatched on the seas. All were outlawed. You've got one prince, whose cousin went behind his back to claim the throne while the prince spent ten years fighting off Damondaen's attempts to extend its territory."

"I hate princes," Fox stated. "With one exception, they are always more trouble than they're worth."

David suppressed the impulse to retort, *And yet you regarded yourself as a displaced king, didn't you?* David was supposed to cooperate, not interrogate. "This prince was sent to sea when young, to keep the royal family from killing him as they went at each other. Eventually there was only him left—until the cousin took the throne."

"Damondaen. In my day that was on Toar," Fox said. "What languages do they speak?"

"All speak some form of Sartoran. Prince Yviski because part of his family had come to Toar from the Sartoran continent—though I'm told he knows little of Sartoran history. The rest are from all over the world, the most famous being the commander who defended the northeast coast of Goerael against the Venn, the Fhlerians, the Chwahir, and all other comers. No one was better—not so much as a rowboat got past her river craft. Which we have a good part of."

"River boats. A prince." Fox waved a hand. "But it sounds like I have little choice. Go. Do what you're going to do. I will take your advice—I've got a vile thirst on me. Wait."

David had risen and turned toward the door, but paused.

Fox eyed him, then said, "I spent years writing a record for Ramis."

"I know," David said, though he suspected Fox's mention was a way into asking what place he had in Marloven history.

"Do today's Marlovans still read it?"

David didn't correct him; Fox would pick up how the language had changed, or he wouldn't. "No one has read it. They don't know of its existence."

Fox's brows slanted in surprise. "Then what did I write it for?"

"For when the truth can be shared." David walked out, hearing the sounds of pouring water behind him.

He'd learned about the capture-spheres when Detlev trained him for the "treasure hunt"—which could not be implemented until Kessler removed the ward from transfer to Norsunder-Beyond. David had only a rough idea how the magic worked, but he did not need to know more. This day, as snow softly fell on the gray seas, he released the last of them.

As the *Treason* sailed with the wind, one by one David tossed the spheres out into the snowy blur, where they vanished. One, two, three heartbeats and with a great surge of foaming waters, a ship—six ships—ten ships and consorts—appeared in a string, the farther ones silhouettes in the snowy air.

David clambered back into the rowboat, along with a pair of strong fishers. These rowed him from flagship to flagship as David repeated the gist of what he'd told Fox, advised them all to drink water and rest.

By the time they rowed him back to the *Treason*, the snow had turned into occasional spits of sleet from clouds scudding across the brilliant sky. The fisher sailed in *Treason*'s lee as David shook off the water and entered the cabin.

Fox was still awake, candlelight gleaming in his eyes. He smacked a hand onto the chart. "I won't sleep until I have some kind of plan ready," he said. "I need more specifics than an enemy with five times what we had in the strait that year."

David nodded, fighting back tiredness. Life was going to continue at the run, it seemed. He dropped down at the table, and when a silent sailor brought him something steaming hot, he slurped at it gratefully, not caring what it was.

Only when he was able to discern taste once the scald died away, he recognized coffee, though with a bitter under-taste, as though the beans had been scalded along with tree bark. He realized he was tasting coffee from eight centuries ago. He shook that off, and pulled the chart to him. "Here's a detailed situation report..."

⁕

Mearsies Heili

Sveneric, safe underground, was asleep when the sun rose. Some of the Irregulars had limped in tiredly half an hour before. He woke briefly, noted where he was and who they were, then sank gratefully back into his dreams.

Dhana—human only in form—woke up an hour or so later, and prowled noiselessly along the hall. She sensed someone in CJ's room as she passed. She poked her head in. She knew that CJ wouldn't mind someone using her room while she was gone, as long as the person didn't mess with her stuff.

For Sveneric, perceiving Dhana in the darkness of the underground distracted him. When he could not see her human form, he relied on his perception in the realm of the spirit, which he could use here within the relative boundaries of safety. Dhana's human form was like the moon eclipsing the sun, a mere shadow, the sun—her other self, blended with shifting non-human forms—a brilliant corona.

Intensely curious, once he passed through the cleaning frame, ridding himself of the last vestiges of that palace in Imar, he left the underground cave to take a walk in the forest air. He knew where Dhana's pool lay, fed by a waterfall from the underground stream that worked its way through the Selenseh Redian above.

Dhana emerged from a morning bathe in a stream that anyone human would find unbearably frigid, to see Sveneric perched on a flat boulder, looking intently into the waters glowing countless shades of blue, from cobalt through aqua to palest dawn blue. The life forms within the water, from which Dhana emerged, were like shifting refractions of light combining and recombining then bursting apart in an endless dance. At the far end, a few rose in huge bubbles, suspended in the air for a time, trembling with rainbow sheen, before falling to the water again. Though he knew it was misleading to ascribe human emotions to non-humans, it still felt as if these were the playful ones. The young ones. Though age, and time, were relative things here.

Dhana plopped onto a rock, ignoring her wet summer shirt and knee pants, and kicked her bare feet in the water, watching the light catch with crystalline shards of color in the splashes.

Sveneric remembered what he had learned of her story: that she had emerged from the waters one day, wearing the form of a girl the same age as Clair and her friends. She had been drawn to CJ's singing, and to the girls' laughter.

Diana had introduced herself and asked her name, and she repeated, "Dhana," which might very well be what someone just getting used to having a voice, and a tongue inside a human mouth, might say. The others had seized on Dhana as a name before she understood what names were, and thus she discovered that she had a name, and a self.

Sveneric looked her way, taking in her expression. While she was human, she reflected human emotions, as changeable as those shades of blue in the waters. "I'm sorry about Diana," he said

Dhana scowled at him. "How did you know?"

"I heard. While I was a prisoner in Imar. I recognized her from the description, but I didn't tell Efael who she was."

"CJ said she's gonna get that slime-faced rot-brained reeker Efael. And I plan to be there helping when she does." A flickering look. "Were you *really* there? In the Host lair?"

"I was there."

She sighed, a short, sigh. Relief or anger? "Detsie getcha out?"

"I got myself out."

"How?" She finally met his gaze directly.

"Not by magic. My own, that is." He hazarded a guess at the real question that lay between them. No, that lay between Dhana and the rest of the world.

Her jaw jutted a little, her expressive face stony. It was otherwise a plain face, freckles across the nose, light-colored eyes, short blond hair barely brushing her shoulders. She was long and light in build for a girl of eleven or twelve. There were signs that she was not human, the most obvious being how comfortably she sat as if it were a balmy summer day, and not very near freezing. But, to Sveneric, that corona shone in the mental realm, searing, bright, and powerful, though she did her utmost to hide it with her human appearance.

Sveneric went on, "I caught one of the Host off-guard. Made her transfer me here."

"Howja get bagged in the first place?" Her hand rose, and a whoosh of bubbles rose into the air, popped softly, and water rained down. She was unable to move ungracefully. That, too, was innate.

"Stupidity." He grinned.

Her gaze dropped from his face to the forearm pressed against his ribs. "Knocked you around? Of course they did."

It was a reminder of how Diana and Troy had suffered under Efael's hand before he abandoned them to die. Sveneric saw the raw grief in her face, and said, "Come on! I've an urge to enjoy as much fresh air as possible, after the stuffy, arid atmosphere of the Host-palace."

"Did it really stink?" She gave a fleeting smile.

"In the realm of the spirit it reeked."

Her mood changed again, as quick as the shifting forms in the water. She was doing her absolute best to remain the eternal twelve-year-old, though Clair's group was changing around her.

She glared at his plain brown high-collared tunic, long trousers, and shoes. "Why are you always so disgustingly tidy? Think it impresses anyone?"

"Do I?" he said, thinking, *you want to hide behind your human self?*

He whispered a spell.

She turned, just in time to meet a very ripe and syrupy banana-cream pie. He leaped to her rock and mashed it in thoroughly.

"Yagh!" she bellowed, and the chase was on.

She vagabonded pies—an easy spell because the matter so quickly pulled together in this form would dissipate after a very short time—and hurled them rapidly, but he dodged easily as he ran.

"Stop!"

"Make me," he taunted.

Then he paused just ahead of her in the path, and seemed uncertain which way to go. Triumph brought her hands up, gathered the magic—

And a net materialized out of the air and dropped over him. He stumbled, then fell flat. She bounded up with her armload of strawberry/rutabaga supremes, swooped down, and rained gooshy pies on him in his net. Sveneric lay tangled on the pathway, making no effort to defend himself. When he was totally beslimed, and breathless with laughter, she dropped down beside him, giddy, her mind full of shifting light and magic—but when her gaze met his, she scowled.

He said, "You are in a net of your own making."

Humor zapped away like fireflies winking out.

"Shut up," she muttered.

He said, "Who are you?"

Dhana glared, her emotions in an angry turmoil.

Through it, clearly, his voice arrowed: "I can feel them, Dhana. Your kind, in the lake. They sense the shadow, and you are their hands and their eyes and their will. Will your hiding out in your underground cave bring Diana back to life?"

She tried to hurl a ball of inchoate magic at him—

But he was gone, leaving the dissolving net and glops of fake pie, which were already beginning to dissipate.

She stumbled, then fell, crying, until she heard Clair's voice. "Dhana? I heard yelling." She pointed up behind her at her room in the mountain, behind the waterfall.

"I hate that stinker! I hate his guts!" Dhana yelled, and kicked at the remains of the net as hard as she could.

"'So there' to who?" Clair asked, running up the path to join her.

"That scum of a Sveneric."

"I thought I heard two voices. He's here?"

"Yeah. Last night. Says he just escaped from the Host. I wish he'd go back."

"Dhana," Clair said with exasperation.

Dhana's mouth twisted into an unwilling grin, then her expression did one of its breathtaking transformations. "I don't like it. I don't understand it, and I want things to go back the way they were!"

Clair thought this over, then said, "To when?"

"When we were all together, having fun!"

"I too would love to have Irenne and Diana back. But would this be before the Shadow was destroyed and Kwenz and Wan-Edhe were constantly trying to ruin the kingdom, or after? if it's after, before or after Mearsieanne—"

"I don't want to be the eyes and the hands," Dhana said loudly. "I want to play, and dance, and I want all the girls to be here again, laughing."

"You want to be your human self?" Clair guessed. And on Dhana's nod, she said, "But your hair is still wet. No human could bear swimming in the stream now. It's nearly freezing."

Dhana turned away. "I don't want to change. I don't want anyone to change."

"What are you afraid of?" Clair shoved her hands deep into the pockets of her linsey-woolsey outer robe.

Dhana turned her back on the lake. "When I am in the waters, I am one with all. When I am human, I am one with all in a different way, but now that all is coming apart, and *they* fear the shadow, and I too fear the shadow. But they want me to act against the shadow as a human, not as a one with them." She spread her thin fingers over the water. "When we do magic as one, it's right. If I do it as me…I don't want to turn into the likes of Mearsieanne."

Clair said, "I guess I'm not ready to talk about Mearsieanne yet. But I will say this. You two couldn't possibly be more different from each other. How do you think you could be like her?"

"She had power. Responsibility. She loved having those things. And she thought she was always right. But we didn't think so." Dhana brooded. "When I came out of the Lake, it was to dance, and have music, and laughter and fun. They are giving me the magic. But I don't want it. What if I do it wrong, the way Mearsieanne did?" Dhana peered into Clair's face. "What if I hurt you more, the way Mearsieanne did?"

"I think I see that. A little. But how does this relate to Sveneric?"

"He stuck his nose in."

Clair said slowly, "How?"

"He sees me in both forms. I *hate* that."

Clair sighed, looked up at the bare trees interlaced overhead and the gray sky beyond. "*I* hate passing on rumors without checking, but I was told that he wasn't just bagged."

"Huh?"

"He, uh, let himself get taken."

"Why?"

"I don't know."

"I asked him how, not why," Dhana muttered. "He said it was stupidity."

"Whatever he did it for might have turned out wrong. But the thing is, no one would do that except because of a sense of responsibility."

"I don't want to change," Dhana whispered desolately.

Clair shut her eyes. "I will fight the shadow for us both."

Dhana looked at her in horror, true emotion welling up, breaking the patterns she had been mimicking from the girls for the time they'd been together.

Overwhelmed with new, painful emotions — regret, guilt, the shock of Clair's willingness to sacrifice herself to protect her and the others — she flickered into a ray of light and vanished into the water.

In the Selenseh Redian, Sveneric collapsed onto a cushion next to the low desk where Siamis had been working. Siamis glanced into an adjacent cave, where he'd spread out a bedroll not far from the running stream that provided the cold, clear water that tasted so pure. Sveneric saw the top of Jilo's black head, and sensed that Jilo was deeply asleep.

Sveneric lowered his voice to a murmur under the rush of the running water. "I spent the night lessoning myself in foreseeing consequences, yet I just came from acting on impulse with Dhana of the Mearsieans." He laced his fingers, turned them palms-out, then flexed them. "Maybe it was a bad idea?"

He looked so earnest. Siamis regarded him with sympathy, trying to remember what it was like to be that age, but for him the After all but overshadowed the vague memories of Before. There was one Before memory seared forever in merciless clarity. His mother had walked with him on the terrace after his tutor had scolded him for a thoughtless error in his work. She said, *Make your mistakes while you are young, my dear, when they don't matter.* A few weeks later, the asters had just vanished and the chrysanthemums began to bloom before he ran down a woodland path, and came face to face with Efael.

With the ease of long habit he shut that away and said to Sveneric, "Dhana has been playing the role of a human girl for so long without actually being one. She loves the role. She loves the camaraderie. But humans are not anything like the lake beings, who apparently live for centuries, as near as we can tell. Dhana is having trouble resolving her dual nature, but the unseen world seems to want her to act as one of their voices. Your instinct was right."

Sveneric shivered; humans could so easily be eradicated, if the world's beings so decided. But Ilerian didn't care because he, too, played a role as a human, and would jettison it at will.

Siamis said, "Leave her be now that you've made your point. Detlev has cautioned Atan and me, in different ways, to leave the Mearsieans to themselves as much as we can."

"For Clair?"

"Just so. Let's go up to the palace and get a solid meal into you. From the looks of you, you're still several meals behind. Then you'll come back here, and I'll fix you up a place to sleep."

They transferred to the palace. Sveneric scanned the kitchen, lit by the low autumn sunrays. A window stood open, letting in cold, pine-scented air from straight off the vast woodland below, but the room—unlike the castles he had been in—was not cold. Staff went about their daily chores, washing, chopping, mixing, and preparing wholesome foods, their chatter easy in tone. All so very different from the toxic elegance of that palace in Imar.

Sveneric thickly buttered a hunk of bread still warm from the oven, and plopped on a cushion. "Is there any word about Imry?"

"None." Siamis poured fresh citrus juice for them both. "He has effectively vanished."

Five

A village high in the mountains of Erdrael Danara

"GRAN! I SEE MURLIF." Tis, a seven-year-old boy who could already do three simple weaves, shouted through the open doorway of his great-grandmother's cottage.

The old woman known all over the mountain community simply as Gran cocked her head, hearing that breathless treble, then examined the room in satisfaction. As well they'd done a good cleaning yesterday. Still, she draped the loom and hobbled about, flecking dust off lamps, and turning the fruit bowl around so that the crack was hidden. Then she checked for the fifth or sixth time that the waiting stock of fronds was thoroughly covered.

Finally, she arranged herself at the loom in time to be "surprised" by the sight of the white-shrouded figure toiling up the road.

Gran pursed her lips as she stared out at the large, handsome woman named Murlif, broad-shouldered and dark-browed, with great quantities of shining dark hair that she wore in complicated braids atop her head. Her sixty-odd years only showed on the rare occasions she was tired, or when she acknowledged defeat, equally rare. Or when she stalked up the mountain as fast as she could, like now.

Gran smiled primly. Thirty-five of her ninety-six years had

been spiced by the enjoyment of an unrelenting feud with Murlif. It was true they'd declared a truce because of the war. Gran looked forward to the rivalry's resumption.

Murlif arrived at the door with a whistle of relief, and dropped her bunched white skirts. Gran rose, and as Murlif stamped in, said, "You look in that mourning like a ship sailing backward in a headwind."

Murlif gave one mighty, slightly wheezy guffaw, then shot back, "I don't see you in colors, you old prune!"

Gran's mouth pursed into a spidery-lined button. "Arlit-Small says the stonebacks don't approve of us in mourning."

Murlif retorted with prompt sarcasm, "And of course the stonebacks patrol up here, every day, just so's you can score 'em off."

"See what happens if they do," Gran said, leaning to pour caif into two tiny porcelain cups.

Caif was scalded and grated coffee that had steeped for two days, then beaten into egg till it was mostly foam. Sometimes cream was added, when coffee was scarce. Gran's precious stash was getting low, and this serving was more egg and cream than coffee, but manners were manners.

Aloud she said, "I didn't expect anyone up here this week." Implying that she drank caif out of four-generation-old porcelain every day.

Murlif snorted, accepted the tiny cup in her large hand, and sipped with a loud, appreciative hiss as she gazed around as if she expected to uncover a spy in the tiny room whose furnishings she had seen for decades.

By chance, of course, her gaze rested last on the muslin-draped stand in the loom-corner and she rapidly assessed its size. Murlif asked bluntly, "You going to do a kingsfold this winter, huh, Gran?"

Gran sniffed, slurped some caif, then said. "Who can afford—"

Murlif sighed, clashing her cup down. "Come now, Gran. First you're rich enough to drink this every day, and now you'll tell me you're reduced to eating grass and weaving with boiled ragweed. I'm too busy to jaw away half the day, even if—"

Gran hadn't thought she'd get Murlif off-balance before getting to the bargaining, but she'd enjoyed trying. "I forget." Her nose lifted. "How little you know of civilized converse."

Snort!

"So I'll talk business now, if you have to have it."

"Chimney." Murlif's dark brows arched. "Saw the worst of it coming up the path. It'll be a long job." She tapped a fingernail against her teeth, looking across the room at the boarded-up hole in the wall and ceiling where the chimney had been.

"Yes," Gran snapped. "A long job, and I know you'll need extra help, and I know we can't go a winter without. But if you try to gouge me, Arlit-Small can bring up some town-jobbers before I'll—"

Another mighty snort from Murlif and a loud finishing slurp drowned the rest of the threat. "That's enough from you, Queen Pursepinch, as if I was some thieving flatlander—"

Their heads turned as Tis bounded into the room, his hands catching the doorframe to keep him from falling flat on the scoured wood floor. His round seven-year-old face was crimson, his eyes wide with amazement. "A man!" he squeaked. "In the carrots!" Rad hair tufting all over his head added to his astonished expression.

Murlif's brows arched. Gran rocked and wheezed to her feet, Murlif following unasked. The women stepped down onto the path around the side of the house.

Tis's breath puffed past his ear as he hopped with impatience. "There!" He stabbed a finger toward the far part of the vegetable garden.

And there he was, lying face down across the last beets and carrots of the season, on the hard, near-frozen ground.

Silence only lasted the space of a few heartbeats, then Gran sighed. Watched her breath cloud, then disappear. "Get him in, I suppose. Saw him come, boy?"

Tis gave his head a violent shake. "I didn't see no one, all day. Came here just now to do my digging." For it was time to bring those root vegetables in, no matter how small they were. The ground would be iron by week's end.

"Coulda been there for candles," Murlif said. "No coat."

"Well he ain't dead." Gran's knees popped as she bent. "I see a puff o' breath. Must be result of mischief from the stonebacks. Though I've never hearda them pulling their magic tricks up in our parts."

Murlif shrugged, and stepped down over the rows. "You each take a leg."

Gran sniffed at being given orders in her own vegetable garden, but she moved out of Murlif's way. Murlif was certainly strong enough to carry the top half. She bent, gripped the man under the armpits, then yanked one hand back and frowned at the smear of blood. She shook her head, bent again, and with a grunt heaved the man up against her. Gran and Tis each picked up a booted foot, and all worked their way slowly to the front of the house and inside.

"My bed!" Gran croaked.

Murlif carefully laid the man on Gran's high-piled pillows, and helped roll him under the quilted comforter. Then Gran sank into a chair, staring bemusedly at her inadvertent guest, who hadn't wakened during the transport. Murlif frowned at the smears of blood down the front of her gown, and plumped her hands on her hips. "Glad I was here, eh?"

"Tis and I woulda managed."

"Hah!"

"By rolling him on a blanket and dragging him. Though I'd as soon be spared washing a blanket when it's near to freezing and no chimney."

Murlif boomed, "Then time to stop your chatter and let's get on with it! I tell ya, after the next show, I'm closing the forge. Seems everyone on the mountain had metal work this summer, and me hardly able to begin a rack—"

"Ho! So it's my fronds you're after. I thought so. And Arlit-Small about to be made journey, the equipment to come from my empty pocket. I'll make you a full length of three-grade, then you won't have to go to the trouble trying to meet my quality, though it takes you all winter!"

"Your quality! Maybe in the ought-years, before any *real* weavers were trained—"

The two women, absorbed in their spirited altercation, had forgotten the erstwhile addition to the vegetables. Tis hovered about, though, staring with interest. Rare was the stranger in his life, and never one in his house. Wouldn't the boys down-mountain boil!

His accumulating catalogue of the stranger's promising strangenesses was interrupted when the man's eyes opened briefly, found Tis's grinning face, and closed again.

"So, Thursday, weather-willing," Murlif was saying when Tis cut in, "He opened his eyes!"

Murlif paused, laughed heartily. "Not for long!"

Behind, Gran's cracked voice wailed, "Still bleeding? My good sheets!"

"You'll have heat by week's end. Now. Let's see what we have here." Murlif bent over the man. "Not very old. Lace-front shirt instead of buttons like toffs wear, but it's good fabric. Made with very fine seam-stitching. Shame it's ruined."

"No knife. No sword," Tis put in, disappointed.

"And what would you do if he had 'em?" Murlif laughed at the boy. "Cut up your peas? I didn't think of weapons. But that might explain the calluses on his hands." Murlif's broad forefinger prodded an upturned palm, then she turned on the boy.

"Tis knows better," Gran stated. "He won't say a thing."

Tis slumped with disappointment.

Murlif gave a mammoth snort. "Or at least you *should* know. With a dead mother, and who knows where your gran is, and your grand-uncle, and all them cousins..."

Tis sighed. "Won't say nothin'." His attitude made it clear: then what was the use of having him inside?

Gran had plenty of decades' practice reading faces. "Huh! That I should live to see kin not willing to help those that need it. I—durse! If that isn't sweat!" She frowned down at the man on the bed.

And she was startled when the closed eyes opened, and the man said, clearly enough, though not very loud, "I've been poisoned."

"Smells funny," Tis corroborated, sniffing at an arm.

Gran surveyed her guest. "Well, if you know that, then you know what of. What do you need?"

"Water."

"That we've got, and aplenty. Tis, fetch a fresh bucket."

The boy whisked himself out. Gran stacked her cups, muttering to herself. She repeated every insult of Murlif's, sniffing after each, and then followed the boy out in order to wash the dishes in the well bucket, which was the only thing left with the clean-water spell still functioning.

The silence afforded Imry Llyenthur a small measure of relief. He knew he was stuck. After the duel in which Efael had used a poison knife, Llyenthur had tried three times to transfer, and each time barely made it a short distance—always to a Destination within sight—before passing out. If he tried another transfer right away, there was a good chance he'd become another mark on a D.I.T. list. Any movement sent blinding white pain through his brain, making it impossible to think or act. But at least he was fairly certain he'd made it over the Chwahir border, and out of range of the Black Knives' search. The Danaran mountains were full of tiny hidden hamlets, a nightmare for a hard target hunt; still, these locals ought to have heard something of a search. Unless Efael had called it off. Only what would cause that?

No knowing. Yet.

He assessed the immediate situation. Propped in a bed too small for him, his top half on this mountain of pillows, bootheels resting gently on the floor. Personnel seemed to be two old women who quarreled about leddas weaving, and a small boy hopping about, staring with the air of a stray dog hopeful of scraps.

They were all three determined to keep him from being discovered by the local Norsundrian command.

Situation: ridiculous. But no danger.

He gave up trying to clear the fire out of his brain. When the urchin returned with water, he drank, then gave up his hold on consciousness.

Six

HE WAS DRIVEN BACK into awareness from time to time by the increase in heat-pain that indicated he needed more water. The bucket had been placed on a stool at his elbow, the ladle toward him. The work involved in reaching for it, holding it so he could slurp up water, and dropping it back, sent him out again, for several repeats.

But the last time or so he noted a few more things. His shirt was gone, an herbal-smelling salve over Efael's cut. The bucket was full each time. The old woman in a corner at a heavy loom, muttering in a singsong as her fingers worked. Once—the window light indicated early morning—the boy sat nearby, and as Llyenthur's hand began its journey bucketward, he eagerly performed the job instead.

The room was dark when, at last, consciousness held. Llyenthur felt the closed windows, the sounds of other breathing, and the still cold air closing in like a smothering blanket. He pushed the quilt onto the floor.

The movement of hand and arm ignited fire along his nerves again. Aware now of a reddish glow across the room, on the tiny makeshift grate, he thought backward, comparing the intensity of this poison-pain with that of his hands being thrust into the fire by his father...

Mathen Erdea's face, when fire consumed his wood-carvings, for harboring a fugitive—

David smiling. Saying, *What the real joke is—*

Imry stilled the spiraling thoughts. The light quick breathing, and the older raspy breathing, the close room, all made sleep impossible.

There was nothing to do but wait until the sun came up.

The room slowly filled with weak gray light, revealing the old woman in the other wooden bunk, under heavy quilts. Above her, the boy lay in a hammock. As Imry watched, the hammock jiggled, then a head and hand appeared.

"Yer awake!" the boy whispered.

Below him, the old woman snorted.

The boy peered down anxiously, waited, then flipped expertly out of the hammock and landed in his stocking feet with no more noise than a cat. He looked at the quilt on the floor. "Aren't you cold?"

"No."

"I hate cold, 'less it snows. We can't have a good fire till the chimney's fixed. Want some more water?"

"Not now."

The snub freckled nose wrinkled appreciatively, the dark brown eyes lively with glee. "You smell kinda like pepper-stew. Izzat the poison?"

"Yes."

"Poison," the boy repeated, clearly impressed. "Was it a real villain, a stoneback?"

"Yes."

"Wha'd he do? Stick it in your food?"

"Knife."

"Knife? Like in a real fight?"

"Yes."

The boy breathed in ecstasy. "I wish—" Then he sidled a quick look at his great-grandmother. "Not supposed to want to see a battle. Maybe I don't want a bad one, like where my uncle and granddad and my ma got killed. I'd like to see a hero, with a magic sword, smashing the stonebacks, and saving everybody! Did you ever see that?"

Imry's lips twitched.

"You gonna go back and get 'im?" The boy made an enthusiastic stabbing motion, at an angle that would have done little damage to anyone but himself. "When yer better, I mean?"

"Possibly."

The boy sighed. "I'd want to, that's for sure." He looked at inward visions for a time, then returned abruptly to the immediate. "Where d'ya come from? What were you doing?"

"Better if you don't know."

"A spy? Are you a spy against the stonebacks?"

Imry was tired of the boy and his questions, and his expression showed it. He reached for the water. Tis was swift to help, then he reluctantly withdrew, with many backward glances. He had to begin his morning chores before the weather struck, he couldn't resist informing Imry before he disappeared.

The sound of the door closing woke the old woman. She and the boy had slept in their many-layered clothes. Still, she moved stiffly as she put water to boil over her little fire. She talked continuously while performing her domestic tasks. Did he want the quilt back on? No? Any food? Even a biscuit? Hers were so good, unlike the rocks to be had down at the forge...

Finally Imry shut his eyes and pretended to sleep.

Gran kept up her muttering, but now it was directed at the loom. When he opened his eyes again she was seated at her place, a clump of long, pliable strands of brownish fiber hanging near her right hand. A thin strip of finished product on the heavy loom was recognizable as what was called khardeg, or leddas-weave, the finest grade. Subtle patterns had been woven into this belt, probably for sale to aristocrats in Colend. Khardeg being finer, less stiff, than the leddas out of which most shoes and boots were made.

The old woman's mind was wholly absorbed in her work. Imry lay passively, watching her fingers.

Outside the wind rose, and rattled the windows.

After an hour or so the door banged open and the small boy stumbled in. "Gran!" he yelped, but his excited face was turned toward Imry. "Arlit-Small's here! She's got news!"

Gran clapped her hands, then covered her work and went to stoke up the tiny makeshift fire.

Imry was silent, gathering what strength he could.

The door banged open again, and a tall girl with Tis's snub nose and dark eyes entered. Arlit, daughter of Arlit, granddaughter and great-granddaughter of two more Arlits, never knew how close she came to death that day. Her face, red-cheeked from a dash in cold weather, turned first toward Imry, but (despite her anxiously hopping small brother) her interest was at best superficial. Her news, then, was not him.

"What's that? In the carrots?" she said absently to her chattering brother, then turned to her great-grandmother as she lowered a heavy pack to the floor. "Guess what! I had to come and tell you, though I thought the blow would catch me for sure." As she spoke the wind moaned and hail rattled against the walls and on the roof. "I've been made journey!"

"Well!" Gran clapped her hands.

"And!" Arlit went on portentously, "What's more, soon's the war's done and the graywits are gone and we can travel again, I'm to be sent to Colend to learn colored glass!"

"You have your mother's eye," Gran said, smirking and nodding. "Runs through the females in my line. Why d'you think I'm still first at the fairs?"

Though this brag had actually been for Imry's sake, Arlit grinned. "Granddad told me *his* people were artists."

"Your granddad talks to weeds, because they are too stupid not to listen," Gran rejoined in a crisp voice. "But what can you expect from a family who'd see a cousin marry a loud, worthless old—"

"Never mind Murlif and the forge folk," Arlit cut in impatiently. "I still have not finished. What I need to know is, will you help me get my glazier tools, or must I pledge my first year's earnings?"

"Of course I'll provide," Gran said indignantly. "Ninety-six years, and never have I let mine go into debt, even in '24, when that—"

Arlit grabbed at Gran's hands and kissed them. "Oh, thank you. Oh, caif!" She sighed as Gran poured a cup. And she took a long, slurping sip.

Tis, who'd listened in silence, pulled at his sister's heavy wool skirt. Arlit looked down and reached to ruffle the boy's thick red hair. "No, I didn't forget you. Go ahead and unpack the bag." And, up at Gran, "I bought some things, but I had to sell my last strip of kingsfold."

"I'm planning a new one," Gran returned, then frowned. "Once that nosy crow is gone for the winter."

Arlit laughed. "Gran! If it wasn't for Murlif, half the village would be dead! And, I'll wager winter's wages it's she who's going to rebuild the chimney. Isn't it?"

"Tomorrow, weather-willing." Tis looked up from his careful unloading of Arlit's shapeless pack.

"She tried to gouge me for my gold-gradation dyes. And dared to hint at my kingsfold pattern—"

"Just to butter you up," Arlit stated. "Hers gets the same

price as ours, down-mountain. I know, because I was with Hass when he sold—"

"Arlit-Small!" Gran was scandalized. "You aren't—"

"Fraternizing with the enemy?" Arlit looked sardonic, then she sighed. "With half both families dead, and stone-wits crawling everywhere hoping to kill the rest of us for sport if we look wrong, the forge folk just don't seem like foes any more. Nor should they be, if you'd just admit—"

"This for me?" Tis had set all the cloth-wrapped little packages out, and help up a plain, short-bladed knife.

"Yes."

At once the boy was up, prancing around, jabbing with inept enthusiasm at an imaginary enemy. Imry, who'd made his first kill at a far younger age, watched in derisive silence.

Arlit knocked Tis's hand aside. "Watch. You nearly kicked over Gran's caif. That's for carving, not fighting. Cousin Mikon said he thought you had an eye."

"You saw Kiref's boy?"

"Yes. He's still running as courier," Arlit replied, some of her humor fading.

"Cousin Mikon! Has he seen the king?" Tis piped up as he reached for a small piece of firewood.

"Doubt it." Arlit shrugged. "We never talk war. Not since Mama died. Durse! I'm so hungry. I was out of town before sunup, so the wall-riders wouldn't see me."

Gran rose, but Arlit pushed her down. "I'll fix it. Go back to the loom. We'll need it. That's so horrid about the chimney. But you need heat in here." She squinted up at the hole where the fire's warmth escaped.

"Was that killer summer storm," Tis said with proud horror. "Took part of the waterfall-miller's roof. Their boys got to sleep in the barn."

"Storm was even worse on the coast, I hear," Arlit said, and began unwrapping her packages. "Coffee, herbs. Some of this pretty blue thread."

Imry's ladle plunked back into the bucket, and the other three froze for a heartbeat. They had forgotten him. They smiled politely, remembering the stranger in Gran's little bed.

Tis said, "You'll have the hammock tonight, Arlit."

Arlit shook her head. "No, soon's weather lifts I'll go back down. I'm on counter tomorrow afternoon. Though business is bad." She was eyeing Imry with more interest now that her news had been shared. "Can I fix you something to eat?"

"No."

"He was poisoned!" Tis put in triumphantly.

Arlit frowned. "Aren't you bloodthirsty, little ant!"

"From a knife fight! With a stoneback!"

Arlit turned a speculative gaze onto Imry. "How did you get up here?"

"Magic."

Arlit studied him a few moments longer, mouth pursed. Then she grunted softly. "I guess I'd rather not know more. There's enough to worry about, the things I can do." She looked over at Gran. "Who knows that he's here?"

"Murlif," Gran said with a sniff. "And she'll bring quiet help."

"You sound like a wet reed," Tis muttered at his sister, sulking.

Arlit looked disgusted. "You just button that lip. When the call comes to rise and fight, I'll fight alongside everyone else, best I'm able. But I don't want to kill anybody, and I don't want to be killed. And I don't want to come up here one day and find that you've all been killed for harboring a fugitive."

"No one's going to be killed," Gran said. "And no one passes my front door that I don't want in. Have to pass me first."

Imry envisioned Efael smiling as he cut old Gran down with one casual strike, then stepping over her body to look for more victims before she'd finished twitching. From Arlit's expression she was having similar thoughts, but she said only, "Let's eat."

The hailstorm ended suddenly not long after noon. Before the sun set, Arlit hefted her pack, settled her dark cloak close about her, and after a kiss for Gran and Tis and a terse "Fare well" to Imry, she was gone.

Gran sat at her loom until late, her old voice muttering verses of ancient songs. Tis was mostly silent as he carved away at his firewood. His red head and clumsy hands reminded Imry of David, at that age, just by the contrast.

He shut his eyes, closing them all out.

The long night, measured by the ceaseless soft breathings, was passed in reviewing logistical considerations in relation to current plans.

There was no point in bothering with conjecture about Larkadhe. He'd find out when he got back.

In the morning, which dawned clear and even colder than before, he discovered that he was hungry. Gran gladly gave him a portion of their tough, tasteless bread, and for a short time he set his skull on fire by chewing it. He finished the bread largely as an experiment; if he could eat it and hold onto consciousness, maybe he could handle magic transfer again.

Not yet, though. He lay like an upended turtle, concentrating on gathering strength, as Gran bustled about, cleaning then preparing a large soup. An hour after dawn voices—and Murlif's booming laugh—were heard outside. None of the people entered the house. Tis was happily engaged on running in and out on small errands.

Gran also hobbled in and out, her high, reedy voice heard over Murlif's deep one. Imry sent his mind out as an experiment. Two men and one woman comprised the help. All mountain folk, busy, limited minds. Limited experience. Silent, unquestioning allegiance to Murlif. The female worker disliked Gran, but kept it inside her head as her hands labored willingly at caulking stones that the men brought.

One of the men fostered the verbal clashes between Murlif and Gran, a mischievous effort making the drudgery lighter. None of them spared a thought to the outside world.

The sense of community reminded Imry, as it must, of his boyhood days in Detlev's group. He acknowledged the memory, then wondered where they all were—the ones still alive. Gathering? Or sent out on runs? The pattern of bids for his attention—each characteristic—could mean anything, though the strangest had been Sveneric's. Nearly disastrous, the pompous young idiot and his big yap.

No current data made speculation boring. Imry dismissed conjecture, touching Murlif's mind out of idle curiosity. Her thoughts ran to the job at hand, and the demands waiting down in the village, and once, in a sudden flare of grief and anger, she wished the husband she'd shared with the female were still alive, but at least she and Lin had each other, and snuffed the grief like a guttering candle.

Bored and restless, Imry withdrew. There were no real parallels; finding in such people reminders of his past meant it was time to be gone.

He was startled by a shout, a shriek, and a clattering roar. Choking dust drifted in through the sudden hole in the chimney-wall.

"Murlif! Murrrr-lif!" Lin sobbed, as one of the men bellowed in anguish. "It's come down on her!"

A blast of fire through muscles and bones, then Imry found himself leaning in the doorway. Pain-fire licked up his spine as he blinked down at a scene of horror-still figures. Scratched hands had just pulled the last of the fallen chimney rocks off two of the people. One of the men, with an already lame leg, rocked back and forth in silent agony. And, lying on her back with her shocked eyes open, was Murlif.

Gran threw her apron over her head as Lin knelt, sobbing, over and over, "Murlif? Can you move? Let's move you, huh? Murlif?"

"Spine's snapped," Imry said, looking at Murlif.

All the heads turned toward him, white faces drawn with shock.

Murlif's eyes read helplessly over the sky. Lynchpin of the little community flattened, like a helpless beetle. If they moved her (and they were about to) they'd kill her.

And that clean break so easy to fix.

Instinct focused the fire in Imry's brain. He didn't even see his hand rise, or the blue fire. He felt Murlif's body jolt and her loud gasp of relief, and then the fire rebounded and hit him.

A brief glimpse of awed faces. That expression, and the fire, and the cool echoing boy's voice *My father saw in you* — all nauseated him and again he acted without thinking, and got himself out of there.

But this time he made it to one of his hideouts. So when the inevitable reaction knocked him out, he was, at least, alone.

Seven

DAWN IN MEARSIES HEILI was a couple hours off. Everyone in the white palace and the Selenseh Redian below it was asleep, except for Siamis, finishing his usual night watch. His eyes burned, and his neck twinged from steady work. He was contemplating walking the spire labyrinth when he sensed impending transfer, and laid his pen down.

Detlev appeared, his expression grim. "You'd better come with me." He flipped Siamis a transfer token.

"Where?"

"To Mondros." Detlev vanished.

Siamis braced. Transferring from the caves was safest to other caves. Transferring to locations that might be warded by Norsunder, as were all the former public Destinations, was the danger, unless one had the latest version of the transfer spell. But there were places Norsunder did not—yet—know about, which had their own protective wards. Mondros's cottage high in the mountains between Colend and Chwahirsland was one of these.

Siamis appeared on a snowy cliff in time to see Mondros recovering from shock at Detlev's sudden appearance.

Detlev was saying, "… Jilo gave me your pass-through."

Mondros ran a massive hand over his face and over his thick black beard, eyed Siamis from under bushy brows, then said in an abyssal rumble, "The two of you turning up together like this has to be bad news."

Detlev did not respond until the three of them went inside the cottage, and at a gesture from Mondros, they all sat at the table. Siamis smelled a berry pie baking, a homey reminder that occasionally regular life did exist.

Detlev laid a battered book on the table, the outer page written in Chwahir.

"That's Kessler's," Mondros exclaimed. "He gave it to Jilo, who copied out the lattice ward spells for me. The rest was evil, and mostly unfinished. Speculation, or experiments. I didn't ask Jilo to toil copying something I would never use."

Detlev said, "The rest is experiments with the blood mage text, to be precise, and some other uses for lattice magic. Yes, abandoned, but I've spent a few days studying it, and believe I've figured out where he was going with his inquiries."

Mondros looked uneasy. "Has it to do with Chwahirsland?"

"It has to do with Norsunder-Beyond," Detlev said. "I believe Kessler's intent is to take Norsunder-Beyond for himself."

That silenced Siamis and Mondros, a silence so tense no one breathed for a heartbeat or two. The only sound was the snow patting the windows; up at this height, winter was already here.

Mondros frowned, saying slowly, "I thought that was always his goal. Well, Norsunder Base, anyway, though I remember overhearing wild talk about him wanting to take over all of Norsunder. But I thought once he left Norsunder, he forgot about it. Especially after he turned up with that boy. Does anyone know how that came to pass? Was he involved with a woman? Somehow I cannot imagine the Birth Spell working for him."

Detlev spread his hands. "If there was anyone else involved, he's kept that secret from Dirk as well as the rest of the world."

"We all assumed his talk about taking Norsunder was just that, talk," Siamis said. And to Detlev, "Did he state taking Norsunder-Beyond as a plan anywhere in that notebook?"

"No. It was the method of his inquiries suggesting this as a probable outcome. That, added to the ward keeping the Host pinned here, makes the probable likely."

"*Why* would he do that?" Mondros said hoarsely.

"That I cannot answer."

Siamis said, "Then he's waiting to see who wins? No. He

wants us to win, if for no other reason than because whenever that ward is broken, the first ones in will be Ilerian and Svir."

Detlev said, "Correct."

Mondros ran his hands over his face, grimaced, then said, "I don't advocate this, but it seems to me that in the not-so-distant past, you've had no scruples about holding someone hostage against someone else to get what you wanted. And you do have Dirk among your followers, do you not?"

"Even if I were willing to brandish Dirk in order to lure Kessler, I doubt it would work," Detlev said evenly. "He'd probably let the boy die—and then he would make it a priority to come after and take out every one of my people, beginning with Sveneric."

Mondros grimaced. "It was an unworthy thought anyway. And I probably shouldn't be flinging your past in your teeth."

If that was an oblique request for clarification—or justification—for Detlev's past actions, it failed. Detlev said, "Kessler does help us now and then, this book being an example. He wants the Host destroyed as much as we do."

Siamis said slowly, "This possible goal of his would explain why his aid is always a lightning strike, here and gone again. Otherwise, why not join us? Plan with us?"

Mondros rocked back and forth on his bench a couple of times, humming under his breath, then he looked up. "And you're here because?"

Detlev tapped the book. "What you haven't seen in this is Jilo's latest work. He's been at it for months, intensively of late. He's found a way to reverse the blood poison spell Wan-Edhe lays on his upper command, and others around him, to control them. At least, I believe he's found it. I need to test it, preferably on a willing volunteer."

Mondros sighed. "And you're not asking Jilo whom to try it on because in his mind, they all need to be dispelled yesterday."

"Right. He'll do what he must, but at this juncture I want to make sure it works, and on the best candidate, one who will not betray Jilo to Norsunder even inadvertently. Wan-Edhe has purged so many of his commanders that I don't know the new ones well enough to judge."

Mondros grunted. "I don't know the naval commanders. Of the army, the best would be Crimson General Furo, commanding the occupation of Colend from Alsais. He's not only favoring Jilo as much as he dares, he looks the other way in the barter system the Chwahir and the Colendi have invented. I'm convinced the only reason there is no bloodbath in Colend, unlike other places, is a kind of wary, distant cooperation between Shontande Lirendi, who is still at large, and General Furo."

"Barter?" Siamis repeated.

"You do know that Wan-Edhe has never paid his army? Of course you know — that's been true for a couple centuries now."

"Right. Back to Kessler; if he turns up, perhaps try to lay him by the heels?" Detlev then indicated the scry stone set amid a jumble of books and papers, turned to Siamis, and said, "Get a report, will you?" And he vanished.

Siamis let out a breath, as did Mondros. "Is that scrystone functional?" Siamis asked.

"Yes."

"I take it you disengaged it from the Scribe Guild's desk before it was brought down?" The spell — as Siamis well knew — that had dismantled the centuries-old communications net called the "scribe desk" had spread to all connected scribe desks and scry stones, so that Norsunder would not be able to use it.

"Early on," Mondros said. "Very early on, at Tsauderei's insistence. It is closed contact, only the two of us."

"Then you are in contact with Tsauderei?"

"Of late it's every night, or most nights," Mondros said, scratching his chin through his beard with his pen. "Tsauderei can't get out of his chair anymore, but his mind is as alert as it ever was." Mondros gave Siamis a pained glance. "Gives him something to live for. Says he refuses to die before Norsunder is defeated. "

Mondros then looked about the comfortable room, crowded with books. "Detlev wants an update? All I can give you is what Tsauderei and I do, and a certain amount of what I can glean of the Chwahirs' occupation of Colend."

"I'd like to hear it."

"Tsauderei digs for old wards. And he completes spell-clusters for me, then gives me the enchantment keys, so all I have to do is shape them for Wan-Edhe. That old snake has to waste a good part of every damn day unraveling the mess I add to his wards in Narad, while I weaken the border wards here and there, in random attacks. It's driving him mad. Madder. Especially as he cannot spend all his time chasing me down. The phantom me. He still does not know who I am. He has to drop everything and do what the Host tell him, especially these past few days. For some reason they've accelerated their efforts to break Kessler's ward."

"I'll pass that on to Detlev. And to Atan, who is keeping a master map."

"Atan?" Mondros repeated.

"In Mearsies Heili. Though she's never lifted a sword, she has turned out to be a superlative strategist. If you'd like to write to her directly, use this." Siamis gave Mondros one of his magic-papers, then explained how it worked.

Mondros laid it carefully beside the scry stone, then said, "Where is Jilo? How is he?"

Siamis told him. Mondros glowered when he heard about the toxic effect that Jilo had endured in his race to master the lethal blood poison spells, but at the end, he was so relieved he could not sit still. He got up and walked about the little cottage, as snow fell softly outside the windows. "I know it'll sound strange, but in a sense he's more my boy than Rel. Puddlenose, too. Not that I don't care for my boy. I do. Always have. But he doesn't need me. Jilo does."

"You will hear no argument from me," Siamis said. "Speaking of family, would you like to hear the latest about your surviving Glenereth relations? I don't mean Rel, who I believe is in Sartor."

Mondros had been fussing in his kitchen corner, but at that he turned, his deep-set eyes wide. "Not if it's ..." He didn't finish that.

"Markham Glenereth is leading the resistance over there. I believe he's got four countries involved, if not more."

"Markham," Mondros murmured. "Little Markham. He was the best of the children, and it broke my heart to leave him, because I knew they would ruin him as they nearly did to me. When I was exiled and disinherited, I swore I would never go back. I would forget they even existed. I've never been back, though I've wondered. I weakened enough once to send Rel in that direction, a few years ago, but he didn't cross over the border."

Siamis smiled. "Markham is not so little. He's as tall as Rel. Leaner. Not just formidable martial skills, but a superlative commander; he and Jason Szinzar learned together, though everyone assumed Markham was a mere liegeman, as the troubles you foresaw did end with him losing name and lands. But he will have to tell you that story when you meet. He has a son. Lexan."

Mondros sat heavily. "Markham. Alive." *For now.* But the information was a gift, and he was grateful. "Thank you."

While Siamis spoke with Mondros, Detlev had come and gone again, the cumbersome transfers a relatively sure method. Of course Norsunder's transfer spell had been changed once Sveneric forced Yeres to send him—but the real threat was the Host's reaction to Sveneric's escape. Ilerian had been prowling the mental realm ceaselessly once he had finished soul-ripping Connanre—which had, as Detlev feared, granted him a leap in power.

But that was no surprise. Detlev had prepared over the years. He had Destinations planted in inconspicuous locations all over the world, and while there was always a chance one or another of the hunters pursuing him had discovered one and turned it into a trap, he would risk it when necessary.

It was necessary now.

As often happens, preparation took far longer than the actual act. He reached Alsais without discovery, and set about making himself virtually invisible: first he located an older healer's home, then stole a worn summer robe that had been cleaned and laid away for the winter.

The merest illusion over his hair was next, giving it a graying sheen and blurring his face to suggest lines. He adopted a bent posture, and walked through the city, listening and observing.

The most frequent publicly discussed topic was next year's Music Festival—so very Colendi. "It wouldn't be a real one," a baker was saying to a customer as Detlev bought a fresh muffin. "How could it be when there are no royal funds for readying?"

"And no foreigners coming," responded an innkeeper with a sigh.

"Probably no musicians, either," someone else offered. "Who can travel, except *them*?"

"Ah-ye, but we! We can make our own music, can we not?"

Through the brightly robed Colendi marched columns of Chwahir, immediately recognizable in their dull, fading greenish-black uniforms, their skin pale and their regulation short hair dark. No one on the streets spoke to them, nor did they speak, or even look when a small boy darted from behind a wisteria-decorated bower to jump with both feet on the last man's shadow.

The Chwahir marched on as a Colendi woman yanked the boy back by his sleeve, uttering a scandalized hiss.

Detlev made his bent-backed way to the palace, which the Norsunder command held. It was mostly Chwahir coming and going in orderly fashion, but here and there gray jackets moved about, avoided by Colendi and Chwahir alike. Very few of them. From this cursory glimpse, Detlev speculated that Imry had been gradually shifting Norsunder's forces out of Colend, needed elsewhere.

Erol, still living as a mole in Narad, had given Detlev the signs employed by the resistance to Wan-Edhe; using those and brief scans, he located Dassler Anjit, a mid-level "pen" — the Chwahir slang for scribe. A pen, who copied records and command-level orders, was regarded above a mere "ink," or a copier of lower-rank orders and lists.

The "hum" sign garnered the eyelid-lift of intense emotion, quickly hidden, and a prudent rapidity. Detlev was ushered along to the general's office, from which drifted the medicinal scent of ginger-root steep.

The general, a harassed man whose jowls were tinged with the sallow color of continuous digestive upset, looked warily at Detlev, who said, "*He* sent me." And the hum sign.

"To?"

"He believes he has constructed an antidote to the blood poison spell. He taught it to me, and I am here to ask if you are willing to attempt it."

Furo's faith in Jilo manifested in the swiftness of his whispered, "I will." Detlev had prepared the complicated spell ahead, so all he had to do is press a token into Furo's dry, slightly feverish hand, murmur the release spell, and watch as Furo jolted. Blinked. Drew a cautious breath. Then turned wide eyes to Detlev as he uttered in an escaping breath, "It's gone."

Detlev said, "It would be best to alter no habits. Keep drinking ginger-steep. It won't harm you. Do nothing that betrays the return of health."

He bowed in the manner of Chwahir servants, and return-ed to the healer's, put the robe through the family's cleaning frame and folded it away in the chest for summer storage, without anyone knowing he had been there.

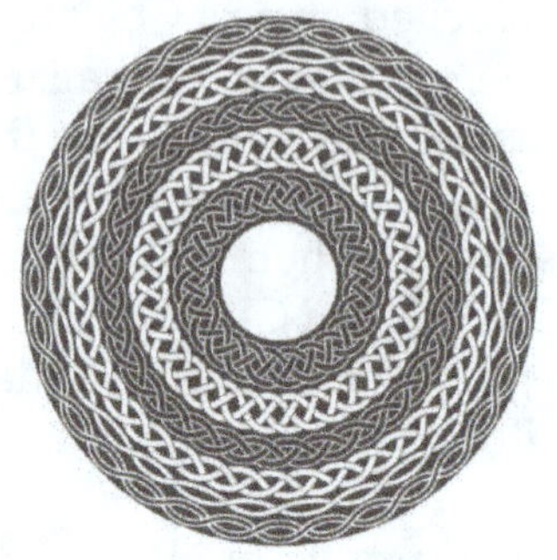

Eight

Mearsies Heili

WHENEVER TEN-YEAR-OLD PRINCESS MERSEDES Carinna Delieth of Everon passed a reflective surface, she forced herself to glance into it as a reminder that, though she loved beautiful things above all else, she was not, and never would be, one of them.

On her way down through the white palace of the Mearsieans, Carl caught her reflection in a window, and forced herself to take in that long, narrow face that looked like someone had clapped a couple of books to either side of her head when she was a baby, then yanked her ears out to fill the space. Lank, dull hair that faded into the darkness behind the window, a thin mouth exactly like Tahra-Mama's, sallow skin, and a scrawny body below.

Carl had once dared to ask Lyren-Sartora, the person she admired most in the world, if she ever looked in mirrors.

"Of course," Lyren-Sartora had said, surprised. "How else would I know if my parting is crooked, or I slopped soup on my front?"

Unsatisfied with this practical answer, Carl had dared edge toward the real subject. "Do you think that … beautiful people … like looking in mirrors? Do they see their own beauty?"

Lyren-Sartora had blinked as though the idea had never occurred to her. "Maybe? Only how boring would that be? If you're staring at yourself, then nothing interesting is happening. You may as well be a statue." Then she'd made a face. "I heard Detlev's boys talking once, when they came to Bereth Ferian. Someone said that terrible Yeres watches herself in the mirror. Maybe she's her favorite person in the world. Or else she's practicing poses. Yuch! Why did I think of her! Let's go out in the garden..."

Ever since, Carl kept her mirror-watching as short as she could, lest it turn her boring as well as homely. But she had to do it. When she was seven, people gave her sugary compliments about how smart she was, how pretty she would be, how clever. Tahra-Mama had said that that was because she was a princess, because they wanted something from Tahra-Mama, and when Carl dared to listen to surface thoughts, she discovered the falsity behind the sugary words. Carl had decided that she must forever remind herself what was truth and what was flattery.

Glance. Still plain.

When she reached the stairs, there were no more windows or mirrors, so no more duty. Much lighter in heart, she slipped down the stairs, peered around for anyone who would feel it necessary to ask where she was going, and then ran for the Destination chamber. Here, she conscientiously did the signs for transfer to the Selenseh Redian.

A small jolt, and cold air that smelled of running water and cedar and pine bathed her face, making her shiver. She'd forgotten that winter was coming. The white palace, though bigger than any palace she had ever seen, was so comfortable, like spring. Every other palace—including the royal palace in Ferdrian, at home in Everon—was either drafty or stuffy, sometimes both.

The whisper of voices down the uneven, jewel-bright passageway drew her. It was guilt, not fear, that kept her steps tentative, but when she sensed her twin's presence among the others, some of the tension left her. Then she saw Sveneric sitting cross-legged next to Jessan, and relief flooded her.

From long habit, Carl reached for Sveneric on the mental plane: *You're truly all right!* In response came Jessan's slightly aggrieved: *I would never lie to you.*

Carl's answer was quick, and contrite: *I know. But you hide bad things from me. Because I'm such a baby. I'm sorry. I can't help it.*

That was followed by Sveneric's reassuring, big brotherly: *You're not a baby, Carl. You're tender of heart. It's a good thing. But nobody wanted to worry you until I got out. And I did. And I won't do that again.*

"Would you like some apple-berry tarts?" Clair asked, pushing a dish toward Carl as she plopped down next to her brother.

Carl took one to be polite, but her attention was riveted to the bright silver cup sitting behind Jilo. He, noticing the direction of her gaze, and asked, "Are you thirsty?"

Carl said, "Where did you get that? They don't have cups like that in the dining room."

Clair laughed. "It's at least four thousand years old, and from another world."

Carl had stretched her hand toward the cup that Jilo help out, but she snatched her fingers back, gasping. "I wouldn't dare!"

"It's metal," Jilo said. "Not glass." He ran his fingers along the uneven surface, on which Carl could see individual hammer strikes. Yes, it truly looked old, but it was so brightly polished that it seemed to be made of a sunlit waterfall caught in metal.

Clair said, "And if you're worried about mysterious spells, it's inert. Jilo's been drinking out of it for days."

"If anything, I think the water is sweeter in it," Jilo said reflectively. "Though that might be only in my head."

Clair passed the cup from hand to hand. Carl thrilled to be touching something so old, and beautiful, and from unimaginably far away. Jessan took it from her and handed to Sveneric, who shut his eyes as he held it. "It's like it's hiding its magic. Sort of an odd feel."

"All I know is, it holds water," Jilo said as Sveneric gave it to him, and he set it with care behind him.

Jessan got to his feet. "Come on, Carl. Atan is on the move. Let's go."

Though they had been born at exactly the same moment, as can only happen with the Birth Spell, Carl was in the habit of letting her brother lead. "I had to see you. I'm so glad you're fine. If only we had Dirk and Ian with us," Carl said to Sveneric.

"They're both right where they want to be," Sveneric responded. "Ian is especially happy among the Goldenwoods."

Jessan waited until he and his twin were on their way to the Destination before he said, "Carl, I told you he was fine."

"I had to see," she said, her voice small.

"But you know Tahra-Mama is going to interrogate us the

moment she sees us again. And you hate lying. Start rehearsing your words now."

Carl's thin shoulders tensed. "I can't lie to Tahra-Mama."

"I *know*." Tender as Carl was, she could be surprisingly stubborn. "That's why we rehearse what we say."

They transferred, and as Jessan drew her down the hall to their suite, he gave her a dramatic scowl. "Did you stay away from that filthy, murdering Detlev and his spawn?"

Carl flinched—but she knew her mother would use those very words, or ones like them.

Jessan said in his normal voice, "Well, what do you say?"

The door banged open, and Madelon Elise bounced out, with white-haired Aurora trotting behind her. Madelon and Clair's daughter had become inseparable. Madelon crossed her arms. "You say, 'Tahra-Mama, Atan made sure that they never came to our wing, ever, ever, ever.'"

"Which is true," Jessan said, but then he frowned at Madelon. "But you don't need to be nosing."

"We could hear you in the hall," Madelon stated. "Huh, Aurora?"

"We could," Aurora said, though with sympathy.

Jessan rolled his eyes, then turned to Carl, and in a sharp, demanding voice, "Mersedes Carinna! Did you stay away from that evil, murdering rotten Detlev, who I will kill if he ever sets foot in Everon, and his evil, rotten son?"

Carl's lips twitched at Jessan's squeaky parody of their mother's voice, but she whispered, "It feels like lying."

Jessan hissed a loud sigh. "Carl. We've known the shrimp ever since we could hear." He tapped his head. "Have we ever heard an evil thought from him? Ever?"

"No."

"Whereas Tahra-Mama—no, don't get upset, I'm not going to say she's evil, of course not. But she hates for the sake of hatred, that's what Atan said when she didn't know I was in the alcove."

Carl jerked her head in a tiny nod, but her eyes sheened. Jessan firmed his resolve, because otherwise everything would be far worse if honest Carl blurted out all the truth to Tahra-Mama. "What are you going to say to Tahra-Mama?"

Carl blinked back the tears of remorse and said obediently, "Atan never let them anywhere near our rooms."

"Good. Keep practicing that."

Nine

IN THE SELENSEH REDIAN, Detlev walked out of Siamis's area and said to Jilo, "Your antidote worked. I gave it to Furo in Colend."

Jilo flushed to the ears — a healthy color — and swung to his feet with a return of the strength he'd learned while traveling with David. "I'll contact Puddlenose," he said on a note that was slightly interrogative and more than a little wary, as if he expected Detlev to try to stop him.

"The sooner the better," Detlev said.

Jilo flashed his rare smile, and ran out, leaving Detlev alone with Sveneric and Siamis. Detlev said to Siamis, "Pull him out only as a last resort." And to Sveneric, who was about to speak, "You need more time." He brushed his fingertips over the top of Sveneric's head, then vanished.

Siamis said, "Can you monitor the southern border for me? The desert has never been attempted, and the north has been quiet since a snowstorm struck there. I'll need to focus on the Chwahir ships."

"Understood," Sveneric said. "I will."

Siamis picked up the Ethe cup and carried it away to be hidden, then vanished as Sveneric settled on his cushion, closed his eyes, and reached southward on the mental plane.

Jilo had prepared a transfer token to take him to Puddlenose's *Lheit,* once a Chwahir transport that been refitted from the keelson up. The ship had also benefitted from Captain

Hereford's tricks of rigging and sail to make it one of the fastest ships on the seas. Hidden by the border ward's vapors, Puddlenose has brought the *Lheit* as close as he dared to the Gold fleet's flagship.

When Siamis arrived, they were already lowering a boat for Jilo. Several had volunteered to put up the sail for Jilo and man the tiller, as they were used to the hapless Jilo of old, totally bewildered on the sea. Jilo was far too self-effacing to point out that he was capable of sailing it himself now; but when Puddlenose gestured for the rope chair to be readied, Jilo didn't even seem to notice it, and followed his volunteer down with an absent sort of ease that rounded more than one pair of eyes.

Puddlenose spotted Siamis and came over to join him, as in the boat, Jilo helped the volunteer raise the mast and sail. "You have anything to do with that?"

"I did not. He sailed to Marloven Hess with David, and seems to have learned a few things while at it. He didn't tell you, I take it?"

"Nope. He barely wrote at all over the past weeks, except something about magic studies. Then he started getting gabby a couple days ago—he wanted to know the Chwahir blockade formation—the names of the ships, and whatever we'd learned of who was still in command. Mog down there got most of that for him."

His brown thumb hitched toward the boat, and the sallow, middle-aged woman at the tiller. "She's half-Chwahir. Doesn't talk much about her story. None of 'em do, but they find me somehow."

Siamis had noted a number of dark-haired, pale crew members before. "They know you were Wan-Edhe's hostage?" he asked. Of course they would—his name would be recognized by the Chwahir as testament to the invisible scars of his having survived, and escaped, The Hate's cruelty.

Puddlenose grinned. He had grown into a tall, rangy young man, his long brown sailor's queue sun-streaked, his skin mahogany. "I told Mog to—ah, there she goes. Good." Puddlenose peered down at the boat, as the woman tied a bright bandana over her head, hiding her fine dark hair. She wasn't quite as pale as Chwahir from the homeland; with the bandana, and her bright blue shirt over striped pants, she could be from anywhere. "They have orders from Wan-Edhe to grab any Chwahir they see, no matter where they come from, flog them a hundred times, and if they survive, put wooden collars on them and make them do scut work."

"Does she know that?"

"She does, but chose to take the risk. The competition among my Chwahir crew to aid Jilo was actually fairly fierce," Puddlenose admitted.

Siamis put his hands behind his back as he watched the boat drift into the vapors wreathing the ship. His mind had been filled with the importance of Jilo's quest to the balance of power in the world, which nearly overshadowed the importance to the Chwahir. They had become so very quiet before outsiders, quiet and colorless. Even their houses were colorless, as painting was forbidden. Which, if you knew where to look for records of the Chwahir, was a profoundly sad diminishment considering how much they had loved color in the far past.

But a last remaining burst of color was the broad red stripe in the white flag that among sea-going Chwahir meant truce and parley.

The little boat was soon swallowed in the real fog that had been generated by the magical fog, so Siamis shut his eyes and followed very cautiously by mind—less than a hair's breadth of a tendril—as Jilo turned his thoughts toward the indistinct shapes looming in the middle distance.

He and Mog didn't speak—they both knew the dangers here. They heard a faint shout from a lookout, followed immediately by the clang of the brass gong that called all to their stations, ready to handle or to defend the ship.

"Boat," a voice called, in Chwahir. "Identity yourself."

"Truce," Jilo called up. "I will identify myself to Gold Admiral Opun."

Most other ships on the ocean would have at least smiled derisively to see a small boat containing two apparently weaponless individuals demanding truce, but no one aboard the *Gold One* flagship even thought of smiling. They all suspected they knew who this was, though he was dressed exactly like them, only without any rank markers whatsoever—something that Jilo had learned from Senrid, who also wore no rank markers that he had not earned.

Opun had come to the foredeck. "Granted."

Jilo, of course, knew all the subtle signs that outsiders found so conflicting in Chwahir. Such as the fact that lowered gaze and humble words kept you alive. And yet, there were the little things that marked the difference between humility and servility. As every pair of eyes on the flagship watched, Jilo ran up the side of the ship with an ease that made it seem he scarcely touched the wood.

He vaulted over the rail to the deck, and saluted the flag, which was a very old courtesy indeed—and one of the few that Wan-Edhe had not countermanded, as he thought of himself as one with the kingdom, and so the salute was to him.

Weapons were still at the ready, eyes tracking as he approached the commander. He stopped out of arm's length, exactly the correct distance, and mumbled, "I bring a dagger." He sketched two edges in the air.

The dagger could mean an actual dagger—which would inevitably carry a message—or a symbolic one. The shared characteristic being two sides, usually taken as both gift and danger.

Opun was a veteran of rough training, countless drills with floggings at the end if the entire square did not move as one, and exponentially more stressful, the climb to command, balancing competence with Wan-Edhe's never-ceasing suspicion. Still, at these words, he had to hide the frantic beating of his heart.

"Speak within the cabin," he said—no terms of respect, as Jilo did not wear rank markers, but neither did he address Jilo in the third-person verb forms that denied him personhood, the way Wan-Edhe required scut workers and women to be addressed.

All those listening heard the distinction, and while it would perhaps be overstating to say that the entire crew held its breath, the tension was acute.

Jilo followed the commander, who he knew had orders to slay him if necessary, but capture him preferably, so that Wan-Edhe could have the pleasure of a very protracted execution.

Siamis, following from the *Lheit*, brushed the surface of the commander's mind as Opun thought of these things, then turned to face Jilo's still rather gaunt, unprepossessing face. But he'd had a lifetime of assessing the countenances of men, first those over him, and then those under his command. What Opun saw there was not Jilo's individual features, but the steady gaze of one for whom actions and tenet are the same. Humility, but no shame. "Speak," he said.

"I can remove the blood poison spell."

"What do you expect in return?"

Jilo shook his head, his matte-black hair brushing over knife-sharp cheekbones — he had forgotten to get a haircut since the one in Marloven Hess during summer, though at least he had new clothes. "No trade. I'll begin as I go on. Or die. It is time for Chwahir to choose their work." He turned a palm out toward the rest of the ship, having used the old word for work — which might be translated as honor or virtue elsewhere.

Opun gazed at those steady honey-colored eyes, and believed that Jilo believed his words. "We've orders."

"Until the sun returns to Chwahirsland," Jilo said, "there are storms that can blow our ships off course. There are necessary repairs to be made." Jilo frowned, and blinked. He hadn't thought of it before, but he began to suspect that Detlev's having turned up like that meant he was running parallel plans. Surely he was. And that meant…

He looked at Opun. "I suspect the shipyards are going to soon be very, very short."

It was only a guess, but he saw the words impact Opun, and then belatedly realized how it must sound: as if he, Jilo, had coordinated a world-wide attack on the shipyards.

The urge to deny, to splutter that he wasn't certain, had to be suppressed, hard. Humility was the Chwahir way, but that was personal humility. The only way to gain the confidence of the spirit-battered Chwahir martial forces was to show that another road was possible, one without Wan-Edhe. No matter who built that road.

Opun took an inadvertent step toward Jilo, impelled by a life of hard punishment for curiosity. For thinking for himself. "If I am summoned to the Presence. He will know."

Jilo said, "But you will not be. He is so suspicious now that the only ones who see him are the minions who relay orders. They bear the poison spell, too. And of course the condemned, when he wants to witness execution or punishment, but then it is already too late."

Opun had heard through the usual labyrinthine conduits that Wan-Edhe no longer permitted any general in his presence. They all had to go to the Hall of Judgment (once the Hall of Justice) and await Wan-Edhe's pleasure, which invariably meant standing at attention while he watched through the spy eyes everyone said he had, until he sent orders via servant.

To shift the subject away, Jilo held out an object. Opun took it, then looked down at an old coin — one that Puddlenose had found in the *Tzasilia* and saved as a memento of the bad old days, from when the Chwahir outpost was located in Mearsies Heili. The coin had been pressed some five hundred years previously, long before Wan-Edhe had forbidden the army to carry coinage, for the usual insane reasons.

Opun saw the worn metal with its square hole in the center as an oblique promise, then a cold shiver ran over his body, as if he had been toiling through the desert, and walked unexpectedly into the fine spray of a waterfall. And the nausea of the threatened poison—deliberately created to remind commanders waking and sleeping of Wan-Edhe's will—was gone.

Jilo said, "You'll need to drink plenty to get the residue out of your body, but he cannot loose the spell, unless you go before him."

Opun said, "And now?"

"You choose," Jilo said. "You know your fleet commanders."

You choose. Who had heard such an order during this reign? Opun knew that Vanguard Commander Korsa of the Fourth Gold regularly snitched to Narad, in hopes of displacing one of his superiors. He said tightly, "I know what to do."

Jilo did not question that. The choice was truly his!

"My gratitude for your work," Jilo said.

The words echoed in Opun's ears as Jilo left the cabin, walked through the silent crew, who had not moved, not even to sheathe weapons, and then went over the side with the same ease he'd shown in coming aboard.

The pirate, or whoever it was down there at the tiller of the truce boat, tightened sail, swung the tiller, and the boat vanished into the eternal fog.

"Back to your stations," Opun said only, but there was that in his voice that caused glances of hope to semaphore from eyes to eyes, as out in the water, Jilo said, "How far is it to the Silver Admiral?"

Ten

Off the eastern Sartoran continent

As soon as the All Captains meeting was over, during which Fox and his new captains mostly fumbled to understand one another's Sartoran—for David did not dare perform the dark magic Universal Language Spell—they set sail for the south.

Everyone understood that time pressed. Fox wondered if the others labored under this sense of unreality. Though the sea was the same, as were the stars overhead, the air smelled different in a way he could not define. Then there was the way he felt, also indefinable.

He shrugged it off, and put his mind to ship maneuvers as they sailed toward the rendezvous. That meant mutual understanding of signal flags (mostly the same, but not altogether), as well as seeing how fast and how well the ships handled.

Though he had no idea how they would fight, at least he had a sense of their seaworthiness by the time the lookout bawled, "Island ahead!"

Buffeted by bands of rain, they performed various maneuvers as they threaded between the small islands, guided by the chart.

Halia – off The Nob

The distinctive profile of their rendezvous poked above the

horizon that day as, at the other end of the strait, the fast tender *Gullwing*, slung by the circling winds of a storm in the sea between Toar and Halia, sighted the Nob. This was a much-battered harbor—by weather and by war—at the tip of the peninsula thrusting into the ocean currents between four continents.

Dour and enduring seemed to be the prevailing mood of whoever held the Nob. Llyenthur had convinced Svir that placing Wan-Edhe's prized Gold Army General Kirech here, not only to hold the Nob, but poised to be launched toward Toar if and when the ward over Mearsies Heili was broken, or toward lower Toar if the barely-held lands around tough Damondaen erupted into trouble, or north toward Goerael to support the Fhlerians, was optimal. Thus overriding Wan-Edhe, who had always kept his prized Gold Army closest to him, as protection and for prestige, and Efael, who relished the chance to point a finger and launch massive fleets to the attack. He had discovered that this was more fun than sending single assassins hither and yon.

Puddlenose had given Jilo the tender, but not before he pleaded, "Don't go. Really. I can find a volunteer to sound the Chwahir around Kirech. You know he was behind at least one of the plots to kill you."

"Because that's what Wan-Edhe wanted," Jilo said. "I never got a sense that it was for bloodshed, like it was with Thiam and Lavit. He's sworn to obey the king, and obedience gives him purpose." Naming two ambitious and bloodthirsty mid-rankers who would have (no, Thiam *had*) killed their own family in order to advance a step, until Kessler took them out in a spectacularly nasty spell.

"Exactly," Puddlenose said. "Kirech might regret it, but he'll collar you just the same, and put you in chains for Wan-Edhe. Jilo," Puddlenose pleaded, "you've got to find some other way. Don't go there yourself."

Jilo shook his head. "That's why I have to. I can't send a messenger, because it would mean I do not have the courage to face him—or else do not honor him enough to speak face to face, just like Wan-Edhe. Either way, he would scorn the message."

Puddlenose had cursed—in Chwahir, which has its own set of expletives—because Jilo was right. That was Chwahir thinking.

Jilo added, remembering what he'd promised Siamis, "If

he doesn't have the poison spell on him, I'll turn around and come back. I won't try to convince him." *Yet.* Because Jilo had to talk to them all, whatever the outcome. But no one needed to know that now.

But they all have the poison spell on them, Puddlenose was going to protest. But Jilo knew that. He expelled a breath. "Whatever you say."

During that trip, Jilo held imaginary conversations with the general, both waking and during restless nights during which he skimmed consciousness and dreams, somewhat like the flying fish diving and spinning in the air around the tender before splashing down into the sea.

They arrived off the Nob in a heavy snow storm, so heavy that only the expertise of the *Gullwing*'s crew kept the tender from breaking up on the rocks surrounding the peninsula. Again, it was Chwahir who accompanied Jilo in the rowboat to a little cove on the lee side, below the city, a cove used by smugglers and pirates for centuries.

They ghosted through thick clumps of drifting snow to the seawall, then over it between sentry rounds. No one was looking seaward, Jilo noticed gratefully as a splat of snow dropped in the tiny gap between his neck and collar. He shivered and shrugged deeper into the borrowed coat as he followed the black head of his guide up the narrow switchback trail.

It was a nerve-wracking stop-and-run trip to the building housing command, their feet sometimes skating over ice between the square stones called whales' teeth.

Here, Jilo made the sign to wait, shrugged out of the coat, and slipped inside, wearing only his high-collared plain black uniform. He reached with his inward sense and made his way along narrow, smooth-plastered corridors. The sharp smell of coffee was ubiquitous; the Chwahir no doubt reveled in the world's best coffee being easily got, and cheap, so close to the source. It tasted good and its effect was so very much better than a drop of deathbrew in hot water steeped in nut shells, which was the usual drink of the flatfoot in winter.

Jilo flattened himself against a wall for support as he listened ahead on the mental plane. Kirech was moving … there.

Jilo opened his eyes and glimpsed the general leaving the mess hall, probably going to his office. Gulping air to slow the sudden thump of his heart, Jilo moved to intercept, gaze searching over the general's heavy-jawed face. He did not see the greenish pallor of the dormant poison. Though that could be deceptive in someone who was naturally sallow. Jilo dared to brush the man's thoughts. And there it was, the seeping discomfort of mild but ceaseless nausea, below the maelstrom of surface thoughts.

Kirech entered the office, Jilo slipped in after him, and Kirech looked up, shock widening his eyes. He stilled. Then his hand slipped to the desk, but paused as Jilo said, "I have the antidote to the poison."

Kirech's breath whooshed out as if he'd been punched in the gut. His reaction struck Jilo: anger, fueled by the utter betrayal Kirech had been fighting against ever since the king made his distrust plain by putting that spell over him. As if all those years of absolute loyalty counted for nothing.

"What do you want?" Kirech said, his fingers resting on whatever token he had to summon Wan-Edhe.

"An end to Chwahir slavery."

Another, shorter breath. "There are no slaves in Chwahirsland."

"Chwahir history is slow. Far slower than Sartoran," Jilo said in a rush of quiet words. "It's older. Much older. And yes, we can say that we outlawed slavery while the rest of the continent, and Toar and Goerael, were still struggling back to a semblance of civilization. We began to erode our own civilization when the people were tied to the land, and the king owned the land. One by one our choices were removed, until we cannot even choose what we wear. What we eat, much less what we want to do with our lives. What is that but slavery?"

"What, then?"

"That, you will decide."

"Me?" Kirech repeated in wary disbelief.

"You, and the other commanders, and the guild leaders, and the clan heads—the elders, the parents, the twis. The people."

"Who can decide anything in all that clamor?" Kirech scowled, and spoke from the experience of his sixty years, "What I trust is the strength of my right arm." He eyed Jilo who wore no armor or weapon.

Jilo said, "Trusting strength is reasonable." He opened the window, raised his hand as snow swirled lazily in, and Kirech started as a firebolt shot from Jilo's hand to the choppy waves some hundred paces below the sea wall, then detonated, shooting a column of steam high into the air. Hot mist billowed, then vanished in the snowfall.

Jilo had only prepared the one fireball—which everyone knew ships had been warded against for centuries. It was still a lethal threat, an impressive sight, and also it was a demonstration of power, as it would seem he had only to lift his hand and will the fireball into being.

He'd gambled on one being enough—and shot to the sea—whereas Wan-Edhe's demonstrations of power always ended with someone dying.

Kirech looked out at the snow, as Jilo turned his back in order to shut the window, another thing Wan-Edhe would never do.

Kirech still struggled with the awareness that the king he had served loyally all his life did not trust him. Would never trust him. Saw him as indistinguishable from the lowest scut worker scraping wax from the streets after a torch parade.

"Your demand?"

"No demand," Jilo said. "A choice. Not now. When the time comes, we will rise against Norsunder. Then make Chwahirsland ours again. Ours. Not mine." He struck his chest. "I have prepared the antidote on this coin, which once we used freely, in trade for our work and our goods. You can use the coin as you choose, to free your division commanders."

"And the king?"

"If we can rid ourselves of Norsunder, we can negotiate with the king. Convince him that Chwahirsland needs a new path."

Jilo laid the coin on the desk, and moved toward the door.

Kirech said, "I will not forget that you removed the poison." The word endings in the verb, and the form of "you", were no longer commander-to-commoner.

Jilo slipped out, listening for the door to open again, the order to go out to capture him. Bracing for magic to seize him, and fling him at Wan-Edhe's feet. But there was only the quiet noise of orderly, everyday activity.

He reached the outer door and leaned against the wall, discovering that he was damp with sweat. Jilo was intensely aware that this was the first deliberate step toward that distant throne, and all its responsibilities.

He found the waiting sailors, and they ghosted toward the seawall, and back to the tender.

Eleven

IN A BAY OBSCURED by the illusion of a wicked reef (dully noted in gray ink on David's chart), the makers of that chart waited in tense expectation; after a year of covert strikes against Norsunder's seafaring force, they had gotten used to being on the run, rarely sleeping twice in the same place.

Between cloudbursts, the cry finally was carried from the hilltop lookout to Jehan and Sasha, the young rulers of Khanerenth, "Here they come!" *Unless it's the enemy* remained unspoken, but everyone was thinking it as they rushed to defense stations, weapons to hand.

A fleet of ships began to emerge from the silver-gray curtain of sleet, at first silhouettes of various sizes. When the details of the lead ship could be made out, first those with spyglasses and then everyone stared, stunned.

"It's like a tapestry come alive," Owl, Jehan's fleet master, muttered hoarsely, as the harbor lookout bellowed, "White flag!"

"Acknowledge," Jehan ordered the signal handler as he swept his glass over the Venn drakan, and up along the black sails. "I can't make out the device on the foresail, except that it's not the Ydrasal tree … are those *runes*?" He lowered his glass and rubbed his eyes, then said to his wife, "I saw runes once, when I was at the Marloven academy. We were getting a tour of some archive. I remember the smell of must and mildew."

"Did the Marlovens have ships like that?" Sasha asked, slinging a heavy blonde braid out of her way; tight as she braided her long, honey-colored hair, in this moist air it frizzled ferociously. She wiped the tendrils back, squinting as the drakan, and the ships behind, dipped their sails in unison, a flash that demonstrated superb skills.

"Here," Jehan said, passing his spyglass to her. As she peered through it at the strange lineaments of the drakan, now drifting in under half-sail, he went on, "No, but the Venn did, centuries and centuries ago. But there was a persistent story about Elgar the Fox having taken a drakan into the Battle for the Strait in 3921."

Sasha and Jehan looked at one another. "Could that be Elgar the Fox?"

"No. Maybe?"

They both thought back to the wintry night early in the year, when the tall, sardonic MV, who had sailed with Jehan's fleet for a time, contacted Owl via the old code words, and then brought a man with him to a singular meeting.

This brown-haired, ordinary-looking man, who seemed of an age somewhere between Owl's forties and Jehan's twenties, had introduced himself as Detlev. *The* infamous Detlev? No one had quite dared to ask. He'd said, "I'll have a chart of enemy installations by midsummer. And when the time is right, I'll send you a fleet."

"A fleet? From where?"

"I've collected them over time." He'd left shortly after, as had MV.

"'Over time.' I thought that meant over the past five years. Since he skipped out of Norsunder," Jehan muttered as Sasha handed back the spyglass. He clapped it shut, and said, "Looks like the past five hundred years might be closer to the truth. Let's get down to the dock."

On board the *Treason*, Fox was also plying his spyglass. He noted with approval the defense—as much as was visible—guessing that the main of the defenders were hidden from view. Good. He wasn't dealing with dolts.

His glass moved more slowly, now picking out individuals. Everyone gave way before an old man and a young woman. No, that man couldn't be old, in spite of his white hair. He moved like a young man—a martially skilled young man.

Morvende? Fox had seen a few in Sartoran waters. A young couple. Not too young, just out of childhood; they appeared to be nearing thirty, a seasoned age. The woman was almost as tall as the man, strongly built, with a hawk nose that gave her the look of a fierce eagle.

The two came down the dock, ignoring the spitting sleet, as the *Treason* drifted in to be moored. By then Jehan and Sasha had taken in Fox's tall, lean form, his bony, lined face.

All three were well-predisposed toward the others, an impression that solidified when they got inside the hut that served as headquarters, and introduced themselves.

Sasha had never heard the Marloven stories. It was Jehan whose nerves thrilled when the tall man with the silver-threaded red hair said, "Call me Fox."

"You're Elgar," Jehan exclaimed. "You're real. I always believed that." Then he flushed to the ears, hearing his words as not only feckless, but probably insulting.

Fox snorted. "There were several of us who traded off being Fox. Ruse of war. The real Elgar, ah, his name was Inda." Fox saw a blink of recognition — and muted surprise — in Jehan, and found himself absurdly glad that Inda was not completely forgotten. Then, wrenching the subject entirely away from himself, "David here says that Ramis, er, what was his real name again? Ah, never mind, I'll never remember it. Our first objective should be the east and north-east shipyards. To which I'd add, let's take advantage of the east winds and sweep a couple of Chwahirsland's three main harbors. I'll take that on," he added. "I also suggest we make this a simultaneous attack. We're supposed to get their attention. Seems to me that would do it."

"We can't coordinate a simultaneous attack anymore," Jehan protested. "The scribe desks are down."

Fox did not know what scribe desks were, but since they were down, he dismissed the term with a wave of his hand toward David, standing silently at the back of the cleared-out room.

Jehan noticed him, then his eyes widened. "I've met you. You're friends with MV, are you not?"

"I am," David said. "I have some papers that will enable communication with the speed of the scribe desk. I'll show you how they work."

"You're joining us?" Jehan asked. "Is MV anywhere about?"

"He's elsewhere," David said. "And I'm only here long enough to make sure there's no language barrier, and to explain these. Though," he grinned, "I can help you with this first strike."

Jehan accepted that; he didn't really know David, but this Fox who sailed in on an ancient drakan might be anyone at all. That seemed easier to believe than that the man had sailed out of history and into this battle at a very convenient time. "Another thing," he said. "I want to put a person on board your ships. Regard them as part of communication. Each will be trained to reef, steer, and fight."

Fox's teeth showed in a brief smile. "You mean spies. That's fine. I wouldn't trust us either, not if things are as bad as has been hinted. Your people can be in charge of these mysterious papers. How's that?"

Sasha and Jehan exchanged looks — both knowing they had little choice. "Agreed," Sasha said. And, "There was a little boy, part of your group. He was an aid to us once. Svenrik, I believe he was called." The second E in Sveneric's name was usually scarcely there, but her pronunciation left it out entirely.

David said, "He's … fine. Now. Related, new orders have apparently come from Norsunder, to triple the building of ships. What that means is, the cutting of trees will accelerate."

"Already has," Jehan said soberly. "We received word on our last supply run, that fresh logs have been floating down the river to Ellir in great numbers. There is no more Wood Guild to halt it."

Everyone looked uneasy, if not grim. Every one of them, ancient and modern, had been raised on stories of the Fall, and how the world had retaliated after the wanton destruction for centuries: long, rough winters, wet springs, blazing summers. Human life had faltered during the early centuries especially, diminished as it was. The Wood Guild was an important part of using only what the world gave. Or had been.

Sasha said, "We know Ellir intimately. We can attack the shipyard there."

David came forward with the chart that Detlev had given him. "Here are all the shipyards at this end of the continent, details noted by MV and another scout who understands what is needed to plan raids. They made this early last summer, but it's unlikely that much has changed, except for the increase in clear-cut wood."

"My guess is," Fox drawled, "these idiots don't realize that wood needs to season before it can be worked into shipbuilding, and it'll take years before they see their enormous fleet. If there are shipwrights enough to build."

Jehan leaned forward. "I suggest we do not make the situation worse by burning the wood. Sabotage ships on the blocks, steal supplies, set back their work so that it'll take all winter to start up again. But no wanton destruction."

"Precision raid," Fox said. "Agreed."

Finding each other both practical and experienced, Fox and Jehan settled the details rapidly. As a pair of former scribes, working from either end, reproduced the chart that MV had made, David then trained the two commanders in the use of the magic-papers. "Don't forget focusing on the person you write to as you write their name," he finished. "You have to have met them first, unless you have Dena Yeresbeth."

"What?" Fox asked, and later, when they made their way back to the Treason, "What was that? I vaguely remember some of the Old Sartoran my sister and I used to trade back and forth when we were being especially obnoxious, but I can't make anything of that."

"It's … something both old and new," David said.

"Wait. Has it to do with magic?"

"It can."

"I don't want to know, unless it's a weapon," Fox said, waving off the subject. "You said you have to leave. Going back to the homeland is my guess?"

"As it happens, yes."

The sleet had turned to snow. Fox eyed him as they leaped over the ramp to the drakan. "You've avoided the subject thus far. We lost?" And as David looked out at the snow falling softly, dimpling the quiet bay before melting, Fox said, "Lost badly, eh? Probably nobody knows how very close we came at Andahi. I expect the ballads still extol Marlovan heroism?" His tone was casual, but his thoughts were intensely vivid, sharp with disappointment, regret, and beneath that, awareness that he and his shipmates might as well have been sent to another world, so unfamiliar had this one become. Why couldn't Ramis have put his invitation to Jeje, at least? But she never would have left Tau or Dasta or those two boys of theirs.

"Some," David said, shutting out the painful intensity of Fox's emotions.

Fox seemed to sense something amiss, for his stride increased as he sauntered down the drakan's companionway. "I wasn't there, but Inda was. The only reason the Venn didn't sweep us into oblivion was because word came the old king had died, and Rajnir was tired and wanted to go home."

It was strange for David to hear these words, knowing that Fox remembered the living, breathing individuals behind the names.

Fox finished mockingly, "I'm only surprised it took so long. Or has Halia been overrun regularly? Don't answer that — I don't want to know. Let's look at that chart again. Whoever drew this knows something about raids. Notice there's not just the number of sentries, but their patterns…"

That was the last reference to Marloven Hess's past, or anything personal. Fox knew that some time or other curiosity might waken, but right now even David's unfamiliar face was a reminder that everyone Fox had known, good, bad, or indifferent, was long dead. Most of them forgotten. Though he still had that magic door in his cabin that permitted him to return to his tower in Darchelde, he had no desire to use it.

But he was alive, and a few days later, he woke to the prospect of battle again. The east wind had stayed steady on their beam, driving them straight past rocky, barnacle-encrusted granite columns, against which the waves smashed, sending water shooting higher than the topmasts.

They slid by in single file, two at the helm on each ship — in the lead those who knew these treacherous waters well. The weather remained perfect cover for a raid, with its wind-whipped snow.

Fox had divided the riverboats among the fleet for this initial venture, leaving the bulk of them, under their Commander Ghaer, to Jehan for the raid on Ellir, and the river full of lumber; Sasha had offered to lay illusion over the timber, if the raiders could shepherd it a ways down the coast to a shallow inlet. Illusion, she explained, was easily broken — but the Norsundrian mages would have to spot it first. And because it was such flimsy magic, the laying of illusion would trigger no wards.

Fox had reserved the toughest challenge, Amfa Harbor, for himself and the man he resisted giving a name to. If he proved his worth, he would cease being merely "the prince."

Under cover of night, as the tide reached full flow, they left barely enough crew aboard to handle the ships and set out for shore, weapons at the ready, talk forbidden. They had sailed in complete darkness once they'd passed the outer rocky ring, in order to thoroughly accustom their eyes to the darkness. Not so much as a single lamp glowed, to keep their vision sharp.

They had their two riverboats, plus their longboats. Fox counted the long silhouettes sliding toward the shore. They drew abreast of the spit of land that divided off the shipyard from the harbor itself. At the right moment, five boat silhouettes began to diminish, the dark sea between increasing, then they bore left toward the spit, and vanished behind it.

Fox shut out the prince and his boats as his party skimmed onward, snow settling softly on heads, shoulders, knees. They slid past headlands. Creeks: one, two, three.

He knocked on the bench three times, the sound muffled by the snow: the two in charge of the sail brailed it up, and the rest unhooked their oars. No one made a clatter as they began to row, the coxswain slapping his knee in a rhythm, the sound no louder than waves slapping wood or rock.

They approached the last natural hazard, speeding with the full tide. They had to round the bluff with its outpost—windows bright, which meant those inside could see nothing but the snow an arm's length in front of them—softly glowing surf raced toward them. The oars lifted.

They hit the merging waters. The coxswain slapped twice. Down plunged the oars, ready to fight a back-eddy, but they caught the narrowed flow and were carried at breathtaking speed toward shore.

Fox shifted on the bench, aware of the ache of cold in his bones. He had fought through much worse weather than this, but he didn't remember ever noticing the cold. You're old, he told himself. Old and slow.

But he wasn't slow as the boats rode the breakers and hissed up the beach. Leaving a guard to each boat, Fox and his company raced up the beach, breaking into teams. Fox fought the instinct to gaze toward the lights of the outbuildings, and forced himself to orient then look away, toward the shadowy figures around him. The snow softened the grunts and gasps as the oblivious sentries were taken out one by one. Gray jackets all: Efael still didn't trust the Chwahir to guard their own harbors.

Up Fox and his teams ran, sand giving way toward soil; with firm footing, they were faster. The warehouse teams peeled off. David had tied a dark scarf over his head, as had the others with light hair; he brought up the rear, Fox leading the way toward the command buildings, all low, built around a square.

Fox opened his mouth so that no one would hear him pant. Old! They reached the outer building. Sentry dropped; Fox caught his breath, annoyed with himself. He used to fight all day and night, and did not remember ever running out of breath. No matter how hard he drilled now …

"Dais?" another sentry called, in Norsundrian. "Hai, Dais? There's mulled punch here. Dais! You better not be aslee —"

Thud.

"They'll be looking for him sooner than later," Fox murmured. "Remember: make your sweep fast, and out. Don't stop to read anything. Take any papers you see, set fire to the room, out."

After that, impressions splintered. David headed unerringly toward the commander's office. How did he know which office to go to? The chart had not marked that. It had to be that mysterious whatever-it-was that made his gaze slacken, then he'd offer an observation that no one else could hear or see.

Fox followed, and they slipped, steel ready, into an empty room. The commander had gone off to bed. The light was steady, blue-white and eerie. Fox had seen glow globes, though not many. These seemed to be as common as lamps had once been. And still were: as Fox swept up all the papers in sight, David found and uncorked lamp oil. The sharp scent tickled Fox's nose as David splashed it everywhere. Then he touched a finger to the oily sheen on the desk, stiffened slightly, and when he lifted his finger away, a lick of flame rose, then spread, blue and hungry.

He looked sharply to one side, then said, "There are prisoners."

Fox swallowed his *How do you know?* "Lead the way."

Splintered impressions again; old habit was faster than thought as Fox took on the two they surprised inside the door of what used to be a scribe house. The fight was short and hard. Anger lent Fox his old speed, but he — veteran of assessing the battle around him — noted that David fought not just superbly, but with an economy of movement that made it seem he knew his opponents' moves before they made them. It was Ramis's style. He took out four to Fox's two.

Then David leaped over the slumped guards, scattering bowls and cups from their spilled meal as he sprinted for what was once a storeroom. Between the two of them they kicked the door in, and peered into the thick, stale air toward people who had pushed to the far wall of the small space.

"Out," David said in Chwahir, then tried two or three languages.

The prisoners stampeded, two or three pausing to kick viciously at the fallen guards, before vanishing into the night in several directions.

Fox's inner sense of the tides tugged at him. Though he couldn't see the moon, he knew it was sinking; some things hadn't changed. It was getting late. He and David ran.

Paper in the single sheet is light. In the aggregate, when one is running full out, burdened further by a sword and four knives, it becomes as cumbersome as a boulder. Fox was gasping by the time they reached the boat, sweat running down his back. But he saw what he'd hoped to see: the hiss of foaming water running short of the high point. The tide was turning.

The others appeared at the run, some carrying things, others with only their weapons. Fox counted: all accounted for.

They pushed off, and for a time everyone gasped and grunted as they fought the surf. They, and the boat, were awash when they got past the breakers, but the receding current then picked them up. Fox worked an oar hard, to keep warm, in spite of his rasping breath.

It seemed they had labored half the night when he became aware of a beating glow off to the right, causing the snowflakes to glimmer around the edges. Then five boats joined them, but there were gaps in the shadowy shapes crouched on the benches, as the sail hoisted, racketing.

That was when the alarm went up on the shore far behind them, the bell clanging frantically as fire beat with ruddy glow through the snow. But by the time a pursuit scrambled, they had sheeted their sails home, and slanted away into the sea.

Messages by magic-paper appeared and vanished through the remainder of the night. Nine dead—two of those the prince's: it turned out that some of the Norsundrians had been using the half-finished ships for trysts and parties, but they didn't forget to take their weapons. There had been hard fighting.

Twenty-eight wounded, the take a miscellany of coinage, food, and papers. Fox blinked at the script, which was Norsundrian, then he pushed the papers toward David, who, curse him, had a youngster's effortless stamina.

David sorted rapidly, then sat back. "It's mostly related to supplies, plus the demands of Efael, some of these orders countermanding earlier ones. We can ignore it all."

"Chuck them into the fire," Fox said, annoyed that he'd had to lumber himself with what turned out to be useless.

David didn't hear him. He stared witlessly at the papers, unmoving, then looked up. He grinned. "Word's going out. Inspections and finger-pointing now. You have everything you need, right? I've just been given the new transfer spell, and I can hide my transfer among all these others."

Fox did not bother asking what any of that meant. He lifted a hand. Then he startled when David vanished.

Same moon, same tides, same seas, but everything else had changed.

Twelve

MEREWEN DEI WAS A weaver.

She had, despite the war and her young age, recently attained mastery. Her house was small and not the least warlike. For months no one had visited outside of local friends or guild-members, and so, despite her connection with the famous Dei family — her father being leader of the Knights of Dei — the overextended, much harassed Norsundrian occupiers had let her slip from their awareness.

Merewen, known to friends and family as Merry, went about her daily occupations exactly the same as ever, as — slowly, tentatively — her visitors began to include not just family members but couriers.

And now that she was back in the country, the queen, Hatahra Delieth.

On this rainy autumn night, Merry sat with her sister and father. They were newly arrived. From her father's expression Merry knew that Roderic understood what he would find within the carefully wrapped layers of cloth in his hands.

She was right. He contemplated history, and how it might affect the present, as his eldest daughter Carinna removed her soggy cloak, and spread it slowly over a bench in front of the roaring fire. She crouched down with her back to the flames and tucked her hands into her armpits. Her dark head dropped forward, and rivulets of rainwater escaped from her pinned braid and ran down her brow. She tried not to think at all. Life was easier if one waited for orders, then carried them out.

Merry studied them both, two of the people she loved most.

Roderic sat down at the broad wooden table, and pulled a branch of candles close. Silence prevailed as his fingers, expressive of reverent care, dealt with the long layers of muslin and the age-creased fine-weave. At last, there it was: he laid the old portrait flat on the table, directly under the light of the candles, and stared at it.

"We're in trouble," he said, and sighed.

Merry looked into her eldest sister's long, somber face. Merry privately thought her sister's clear gray eyes, and her rare smile, beautiful. Though Carinna hadn't smiled since she'd been Knighted, nearly a year ago.

Since no one seemed yet inclined to speak on the subject of the portrait, and what it meant, Merry said, "I've mulled some wine. Would anyone like some?"

Carinna looked up quickly. "I would indeed. Thanks, Merry."

"Was it a horrid ride?" Merry was glad to break the silence—and glad Carinna seemed, for once, disposed to talk.

"Sleet." Carinna's eyes narrowed with fleeting humor. "Horrid indeed."

"How did home look? Have *they* done anything?"

"Deserted. Some weather damage, where their searchers had left doors or windows open. There was a nest of owls, of all things, in the library alcove."

Roderic looked up. "You altered nothing?"

"As you desired." Carinna's avowal took on the formality of orders carried out. Then, her lips curving a little, "The owls nest in peace."

There. That was a smile. Merry was relieved as she poured out three cups of wine and covertly studied her sister. She'd seen so little of Carinna since the war began and the Knights had been forced to go underground. But it was the quick smile of gratitude. All the joy had gone out of it.

"Here you go," Merry said in her brightest voice. "Peace-with-Spring." And she put a cup into her sister's long, capable hands. Then, turning to Roderic, "Papa. Yours."

"Peace." Roderic lifted the cup, but his eyes and mind were

on the portrait.

Merry moved away, and the candles on the table flickered and streamed. The uncertain light gave the vivid ancestor-face on the table a semblance of movement for a moment, and Merry shivered and drank from her spiced wine.

Carinna had yet to sip from hers. Staring down into its depths, she murmured, "Isn't the queen coming?"

"She'll be here." Merry nodded. "Probably the weather making her late. The mountain roads are all awash, the courier said."

Roderic glanced over. "The Norsundrians have been destroying bridges."

Merry winced. "How terrible!"

"We've told those youngsters up there to hide for now," Carinna said, her smile wintry. "They don't consider orders to preserve their lives any favor." And, at last, she drank.

Roderic's fingers tapped on the table. a sure sign his mind was on something he disliked. Merry watched both, distracted, and turned her thoughts to her sister.

Merry first saw her sister's face reflect this pain when? At the Knighthood ceremony?

Carinna let a quiet sigh escape. "This is so good, Merry! I feel less like last winter's mud. How are Mama and the girls?"

"As well as can be," Merry reported. "And all send their very best. Or would! I have not seen Theanra, but I hear she's working hard."

"Remember to give them all my love," Carinna said, and drank again.

"I have some dry clothes, if you like, though they will be short," Merry said.

Carinna's lips quirked. "That's all right, thanks. I'll have to go out again anyway. And I'm warn enough here by the fire."

Silence fell.

It can't be the Knighthood, Merry thought. The only one of the five of us ever deemed close to being worthy, and recommended for his own place on Carnold's dying breath—

Memory stirred.

Carinna lifted her head to address their father. "Have you decided to tell the queen?"

Roderic stroked his chin.

Merry said softly, "About poor Troy?"

Roderic's eyes turned her way. "She must be told. That is

one of the reasons for this meeting. But in addition—" He paused, listening.

They all heard the sounds of arrival, faint over the roar of the rain.

Merry scolded herself—it had to have been Carnold dying. How could she be so inobservant? Carinna and Carnold had first started flirting as teens, but once Mama said that Carinna was incapable of superficial relationships. Now Carinna had only his place, and his sword.

The door opened, sending flames leaping as cold air swirled through the room. Entered a short, golden-haired boy of sixteen or so, and behind, straight and tall in her wet cloak and battle tunic, Hatahra Delieth. The dawnsinger boy grinned in greeting at the three in the room, and moved to sit next to Carinna before the fire.

Carinna raised her hand in the Knights' salute, and Merry swept a curtsey.

"No protocol." Tahra shook her head as she put back her hood. Like Carinna, she had curling dark hair, subtle evidence of the occasional cousinship between the Delieths and Deis. But her thin lips, the shape of ears and eye sockets, her narrow features, were all Delieth. Her only resemblance to her mother, gone these ten years, was in certain expressions, no more than a trace, sought for by the older generation who had loved the queen, many of them dearly. "It's good to see you, Merry. Oh, thank you," she added, as Merry put a cup of hot wine into her hands.

Roderic had laid a fold of cloth across the portrait as Tahra and her aide entered. Tahra sat down across from Roderic, frowning slightly. "Commander. You requested a meeting. Bad news, then? You would smile if it were good."

"Morgeh Troiad is dead," Roderic said gently.

Tahra's breath hissed in. "Norsunder?"

"One of the Host. Apparently found them when chasing after you."

Tahra's hand tightened on her cup, spilling wine onto the table, the red looking for a moment like blood. Merry hastened to clean it up with a quick swipe of her apron as Tahra said, "I did not know Troy was even in Wnelder Vee."

"He was traveling with a Mearsiean girl," Roderic said, his voice gentle. "Also dead."

Merry, who had known for a day and a half, wiped her

burning eyes. Troy's music—gone! She saw the dawnsinger's face then, stricken as if he'd been knifed, and her eyes filled anew.

"Troy—Morgeh. I kept trying to get him to use his proper name. A good name. To begin to think like a king. The world is filled with bards, but there could only be one king in Wnelder Vee." Tahra's voice was a breath of pain. Then she looked up, the faint lines in her face pulling tight with tension. "What happened exactly?"

"It was Efael of the Host. Sported with them. One of our northern contacts was one of those who found out they were looking for a vessel, and tried to ride to the rescue. She was too late. At least they were not killed with cursed knives."

"The source is reliable?"

"Yes. She rode here and told me in person, as soon as she received the information."

Tahra knew Roderic. Said sharply, "From?"

"Laban."

Tahra put her hands flat on the table, visibly suppressing an angry exclamation. Presently she said, "That's what, the fifth or sixth time he's surfaced while interfering in our affairs? Unless—"

Carinna spoke up, voice calm. "He did not kill them."

Tahra shot her a cold look, then murmured, "I made it clear years ago he is not welcome in Everon. Why is he here?"

"I may have an answer for that," Roderic said slowly.

"And it's something I will hate," Tahra said. "I can see it in your face. What is it, Roderic?" Her voice was sharp.

Merry's heart hurt in pieces. For Troy—who had at last escaped the kingship he had loathed—for the dawnsinger's silent, sad face, for her father who looked so old. He'd wanted to retire from duty and live in peace ten years ago, she thought. For Carinna.

For the queen.

"Have you seen him?" Roderic countered.

"No. I'd like to say he wouldn't dare, but effrontery was always a particular hallmark of Detlev's assassins," Tahra said. "I take it you have? And?"

"There was little speech between us, and none of it to much purpose. It was just after Llyenthur defeated our last uprising, the mountain teens. Laban has grown in these years between this war and the last."

"And?" She sounded rude because she was anxious.

"I recognized him," Roderic said gently.

"You—" Tahra cut herself short. One of her hands closed into a fist. "You are not telling me you believe his ridiculous claims?"

Roderic set aside the cloth and with careful fingers lifted and reversed the portrait. Tahra glanced down at the familiar painting, a couple of centuries old, one of the more famous members of the famous Dei family, descendants of the Dei branch in the Eid, former principality in Imar, reaching into Everon. "My mother used to call him Grandpa Saddlesore because he—" She slapped her palm on the table. "He can't be."

Roderic nodded. "His image. As was Harold. Except Laban's eyes are blue, and Leskandar Dei's were gray. And Laban's hair is not completely black, though that might come with age. If similar features are anything to do by, he is a Dei."

Tahra's mouth twisted with nausea as she glanced down at the dashing face framed in long courtier locks, black as a moonless night. At the old-fashioned lace-edged collar and gold-embroidered, extravagantly cut doublet. Back to the rakish smile—

"I've been through the records," Roderic said. "After Harold was outlawed, he went to Geth with the two children, then produced a third while he was there."

"Laban. Pronounced Lah-BAHN, it is a Geth name."

"The younger Knights—the ones around Glenn—said he claimed to have been born on Geth, when he first came."

Tahra said flatly, "Harold Dei was a criminal. How like Detlev to search worlds just to fling the spawn of criminals in our faces. He knows there is no possible welcome for him here. Why was he lurking in Wnelder Vee?" Her brows contracted. "Of course. He wants the throne. Hah! Only after I'm dead!"

And Carinna, who had clearly been waiting for just this moment, said, "I have questioned directly the individuals involved. He did not betray King Morgeh or the Mearsiean. He did not arrange their deaths. He's been training the resistance in the western mountains."

Roderic said, "You must remember there is always the possibility he does not know his great-grandmother was connected to both the Troiads and to the Delieths—"

"Does not know," Tahra cut in, her voice derisive. "Of course he knows. When he first polluted my palace six years ago, he told me of the connection, as if that would mitigate all the evil they've done! Remember who gathered those assassins, trained them, and inflicted them on us—but ah! *You* did not know!" She swung back, addressed Roderic with false affability. "You did not know that Imry Llyenthur is none other than brother to our old 'friend' David, of the black sword. That came out last summer. And do you know where Detlev found them? In Llyenthur, at the other end of the continent, with their father who'd become a pirate after being exiled from Marloven Hess, and took the name of the land for his own. I wonder if Senrid Montredaun-An found out about his new cousins before or after Llyenthur knifed his four-year-old daughter?"

Merry gasped, hugging her chilled arms close.

"Detlev probably set out deliberately to locate every brigand who has a blood-claim on a throne somewhere in the world. What a sporting new game this would be, empire-building directly through the ruling families."

Roderic said, "So if Laban does claim the throne in Fortnyal Roth?"

Tahra glared across the table at him. "You're challenging me!"

"I'm reminding you that in thirty years, we've suffered three major wars. More than half our population is under the age of twenty, and a good portion of the rest are ineffectual oldsters my mother's age, and I will soon be. If I live. Those young people want to fight, some of them like to fight, and if any of them are left after we do rid ourselves of Norsunder, they'd been easy to mobilize yet again for whatever cause anyone wants to put forward. But how much good will it do the kingdom—both kingdoms—to gather the remnants of the populace and sweep them into yet another civil war?"

"You dare to suggest that I stand by and do nothing if this felon steps up to Morgeh's throne and decides he likes the view?"

"There is no designated heir," Roderic reminded her, as he carefully began the process of rewrapping the old portrait. "For those who regard blood as the standard for inheritance, his sister would come first, then him. And from anything I've learned, the sister regards Geth as her home world."

Merry remembered her wine and picked up the decanter. She moved to the table, where she was able to see Tahra's face directly, and the gleam of gathered tears in her eyes. They didn't fall, though, and Tahra's voice remained steady. "And if I do nothing, and he sets himself up as king in Wnelder Vee — and it transpires it's yet another plot of Detlev's?"

"If the people follow him willingly —"

Suddenly Tahra's anger disappeared, as if another chill wind had blown through the room and taken it. "If the people follow him willingly then he has the right, and if he employs arcane powers to enforce his claim then I'm not strong enough to fight them. How I detest impotence!"

"To be aware, and ready to act when action becomes necessary — if it becomes necessary — is your wisest course."

"Yes. So I see," she said listlessly. "Where is he now?"

"No one knows. He might have been involved with the escape of Detlev's son from the Norsundrian headquarters in Imar."

"Detlev's son," Tahra repeated, passing a hand over her eyes. The hatred eased in her face, just for a few moments, changing to a strange expression.

Merry had heard about Sveneric, Detlev's son. Not much, but the little she had heard redounded to his credit. And even Tahra, who reviled freely against Detlev and his gang, had never said a word about Detlev's son, who she knew very well was a friend to her eldest twins.

Tahra's hand dropped. "Who else is aware of Troy's death?"

"We have told no one. The messenger also, and his friends. We do not know who Laban or the Mearsiean might have spoken to."

"A Mearsiean." Tahra's hand slipped into her pocket. "I wonder if Atan Landis knows. No one has written to me." She turned to her dawnsinger aide, who looked up silently. In a kind voice, she said, "You are free to go to your people, DarAndar. They'll want to sing tribute for Troy." She didn't bother with his royal name anymore. What purpose now?

"Will you come to us?" The dawnsinger stood up, raindrops falling from his tunic and hair.

But Tahra didn't hear, just stared into the fire. He left, silent of voice and of step.

Tahra said presently, "Merry, may I sleep here? I don't think I can do any more. I keep seeing Troy's face, acting the fool when they tried to betroth him to Cassandra, and I think —" Her mouth opened, closed again. "How I hate Detlev," she said in a low voice.

She turned to stare at the fire. After a time Roderic signaled his oldest daughter with his eyes, and they departed noiselessly. Merry went upstairs to put a hot brick in the best bed, and to lay out her warmest nightgown, then she trod soundlessly back downstairs to wait until the queen should want her. But Tahra, wrapped in memory and grief, did not go to bed that night.

By the time darkness had grayed into another cold, drenching day Tahra was gone. Merry, now alone, carried the portrait upstairs to be stowed away, then she climbed into the cold, empty bed and fell into exhausted sleep.

Thirteen

ADAM FELT AS IF he'd just fallen into dreams when he was startled into wakefulness by a hand on his shoulder. The chamber in the Darchelde Forest underground hideout was utterly dark, but he recognized MV's touch.

A whisper: "Detlev's here."

They all slept in their clothes these days. Adam flung off his blanket, shoved his feet into his waiting shoes, and followed MV noiselessly out, the cleaning frame in the doorway zapping sleep frowziness from clothing and skin. Alas, it did nothing for shorted sleep. They trod fast up the tunnel past two rooms of slumbering Marloven teens.

Detlev had apparently contacted someone first, because he wasn't actually in the hideout yet. David, a few days back with them, looking tousled and heavy-eyed, was in the kitchen starting up something hot to drink—obviously he hadn't been to bed yet. MV prowled around lighting extra lamps, then he stoked up the vagabond fire with a wave of his hand.

Adam dropped onto one of the floor pillows. There was a swirl of raw, cold air down the main tunnel as the door opened. MV snickered at the heralding smell of horse and wet wool.

Then not one but two figures entered. Adam started up, delighted when he recognized the long, narrow face following Detlev down the tunnel. "Roy!"

David's head poked out from the kitchen. "Long time!"

MV drawled, "All we need to complete this merry band is—"

"Erol, Ferret, Vana—" Adam began.

"—is Imry," MV finished, before Adam could get to Leefan.

Roy raised his hands. "Just keep him away from Fhleria, if you can, and I think we've set up a suitable surprise."

Adam turned from assessing Roy's appearance and manner to address Detlev. "How is Sveneric? Siamis has written nothing beyond the fact that he safely escaped."

Detlev removed the brown cloak he had been wearing. David handed him a steaming cup, then took the cloak to a peg. The room filled with the summery aroma of Sartoran steep as Detlev said, "Sveneric can give you the details. He should be here in a few days. As for how he got out, he took advantage of Yeres being careless." He sat on the bench.

"He got caught how?" MV asked from where he was crouched before the fire.

"In Larkadhe," Detlev said, leaning back with the cup in his fingers.

MV whistled. "Went after Imry, eh? Why?"

David grimaced, handed Adam a cup, and flopped down beside him. "Because you did?" Adam asked David.

David turned an inquiring look to Detlev, who appreciatively sipped the warm steep, but (typically) said nothing.

"And Imry?" Adam went on, when it was clear that any answer would have to come from Sveneric himself.

"No one knows. He's very well hidden."

"I'm up for some fun with Imry." MV grinned across the chamber at Detlev—then the wickedness gave way to a sort of appreciative surprise. Not that Detlev looked any different to the casual glance; as usual, he wore a plain long tunic with a high collar, over riding trousers and forest mocs. But MV's expert eye noted a stiff shoulder, and the bulk of a bandage there and around a knee. "Been stepping out a little?"

Detlev said, "I met Erol on the Chwahir coast, to hand off a token with Jilo's antidote to Wan-Edhe's blood poison. It appeared that Jainek had caught wind of him, and Erol couldn't quite shake him."

"Jainek," MV said, hawked and spat into the fire. "What

does that make, six Black Knives down now?"

"Not enough," Detlev said evenly. "Not enough."

Adam murmured in a flat voice very unlike his usual, "Jainek ought to count for two."

"We'll call it seven, then," MV said. "But next time, I'm in."

Detlev lifted a hand in acknowledgment, then said, "In the meantime, concentrate on the circle."

Senrid drifted into the room, looking neat and very much awake. "Detlev." He flicked out a hand. "Poopsie confab, eh? Roy!"

Roy grinned. "Been a long year, what?"

"Long and a few other things," Senrid said. "Where's Sveneric?"

David gave Senrid a swift rundown; MV turned to Roy and asked a couple of low-voiced questions about the Fhlerian situation.

Detlev said to Adam, "Laban?"

Adam smiled. "Patrol."

Detlev turned to Senrid. "Have you room for one more?"

"Sure." MV broke off his conversation to offer, with characteristic generosity, "You can have Andri's bed."

"But Andri's in it." David laughed soundlessly, leaning on the back of Detlev's chair.

"Won't be, after we go down and bounce him out," MV returned reasonably. "Be nice and warm. He's gotta take off on the supply run in a little while, anyway."

"How about your bed?" Mildred spoke up for the first time, her cat eyes slitting with wickedness.

"Nope. If I'm going be leading drills, I've gotta rack up some sack time."

Andri got to sleep peacefully on until a slothful pre-dawn watch change, as very little arranging was necessary in order to accommodate Detlev. Senrid even managed to give Detlev a room to himself, so he wouldn't have to block out the noise of a roommate coming and going.

At noon, Marend Ndarga, who'd (rather heavy-handedly) arranged her own group's activities around her desire to meet the Mighty Detlev, was waiting when the latter emerged to claim his share of the shirred eggs and crisped, seasoned rice that Kelsan had cooked up. Marend was seated in her usual spot, back to one side of the hearth, when Detlev came out of the kitchen. And she stared in silent dismay: what she'd envisioned had been a powerful "inda" of the olden days, biceps and triceps rippling at every stomp, myriad weapons clanking and clattering about his person, who'd stalk out and begin issuing orders in a field-command voice. Instead she stared up at a very ordinary looking man whose hair was courtier length (though tied in back) and who dressed more like a merchant than like a warrior. His voice was on the quiet side of ordinary — and he was not talking about war, but complimenting the stupidly grinning Ramond on some of his pictures that he'd hung from roots overhead.

But this was the one who saved her life! And Retren's. And he was the one who trained MV!

Marend fought disappointment, stood up to greet the illustrious newcomer, and followed it up with a polite request: "Before you depart would you benefit us with your expertise in a weapons-training session?"

"*Mar*-end," Ramond groaned, eyes rolling up. "Don't we get enough of that already?"

"She can be forgiven for that, these days," Detlev said. His tone somehow defused the two long-time rivals. Then he looked at Marend, and she obtained a swift, half-conscious impression of subtle observations as he said, "If there is time, I'd be honored. But you know, there really is very little I can offer beyond what MV and David must have been showing you."

"Tell us something about the Ancient Sartorans!" Ramond could barely contain himself. "Was their art—"

"Let the man eat his meal before those eggs congeal," Tdor cut in from behind. "What a bunch of bloodlusts he must think us!"

"But!" Ramond flung his hands wide. "When will we ever get another chance—"

"C'mon, help me unload these supplies. At least until he's eaten." Tdor met a stony-eyed glare from Marend, and she shook her head, twitting loudly as she moved away.

Ramond got up with reluctant slowness. Marend promptly turned her back on him, preparing to have Detlev all to herself. Fuming, Ramond sat back down, but just as he opened his mouth to vent some fairly hot feelings, Senrid silently appeared. Ramond and Marend froze, one face flaming crimson and the other tight with guilt. Senrid snapped his fingers at them and jerked his thumb toward the kitchen, where Tdor and Kelsan were laboring alone.

Four eyes tracked from the thumb to Senrid's cold gray-blue gaze—then the pair retreated in haste, and teamed up to dunk, dry, and stow the dirty dishes, which allowed Detlev to finish his breakfast undisturbed.

Senrid dropped onto Ramond's chair. "Been a couple of days since you've eaten last, eh?"

Detlev chased a last bit of egg around on his plate, and ate that, too, then reached for his steep. "Seems like months."

MV said, "We've heard nothing about Aldon, but the local garrisons get their news at least a week late. Now that winter's here, it'll be longer."

Detlev flicked his fingers up. "Aldon is still in Sartor. I've shifted Ferret to Larkadhe, now that Imry isn't there. If he returns, Ferret will fade. Until then, once he works his way from his inn to the castle kitchen, we should get a better stream of immediate news. For now, we've got two items."

He smiled slightly as he held up his hand. "First, Aldon was told by Efael that if he captures Rel, he can name his promotion. Which of course will bring him here, so Senrid, prepare accordingly."

"Already doing that," Senrid said.

"We are as well." MV rubbed his hands.

"Second, Efael has put a bounty on Jehan of Khanerenth's head; from the gossip in Imry's tower, Svir seemed to think that the attack on the shipyards was Efael's fault. That is, he ought to have increased the defense when he handed down his order for a thousand ships to be built as soon as possible."

That caused the predictable laughter, amid outbursts of opprobrium against Aldon and Efael. When the cursing and insults died down, Detlev said, "Where's Zairna Raadi?"

"I am here." Zairna's voice came from behind as he and Rolfin appeared, all carrying plates of food. Mildred shifted over to make space, and they dropped down, sitting elbow to elbow. Mildred and Rolfin, tall and black-haired, made a striking contrast to Zairna's slender, pale-blond, pensive self, his movements unobtrusive—surprising in someone wearing diamonds in his ears, with thorned dragonflowers inked into his skin from his neck up over one ear.

Detlev said to Zairna, "Your guesses about Imar's defensive magic turned out to be an accurate assessment, corroborated by Sveneric. But ever since Ilerian killed Connanre, it has intensified exponentially. We might not have until summer."

That silenced everyone.

Detlev shifted to Sartoran. "The circle is now your priority. Concentrate on eradicating identity borders. Those who can't must be able to deflect prowlers." Detlev set his empty mug down, and turned to Andri. "We will not constrain you if you wish to return to Enaeran."

Andri's generous mouth twisted, the deep dimples at either side pronounced. "Why do I hear a *but*?"

"But we desperately need your talents," Detlev said.

Andri's grin faded. "Then you ought to swap me for Liere. She's the one with the strength."

"You actually have the same potential. Surely you understand that after your experience in the Selenseh Redian?"

Andri didn't deny it; the extraordinary leap in his sensitivity had not faded, though he'd expected it to. "But I'm pig-ignorant," he said. "Liere's the one with all the training."

"Liere is an excellent mage, and skilled in many ways," Detlev said. "But she actually has little training with Dena Yeresbeth. Her gift is idiosyncratic, after a lifetime of adapting on her own. There is nothing wrong with that. It serves her well. But this circle we are forming would require her to unlearn certain patterns that have become habit, whereas you have not formed those habits yet. Your training would progress rapidly. But again, that is by way of explanation, not coercion, or even moral suasion. There is no 'righter' choice here. You don't have to decide this moment," he added. "Take your time, while we have it. But I suggest you do continue training with the others. It might serve you in other ways."

Andri shut his eyes, wanting to go home so badly it took an effort to remain silent. He knew that Liere was doing well. In some ways it was actually better that he was not there, not just because Adon Marsael would rip apart the city searching for him if he had any idea Andri might be present. Andri also knew that Gared, so badly wounded in Adon Marsael's torture chamber, had recovered largely because he had purpose as Andri's chief of operations in Enaeran's resistance. If Andri showed up again, Gared would defer. Whereas Liere's letters made it clear that she and Gared were an excellent team.

While Andri brooded, the others began chattering until Kelsan emerged from the cooking nook.

"Want some more?" Kelsan pounced on empty plates; like most to whom a foreign tongue is so much babble, he didn't think he was interrupting as long as he didn't cut anyone's words off.

"No thank you, Kelsan," Detlev said.

Kelsan flushed with pleasure at being addressed by name by The Infamous One, and as he carried his stack into the kitchen he passed right by Marend without noticing her contemptuous glare.

The clattering of Kelsan gathering dishes broke up the meeting. David yawned and rubbed his eyes, for he still had not been to bed. "Well, that's it. I'm out. If Imry shows up, you people will have to entertain him." And he wandered off to sleep.

Some followed David off to bed and others started on chores, everyone talking, except Laban, who had returned from patrol. He'd greeted Roy with a surprised smile and lift of the hand, but when he saw Detlev, his expression changed. This was not missed by David, MV, or Adam.

Laban and Detlev were long overdue for a talk. Time to make certain they had it.

Fourteen

ADAM AND MV DIVIDED up those with nothing to do, leaving Laban alone, his shoulders tense as he gazed into the fire.

Detlev said, "Has the rain lifted?"

"Briefly."

"Then I'll make my essay into fresh air brief."

Laban watched him go up the tunnel toward the entrance. He hesitated, then plunged after him.

Up in the forest a cold, strong wind blew steadily from the northwest. Bare tree branches dripped dismally. Detlev contemplated his boot squelching into a wide puddle, then he looked up appraisingly at Laban. "Don't you want a jacket?"

The wind sent ripples through Laban's white shirt, but he gave his head an impatient shake. Detlev was silent under the other's sidelong scrutiny, his attention on avoiding the worst of the soggy ground. Laban paid as little heed to the mud splashing his legs as he did to the biting wind.

Finally Laban said, "Where's the shrimp?"

"Mearsies Heili."

"Bad shape?"

"Recovering rapidly. You should see him here in a few days."

Laban's expressive brows met in a dark line as he ducked a low, wet branch. They emerged in a clearing. Here the gray light, unshadowed by trees, was silver. Detlev spotted a mossy rock jutting up from the broken ground, made for it, sat down, and looked around appreciatively.

Laban swung around to face him, and propped a foot on a low shelf of stone.

Detlev smiled up at Laban's fierce blue gaze. "Well?" he offered. "What is it you wish to ask me?"

But Laban seemed unnerved by the openness of this invitation.

Detlev's smile increased faintly. "I'd hoped you'd finally forgiven me for not being omniscient."

Laban's breath whooshed out.

Detlev continued, "The fact remains that I did not know about Kessler until he was already allied with Dejain. His mind-shield was instinctive, and impervious. By the time I learned of him, he was beyond my ability to control, or even influence. I did what I could to isolate him. I got Siamis to alienate him, but nothing swerved him from his goals."

Laban did not see the sodden ground and dripping trees of the present. He remembered his single glimpse, as a small boy, of the terrible destruction of Ferdrian in '42, under Kessler's command. "He acted on your orders."

"Yes."

"You knew what was likely to happen."

"Yes," Detlev said. "Henerek was already there, and so incompetent a commander that Bostian and Aldon were poised to go there and rival one another showing him how to do it right, and the scorched ground strategy would have happened anyway, but with them there would have been no way to avoid it taking up half the continent. Everyone at Norsunder Base hated Kessler. They wanted to see him lose. After Kessler smashed through Everon so fast, Henerek went whining to Yeres — you will remember he was her favorite at that time — and it was she who pulled Kessler. All I had to do was make certain neither of them had the supplies to get through the winter."

Laban glowered. "I understand all that." Another fierce blue glare. "You wouldn't be trying to warn me off?"

"Tell me about Morgeh Troiad," Detlev replied. "That was another situation I did not know about, or I would have done my best to draw them off."

"I was too late, too," Laban admitted, and added with grim distaste, "Efael made certain there was little left when he abandoned them. What else is there to know?"

"How Morgeh died."

"Why?" Laban flung his head back, hot and haughty. "Adam asked me that as well. Did the pair of you imagine that I carried on where Efael left off?"

"Yes, we did," Detlev said. "I'm consumed with curiosity concerning the details."

Laban's expression cleared suddenly, and he laughed, but did not immediately answer.

Detlev added, "If you decide to make that land your life's work, you will never cease to feel the repercussions of Morgeh Troiad's death."

Laban did not at first comprehend Detlev's full meaning, he was so disturbed by memory. "Repercussions ... yes. Troy's friendship with the various nonhuman races."

"In part," Detlev agreed.

"I hadn't realized the extent of his connections until I went into his mind, to ease his end." Laban's expression changed again, sober, distant-seeing. "I don't think he ever knew who I was. He was completely lost. When I touched minds there was no resistance whatever. He was too weak for any kind of focus, but if I had to describe what it was of him that I sensed it would be expectancy of kinship. I looked for a memory to encompass him with—and found..."

Laban's words failed him at the vast echoing of music-wreathed celebrations of which Troy had been a part. Laban had experienced in Troy's mind a Sartorias-deles that had little to do with political paradigms, and thus he could never again think of him as merely a failed king.

He shook his head slowly. "So I drew him back a year or two, to a festival with the dawnsingers. Dtheldevor's gang was with him that time. He recognized them all, without seeing that it was mere memory. Quite happy. A little confused. Then he slipped away."

Laban looked down, and discovered that he was shivering. He flexed his hands, exerting control to bring up inner warmth. Then he turned Detlev's way. "Want to hear about the Mearsiean girl's death as well?"

"Do you want to talk about it?"

"Not particularly. CJ showed up. Seeing her calmed Diana." Laban's hands flexed once or twice more, then he smiled a little. "I realized I missed that kind of kinship. What's more, I think Imry does as well."

"Tell me about that meeting."

"There's little to tell beyond the fact that I came off like a fool." Laban grimaced. "Mountains of western Everon. I'd stumbled on a forming resistance group made up of some morvende, some refugees, all young. Got 'em organized. Drilled. Second or third strike—just as they were pulling together—Imry hit us. Cut me out from the scuttling retreat. Taunted me a little, promising to come back for me. He even offered me a transfer spell to join him. It was all an exercise in humiliation."

"What makes you think he misses the group?"

"The way he flung it in my teeth. He could've thought of plenty of other ways to mortify me."

"Here comes the weather." Detlev's eyes lifted westward.

Laban glanced impatiently over his shoulder, and followed as Detlev got up and began walking back. They had left the clearing and were winding their way among the trees when Laban spoke. "Afterward. Are you going to stand in my way?"

"If?" Detlev prompted.

Laban said it straight out. "If I lay claim to the empty throne in Fortnyal Roth."

Detlev responded mildly, "It seems to me you should be addressing this question to Hatahra Delieth. And your sister. Once the two of you meet. Though I suspect she desires only to return to Geth."

"Why should I try to talk to Tahra again?" Laban retorted with grim humor. "It won't be any different than when I went to her after we hopped the fence, will it? Only this time she'll meet me—and my humble petition—with a noose and a posse of Knights."

Detlev smiled. "The young ones, perhaps. It would be unwise to underestimate old Roderic."

Laban thought that over for a long moment, shaking his head impatiently as snowflakes drifted around them both. "So it was by design, and not by accident, that Roderic Dei survived when Henerek took Mersedes Carinna as a prisoner."

"I tried to stem the extent of Henerek's stupidity, but Yeres was actively interfering, and it was Efael's Black Knives who captured Mersedes Carinna. Siamis managed to sniff out where Henerek held Roderic Dei; we thought the queen was dead, as Yeres created a cache for Henerek in the Beyond so he could carry out his cruelties undisturbed. They also had your brother. By the time I found out, I could not interfere directly—I had to find a way for Roy to discover them while I laid some lures to distract Efael and Yeres."

"I know the details from the point-of-view of your personas," Laban cut in sharply. "Don't attempt to deflect me with perceptual pyrotechnics. What you mean is you won't tell us—me—what your real strategy was?"

"Not yet," Detlev agreed.

"Why?"

Detlev was gazing off through the winter-bare trees. After a silence during which an unforgiving wind tugged at their clothing and hair, and sleety rain spattered with soft thuds and plunks into the mud and puddles around them, Laban burst out with deep-felt bitterness, "How can you expect us to work for you for the rest of our lives?"

Detlev stopped, despite the snow that had begun to fall. "Laban. What did I say to you before I released you a few years ago?"

Laban's brows tightened. "You said..." A gesture, quick and sudden smile. "I was not really listening. I was too angry. I just wanted to get out of that house to go to Everon." A rueful grin. "And after that spectacular failure, I wanted to get away from this world altogether. I don't remember what you said."

"You weren't listening because you'd decided not to believe anything I said."

Now Laban's thoughts invoked with vivid immediacy those last days, specifically the emotional whiplash of being told they were leaving Norsunder—every one of them knowing how ill-received they would be by the rest of Sartorias-deles. "The contradictions ... David and MV, and Sveneric, even, thinking you wanted a place among the Host in Norsunder, and you were going after Efael and Yeres to get it. And then trying to guess how far back you decided to hop the fence... And you talked to them separately, but I—" He looked up, his face expressive now of amusement. "I see. I avoiding talking to you because I was afraid of being talked into obedience, and didn't see that freedom of choice right there proved that you really were cutting us free."

"Second thing," Detlev said. "I trained the group to work for Sartorias-deles. Not for me."

"But I—" Laban stopped, then started again, forcefully. "So what? That can be done from a throne as well as from a magician's cottage in Delfina Valley, or by a wanderer—" And then he laughed. "Oh, damn. It can, can't it? 'If you take up your work in that part of the world...' What is this, you've roped me back in, haven't you?"

"Will you need help?" Detlev motioned toward the path, but Laban stood where he was; not until later, after hearing an unrelated remark of David's, did Laban see the question as a double one.

"I don't think so," he said, after a long pause, as snow began to fall faster. "Not unless Tahra mounts an invasion in order to throw me out. The people of Wnelder Vee are in a desperate way. Defeated. Confused. The treasury empty. No leadership save sporadic messages from Roderic across the border. Just setting up a courier and refuge relay inspired them to look to me for hope."

"There has been little resistance to the Norsundrians in Wnelder Vee."

Laban nodded. "They don't want to fight. Don't know how to fight. Most think the only alternative is to become a province of Everon, and Tahra will just use them as a supplier. They will never have equality, or any voice in her decisions. Until recently I wondered if my background — the Deis as well as you — would mark me out as suspect, for my father left as a criminal. But the oldsters remember my great-grandmother, and my being a Dei would provide a semblance of the continuity everyone craves and no one has had for two, three generations."

Detlev said, "The snow's starting in earnest."

Laban signified assent, but then swung around again, snowflakes flying off his hair. "Did you know about our speculations?'

A laugh escaped Detlev. "I suppose it was inevitable, don't you think?"

Laban paused before the entrance to the hideout, his foot against it. They were both damp now, but Detlev waited patiently while Laban gazed somberly downward. Finally Laban looked up. "Meaning they don't know either, eh?" And, as Detlev said nothing, he went on, "Will you tell me, now, when you turned against the Host — and why?"

He stepped toward Detlev. He was Detlev's size — taller, actually — and so was thus able to stare straight down into his eyes. And though Detlev's expression of mild humor hadn't altered and his gaze was unwavering, Laban perceived about as much of his psyche as one would see of a clear, placid lake whose depths were hidden.

Detlev said, "Why do you want to know?"

Laban sighed, and turned away with an extravagant gesture. He felt all his energy dissipate along with his residual anger. "I don't know. And I don't know why it should make a difference, either. But it does."

Detlev gestured toward the door, and Laban stepped aside. Detlev stooped down to pull the cleverly made hatchway, but paused. Looking up past his shoulder at Laban, he said, "When it no longer matters, if I'm still around, then ask me again."

Laban had to laugh. They entered the tunnel on that sound.

Fifteen

NO ONE MOVED. NO one breathed as, across the river, a man picked his way slowly down the embankment. It was difficult to descry his moving silhouette from the dark-obscured riverbank.

For a few heartbeats the watchers lost sight of him, but sound carried the scrabbling of his progress over the rush of the river. A scrape, a hiss, the clatter of little stones against greater ones, then a blurred whitish shape flickered: a hand pumped up and down, a deliberate signal. For an instant the pale blob of the man's face turned in their direction to scan for followers — witnesses — betrayal of his own betrayal.

Satisfied that he remained unseen, he turned away again.

Above, hidden in the narrow opening between two houses, waited Liere and Marga Fer Eider, and one of Andri's oldest friends, Marten Eldias, alongside Gared, who still wore Andri's signet ring. On Liere's other side trembled the wife of the wife of the man below.

More silence, then the splash of an oar. Plash, splash! Again. A small hiss of wet gravel falling as the man on the bank scrambled down to the edge of the water.

The rowboat stopped directly under the old, high-arched bridge. Liere and her company were only able to make out its bow. Gared shifted to better his view, but Liere touched his arm warningly.

Over the water certain noises carried clean and distinct, others were blurred by the wintry breeze moaning around the eaves of the riverbank houses. The clink of coins in a cloth bag. A bootheel on the wooden planks of the rowboat. A low, monotonous voice not quite a whisper.

The stocky figure of Nac Parlion was stiff with tension. Liere, her companions, and Nac's wife Lantra watched his pale blob of a face nod jerkily several times, then he began to climb back up the riverbank.

The movement this time came from Lantra Parlion, and once again Liere gave Gared a warning press.

The woman's clothing shifted, and her breath warmed Liere's ear. "I want to see which one it is."

Liere made mental contact: *I know which one it is. Quiet. We are not out of danger.*

The older woman stiffened at the mind-touch, and, as Liere intended, stilled her anger-boiling questions.

Below, the rowboat sculled up the river. Then, after another long wait, three figures emerged out of the darkness not four houses away, and marched up the street.

Marten let out a soft sigh.

"Told ya," Gared muttered with grim humor.

Liere's attention was wholly on the plump, trembling figure next to her. Pity suffused her. Pity, and guilt. For it was she who had arranged this gathering, but if she read the woman right this was the only way she could be told—convinced—that her husband of thirty years was a Norsunder collaborator.

"He's betrayed us," Lantra muttered.

"He's bought your family a semblance of security. He thinks," Liere murmured.

Lantra's head came up sharply. Liere saw the water standing in the woman's eyes, sensing her anguish, humiliation, and rage as Lantra demanded, "You seek to excuse him?"

"I'm reminding you that he's not evil. Weak, possibly. Misguided, certainly. But an evil man would not care what happens to his family."

Lantra's voice was still low, and thick with emotion. "Think you the king would excuse treason?"

"The king," Liere permitted her voice to go cold and emotionless, "would expect you to carry on exactly as usual. A known spy ceases to be a danger, and becomes an advantage, if left alone."

Lantra studied the river below them, then lifted her head. "You said you know the Norsundrian responsible for suborning him? Shall we leave them alone too?"

"Until the time comes," Liere said, a calm command. No hint of her own doubts must escape, or she would not be able to overcome the humiliation Lantra fought against, and the entire family would be brought down. And Adon Marsael's chief spy would just find another victim. The only way out was to make them conspirators against Nac Parlion—as special emissaries of the king.

Liere said, "The fellow in the boat is just a flunky of Wilsar's. And Wilsar is Adon Marsael's head spy. Very effective—and very hard to find. He will be our first target, when the signal comes. We can weaken his position until then by identifying his informants, and slipping him tidbits of false information."

A sharp breath—not quite triumph, or pleasure, or relief, but near all three. "Through Nac."

"And others. Can you do it? No one—at all—besides you and your oldest daughter to know."

"We can." It was a vow.

"Then we will be in contact." Liere stepped back so the woman could move down the steep stairs to the cobbled street below. Unbidden, Marten slipped after her in order to see her safely back.

But then they heard a short gasp, a curt "Halt!" and the quiet street exploded into noise and whirling blades.

: Get Lantra free!

Liere sent the thought to Marten, and was startled when her niece Marga sang out mind-to-mind: *I'll divert them!*

She blurred into a bat, wings whirring on the cold air. Liere whipped out her blades and ran down the stairs while assessing the situation. Five, six Norsundrians? Trap? No, a patrol. After all their care not to be seen from the river, they'd blundered directly into the path of a regular patrol. At least Marten and Lantra were melding into the darkness in the other direction, and poor Nac was far down the river.

When Liere ducked through an archway that opened onto the street, a horse's hindquarters lurched into her way. Its rider was trying to hack Gared's long sword from his grip. She ducked; a whirl, a well-planted foot and the mounted Norsundrian tumbled out of the saddle. Liere leaped into his place, legs clamping to the horse's sides and mind brushing the creature's with wordless calm, and direction. Then Andri's days of drill took over her wrists, shoulders, and eyes.

Watchers from behind windows saw her long golden braids swinging in the ruddy torchlight, her fine-featured face turning this way and that as her thin-bladed rapier hummed, struck, sang, struck again, this time with a coruscation of blue sparks. She, Gared, and Marten dropped the last of the Norsundrians—Liere preferring to take out knees rather than lives—and retreated, leaving a deserted street.

Marga rejoined them a block or two over. Her bat blurred and elongated into a slim figure of ambiguous gender, wearing a light summer tunic, kneepants, and mocs, in spite of the cold. "No more of them near," she breathed.

They reached the bakehouse that was their latest hideout, and climbed gratefully into its warm attic. Gared lit a candle, then whistled when he saw Marten sink down silently, clutching a bloody arm. The trapdoor lifted and an old man looked in, his bristling eyebrows, curled mustachios, beard, and hair glistening white in the candlelight. "Serious?"

"No." Marten grunted.

"I don't know," Liere said as if Marten hadn't spoken. "Can you bring us some hot water and clean cloth, please?"

The trapdoor banged shut, and soon reopened again, this time for delivery of the requested items.

> *Between Gared and me, we got Marten's coat, vest, and shirt off* [Liere continued in a letter later that night] *and patched him up. Gared made sure he was comfortable before he'd let me look at the cut on his back. But he worried about Marten, and when Marten got feverish and muttered about his bad defense, Gared only said that we could drill on fighting against mounted some more, once Marten heals up.*

> *Gared has such a good heart! Not a hint of superiority, though I know some who might have smirked at the aristocrat admitting weakness to the son of the former Master of Horse. But it seems to me that Gared's popularity stems from the way he accepts everyone the way they wish to be perceived. And it helps that Marten is much the same way, though his family is connected to*

one of the highest noble families of Sles Adran.

*I know that Gared dislikes being mewed up as well,
especially since his recovery, and yet when I suggested
that because of the blunder with the patrol we ought to
consider holing up, just the four of us, until the
inevitable search dies down, he accepted it with that shy
smile of his. Not a hint of argument. Perhaps that cut
across his back was worse than I guessed...*

On the other side of the mountains in Darchelde, Andri sat back, glad that a blizzard had pinned everyone down for a time. He was alone in the secondary Darchelde hideout with Crow, who never talked if he could help it, and Zairna, also quiet, deep in some book of magic studies.

Andri began running the quill through his fingers as he considered Liere's words.

First there was her blithe assertion that Gared's smile was shy, and that he was helpful to all. Ah, that last was actually true, but Andri would never have described Gared's grin as shy. Nor was Gared particular reticent — the two of them had shared lovers since they hit the age of interest at about the same time: it was Gared who used to say to anyone who would hear that a day wasn't good without a fight and a tumble.

But reading about all the little ways Gared was striving to do what would please Liere, it was clear that Gared was torching for her. Hard. And — as usual — Liere, so sensitive when it came to other people, couldn't see it. Andri had suspected for some time now that she was by nature monogamous, but when he'd written to her, offering to try being monogamous, her answer had totally taken him aback — instead of being pleased, she'd written hastily, *Oh, don't do that! You're sure to get bored with me, then you'll hate me. I like all your favorites. I'm happy to share you with them!*

He was beginning to understand that, though her graceful, golden beauty nearly made people walk into doors, her inner vision of herself was still a scrawny, homely, and hapless bore.

Andri considered dropping a hint by encouraging Liere to take Gared as a lover. It would be good for them both — the more love in the world, the better — except he'd learned that that sort of thing was better left to happen naturally. Telling people that someone else would be good for them seldom resulted in much besides awkwardness, even resentment.

Poor Gared! At least it would burn out as suddenly as it had ignited. Andri had seen Gared fall in and out of love a dozen times since they reached the age of interest.

He held the paper up to the lamp again and read on.

My main worry is still Marga. There is no use trying to keep her mewed up, much as I wish we could. She vanishes suddenly, and reappears a day, or three, or four, later, having changed to beast or bird. But then the danger is less her discovery by some roaming spy, and far more her being found by Ilerian prowling the realm of the spirit. Especially as he has become so much more powerful, just in the past week or two. Though I remain shielded, I can still sense it, the way you can feel the heat of the sun through thick curtains in summer.

Marga tries to be no trouble, but things she does and says are unsettling. Not an hour ago, Gared and I were eating the supper the baker brought, when I saw Marga sitting with her spoon in the air, staring at Marten's bandaged forearm, her thoughts clearly distant.

When I asked if something troubled her, she apologized, and then stunned us by saying that she had recovered the bits of her missing memory, as if she were mentioning finding a missing pair of mittens. She was unshielded to me, her memory very vivid as she stared at a man's forearm, a man with bright green eyes — and I recognized Imry Llyenthur.

The memory caught me as if I had been thrown into the rapids of a river, the two of them facing one another on an island far out in the sea, no humans within days of travel. Faster than the circles that spread and intersect when rain drops into a lake, memories interconnected.

She looked up at me, and said, "Except he is not so much my enemy as that one in Imar whose presence I feel waking and sleeping."

What to say to THAT?

She just laughed, then said, "I believe I gave Imry

Llyenthur the fidgets, for my mind was as empty as the sky, and all he did was gawk at me helplessly. My memory just took its time coming back."

The trapdoor opened then, and we handed down the empty trays, and the baker offered more blankets as his wife said she smelled snow on the wind. The others settled to sleep, probably to escape the pain of their hurts, which is why I am writing to you now.

Thinking about Marga and her place in the world brought my mind to Detlev, my old puzzle. He's become less puzzling since I figured out that he doesn't always address the immediate subject, but other subjects <u>behind</u> the immediate subject. Except I still cannot figure out what other subjects there might be when he asked me if I had met Chantala Shagal's "other friend." He had assured me that he did not suspect Norsundrian shadows touching poor Chantala, so I'd dismissed the matter at the time, but it keeps coming back to me.

Are you finding something similar, with him there in your midst?

Liere sent that, and then shook out her fingers after so much writing in the tiniest handwriting possible. She yawned, and was about to spread out her bedding when the words, which had been fading, vanished altogether, were replaced by Andri's hand:

Liere: You never told me that. What exactly happened?

Liere looked down, startled. Of course she had. Hadn't she? No, actually, she hadn't. That conversation with Detlev had occurred right before she discovered that Andri had been taken prisoner, and then events had moved so very fast. She thought back carefully, and realized that all she'd mentioned to Andri was that she had met Chantala on her journey to contact the Sles Adran resistance, and that she was fine.

Fighting back tiredness, she dipped her pen in the ink, and scrawled a quick precis of her conversation with Detlev.

On the other side of the mountains, Andri waited impatiently. Was this something he needed to return home for? Except that Detlev had not suspected Norsunder involvement.

If that had changed, surely he would have told one or the other of them? Andri really did not want to get mixed up again in Mariana's plot to marry off Chantala to him. Though he was safely married to Liere, you never knew what political plots would mire your boots if you weren't nimble in sidestepping.

Words appeared on his paper. He read swiftly through, and then sat back, frowning. If the friend was an Adrani, then that would be the best outcome. Finally he wrote:

> *Liere, anything to do with Sles Adran worries me. Enaeran is in bad shape. Sles Adran isn't. If we manage to rid ourselves of Adon Marsael and Bartal na Shagal, that will remain the same. It's better if we know. Since you have to sit tight to let the searches die down, can you sit tight on a horse, well away from Shiovhan, and check on her once more? Or Gared could go. Or even Marten. Though not if they are badly hurt.*

Liere read that, and looked at the two sleeping men. Of course both of them would instantly claim they were fine. But she knew they weren't. It didn't take much to sense the pain they were hiding. Besides, how would they find that artists' colony? It was so very remote.

Ah, this is what being married means.

> *Andri: I'll leave tomorrow.*

Sixteen

SASHA TOOK OVER COMMUNICATION for Khanerenth's fleet, and sent Fox a tough old character named Sage, who handled the magic-paper for him. Fox found modern script maddening—familiar yet not. He spent most of his time either poring over the chart, or drilling on the foredeck, counting under his breath the time between signal flags going up and the flash of sails along his haphazard fleet.

David wrote to both; he was in steady contact with Ferret in Larkadhe.

Sage fitted in well with the drakan's crew, but tended to be succinct, if not cryptic. Sasha, who liked description, ended up sending longer reports to David, who then collected appreciative comments from those in Darchelde who knew the sea, and passed them back. Encouraged by these, Sasha began to get creative with her reports.

> *… Jehan is calling this last one the Sleeper Raid. I don't know if that sounds sufficiently badass — ah, that's a word from my world, for which Jehan suggests as a definition, "Think of MV on the deck of the Mule Kick, cutlass in one hand, dagger in the other, fighting off five pirates" — ah, I lost track of my sentence, and this weird paper makes it tough to edit.*

I'll start again. The Sleeper Raid. Not nearly as badass as Fox's raid on the Chwahir coastline, but successful as a one-time thing. I took a team up into Ellir, a harbor city I know very well. Jehan says that he met you there. Then I don't need to describe it, except to say that we used one of the passages to get up into the garrison on the escarpment.

We came out by the lazarette, which is usually the least guarded. The watch bell was about to ring, and we were waiting for that so we could mix in with the noise and movement of the watch change. But Lesi Valleg, a young captain who was stationed at Ellir before she was shifted to ship duty, said that she smelled pepper-bean soup, which is often served with bread for winter dinners. When I remembered that the dispensary is on the other side of the kitchens, I got an idea.

We tried the passage behind the row of rooms, and as expected, Norsunder hasn't yet discovered it. Nobody's told them. I was able to get into the dispensary to grab the jar of sleepweed, which was nearly full.

From there it was a matter of distracting the cooks long enough for me to slip in and add the entire jar of sleepweed to the two big tureens. Since the soup has, besides the beans and onions and corn and pepper, shredded spinach as ingredients, I didn't think anyone would notice extra green bits. I stirred in more sweet pepper to mask the taste, and slipped out just in time — the watch bell clanged right overhead, and the kitchen help, who had mostly been fussing over the bread coming out of the ovens, stampeded to serve the food.

I hotfooted back inside the passage to my team.

"Let's wait," I told them — though we were supposed to disperse in the watch-change stream in order to map sentry numbers and positions, in case there were substantive changes from when we held Ellir.

We waited what seemed like a hundred hours — probably the turn of the half-hour glass, if that — and ventured *out, to find pretty much the entire fortress snoring. That is some <u>strong</u> sleepweed! Too bad this sort of thing only works once. I'm sure the next orders your friend at the capital will pass on will be for tasters.*

But it was so good while it lasted! The few who didn't eat the soup were easy to overcome. Jehan has left it up to people's consciences whether to kill or preserve lives; more than a few were well tied and gagged with sailors' knots for the duration, in particular, I noticed, the very young and the very old. I think one of the most grievous aspects of this invasion for Jehan are the people who join the other side mainly to survive.

Jehan and Owl led their teams down to the barrier, and though they were prepared to fight, they didn't have to. They dismantled the barrier, and decided to tote that wood, too, as the logs jammed behind the barrier began rushing out to sea.

Captain Gliss, who has been attached to Captain Ghaer's river boat sailors, reported that the guiding of the logs went swimmingly, ha ha. The bay we'd picked was full of timber by the time I got there to lay the illusion over the entrance to the bay. I created a very threatening-looking reef, and we sailed on the turn of the dawn tide...

All the fleet commanders agreed that a lightning strategy was best—striking here, there, never predictable.

After hearing a little about Wan-Edhe, Fox figured that this mad king would demand the coastal Chwahir to sail west to Narad to protect him. He was right. Thus, Fox's next raid was at Essla, the east-most Chwahir harbor. At the same time, Jehan's people rode a storm down to a small, isolated harbor on the coast of Sarendan, where they discovered a single ship that was nearing completion, its mainmast newly settled in. This, Sasha's group stole, while Jehan's lured off the main of the defense—mostly a mix of Bostian's least effective, eked out by some raw Adrani recruits.

Sage went to Fox. "David reports that Efael himself went down to Sarendan to investigate, but all he got was blizzard in the face. Not too happy."

Sage paused as those crowded in the galley made crude suggestions about Efael, and enjoyed a good laugh at his expense.

Fox was scarcely listening. When he got that narrow-eyed look, his crew knew they were soon going to be up on the spars, squeezing every bit of speed out of the drakan as they slanted against the icy winds. Laugh while they could.

"Let's set sail for Drael," Fox said finally.

His first mate scowled. "We're going to raid Jaro?"

"No," Fox drawled. "Why would we attack a harbor that already has a division of warriors waiting to welcome us? Probably more, by now."

"Then … up north?"

"Perhaps. But first, we'll raid Beila Lana. Ah. It seems to be called Beilann or Belann, now, in the language of something called Everon. Ymar in my day." He lifted a shoulder, shrugging off political and language shifts. "Looks to me from this chart like all the shipbuilding in southeastern Drael goes on there."

The third mate elbowed her way in. "Which they'll be expecting. Half of that division at Jaro is probably just arriving right now, in time to sharpen their swords and making bets on how many of us they can kill."

"I know Beila Lana," the first mate put in, stabbing the chart with a blunt, gnarled finger. "That passage is so narrow you can throw a stone across, or near as. They won't even have to run. Just stand on either side and shoot us down as we come out—assuming we get past 'em to go in."

"Of course." Fox's green eyes were lambent in the glow of the lantern. "But we're not going to take out those ships. Not this time, anyway."

"What?"

"What?"

"What?"

Fox's grin was exactly as nasty as it had been when he was twenty-five. "I've got another idea," he said.

Sles Adran

A large, cold-white moon drifted low over the distant line of northern mountains, the clouds high and insubstantial in the west.

By now Liere was an expert in gauging how far and fast a

single horse could go. The great rivers had turned to ice, which meant she could avoid bridges that were likely patrolled.

She knew the way now, and once she was on the road in a beautiful, exhilarating world of white, she enjoyed the trip. Alone with her thoughts, she watched her own and the horse's breaths puff in fragile white clouds and disappear. Sounds were crisp and loud. Winter had set in hard, but her blood raced faster than the flashing hooves of her frisky mount.

As the days drifted by, and she scanted sleep in order to hasten her journey, she caught her mind flowing along familiar channels. It was still a habit to reach for Senrid. Every time she recognized it, she pulled her thoughts back. Even if they hadn't had that awful argument the winter previous, farsense was far too dangerous.

She still felt uneasy, not quite guilty, but something like it, whenever she thought about Senrid. But what possible use was that? There were too many other problems to consider, ones she *could* fix, like repairing her communication with her daughter. She still checked on Lyren-Sartora every night, and knew she was safe, but so far, Lyren-Sartora refused to write back to her, except the briefest line to say she was perfectly able to be independent.

Late in the afternoon the next day, Liere reached the secluded artists' colony hamlet on the edge of the lake below a huge, snow-crested mountain. Here there was little evidence of war. None, if one overlooked the children who spotted her tired horse plodding up the last steep switchback on the trail the locals regarded as the main road, and scampered back up the hill to warn someone as soon as they saw her choose the turnoff.

The little hollow, sheltered from winds and winter, afforded an unexpected burst of late-autumn beauty here and there: trees and wildflowers reflected in the tranquil pool at the bottom of the hollow, creating a doubled glory of crimson, gold, amber, cinnamon and yellow around the hot spring that fed the pool. Liere rode past a sweeping row of bare, silver-barked ash, and gazed with pleasure across a protective wall of whispering evergreens, with their contrasting carpet of brown and rust-colored leaves. The place was exactly as beautiful as it had been late in the spring when she'd first come here. Only the colors had changed.

The hamlet consisted of a half-circle of stone houses set on the slopes. The Harieses were nearest the top. Their house had

begun as a way station on an ancient trade-route, and had been deserted and rediscovered four or five times since. The hamlet was now inhabited mainly by artists who, in catering to the never-ending demand for decorative art by Sles Adran's wealthy citizens, felt it necessary to live close to the source of inspiration.

Three tall, soughing evergreens sheltered the house of the couple who cared for Chantala. As Liere rode up, a woman came out, small and rosy-faced and smiling, wiping her hands on her paint-smeared apron. At the same time a small boy shot round the side of the house and pounded up.

"Good day, Honor," the woman greeted Liere. Squinted more closely. "Do I not know you? Oh, yes! Welcome back among us! A long ride?"

Liere did not yet realize how diplomatic the question was, for she rarely paid any heed to her appearance, except when trying to disguise herself. But there was no need to here. Politely turning aside offers of food and drink, she scanned as much of the wide-windowed house as she could see. The winter shutters were not yet up; inside a man worked away at enameling a table. As soon as she could interpose a word into the gentle flow of questions and exclamations, she asked where Chantala was.

"Oh, they walked up to the winter garden." Lies Haries nodded beyond the top of the slope.

Liere dismounted, and thanked the child waiting to see to the horse. She set out through the crackling frost-topped snow toward the winter garden, her legs watery and her knees stiff after the long ride. She lengthened her strides, kicking her mocs vigorously through the snow.

She rounded a ridge marked by firs. Below lay a sheltered cove, through the middle of which, in springtime, a mountain stream had chuckled and splashed. Now it was an ice sculpture in myriad shades of blue. At one side was a mossy, rounded rock into which someone centuries ago had carved a bench. Behind grew a bank of hardy evergreen shrubs, and in spring a hedge of flowering shrubs, now bare. On the bench sat two figures, at this distance as handsome as a painting in a royal castle.

Chantala looked healthy and smiling, the thin, chalk-pale face that Liere had first met now glowing with delicate color. Her pale, thin hair was braided into a coronet on her head, and about her neck was a soft ruff of woven yeath fur the exact shade of her light gray eyes. Liere took in the rest of the beautiful silver coat, and the heavy watered-silk skirt billowing in rich folds round Chantala's feet. Woven yeath-coats of that color, and that fine make, were spectacularly expensive, even for aristocrats of the highest degree.

Someone had been taking very good care of her—far more than one would think the Harieses could afford.

Liere's gaze transferred back to the tall, broad-shouldered man who stood at Liere's approach, dark hair waving down over his shoulders from a high brow. Clean, ordered hair. When did she have clean hair last? she thought hazily, as her gaze traveled down the exquisitely tailored dark gold riding tunic that enhanced a splendid build. The robe was long, the hem ending at his boot tops, split up the side, showing dark green trousers. Fresh lace at the wide wrist cuffs made aristocratic framing for a pair of beautiful hands.

His head turned. The strong bones were immediately familiar, though his nose was straight, his lips cut in the Elsarion curve. As she neared, she saw details—arched brows, long black lashes framing eyes the blue of a winter sky.

Chantala rose, then stumbled on the hem of her gown. There was no mistaking the concern, the care, of his quick gesture as he caught her arms and righted her before she could fall. Chantala smiled up at him with the ease of one used to his company. His proximity.

"Liere?" Chantala cried, clutching her thin hands close to her frail chest. "Is that Liere?"

"Chantala," Liere said, then turned her wide golden gaze to Chantala's companion. "Trevor Macael Elsarion, I'm guessing?"

He bowed. "Am I to understand that I am—at last—meeting *the* justly famed Liere Fer Eider?"

For the first time within living memory Liere was suddenly and acutely conscious of her appearance. A swift mental assessment was sufficiently dismaying: gritty hair, an ugly, tie-less brown cloak, ravel-edged as an old horse blanket, pinned haphazardly at her shoulder by a gaudy gold-and-ruby brooch that Gared had unearthed from his and Andri's former light-fingered days; a shapeless, filthy brown coat over equally grubby green tunic and riding trousers—for cleaning frames were rare in war-devastated Enaeran—belted with two weapons; mud-caked mocs and scruffy stockings falling down about her ankles, with the hilt of a stolen Norsunder dagger, visible to all, sticking out of the top of the left one. She was road-grimed to the fingernails, and probably whiffed of horse. No, make that surely.

There was only one thing to do. Performing an even more elegant bow than Trevor Macael Elsarion's, she replied, "You are."

Chantala beamed at her with delight as Liere said to her, "I came to see that you are still safe."

"I am very well." Chantala held out her hands in welcome. "So kind of you to come to me again! Will you stay with the Harieses? You know there is room, and you are very welcome."

"Weather on the way." Macael glanced up at the sighing fir tops, and beyond to the now turbulent, steely sky. "Perhaps we ought to get inside."

A cold, damp wind was already fingering at their faces and clothes, and Chantala's thin fingers groped at the opening of her cloak to pull it close.

As they started down the path Macael said over Chantala's bent head, "Is Andri behind you?"

"No. I came alone," Liere said.

"Had you received some sort of word of sign that there might be danger nigh?" he asked, his voice low.

"No. Andri asked me to stop by if I rode near the area," Liere finessed, with a glance toward Chantala, who was tracking a pair of birds fluttering about the top of a pine.

A gust of wind took a swipe at them, bringing a whirl of snowflakes. Even buried in her fabulous coat Chantala shivered, and Macael's hand moved to her elbow.

No one spoke until they reached the relative shelter of the Harieses' doorstep. There Chantala looked up in question at Macael. "Perhaps you should come back for dinner?"

Macael smiled reassuringly. "Why increase Aunt Thi's domestic cares? I think Fan and I can contrive a supper for three."

Chantala looked relieved. She turned to Liere. "Macael was going to arrange dinner for us tonight, so that the Harieses could finish some work to go out before New Year's Week. Will you join us?"

Macael said, "Please. I would like very much to hear the news from Enaeran."

"Very well," Liere said.

Chantala's sincerity was real, and Macael's manners

perfect; he opened the latch so that Chantala would not have to put her hands out into the cold and then he walked off into the rising wind, his long, glossy dark hair streaming.

Inside, the air was warm, and still, and smelled strongly of paint solvents. Maybe it would mask Liere's contribution of old horse blanket, she thought with reeling hilarity as they closed out the weather and entered the big main room. Stav Haries's aunt, who was their housekeeper and cook, was just setting another lamp down around the cluster already circling the working artists when Lies' hand jerked.

With an exclamation of dismay she dropped her tiny brush into the murky water and daubed with her apron at the porcelain vase she'd been painting. Then she looked up, and smiled a distracted welcome. "Oh, good. You found them. I'll take a brief break." She yawned, wringing and flexing her hand.

Stav Haries worked on unheeding, his beak-nosed face obviously unaware of the existence of extra people in his home, even filthy ones who reeked of horse. Liere passed by, admiring his deft touches on the fine enameled gold scrollwork and tiny emerald leaves in an arabesque pattern that his wife was reproducing in miniature on the vase.

Fashion. Liere embraced its frivolity, its total irrelevance to the realities of war. She resolved that she would never sneer at it again.

Stav's aunt pressed steep into her hands. "Honor Chantala's got three trunks 'o dresses now, so you go up and pick one, and I'll have yours fresh by morning."

"I can bed down with the horses," Liere said. "They won't mind how ripe I am."

"No, there are so many empty rooms," Chantala said. "It is so nice to have a visitor."

Aunt Thi put in succinctly, "*Your* clothes won't be no trouble. Boil 'em."

Liere glanced at Chantala's lace and embroidery decorated silk, and guessed correctly that, without a cleaning frame, laundry would keep an army of servants busy. But she also knew that Chantala was not the kind to change with careless frequency, though she'd been raised by a duchas and was now heir to the kingdom of Sles Adran.

"We have a bath, brought down from the hot spring. With water that cleans by magic," Aunt Thi added. "Young Macael brought the wand back from his place last summer. Said they have extra ones at Elsarion."

A bath? In hot, clean water that would not have to be hauled in, bucket by bucket? That was the clincher. Within a short time Liere sank gratefully into the extravagant tub upstairs, full of steaming, herb-scented water. All the tension melted from her bones, so warm, so pleasant—

Sleep almost took her, just like that. She sat up, thinking, how typical. The great and mighty Sartora, drowned snoring in a bathtub. As she scrubbed her scalp vigorously, her gaze rested on her three weapons sitting on the stool. What a strange turn her life had taken! The mental contrast of her appearance with the well-groomed pair she'd met in the winter garden—the obliviousness of the uncle—the relief that the mysterious friend was Andri's cousin, and no sinister spy, all made her feel as if someone had replaced her insides with bubbles.

She needed sleep. Well, after this dinner she would get it, and in a clean bed.

But first she finished her bath while Chantala happily pulled apart her trunks, with many considering looks in Liere's direction. At times she seemed as unworldly as a small child, but now she was in her element. When had that happened? The Chantala Liere remembered from spring had seemed too vague to take any interest in clothes. Somebody cared. And, it seemed, she cared for the opinion of that somebody.

Blue, brown, green, wine, violet, colors rich and rare, and selected to make the most of Chantala's faded sallow coloring, were pulled this way and that. All new robes. Liere liked the over robe that Chantala finally chose; she had an exacting eye. As might be expected from the writer of the Cabriol poem, and its appreciations for the beauties of nature. This outfit was a soft light blue that had a silver sheen, worn over a pale, eggshell blue under robe, the front tied with ribbons of the same eggshell blue. "Your golden hair and this blue is so pretty a combination," Chantala said. "Ah, yes. A gold silk sash, to match your hair."

Liere was in the process of combing the knots out of her wet hair. How long had it been since she'd had it unbraided and washed? Too long; and the last time she'd worn a fine robe was when she had visited the resistance in Sles Adran in spring.

But at last her hair was free of tangles. She glanced at herself in the mirror to see that she was tidy, and paused, surprised at the difference being clean made. "Oh." The blue robe was really quite beautiful, and how had she managed not to notice how long her hair had grown, waving in a fall to the tops of her thighs?

She moved to sit by the fire in hopes her hair would dry a bit faster, as Chantala folded the silken robes away again. But that did not take long; Liere grimaced, knowing that if she braided her hair now, she would wind up sleeping on a wet braid. She let it hang loose, in hopes more time might dry it better.

They went downstairs, Liere too busy finding Chantala's yeath-fur coat to notice the stares of the two older women, or Stav groping for his chalks as he goggled at her. She helped Chantala into her yeath-wrap, insisting she'd be fine without for the short walk to Macael's cottage.

The outside air was cold, but at least the snow had stopped. Liere shivered, wondering if her layer of grime had provided insulation. Or maybe she'd scrubbed too hard, and her skin was sensitive? She was glad when the door to a small cottage at the end of a narrow pathway opened, enveloping them in light and warmth. Macael stood there in dark red velvet embroidered with gold and green intertwined leaves down the front and the sleeves, fine lace at his wrists, dark trousers worn over his exquisitely made riding boots.

For the space of a breath the three of them stood there as Liere tried to catch at her blowing hair to keep it from becoming a hopeless tangle.

"Dear Macael," Chantala said. "It smells so welcoming."

He held the door wide. "Please, come in."

Seventeen

"WHAT'S DAVID SAY NOW?" Fox asked, as the Ydrasal chandelier swung and swayed in the cabin. He'd noticed that, no matter how high the waves, the chandelier never struck the bulkheads. Magic or ancient Venn shipwrights' design? Another question to ask Ramis, if he turned up again.

Sage waved the limp piece of beige paper. "More gossip from Norsunder HQ at Larkadhe. The Host endorses Wan-Edhe's command to bring the two main Chwahir fleets home. They expect to break the world ward, after which the ward over Mearsies Heili will be simple to destroy."

Fox didn't know what wards were. He didn't care, unless they interfered with him directly. "Make sure Prince Yviski knows about the movement of the Chwahir fleets. Though my guess is, they'll be under orders to stay in sight of the south shore. As long as he sticks to the north shore, he should get by unseen."

Prince Yviski, a middle-aged, somewhat morose-looking man, had proved to be an innovative commander. Ghaer as well. It was her boats now shepherding the barely-seaworthy tub they had cut out at Essla, which had been in the process of being gutted for the few sound timbers left in it. That tub might even date back to Fox's day—the shape of that round hull was certainly familiar enough, and he knew that the Chwahir, along with other kingdoms, had been in the habit of preserving ships' wood through magic.

Fox sat back, frowning at the door through which—if he used the magic he'd been given eight centuries ago—he was able to move back and forth from the drakan to his family castle in Darchelde. He was not certain if he wanted to see what was there, or not. It certainly wouldn't be prudent, if his homeland's descendants had lost badly. And there would be no one he recognized.

He turned his back, and bent over the chart once again; they ought to spot land by nightfall, and if weather and wind served them, why wait and chance being discovered?

Artists' Colony – Sles Adran

"You don't stay with the Harieses?" Liere asked Macael.

"I wish he would," Chantala said softly. "I don't think this cottage is warm enough in winter."

Macael smiled as a quiet, soberly dressed servant took Chantala's wrap, and then brought out hot mulled wine. "For a few days, perhaps. But any more than that is a disturbance. And I must return to Elsarion for the turn of the year."

They sat on cushions around a little table before the fire. The servant brought out a tray and set it down; Macael uncovered each with a smiling, graceful flourish.

The warmth, the wine, the anticipation of a pleasant evening put faint color in Chantala's cheeks and a happy quirk to her shadowed gray eyes. There were a few cheery comments about the weather and the walk over, then Macael gave a mock-lordly gesture. "Help yourself while it's hot—"

A sudden gust of wind drummed at the window, which blanked with thick snow. "You planned your entrance well," Macael said.

Chantala chuckled—this was exactly the sort of very mild joke she enjoyed.

The food was simple: a fresh-water fish poached in wine and shallots, rice cooked with slivers of almond, buttered carrots, corn-biscuits, a spray of grapes. When Liere had filled her plate, Macael served Chantala before himself, then they ate.

Conversation was much like his joke—pleasant,

observations of the obvious: weather predictions, what the children had been playing, the art the Harieses were making. Under the influence of wine, warmth, and this easy dialogue, Chantala was at her best.

When such topics appeared to be exhausted, Macael turned to Liere. "How is Andri?"

Liere's gaze slid thoughtfully toward Chantala, then she said, "He's very busy. He will be glad to hear that we met, and that you are well."

"Please give him my greeting, too," Chantala said. "He was so kind to me. Mariana liked him, though I do not think my uncle did, even though they had never met. That puzzled me. But many things Uncle Bartal did, and said, puzzled me. It was the same with that Commander Mandracar he wished me to marry. I am glad that Commander Mandracar seems to have stayed away from Denwy, ever since I sent divorce papers to him."

Liere felt that it was safe to say, "The king appears to have had more troubles to think about, specifically with the kingdom being largely governed by Kinarde. Though now, with Llyenthur out, who knows what will happen?"

"What's that? Llyenthur deposed?" Macael said lightly, like Liere sending a quick look at Chantala to see how she took this news. "When was that?"

"Recent—a week or so ago, from my understanding."

Macael's eyes narrowed, as though he was silently appreciating a very good joke. But he only turned to inquire if Chantala had had enough, and was it to her liking?

From there the conversation strayed to the Harieses' latest stylistic twists, and from there to current styles in Nente. Talking about art inspired Chantala almost to animation; if a reference veered war-ward, she listened, but quietly. Macael always adroitly shifted the talk back into safe topics.

Liere remembered that Chantala had enjoyed talking about her mother and nurse, both beloved figures. She listened, and even asked questions, giving no hint that she had heard it all from Chantala months ago. Other than that one mention of her divorce—apparently a princess did not have to get the king's permission—Chantala made no other reference to her month-long marriage to a Norsundrian-allied military commander. The man, Liere knew, who had commanded the slaughter of Andri's newly-formed, barely trained King's Guard. They needn't have done that. It would have sufficed to disarm them and chase them back over the border. But the single witness had been graphic in describing how much he had enjoyed leading the slaughter.

When the meal was done, Liere helped Macael to move the table back as the servant carried the tray of dirty dishes away. Snow thrummed against the windows as they gathered close to the fire. Macael leaned out to wave the firestick higher, a brilliant flash from his little finger drawing Liere's attention to a gold ring with a sapphire set with three diamonds. Something was carved into the face of the sapphire.

She was not aware of staring until he glanced up. The question in his gaze made her feel as if she had trespassed into personal space. But he resumed his seat, as Chantala said, "May we have music?"

"Whatever you wish."

<hr>

Off Beilann Harbor - Everon

All titles were absurd, Fox believed. Including the ones he had inherited, as well as the ones his ancestors had lost with a stab in the back. But when did a title go from absurd to risible?

When there was no land or holdings or power to go with it. Prince Yviski might or might not hold similar notions — at any rate, it was not he who insisted on his title, and its honorifics, but his ardent followers.

The displaced prince bent over the drawing that Fox had made of Beilann harbor, which was a blend of the sketch on MV's chart and his own memory of the Beila Lana of eight centuries previous. So far, the only recognizable parts of the world had been mountains, rocky formations such as The Fangs, the moon, and the movement of the seas.

"Got it," the prince said. He'd never been on this side of the world. "I'll take the tub."

"I can do that," Ghaer said, crossing her arms.

She reminded Fox a little of Jeje — her brisk attitude, and the way her black brows lowered to a line over her nose. Though Ghaer was thin and tall, instead of short, and she had a mouse squeak of a voice instead of the low growl like a hunting cat that had characterized Jeje.

Fox shook his head. "I need you watching those boats of yours. You know how to signal them. What speed you can get out of them. The boats are crucial—the timing has to be perfect, or all the risk will be for nothing."

The prince said to her, dryly, "They'll be shooting at you, too. I just need to get off the tub and out of the water."

Ghaer lifted a shoulder. Then eyed Fox. "You?"

"My people and I are going to be the goat in this game. Word has to be going out about *Treason*'s distinctive silhouette." He leaned out and smacked a bulkhead. "Let 'em think we're going after the ships on the blocks. We'll go over land. Come around from behind. If we actually get close enough to start some fires, great, but I expect we won't get within spitting distance. What we really need is to draw off their people in a good, long chase, over marshy land. I've already sent someone ahead who knows marshes, to pick out a path for us..."

All three heads came up, Ghaer sniffing the air, Prince Yviski cocking his head to listen to the song of the wind in the sails, and Fox evaluating the feel of the ship beneath them. "Tide's out," he said to their knowing faces. "Let's go."

Artists' Colony – Sles Adran

Macael retreated to the far room, and returned with a very well-made twelve string lute. Then he gestured for Liere to take the second upholstered wing chair, and he sat on the plain wooden stool he'd used at dinner. He ran his fingers experimentally over the lute, tightening and sounding it again several times; his hearing was much more acute than hers, for it sounded fine to her. Finally he sent a chord shimmering through the noise of the storm, and Liere was surprised to discover that he was not just musical, but played very well. As one might expect of someone who had spent many winters in isolation.

Macael never made a mistake, even with the most intricate melodies, and during the long evening he never had recourse to music notations. He repeated a song only twice, at Chantala's request.

He sang, too. Sometimes alone, but only when Chantala asked, mostly accompanied by Chantala. Her light voice had been well trained, and he sang softly, harmonizing well. The songs were all peacetime ones. Tiredness, wine, and comfort carried Liere's thoughts down a shadowy stream, caught now and again by bright images from the music.

The twice-repeated song was "Two Travelers from Cabriol," Chantala's poem, recited while she and Andri stood on a cliff edge staring out into a snow storm. Andri had experienced an overwhelming shift in perspective when he'd seen that valley not in military terms, as he'd been accustomed, but as scenery, beautiful scenery at that. When it ended the second time, Liere saw Chantala looking her way, her expression one of question, perhaps hope.

"That's beautiful," Liere said. "Andri recited a bit of the poem to me once. Macael, I take it you set Chantala's poem to music, then?"

"You know my poem?" Chantala pinked with pleasure. "Andri remembered my poem?"

"Just bits of it," Liere said, again not mentioning that they had had this conversation during the dinner, as well as last spring. "He regretted not having remembered it all, he was so impressed by it."

"He did? He did?" Chantala's face lifted, expressive of delight.

Chantala began to speak of Mariana, her voice ever softer. When she rubbed her eyes twice, Macael said, "Here, you must be tired from sitting on that cushion. Would you like to stretch out on the sofa there, until the snow stops?"

Chantala agreed, and moved to the comfort of the three-cushion recliner. Macael brought some shawls to cast over Chantala, who curled on her side, her fists under her chin. Her eyes drifted closed.

Macael returned to his cushion and began to play very softly; gradually the soft sounds swelled into long, intricate melodies that moved through changing chords, evoking a complexity of emotions and memories; Liere had always liked music, but until that night, had never equated music with passion.

Eighteen

Beilann Harbor

ONE OF THE THINGS Jehan had said to Fox was that farmers in Khanerenth had been insisting it was going to be a rough winter—judging by the thickness of animals' coats, and other such signs, one of the roughest in memory.

This was exactly what they needed.

Under cover of spears of sleet that slanted nearly horizontal, the riverboats shepherded the waterlogged tub they had coaxed out of Essla Harbor. It was listing badly, the hold taking in water. Until they reached the long, narrow passage leading to Beilann Harbor, they'd rotated teams of sailors from the entire fleet to bail constantly, lest they lose the tub in the middle of the ocean. As soon as they started into the passage, the signal went out: cease bailing, and get off the ship.

The sails were made fast; the prince's mariners withdrew in their own boat, which slanted into the wind, carrying them past the loaded river boats and back to sea. Only Prince Yviski remained at the tub's helm, hauling with all his strength against wind, water, and the saturated, sagging ship's own tendency to crab.

The river boats carried on with their orders. Each had taken aboard as many boulders from one of the countless rocky islets off the shore as possible, and under Ghaer's eye, the boats wallowed alongside the tub, only slightly faster. Teams climbed rope ladders to the tub's deck, and began throwing the boulders down into the bowels of the leaking ship.

The prince directed them to begin on the side that was listing, which caused a balance for a brief time; it was about then that a miserable sentry on one of the passage spits spotted the silhouette bulking up a passage that only permitted fishers, yachts, yawls, and other small craft. No larger ships sailed into Beilann. They had all been directed to Jaro.

The sentry rang the alarm, unheard over the howling wind. After a roared exchange with his partner, whose eyesight was not as sharp, one remained there and the other ran to report, while out in the passage the boats kept bumping up against each other as mariners swarmed up, lugging rocks.

The first sign of defense was one of the river mariners jolting upright, then falling, an arrow in her chest, as the heavy stone she'd been guiding in its sling dropped between her boat and the tub.

"Shields!" Ghaer's voice was lost in the wind, but her signal wasn't. All the coxswains under her command had been trained to watch for signals; on every boat, shields rose above the gunwales, mariners ducking down.

The prince hunched over, one hand in a death grip on the helm. Almost there … almost there …

The hiss and zip of arrows began from both sides of the passage—just as the tub reached the narrowest point.

Which was Prince Yviski's sign. He cut the rope holding the helm. It spun—the ship's rotting timbers groaned and graunched as the tub listed, turning broadside to. The prince yanked another rope, which had been bound to a pulley; one of the boulders dropped into the ocean, yanking a huge piece of wood that had corked a hole in the hull.

Water began to flood into the hold, the boulders pulling the old tub down.

Yviski crept on hands and knees across the deck as a lethal canopy flew from both directions over him, and he dove overboard. A heartbeat after he plunged into the icy water, the masts toppled, and crashed to the deck, smashing splinters in all directions, as lethal as the arrows.

"Sails!"

The river boats, one by one, stepped their single masts, and raised sail. The sails had been dyed gray and brown to be more difficult to see at night, but still arrows flew at them. Mariners watched anxiously as holes appeared in the belling sails, but their lightness, the current, and the wind that they had fought against while following in the tub's wake now worked for them. One by one the river boats picked up speed, surging down the passage toward the open sea, as the enemy ran stumbling along both sides, slipping on treacherous, icy rocks as they tried to run and shoot.

The last boat was Ghaer's. She and her coxswain pulled the prince out of the water. As the boat's crew shielded him as best they could while tending the ship and shooting back, captain and coxswain stripped the prince unceremoniously down to the skin. Shivering violently, he made no protest; he was already blue at lips and fingers.

They wrapped him in sacking and extra cloaks, as behind them, the tub sank rapidly to the bottom of the passage, thus blocking it thoroughly, and bottling up all Norsunder's vessels in the inner harbor. The sleet was turning icy, and then the clouds vanished, leaving a frigid wind that promised ice filming rocks and water by morning. None of those ships was going anywhere anytime soon.

The prince huddled on the bench, laughing at himself. For a man who had accepted the bargain to sail into Norsunder, not caring if he lived or died, he'd certainly fought hard enough to survive. Hope, or cowardice?

A hand landed on his shoulder.

He turned his head, though it took effort, to look up at Ghaer's profile, side-lit in the cold bluish starlight. "Look, my friend," she said in her wretched Sartoran. "Look."

The entire crew paused to stare to the northwest, behind them. And saw the ruddy beat of fire, where Fox and his followers had gotten to the most finished of the ships on the blocks, before melting into the darkness.

"It's never going to be this easy again," Ghaer said at length.

"P-p-p-probably n-n-not," the prince managed past chattering teeth. "Hah!"

"Hah!" the crew echoed around him.

⸻ ⦂ ⸻

Artists' Colony – Sles Adran

Macael played until Chantala's hands fell loose in the obliviousness of deep slumber, then he set aside the lute.

"That was wonderful," Liere whispered. "The best I think I ever heard." There was no mistaking the sincerity in her voice.

Macael bowed, his attention on Chantala.

Liere ventured a cautious remark, though it was innocuous enough: "Chantala seems much happier than she was in spring."

Macael sent Liere a composed, though unreadable glance, then said, "She does not know this, and I hope never will, but her mother was poisoned."

"Poisoned?" Liere repeated, shocked. "You must mean slow poison."

"Slow indeed. Until the end."

"Was it King Bartal?"

Macael smiled slightly. "It seemed so, until the end, when someone got impatient. Now the Nente court gossip blames Mandracar, Chantala's husband of one month, who it is said would have killed his own mother for rank and title. No one knew that Chantal and her daughter often shared their food, as had been their habit all Chantala's life. Chantal died, and Chantala's health was broken. She lives only because she ate so little."

That, Liere thought, explained a lot about Chantala. "You knew her before," Liere hazarded.

Macael's lips curved in brief amusement. "That's surprising?"

Conjecture was now too rapid to dismiss. "So—then—it was you Mariana had in mind to harbor Chantala, before Andri came along?"

"I expect so. There had been talk of a betrothal when we were both young; there are some connections through our respective elders, and I spent some summers in Denwy, at the duchas's invitation. Though the invitations ended when King Alored, Andri's father, was overthrown. Our position—the Elsarions' position—became somewhat anomalous."

Tired as she was, Liere found her thoughts running headlong. "The resistance. Andri ..."

"You must not blame Mariana for trying to get a king for her charge, rather than an unsworn Enaeraneth duchas whose lands in Sles Adran are not extensive. I inherited a modest holding through my grandmother." Macael's unruffled, amused countenance nearly drained his words of personal consequence; they might have been talking about people who'd lived long ago and far away.

Liere winced. How odd, that someone who betrayed so little emotion about life-changing events could wring the heart with such music.

"Are you imagining two lovers cruelly separated? The truth is—"

"You don't owe me any explanations," she cut in quickly, wishing she was asleep in someone's attic, filthy but tranquil. She was as unsettled as she had ever been in her life—the more because she could not define why. "This is really Adrani politics, to which you, at least, have a family claim. As well as this long friendship. I have no claim whatsoever, and I'm also ignorant," she said quickly.

"But Andri will want to know what I'm doing here, will he not?"

The question was uninflected. The wind thrummed against the window as Liere met Macael's steady blue gaze. She felt even more off-balance, though she still could not define why. She certainly sensed no threat, or even resentment, much less anger. His manner was patient. Forbearing. His gaze shifted to the fire, then he picked up the lute again, the ring glinting on his hand. The diamonds flashed, dimmed, and Liere recognized the Elsarion device carved into the stone.

He said, "In some ways Chantala is the same as that dreaming girl of ten with whom I wandered through the gardens when we were children. It might be the poison. She might never change. She is happiest with familiar faces around her, and no raised voices. There are those in Sles Adran's court who care for her welfare very much. They were appalled when Bartal brought Chantala to Nente, and tricked her into marriage with Commander Mandracar."

Liere said, "In spite of Mariana's wishes, Andri hasn't the least idea how to save Sles Adran. I'm sure he must have told you himself. Enaeran is going to be challenging enough to wrest from Norsunder when the time comes. He could really use your help," she said. There, it was out.

Macael looked up briefly from the fire, and again his eyes narrowed with suppressed laughter. "Then you didn't hear from Andri about my lamentable awkwardness on our journey together?"

She remembered quite clearly how badly Andri wanted to find an ally in Macael. "So you've had little war training," she said stoutly. "Andri thought rather highly of your courage in action. He said that much."

"The issue is a matter of trust," Macael said gently. "Andri did not like my method of inviting myself along on his journey."

"There are some rulers," she responded, feeling her way with care, "who distrust until someone proves they can be trusted. Such rulers are reluctant to arm their populaces against Norsunder. They think, once Norsunder is gone the masses will have a taste for fighting, or will have a taste for settling their own problems, and will decide to meddle in government. Andri is the opposite. He wants to trust, until someone does something to prove untrustworthy. And we are trying to arm all of Enaeran, so that if and when the world rises against Norsunder, diminished as we are, we can prevail against the invaders."

"We," he repeated. She understood now why she was unsettled; it was impossible to read him. She did not even know if Macael had Dena Yeresbeth, he was so reserved.

He smiled. "I'm acquainted sufficiently with Andri's style. I recognize your generous invitation to prove myself, and I do thank you for it. The fact remains, I am by nature more of a seneschal than a war chieftain."

"You would be welcome," she said, lacing her fingers loosely in her lap.

Macael's gaze lifted from the fire again, warm and friendly at her sincerity. His glossy head shook. "So far I am merely a liability."

"You could gather weapons for us."

He looked perplexed. "You mean, buy them for you?"

"If need be. But I was thinking of your connections among the Adranis, which I expect are far greater than Andri's, given that you used to spend time among them."

"I do know some of Bartal's chief opponents..." His gaze was again on the fire. "My contacts are mostly old friends and relations, but I will do my best to exploit these as well as I can for weapons. Where ought I to send any I do manage to gather?"

She thought. "Would you object to your old home, Elsarion Castle? Andri said that Norsunder ceased to disturb you there."

Macael opened his hands. "No objection at all."

"Then I'll see to it that you get some kind of message."

"Question," he said.

"Yes?"

"You said we. Your devotion to the affairs of Enaeran..." He said it delicately.

"It's my home now," she declared, in the stout tone of one who'd never felt at home anywhere, really, except—

No. That was when she was a child of eleven, too ignorant to comprehend the notion of home. Senrid had given her a place to stay where no one either criticized her, or expected her to be Sartora, the Girls Who Saved the World.

"I did wonder how Andri's quest ended last winter," Macael said.

"We married, Andri and I, and I'm adopting into your family." She grinned. "Which I guess makes us cousins-by-marriage, all working for Enaeran's future."

"Indeed," he said, rising to pour out more wine. He brought the glasses back, and handed one to Liere. "To Enaeran's future." He raised the crystal and touched it to hers with a sweet ringing tone.

She sipped, meeting his dense blue gaze through the crystal, the color echoed in the cobalt glitter of the ring on his hand. The wine was warm and savory.

He emptied his glass, and with a sudden turn of the wrist flung his empty crystal into the fire, where it smashed into glittering shards.

PART TWO

OF EVERYONE HIBERN OF Roth Drael knew, she would have thought herself the least likely to survive being forced into Norsunder-Beyond. How ironic that, so far, it seemed she was the best prepared.

As a child with weak knees, she had learned patience. Poring over her father's books for something to do, she had learned something about magic, and history. Her mage tutors' books had shown her that her father's books presented one theory and one point of view. So she had learned about paradigm.

She'd tested personal variations in perception when she tried to understand her mad brother — and to explain him to the rest of the household. Wider experience of the worst and best in the Marlovens' martial attitude toward life had come when she'd listened in on Tdanerend's visits to her father, and later, when she became friends with Senrid.

Growing up in Latvian Askan's crazy household had guaranteed that she knew how to take care of herself when the world seemed to explode into meaningless chaos around her. Not just take care of herself, but persist in her studies. Because above all, she was a scholar, trained to winnow out clues in solving puzzles.

That meant *perceiving* puzzles.

Because the lies in Detlev's reports were a puzzle. Or, another way of looking at them, they were a pattern. Fending off the prowling Theronezhe while pursuing these clues was akin to fending off her brother at his most splintered without losing momentum in her studies, now that she understood how to move in the Beyond. Theronezhe had his own patterns; it seemed he could not figure out what she was doing, as he kept circling back to that library, without perceiving that she had figured out how to summon what she wanted from the library to her.

Also, he hadn't read all those reports. Either that, or he did not know Sartorias-deles history well enough to spot the lies.

Much less how these, too, formed a pattern, she discovered while shifting levels outward from that central garden. Detlev's lies all matched with thorns worked decoratively among the … oh, call them the trellises of the Beyond's structure. Let's impose more garden imagery, she decided, though that was as far as she would cooperate with the malevolence that had wrought this abomination into being.

Hibern took a deep breath.

"Not much I can do about the air," she said, for she was now thoroughly in the habit of talking to herself.

She stood, at last, in the eye of the hurricane. This garden, its exquisite trees and ferns and flowering vines, had been ripped from time and space during the height of spring, and frozen here at the point of death, to exist unchanged for centuries.

This garden was Ilerian's inner citadel in Norsunder. It no longer mattered who was the more arrogant, the Host in designing this place and designating it the center of their power, or Detlev by his many, apparently careless references to these interrogations and displays of power, almost always after one of the reports with the thorns—the lies—embedded.

All the lies in the records twisted around and around to this spot, in patterns not unlike the interlocked patterns in humble objects found readily in nature—in shells, and seeds, and tree branches.

Once she saw it, she wondered if this same pattern underlay that beautiful labyrinth in Atan's garden, which Hibern had found soothing to walk, even kicked apart by Bostian's followers, when she and Liere fought against the enemy in Sartor's capital.

All the reports led to this garden; writings from those living and dead made reference to "I stood before Svir in the

Garden," and "Yeres summoned me to attend her in the Garden." More sinisterly, "They interrogated him in the Garden, which they required us to watch but then Ilerian took him and we never saw him after."

Not all Detlev's reports bore the obsequious knee-bendings to the Host's power; that was common to the earliest reports, and persisted in those with the lies embedded. Were these paired lies and flatteries signs of the birth of his dissatisfaction? But who would know, unless you knew the history?

To test herself, she read farther back, before her birth, choosing records of places and times that she had studied so extensively that she was fairly certain she would catch a lie. But she didn't see a one. What she did see was that seemingly endless wall of reports, going back and back for centuries. All in that handwriting that changed very little over time. Every ten years, ten times a century.

Further—she sensed Theronezhe and shifted… sideways—the lies seemed to group. She had seen that one set encircled Eidervaen. Another Ferdrian, capital of Everon. Here was the labyrinth, if you knew your map, its pattern a palimpsest over the circles within circles that formed the, oh, think of them as pillars, supporting the structure of the Beyond.

But though the labyrinth was overall a circle, the patterns within were not, creating tension points. And these, she discovered, flashing from one level to another, insinuated a lattice. Within the actual lattice.

A lattice is a structure.

She circled around one tension point, examining it…

One

Artists' Colony – Sles Adran

THE PERSISTENT ACHE IN the back of Liere's skull at last forced its way into her consciousness. She opened her eyes, sat up, and saw that the fire had been diminished to a low flame to retain the warmth of the room. She flexed sleep-stiffened muscles in her back, neck, and arms; she had curled up on her cushion.

Memory returned: Chantala stirring at the sound of the crystal shattering, which had startled Liere. She knew that some of the Sartoran-influenced cultures did that after making a vow. She'd never heard of smashing a glass after a friendly toast. But she knew she was still terribly ignorant, especially about things nobles did.

While she'd blinked, Macael had gone on as if nothing was amiss; seeing Chantala stir, he reached for the lute and resumed playing, a cascade of sound even more intricate and expressive than previously. Liere closed her eyes, the better to enjoy his expertise, but tiredness and the brilliance of the imagery the music evoked together lured her into dreams, thence to sleep.

She'd fallen asleep! Had she snored like a bear? Drooled all over? Remorse at her inadvertent rudeness prodded her into wakefulness. Chantala was missing. Macael and Fan must have put Chantala in the bedroom; however close Macael and Chantala were, apparently they did not sleep together, or at least not with someone else present, for Macael had laid his crossed arms on the table, resting his head on them.

Liere got up, moving as soundlessly as possible. One of Macael's hands had fallen loose. She glimpsed moon-slivers of dark red under his fingernails, which shocked her into a short intake of breath. Soft as it was, it woke him, and he lifted his head, his blue eyes very tired-looking but alert.

She gave him a grimace of apology and motioned toward the door. She heard him get up behind her, as Fan, the quiet young man who waited on Macael, emerged from a far room and soundlessly began tidying. A rush of cold air smote their faces as they stepped out onto the flagstones.

Macael pulled the door nearly closed, and Liere whispered, "Thank you for the dinner and the music. I'm sorry I fell asleep. No reflection upon your playing, I assure you."

He smiled a little. "No offense taken—Chantala likes to be serenaded to sleep. Those pieces were chosen for it. Thank you for joining us. Any message for Chantala?"

"Just my best wishes for a happier New Year. I will see that you get a message with our signals and so forth. We really could use your help."

"I promise I will aid you as much as I can. Send it to Elsarion; I'll need to return before the new year."

"Very well." Liere picked up robe so it wouldn't drag in the snow. "Andri will wish me to convey his best greetings."

"And mine to him," Macael said. "Safe journey."

She waded out into the drifts of fresh snow; half a glass later she was riding on her fresh, frisky horse. As she watched her breath plume and stream her mind filled with images of Macael's quiet manner, characterized by a difficult-to-define combination of patience and latent strength. What to make of those bloody fingernails? She had no idea what to make of that. Like his music, Macael was endlessly complex, yet offering no single clear emotional clue to the thinking brain behind it.

Darchelde – Marloven Hess

Sveneric slipped noiselessly into the Darchelde underground a couple hours before dawn. He found David, Adam, Rolfin, Laban, MV, Roy, and Dirk waiting—Senrid's Methden teens were all still asleep, or else on night maneuvers.

Roy's grin was real, happy, unshadowed, and Sveneric went straight to him. A brief, fervent clasp of hands, a swift mental exchange, and then Sveneric turned to Laban, the pleasure of reunion unguarded.

"Patrols stepped up at the border," Sveneric offered, meeting the rest of their gazes.

David gave him a friendly nod of acknowledgement. "Recovered?"

"Enough." One of Sveneric's hands sketched a dismissive gesture, then he straightened up: time for the consequences.

At Sveneric's entrance MV, who'd been wall-propping, strolled a leisurely perimeter of the room. The two stood face to shirt-front. As Sveneric tilted his head back, MV smiled a nasty smile and with a thoughtful gesture took hold of Sveneric's collar between thumb and forefinger.

"And now," he drawled, "for a tale of such surpassing fascination I'll be too stunned to land you back in the rack for a couple more weeks."

Though the welcome was genuine, Sveneric had known on his entrance that the group gathered here was also a kind of inquest. No accident that only Detlev's gang (excepting only Dirk) awaited him; it had, in fact, been in a spirit of facilitation that Sveneric had contacted David by farsense as soon as he'd crossed the border.

"Unless the recounting of fiascos fills you with amazement, I'm resigned."

Over Sveneric's head, MV's gaze touched David's. Then MV's hand came up, but only to grasp the boy's shoulder and thrust him into the earthen bench carved into the wall.

David drifted to the other side of the chamber and seated himself on the edge of Senrid's desk, from which he could command a view of the room. His expression was thoughtful, patient; no one would know from looking at him how little he liked the minor drama now playing out before him.

MV reached lazily and jerked up Sveneric's chin. "Not a bad job." He grinned, turning Sveneric's face from side to side before releasing it. Then he doubled his hand and dealt Sveneric a light blow across the ribs. "Here too, eh?"

David watched Dirk. This scene had to be gone through for Dirk's sake, and for those waiting to hear what Dirk reported. The Marlovens would soon contrive to pester Dirk when they thought they weren't overheard; far from here,

Julian Landis, Darian Selenna, Lyren-Sartora, CJ of the Mearsieans and through her Randon Amdrelya and others who fretted under the constraints of cooperative waiting, all were impatient for word on what Detlev's boys did to Sveneric for breaking orders and running off.

MV straightened up casually. "I hate to debase my artistry with someone else's set of lumps. Who was it? Imry or his grunts? Start warbling, little shitbird."

Beyond a faint, persistent brow-quirk of humor, Sveneric's expression was impossible to read as he stared up at MV. "The grunts," he said. "Imry couldn't be rid of me fast enough."

And of course the Grand Inquisitor had to be MV. The lesson had to be played out, and David had to watch in order to determine (if he could) whether Sveneric had arrived at his acceptance of the inquest's necessity after sober reappraisal—or whether he had taken its probability into consideration from the start. Which would give a clue to his true motivation.

"Well, well! But we're a little ahead, aren't we?" MV said, the fitful firelight below and to his left heightening his expression of sardonic amusement in a most unpleasant way. "Let's backtrack a little. You got up one day and decided to prance off into new dangers—by the way, we told the Marlovens that Detlev sent you on a secret mission, thus affording our reputations, at least, a little protection from the tarnish of rank stupidity—and then what? Imry and his boys found you contemplating lilies at a roadside? Or did you walk into Imry's HQ and say, 'Here am I—quail at the Greatness of my Famous Name!'?"

Dirk's shoulders tightened, a barely perceptible alteration of his posture, but Sveneric's gaze shifted to him. Then MV stepped between them, and Sveneric said, "Detlev came here after. He did not give you a report of my experiences?"

"No." MV smiled, his voice cuttingly rude. "Do you blame him for wanting to hide how stupid you were?"

Dirk rose from his chair. MV made a half-turn and rammed him right down again, then inquired with knife-edge politesse, "Have you a lesson in group action to offer, Dirk?"

And, inwardly, to David: *Enough?*

David replied: *For Dirk. Let Sveneric talk now.*

MV rounded on Sveneric. "Let's hear it."

Sveneric began his narration at the point of his arrival in

Imar. He knew how to fit the narrative to the audience, giving a vivid description of Efael's face when Svir apparently changed his mind about his promise that he could have Sveneric for his very own plaything whenever he was run to ground.

No one interrupted, and at the end, when Dirk asked, "But what about Llyenthur? How'd that happen?" Sveneric gave a succinct, funny, vivid account of his capture, and what he'd glimpsed in the Larkadhe map room, without any mention of why he'd gone there. Dirk, as everyone expected, assumed that Sveneric had been taken by the desire to make a scouting run himself.

When Sveneric finished with his encounter with Yeres, and what he learned, most went back to bed, Dirk with some muted, resentful looks at the sublimely unaware MV. Despite Dirk's very real tiredness and a need for sleep, in the privacy of his chamber, he set up a candle and vented his anger on Sveneric's behalf by firing off some scathing notes to Darian Selenna, Jessan Delieth, and Lyren-Sartora about MV acting like he's in command of the world. The message thus went out, with unequivocal clarity, that Detlev's gang would land hard on anyone who took off on individual missions.

Not everyone retired. Adam went off and brewed some coffee as Senrid drifted in, having listened from the passage. The Methden teens soon tumbled up, still frowsy from sleep, and discovered to their surprise that Sveneric was back.

All he said was, "I went on a mission." The healing cut over his eye, the multi-hued bruises, and his complete silence about that mission caused the subject to end. Except for sixteen-year-old Marend, who was desperate to be accepted in among Detlev's Own. Like Sveneric and Dirk, who were younger than she was!

People left the hideout to patrol, to drill, or to make a supply run. Senrid remained where he was, frowning over his map with its notations about numbers and weapons, until one by one, Andri, Mildred, Zairna, and Rolfin appeared. Adam handed around hot drinks as he said, "Take your positions."

Dirk was the last, dropping down beside Sveneric with an air of challenge, but he took his cue from Sveneric, who sat cross-legged, hands on his knees, eyes closed.

The group formed a loose circle, David and Adam sitting opposite one another. All had been chosen for the strength of their Dena Yeresbeth, though too few of them had had any semblance of training. Adam had been trying to repair that ignorance as much as he could, both individually and in group, but first they had had to learn to shield themselves as a group — in spite of many — too many — interruptions.

MV sauntered down from overseeing the morning drill and dropped between Mildred and Rolfin as Adam said, "Ilerian is gaining power. We have to work on blending, for our attack has to be as one to be effective."

Zairna couldn't completely blend with the others, and Senrid wouldn't. No one asked why. It no longer mattered. They needed more people whose Dena Yeresbeth encompassed powerful farsense, but it had become clear that they were not going to get them.

Senrid in particular loathed, with his entire being, the idea of going to war solely with his mind, while someone else led the military resistance in Marloven Hess. His gaze rested on Dirk, the youngest there. Dirk was evidence of the desperation Detlev had to be feeling, relying on someone even younger than Sveneric to aid in attacking an ancient evil like Ilerian. However, age and size did not limit strength, and Dirk would not be leading. Each person there had some quality that Detlev needed: Senrid suspected Dirk's was the same innate natural shield that his father had. Senrid guessed Dirk would survive longer than most of the rest of them, if Ilerian got the drop on them.

As for himself...the only claim he made for his own untrained Dena Yeresbeth was the habit of self-discipline. He did not want to be part of this circle, but he'd decided that he owed Detlev, and as for the ground fight, he'd lost the first war. Van Stad would no doubt be a better commander.

Artists' Colony – Sles Adran

When Macael and Chantala stepped into the Harieses' warm stone house, they found the three older people sitting down to breakfast. Aunt Thi got up to serve Chantala and Macael, exchanging small talk about the first significant snowstorm of the season, and storms of the past, as Stav sat on his stool sipping coffee and frowning into the kitchen fire, eyes abstract.

"I told ye," Aunt Thi proclaimed, not without triumph. "I told ye, it'll be a rare winter, this one. You can always tell when the late vegetables have tough skins. And those carrots — tough! Rarely seen tougher."

"Oh, I hope not," Chantala murmured, warming her hands on her steep.

Lies frowned, tapping her fingernail on her spoon. "A sled," she said to Macael. "Do you think? We'll need supplies, and we've four deliveries promised between now and spring season, not counting the one going out today."

"Then you'll need a pair of heavy horses," Macael said. "And feed enough for winter. I can see to that while I deliver your art."

"The things in there can be first load in," Lies said, pointing back to the big room. "Plus! Some —"

"Who *was* that?" Stav spoke suddenly. And, as all eyes turned to him in surprise, he sat up a little straighter and rewrapped his long legs around his stool, then made the supreme effort to get out a few more words. "In here and out. Blue of a summer dawn. Gold and silver."

His wife burst out laughing. "So you noticed we had a guest, eh, Stavo?"

"Guest?" her husband replied blankly, then he frowned. "You might've told me. Perhaps she would have posed before lighting out again."

"She did go?" Lies turned to Chantala, but Aunt Thi spoke up.

"Early. In and out again with her near-dried clothes, while you were still abed." She smiled suddenly. "I must say, you could've puffed me flat when she floated downstairs last night in that blue robe —"

The women smiled reminiscently.

"She is truly beautiful," Chantala said with heartfelt pleasure. "There is no one like her at my uncle's court. Not just beautiful — we have many who are thought beautiful — but graceful, and the kindest heart. I wish my mother could have met her!"

"Could've stayed long enough to pose," Stav grumbled irritably, still actually following the drift of the conversation.

"See here, Stav, if she comes again you can ask her," his wife said with her usual good nature. And to Macael, "If it does not put you to too much trouble, I suppose I'd better write notes to all the relatives as well." She pushed her dishes aside and began to scratch out a list with the pen and paper already on the table.

"I intend to visit several friends in Nente, so your errand will not trouble me in the least. I'll go speak to Koldner about space in the stable," Macael said, rising. And as Chantala looked up uncertainly, he reached to touch her hand. "Why don't you stay and finish your meal? Warm up. I'll come back in before I leave for Nente."

Chantala sank back in her chair and sipped her steep.

As Macael turned toward the door he noticed Stav's beaky-nosed frown, and he laughed. "Why don't you use the after-image?" And went out.

"What?" Aunt Thi spoke up as she brought in more steaming water to the steep-pot.

"Liere," Lies said, rubbing her pen-quill against her cheek.

Stav's brow cleared, and he grunted in agreement. "Sun," he said, nodding. "And moon."

Aunt Thi threw up her hands and moved to the stove; Lies smothered a laugh and began to write rapidly.

Chantala smiled as she stared dreamily at the fire. Her mind drifted to those realms where the sun always shone bright and warm, and where people never had reason to stop dancing, singing, and laughing.

Two

A WEEK PASSED, AND half of another.

The two most formidable of the Chwahir fleets tacked against the current and the wind up the strait, to answer the king's command.

That is, they tried to. Two harsh storms racing down the strait from the east blew them right back out to sea at the other end.

Once, Prince Yviski caught sight of them, old ships with layers of wards coaxing another century out of the aging timbers, decade by decade. They were like a line of ghost ships, half-perceived in the wildly whirling blizzard. His fleet hauled up into the wind, sails slack, though that did not guarantee they were unseen. But the Chwahir never broke formation to investigate.

As well, because Yviski, armed with the latest intelligence from Ferret in Larkadhe ("Veteran commanders were summarily being sent to eastern Sartor, by Efael") had on board a load of stolen Norsundrian uniforms.

According to Ferret, the garrison, which supplied warriors to reinforce the west end of the strait, was manned by Fhlerians, Chwahir, and Norsundrians from Aldon's old company, three wildly disparate military groups jumbled together by Efael. The new Norsundrian commander and the latest Fhlerian captain loathed each other. The Chwahir, despised by all, lived strictly apart from everyone else, doing everything stringently according to orders—which the Fhlerians saw as reproach.

The Fhlerian and the Norsundrian commanders each kept crucial intelligence from the other, in hopes of dislodging the unwanted interloper; their communications, when they had to communicate, were full of innuendo as well as overt insult. The result was a seething struggle for ascendance, right down to the stable hands and the dockside barnacle scrapers.

In the boldest ruse yet, Yviski and volunteers whose accents sounded modern put on Norsundrian gray. A river boat ghosted them up the coast and into the bay of Nelsaiam, and landed them outside the main garrison. Yviski and his three volunteers offered the latest code words from Larkadhe, claimed they were special agents sent by Efael, and spoke the words everyone had begun dreading to hear, "Surprise inspection!"

That shit Llyenthur had been bad enough—but at least when he purged someone it was for stealing, drinking, goldbricking—and getting caught at it, idiots! Efael landed on people who forgot to bow.

So much Ferret had gleaned, and Yviski used.

He was awash with sweat despite the bitter cold as he marched up to the command center, and, using his tyrannical grandfather's hated manner, bawled, "Everything is to be inspected! Everything! There will be order! There will be discipline! If another raid is successful, you will all be in the execution yard..." Oh, he remembered every word of those abominable speeches.

The two commanders, for the first time ever, looked at one another in terror and bewilderment, then ran to summon their respective commands.

Ghaer and Fox's people, who had followed up under cover of a storm, mixed in with the thoroughly upended garrison, which scrambled about trying to ready—hide evidence—and, in forming helpful tidying parties, cleaned out supplies, while a team of scrubbers and sweepers sabotaged the ships waiting in the dock.

This scene of madness lasted through a lull in the storm. When an angry gust of wind brought a white wall of snow, Yviski and Ghaer signaled for retreat, not without exchanging glances of amazement that so far, they'd gotten away with it.

Fox and his broom squad flanked them as they vanished, lifting everything they could carry, leaving the angry, harried commanders to write a report that wouldn't get them killed.

Efael only read a few lines of the much-debated finessing and finger-pointing. "We've got a mole," he said to Yeres—once he was done cursing.

She looked at the reports, annoyed that she hadn't figured it out. Nor had that nasty, back-stabbing Hyath, who prided herself so much on her cleverness and discernment. Hyath had failed a lot lately, from keeping the transfer spell changed to winnowing out moles. Too busy chasing Connanre—not that that got her much benefit. Time to be rid of her.

Yeres drank a fresh infusion of poppy elixir and went to oversee the fun. Efael transferred to Larkadhe, as always his appearance causing a shockwave of reaction, which he relished far too much to ever consider the consequences. Such as Ferret, sensitive to the slightest change in atmosphere, getting through the gates, driving a cart full of empty beer barrels, just ahead of the orders to lock down the castle for a thorough search.

Efael rampaged through yet another purge, and when that tired him, new orders went out.

Sage came to Fox. "David says, we no longer have ears in Larkadhe, but the Chwahir are now on the move."

"We're facing off the Chwahir?" Fox asked grimly.

But Sage shook her head. "I'm to shift back to the *Mule Kick*. Detlev says, you withdraw to deep seas and come around Sartor, through the land bridge, to the waters off Halia, to be ready for the combined force attack."

She laid down Fox's magic paper, effaced herself, and went to get her dunnage.

Fox picked up then tossed down the paper, and went to signal his fleet. Like it or not, it seemed he was heading to the homeland.

There was no triumph in Darchelde. Detlev's people carried on tight-lipped until a brief note came that Ferret had managed to go safely to ground. That was right before one of Senrid's couriers turned up, overheard saying something about trouble on the coast.

That same night, Adam woke abruptly—and though he was shielded, the others in the circle, now sensitive to one another, woke to discover him scrambling his things together.

"You're leaving?" Sveneric asked.

"It—my cousin," Adam whispered. "I told him not to try contacting me. He barely knows how to…" He looked away. "I might be too late, but I have to go."

Senrid appeared out of the shadows into the fitful light of a single candle. He was fully dressed, his eyes marked with exhaustion. His sashed coat, tight from shoulders to waist, the flaring skirt flaps reaching to his boot tops, made him look as if he'd walked out of a tapestry. "I was going to leave in the morning, but I can't sleep. My relay can get you as far as Sindan An."

"I'm ready," Adam murmured.

They were gone almost in the next breath, leaving an atmosphere of tension as the candle streamed.

Later that next day, sitting in the main chamber of Darchelde hideout, Marend Ndarga dropped her pen and rubbed her fingers to restore circulation, then stretched her stiff back. When that was done she suppressed a sigh and looked round the chamber.

Sveneric was over there now, bent over the large sheet of paper on the king's desk, the curled edges of which were weighted down by a candlestick, a knife, a book, and a rock. His light brown head was bent near Zairna's pale one as they studied the map. No one would say where Sveneric had gone—and she *hated* that. She had only muttered something about distrust (perfectly justified) and the king himself had stuck her with copying lists, to be sent out by courier the next day.

This just before he left himself.

Marend's fingers fussed moodily with the pen as she watched Sveneric and Zairna. She picked up the pen, and dropped it again when she heard the trapdoor open. Multiple footsteps approached, nearly smothering the hissing breathing of someone in pain.

Fight? She longed to be up, armed, and into action.

It was just Crow, his face whitish-green. No blood. His bony right hand clutched stretch-knuckled at his left shoulder; she recognized MV's stride coming down the tunnel just before she heard him call out in his breezy way, "Who's here? Ah! Just who I need. Roy! Get up here!"

"What's up?" came a voice.

"Torture session," MV called with grim humor.

"Argh," Crow muttered, hoarser than ever. "I'm fine—"

"Face down. Now."

Crow's breath hissed as he eased himself to the ground before the fire. Roy appeared, obviously just out of bed, and gave Crow a sympathetic smile. MV plumped himself down so he was kneeling on either side of Crow's lower back. He grasped Crow's left arm and stretched it straight out to the side.

Roy rubbed his hands, then laid his palms experimentally over Crow's shoulder blade before he hooked his fingers and began to work at the terrible knots.

"Pulled muscles are forbidden, I told you that before," MV said to Crow. "Tonight, tomorrow, tomorrow night, a double set of those loosening moves I showed you. And a hot rock tucked up against your shoulder blade after."

Crow groaned as Roy's fingers slowly worked away. Two muscle spasms shook Crow's skinny frame, but MV held him firmly pinned to the ground. Roy said nothing as he worked slowly, steadily. MV kept up a running commentary of pungent insults that masked the alteration of Crow's harsh, pained breathing to the sonorous half-sleep of euphoria as the knots began to loosen.

Once Sveneric looked up, smiled across the room at them, then returned to his drawing. Marend gritted her teeth, and snatched up her straight-edge to measure off a few more lines. The worst thing was, there was no explanation for those margin notes. No doubt those made a point of this mess — would make it bearable, if she could just see how the list fitted into the king's plans. That would be high-level work, and she certainly wouldn't object to acting desk-jockey for the king! An agreeable inner vision of herself privy to kingdom-wide war plans — discussing, arguing — lit her mind, to be snuffed. She wasn't a desk jockey. She had been given this task because she had been arguing with that goat Ramond. For perfectly justified reasons — if only the king would *listen*.

Marend dropped her pen when MV stood up and pulled Crow to his feet. No doubt about it, the foreigner really was standing a lot straighter these days. And his face seemed younger — less like a crabbed old man.

"Awright, enough loafing. Get back out there," MV said, and Crow took off up the tunnel. Then one by one, Detlev's Own vanished, except for Sveneric still writing. And Zairna, who had been up all night and all day as well. He went off to his overdue rest.

Marend sighed, finished the lists, and then, since it was clear she wasn't going to find anything out tonight, she withdrew with lagging steps. She had tomorrow's pre-dawn run.

David emerged from the other direction. He and Sveneric were alone. David lowered himself onto a broad cushion, giving a loud sigh of relief. But Sveneric knew him; MV's interrogation had been public. More than a week later, this was David's.

Sveneric stood before him. "Ask your questions."

"All answered."

"By whom?" Sveneric asked after a moment or two of silence, during which he continued to walk restlessly round the room. "Detlev did not tell you why I went to Larkadhe?"

David grinned with tolerant scorn.

"Then—?" Sveneric persisted.

"You did." David sighed. Then smiled again. "I suppose you thought, like most of the others, that I went after Imry for purposes of assassination?"

"Senrid said you were wasting your time. He wouldn't think Imry's assassination a waste of time. Detlev and MV said nothing."

"Ah, secrets!" David laughed silently. "It appears we had the same thought, you and I. No. Emendation: the same intention."

Sveneric's eyes were wide, and dark as the sea just before a storm. "I thought he chose Larkadhe because of memories. How Detlev used to use harpwinds to calm him. Though he'd stopped by the time you were two or three, but did you remember it—"

"No," David said.

The fire crackled. Sveneric pressed fingers to his eyes. "I said to Imry, *His plans were made in the beginning,* by which I meant when he adopted everyone, as a preface to the other observation, that he saw the healer's talent in him. I thought it would matter, that he would want to know. But he doesn't. He just looked at me as if I'd farted on his dinner, and called me a pompous twit—which I guess I was. He doesn't *care.*" Sveneric's voice husked. "He doesn't care. I was so stupid. He doesn't care about anything."

David knew by now that Sveneric had thoroughly learned the difference between theorizing and the messiness of real life.

"Oh, he cares. But in his own way. Imry wants to measure himself against Detlev."

Sveneric wiped his eyes on his sleeve, then tipped his head. "I think. I see that. He stilled, when I said that Detlev's plans were made in the beginning. But it wasn't until I was writing to Ian that we both figured Imry might have seen that as a claim about Detlev's motives for … everything." Sveneric peered anxiously at David. "Do you or Adam know?"

"You mean—" Amusement quirked David's eyes. "—has anyone else actual facts about what really happened four thousand years ago? Not to my knowledge."

Sveneric sighed.

"So..." David clasped his hands behind his head. "Not even to you, eh?"

Sveneric whispered, "I have never asked."

David's smile warmed into another silent laugh. "Laban did. Quite recently." And he repeated the gist of Laban's conversation with Detlev, which Laban had poured into David's ears half a watch after it took place.

Sveneric listened, face thoughtful.

After a time, David said, "Well, why not?"

"Because he might answer." Sveneric smiled reluctantly. "And I'm not sure I'm ready for that."

David slid a hand over his eyes as he went into silent convulsions. "He must think we're as good as a play," he said finally, wiping his eyes on his sleeve.

"A farce," Sveneric said with admirable voice-control, but David was undeceived.

"Sit down." He pointed. "You've got to be even more tired than I am, and besides you're making my neck ache, standing behind me like that."

"I *am* tired," Sveneric admitted. "I'm trying to catch up in circle. Zairna's a big help with that. Challenging. And I'd promised Rom and Sindan that I'd drill with them, and go on scouting runs with their team. I have to make it up to everyone I disappointed, and I'm afraid if I sit I'll never rise again." But as he spoke he took one step, another more quickly, and then he sandbagged onto the cushion next to David.

And David's arm moved instinctively, dropping around Sveneric's thin shoulders and pulling his trembling body up against him. He hadn't made that kind of gesture since Sveneric was very small—before David vanished for several years into the Beyond to learn the treasure hunt. But now, this reassuring hug was exactly right.

When, at last, Sveneric's shuddering ceased, David lifted his eyes from his contemplation of the steadily burning vagabond fire. He knew now what had most deeply upset Sveneric: not his experiences in Imar, nor his realization that he'd misjudged Imry, with serious consequences. He'd escaped Imar. Misjudgment was not new. And those consequences would have happened sooner or later. It was Detlev's displeasure that had devastated Sveneric. Even when brief, or even feigned, it was a reminder to his son of his mortality.

David said, "It was bad, eh?"

"He looked so *tired*. I was so *stupid*."

"I'll tell you this: at least you've got the relative comfort of still being in training." David laughed, squeezed Sveneric's shoulder, then he stood up to stretch. "C'mon. I hear my pillow calling to me, and if you don't hear yours then we'd best get you a hearing horn."

Three

WHEN IMRY LLYENTHUR ENTERED the old tower, he first noticed the silence. And underneath, the unheard but felt resonances from the far towers. The air in the chamber was still, cold. Around the tower wind blew, strong and ice-laden.

He moved from room to room, looking silently into each, listening to the sounds of his steps on the weird white almost stone of the tower, and then, as he ventured into the rest of the castle, on marble, stone, tile. Softened on carpet. Marble again.

The maps were gone, the weapons-arsenal. Empty even of furniture.

At last he returned to the tower room that had been the center of his command, and listened for a time to the distant winds high on the mountain.

Then he transferred himself to the palace of the Host of Lords in Imar.

It too was empty, or nearly, but this emptiness after that in Larkadhe was impending thunder after clear-skied winter stillness.

Yeres was there, alone. Imry found her in the library room that Svir most often chose to sit in. She hunched forward in one of the wingchairs, staring at the fire. Since he was approaching from behind he could see little of her face beyond a taut cheek. Her pose was intent, her hands clasped lock-fingered in her lap—without rings, for once. She'd always worn rings because she admired her hands with rings, especially when the rings gouged the flesh of her victims when she slapped them.

He sensed her mind was engrossed in one of her magically induced memories, sped by poppy-juice, and—from the smell of it—deathbrew. He suppressed a shudder of revulsion—he was still working the vile poison out of his joints—and moved into her range of vision before seating himself in the empty wingchair.

Her head jerked up and she blinked hard. He saw dark bruises on her neck. Her face was tense, her coloring ill. She said in a sharp voice, "It's about time."

"From the looks of things they've been carrying on without me," he commented.

She studied him, her foremost emotion clearly annoyance. She either didn't notice, or care, that her next statement was a direct contradiction of her friendly greeting: "You certainly seem to have recovered fast."

"You might follow my example," he responded, on the verge of a laugh. And because she wasn't now fair game—obviously really did need some R & R —he went on, "What happened?"

Her familiar sneer, superimposed on that tight face, made her look like a rodent. "There was a mole. Of course everyone thinks it's Detlev, as usual. I thought it was Hyath."

Imry Llyenthur looked askance. "Hyath? She hates the lighters. Ah, you needed an excuse to kill her." So predictable—any woman who managed to be clever enough to advance to the Garden of the Twelve, Yeres invariably backstabbed her. She liked being the only woman.

Yeres lifted a shoulder, watching a fold of her garment slip down her arm. She eyed her bare shoulder complacently as she said, "She was so eager last year. Did anything I asked. But that sure ended fast. Do you know she dared to blame *me* for Connanre's end? Turns out she was sneaking to his place up north when I thought she was working on changing the transfer wards. No wonder they were always lagging." Yeres scowled, looking more like a rodent than ever. "*Nobody* plays with my toys until I'm done with them."

Llyenthur had no interest in the tangles of the twins' sexual affairs. He said patiently, "Svir and Ilerian tried to break Kessler's ward, that much I understand. Using Connanre?"

"You really didn't know?" Yeres leaned forward.

"No." He spread his hands. "If I had, do you think I would be sitting here chatting so comfortably now? And, I'm guessing, Ilerian added to his fun by requiring your presence as witness."

She nodded, her face waxy at the memory. "Took his mind. Not at once. In pieces." She'd watched before, always with enjoyment; this was the first time he'd devoured one of *them*.

"Mmm," Imry said. "And so the power surge we all sense."

The silence in the Dei manor was so profound, so enervating, one did not even hear the fire. Instead there loomed just beyond superficial sight and hearing an increasing darkness. It bled into the shadows, leaching away object outlines. Their voices sounded flat. The air was very nearly the same stale non-air of Norsunder-Beyond, but still Yeres shivered occasionally. Not just reaction, but cold: the effect of time, whose weight even Ilerian could not ward.

Yet.

He has not found the girl.

"If you didn't know about Detlev's game, how did you figure out that it had to do with Connanre?" Yeres asked, eyeing him narrowly.

"Well, I don't have it all, yet," Imry admitted with a conspiratorial air. "I knew Connanre had plans. You'll remember: my part was to serve as bait. Obviously Connanre thought he could trap Detlev when, actually, the trap was closing in on him. A trap of Detlev's devising, made—let us conjecture—a while ago."

"In the beginning, that's what *they* say." She shrugged, and grimaced. One of her hands came up to finger her neck as she went on crossly, "Which is stupid. We had him, all right. We were there. Had him so tight he couldn't even squirm! Ah, that was fun! The brat was ours absolutely, too. When we were done with him he'd do anything for Efael, anything at all, and beg for the chance." She sneered. "I watched."

'The brat' being Siamas Y Reverael, twelve years old. But then Efael had never had any concept of justice, fairness, or decency. Siamis's youth would make the violation all the sweeter.

"What precisely did Connanre discover? Or think he'd discovered?"

"Oh, he discovered it, all right. The arrogant fool," she added corrosively. Gone from her mind was her centuries-long flirtation with Connanre, and the fact that he had followed her into Norsunder to win her away from her brother; gone were the occasional dalliances, her intermittent toyings with the prospect of running off with him to some other world and there to use their considerable skills to play without competition. He had dwindled in her mind to the fool who had given her some very bad days by trying to involve her in his worthless plans.

"Detlev had written his most recent general reports around certain blinds, apparently. I don't know how. His stuff was so impossibly dull I avoided reading any of it, but Efael had read 'em and he told me what he thought about them..."

As she rattled on, Imry tried to remember the reports. He'd been forced to read them — as were all the boys — when they were instructed in the proper composition of status reports. He'd been scornful at the time and had paid little attention; there'd been nothing remarkable at all about those reports, nothing that couldn't have been written by any flunky with a modicum of intelligence.

So he'd thought.

"Form, not content," he said with a sudden laugh, when she had finished. "Seems to me he forced his various lieutenants to read 'em as well." Obviously there'd been another level altogether below the bland objectivity; surmising how much Detlev must have enjoyed this race between either side to figure out what he was doing, and all along his plans were housed right there in the Host's own private archives, Llyenthur laughed again, with such appreciation Yeres glared at him with unconcealed hostility. "I wish I'd known," Imry said, trying with difficulty to dampen down his hilarity.

She thought this a stupidly obvious remark, and said so. He agreed with such alacrity (while thinking, *Next time, Detlev, I'm going to have to guarantee there are no interruptions*) she seemed about ready to take up a knife so he said, "You've been waiting here for me to slouch back in, have you, so you could tell me Efael has dismantled my command? Come! Cheer yourself by telling me whose stables I've been elected to sweep and we can both get back to the action."

A little of her customary energetic malice was back in her voice. "Efael's shifted your HQ to his place, just yesterday. Well, and some to Aldon in Sartor. He thinks there are spies breeding like rats all over Larkadhe. He was going to kill them all, but Svir insisted they are well-trained, and merely to split them up. Efael says you are welcome to come back and talk to him about it. Any time."

Imry grinned. "I see! Yes, I will. Presently. Svir?"

"He's said nothing to me about you at all."

"So, in fact, you're here to convey Efael's comradely invite? How cooperative!"

She eyed him with dislike. "I'm here because I'm cold."

"Cold?" He sat back, miming surprise. "Cold—outside?"

"Yes. Everywhere but here."

He received this statement with bland query. "The atmosphere here is really rather poisonous. Those marks on your neck ought to be gone by now."

"I can't leave. It's too cold," she snapped. "Poppy elixir only makes it bearable. I want some magic that won't leave me half-asleep for weeks. Idiot." She added abruptly as he got to his feet, "Efael will be expecting you."

"Meaning: where am I going?" He smiled down at her. "Well, I thought, seeing as I've been gifted with some free time, I'd relearn the steps to Detlev's dances."

She laughed suddenly, remembering that Imry had never betrayed the least sign of being afraid of Efael. "Why?" she demanded, as she realized she'd be bored without someone to throw at Efael occasionally, now that Connanre was gone.

"To change them, of course," he said, and transferred out.

She smiled thinly at the place he'd been. The answer was exactly what she'd expected. And, really, was most satisfactory. Imry was going out to do some spying; he wouldn't hesitate to stand up to Efael; he'd known Detlev, didn't just talk about him. Really, if he lasted, he'd make a more satisfying plaything than Connanre ever had.

"Besides, Connanre was so very tiresome about that stupid music of his," she said to the fire.

Which was all the epitaph that Connanre ever got.

⸻⸻ ⟜⟜⊷⊶⟞⟞ ⸻⸻

In the realm of the spirit, Ilerian watched and waited.

The physical limitations imposed by Kessler's spell required an occasional exchange of places with Svir, but these were rare enough. Ilerian didn't eat much, needed little exercise, and lying as he did at the center of his strengthening powerbase, he was able to range nearly as freely in dreams as he did while conscious.

To those who ventured into that realm he was an unchanging white light like a storm that spiraled slowly outward. To perceive the storm was to feel an increasing pull toward its center.

He fashioned that image deliberately, knowing that the girl who had awakened as a sirei-atanrial would eventually respond to that light. But first he must break Kessler's ward. He knew now that that would require an exponential power increase, one that could only be afforded by someone like Detlev. Svir wanted Detlev for vengeance, which was entertaining in its way, but Ilerian had shrugged off the betrayal. He recognized in Detlev a rival worthy of the game.

They both had different styles of hunting. Svir amused himself by pouncing on occasional lights of green, or blue, or gold, that arced with meteorite desperation from place to place in the mental realm. Pounced, ripped through mind and memory. When they disappointed him, he snuffed the light—the life.

Ilerian was more patient, lying in wait for connections that would lead to Detlev. Then struck.

He appeared with no warning in the locked and barred cellar of an ancient inn high in the mountains of eastern Shingara. He ignored the shock-rigid circle of people who stared without comprehension at his light-amber eyes and drifting white hair, and he advanced in two unhurried steps on the dark-haired young man who sat cross-legged and straight-backed against one wall.

The young man's face paled, but otherwise he gave no outward sign of the lost race to drop from the mental realm to the physical before Ilerian's strong white fingers closed round his throat.

Even the head-blind witnesses endured the ferocious stoop like a dark-winged raptor onto the spirit of their second young relation who seemed to have that mysterious mind talent. They were battered by the unvoiced but high-charged anguish of the victim's identity being shredded as they helplessly watched the physical agony of life being choked from heart and veins and flesh. Death came first to the once-strong body, after which the mind was consumed with outward-crackling emanations of cruel exultation.

Then, suddenly, they were alone.

And a moment later Ilerian walked into the library of the Imaran citadel. As Svir opened his eyes and looked up expectantly Ilerian said, "He was not the one Detlev trained. But he knows the one."

Svir said in his mild voice, "You are going to have to learn their names."

"Adam," Ilerian said obediently. "This was a cousin to Adam."

Ilerian returned to the contemplation of his targets. For there were two in the immediate sense. Either would serve: both would, in breaking, easily break Kessler's hold, so that he could go after the third.

Identities were what he sought. Ilerian seldom paid attention to the names and appearances of individuals. Those things could be changed so easily, he had discovered, in contemplating Detlev's long-hidden scheme. But if Svir said it was important, then he would do so.

First of course was Detlev. The second, Clair, whose will held the key to the ward round the single resisting kingdom on the world.

And the third, most important of all: there was no identity as yet. Only the physical image, as supplied by Imry Llyenthur, of a young girl with wide blue eyes and sun-bleached patches of curling hair. That form had probably changed; in his own accustomed realm he would immediately know again the silver-white star that was a match in intensity for his own.

This search was to be savored.

Four

RIGIDLY GRIPPED FURY COOLED and then evaporated for the first time in eternities when Marend Ndarga saw the footprint.

No more than an edge of a bootheel was visible in the ooze of mud and moss, but that was enough. A man's bootheel. None of the man-sized feet residing in the Darchelde hideout wore riding boots for forest work.

She looked up, grinning, about to call to the rest of the patrol. And there she saw that exasperating twit Ramond, red-nosed and red-eared from the cold weather, gazing raptly into a tree and gabbling clapper-jawed to one of his twit friends.

The two idiots were looking at the same thing, and Marend could tell from Ramond's excited, jerky hand-movements that he was blathering about something artistic.

Her lip curled. She turned her back and pushed on, looking for one of Detlev's Own to tell. How perfect it would be if she discovered something new—wouldn't that negate Ramond's idiocy, and bring her, and her gang, she amended quickly, into *Them*? Of course it was Ramond's fault that Detlev's Own stayed aloof as far as their plans went. She hated it when they all went silent—she knew they were talking to each other in thought form. Which they wouldn't teach any of the rest of the gang.

She looked around for MV, or Roy, or any of them … and

saw another print.

Same foot.

Giving her a vector.

She eyed the print, then sent a hot glare through the tangled wintry branches at Ramond, who was now crouched over some plant. Then she made a daring decision: she would be faster on her own.

She patted out the print, retraced her steps, and did the same with the first, careful as always not to leave prints of her own. It was harder because of the thaw of the past few days, leaving squelching mud where the sun shone, and snowdrifts in the shadows. But there were plenty of rocks to step on, and where she had to venture into mud, she had found a long branch with twigs that had fallen from a tree in one of the storms, with which she could smear out her own prints.

As the patrol finished the route and returned she was silent, imagining her appearance with a prisoner. Some Norsundrian spy, of course. Had to be—and a fairly good one, too, or their patrol would have caught him. Or her, though that boot print looked like it belonged to a fairly tall man. And to MV's question on why she'd countermanded the standing order about no groups with fewer than three she'd have—at last—her opportunity to give her opinion on a number of things. She just had to make sure she took the spy, or whoever it was, by surprise, so that she retained the upper hand. And after months of drill, she was confident she'd win.

So involved she was in the wording of her speech about Ramond and his paying attention to plants while on patrol, she had little attention to spare for her surroundings until she was startled by Tdor's brown face poking close to hers as they stood outside the little kitchen nook in the big underground hideout.

"Marend!" Tdor exclaimed. "You all right?"

"Of course," Marend snapped.

"Then here," Sindan spoke from behind his sister. "Unless you expect me to stand here and hold this plate all night while you contemplate its worthiness for your innards?"

Kethadrend guffawed loudly.

"Shut up, Rat," Tdor said good-naturedly. As Marend took the plate Sindan was holding out to her and elbowed her way past the others in the Methden gang, Tdor sent a sharp, slightly perplexed look after her sometimes exasperating friend.

Then was startled by a murmur at her shoulder, "Patrol went well? Nothing to report?"

It was Sveneric. Tdor liked him. She knew immediately that he was asking in an indirect way about Marend. She hesitated, but loyalty to the Methden gang, plus a healthy respect for Marend's temper, prompted her to say stoutly, "We went all the way to the south road fork, leading to the ruined castle. Nothing to report."

Sveneric nodded, smiled, took his share of the dinner, and moved away.

After dinner, Tdor decided to consult a couple friends. If the outsiders were beginning to notice Marend's latest brooding, then maybe it was time to do something. But what?

They'd talk it over and decide among them.

Which meant that no one was around in the big chamber just before sundown, so Marend was able to fetch her bow and knife and slip away long before she'd let herself hope for a chance.

Once up in the silent forest, she sped swiftly for the bend in the stream where she'd seen the prints, hardly noticing the cold misting drizzle on her face. "Be there," she murmured in supplication and challenge to the unknown intruder as she ran. "Just be there."

She ran alongside the south road, tightened her bowstring, and set off on the hunt, trying to keep elation, conjecture, even anger out of her mind. Six months of intensive training did not make her an expert tracker — as MV and Rolfin kept reminding them — even though she knew the terrain very well indeed. She must keep eyes and ears and mind alert for all the subtle signs...

And she found another one! The spy had turned toward the castle everyone insisted had once belonged to the king's ancestors, before they became the kings in Choreid Dhelerei. No one ever went to the castle, which (everyone said) had evil magic lurking.

Triumph burned through her veins, chasing away mere cold and hunger. Bending slightly in the fading light, she doubled her speed — and found, this time, a broken twig from a wiry bush. Caught on a cloak? She found the twig fragment ten paces farther on, and so she kept up her run.

And nearly danced with glee when she came across the signs of a clumsily eradicated camp. Fresh!

She was running hard now, so hard she nearly ran smack

into her quarry. She'd tracked him up into the rocky hills that led toward the border, and in her excitement she forgot the tiny river that cut through them, leaving high and impassable rocky palisades on either side.

And so—she stopped just in time—she found him, and he was boxed.

Her fingers trembled, stilled with fierce effort as she drew an arrow, nocked it. Readied it. Stepped forward once. Twice.

Her quarry stood at the very edge of the rocky cliff, staring down into the gully. Not much could be told from his back; he was tall, dressed in a heavy forest-green tunic, dark trousers, riding boots, sword across his back. His damp hair was longish, color a dull light brown. Her heart thumped hard against her ribs.

"If you're going to jump," she said clearly, "you'd better do it now."

The man turned around, and even in the weak light she easily recognized the facial bone-structure, the lounging attitude, of Imry Llyenthur. Her triumph lurched unpleasantly until she remembered the bow in her hands. She resisted the impulse to aim at his face, and kept the arrow trained steadily on his heart as he stepped toward her. Once. Twice.

Perhaps fifteen paces lay between them. She dismissed an instinctive urge to retreat and said hungrily, "I'd love to shoot you."

"But—?" he prompted, the planes of his face changing from curiosity to amusement.

"There are some who'd consider you a prize. Alive."

"You're probably right," he agreed—and she realized he was looking, and listening, behind her.

Convulsively she swallowed and steeled herself. All right, she was alone. To capture Imry Llyenthur alone would earn her kingdom-wide renown. It would reach the king's ears even in Choreid Dhelerei. Would even force praise from MV...

But then he took a step. And another.

Marend stiffened her legs and said, "One more and I shoot."

"Shoot, then!" Llyenthur laughed, and advanced.

Suppressing regret, she let fly—and watched in dismay as his right hand jerked up, a hereto hidden blackweave-and-steel-ring wrist guard flashing as it deflected the arrow. His hand dropped and his sleeve covered the wrist-guards.

Furious, she grabbed for another arrow, but then he was on her. His hand wrenched the bow from her fingers. Giving in to rage, she yanked out her knife and launched herself to kill. Some of MV's constant drills gave her enough power and speed to score her point heavily across one of his hands before the world crashed and splintered and then coalesced again with her face down in the cold, gritty forest muck, her hands being bound behind her with her own bowstring.

She saw the splintered remains of her bow lying an arm's length away, and then she gasped as she was hauled up by her scruff and set on her feet.

She shook her head, trying to clear her swimming vision, as Llyenthur peered down at her. One of his hands, she noted numbly, pulled a handkerchief from a tunic pocket. He twisted it around his dark-smeared other hand as he said, "I thought so. Marend! So this is where your group of Methden urchins scuttled to. Why here? And—did my brother teach you that particular move, or has Senrid managed to garner a few of our old tricks?" He paused, and as she remained silent—remembering her mind-shield—he went on, "Who's here with you?"

"No one," she said shortly.

"Well then," he returned pleasantly, "perhaps the birds and butterflies will come to your rescue, eh?" He grasped her arm, spun her about, said cheerfully, "March!" as he gave her a prod between the shoulder-blades.

Five

MAREND STUMBLED FORWARD INTO the gathering darkness, remembering MV, David, and Adam giving a demonstration with wrist-guards. Remembering her own bitter disappointment when MV refused to train the gang to use them until their reflexes were fast enough ... Imry used to be part of MV's gang ... Clumsy in forests?

Then she realized that the footprints, the half-smeared campsite, had all been a trap.

And instead of scuffing up a trail, she forced herself to tread as carefully as possible. Behind her, Llyenthur walked silently, but she could tell by the sounds of his breathing that he was looking and listening this way and that. Rage welled up inside her again, hot and choking, but this time directed against herself.

They walked on for a time, until the darkness around them was nearly impenetrable, then he said, "Well, that little stroll ought to draw someone, mmm? Here, let's provide further encouragement by setting up a camp."

He put a hand on her shoulder and steered her to a slight rise. Then he stopped, made a gesture, and a bright orange fire leaped into existence. Not a vagabond one—a real one, burning the duff from an old log, giving off a cloud of white smoke.

She looked up into that familiar face and all her problems of the previous spring crowded back into her mind. Scowling stonily, she turned away—to be yanked off her feet by a tug on her tunic hem. She plunked down in the mud. Squelch.

He sat on a rock next to her, giving a soft laugh. "The idea is to provide bait. So, what have you been doing since our short-lived alliance?"

"Nothing," she said curtly. Then, remembering recent events, she added nastily, "But I hear you've been rather busy losing a duel, and your command." Then felt a moment of panic when she thought, Should I know that?

But he only laughed again. "That gossip has even reached the backwaters, eh? Yes, you see me here, acting on my own. Which of course can have its own rewards."

The coldness of the wet mud had seeped into her clothes, and was numbing her legs, hands, and back. She clenched her teeth to keep them from chattering, and resolved on saying nothing more.

"One side benefit is that I now have time for personal projects. One of these is to find my brother and restore his sword to him." He slapped the weapon lying on a flat boulder at his side.

Marend's attention was caught by the gleam of firelight on gold, the glitter and flicker of reflected flame on obsidian. Unwilling admiration surged through her at the sight of that weapon but she kept her face, and mind, closed.

Llyenthur smiled. "You won't talk to me anymore? And it seems you've learned a mind-shield. Well, let's see what emerges from the woods, shall we?" And he, too, fell silent.

She tried, once, to squirm into a better position for instant flight but when bade "Sit still!" gave it up. And stared morosely into the fire, trying not to think what the others would say—if—when—

I hope he kills me, she thought miserably, and forced her mind to abandon conjecture.

And was wrenched from black abstraction when, without any forewarning, his hand came out of nowhere and smacked her head up against his side. One of her elbows ground pain-fully against the rock as she struggled, totally off-balance. His palm pressed across the back of her skull, two fingers jammed into the soft flesh under her jaw so that if she moved, knives of agony stabbed through brain and eyeballs. One of her eyes was smooshed against the rough green cloth of his tunic, the other saw only the haze round his fire. A final affront was the sound of his heart beating, slow and steady, under her head while her own was thumping crazily somewhere near her throat.

For her this was death and for him just a game he was playing with Detlev's gang; she closed the one eye, and willed him—or someone—to slide in the knife now.

Instead, quite suddenly, she was thrust away to land sprawling face first in a puddle of liquid sludge while behind there was a confusion of voices.

Then hands picked her up, a knife freed her wrists, and Ramond peered into her face, his own wildly side-lit by the leaping flames. "Marend? Are you all right?"

Her jaw was clenched; she could only jerk her head.

"Then let's go."

Behind Ramond, Rom and Sindan stared at her. And behind them, the rest of the Methden gang.

Beyond being able to question, she followed.

No one spoke to her on the long walk back.

When they arrived, Sveneric was alone in the big room, waiting. He looked up at their arrival, and Marend, meeting his eyes briefly, saw only question. She turned abruptly to the fire, held her hands out, saw with blank surprise that they were crusted and smeared with mud. So, in fact, was she.

"Well? Did he follow us?" Ramond's excited voice chattered behind her.

"No. At least, not that I can tell. The others are still scouting," was Sveneric's calm reply.

Ramond, Rom, and Sindan withdrew to the kitchen, whispering among themselves. Marend felt quite suddenly as if an invisible wall had formed around her. She was alone. Alone—and awaiting trial.

Her brain refused to advance past that, her few thoughts buzzing a little, then bumping, like dying flies. Little remembered things: Llyenthur's *One of them is to find my brother and restore to him his sword.* Brothers. Retren. When he said—*no, I can't think about Ret, I can't.*

But hard on that, MV's voice, weeks ago, *And if any of you blundering shitbirds forget that order and decide to go out strolling alone, I'm going to pound the remains into a rug. At least then you'll be of some use.*

Her guts knotted suddenly and she twisted away—and heard, up at the top of the tunnel, the sounds of arrival.

Foremost was MV. Right behind him were Andri, Mildred, Dirk, David. All were heavily armed. Rolfin closed the tunnel, and came down last. David said to them all, "He's gone."

"First, let's find out what he knows," MV retorted, and advanced on Marend. "You. Start talking."

She worked her lips, her throat. She managed to say, "I told him nothing."

MV replied, "You're too stupid to know what you told him. I want a detailed I-said he-said account. Very detailed, right down to farts and sniffs. Now."

She went through it, in a flattened, curt voice, the last shreds of her self-control focused on hiding how the humiliating story scraped over her nerves like a flaying knife. Further laceration came in the form of laughter from those gathered in the background at some of Llyenthur's words. But she refused to turn, or acknowledge it in any way.

"... he suddenly flung me face down in the mud, and I saw nothing more." At last it was done.

MV had listened silently throughout, neither laughing nor frowning. He looked up at the others of his group, to David (who was having difficulty controlling yawns), Sveneric, Roy, Rolfin, and to Laban, who had just come softly in from the regularly scheduled forest-border patrol.

David shrugged. Sveneric said, "What this means is, whether or not he learned of our presence from Marend, he will be back. He suspects, or he wouldn't have been here at all. Am I right?"

"Unless he experienced a sudden desire to personally tour the ancestral home," David said. "But why would he trouble to lay a trap? No, he's niffed some sign that we might be around, and he will return."

"With or without backup." Laban spoke up from where he was lounging damply against a wall.

Rolfin moved slightly then. No more of a glance Laban's way, but MV took that for consensus, and he said, "That does it. We're out of here. Someone write to Senrid, Adam, and Zairna?" The latter having vanished a couple days previously on assignment.

"I will," Mildred volunteered.

MV turned to Marend. "Now, what to do with you." Hands on hips.

She said, stiffly, "I'd as soon get the thrashing over with."

David shaded his eyes with one hand and turned away.

Laban, who understood Marend better than anyone, winced with a sort of rueful sympathy, and decided to go off in search of dry clothes.

On the other side of the room the Methden teens and Dirk and Crow waited in total silence.

"What?" MV drawled, with patently fake surprise. "A thrashing? But that would make you feel better!"

The silence intensified.

He went on affably, "You might have noticed on your previous encounters with our old friend Imry that he's not got eight arms and he's not made of brick. He was here looking for information, which is why he let you find him. Three of you, moving the way I've taught you, could've brought him down. Instead..." His hand came down on her shoulder, the heavy, wet smack sounding to her like the harbinger of the end of the world. "No, what I'm going to do is tell you just what I think of you. But in private. Because I want your few wits to be all on me, and not wallowing in public self-pity."

He spun her about, and gave her a prod between the shoulder blades. "March," he said cheerfully, in unconscious but devastating echo of Imry.

It was even more devastating.

It was, in fact, the second worst experience of Marend's short but intense life. Only the moment when she nearly had her brother's life ended (relived since countless times in nightmares) matched the misery of MV's utterly merciless critique.

Of all the people in Marend's life right now, MV was the most important. She rated him just below the memory of her father, second only to the king; that was a conscious rating, but in reality MV was the living embodiment of all she admired most. He was a true inda: taller, stronger, faster than anyone — including the king — and he was completely emotionless. Solo operations came as easily to him as field command. He was such an inda that he didn't ever spare a moment's thought on others' opinions of him.

She'd had reprimands from other people — including her father, and the king — but somewhere in the back of her awareness had always been the secure notion that the unpleasantness, commander to commander-in-training, was in her best interest.

MV discussed, with clinical objectivity, her attitudes, her

actions and their motivations. His accuracy was undeniable. She felt as if he'd opened her brain and dragged out fistfuls of thoughts and memories, and after looking at them in visibly measurable increments of disgust, dismissed them with contempt. She was thus forced to look at them as well, and saw in the impartial light that everyone shared that what had looked so fine and steely when locked inside her skull was in reality only weakness blown up by the false hot air of pomposity and self-delusion. And the worst of it was, among her many shortcomings, he made no reference to her size relative to everyone else.

The critique, coming as it did from the person she'd been straining for six months to impress, was paid for by the last of her self-respect.

She did manage, just barely, to keep her reactions from visual display or it's very likely that when he finally left her alone she would have found a knife and plunged it right into the center of that terrible pain in her heart. But by locking her jaw and freezing her muscles into rigidity she neither moved nor made a sound.

An eternity of agony later, Tdor's face hovered near, eyes trying to catch Marend's eyes. The brief contact was unbearable, like fire on flayed skin, and consciousness returned long enough for Marend to jerk away and cover her face with her hands.

"Tsk!" Tdor clucked. "Marend. You are covered head to heels with prime forest loam. If it dries and drops off, we'll have to dig the tunnel out all over again. Look. Let's step through the cleaning frame, and I have your favorite tunic all ready..."

The words made no sense but the cheerful, practical tone somehow got Marend out of her wet, gritty clothing, and into dry clothes. Then hands pushed her down onto her bed and she obediently stretched out—

—and out of the blackness came a touch on her shoulder, and a cool, soothing voice, "Marend. I want to show you something."

She turned her head. Sveneric knelt beside her bunk, a candle in one hand. From the bunk above came Tdor's slow, even breathing.

"Time is short," Sveneric murmured. "You must come now."

Six

MAREND MET SVENERIC'S EYES. She saw no question, surprise, anger, disgust, or pity. No judgment. They were just eyes, gray-green and steady.

Slowly consciousness seeped back, and with it awareness of light. Ordinary eyes in an ordinary face. Her gaze took in her room. Back to Sveneric, whose one hand held the candle so still there was no eye-worrying flicker. He was not shrouded in his usual tunic; he wore only a white shirt above the usual dark trousers and forest mocs. Past his face again—still waiting—to the other hand, which gripped the hilt of a heavy cavalry saber.

My execution, she thought. And, bitterly, I hope.

It was this hope that sent her feet swinging over the side of the bed. Sveneric rose to his feet and stepped out of the way as Marend pulled on her waiting mocs and laced them up.

Sveneric led the way out. In the tunnel the blackness threatened again at the thought of eyes in the main room—but then they were there, and they were alone.

They did not detour for cloaks or coats. Marend's gaze took in his plain white shirt, as her arms registered the increasing chill, but she said nothing. She was beyond questioning. She just followed.

Outside, the cold air of dawn smote her face. Her skull ached. But she followed Sveneric out, then bent to secure the hatch with nervelessly careful fingers, her breath clouding. Tiny noises sounded loud and distinct: the crunch of their feet in the thin frost layer covering the ground; the hiss of fabric brushing against winter-hardened twigs; farther away, the sudden whir of wings.

Sveneric waited until she straightened up, then said, "This way." And fell in step beside her. She glanced once at the sword, which was an ordinary rider-rank saber with a worn hilt. He was using it now as a walking stick. She wondered how the dully gleaming edge would feel on her neck.

They reached a clearing. Fog obscured the sky at treetop level, taller tangles of trunk and bare branches just discernable, ghost-etched against the fading gray background.

"I'd like to show you something," Sveneric said. His voice wasn't loud, but it seemed the only one in the universe right now. No. Not the only one, there was another soft boy-soprano that Sveneric's voice reminded her of. Voice, and window-eyes—

She gritted her teeth.

"You'd get the best view if you sit on that rock right there," Sveneric said.

She stepped back, dropped onto the cold, mossy rock, and looked up in numb misery. Her head pounded, at first with sickening and almost blinding intensity.

Sveneric stood in the center of the clearing, not looking cold despite the thin shirt, his breath puffing little clouds. There was a sort of relaxed alertness to his gaze. For a few more breaths he stood there, feet slightly apart, blade just touching the ground before him, both hands on the hilt. Then he lifted the blade and started to swing it.

"Against one, on foot," he said.

The blade arced, reversed, arced again. Offense, defense above; offensive glow, defensive parry from below. From the sides. Left hand, right hand. The blade never stopped moving.

"Against two, on foot," Sveneric said, and the speed of the whirling saber increased.

Marend's eyes followed the silver blade—now dull, now gleaming in the pale haze—in its unhesitating, hypnotizing pattern.

"Against three, on foot." And now the pattern was even faster. She followed enough to see that he made no slips, no shortcuts; his shoulders and wrists took the halts and turns with precision.

"We call this the warmup." Step step, turn, down-thrust,

parry-to-left. No pause: repeat of the pattern to the right. "Detlev learned something like it when he was young and he refined it. Taught it to us."

Step-step-feint, step-step-thrust. Now he covered the whole clearing, and the heavy blade hissed and hummed. But his breathing was still steady, and his voice showed no effort. "Against four, on foot."

Again the increase in speed, which she would have thought impossible. The blade sang, like someone unseen playing a war dirge on a crumhorn.

"Against two mounted." The angle shifted; the speed did not abate.

"…and against four mounted finishes it. Though we sometimes combine patterns, such as two mounted and two on foot, and so on."

The incredible pattern altered now between the upper and lower angles, then, with no flourish, Sveneric stopped in the exact spot he'd begun in, and he lowered the sword blade so that the point rested on the ground. His cheeks glowed, but his breathing was only slightly quickened. He smiled. "You see it's only a pattern, don't you? What would you do if more than one foe came at you?"

"Back to wall, tree, or partner," she said instantly. Once she would have added scornfully, "I knew that before my fourth year," but now she returned his smile, a little, and waited.

"The warmup does several things. Besides the obvious," he added with another smile as he wiped his forehead with his sleeve. "The individual patterns will become automatic should you need them. And your eyes, and arms, will respond with the necessary speed if you practice every day. The other lesson, though, is the attaining—and sustaining—of focus."

"Concentration?" she asked.

"Not quite." He moved forward a couple of steps and began to swing the sword in a lazy arc back and forth. "Some don't need to practice it every day. Likewise some have a great deal of natural strength. Rolfin, for example. MV, too. Adam doesn't. Neither do I—and I probably never will, I'm built too light. But it doesn't matter, because when it's necessary I have access to all I can use—"

Suddenly the blade swung up and down, too fast for her to see more than a steely flicker. Once again she heard that scalp-prickling hum and then jumped as, with a sharp *Crack!* Sveneric sidestepped and brought the sword blade down across the mossy top of a tree stump. The saber had buried itself completely in the wood. A thin smell of hot metal and crisped tree-bark tickled her nose.

"Pull it out." He gestured.

She tried, silently exerting all her strength until the headache came crashing back. She couldn't budge it. Then Sveneric closed his hands around the hilt. She saw the effort, but it wasn't undue, and the blade was free.

"Some learn focus naturally as well. Imry was one, I'm told. But, like natural strength, it matters little how or when you learn it. If Adam found it necessary to go up against Imry I wouldn't place any wagers on the outcome."

Marend stood for a time, looking down at the deep line bisecting the tree stump. And then, reluctantly, lest she misunderstood, and was going to be humiliated yet again, "I'm to learn it too?"

Once again Sveneric surprised her. "Well, we are fighting Norsunder, aren't we?" No warnings, reminders of responsibility, or even pity. "Chances are you're going to find this stuff useful some time or other." He put the sword into her hands. "Take up your stance. Notice where your feet are. Part of the control is in returning to this same spot, which means being aware of you in relation to your surroundings. All right, let's begin with the breathing while you warm up your arms..."

<hr>

While the two in the clearing began their lesson, Mildred woke out of jumbled dreams, and heard Crow whisper, "Something's up. Meeting in Andri's and MV's room, right now. Don't waken the locals."

He vanished in the darkness. Mildred rolled out of bed, cursed at the freezing air, and with foresight borne of experience she dug in her stuff, pulled on her warmest shirt, tunic, and pants. Two pairs of socks before lacing up her mocs. Traveling clothes.

She slid into the crowded room just behind David, whose wet head indicated he'd been forced to shock himself awake with cold water. The marks under his eyes were very pronounced in the light of the lamp Andri had put on a chair.

The resemblance to Senrid increased proportionally; he looked awake and alert, though.

MV and Andri were sitting on the top bunk, one dark head and one blond, long legs dangling down. MV looked grim. Andri sneezed.

"Bad news," MV said as Mildred pulled the door shut behind her. "Adam just found out that Ilerian nailed his cousin. No way to find out how, why, or what Ilerian learned, but there is one thing we're going to have to manage somehow. Find ourselves a hide far from any kind of civilization."

He paused to let the implications sink in. A quick glance around at grim faces showed they had. "Adam's heading straight for Ghildraith to lose himself. We're going to disperse and make separate runs that call attention to us not being together, or coordinated. And then—"

"If," Laban interjected sardonically.

"—assuming we survive that, we'll form up again, and Detlev will join us for the strike. Siamis is staying in Mearsies Heili, and through him and Atan we'll be coordinating the field action. Final phase now, shitbirds."

Silence again.

Then Andri sniffed, coughed, said, "Runs?"

"David's gotta stay here and play tag with Imry since he knows he's around—" MV paused to skewer David with a fiery look.

"Now, now," David said soothingly. "Knowing Imry, the chances are very good you'll get your turn with him. And I'm tolerably certain he's looking forward to it as well."

Grins lightened certain faces.

• • •

"...That's right," came Sveneric's voice. "Eye to mind to hand. Working together as a practiced unit, a ready conduit for the flow of focus."

Marend's head was pounding again, but it was the painless thump of exertion and of ignored hunger.

"That's it," Sveneric said, sitting down on the rock. He looked much the same as he had earlier, damp hair on brow. Marend was wringing wet and flushed, and her legs and arms felt like they'd been exchanged for those of a rag doll. No. A rag doll's wouldn't ache. But it was a good ache, and her brain was singing faintly as she plumped weak-kneed on the rock next to him.

"You'll remember it now," he went on. "Do it every day, and I think you'll find the focus coming to you fairly quickly. Detlev once told me that if you can remember and recite a poem during four and two-two, then you should be feeling the potential ready to hand."

She lifted a hand to wipe her damp black curls off her forehead, froze as she noticed movement in the thickening white fog.

A shifting of shadows resolved into figures. One, two, five tall human shapes entered the clearing. They came near and she recognized Mildred of the glossy black braids, then Andri's long yellow hair. Rolfin, Laban. MV and David just behind, all of them carrying travel gear.

"Done?" Laban said to Sveneric.

"Done. She picked it up fast," Sveneric said.

Marend was so shocked by the sight of them with knapsacks and weapons that she didn't register the compliment until much later. "What's this? A patrol? Llyenthur out again?" she asked, eyeing those packs. Her new contentment dissolved into chill, like the fog around them, and a reprise of that sick feeling of the night before.

"Nope," Andri said. "We're off!"

"I wish we could stay and chase Imry a little while longer," MV said, strolling forward. "But we're moving on."

They were all there now, Mildred and Crow with them. The sense of impending loss was so great that Marend felt her heart, her spirit, crushing under the weight of guilt. *My fault, my fault, no matter what MV says.*

"So instead of having a little fun, we're leaving Imry to you and the rats," MV said. "If you want my advice, play least-in-sight a week or so," he added.

"Actually, that pretty much sums up the first part of Senrid's orders," David spoke up. "Just got a note back from him. Marend: he's not sure when he'll get down south again, but for now the old refugee plan is in effect. Continue to funnel 'em into the hills. And when the Signal comes, if he's not back, you're to place yourself and your people under the command of Mordan Nauldra. Says you know him."

"Our old Desk Jockey," she whispered.

"Says Mordan knows you, and will be counting on your

band. That's it!"

David smiled over her shoulder at the rest of the Methden people, who had gathered silently behind. It wasn't until later that Marend understood partly why Senrid's last communication came in this form—by addressing her thus before the others, David had reestablished Marend's authority in their eyes.

Now, she could only think: They're leaving. And it's worse than when Ret left because I thought he'd be back soon, and I know they will never come back here.

Why should they? There was nothing here for them. They were going out to save the world.

As the two groups said low-voiced goodbyes and exchanged a few muffled, quick laughs, her aching eyes went from MV's tall form in his accustomed black to short, tense Dirk who dug an elbow into Rom's side as they exchanged a private joke. Andri caught her attention with another sneeze; Roy did as he accepted a wrapped package of hot rolls from Kelsan.

He belongs. I don't, she admitted to herself. And in the absence of anger, she tested the idea that that was part of their greatness: they were together. They belonged, even when they made mistakes, like Sveneric did. But she didn't belong.

The sense of loss had never been so sharp, but without the cloud of anger she was able to recognize it for what it was. Her head dropped forward a little because she could not prevent the sting in her eyes, and she saw the saber lying at her feet.

Remembering the feeling of strength, of integration, she'd felt while working under Sveneric's direction, she wondered if what he said about unity held for other things. She'd never be part of their circle. But she had her own.

She looked up at Ramond's familiar red nose as he sneezed again, and at Tdor's brown braid. Kelsan's round blond head. She had her own circle, and they would free Marloven Hess. That was what mattered most.

Silently, unnoticed, Sveneric got up from his place at her side, and moved to join the others. Laban handed him his tunic, cloak, and pack, and Dirk his knife.

The two groups separated as the last good-byes and spirit-raising Norsunder insults flew back and forth, and then David and MV exchanged a look and the Host-harriers formed into a rough line and disappeared swiftly and silently into the fog.

The Marlovens watched until they were gone, no twig or

needle to mark their way.

The forest had been silent for some time when at last they looked at one another. Marend saw traces of her own emotion in the faces around her. What friendships had happened that she was entirely unaware of?

She sat on her rock. Her authority had been reestablished in the others' eyes, but not in her own. But eventually she'd get tired of waiting for someone to make a workable suggestion, and habit would prompt her to offer suggestions for plans, for drill, for action. These would be good, and the others prompt in acting on them, suggestions would give way to another, older, habit: giving orders. But the balance of power had been forever changed—and in changing it, she began a new path through life.

At that moment, Sindan put his fists on his hips. "I think we better all have a talk first," he said. "Why don't we all go back into the hideout?"

"Right," Marend agreed, and bent to pick up the saber.

Seven

First of all, though he'd personally inspected every face after locking down various headquarters, he couldn't be certain he'd caught the mole.

At least the attacks had lessened—but that brought him to what really irritated him: Wan-Edhe daring to break the blockade that he, Efael, had required around the northeast corner of Toar. Wan-Edhe could parade around being King of the Chwahir all he liked. But he did not appear to truly comprehend that it was Efael who let him do it. Only because Efael had no interest in being mere King of the Chwahir.

He prowled around scowling, until a report arrived from Alsais that his commander there had caught one of the mid-ranking Chwahir skirting orders, and there was to be an execution to make an example of him—and to remind the Chwahir who was subordinate.

Efael's mood brightened. Here was an excellent opportunity to remind Wan-Edhe who held the whip-hand. Oh, this would be fun.

He shifted to Alsais, and then, making as much parade as possible, required the elites of both Norsunder and the Chwahir to attend him as he was conducted to the primary silk warehouses so that he could choose bolts of fabric for his sister.

He signaled what he liked by requiring the attendants to

carry what he pointed at. If he didn't like something, he tossed it onto the floor. Colendi in the background cowered, one or two even moaning as the silk rippled like some live thing, shimmering as it slid along the ground. Efael knew very well that that was no way to treat silk — as a small boy in the brothel, when he wasn't servicing the customers, he was supposed to help with the silks. Oh, so many beatings for uncareful hands! It was thousands of years and worlds away from the hecatomb he and his sister had left of that place before Svir found them, but he still took vicious pleasure in grinding the beautifully woven fabric under his iron-shod heel. Even sweeter was every flinch of those Colendi merchants as they bowed like weeds before the wind.

When he was tired of that, he waved carelessly. "Send the stuff to Imar. My sister will decide what to do with it."

And now, it should be time for the execution. He walked back to the royal palace, relishing everyone scurrying out of the way. But when he got there — where was the whipping post? The garrison all lined up and waiting?

He turned to Norsundrian Commander Nayan. "Where's my execution?"

The Norsundrian captain's thin mouth tightened to a sneer. "Have to ask Furo. He dismissed the charge."

"What?" Efael turned to Crimson General Furo, who stood at strict attention at the side. "Explain."

Furo faced straight ahead, saying, "I am required by my king to investigate all charges against Chwahir."

"Go on."

"There was no evidence. Therefore, as directed, I dismissed the charge."

"Nayan?"

"Anjit was seen making trade, which we have forbidden, with a local," Nayan said.

"Hearsay, from one source," Furo stated. "No corroboration. And totally against orders as well as character."

"Character?"

Furo hesitated, then said neutrally, "We are not trained to take initiative. Anjit is a scribe. His testimony makes it clear he was obtaining end-of-year lists, required by our king. All inventory in the royal treasury to be itemized."

"That might be true," Efael said, drawing out the moment. "We know Wan-Edhe thinks everything in Colend belongs to him."

Furo stared straight ahead as Efael prowled around him,

heels ringing, the stink of leather causing a roiling echo of the blood poison spell. "If. I permit."

Another circuit.

"You Chwahir are good little beetles, are you not? Isn't that what we call you flat-faces? Slugs would be more to the point. Obedient, and oh, *never* would you take initiative."

Nayan, who had survived Efael's much-purged chain of command so far, held his breath until that moment. Hearing the acidic drawl in Efael's voice, he knew instinctively that Efael was leading somewhere, but he was not the target.

"And yet," Efael drew the word out. "I came here not only to see a demonstration, but to make one."

Silence. Furo didn't even blink.

"You should be asking, what demonstration, my lord?"

"What demonstration, my lord?"

"I will tell you. A demonstration to your king. A reminder who issues commands to our armies. Someone has to serve as a reminder, eh?"

At that point, Efael paused—looking around. He was not the only one to recollect the single order that Svir had given, which was to the effect that no one in command was to be done away with before he investigated the situation.

Efael snapped his finger and pointed to one of the Black Knives flanking him, then indicated Furo with a flick of his finger.

The Black Knife, who carried a transfer token, slapped it against Furo. Who vanished to Efael's lair high in the mountains between Erdrael Danara and Chwahirsland.

Marloven Hess

The beginning of the last journey of Detlev's circle was enlivened by gossip.

Mildred walked alone for a time into the thickening fog. She quickened her pace until she caught up with MV. Breaking unceremoniously into his low-voiced conversation with Andri, she said, "You were pretty nasty with the little one."

MV shrugged one shoulder. "Had to be."

"You had a reason." Mildred became aware that conversations behind had ceased. Everyone was listening now, though they all continued walking.

"We didn't have the time to straighten her out easy and slow. Senrid—for whatever reasons—wasn't doing it. Then he took off. If we'd left her like that, they would fracture in a week. And get 'em all nabbed."

Mildred saw Andri grimace in agreement. Behind, Laban said softly, "That's true. Poor little sod."

MV added, "I took her apart and the shrimp put her together again, leaving out some of the rot she'd picked up along the way. She'll be all right."

"When she's had a chance to sort it all out," Laban said. "Thwarted ambition set up against conviction she'd never be good enough. Residual guilt about the brother."

Mildred sighed. "Just so you had a reason."

MV grinned. "I wasn't mad at her. I was mad because I thought we might lose a chance at some fun with Imry. But we were gonna lose it anyway."

Mildred laughed, watching her breath puff. "Why you want to tangle with that twit—why you'd think it fun—is beyond me."

MV's black brows shot up in exaggerated astonishment. "But that's obvious!"

"Spare your breath."

A consequence of their intense melding of mind was learning new ways of coping. Mildred believed that problems were best addressed right out, and aloud, not mind to mind with its enforced intimacy. Living together, working together, then joining minds at increasingly frequent intervals had fostered in them all an acute awareness of the importance of harmony and balance in communication. And, what very hard work it was to maintain it.

Which was one of the reasons why Detlev had assigned them this last chore before the final assault. They needed time away from one another. Dangerous as it was, they all looked forward to it. By now even the thoughtful ways one's companions respected one's barriers without touching them were unnerving because one knew they knew what it was one protected.

"Curse it," Andri said agreeably. "Fog's worsening."

They began to argue vigorously about what weather was worse for fast-travel sneakery. Laban and David lagged their steps, walking side by side. David looked heavy-eyed and he yawned frequently. Laban frowned.

After watching Laban glance back twice, David stifled what felt like his thousandth yawn and said, "Clumsy, wasn't he?"

Laban glanced yet again at Sveneric, who was now walking with Dirk, both mist-shrouded.

"Right." Laban's voice was soft but still managed to convey oceans of irony. "Can you match what we just saw?"

"Not I," David admitted, smiling.

Laban snorted. "It would have been so easy to give Marend a new hero to emulate, especially as she was still reeling from the burn of MV's tongue."

"The hand through the water," David murmured. Then he squinted. "Either the fog is thickening or my eyes are going to desert me at last."

Laban cocked a brow. "It does seem that everything happens just before your sleep shift."

"What sleep shift?" David queried grimly.

"What're you going to do with Imry?"

"I'm not doing anything with anyone besides a mattress and blanket in the foreseeable future. I can't see — *is* that fog? — and I can't think. Imry," David laughed softly, "will have to practice patience."

They walked in silence for a time. David was content to follow mindlessly, leaving the immediate planning to those up front. Laban thrust his hands into his coat pockets and sank into a reverie.

Detlev had never begun serious talk about dyranarya training until after the switch, when they were all living cooped up in his house. Laban wondered if David remembered how, after the introductory talk about the concept of the hand passing through the water, Laban had loudly and scornfully rejected the whole process.

At the time — so long ago it seemed! — he'd deemed it typical lighter hypocrisy, the metaphor of the fingers dipping into the water, moving through, then lifting, leaving no trace of their presence beyond the widening eddies. Now that he'd watched the process in person for the first time, he could see that Sveneric, who was obviously still euphoric over a job well done, did not require, much less desire, Marend's gratitude or emulation.

Since that first conversation with Detlev, he'd been too busy to brood over that empty throne in Fortnyal Roth and the deadly enemy in Ferdrian.

He considered the house that Curtas had made, sitting on uninhabited land. No titles, no ownership, even, attached. Land undisturbed except for the house. The house itself, though designed and built by Curtas — still much missed by the entire group—had so little of Detlev in it, Laban guessed (correctly) that the Norsundrians who knew Detlev personally had not bothered to seek the place out to molest it. They'd know that Detlev would shrug and walk away.

Sveneric was shaping up to be just the same: his perception of home constituted something very different from a structure built on a specific piece of land.

The establishment of a home was a part, but not all, to Laban. *Do I desire to win adulation in the eyes of the people? Is that it?* He laughed to himself. Of course it wasn't. But, he suspected, some were likely to think so.

"A joke," David's voice splintered his thoughts, "would keep me awake."

"How much do you know about the Deis?"

"Less than you, I'm sure," David said, with an enquiring look.

"Remarkable. For all their exploits, and their supposed charisma, they've never been able to hold a throne. Not as a family."

David shrugged lazily. "From what I remember, some of 'em did pretty well in that regard as individuals."

"When joined with other families."

"And the punchline is—?"

"That will be me," Laban said, "when I confront our old friend Tahra with my plans." In his coat pockets, his hands were suddenly clammy with sweat.

"Main road," MV sang out.

He and Andri waited until the rest of the group straggled up. They gathered in a circle beneath a dripping tree, the fog dampening hair and reddening ears and noses.

Eyes turned expectantly from David, who smothered another yawn, to MV. Andri snuffled, then sneezed.

MV said, "Either Zairna or Adam contact you, by whatever method, come on the double. Make sure you're seen first, then go to ground. No trace." He smiled.

Various grunts and nods of agreement.

He met everyone's gaze. "All right, then. This is it."

"Catch you in a few." Andri, seeing others reluctant to break the circle first, flung up a hand and started trudging eastward.

It worked. The group broke up, moving in several directions, some exchanging last cracks over their shoulders. David watched, smiling, then turned the disintegrating remains of his energy to finding somewhere warm to hole up. Within an hour he was blissfully asleep.

Mildred had been the second one to break the circle and start walking. Her spirits were high, and after a couple of sulfurous insults from Rolfin (no doubt for the acorns she'd slipped into his shoes while everyone was rushing around collecting gear), and an unrepentant grin on her part, she strode fast, hoping to warm up. Her plan was to find a nice, warm, dry spot and write some last letters, beginning with *Now that I'm on my own again*, which was in strict accordance with the new orders, yet would give her the chance to catch up with everybody from Geth.

And after that she might as well apply to Atan and find out what sort of harassment duty to take on. She was philosophical about that part—didn't matter much where or what.

Well, her plans were smoked when came a familiar dry voice, "Hey, you two."

That was MV.

Mildred spun around to discover Crow's thin, triangular face some thirty paces behind her. He halted as MV, flanked by Rolfin, ambled up the road toward them, dark-clad and dangerous.

Rolfin grinned without speaking. MV said, "One at a time, one at a time, and we're glad to see you, too."

Crow's twisted smile flared briefly. The fog almost smothered his hoarse rasp of a voice, "Thinking about home. Want to get there."

"Can it wait? It should wait," MV said, surprisingly. "Since you can trust your second-in-command, a short visit won't accomplish much. You!" This last was to Mildred; he pointed to her and jerked his thumb toward the ground in front of him.

The first step or two were automatic, habit after all those drills; the rest were because she was curious.

"Those acorns," Rolfin said, with foreboding promise. "How'd you get 'em in?"

Mildred cackled.

MV said, "You two. Truce. We need to be fast, if we do it at all." To Mildred, "Where were you headed?"

Mildred shrugged. "All the same to me."

"Thought so. Thing is, Host has never heard of either of you, so it doesn't matter where they see you. What does matter is that Efael think he's our next target. Need more'n two of us for that."

Mildred wrinkled her upper lip. "For what? Attacking Efael?"

"No. He's going to think so. Much as I want to face him with knife in hand, he'd cheat, and he knows far more magic. I promised Detlev we'll only hit his stronghold, which will make him madder anyway."

"We're going to attack his stronghold?"

"And if we take out one or two Black Knives, it's a benefit to the world. They don't know any magic. Or much — Efael would never trust them that far. You in?"

Crow's thin cheeks flushed with martial pleasure.

Mildred sighed. "All right. If you'll let me kick him." Pointing to Rolfin. "Just once. A gesture of consolation."

"If we survive," Rolfin conceded handsomely. "*After* I pay back the acorns."

Eight

YERES LOOKED UP FROM the fire when Efael stalked in. His eyes flickered in a wary scan. He noted that she was alone, and then he said impatiently, "Did you have fun with your silks?"

She shrugged. What was the point of a lot of fabric unless someone was admiring its slither over her flesh?

Her pout made it clear she was going to whine about cold again. Forestalling her, Efael snapped, "You've sat here doing nothing long enough. I need you. Everyone who is not busy is worthless."

"What do you want me to do?" She added, "It better be something I like."

His nasty grin promised it would be. "I want you to find Imry for me."

"He said he'd go talk to you."

"He did. But managed somehow, the squirming coward, to corner me on neutral ground. I don't know how he managed to find out my intentions—"

"Wouldn't that be rather obvious?"

"Where I was going that day," he cut in. "Did Detlev's crotch-dropping empty out your skull completely? Go find Imry."

"Then what?"

"I'm going to play with him a little. Play with him a lot," he corrected, grinning again. "He needs the experience."

"Svir doesn't want him dead. Has something in mind concerning Detlev."

"So he said. And?"

"So at the right moment, I shall rescue him from you!" She fluttered her hands in much the old way.

Efael rolled his eyes in disgust.

"I like having someone fetch for me, and submit when I'm amorous, and he has to be someone you don't like. So much more fun."

Efael laughed. "He will submit to me, first. Then you may have him."

Svir appeared in the other wingchair.

Yeres jumped, then grimaced as black spots swam before her eyes.

Svir said, "Two errands more and then Ilerian will be ready to exert himself on the matters awaiting our attention here."

"That girl." Yeres flung back her long curls. "He's *still* looking for her? The bald one that thinks she'll take Ejhir's place?"

"She *has* taken his place. For some reason, probably fear, she's done nothing with it. But the power is there. That will suffice to gain our egress."

Efael made a gesture of impatience. "But first Ilerian has to find her. Little we can do about that. What else?"

"Little you can do for either errand." Svir's amused and non-complimentary tone suggested that they might have tasks they could see to. And should. "In any case, that girl will require sustained effort, which must wait on certain preliminary ... let us term them vexations. Yes. Ilerian's current exertion is confined to breaking the ward over Mearsies Heili, and retrieving the Alshi cup."

Mearsies Heili

With snow falling softly and steadily, morning court was often comprised of those who gathered there to listen and to talk — anywhere else they would be courtiers, except that these refugees came and went as they would, they came from all walks of life, and they offered their opinions if moved to do so.

Clair forced herself to concentrate on listening, but it was so very hard when she was so, so tired. So very tired…

But she dared not sleep.

Her eyelids burned, a warning. She slid her fingers within a fold of her robe and pinched the skin of her leg, hard. Pain blurred her eyes, but at least she was awake. And she had to concentrate. She'd learned from Atan how to curb those who seemed to find it necessary to comment—lengthily—on everything, including the weather.

Atan could be quite intimidating when in the mood, but that aspect she confined to what she considered personal interference. In Clair's throne room, she skillfully deflected the blabberers by interposing questions when the person paused for breath, or turned toward someone else with a question. Atan had during the past year not only trained Clair—she trained the gathering, though she firmly held off from organizing a court in the usual sense, in a kingdom that was not hers.

Clair was startled when a small body collided with her knees, then caromed on, leaving behind the distinct odor of a small person whose grasp on the Waste Spell was still shaky.

A parent or guardian dashed by, muttering, "Sorry!" before swooping down and swinging the child into the air. "Time for a bath," he said.

"No bath! No bath!"

"Bibi is in the bath."

"No wash hair," the little voice countered, before adult and child vanished behind a mass of people pressing toward the side hall set up for meals.

Voices reached Clair again, overrode by a shrill woman, who talked on: "… not that anyone asked *me*, but the last *I* heard, a body has a right to speak up, especially when she has the benefit of experience to offer. Now, we all know that New Year's Week is a full month away—but let me tell you, thirty-six days passes as fast as six days if you don't look about you. If only for the sake of the children, who are guests in our kingdom, it might best to hire…"

"Liberty!" The teenage daughter of one of the palace servants bounced in, ignoring the woman trying to extort gold from Atan. Ordinarily Atan did not approve of servants elbowing their way in and taking over the conversation, but this was Clair's kingdom—and she smiled secretly at the scowling would-be extortionist. "My big sister turned up last night, off the *Lheit*. She says the last of the Chwahir blockade is moving out!"

"Going back to Chwahirsland like the rest?"

"The *Lheit* means to find out, after tomorrow. Today they get liberty!"

That roused Clair. "Will Puddlenose be coming in then?"

"No, he is having a meeting with the Chwahir in the crew. My sister thinks some of them are going to sneak into the homeland. Whew, better them than me!" She bestowed a smile on everyone and ran out again.

The woman cleared her throat, and started in again. Clair's attention wandered to Dhana, prowling along the windows. The girls—except for Seshe—usually avoided court, busy as it was. Dhana especially hated it, but she knew that her presence was comforting to Clair.

Clair tried to shut out the second attempt at charging Atan twelve gold pieces for some kind of organizing that the girls usually handled. Clair swayed, her eyes closing—and she saw herself standing up and sinking a knife into the folds of the old woman's neck, and laughing as blood squirted all over the white floor—

Clair's hand tensed, as though moved by someone else.

Dhana frowned. Clair's eyes had gone so *weird before she closed them.*

"Your majesty?" the woman asked. And then a sniff. "I do not feel you heard me. I said, in addition, this new edict forbidding landowners to raise rents cannot be well considered—"

Clair's fingers hooked, her mouth drew into a weird grimace—

And Dhana's body acted before her mind made the decision to act. Her feet propelled her forward, and her hands flattened at either side of Clair's face. "See me! Hear me! Wake up!"

"Dhana?" Atan gasped.

"What do you think you are doing?" the woman shrilled.

Dhana grabbed Clair's clammy-cold hand. She transferred to the caves, where Clair sagged to the rocky ground.

"I'm sorry, Clair," Dhana muttered hoarsely. "I'm so sorry."

Siamis arrived, his hair messy and clothes rumpled as if he'd been asleep. He knelt down, and Dhana moved aside to let him look. "Tell me what happened," he asked. "Though I think I know."

Dhana described what she'd seen, her voice going wobbly.

Siamis expelled a breath. "That was Ilerian," he said.

"Yecch." Dhana shivered with revulsion. "In her mind. In HER mind. That—" She frowned. "What's he look like?"

"Look like?" Siamis repeated, sitting back on his heels.

Dhana grimaced. "You can talk about your mental realm and spirit all you want, but to me, villains are a human thing. Humans have faces. He needs a face, so I know who I'm fighting against."

Siamis touched her arm. The contact was brief. Dhana's recoil was both from the face she saw, and from the contact itself. "He looks like *her*," she whispered in voiceless horror. Then, with an almost comical recovery, she gasped and exclaimed, "No, he doesn't! But the white hair—"

"Ilerian's human form is a morvende. I thought you knew that."

"Maybe I did, but couldn't really believe it. Hearing something's not the same as believing it. But, he couldn't—" She swallowed, unable to continue.

Siamis smiled a little, despite the tension. "Not what you think. Clair's family has had a long and varied history—including a morvende out of Sartor—but she's not about to sprout long-denied cousinship with Ilerian. When he took that form centuries ago, he murdered his entire family. None of them survived. There is, however, enough of her morvende ancestor in her to enable him to get at her the more easily."

"Yeah ... I've seen morvende talk mind to mind," she muttered.

It didn't surprise her that Siamis knew something about Clair's family that Clair didn't know. After all, he was an Ancient Sartoran; he'd been around, presumably, when that stuff was happening.

She said, "Well, he's too old to be a wicked uncle, which is a comfort. After old creepy Doumei, she doesn't need any more of those. What now?"

"Keep her here when she wakens. I'd better go back, in case he can reach anyone else in the white palace. I have an idea that might help."

<hr>

Liere to Clair:

> *... and I found it to be one of the most peaceful places in the world.*

Liere dipped her pen, formulating the words to describe her

experience with Marga, but before the pen touched the magic paper, she halted. Everyone in Mearsies Heili's white palace was worried about Clair. If there was anyone in more danger from Ilerian than Clair, it might very well be Marga; Liere shook her head, and reframed her words, sorrow in her heart at this realization that she could not trust Clair.

> *If Siamis wants to take you there, you ought to go. Also, I understand what you say about not wanting to trouble him. I felt the same way when he offered to take Tahra and me away from Sartorias-deles for a time. The journey was good not only for little Lyren, it was good for Tahra and for me, partly because of Siamis himself. He seems to like to teach. I know he's good at it.*

> *You might remember how wild Lyren was at that age, but he managed to get her to listen without subjecting her to any of the terrible things I endured from my father — which was the only method of child-raising I knew. And I so loathed myself for doing nothing to teach or correct Lyren, but I was not about to constrain her with my father's corrosive rules. Lyren-Sartora, I should say. All those lovely manners everyone comments on about her? She did not get those from me.*

> *Also. You know what happened to Siamis when young. There is no one we know who will better understand whatever thoughts the enemy is pulling in your head. Don't feel you have to hide it.*

Clair read the last two lines over and over, until they blurred before her burning eyes. She knew she had to do something — she was so very tired, but far worse was her fear of falling asleep. Because of those dreams.

She shook the words from the paper, steadied her breathing, and left her little cave within the cave.

"Very well," she said to Siamis. "Tell me what to do."

Siamis had been writing his own letter. He set down his pen and explained the Destination to the Sartoran Selenseh Redian, his profile invariably patient. Kind. Clair had overheard gossip about how handsome he was, but looks meant nothing to her. Kindness — doing what you said you would — were everything.

But kindness surely had a limit, and she knew she had done

absolutely nothing in trade. Though Clair knew it was rude, she turned away, shut her eyes, and transferred, before the insidious doubts could whisper through her mind, like a reek of rot not quite masked by fresh flowers.

The transfer from one cave to another didn't hurt. She contemplated that for a breath or two, and then looked around. It was strange, how each Selenseh Redian differed in subtle degrees. How could one describe it? They were all openings in rocky mountains, the inner portions of which created tunnels of fabulous colored crystals that looked like gems with lights inside, and sounded in the back of the mind a little like when you ran your wet finger round the rim of a crystal goblet.

They were all places where something was alive, though you didn't see the life. You felt it. Yet the one in Mearsies Heili was different than this one.

She stepped out onto a path. Who had swept it? No, this was not swept. This had to be ancient magic, keeping snow from piling up. Clair listened to the soft crunch of her footfalls on the path as she took in the thousand shades of white and blue and silver along the Sartoran mountainside.

There was an ancient pathway lined by very, very old trees, just as Liere had described. How long a walk would it be? The outer parts of her arms chilled, along with her neck and her lower back where air came up between her shirt and trousers. She glanced down at her shirt, and realized she wasn't really dressed for winter. Her decision to come had been too sudden for practicality.

But then Detlev's contact came: *Here's your Destination. Go back inside and transfer.*

He knew she was coming. So what? What did anything mean anymore? Oh, things still mattered. Or did they? Yes. Yes. Friends. Her kingdom. They mattered. She wasn't sure of anything else, but those, she held to, with all her dwindling strength.

She walked away from the questions as if they were rocks lying there in the snow, retreated into the cave, did the spell, and found herself on a cliff overlooking a vast panorama of white and gray and blue-white, under a milky-blue sky scattered with clouds like washed wool.

She turned around, blinking away the transfer-dazzle.

Detlev sat alone before a campfire. Weird. The only sound was the wind soughing through distant high-reaching firs, that she could swear, yet she sensed another sound, a constant sound, almost like a great choir was singing, but it didn't quite reach her ears. It was more like the echo just after they sang, when the music is still there in the air.

"You are sensing the disirad," Detlev said, opening his hand toward a dry place next to him. There was a small space free of snow; old summer-dry grasses surrounded his campfire. He had a couple of camping pillows to sit on, a bedroll, and a few dishes on the stones ringing the fire.

"Disirad," she repeated. "The stuff that the dyra are made of."

"Yes."

She didn't know what to think of that, and anyway it didn't really matter, did it? "Is this where you sleep?"

"When I can." He smiled.

"But don't you have to move around, like all the others? I thought the Host were searching for you."

"They are. As yet they cannot perceive this place."

She drew in a deep breath. It was peaceful here, like the inside of the caves. She frowned in wary disbelief. "You'd think they'd know right away. I mean, you can really feel the magic. And you certainly did magic to make this dry spot here."

"It's just the opposite," Detlev explained, calm and unhurried, as if it was an everyday thing for her to come here, and for them to chat of this and that. As if there was no war, and no —

Her shoulders hunched up; her neck twinged: she was turtling again. She hadn't even known she was doing it until she'd noticed Dhana flinching, and finally comprehended the cause.

Detlev went on, "This place is like an absence in their awareness, an anti-awareness, if that makes sense. They will only be able to find it if they physically search over the entire world, something they won't be able to do with any kind of ease until they break Kessler's spell and regain their powerbase."

"I thought their power was plenty strong," Clair muttered.

"It is, for many purposes. But it's finite, and it's costing them, while at the same time they are feeling the pull of time again, something they could successfully ward in the center of Norsunder."

Clair nodded. "I think I understand that. Dhana said that you never have to eat or drink there, or even sleep, if you don't want." She frowned at him. "But don't you feel it, too? You're as old as they are, or nearly so."

"Yes, but I stayed out of the center as much as I could. And I balanced my existence within and without Norsunder, though it took more effort; one must address the needs of the physical self. I aged some, as one must, however long one hides from the inevitable. In the center, they did not. So the cost for me in the physical world is light, no more than the return to natural rhythms. It is far worse for them. Though they are doing their best to ward that."

Clair sighed. "And so I'm safe here. But not forever?"

"You are safe here, for a time," Detlev repeated. "They cannot hear you as long as I can keep the ward strong. I wish I could stay here for the duration—"

"No, no, I would never be so selfish," she cried. Then, in desperation, she dared to come close to what she wanted—needed—to say, "And I cannot hear *him*."

"No."

Her chest squeezed, as if her physical self wanted to weep, except her spirit was far beyond the easy release of tears. "Siamis," she said, wringing the name past her closed throat. She fought, and won, a deep, shuddering breath.

Detlev waited.

Another deep breath, then she said, "I know that he's there to search by Dena Yeresbeth for enemies trying to get past the magical fog protecting the border. Everybody knows that, and I think most now understand how much work that takes." There, that was easy enough to say.

Detlev made an encouraging gesture, palm toward her.

Clair took a third deep breath. "But I think he's really there for me. Is he?"

"Yes," Detlev said.

Clair closed her eyes. "I need help." The words wrenched themselves out of her. For a time she sat there, fighting the trembling, the ache of tears that couldn't come.

And when she opened her eyes, they were both there. Siamis held out a cup of hot chocolate. It was so simple a thing. But so comforting, in a way that nothing had been comforting, not since she was very very small. Why? It was just chocolate, but it smelled good, and the warmth felt good on her hands, but more than that, he knew what to bring. One of the girls might have told him to bring it, but he still brought it. This simple gesture had come to pass because others cared about her comfort.

Siamis and Detlev sat there, and she knew that they were extremely busy—needed elsewhere—but they had taken time away from protecting the world, for her. At this moment. She must honor that sacrifice, because she knew it was a sacrifice, with trust. She said, "He's in my dreams. I do all the things you taught us about shields, but he's there anyway. Not all the time, but I know it's going to come to that. I do things, terrible things, in my dreams—"

The images were there, though drained of some of their immediacy. The echo of music seemed to put a distance between Clair and the nightmares, though she knew that that was only temporary.

Contact was easier here, but it went both ways: she heard Siamis's mental voice: *Things no child should see.*

Some of those things had happened to Siamis, and when he was no older than she had been when she did the Child Spell. Physically, she was still thirteen. He knew she had seen those things. Clair covered her face.

"There's a way I can help a little, I think," Siamis said. "You know what the Sartoran Napurdiav is?"

Clair wearily searched her memory. "Purrad. That maze thing behind Atan's palace? Should we make one in our garden?"

"It's a labyrinth rather than a maze, and you do not have to lay one down in your garden, unless the patterns give you pleasure. Your palace was built on the Napurdiav pattern. I can teach you to walk it, and the meditations that used to be common when persons were disturbed in spirit. It will not banish Ilerian's attempts to get at you, but it can soothe your spirit."

"Yes. Please," Clair said.

Siamis smiled. "When we return. For now, I brought this bedding. Sleep. Between the two of us, we can give you a night of peace. And when you dream, find me, and I will teach you some ways to shut Ilerian out."

Clair looked away. "But you might see … things. I would never do. Things I never thought, but they are there."

"Old tricks," Detlev said, with a dismissive wave. "Filthy tricks. Meant to cut you out from your support."

The utter lack of surprise in their two faces caused her to shudder with relief, and then shudder with the sobs she had valiantly suppressed for too long, but she sensed that Siamis understood, for he too had cried, only he had been alone.

Nine

FAR TO THE NORTH and east, Lyren-Sartora, Liere Fer Eider's daughter — no longer a child, just barely a teen — was far more comfortable in body, but her mental state was much like Laban's.

She sat high in a dawnsinger tree platform, sheltered from the thick snowfall by protective boughs and woven mats. In her hands she held a round, handle-less ceramic cup full of a hot aromatic liquid. Something distilled, with apples, and raisins.

She was alone, listening to the sound of the storm and feeling the sway of the platform. She'd crossed the border under cover of the rising tempest, but almost immediately had lost her way, and had endured a terrible time of stumbling around in the white-ice whirl before she'd finally found a Sign.

But that wasn't on her mind.

The entire journey from Imar had been rough. She had endured that, too, each day's struggle forgotten when she successfully got to the next, because she had known it would be rough but she'd chosen to make it. No one had made her.

No, what made her wince as she stared down into the cup was the realization that the very day she'd seen that she'd managed to successfully charm the last of her Fer Eider relatives and their friends, she got bored.

There was no escaping the truth.

She'd stayed in Belann, at first to relay messages about

Marga. After Marga was rescued, Lyren-Sartora had lingered, finding a challenge in winning over her morose grandmother, skeptical cousins, and the mistrustful baker's girl Tolia. Lyren-Sartora took over Marga's chores, showed an interest (and of course an aptitude, for Siamis had trained her well to listen and to be deft with whatever she turned her hand to) in the shop, and generally made herself both useful and ornamental as one by one she caused them to smile when she came into a room, instead of frown and stop talking. Even Tolia, the baker's girl, had changed from a dead distrust to a sort of shy truce that in no way eased the burden of her grief for Marga's absence.

It was seeing this turmoil, actually, that made Lyren-Sartora suddenly hate the role she was playing and leave Tolia to the inarticulate but comforting company of Marga's brother Milnat.

Because it was a role. For them it was life, for her it was no more than a play on the world-stage, a challenge, an inner wager. And at the end, when she won, and declared that she had to return to the war effort, they gave her a huge party, though resources were scarce. She smiled and laughed and exchanged fond nothings while hating herself for hypocrisy. Because she realized that Liere was right—they really were provincial, petty in outlook, thinking their internecine squabbles of far more importance than world events. Liere would never go back because she could never pretend to be anything but what she was: Lyren-Sartora was too good at role-playing.

She stared off into the snow. "I didn't hurt anyone," she said, glad to be alone. To be surrounded by trees and quiet snow. "That's all I can say in my favor."

Was she really as frivolous, superficial, and wayward as they all had believed her to be?

"I can't be," she whispered. "I don't want to be. Don't mean to be."

Which is why, when the snow ended, she did not face west and make the long journey back toward the safety of Mearsies Heili.

Instead, she turned to the north and a much shorter journey. Everon was only a couple days away, a much tougher challenge.

Norsunder HQ – Eidervaen - two weeks later

Duin shifted in his chair, s-l-o-w-l-y rubbing the portion of his back below his shoulder blade against the carved whatsis on the chair back. Ahhh. Ungh. Careful. Right. That's the spot that's itched like a summer blaze all morning.

When he was done he leaned forward on his elbows and frowned at the pile of paper lying before him on the table, then sighed. Under the table, his feet now began to ache with renewed insistence. Duin stamped them, and glared at the flickering candles on the table. Surprised the damn flames hadn't frozen.

If he'd known what was coming next, he wouldn't have laughed so damn hard when the word came in on Llyenthur. Ousted. Just like that! Well, wasn't it always that way? Except Duin and the desk jockeys thought their boy was faster.

No one really knew what the real circs were, only that something happened up north in the old Sonscarna castle Efael had taken over for his own (and Duin shuddered, remembering what that place was like), following which Efael had sent out armed parties of hunters to search the immediate vicinity. There were plenty of people, especially those still smarting from the last shakedown, who thought it a joke of surpassing richness that Llyenthur should be deposed with such ease and speed.

Duin, of course, had laughed right along with the rest. That is, he'd laughed after he'd recovered from being singled out to give the Host a tour of the Larkadhe HQ. Damn, that had been a nasty surprise, and he could still recall the looks from the rest of the desk jockeys that said, better you than me!

But They hadn't done anything to anyone, just poked about, then vanished. After that, Duin got back to the relay desk while waiting for the promotion sure to come.

When Efael finally came, it was to get rid of them all.

Duin fiddled with his pen, frowning down at the papers in front of him without seeing them. Instead he saw that bony dark-eyed face, so like a hungry rat, while Duin tried his best to explain the system. He'd tried to be as brief and concise as possible, but how could anyone make communications and logistics quick and interesting?

Duin hadn't known until that bootlicking Tschem explained it to him that Efael didn't concern himself with that shit, and he got bored with anyone who did. He didn't give a damn that the Norsunder-supplied gear was down to stuff of decidedly poor quality, that either they needed to scout handmade stuff or make it themselves. He had no interest whatever in the dismally hard-won fact that a steady diet of bad food sapped strength and health, here in the time-bound world, and he didn't even care to know how regional commanders carried out general orders.

All he wanted to know was that *his* orders were carried out. And if someone failed his orders, he was trashed. Simple. Did you do it, or not? Do it, or die.

Now Aldon was busy filling the power void in the south, and Efael didn't seem to care about that, either, as long as Aldon bootlicked him when he turned up. Efael didn't seem to know, or maybe didn't care, that Aldon cursed him the moment he left.

Since Aldon's taking over. Duin had found himself, Bergan, and four or five of the other Larkadhe desk jockeys shifted here to Eidervaen to do much of their old job.

Only what a difference. Duin probed at the sore memories, getting angry all over again. Oh, he'd always enjoyed a good flogging. Not buddies, and not even people in his company, because the eye might fall on you next, but those he hated. Or lighters. They were always good for a show, especially the ones that begged and pleaded. He never thought he'd be the one at the post as the "example" of lack of discipline, insubordination, and sloppiness.

And all for just using his own initiative, the way Llyenthur had expected him to do.

He still wasn't sure how many days he'd lain face down on his bunk with back and brain on fire, but after years of misery, someone had put a hand over his mouth to keep him from making noise and then had slapped some strong-smelling, cold goo on his back. Bad, at first. It burned, but when the fire died down he'd been able to sleep for the first time.

And the very next day Aldon was down in the barracks. On your feet. There's work to be done. Any more trouble out of you and next time we'll have your back to the wall. That meant death.

Duin rubbed his shoulder blade against the chair once more, wincing as he remembered how he thought he'd die without even being shot, having a shirt on again. But he'd made it, somehow, with some help from a couple buddies. Oh, he'd remember who helped — and who gloated.

And he'd kept his head down since. Stand and salute when Aldon came in, something Llyenthur had never given a damn about. Kept his mouth shut and opinions to himself, even when he heard something he knew was wrong. All he did was try to find out who that hand had been in the night, slapping that goo on his back. He owed whoever it was.

Though maybe it was just someone who wanted a target between them and Aldon; he brooded on that, toying with his pen. A theory, anyway. Certainly Aldon had been even nastier of late, when he'd discovered that Llyenthur had been in and out of his own rooms three or four times, then vanished with either papers or a couple of his prime men.

Duin thought with nostalgia of the old days. Rumor had it Llyenthur had orders to concentrate on hunting down Detlev and his boys, and so he was all over the world, staying nowhere long. At any rate, just recently he'd walked in, calm as you please, when Aldon wasn't around, got what he wanted (and knew right where to find it, too) and no one had stopped him.

Tschem had told Duin in the mess-line that Aldon had gone to Efael and said What about Llyenthur? and had been told *Do what you like, short of death. Svir still wants him.* So they all now had orders to disarm-and-secure if he showed up again.

Duin sighed. That was the problem, wasn't it? Would he even try to stop him, if he did show up in Duin's area? He'd hoped next time Llyenthur would come for him, and get him out of here. For anything. Even running supplies, or picket duty, was better than being stuck here under Aldon's blood-lusting eyes — the shithead seemed to find watching floggings more fun than anyone else found food, or sex, or drink.

Surreptitiously Duin tried one of the old signals.

Nothing.

Of course someone had done whatever it is they do to magic spells.

Probably in for years of this horseshit.

He scoured his back against the chair again — and flinched as the noise out in the courtyard below resolved into the familiar sound of some poor shit at the post. The drill units shouted the count. What, third this week?

There were definitely worse things than Llyenthur's ready sarcasm when he was in a temper. At least you knew what to expect: you do what you're told, he left you alone.

Duin stared down at his papers, thinking, *What if? What if?*

He sorted them slowly, turning ideas over in his mind. Supposing he could wangle his own way out?

Everon – Merry Dei's house

Once Lyren-Sartora arrived, everyone's mood brightened.

A couple of weeks after her arrival, she laid aside the lute she'd been strumming and looked across the low-ceilinged wooden room to Tahra, who had just stood away from the table.

"What does Atan say?" Lyren-Sartora asked. "Anything about the wedding plans?"

"Nothing about that." Tahra came up and sat down by the fire. Her eyes were dark and unreadable, her mind, as always, guarded. "It will probably happen New Year's Week some time, or the new year's Firstday, unless something occurs to ruin the symbolic effect."

"Of course Rel and Atan will make it as symbolic as they can," Lyren-Sartora said.

"Yes," Tahra agreed, without taking her gaze from the fire.

Lyren-Sartora studied her. She had spent most of the past couple of weeks in Tahra's company, exerting herself to entertain and to charm, because here she knew that diversion was needed. One night she'd gone to bed with a sore throat after singing silly songs for most of the evening, and her reward had been a sunlit smile from Merry Dei and the wondering observation, *You made her laugh!*

The gratitude in Merry's eyes had made Lyren-Sartora try again, and again, thinking, even a clown has a place in the world.

Now she was serious, though she knew being serious carried terrible risk. Tahra's anger was like hidden fire, liable to erupt unexpectedly. Her people loved her for how hard she worked, how devoted she was to Everon—but they were also afraid of her.

Well, clowns not only had a place, they weren't afraid.

"Why should there be a problem?" Lyren-Sartora asked, getting up and spinning around so that the ribbons she wore in her hair and binding her upper sleeves streamed and fluttered.

"Because," Tahra said, "I'm wondering if those who are so diligent fostering that inspiring illusion of unity will turn their busy little minds to the empty thrones on either side of me."

Merry Dei gasped. Lyren-Sartora drew Tahra's attention safely back to her, dancing before the fire. "What's that supposed to mean?"

Tahra said, "One of the reasons I like having you around is because you don't know." She got up and moved toward the stairs, leaving Lyren-Sartora grimacing in rueful regret.

"I think that went wonderfully," she joked.

Merry gave her a kindly, patient smile. "Was there bad news from Mearsies Heili?"

"No, not in my note, anyway," Lyren-Sartora said. And she told Merry the little bits of news that Atan had written; as she did, she watched the subtle change of emotion across the broad brow opposite her. Merry sat at her loom, listening carefully. She was very few years older than Lyren-Sartora, and in the few days Lyren-Sartora had known her she'd seemed at times young as a child, and at others older than old. Lyren-Sartora found her puzzling, but respected her; she was beginning to perceive why Tahra had made this tiny house her unofficial headquarters.

She finished up, "And so why should she be worried about the thrones of Imar and Wnelder Vee? The way things are, the danger from Norsunder is the greatest concern, and afterward there will be plenty of candidates for those thrones."

Merry folded her hands and leaned her chin on them. "I think that the problem is that the most qualified candidate for Wnelder Vee is Laban."

"You don't mean Laban the poopsie?"

"Poopsie?" Merry blinked in confusion. "I refer to one of Detlev's former gang of assassins."

"The very same. Some friends nicknamed them poopsies, which I think it hilarious."

"Oh." Merry's smile flickered. "Well, it seems that he has a blood claim on Wnelder Vee."

"What?"

"He's another of us Deis. It seems," Merry said, with rare irony, "that we are somewhat difficult to stamp out."

"But if he has a claim, don't you, or your sister, or your father, certainly, have a better?"

Merry gave a soft laugh. "Shall we go into the twists and turns of family connections? That would take half a day. Or a year, if we include personalities, and not just incidences of kinship. Besides, there is the vow the Knights take to never marry while in duty, and the Everon Deis have captained them in a straight line ever since Leskandar Dei."

Lyren-Sartora whistled. "Go on."

"The important thing is, if Laban is indeed the son of Harold Dei of Sartor, then he, and his sister, have the best blood claim on Wnelder Vee. He's even got strong ties to the thrones of Sartor, Everon, Imar and Colend!"

"Colend? I don't know anything about that place, except that the Lirendi family has had it for a few zillion years."

"But the Deis have intermarried with them, don't you see?"

"Oh, of course. As they have with the Landises."

"Yes. And Atan as well as Shontande Lirendi of Colend must know of Laban's background, and they'd know the legitimacy of his claim. So if Laban is capable, and the people like him, it would be difficult to oppose him."

Lyren-Sartora listened in silence, mind working rapidly. "And Tahra hates him for something he did, or just because he's a poopsie? She keeps saying that she thinks Detlev isn't really on our side. Ah! Laban must be the 'outlaw' she's made mention of a couple times — and that's the nicest word. I thought she meant the local Norsunder commander!"

Merry nodded, her brow puckered. "She has forbidden any of us to communicate with him at all. Lest he betray us to the Norsundrians. She has sent spies, but they don't seem to be able to pin down his location. Yet my sister told me that Laban has gained support with amazing rapidity."

Lyren-Sartora tapped her fingernails on the table. "How many know of his claim?"

"Very few. We've told no one. And, it seems, he hasn't either. No one knows the reason for that as well. Ah, the dawnsingers might know, but of course they never interfere in political matters."

Lyren-Sartora nodded. Any attempt to involve dawnsingers in what they'd term a land dispute would have one result: they'd disappear. "No communication, eh?"

Merry shook her head. "So we do not know if he's ally or enemy."

"When we desperately need allies," Lyren-Sartora said. She snapped her fingers. "I know what to do. No one has forbidden *me* to find Laban and have a little talk."

Merry gasped. "Oh, I wish you wouldn't—"

"Why not? I don't believe for one moment I'm in any danger from the likes of him. They sure never laid a finger on me when I was two, and that was when they were at their nastiest. Sveneric would have something to say if they even dared."

"I do not think you could find him, for our best trackers — even among the Knights — have had no success."

Lyren-Sartora laughed, an engaging, dimple-framed laugh, and Merry felt some of her anxiety vanish before the assurance of this sunny, charming girl. "You think not?" Lyren-Sartora asked, dancing lightly down the room. She whirled around, struck a pose, then added, "So we shall have to make certain that *he* finds *me*."

Ten

"… AND DOWN THIS ROAD, we've got a school for teachers. It's mostly women. If there were men, they're gone. Probably serving us." The Norsundrian patrol captain paused to snicker. "We've been bypassing it, mostly, except a sporadic check. Not that much ever happens this close to your mountains, beetle." The captain waved a hand at rank on rank of blue-white mountains running east-west as far as the eye could see.

"Hesan," Squad Captain Nine Hesan, Fourth Company, Fifth Brigade, First Division, Crimson Army, to be correct— though she didn't particularly want this no-twi grayback to sully her rank with his no-family mouth.

But she had a name. And since she was now assigned to share a patrol, she would see it used, instead of the ubiquitous "beetle" or "platter-face."

The Norsundrian, secure in his superiority, snorted, but then remembered that any troublemaking had to originate from the beetles, at a cost of fifty at the post. "We may as well ride in. I'll warn you now, this time of year, the place stinks like a thousand barns unwanded, when they start up with the dyes."

The Norsundrian raised a hand, turning his palm toward the road. The two squads, riding side by side in the merest semblance of cooperation, obediently turned up the path, no one paying much attention to the thickets and the stands of larch, some still holding onto their golden needles. No one saw dun-clad figures slip away over a ridge hidden from the winding road.

The two patrols proceeded through the open gates of a community of pleasing, whitewashed Colendi cottages built around a square, with outbuildings beyond on three sides. The distinct, musty-mulch smell of indigo dye became increasingly strong as the patrol entered the square, where a lot of girls gathered around a wizened, white-haired woman. All wore splattered aprons; they looked up, then went back to stirring gigantic cauldrons with sticks.

The patrol gave them wide berth and kept riding. The cottages around the square appeared to be classrooms. They glimpsed more girls seated on benches. In one classroom, a tall, willowy teacher pointed a stick at something on a slate board, and the girls began reciting cadenced words.

All very orderly, open, and, as the Norsundrian captain muttered, "Once a month does it." Boring.

To Hesan it looked exactly like the village displays when The Hate's spies came through, so open it was staged. But she said nothing. Her orders were clear, especially since The Stench Named Efael took away their General.

She held herself in the grip of control when, toward the end of the circuit, they rode past the barn, where she caught sight of a shambling fellow barely on the verge of manhood, his lank hair overlong, his chin receding —

Could it possibly be ... Him?

But not so much as a blink escaped her. The sudden fierce hope that she had truly seen Him nearly overwhelmed her, and for a short, desperate time she didn't hear a word the other was gabbling. But she caught up quickly, and grunted a corroborative before the Norsundrian could get annoyed at being ignored, and wonder what had caught her attention.

They rode away, and behind them, the school reverted to its usual mode, which began with Shontande Lirendi personally letting his cousin Nash — who, built along heroic lines, was not easily disguised — out of the huge ceramic pressed oil jug that was his hiding place anytime anyone came up the road. Two more of Shontande's nobles hid up in the rafters of the pottery, otherwise everyone else was disguised as a girl.

As thick white clouds slowly descended, obscuring the mountains, they gathered in the back kitchen, where it was warm and the comforting smell of baking biscuits enveloped them.

They waited until Jilo slouched in, shedding bits of hay, Retren Ndarga—who hitherto had been the pretty, curly-haired girl feeding the cows—at Jilo's heels. Jilo slumped down, disconsolate still in his worry about Crimson General Furo.

"That was someone new on the Chwahir side," Shontande observed, looking concerned.

Though a young man, his slender form and fine features made disguising as a woman easy. He knew exactly how to dress to draw emphasis away from his shoulders and neck, and his glossy auburn hair was elaborately done upward to keep the eye to his long, intense blue eyes and his winged brows, and away from his jawline.

He could not have made more of a contrast with Jilo, whose unprepossessing features and flapping clothes seemed to emphasize his awkwardness. And yet the stylish Colendi took their cue from their king, who said. "Have you a conjecture what it might mean?"

"N-no." Jilo winced as he stumbled over the word. He knew that the Colendi preferred to avoid blunt negatives, but he never seemed to be able to remember. He flushed, then said, "My guess is, internal shifts. Here's what's important: if Furo talked, all of upper command would be summoned back to Narad, and surely purged. Wan-Edhe hasn't sent for individuals. He seems more obsessed with being protected by entire fleets and armies. What we don't know is if Furo's alive."

Alive. The word had been echoing through Jilo's thoughts for days. But what could he do; he slept badly, instead turning over increasingly wild plans for trying to rescue the general. He even knew that castle, and all of Wan-Edhe's traps. But how would he get the general out again, assuming he could even get in?

Three, four days passed with him increasingly stressed. That night snow closed them in, or he might have chucked everything and run, just to be doing something.

Exhaustion finally weighed down the jittering thoughts, covering them as the snow covered the school … until Detlev's voice emerged from the dream: *Jilo. I'm sending aid.*

And that was all, barely a heartbeat of time. But those four words arrived with the distinct image of Efael's castle.

Jilo dropped into dreamlessness.

The next morning, they woke to a white world. The Colendi gazed in well-bred surprise as Jilo entered with a brisk step, rather than slouching in. "Detlev came in a dream last night," he said to Shontande.

Whose face tightened at the mention of Detlev, but otherwise he made no sign.

"He said there will be aid. And to come."

"He said this in a dream?" Shontande's very polite tone did not mask his skepticism.

"Yes," Jilo replied as he stuffed a biscuit full of egg.

"Do you trust that?"

Jilo mumbled past a huge bite, "If he wanted to betray me he could have done it a hundred times by now. And I really want to free Crimson General Furo, but I can't do it alone. I want to believe him. I'm leaving as soon as I can."

No one argued, of course, though many sent inquiring looks toward their king. It was Shontande Lirendi who had told his people that Jilo was to be regarded as a fellow monarch, and his words about the Chwahir were to be accepted as royal decrees. So no one said anything.

But later that night, when the clouds had cleared, leaving enough light to travel by, Jilo found Shontande Lirendi dressed in dark clothing, carrying a knapsack of provisions.

They looked at one another. "Jilo, did you forget to at least pack a loaf of bread?"

Jilo blushed. "I'm a guest. I still don't really understand how to be a guest, except I know you don't demand stores from those who invited you. Why, uh, what are you dressed for?"

"I am going with you, of course," Shontande said.

"You are? Why?"

Shontande overlooked the rudeness of the question, comprehending Jilo's worry on his behalf, and his puzzlement. Also, his total lack of distrust for mysterious messages from Detlev. Shontande still hated Detlev for what he had done to Shontande's father, locking him in a dream world for decades. But he'd spent years hating Curtas by extension, when they could have resumed their friendship but for that hatred. Curtas had believed Detlev had good reasons for what he did. Believed it so strongly he was willing to give his life.

Shontande was willing to ... reserve judgment.

He murmured, "You once said it's possible that place is warded against you. I am absolutely sure that it is not warded against me. And I, for one, would like to see Furo free." *If he's even alive.*

"But you're ..."

"King?" Shontande laughed. "Where is my throne? Jilo, go

get your coat. We will leave Retren Ndarga safely here with my cousin Nash. I've plenty of stores for the two of us, enough to get us up to Terry's hideout, where I believe Halad is still watching things. Let's go while we have relatively good light."

Eleven

Choreid Dhelere

DAVID DRIFTED INTO THE cabinet-maker's shop, where no lamps or candles had been lit, but the people were waiting for him. The ancient man peered at him wordlessly, bright old eyes discernable in the reflected light from street torches, then pressed a heavy mug of hot cider into his hands before letting him down into the secret room.

David descended slowly, shifting the mug from hand to hand and pulling off his gloves with his teeth as he did so. There was a fire in one corner of the underground room, but the air was not any less cold than that above, suggesting that the present occupants had arrived only slightly in advance of him.

Two men and a woman sat around the rough-made table with Senrid. The men wore Marloven cavalry tunics. The older man sported the rank insignia of a cavalry wing commander, the younger a captain of foot. Senrid's was bare of markings, and was half unbuttoned besides. Underneath it he wore a civ tunic, laced up to the throat, and a heavy linen shirt collar showed at the neck of that. He'd been riding hard, eh?

David exchanged greetings with the cobbler Daltan, leader of the civilian resistance in Choreid Dhelerei. Her son brought in food as Senrid waved David to the empty chair, and said, "David, Asservend, Mordan Nauldra. Nauldra wanted news of Marend Ndarga and the Darchelde group, if you have any?"

"Nothing since we left them last month."

"We don't know the details of the incident with Llyenthur."

"Ah." David gave them a brief outline, winding up, "Marend will keep up the drills, and when you send the signal, she'll have her people ready and willing."

A slow flush came and went in Mordan Nauldra's face. He said nothing, but appeared to be relieved at these words.

Senrid then took over the meeting. He asked for, and got, reports from Daltan and the two officers, and after some free-form discussion (David remained silent) he gave orders. The three then left.

Senrid had said nothing before David and the others about why he'd invited David to this meeting.

When the hatch shut behind Daltan, leaving him alone with Senrid, David drank his cider, now lukewarm. But he discovered that a potent whisky had been thoughtfully added in, so it was internally warming. Senrid poured some into his own mug from the stone jug on the table, and settled back.

"Eat. Well?" he said, stretching his booted feet out to the arm of the adjacent chair. Klunk, klunk.

David had already attacked the stale bread stuffed with excellent cheese. When he came up for air, he said, "I think you're right about Perideth. Might even speed things up with the rest as well, if I don't confront them as a civilian. Therefore I humbly request you grant me suitable rank in your esteemed army. Real rank, not the pretend we've used before, to finesse people; too many know the structure of your army, even with all the deaths. I promise to relinquish it the very day we get rid of—"

"What rank d'you want? Foot, cavalry? Cavalry has the prestige. Better, tell 'em you're my heir."

"But that would entail so many explanations!" David spread his hands. "Grant me some suitable rank, not too modest, but low enough that I don't have to constantly prove myself with duel-challenges from your hot-blooded commanders, and I can then go forth and garner some glory for them."

Senrid laughed. "Glory. Right. Then tell them you are a scout captain under Jan Senelac. Everyone knows they have special status—and a short chain of command. Directly under me. No one can interfere with you that way. Including Crown Prince Valta down south, should you meet him. Perideth father and son hate my guts anyway, so your promotion won't make things worse. Only reason why he's stomaching this army-alliance plot is because it's in the name of the King and Queen of

Sartor."

"You seem to have been a trifle abrupt with the Pride of the House of Perideth recently. Richly deserved, but not very diplomatic."

"Didn't say a word out of line," Senrid murmured reminiscently. "He wanted to 'train' with us. Fine. We sent him out for a two-week run with Marend's pack—made sure that all of them were younger than our army-mad Crown Prince Valta of Perideth. He grassed himself at the outset..." Senrid went on to outline the puncturing of a potentially pompous windbag.

As he listened, David noted subtle changes. Senrid was obviously very much in command of himself now. Holed up in Darchelde, with the forbearing Andri living there (though Andri had volunteered for as many supply runs as he could without drawing attention to the doing) Senrid had chosen to resolve his emotional troubles by resorting to drink. Strong drink, sometimes beginning early in the day and continuing through to late at night, until he was able to fall asleep.

Though the whisky-laced cider sat in a jug at his elbow now, he had no more than two cups, as did David. His eyes were clear, hands steady, but there was a tightness to the corners of his mouth, and edging his words, that indicated a new hardness. It was difficult, looking at Senrid now, to picture him dropping everything to play pinchies and nuzzles with a four-year-old as he'd done a year and a half ago.

Impending action gave Senrid purpose; he had shut away his emotions within an inner citadel, and had no intention of letting them out again. His success in at last getting the separation complete was no doubt a relief. David suspected, sadly, that if anyone were to see any glimmerings remaining of that side of Senrid, it would be himself.

David strongly suspected that Senrid's dealings with his people would by steady degrees confine themselves within the orderly context of military hierarchy, closing out the risky social arena. Like Marend Ndarga, who had worshipped her father as a hero, but he'd died. Then she'd transferred all that intense and unwavering devotion to MV, who had swatted it away again, leaving her looking for a new hero. Had the teenaged girl already unconsciously chosen Senrid for that role, or was Senrid ducking her so that it wouldn't happen? Either way David foresaw more trouble for poor Marend in the future—but it was not, even remotely, his place to tell Senrid how to handle his own people.

"...and so we sent him back down south. He was fuming,

but at least he's got an even chance now of living through any weapons encounters with weak or shortsighted or soulbound Norsundrians. You're doing well with what I asked you to see to. What about Detlev's orders?"

David made a gesture indicating much activity to little purpose.

Senrid said, "Why? Reports I've had recently, Llyenthur's been nosing around frequently enough. Either here, or near here, or in the hills." He tipped his head eastward.

"Yes, I know. But can you tell me precisely what he's been doing?"

Senrid hesitated, and frowned. "Not much of anything, really, and I confess I keep expecting him to show up and sting me in some way. He's got to know where I am, at least some of the time. Though maybe he can no longer whistle up a sufficient strike force for—" He stopped himself. "Why?"

"Would you call that characteristic, judging from his past behavior?"

Senrid said something succinct about Llyenthur's characteristic behavior; David smiled appreciatively, but waited.

Senrid said, "No. He's up to something besides trying to run us to ground, then?"

"I'm wondering."

"What do you think?"

David grinned. "I wonder if he's doing just what Detlev is having the rest of us do—being seen in one place while plotting elsewhere."

Senrid looked disgusted. "Well, why doesn't he go plot in Imar, then?"

"This is only conjecture on my part, Senrid. And it might work to our advantage to keep it strictly to ourselves."

Senrid's expression of disgust deepened, but he said, "As you wish. Going to try to find out?"

"It might be interesting," David said, still smiling.

※

For the two weeks David had been traveling around on Senrid's errands, Dhana, in Mearsies Heili, watched silently over Clair.

Clair seemed to be holding up all right, and Siamis stayed there with them day and night, never leaving, his presence a comfort because he just sat around, reading or talking, and never gave orders, or interfered with Clair's work.

Dhana comforted herself with the thought that Clair was perfectly all right, and that work was good for her. Steadying. There was certainly plenty to do, with all those refugees in the kingdom—and more being sneaked in all the time, despite the winter weather and the remaining Norsundrian patrols.

Until one night, in the library, when Clair thought she was alone and Dhana soft-footed in looking for company. She saw Clair's face, and the tear tracks she could not hide, then left again.

Next morning she drifted in when Clair and Siamis and Atan were eating breakfast. Outside they could hear the distant shrieks of the little Delieths and Aurora, who were enjoying the fresh snowfall.

Siamis said, "The range is narrower by day now. Another couple of weeks and we will have difficulty transferring anyone at all, expect perhaps sunrise and midnight at the destination, when natural magic is still strongest."

Dhana heard herself say, "I can do it."

All three looked up.

Dhana's stomach scrinched and her heart galumphed, but she knew, now, that it was right, that to not do her duty was the same as sending a message to those stinkards in Imar offering her help.

She cleared her throat. "I can send anywhere. Any time. I—I've already been to see Puddlenose twice, when—" She glanced at Clair, and changed her words to, "when I was in a bad mood, and needed some jokes to cheer me up. I don't know why it works—I guess I have some of the magic of my people, even though I'm wearing my human self—but it does." She shrugged, and turned away to look out the window.

Siamis had to hide the vast surge of hope that these disjointed words raised. It seemed that the indigenous beings were offering aid through Dhana. A very volatile, even flimsy vessel, but to them did all human forms seem much the same? Impossible to know. "And so?" Siamis asked politely. "What does that mean? This matter is too important for me to not understand what you are offering—or to refrain from asking if you understand what you are offering."

Dhana flushed, hating the hope in Clair's face because it carried such quiet pain. "And so I'll send people. Whenever you want. Our magic ... it gets past whatever Norsunder is doing. Trying to do. Messing with their transfer spells and everything."

Siamis contemplated this astounding offer, and through him, Detlev: *It means that this time, they understand that Ilerian is not human, and threatens destruction of humankind as well as the world. They won't take life — this appears to be their way of allying.*

Outside an icicle dripped, crystal water catching light and falling. Beyond that, Aurora's happy voice, shrieking, "I'm gonna getcha, Svir!" And Madelon Delieth growling threats.

Siamis said, still politely, "Dhana, we'll need to be able to rely on you. To be able to find you at any time, even mid-watch in the night, even if you're in a bad mood and think us adults are all idiots and interferers."

"I said I'll do it. So I'll do it."

Clair spoke, so soft it was hard to hear her. "Dhana always keeps her word. All the girls do."

"I know," Atan said, her hands on the table, tightly clasped. "I've always trusted you Mearsiean girls, ever since I first knew you. That has never changed, though everything around you has changed."

Clair's unwinking pale green gaze met Atan's dark blue one, a long look, one that Dhana felt in her heart, though she couldn't define it in any terms that made sense.

Siamis smiled. "Very well. Thanks, Dhana. This will be a very great aid. Perhaps the greatest."

He got up and left.

Atan leaned back in her chair, her face now bland.

Clair turned her haunted eyes up to Dhana. "Thanks," she whispered.

Dhana forced a grin, but she really felt like crying, which was useless and stupid, and so she slipped out to go dance out her feelings in the softly falling snow.

Twelve

Wnelder Vee

THE WATCHERS, THERE IN the southern river valley, weren't necessarily callous or stonehearted people, but events had forced them to adopt a certain amount of distrust, and therefore distance.

So they laid wagers as they watched the four Norsundrians chase a rider up the valley and over a hill. If the Norsundrians had gained and attacked—if the quarry had been less skilled— maybe they would not have stayed, prone among the thick fir branches, watching the spectacular cross-country chase and hoping the rider would get near enough for them to determine who was to provide the next round of toddies.

A dawnsinger? Naw, a boy. Same size, at least, as my brother. Your brother doesn't ride like that or he'd be with us now! A dawnsinger, I tell you. No, he don't ride like that, but my Everoneth cousin, Reed, named for old Nelvarias of the horses, does, and the Knights were said to be scoutin' him—

"Shut up, clapper-tongues, here they come again!"

"Damn, and there they go—look at the snow fly!"

The next day, when the mystery rider was again seen in the adjacent hills (this time with two pursuit parties), the word came down to intercept.

The rescue was aided considerably by the skill of the rider, who was on (they saw in amazement) a hide-dyed Knights' white. Tired the horse was, and the mud-brown mottling smeared, but no mistaking the breeding. Blowing, wet and foam-flecked, the horse rolled intelligent eyes in fiery threat when anyone rode too near.

They used one of their camouflaged paths, and after the Norsundrians rode by, chasing the detour detail, the rider was flanked in a wordless, businesslike way, and led back into the hills. Way too many of the outer perimeter riders were in sight to wave them on; they thundered into camp just as a heavy snow began to howl through the trees again.

The four watchers made sure they were on hand to witness the rider's dismount, and four tongues tasted wager-won toddies...

Then went stone cold with jaw-dropped astonishment as the enveloping black scarf was thrown back above the anonymous gray cloak and a pair of laughing gold—and feminine—eyes emerged.

"Well! It's about time," a clear, high voice said breathlessly. "Though it was fun, I must admit."

An elegantly-clad leg was thrown over the disguised white's back, and a girl leaped lightly to the mushy ground as though she'd just returned from a refreshing canter through the gardens of some palace.

She was short. And no more than thirteen years old.

The four stared until a practical elbow thrust aside their leader: "Take root somewhere else, mallet-heads. Here, you. Come this way."

"As soon as I see to Danwen," was the smiling reply.

"We'll see to the horse. Now, in fact." A meaning look at the two on stable duty.

In scrambling haste five now accompanied their surprising guest down into the tunnel to the abandoned way-post morvende geliath that served as their stable. There the horse was made comfortable, and then the girl smiled sunnily on the knot of tall young adults staring at her, and inquired kindly, "May I have something hot to drink before I meet Laban?"

How did she know—?

She was led to the caves that Laban used, where she talked about the weather while she delicately sipped cream-laced coffee.

She wouldn't give her name, nor her reason for being chased back and forth across the valley, and despite her diminutive size, and unmilitary grace, and unthreatening stream of pleasant babble, the watchers were relieved when Laban himself appeared, boots and the lower half of his cloak snow-crusted from a long ride. They effaced themselves, leaving Laban staring in mute surprise.

"I wouldn't tell them who I am because I wanted to see if you recognize me," said the brightly smiling figure in the tailored green riding clothes.

"Lyren-Sartora," he said slowly, and in question.

She clapped in delight. "Wonderful! Though I don't think I would have been insulted if you hadn't, because I really don't think I would have recognized you. Last time I saw you, you were about my size now, and your hair was lighter, and not so long and curly, and—well, to tell you the truth, you do look like that portrait of Leskandar Dei that Merry showed me, but to my mind you like nicer. There's something snooty about those old courtier portraits. I wonder if they really were as haughty as they look in the pictures? Of course, the pictures might look worse because they're usually high on walls, which makes it seem the people in them are looking down their noble sniffers at you."

Lyren-Sartora stopped, and gave Laban a jubilant smile.

Laban's hair was wet and stringing from his ride in the brewing storm, his fingers, toes, and nose were numb, and he was gnawingly hungry, having elected to skip breakfast before dawn—and dinner the night before—but all that was forgotten as he stared down at Liere's daughter. How could this be Liere's daughter? Or had Liere changed, too, during all those years he was gone?

He laughed. "Spare me the flattery, at least until we've known one another half a day. Or is all that about my snotty ancestors meant to unman me? We did rescue you, after all, and at least *you* cannot claim a grudge from the past."

"Not against you," she conceded, dropping down cross-legged onto one of his pillows. Her brow furrowed, radically altering her expression. "And you didn't rescue me, you noticed me. Finally, I might add. You're wet, you know. Don't you want to get on some dry things?"

He slung off the wet cloak, and shrugged out of the spattered heavy tunic beneath, then dropped down beside her in shirt, breeches, and boots. "This'll do for now." He made a gesture of dismissal. "Who sent you?"

"Self-appointed mission." Lyren-Sartora grinned conspiratorially.

"Tahra know?"

Lyren-Sartora shrugged, still grinning.

"But you were with her. You mentioned Merry. That would have to be Mersedes, Roderic's daughter. Who else would have a portrait of that old court card — outside of Roderic Dei?"

"All true."

"Why?"

They studied one another with interest and appraisal. This was one of those crucial moments, wherein any reaction would set in motion an accumulating train of events — one possible outcome diverging with kingdom-altering difference from another. Neither realized this, as yet. Their focus was equally absorbed in the immediate.

"Because ... she wouldn't come herself." Lyren-Sartora shrugged ruefully.

They were enough alike — intense, mercurial temperaments protected by an arsenal of charming deflections — that it would have been easy to take an instant dislike. But at exactly the right moment she hadn't been flippant, and so, at exactly the right moment he wasn't, either.

"To my everlasting regret," he said, honestly, without sarcasm or irritation or condescension.

"I'll help. If I can," she promised. "With Tahra, I mean."

"Ride with us a few days," he offered. "See what I'm doing. See what you think."

⸺⸺⸺◈⸺⸺⸺

Efael's lair – Chwahirsland border

Four heads lifted cautiously over a rim of granite and stared across the chasm at Efael's stone fortress.

The light was fast fading. The four lay flat on their rock, shoulder to shoulder so their voices wouldn't carry on the icy wind, then MV shook with silent laughter.

Mildred felt MV's laugh in the tremble of the hard arm pressed up against hers. She secretly enjoyed the inner heat. But she wasn't about to let him know. She eyed his profile, noted his grin, and muttered in disgust, "Think it's pretty?"

"I think it's an almighty pile of fly-buzzing dunk," MV answered promptly. "Isn't that just like Efael to pick this shit-pile when he can have any place in the world."

Until lately, Mildred's occasional crushes had all been women, and all were crushes of admiration. She didn't admire MV. It was just heat.

The flare of attraction was nothing to the fierce, hot pleasure deep within her at the thought of thumbing her nose at Efael of the Host, who surely believed himself safe inside his impregnable citadel. She'd seen memory-images enough, during circle rapport with Detlev's boys, to give her more than a lifetime's cordial hatred of Efael and Yeres

"Here's what we do," MV murmured. And he pointed out landmarks around the castle that roughly divided its circumference into quarters. "Each take one. Map your terrain and take note of whatever movement you see, within and without. Guards. Weapons. Lights. We meet here at sunset in two days. Compare."

Like melting shadows they slid backward off their cliff, and dispersed.

Thirteen

Aurum Hills – west of Crestel

DAVID WAITED PATIENTLY BEHIND a smooth-barked tree while the Norsundrian patrol emerged from the little shack below, and mounted up. Four... five... six. David watched the last three check weapons as they joked back and forth, breath streaming. They got on the waiting horses and rode out.

Six.

Leaving one horse still tied to the rail, and the seventh inside.

Soft flurries of drifting snow dusted David's shoulders and arms as he left the shelter of the tree and moved cautiously down toward the shack.

The hut had windows either side of a central door. The windows were hinged, and the one on the right was, of course, partly open. Of course, because Imry couldn't abide stuffy rooms, no matter what the weather, and David was quite certain that Imry was in there.

David ghosted up next to the open window.

Inside was Imry, all right, and he was alone. David watched as his brother gazed at the fire.

"Imry."

He turned fast—and grinned when he saw David half-sitting in the window, folded hands on a cocked knee.

David watched Imry's eyes register the black-and-tan

Marloven cavalry tunic and accoutrements—two visible knives—then rise to meet his own. He saw a certain speculative appreciation, twin to his own, narrow Imry's gaze.

David said, "You've been looking for me?"

"You're playing army? How very predictable of you." When David didn't take the bait, Imry strolled along the opposite wall, two, perhaps three long paces between them. "I'm not here to interfere with Senrid—though I am tempted to test our fierce cousin a little. I have something for you." He gestured toward the far corner, where leaned the black sword. Firelight flickered on the gold-leaf trim like a fitfully beating heart.

"I thought that might be it. Well, here I am to get it. Also, to find out why you're here in Marloven Hess spoiling sport. Have you decided to cut Senrid out after all?"

"Have you?" Imry canted a glance at the uniform.

David shrugged and smiled.

"I'd half believe you, I think," Imry said, "if you said yes."

"Half? Detlev's not here," David said. "Haven't seen him for weeks."

"Those field-report blinds," Imry responded, hands gesturing wide. He was wearing only a shirt, trousers, and boots, cuffs outside. Two wrist knives, then, and a third in a boot, but he'd have to yank his cuff up to get to it

David gave a quick, silent laugh.

"You didn't know about those?"

David's grin widened. "We put the last of 'em down in '53, just before we hopped the fence."

Imry grimaced.

"See what fun you missed?"

"Ah, but at what a price! Why are you really here?"

"I'm here to get my sword back," David said reasonably. "You're around, so I'm around. Then ... I thought I might head east and bait Efael, since you seem to have stepped aside so cooperatively."

"Efael is annoyed that you've ignored him thus far. He livened an otherwise dull summer by trying to build a case for our being allies after all."

"Dull? You're still smarting from Detlev's attentions?" David smiled. "You should be grateful he's still willing to tutor."

That one got home. Only for a heartbeat, but David saw it in the sudden narrowing of Imry's green eyes.

Imry said, "You do keep twanging that same tune, don't you? I wonder if there can be anything in it?"

"Let me know. " David's tone, and smile, were mocking. "I want my sword back."

"Come and take it. " Imry gestured invitingly.

At that very same moment, far to the north and east in the cold spring land of Fhleria, Roy sat down with a couple of old friends. First they had to drink the ritual mug of spiced coffee, because even on the run, during the middle of the night in a time of war, Fhlerians' lives were bounded by custom.

In truth, Roy was glad of the coffee. It warmed him, and gave him time to study their faces. Damientsi Lathriamara — Dami the Scribe — looked smaller and skinnier than ever, his fine black hair as usual falling into his eyes, his wrists inside the embroidered blue cuffs of his uniform looking impossibly bony. The pinched, hurt expression Roy had seen in his eyes before was now gone, however.

The one blond, Halvarzias, looked much the same as ever, stolid and pleasant-faced, and the guild auditor's dark, slanted eyes showed definite pleasure.

As soon as the exchanges of courtesy were over, the auditor said, "I reserved for myself the pleasure of telling you that we have accomplished our aim."

Surprise silenced Roy, then he laughed at her. "What? You have managed to disenchant every single warrior?"

She made a complicated gesture, like a waterfall, and the others smiled. "Great would be our credit to say yes, would it not?" Dami spoke. "No. The progress was at first slow, but steady, much as you promised before you left us last: person to person, and they have to truly see us, eye to eye before they can hear. Until a week ago. Then it became easy, so suddenly easy we suspect someone else came to our aid. In fact, we thought it might be you."

"Not I," Roy said. "Though I would have liked very much to have found the way. But my knowledge of magic just is not that great."

The auditor said, "It is no matter, for you still set us on the path to regaining our honor. And we remember our debts. So, have you words for us of plans in the south? Is there a way we can support the alliance you proposed before you left?"

Roy said to her, taking in the other young conspirators, "I do indeed have news, and I hoped that you would be able to join the battle against the enemy. I go to join the Sartoran army at year's end. Look for the signal to strike any time after that..."

Imry and David strenuously and enthusiastically wrecked what little remained of the hut's furniture.

They found themselves evenly matched, as they had assumed the summer before when they first saw one another after more than ten years' separation. Now neither of them was ill, or weakened by wounds or poison; they were both in excellent condition, with training methods to drawn on ranging from subtle martial arts to dirty street fighting, practiced in countless lands on at least three different worlds.

Imry was in a good mood. He appreciated David's curiosity and enthusiasm, and he fought to subdue, and not to maim or to kill. He deliberately kept his temper leashed. To let go would guarantee his winning, probably at the cost of David's life —

A grunt of surprise escaped him; David very nearly had him pinned down. He glimpsed the exertion-flushed, grinning face. Hah. Can't have that.

The action intensified, then they flung apart, and an oak table crashed between them. The lamp smashed, sending oil and a runnel of flame spreading toward the door. Imry snuffed it with a casual gesture.

The door slammed open. It was Imry's second patrol, returned as expected — which was why Imry had done his best to delay David.

The leader stood like stone in the doorway, and he and the guard at his shoulder gawked egg-eyed at the shambles before them.

David's head turned. His eyes met Imry's, and both choked on sudden laughter. Imry leaned against the overturned table, the black sword resting unmolested in the corner behind him, and began unhurriedly to straighten his clothes as his hand-picked patrol started in. Contest over.

David took a step, then flowed into a lightning blur of movement. A palm under the chin of the lead man, who fell back into number two, a half-turn and precise and deadly kick at the third that sent her head back with a snap. She fell right in Imry's path. Imry leaped over the falling woman as the last of the patrol dodged and dove aside —

— And those still standing were on their feet in time to meet a rain of glass from the swinging window, propelled by a well-placed punch.

Then David was gone.

Of course half the patrol stampeded out the door at a dead run, to see David fling himself on the back of Imry's fresh horse, his fingers finding the saddle-sheathed knife and bringing it down on the tied reins in one smooth stroke.

The horse leaped into a gallop — and the tired mounts who'd just returned all suddenly went mad, plunging and kicking.

Imry leaned in the doorway, watching the patrol try to calm the frenzied beasts, and wiped absently at a cut on his temple from when he'd landed on a fallen shelf of smashed crockery.

He glanced back inside at the room that looked like an army had swept through in a charge. His gaze took in the guards who had fallen, still lying where they'd dropped. He recalled that sudden, deadly and intense focus of David's. So there was a level of training above after all. He'd always thought Siamis had lied.

What it meant was, David could have killed *him*.

Laughing to himself, he picked up the sword and went out to help catch horses.

Fourteen

Mearsies Heili

THE CLOCK UPSTAIRS HAD just chimed softly four times when Clair's long vigil was rewarded by the sight of the border runners straggling in toward warmth and rest.

Clair stayed in the shadowy archway until she recognized June's silhouette coming slowly down the hall.

Clair stepped out, slapping her feet down on the cold white floor so as not to startle June, whose head came up abruptly.

"It's Clair," Clair said, not knowing how her identity was immediately revealed by her proximity to a window. Even weak moonlight touched her white hair with a ghostly glow. "May I speak to you a moment?"

"Sure," June said, leading the way to her room. "Light okay?"

"Please."

June snapped her fingers and the glowglobe flared to life, golden and welcoming, revealing the pleasing but impersonal room. June had done nothing to make it seem her own; she still regarded Sartorias-deles as a way-station in her life. Though it was beginning to feel more like a school, only in a good way. One that she had resisted, but had unexpectedly turned out to have something to be learned after all.

Clair sat on a chair as June took off her knife belt. Clair said, "I'm sorry to keep you even a moment from rest, but I wanted to speak to you privately, and I'm seldom alone these days."

June nodded, blank-faced, her gaze going to the fake silver cup on her bureau, and she thought of the real one hidden in her old Earth jeans, at the bottom of her trunk. But Clair didn't even look that way.

Sturdily built, browned by the sun, June had found purpose on this world. It might not last, but it was good enough now. And though her expression rarely showed any of the warmer emotions, she had gradually become less sulky and sullen in demeanor.

Clair said, so that she would not be misunderstood, "Which is the only thing keeping me alive, I think. I know I can't stand up to Il-ilerian," she stumbled on the name. "And I need the help warding. Siamis is monitoring right now, but I've closed him off for just this short time, and he seems to have figured out that I w-wanted some privacy."

"What can I do?"

"I haven't told anyone what Ilerian wants. Besides getting me to let him into the kingdom. It's not just the border wards." Her gaze now shifted to the false version of the silver cup Ethe, the fifth protection of the world of Alshea.

June didn't look surprised. Her expression soured.

"I was hoping that you could help me on a plan to decoy him. It won't work for long. But if we're careful. And if I can manage it here," Clair touched her taut forehead, "it m-might buy us some time. But even talking about it is dangerous. I have to time it for when his attention is otherwhere."

June snorted. Danger? Bring it on. She crossed her arms. "When do we get started?"

Clair smiled, got up, and moved to the door. "I'll let the others know what we've got in mind." She gave June a brief smile of relief and gratitude, and went out to try to rest, surrendering to Siamis's silent but watchful awareness.

⁂

Dawn was bleak and cold. Despite very old and strong insulating magic that was bound right into the glistening white stone of which the palace was made, air currents from Clair's open window drifted like invisible ghostly fingers to trail across her neck.

She shivered, then rubbed her hands and tucked them into her armpits. No one stirred yet, for which she was thankful. She sensed June fast asleep.

She couldn't keep her expression calm before Gwen or Seshe or the others, besides Dhana, not any more. She couldn't bear the helpless pain she saw in their faces. Nor could she bear to be polite and nice to yet another pair of searching eyes from the refugees. Even from friends. Oh, friends were the hardest. She was so grateful that CJ was up north in Land of the Venn, and not here, crying in rage every night at her inability to fix things.

Clair walked through her cleaning frame, and even that failed to make her feel better. Just clean in her skin, though she wondered if her mind would ever be clean again. She slipped out of her room and rounded the corner to where Siamis had begun staying. His door was open, and it looked as if he, too, had just been through the cleaning frame, though his face below the ordered blond hair was marked with tiredness.

"Bad one, eh?" he said, before she could speak.

It was a relief, because sometimes she felt as if she'd scream if she had to force one more apology out.

"Very," she said.

She was no longer sorry he had to stay awake all night, and most of the day as well. She was no longer sorry that he was sometimes found with his head on his arms, catching little naps. She didn't have any sorry left in her, not a drop.

Was she shielded? Even that no longer mattered.

"Am I turning evil?" she said.

"No," Siamis answered. "If you have to ask, then you are not."

She tried to hear sense in what he said, but even thinking was too hard. "Go on."

"Evil is either embraced, or else becomes a habit, slowly, inadvertently. Perhaps rationally, for there is always someone or something convenient to blame for one's difficult choices." He paused.

"Go on."

"Till at last one stops making choices, and evil is always there to take over that which the will surrenders."

She went to the window. Didn't want to see his face. "When did you know? When they got you?"

"That I walked the designated path toward evil?" He didn't sound angry, or even surprised.

She half-turned. "You were even my age—the age I stopped at. No. Younger. You must know what it's like."

"Yes. And it's a difficult question to answer, for many

reasons. Suffice it to say that I never regarded myself as evil. First I chose the way to survive unending pain. Then the way to avoid more pain. Then the easy way, then the expedient. Then the logical, the rational, without the foolish sentimentality of the weak—"

"Such as loyalty, or honor, or truth."

"Oh, but there is no truth. At least, you create your own truth, that's the first thing they will tell you. And then show you, over and over, proving it first on you, body and soul, if they can."

"Yes." Clair's voice thinned. "Yes." Her arms hugged tight against her.

"Until you lose sight of the greater truth, because you are so very finite. And it seems that they are not. Because their power seems endless."

"Yes." She was weeping now, the dry, shuddering sobs that usually he only heard at night. But she could not bear to be touched, and so even the simple, wordless comfort of a kind embrace was denied them both, he to give, her to accept. His arms were empty, as they had been since his daughter Yanli had decided she was too old for hugs.

He slipped out of the room, with quick, quiet step, found Dhana's room, entered unceremoniously and shook her awake. And when she sat up, messy-haired, her nightgown awry, he said, "Get her to the cave. Now."

Dhana was out the door in three steps. He felt the transfer, then returned to his room, dropped tiredly into the chair, and reached for the beige paper.

: Detlev, Clair is breaking.

His own sense of failure made him feel physically sick.

The answer came back almost immediately: *Will she stay in the caves?*

: No. After a time she says she is suffocating.

Not surprising, of course. The caves were at best an interface between non-human life forms and humans, never meant for sustained dwelling. And it was too dangerous now to take her to the disirad, unless both of them could remain with her, actively warding.

Detlev responded, after a very long wait, during which Siamis dealt with the inner turmoil Clair's misery stirred up. Every time the tireless Ilerian broke past her guard, and his guard, there lay an ugly memory, a shock for them both.

Detlev's handwriting appeared: *I've given my circle until the 25th-35th of Twelfthmonth. Hold her, any way you can. But don't let her find out about our gathering.*

Siamis wiped sweat from his brow, and from his hands. He went to the window, threw it wide, and breathed in the frigid air. Then he did a mental check: Clair and Dhana were in the cave. Time to get to work.

He found Atan heading for her daily walk up the spires of the Purrad, but as always, it took only the briefest glance for her to understand that he needed to speak in private. As soon as he shut the door he said, "Detlev will summon his group by year's end."

She showed little reaction, despite a sharp pang. *So it begins.* "How long does he propose to spend on whatever it is that group is doing? I take it he wants to protect knowledge of the cave transfer even then?"

Siamis nodded. "As long as we can. We'll have until those of his people farthest away make it to Ghildraith."

Atan said, "All right. Thanks." And understood that the conversation was private for a reason — they could not tell Clair, which meant they also had to hide it from the girls.

Atan went to the library, wanting to stand before the fire and think. But she found it occupied by a furrow-browed Delieth child, studying. She backed out, her skirts hissing on the floor, and she crossed the gallery and pressed her forehead against the wall: I, who hate war above all things, shall be married on a metaphorical battlefield.

Weak sunlight slanted in through the hall windows. She straightened up, lest someone find her there, and worry, or question, or go off and comment to someone else, starting a flurry of rumor in this palace that was becoming too crowded. She walked along the hall past the high windows. Brief, dazzling light. Shadow. Light, and warmth. Shadow, and chill.

Memory, so unforgiving, brought from the past another time when she had walked down a hall, seeing intermittent shafts of light. How long ago, when she went to confront Peitar Selenna? Almost ten years. Seemed more like a century.

Peitar had been so very strange, sometimes seeming to be half of this world, and half of another. Darian was occasionally like his father, so studious and unworldly, but unalike as well. Darian loved to laugh, and Atan could not remember Peitar laughing, though surely she must have seen it. He had never been stodgy. But he'd been oddly stubborn, even driven, in a way that Darian wasn't.

That time rumor had begun coupling her name with Peitar

Selenna of Sarendan, originating in her own court after a visit from some aristocrat from Sarendan. Atan winced as she remembered transferring from her capital to his, and confronting him, while she seethed with righteous indignation.

Peitar Selenna had looked so strained and tired when she appeared, she'd felt her silly indignation vanish. What was it, four months later when Detlev's bully assassinated him in cold blood?

He wouldn't tell her what his great magic project was, yet Tsauderei knew. It had something to do with Detlev, and that made Atan furious.

She'd said: *Do you expect to marry me and join the kingdoms, or not? Everyone else seems to think so!* How stupid her indignation seemed now!

Peitar had replied: *I will never find the time for marriage, I suspect. And though it might be a battlefield that finally sees you marry and raise your family standard, the gesture will serve as a signal for hope.*

At the time she'd been merely embarrassed, as if he implied that it would take a war before she'd cross the threshold to adult, and accept its emotional responsibilities.

But now...

Did you know, Peitar? she asked the silent sky.

Sarendan

While far to the east, in Peitar's old kingdom, Dirk Sonscarna paused in the doorway of an old house. Newly arrived, no one was aware of his presence as he peered in at Peitar's and Detlev's sons.

He seldom gave a moment to the sorts of personal reflections and ruminations that seemed to run unceasingly through the minds of Darian and Sveneric. When they did occur, the effect was often nearly paralyzing.

Such was the case now.

The two boys, newly arrived themselves, sat in a long corner salon with tall windows above a curved bench. The windows faced north and east. Wintry light streamed in, silvery-gray, catching and illuminating in thousands of tiny white blazes a cloud of dust motes. And there were the two figures, one fire-lined by light, the other no more than a silhouette in the diffuse shadows by the long black drapes.

It was Sveneric in the light, his profile turned directly up into the slanting rays. Silver glowed in his hair and clothes as he listened to Darian describe life in the Goldenwoods. Behind, Darian bent over, digging through a worn knapsack, his body lost in shadow as he spoke. They were both, at this distance, miniatures of their fathers. One in the light, one in the dark. One still alive, one dead, those fathers. Dead on the order of the other.

Ah, I hate that kind of crap.

To break the thought, and the spell, Dirk walked with heavy step into the room.

Both looked over. "Dirk!" Darian exclaimed. "Here you are at last!"

Sveneric said, "Get some sleep? I can't tell whether those clouds out there are coming or going."

"Bother." Darian grunted as he inspected the winter tunic he had just pulled from the knapsack. "All the thread has rotted. I've got to learn to carry some with me. Why is it always me who gets the ripped seams and lost buttons?"

The question was rhetorical, but as Darian hunted through a cabinet behind him, Sveneric said gloatingly, "Because you never pay attention until it's too late."

Darian threw a look of superior scorn over his shoulder. "Nag." And, to Dirk, "Ready to ride?"

"Not yet. You hear from Detlev last night? About the counterattack?" Dirk asked Sveneric, whose face sobered at his father's name.

"Nothing last night," Sveneric said informatively.

"Why do I even ask? Eh, he just wrote to me on this paper thing. Says, finish up by year's end, if we can. Adam and Leander got us a place."

Darian and Sveneric both knew this wasn't his big news. "And?"

"Just got done writing to Kessler—"

"What?" Darian laughed. "Kessler? Actually answered one of those?"

"He has one?" Sveneric asked, greenish eyes wide.

"I gave him my old one," Dirk said, equally informatively — aware that he was sitting on his own secrets. Actually his father's. Though he didn't know why his father was hiding from everyone. "—and when we give the signal he'll attack the Dei Manor in Imar."

Darian tossed a ball of thread in the air. "Hurray!"

Sveneric said: "The others?"

Dirk shrugged. "Business as usual. Oh! Except you'll enjoy this one. Lyren-Sartora has apparently decided to take on Laban's cause—and is doing it in Everon, in all probability in Tahra's camp. Why, I dunno, not that she ever needed a reason for any of her whims."

Darian chuckled.

"She does," Sveneric said. "But as yet her reasons have been too insufficient for anyone to know she has 'em."

Dirk said bluntly, "Seems to me her readiness to blame Detlev for whatever she doesn't like in her life has indicated a fairly sufficient reason."

"It's been decreasingly sufficient," Sveneric murmured, looking quizzically at Darian. "Which is why you've heard more of it in recent years. What are you laughing at?"

Darian was still chuckling. "A sudden image. Lyren-Sartora and them."

"Lyren-Sartora head-to-head with Tahra over Laban's claims?" Dirk rolled his eyes. "Fire and sword!"

"Not Lyren-Sartora," Sveneric said. "No fire, no sword. That isn't her style—you know it, both of you. For fire and sword, try Tahra Delieth and Laban."

Darian whistled.

Dirk snorted. "Let's ride. Aldon's courier relay awaits our attentions."

Fifteen

The ridge above Efael's HQ

SNOW WAS STARTING TO blow westward in deadly earnest when MV, Rolfin, Crow, and Mildred met at their appointed rendezvous. They'd seen the heavy weather developing, and had decided to cut their recon work short. So when each saw the three other moving silhouettes in the gray-white gusts of wind, Rolfin made violent *Follow me!* arm motions.

After an increasingly nasty interval of icy climbing they squeezed through a slanted fissure between two great stone slabs. Abruptly the howl diminished. Ice crunched under their feet for a ways up a twisted tunnel, and then they entered a huge cavern with a running stream. Somewhere, the stream was fed by a hot spring, for the water was summer-warm, and the air of the cavern was, if not balmy, at least not icy.

MV snapped up a vagabond fire, took one appraising look, then said, "Even if you found nothing else, Rolfin, this beats me."

"S-same," Crow croaked, watching his breath freeze and fall. It never got this cold in Ama Hazanth.

Rolfin grinned at Mildred, a scrap of white between his hat pulled down to his nose and the collar of his coat pulled up to his ears.

She said, "I'll walk on acorns if you put 'em in my shoes. I saw nothing as good as this."

Rolfin said, "I think, if we go back far enough, we could

even bathe. Though it might get too narrow. Didn't get that far yet."

———

Ghildraith Mountains

The same day Rolfin found the hot spring fissure above Efael's HQ, far to the west, in the northern portion of the great Ghildraith Range, Adam perched on a branch of a venerable pine, peering down.

By riding hard, he'd managed to reach a point in the wooded hills below the mountains, two days from his family when Detlev blew through his dreams with the shocking news that Ilerian had struck. Adam's cousin, excited about his nascent Dena Yeresbeth, had ignored Adam's cautions, and now Ilerian was hunting Adam: *Go to ground,* Detlev said, and was gone.

Adam's version of going to ground had always been to take to the air — that is, up into trees. For a day he had been riding through a vast forest of venerable cedar.

He set the horse free, chose an older tree, its branches flat in a spiral, and swarmed upward, snuffing in the sharp scent of crushed cedar needles in the vain hope of vanquishing shock and grief. Then leaped to a nearby tree, and thence to another.

When altitude thinned the cedars he climbed into the branches of resinous conifers until he gained enough height to drop to goat trails. When he dared a contact, there was another command, then silence: *Watch for Zairna and Tarael.*

So that was Zairna's assignment! Tarael, a morvende elder, had been a prisoner of the Host; the only person he had spoken to after his rescue had been Zairna Raadi, from another world entirely.

The best anodyne to grief, Adam believed, was purpose. If the pair was being chased, the simplest way to discover where they were and how many in pursuit would be to cross from east to west, looking for any sign of pursuit running north and south.

Fourth day in, he found dimples in the snow that had been footprints. They were partially obscured by fresher ones. He paused, studying them. He was only certain of one set. But they could be going single file, the one with the larger feet following, to hide that they were two. It — he, or a she near Atan's height — or them, were chased by eight, perhaps a day and a light snow apart.

Adam considered the rough landscape, with escarpments thrusting up like thorns, the uneven ground obscured by snow, then began to run a parallel track, pausing only long enough to break up his own trail when he couldn't use tree branches, boulders, or the thick, snowless duff beneath the heaviest-laden trees.

As he ran, he watched the character of the tracks. There was at least one animal that seemed to be with Zairna and Tarael. A dog of medium size, from the looks of the paw prints. This dog's tracks zigzagged back and forth, as if the animal had burst through brush, which obscured the human tracks for a time.

Each of these caused a trampling hither and yon by the pursuit, until they caught the footprints again farther away. Adam noted discarded items, and the character of the pursuit prints. He needed Ferret to make sure, but he suspected that one of the chasers was a steady drinker, and at least two had not been taught long hunts — these two were getting rid of items deemed excess weight, mostly extra weapons. He annexed a couple of these.

The hunters were not moving fast. But the two being pursued had not lengthened the distance. As the prints sharpened, indicating Adam was catching up, he noted that one foot seemed to be coming down more heavily, and sooner. A limp?

A lance of awareness from overhead shocked Adam; he froze under a tree, not daring to move. Once he sensed the sweeping awareness moving on, he glanced through the pine branches to spot a peregrine falcon drifting overhead.

Bird spy.

He'd been about to force down more of the very stale honey-sweetened travel bread the Marlovens made. Adam loathed the combination of rye and honey; until he saw that falcon, he'd been thinking wistfully of the far better morvende waybreads, hoping that Tarael might have some.

He began to run. As he closed the distance, the prints became more erratic, then it appeared that a second set peeled off. Adam wondered if Zairna and Tarael had split up. In which case, which set ought he to follow? But then he could hear Ferret whispering in memory, "Observe. No assumptions, or you will be following a false trail instead of laying one down."

He made sure he was under cover as he examined the topography. This side of the mountain had worn away toward a waterfall that fed a river below. One set of footprints seemed to go in that direction. The other set climbed toward a peak now hidden in cloud.

Instinct clamored to follow the second set — and before long, there were the dog prints again, crossing the trail, then further on, the prints vanished. Again —

Ah, the peregrine was returning.

Adam scrambled for cover and stilled, breathing fast. The clouds were thickening; the bird flew away, and vanished. Adam ran on, hard. Now he could hear the pursuit. They cracked and snapped through underbrush, calling back and forth, occasionally cursing, with the ease of those who know that the biggest danger on the mountain is themselves.

As drifts of fog began chilling the air to ice, Adam ran parallel to the Norsundrians — he could hear the language now — until they called for a camp. "Anyone running in this soup will end up diving off a cliff," a voice declared.

Not untrue. Adam waited until the Norsundrians had made a circle around a fire and were passing out what smelled like spiced dried fish and pickled greens, while sweet potatoes roasted at the edge of the fire.

Once they were busy eating, Adam drifted away, bending close to the ground until he picked up the quarry's footsteps again. Still one set of human, and dog. He pulled off a branch of fir and obliterated the sharp, fresh print, and then made a new set, doubling back around, leading to a frozen stream. Let them think the runner had slid along the ice for a time.

Then, moving slowly, bent almost double, he picked up the trail again, smoothing out the prints behind him. When fog and darkness made it impossible to see, he camped where he was, and at the first lifting of light he set out again, the ring of voices echoing against the hills behind him.

He had not gone far when a rustle in the blackberry shrubs alerted him, and a long-legged black dog emerged in a leap, tongue lolling, mind reaching. This dog had canine Dena Yeresbeth.

Adam dropped his shield, to be hit with an overwhelmingly alien world of scent, so intense he lost grip of his own leading sense of sight, slipped, and fell flat in the snow.

It wasn't that he didn't know how to filter. He'd actually learned it by instinct in a simple way when young. Then, later, when the boys hit their late teens, and as usual, when reaching their adult height and requiring the beard spell, the flickers of sex-feelings had roared into inferno through approximately nine tenths of the day. At that time Adam was too focused on recovering from a variety of traumas, such as regrowing a set of fingernails, to share their appetites and so he had learned to filter all that out, though otherwise listening.

But the dog had come on him suddenly, and he sensed its protective intent and suspicion. He lay in the snow, blinking snowflakes off his lashes as the dog sat nearby, alert but not menacing, panting gently.

And then a face hove into view, bending to look down.

Adam gazed up, to meet vivid green eyes framed by curling dark hair in a face to make painters weep. He stilled — they both stilled.

Painters, and poets, balladeers and courtiers, through the centuries have expressed in a variety of metaphors that rare moment when eye meets eye, and each finds self catapulted to an entirely different realm, where the sun of midsummer burns eternally, and body, mind, and spirit know one another once and forever.

"Adam?" Leander said, on a note of wonder.

Adam gazed up at Leander Tlennen-Hess, who had changed so very much since the last time they had met, as boys.

"Are you all right?" Leander asked, extending a hand as he glanced around. "There's a patrol…"

Adam took that hand, not that he needed it, except to reassure him that he had not, after all, stepped out of this world.

With awareness returned, he made a discovery: that bird was back. "Let's run," he said.

Above the crags of Ghildraith

The strange, air-sensitive eyes flicking back and forth across the shadow-slashed peaks and canyons fixed on a soaring black speck, and the sudden surge of red-hot adrenals nearly dislodged Imry.

Mind-rider notwithstanding, the peregrine falcon was on the hunt.

The great wings beat hard and fast, uncannily sharp-sighted eyes fixed on the unwary prey. Imry resigned himself for the time being; he really wasn't all that interested in this search for Adam, supposedly somewhere in these mountains, but Ilerian had ordered the chase, and so here he was.

Instead, he prepared to enjoy the stoop and strike before he could direct the bird's mind again. The day was late anyway, the shadows beginning to obscure land distinctions; maybe it was time to have this last bit of vicarious fun and then get back to his own pursuits.

Meanwhile the peregrine folded its wings and began the long stoop. The insane speed exhilarated Imry. Rocky scarps blurred at either side. Air roared like thunder. The falcon's eyes stayed on the prey, which increased rapidly in size.

The prey resolved into a long-tailed, sooty-colored white-throated swift, changed direction with a sudden twitch of a wing, and swooped round a tower of weather-carved rock, disappearing as the falcon's wings spread. It banked. The swift reappeared beyond a tumbled cliff, dashing away at tremendous speed. As the falcon shot around the cliff in blood-mad pursuit, a fall of shrill notes tumbled back through the air. "He he he!" Like human laughter —

Instinctively, quicker than conscious thought, Imry touched minds with the small, black-feathered bird winging away. And caught the briefest glitter of exultation, a bright flash of laughter —

"Human," he thought, surprised and intrigued.

And it was gone.

Someone mind-traveling with the swift, as he was with the falcon? As the two birds began a spectacular, sky-traversing chase, he was more deliberate about contact and this time found himself stonewalled.

He was content to enjoy the ride.

The sky-piercing peaks of Ghildraith sped by beneath and beside him like passing storm-whitecaps on the ocean as two of the world's fastest breeds of feathered creatures stretched wings in a death-chase. The falcon arrowed after the swift like a bolt from a crossbow, but the smaller bird showed itself intriguingly adept at evasive action — wheels, dives, turns — always, though, it fled westward.

Time seemed to pass as rapidly as the birds in flight. Now they flew in cold, snow-blue shadow, now they passed a rocky precipice and sped straight toward the fiery glory of the sinking sun.

The peregrine never shifted gaze from the small black speck, so when, with a flick of far-off wingtips, the prey suddenly disappeared beyond a long, dark-veined slab of ancient stone, the falcon screamed and stooped again, shooting straight for the place where the swift had been.

Just before reaching it, there was a tiny flick at the edge of its vision: the swift rounded a cliff, high up, and once again winged westward. The falcon abandoned its dive, swooping upward on a draft of air above the snow-packed mountainside and once again took up the chase.

This happened twice more until Imry, until now content to be a passive observer, invaded the falcon's tiring mind and took control. The swift, also tiring, provided a vector that it took a human to follow.

Time to investigate.

A little time was spent in accustoming himself to the feel of wings, the alignment of bird-body with wind, and then he began to gain altitude while continuing with the chase. The next time the swift disappeared he scanned the surrounding geography, estimated speed, and fled northwest. When the swift emerged not two-hundred paces distant, he was nearly on top of it before it spotted him.

Once again a spectacular veer, dive, lift—and another disappearance.

This time he began the stoop just before the swift reappeared, and the falcon regained control of its body as it went for the kill. The swift's eyes briefly glowed like rubies, reflecting the sinking sun, as its head swiveled.

The bird then veered desperately just as the powerful clawed feet struck down. One missed. The other caught the swift a blow across the back. The swift faltered and fell as though stunned, then as the falcon gave its triumph-cry, the prey copied its own tactic, folded its wings close, and dropped straight-shot toward the shadow-obscured spires of stone below.

It twisted and fluttered into a cave; the falcon, tired, gave up the chase; it hated caves. Imry stayed with the falcon long enough to mark the cave, then left the falcon and returned to his body.

As soon as he recovered, he transferred back to that fissure.

The other mind was blocked. He heard human breathing, and walked into the cave. He found a thin figure of medium height standing just inside the rocky entrance, leaning heavily against the uneven stone, breath puffing white. Her feet were bare, despite the cold, her tunic and riding trousers old and worn, made for a body much larger than hers.

He raised a hand and a torch burst into reddish-gold existence. Its light painted warmly over the features of a slender girl of sixteen or seventeen with a cap of short, curly dark hair. The wide blue eyes, the pain-drawn face with its reckless smile distracted him, briefly calling up memory of Laban many years ago. Chance resemblance; only their coloring was similar, not their features. Laban used to affect just the same bravado when in the most pain.

Bravado indeed. One of her hands clutched tightly at the opposite shoulder. The other hand hung limply. The breast of her tunic moved with her hard breathing; despite this fight for breath, and despite the heavy blow she'd taken her eyes were alert, wary, and not without a certain muted humor.

She said in Imaran, "That was quite a chase."

Even more surprised now, he recognized in her his mindless prize of late summer.

Sixteen

AMUSEMENT AND INTEREST SPARKED a laugh. Imry Llyenthur stepped up and jammed the torch into a crack in the stone roughly halfway between then.

His quarry watched, unmoving.

He said, "Who are you?"

Her lips parted, her brow considering. That expression in the flickering light introduced another resemblance, but this one was far stronger: Liere Fer Eider.

She saw the recognition. "Marga Fer Eider." She added blandly, "I left home six months ago. Quite cast off by my family, in fact—"

"Your efforts on their behalf are a waste of time. I leave reprisals against hapless families to Efael."

The torchlight in her unblinking eyes made them glitter brightly. "Except," she said gently, "your own?"

He received that with a sudden lift to his brows, then he retorted, "I've called Senrid Montredaun-An a number of things, but never family." As he spoke he noticed the tightening of her jaw muscles, her convulsive swallow. "Broken?" He glanced at her shoulder.

"I don't know," she admitted. "I expect I'll find out soon enough." Then grinned. "Now who's to ask the other first why they were birding over these snowy mountains?"

He gave a dismissive shrug. "Shall I provide the expected answer: to enjoy the view? I'm more interested in your importance in the general scheme of things. For someone whose appearance last summer agitated our mightiest captains on either side, you've been little heard from."

Her laugh was slightly breathless. "Ah, well."

He moved. Her eyes tracked, but once again she remained motionless.

He stepped sideways once, twice, and sat down on a rock inside the cave on the opposite wall from her. The black-and-gold chased hilt of Adamas Dei's black sword was inches from where his left hand rested, but her gaze never lowered from his face.

Neither had a cloak, yet neither noticed the cold.

"Tell me something," he invited.

"If I can." Her bright eyes, head tilted a little to one side, reminded him of the bird shape she'd worn so recently.

"The connection with Ilerian."

Her tunic shifted as, at last, she succeeded in getting control of her breathing. Her body under that ill-fitting tunic was slim, strong, a graceful line from neck to hip. Already the flush of overexertion was fading from her cheeks, leaving them pale. He waited silently, watching with bland interest as her gaze drifted out to the star-glowing western sky. Thin streamers of fog blurred the escarpments, glowing with a wash of predawn color.

Finally she looked back. Her lips were now pale, but the expression in her wide blue eyes remained steady and lively. Her head tilted a little more, the tick of her heartbeat in the curve of her throat. "You could ask him."

"I could," he agreed.

Another convulsive swallow. She was afraid. Naturally. Who wouldn't be? Also, no doubt the numbness that had muted the blow from the falcon's foot until now was giving way to pain. There were obviously no weapons hidden in that rumpled tunic or the saddle-worn summer trousers. And even if she'd had a weapon, she couldn't move very fast now.

But she smiled, with a recklessness that intrigued him, though he usually found teenagers boring, and those smooth, round cheeks, the still-childish chin, indicated she was no older than eighteen, if that.

"Then why don't you?" she asked, her voice light, timbreless.

"Because, right now, I'm not interested in contributing to anyone's efforts but my own, unless ordered."

Her brows twitched up; though his orders had been to hunt down Adam, they both knew that Ilerian would give anything to get hold of her.

"Why does Ilerian want you? What is it that marks you apart from anyone else? You were singularly useless the last time I bestirred myself on your behalf. Of course you've regained your wits since then. And, it seems, your memory."

"Yes." A laugh flickered in the corners of her eyes and her mouth, a subtle change of expression. Her jaw was too tight to give it sound.

"That storm. You remember it?"

"Very well." Once again, fainter, the laughter.

"What exactly did you do?"

"End it."

"That much I gathered. How?"

Her eyes focused for the space of a breath on a point far distance from this little rocky crevasse. "It took a bit of effort," she said finally, seeing he was waiting. "Which is quite beyond me now," she added, with a slight grimace.

He rose suddenly. The steel-reinforced point of the sword sheath scraped against rock. A step, bootheel grinding in gravel. Another.

Her face did not change, or lift, as he stopped directly in front of her but her fingers tightened on her shoulder. She was still, not even breathing as he lifted a hand — and only brushed it lightly over the back of her shoulder beyond her clutching fingers. Then he turned away and retreated to the other side of the cave, and she watched him reflectively until he sat down again on the ledge of rock.

He said, "Not broken. But you're going to have a prime bruise for some time."

Her head dropped back against the stone wall, expressive of relief. "The distinction," she said, "will one day no doubt be perceptible."

Laban was back, in the drawl, the reckless smile — Laban after a spectacular failure. And suddenly various clues observed during this surprising episode added up. Another surprise.

"It wasn't a chance encounter," he said. "You knew I was riding the peregrine. Were you by any chance running as decoy? You've got to know that you're a far greater prize than Adam."

She gave him a big, lopsided grin, and again there was the old reckless Laban of Imry's youth. "Wanted to meet you," she said. "This time in possession of my wits. It seemed as good an opportunity as any."

"And then?" he prompted.

Her good shoulder shrugged. "If I survived the encounter, hole up somewhere and sleep." She grimaced.

"And if I decide to take you to Imar?"

That smile flashed again. "They won't have any beds?"

"You *are* deflecting me," he exclaimed, rising to his feet. Ambivalence was unexpectedly strong—but if Ilerian turned up—

"He cannot see me," she said. "And at this moment he is looking elsewhere."

"You know that?" Imry asked.

Her head tipped a little. "I always know where he is. Where he looks. Always."

Imry hesitated. He had no particular desire to please Ilerian, but to cross him in this was to invite a protracted death.

In the heartbeat that he hesitated, he lost the choice: she blurred and he found himself looking at the stone where she had stood. By the time he spotted a bee at an altitude no bee was ever found, it was already leaving the cave, whereupon it vanished from sight.

———◈———

Adam sensed the peregrine flying rapidly away, chasing a bird he could not see, except as a shooting star in the mental realm. He shielded his mind, laughing. "Spy's gone. Shall we run?"

He assumed that he would lead, for he'd been trained, and he remembered Leander as a serious mage student, his fingers invariably covered with ink. But Leander—in spite of a slight limp after a painful fall on unseen ice—proved to be exactly as adept as Adam, especially with Rori, the dog, running as their scout.

And so the journey became one of dazzling laughter, both courtship and challenge: a swing over a treacherously icy stream via a tree branch, a leap from rock to rock over a dizzying fall, a dash along a broken ridge no wider than a fence. These daring exploits did not leave prints. When they ran in snow, they traded off using the fir branch to obliterate prints. Even Rori seemed to be contributing by leading them to where other animals had crossed, creating a pattern of different prints.

They ran through the day as the sky clouded, dappling the world with whirling flakes, then brightened again.

Questions piled up, but each waited for the other to begin. The shadows had begun to lengthen when Leander exclaimed suddenly, "Ah, we're almost on it."

It?

Had to be one of the mysterious signs indicating a morvende entrance. To which sunsiders were not welcome, except in very rare occasions. Sharp disappointment was Adam's first reaction, but he smothered that, determined to remember this run, whatever it led to.

As it happened, he did not have long to wait. Leander halted, looking around. Adam dared a swift search on the mental realm, for the pressure of that terrible probing, searching white light that was Ilerian in that realm had turned northward.

The Norsundrian patrol was at least a day behind, and weather was moving in.

"Can you turn your back?" Leander asked.

Adam did so, without asking why.

Leander sketched the sign against a glowing mark in a rock, and a short time later, the rock slid silently, as two cobwebby white heads looked out.

"Leander!"

"Elkan," Leander said. "There's enemies on the chase."

Elkan's smile smoothed to blandness when he perceived that Leander was not alone. "Who is this?"

Leander glanced back at Adam, who stood there politely, hands clasped behind him.

"He is with me," Leander said, and then, in a slightly stronger voice, "If he cannot pass inside—I remember your rules—then I will rescind my pass sign."

Elkan exchanged a glance with the other morvende. She looked past Elkan, saying coolly," If you will wait?"

The stone closed.

Adam did another sweep, then said, "I don't want to cause trouble."

"Sit down." Leander indicated a lichen-covered flat stone nearby. "You disappeared for years. What happened?"

Adam tried a smile, having no idea how little mirth was in it. No anger, only the patience that Leander remembered from boyhood. "Some travel," Adam said. "Off-world."

Rock rumbled and grated, and Elkan was back. "There is a gathering place," he said, his voice full of question. "Tarael of the north has spoken for you. I am to give you both the transfer."

Then Zairna had reached safety.

Adam rose, and this time it was he who extended his hand, encased in its glove. Leander closed his fingers around Adam's, feeling the latent strength there, and in the firm grip a hint of promise.

They took the first step on a new road, Rori prancing at their heels.

Toth

The sun came up on David and Senrid riding side by side across the winter-brown, misty plains where eight centuries ago, the aging Adaluin Inda Algara-Vayir had completed his yearly ride of his lands. Having dealt with the difficult crown prince of Perideth at that kingdom's border, Senrid and David were riding toward the southwest of Marloven Hess.

Their horses raced headlong at the gallop, so neither spoke. David looked around in passive appreciation of the subtlety of wintry field colors. Senrid noted another a plinth carved with town names and directional arrows, a thing not to be found in Marloven Hess. He eyed that plinth as they passed; so much for generations of Marloven belief that directional signs would only aid invaders. Norsunder had not been troubled by the lack. Bleakly he imagined Imry Llyenthur riding about unnoticed sometime during the past five or ten years, creating military maps with landmarks as guides. That, Senrid knew, was what he himself would have done.

David carried Senrid's beige-paper. He'd used it relatively frequently since Senrid tendered it to him, which if Senrid noticed he never said. From time to time David gave Senrid status reports on the doings of others. Senrid very rarely returned comment, and never asked. To all appearances he cared very little about anything beyond his immediate concerns; his attitude about the eventual summons by Detlev for the final trial seemed to be a fatalistic unconcern.

When David suddenly reached into his Marloven army winter coat and pulled out the battered, fluttering magic-paper, Senrid sent a fast glance. As soon as he saw the paper in David's fingers instead of a weapon he returned to his own thoughts.

David slid the paper back into his pocket.

Midmorning they neared the border hills and slowed their pace. David said, "Message from Detlev. He's giving us until the 25th, 35th at the outside."

"35th," Senrid repeated, his thoughts rapidly sifting

through evolving plans, adjusting and rearranging.

After a lengthy pause, David said, "Lest suspense consume you, I hasten to inform you where we're going."

"Hmm—what?" Senrid eyed David's smile. "Yes. Suspense. Where?"

"Ghildraith."

"Ah."

"Which doesn't surprise you, it appears."

Senrid's lip curled, then he turned his head scan a low patch of evergreen shrubs. "By the way. Did I tell you that you're also heir to Vasande Leror?"

David thought of Leander, and how much he had loathed the responsibilities of kingship, even over such a tiny polity as Vasande Leror. It would have been a relief to abdicate, if he could surrender his duties in good conscience. "I expect Leander was glad of his escape."

"Yep," Senrid said. "He did say he'd try to win us some aid in the greater cause. Which is why I'm not surprised about Ghildraith."

David waited for Senrid to enlarge on what to everyone else had been a surprise, to discover that there was one of the most ancient morvende civilizations on the world in those formidable mountains—and that Leander Tlennen-Hess had been accepted among them, a rarity indeed. Or, to express his relief at having Vasande Leror reunited with Marloven Hess again. But of course Senrid said nothing, because Senrid no longer had feelings.

David sighed inwardly. "It appears that the credit must be shared with someone else, for Adam and Leander were apparently in some danger there at the end, before they reached the Ghildraith entry-point."

And paused, leaving this promising opening for the story of the world-wide search for Marga Fer Eider.

Senrid flicked his palm up. "We'll probably have to hear more than we want about it when we do report in. Need lunch before we cross the border? Time to water the horses."

"Your wish is my command, O mighty monarch," David said.

"When you talk like that," Senrid said cordially, "I want to break your teeth."

"When you talk like nothing else matters outside of the midden-pile made by our ancestors," David retorted, equally cordially, "I want to break yours."

"But nothing else does matter," Senrid said so blandly that

David gave up.

They stopped and ate the cold remains of a predawn breakfast while their mounts rested. Then they followed an old horse thief path to slip over the border. There they parted, each to pursue individual chores in the time they had left before Detlev's summons.

Seventeen

A campsite in Enaeran

THE SUN CAME UP on a steel-gray day of bitter cold.

Andri Malcolm Elsarion reluctantly opened his eyes and looked up at the roof of the tent. Little ripples. No snow weight. That's good. But a nasty, icy wind. That's rotten. That's damned rotten.

He lay without moving, his mind ranging freely. It was the first chance he'd had to think since he'd arrived back home after the long stay in Marloven Hess, but he was used to living on the run, and so he rapidly reviewed his reunion with Liere (that made him grin) and his welcome from his own friends, all of whom had been eager to tell him, in private, just how amazing — how skillful and graceful and quick — Liere was.

His entire kingdom seemed to have fallen in love with her as she had adapted to his rough-and-tumble, war-torn, easy-to-ignite people, smilingly getting them all pointed in the same direction when usually if you managed to get five Enaeraneth in a room, six plans would emerge. What was more amazing, it seemed she'd even managed to rope in from a distance his enigmatic cousin Trevor Macael — and that after Andri's own disastrously inept beginning acquaintance. At least, Macael had been sending a steady supply of first-rate steel, along with communications breathing of alliance.

Heh. Ready warmth kindled inside him; time to wake her

up, and kick up some—

He turned, reached, then snapped his hand back, getting a shock that made him forget the cold—and that inner kindling. Instead of one slender lump next to him under the shapeless gray comforter, there were two.

He could have sworn Liere was not the sort for threesomes—

Just then two heads popped out from the comforter, next to him one golden, and next to her one covered with short, silky dark curls. Two pairs of eyes shaped exactly the same regarded him, one golden, one blue.

Liere smiled. "You're letting cold air under the blanket."

"Huh?" Andri contributed, with grace, intelligence, and tact. "Who is this?"

"Auntie Liere told me I could crawl in here," the newcomer said, apologetically, with a blithe, sunny smile. "I arrived when you were asleep."

"Be my guest." Andri waved a mittened hand, trying for suavity. "May I ask your name?"

Liere grinned at him, and turned to pat Marga's shoulder. "You've already figured out she's Marga. I—oh, no, what is it?" Her tone sharpened into worry when Marga winced and went pale as paper.

Marga's smile flickered back. "Bit of a miscalculation," she said rather breathlessly as Liere lifted the edge of her tunic-neck and gasped at the bruised flesh beneath. "You might say I 'ran afoul' of someone—"

"Marga, that bruise looks terrible! And is that—did you get clawed?"

"Oh, it hurt for a day or so, but not so much now. And I got here safely, didn't I?" As Marga spoke, she eased out from under the covers and pulled on a shapeless coat. She patted her sash into place then said in a brisk voice, "Uncle Andri, did you know that Benefactor Detlev will be expecting you by the 35th? In the Ghildraith mountains, almost directly west in a line from us here."

"I know," Andri said. "What I'm wondering is how you know."

"Have you been mixing with Detlev and the Norsundrians?" Liere asked Marga, not accusingly, but more helplessly.

Marga smiled and shook her curly head. "Not Benefactor Detlev, and only briefly some Norsundrians. Though that was almost too much for me! But I was able to help some other friends of yours, and I also met the morvende, and other folk of songs and stories."

Liere opened her mouth, hesitated, exchanged a look with Andri, whose thought was clear: *This one's yours.*

So she said only, "I think we could all use something hot to drink. Let's rouse the camp."

Near Efael's lair

Detlev brought in not two, but three.

MV, Mildred, Rolfin, Crow, and new arrival Yanli gazed from Jilo—taller, still gaunt, his lank hair unkempt and his cloths flapping—to Shontande Lirendi, neat even when travelworn, to the small figure with them. Unconsciously the kings of Colend and Chwahirsland closed protectively—and guiltily—in on either side of Retren Ndarga.

Though Jilo and Shontande had both been learning road-survival at an admirably rapid rate, they had not been trained to spot a shadow; when Detlev caught up with them at the corner where the borders of Colend, Chwahirsland, and Erdrael Danara met, he flushed Retren, at that point half-starved, shivering with cold, and chattering incomprehensibly about a singing mountain. He had followed them all this way on his own.

Detlev had traveled with the three of them the rest of the way.

Before Detlev could speak, Yanli bounced up, arms wide. "Welcome, welcome. Siamis sent me with stores—which includes hot food. Looks to me as if you could do with some." With an assurance that sat oddly on one not much older than Retren Ndarga, Yanli introduced everyone, then said, "Jilo, I think Crow will be an immense help to you one day, and you to him." Yanli's wide-set eyes were crescents of mirth as she briskly combined the two parties into one, while making sure the newcomers had hot pear cider to drink.

Detlev stepped back to watch it happen.

Yanli's personality dictated the same ferocious focus, not on the bonds of kin or friend, but on other things, which reminded him of Sfenrael, Siamis's mother. He knew it was fanciful. These many millennia later, finding traces in today's generation of those he had known and loved back then was akin to seeing writing in the shapes of clouds. Even so, Yanli's concentration was on the process of humans mastering magic, and long ago, Sfenrael's on her home and lands, growing up to demonstrate a lightning brilliance that had protected her home and its vital legacy for centuries—millennia—though she could not protect their lives. That monument to her care stood yet on its mountain above the mysterious caves, though every other disirad structure was in pieces, or destroyed entirely.

That much, Detlev had been able to preserve for Siamis.

But Yanli was very much her own person, small, round, neat, and eminently practical even at that otherwise difficult age, early teens. Utterly unlike tall, graceful Sfenrael had been.

Detlev had said before transferring her from Roth Drael, "Shall we visit Siamis first?"

Yanli shook her head decidedly. "Not now. I'll only distract him. And I don't like how he's reliving his boyhood under the psychic knives of the Host while watching Clair go through a similar kind of torture. If I could do anything, I would."

Detlev watched Yanli chatter away at high speed at her little circle of oddly matched people, ignoring Rolfin and MV, whom she had known all her life.

MV turned to Detlev. "Why is Jilo here? Surely he didn't think we'd leave that Chwahir general to Efael?"

"The Chwahir," Detlev said, as usual answering the question behind the question. "are on the move." He went on, "Jilo knows that castle from Wan-Edhe's day. He can run the rescue. You confine yourselves to defense. This will be a distraction for him."

With an internal shrug, MV abandoned the plans he'd been forming—they had not managed to glean much about the castle. Now, it seemed, this raid might actually work, whereas until this moment he'd given them a fifty-fifty chance—reserving going inside solely to himself.

"And Lirendi?" They turned toward where the handsome Colendi king stood near Jilo, his profile sober.

"He ... decided to come along."

MV grunted, sending a thought to Mildred and Rolfin: *That boy. It's the brother. Has to be.*

Mildred responded: *He looks like Marend, but in three heartbeats of conversation he's already as unlike her as anyone could possibly be.*

MV said to Detlev, "What about Imry?"

"He's gone renegade, more or less," Detlev said. "Oh, he's hunting us, as ordered, and he heels when they snap their fingers, which is increasingly rare as they turn more to magic. Meanwhile he's snapped his own fingers in Efael's face, and Yeres is apparently on his tail."

MV strolled out into the main part of the cave, heels ringing on the rocky floor and hands on hips. "What kind of worthless laze-offs have you dragged up here? Lirendi, you're looking disgustingly overfed. And you! Jilo! Have you learned yet to pick up those flat Chwahir feet when you lift a sword?..."

He went on to insult them all, until they were laughing, or at least smiling—Shontande Lirendi—and then in one smooth, fast transition the insults were turned against Efael and intensified to a report on what the Host's resident dungeon master had been doing for entertainment of late, and so though everyone needed rest, they found themselves forming into a circle and planning instead.

Jilo watched, as usual lost in admiration of MV's effortless style in leadership. On their arrival they'd been an awkward combination of people, some of whom had at least hidden dislikes of others, but now quite suddenly they were a twi. MV walked back and forth shooting questions at them, finding out what strengths they'd developed since he saw them last, what weaknesses might have accrued and why.

Probably everyone knew what he was doing. There was Shontande, polite, bland. Overfed! He'd probably never been this thin even as a small boy. But centuries of Lirendi ancestors holding a far-flung kingdom by virtue of brains, charm, and beauty prevented a single year of wartime living from marring his astonishing good looks.

Retren answered, loud and clear. There was enough Marloven training in his background to make him respond instantly to this kind of handling. What's more, though Jilo knew that MV had spent some time in Senrid's kingdom—and that recently, too—MV did not make the mistake of mentioning the sister.

And there was Mildred. She'd changed a lot since Jilo'd seen her last. She'd always been as active as she was good-natured, but now she was as lean and straight-edged as a knife. To be expected, if she'd been mixing with the poopsies of late. And this squinty-eyed, silent Crow, same deal.

Rolfin hadn't changed much. And of course Detlev never does. Do they look at me, Jilo thought, and see any change?

"...so here's our idea," MV was saying. "We need to rescue the Chwahir general, while making it look like a hasty scouting run—grabbing communications, magic books, the like. Efael's got to think we're setting up for a major attack, which will set off a tantrum. According to Erol, you've been leaking false info through the army, Jilo?" MV whirled and pointed.

Jilo turned to Shontande, and gestured 'go ahead.'

Shontande Lirendi said, "Since summer, our resistance, and General Furo's secret resistance within the Chwahir hierarchy, have both been slipping Wan-Edhe and Efael's spies false reports about resistance groups hidden in the eastern mountains. Any attack either by the Chwahir or by Colendi has been attributed to renegade Norsundrians. We've coordinated reports so there's been enough hard data on dates and locations to send Wan-Edhe into a frenzy of searches. This was before Efael seized Crimson General Furo."

MV clapped his hands, a sharp sound that echoed faintly back in the shadowy tunnels. "Right. Mountain base." He turned an interrogative look to Detlev, whose thought came back: *Siamis is aware.*

MV said to the group, "What we four have mapped out is the defense. Though no one except us has ever come here, there's Efael's paranoia, which makes Wan-Edhe almost look sane. He has wards set up to prevent anyone at all—outside of the Host, or specifically coded and warded runners—from magic transfer directly into the fortress. Everyone else has to ride in from two designated transfer points half-an-hour ride from the citadel. Also in our favor is his arrogant assumption that no attack can break through his outer perimeter. He's got very little staff inside—the inner perimeter is mostly him prowling around all night and day, guarded by whoever of his Black Knives is not spying elsewhere, like interfering with Aldon down in Sartor."

"Time malaise is making it worse instead of better," Detlev murmured. "Not that you can count on that to diminish his strength or his ferocity if cornered. What it will do is engender more random and drastic reactions."

MV saw the group absorb this, and then he went on. "He's got the pick of Bostian's old strike troops on guard duty, though they all hate it..."

Part of Jilo's mind listened to the details of MV's report of the defensive perimeters. He paid minimal attention because he wouldn't be going against any of those. He'd be going inside, because he knew the layout of that old castle, and its traps. Except for anything Efael might have added, but MV wouldn't know those, either. He had to trust his own magic senses, honed after all that time in the center of Wan-Edhe's citadel, to sniff them out.

He watched the others listening. Shontande's expression had shuttered completely, throwing Jilo back to summer right after Conrad of Imar had hanged himself. Jilo knew that the shock of that gesture of despair on the part of the difficult, conflicted prince had hit Shontande just as hard, making him feel they had failed Conrad. *Why couldn't he talk to us?* Because he admired Shontande too much—and the damnable humiliation of the Host choosing his land to destroy with their presence…

"…when Efael leaves next, and we'll strike then."

Mildred fought off an increasing sense of unreality as she turned her hand to serving the newcomers from the crocks of hot food that Detlev had brought from Mearsies Heili on the other side of the world, via the cave transfer. *It's real,* she kept thinking. *This isn't a drill, it's real.*

Then she laughed at herself: *Or maybe she wasn't real,* standing there staring at a bowl of fried potatoes as though they were about to take wing and fly off. Or as if they were about to speak to her, *Mildred! If you had the sense of a potato you'd be wrapped up in your jacket and sleeping, instead of preparing to go out and jump Norsundrians…*

She shrugged off the absurdity, and caught an appraising glance from Rolfin's black eyes. She raised her voice, "Come on and get it while it's hot."

MV continued, "We have to assume that any magic attack's going to set off the wards and bring Efael back —probably with Yeres, and maybe with Svir. You've got to get in unnoticed, which means we've got to keep the roads clear until you get out. Get Furo, and any other prisoners. Get out. Arrivals on the road, spotted from the castle, will mean Efael gets a message and transfers back."

"Got it," Yanli said, and bit into a roll.

"Well, Lirendi? You've said nothing."

Shontande's eyes had been on the bowl in his hands. He drawled in the Colendi courtly singsong, "It appears your plan must run smoothly, as long as the weather holds steadily bad, blinding us all, and as long as Efael is not nipping out to fetch fresh flowers for his garland, and as long as we stumble over no new wards, and enter and exit unseen, and there are no reinforcements sent by Wan-Edhe. Quite a comfortable margin for error indeed, and who could possibly object?"

During the scoffing and cracks that followed, Mildred saw a faint line crease Detlev's brow. He reached into his coat and pulled out a beige paper. As he read it, he got to his feet and moved a few steps away. Then he pulled out a pencil, leaned against a rock, and wrote swiftly.

The joking around was a good tension release. Through it, Mildred watched Detlev read his response and then stand motionless by the cave wall, leaning against it on one hand, his gaze on the ground. She wouldn't have watched had she not become so sensitized to Rolfin and MV, whose focus had sharpened when Detlev moved.

Detlev looked up, and his gaze found MV. Mildred felt the exchange, though she didn't hear it, for both Detlev and MV were expert at single-identity-focus contacts.

Then, without warning, MV was in her mind: *It's you and me short one if he goes on an emergency errand. What say?*

Mildred's first instinct was to ask if it were a life and death matter, but she squashed it. Of course it was. Everything was, these days, and if it wasn't, he wouldn't even have asked.

So what was it? She knew instinctively that she'd be told if she asked. But somehow that made it impossible to ask. And what did it matter, who was at the other end of the emergency? He was going to do what he believed he had to do: *No problem here. But who'll tell us when Efael goes?*

Detlev replied this time: *Yanli. I will return as quickly as I can.*

And with his thought came wordless gratitude.

As MV turned to tell the others, Mildred glowed inside. Whatever you had to say against Detlev—and she knew there was plenty—he did know how to say thank you. And mean it.

Detlev was transferred out.

Aldon's HQ in Eidervaen, capital of Sartor

Duin saluted smartly, his face wooden, until the moment his superior had gone out the door.

"All general orders to be logged," he muttered to himself. "Order: Aldon, to all communications units, as of today, you will travel in doubled columns, until further notice."

Duin chuckled inside—while keeping a zealously straight face even though he was alone in the dismally cold room. He sat down to inscribe the order in the log book, in his neatest and clearest hand.

Then he laid aside the pen to savor again the blood-red fury in Aldon's face at the latest reports of damage done by what appeared to be three brats. The Selenna urchin for certain, and rumor named his companions as Detlev's and Kessler Sonscarna's litter. Maybe. If the word was straight on their exploits, and not magnified to cover time-malaise, or drunkenness, or inter-unit squabbles and lack of communication—all incompetence. Duin had his doubts. He remembered what the Detlev boy had looked like, before they sent him to Imar. Knew there'd been an escape, but he thought it unlikely a brat in that bad of shape could race about in rotten weather, striking at courier relays, and never get caught.

Not that it mattered much either way. The facts were that *someone* was ambushing communications riders, leaving them frozen, someone shooting fire-arrows through outposts and burning the papers, and someone had even hit a garrison south of the city—after patrols had made certain all local citizens were locked down—and stolen orders off the dispatch desks.

The rich thing was, Aldon had to investigate himself.

Meanwhile...

Duin's inward smile turned to gloat.

That order. And the weekly report to go to Lord Patience in his fortress on the border of Chwahirsland tonight, and the only escort left unassigned, the Black Knives. Who would be insulted and furious to be sent on escort duty. Especially escort for a piece of paper.

"Insubordination, that's what he called opinion. What would he call countering general orders with specific overrides?"

Duin crossed his hands behind his head, and laughed. Twice, now, in the last weeks he'd been able to drop some acid into the pot—strictly obeying orders—and watch the resultant confusion. This one promised to be the richest yield yet.

If Aldon didn't remember Efael's order, and countermand. But he wouldn't remember. It was Efael himself who had insisted he personally conduct the search for those phantom boys.

Duin sat back and contemplated the ceiling. Two watches until the report was to be sent—oh, he wished he could be there to see the Black knives' fury. And Efael's fury at Aldon's messing with his Black Knives...

He could hardly wait.

Eighteen

AS SOON AS CJ saw Detlev's neat handwriting promising to come, she tucked her pencil stub back into her pocket and looked over at Erenlara's still form.

She rocked back and forth on her heels, her emotions reeling between worry and profound relief. She tried to talk herself into the relief. Of course no one wanted to ask any grownups to walk in and take over, but it wasn't like she hadn't been trying to solve things herself.

She held her fingers out to the candle flame to warm them. It was spring, here in the Land of the Venn, but you'd never know it. Eren had said it was a cold land, with much bad weather, and she'd been right.

CJ worriedly checked Eren's still, pale face. She'd pillowed her on a bag of rotting chicken feed in this chicken coop that they'd adopted as their latest hidey hole. Eren's hands, under her cloak, had both girls' pairs of gloves on, and Eren's feet inside their mocs had three pairs of socks on, the third being CJ's extra pair.

She crouched, hugging her legs to her chest and grinding her chin on her knees; the night was so quiet here, except for night birds, or a breeze through the new grasses. Eventually she felt a contact, and then she heard a quiet step, then another, and he was there.

He pushed aside the door of the coop, came in at a crouch, and carefully closed the door. CJ had found some mats and part of a children's table in an empty house; she pushed the mats over, and Detlev sat down, attention entirely on Eren. With a wave of his hand, he increased the intensity of CJ's candle flame.

CJ sighed. "I wish I could do that."

"Want me to show you?"

"Ah, Dhana has. Sometimes I can do it. Other times it's like trying to catch raindrops. I guess there has to be lots and lots of magic in the air before I can gather it. Wow." She looked at Detlev critically. His clothes looked rumpled and slept-in, with a few slices here and there in his long riding coat—sword-cuts. "Don't you ever sleep?"

He smiled. "Whenever I can. Which isn't as often as I'd like." His face looked much the same as usual, but the skin around his eyes was tense as he regarded Eren. He touched her forehead. Five, ten breaths passed.

"I tried that. Bunch of times," CJ said at last. "All I could get was a weird feeling, like being in a giant cave, one that echoes." She grimaced. "Be okay?" She finally forced the question out.

"I think so." Detlev's tone was reassuring, and CJ's shoulders dropped as Detlev lifted his hand. "What's wrong?"

CJ's chin ground against one knee, her face burning. Finally she gave him a terrible grimace, and said, "You're not going to, like, switch back?"

"No."

"Um, I didn't think so. Whatever I thought before you rescued ol' David, afterward I was pretty sure you guys are really and truly on our side. But Dirk said..." She shrugged sharply. "I hate bullies, and meanness. People have been saying all these nasty things—though it's all guesses. About your past. And why you so suddenly switched a few years ago." A quick look up. "Though I happen to think that a person ought to get a chance to fix mess-ups, and start over. But, um, I guess I don't see why the poopsies—MV— had to act so rotten to Sveneric. It sounds just like they went right back to being Norsundrians."

"Perhaps you should ask Sveneric about that. Or MV."

"Write to MV?" CJ's grimace was even more fierce. "With my luck he's figured out a way to stomp people via paper."

"That interaction between MV and Sveneric was very brief, vocal instead of physical, and it served a purpose."

CJ sighed. "I should know better than to believe stuff third hand." She looked up. "You do know, don't you, what the poopsies are doing?"

"They, like you, are doing their best to carry out their part of the general plan."

"But you're directing them, right?"

"To a certain extent."

"Why didn't you take over command of all of *us* last summer? Everyone was ready for that. It woulda been okay. Except maybe with Tahra."

"There was no need," he said. "People are doing well on their own. In the meantime, I offer you a promise—for whatever value you place on it—that neither I nor Sveneric, nor David, or any of the group, are doing or will do anything to aid Norsunder. Our goal is the same as yours: to defeat the Host and their allies, so soundly they will never be able to act again. How is that?"

"Plain enough. And I believe you, too," she said, gratified and a bit overwhelmed at Detlev's handsome speech. She felt as if she'd grudgingly asked for a glass of water, and had been offered a waterfall into a crystal lake.

Detlev killed the fire with one of his gestures, then said, "Let's get Princess Erenlara to a safer place, shall we?"

"Okay." CJ picked up and pocketed her warm candle. "You know of one, I suppose."

"Did she show you the Hall of Ancestors?"

"Nuh uh. Mentioned it once."

"It might be the best place for her, though it's a bit of a ways from here. On second thought, I know a better."

CJ was not enthusiastic about the prospect of walking all night in the freezing air when she'd had horrible sleep and only one wen-cake since she found Eren, but she said nothing in deference to that assurance of his.

Detlev wrapped Eren securely in the quilt and cloak CJ had scouted out from the empty house, picked her up, and began walking northward to where one of the many Venn mountains bulked against the horizon, blocking the stars.

They walked for a time, until they were well past the riverside village, and then Detlev put Eren down, left CJ to guard her, and vanished into the night, to reappear a short time later with a horse.

The journey from there was a decided blank, as far as CJ was concerned. First she had to ride behind Detlev, which meant she couldn't see where they were going. After a time she felt they were going up, but where she had no idea.

Then, after they dismounted, she realized that sightseeing

was not going to improve. Somehow they found themselves in a tunnel. She was never sure how Detlev did that, between dismounting, picking Eren up, and sending the horse off. The tunnel was utterly dark, miserably cold, and smelled forebodingly of damp stone. Memories of dungeons crowded into CJ's mind.

"Can't we have a light?" she finally ventured, after a long, stumbling walk in thick darkness.

"There might be wards against that," came the answer. "There used to be, centuries ago. Go ahead and grab my coat, if you like."

"Groanboils," she muttered—but her hand reached, knocked into Eren's blankets, moved back, located a fold of Detlev's long coat, and she hung on.

And was glad. That was a *very* long walk. And it's all very well to say *Use your other senses*, but what's to rejoice in hearing the occasional moans of wind in unseen tunnels, or smelling different cross-draft mixes of moss and wet stone?

After a time she became aware that the air, though still cold, was much more bearable: still, but dry, and neither warm nor cold. They had to be a ways inside a mountain.

Golden light flared, and Detlev stopped walking.

"Wow," CJ said inadequately.

They'd arrived at a long room carved out of rock. Three levels were visible in the light of the fire that Detlev had brought to life. Above arched stone accesses the smoothed walls were painted with beautiful patterns, mostly stylized spring greenery highlighted with softly glowing gold leaf, everything leading to a vast mosaic, made of glittering pieces of rock and hammered gold, of a great white tree with interwoven roots in knotwork, and equally interwoven branches formed around a crowned sun. Ash and elm had been carved into the surrounding walls in silver patterns of knotwork.

"Wow," CJ said again, following Detlev up some wide, shallow steps that had been decorated with tile in mosaic.

On the upper level there was a softly rushing stream that emerged from the wall, fed a wide pool, fell plashing down a stone parapet, and disappeared in a narrow causeway. Detlev lowered Eren to the tile flooring beside the pool, and made sure she was still warmly wrapped.

CJ flopped gratefully down at Eren's golden head as Detlev sat at Eren's other side.

"Now," he said. "Tell me what happened."

Perimeter watch at Efael's HQ

Mildred jerked soggily out of a heavy sleep when knuckles rapped on her skull.

Her eyelids peeled unwillingly open. She found MV's eyes, merely dark lines in the weak light. He had a gray muffler wrapped around the upper and lower portions of his head. The cold was bitter, the snow coming down as hard as ever.

She stretched up slowly from the rock she'd crouched behind, and glanced skyward. Only the faintest glow in the thick clouds indicated where Erhal was in its daily path, far to the north.

They'd got into position just after dawn, and MV had let her have first rest. Noon, now. She'd had a full watch. Why did it feel like five heartbeats?

She swung her arms, and nodded at MV indicating she was awake. He promptly slid down into the spot she'd just vacated, folding his long length and resting head on knees.

She stared down at the curve of road below. It was barely discernible in the driving snow. South road. Used fewer times than the east, according to their observations. She, Detlev, and MV had been slated to take the east, but with Detlev being called off on some emergency, they'd switched around.

Somehow, having Detlev gone felt like half the group had abandoned them. For all she knew he's great with the talk and magic, and slow in action... Yeah. Right. She didn't believe that for an eyeblink. Though she'd never seen Detlev so much as touch a weapon, his boys all insisted that he was the best, so much better that the only one he could truly spar with was Siamis. Everything else was merely teaching.

Just let this be a long, cold, wet, dreary wait.

Though—this was jolting to think of—not everyone was waiting. Jilo, Yanli, and Shontande had to be inside right now, taking the biggest risk as they searched for that general.

She did not let herself consider the alternative, but glanced behind her, though she knew that the huge fortress was on the other side of the huge slope beyond her right shoulder. And— over that way—Rolfin, Retren, and Crow lay freezing behind some rocks, looking down on the eastern stretch of road.

Mildred turned her attention to the south road.

Maybe it was worth it after all, though when they'd finally

slogged into position, she'd just wanted to collapse. Instead, MV had made her help him tie a thin line of twine around two rocky spires, at riders' neck height. In the snow, the cord was totally invisible.

Conserve strength, she scolded herself — aware of that sense of a stone of granite right below her ribs. To dismiss it, she pulled a chunk of wrapped waybread from her inner pocket and began forcing down bites with mouthfuls of fresh snow.

The sun moved a couple finger-spans.

A couple more...

The snow began to intensify, and she could no longer see the sun's position at all. A tall gray shadow loomed next to her. As it sank down to her level, she peered through the flocking flakes, and saw MV's eyes squinting rearward.

"It's quiet," she said, lifting her voice over the moaning wind. "Go ahead and sleep. You've got time till sundown."

"Can't." She felt rather than saw his grin. "Snow keeps melting down my damn collar, and my butt's frozen." He squinted upward. "No sun anywhere. Guess at the time?"

"Four. Five, maybe." And, after a stretch of silence, "Tell me something."

MV gave an interrogative grunt.

"MV initials?"

"Yep."

"What do they signify?"

"Mal Venn," he said, clearly surprised that she'd ask.

"I wondered," she said, "if you were capable of any kind of conversation outside the cut and the thrust."

MV snorted a laugh. "Want art, go talk to Lirendi."

"What I want is to stay awake. Look! Sun's gotta be going down. Light's going blue."

He shrugged.

Taking that as permission to ask further questions, she said, "So you come from Erenlara's country?"

"Nah. Well, ancestors did, but eighteen hundred years ago. Mal Venn's usually a surname. Used by people outside the homeland. Mark their proud origins. In my case, Geranda."

"Do you remember Geranda?"

"All I remember is the stable," he said with a reminiscent laugh. "Royal stable. Several hundred horses. My job was to pitch hay, and wand shit."

After a moment of silence, she said, "Go on."

"Not much to tell. Father was related to the king, second

heir. Had me as part of a plot that didn't work. King put me in the stables—I was four at the time—until he could decide what to do. Capable of killing brats, but not royally born ones. Might give the disaffected ideas. Detlev came along. Took me off his hands."

"Have you gone back?"

"Once or twice. Visit. Cousin's a good hand at ruling. Don't want to make problems for him."

"That's how I feel about my homeland," she said, surprised. "Of course the place never did feel like *home*, since I was a prisoner for most of my time there."

"Home?" he asked, surprising her again. She wasn't sure he'd even listened.

"Eh, I discovered it's people more than place."

"Yep."

"That the way Detlev raised the pack of you?"

"More or less. Some have relations. Makes a difference. Don't know why. Not David. He likes Senrid, but he has no ambition in Marloven Hess. That never worked with Laban. We tried to beat it out of him, scorn it out of him, but he's always been loyal to that scrap of land at the southeast end of Drael. What about you? Say we live through this one. You going back to Geth?"

"Don't know."

"Ought to world hop a little. Look around."

She laughed. "Truth is, Dak talked me into trying to learn magic, but the Geth mages didn't like my background. So I came here."

"Prejudice?"

"Prudence," Mildred said with a shrug. "I can see their view: deposed princess. Martial skill. Suddenly wants to learn magic? Not a promising combination, if nobody believes me when I say I don't want to be tied to governing."

MV snorted his version of a laugh, then said, "Tell me about this guardian of yours. What styles did he teach you?"

Mildred groaned. "As if I didn't get enough of that back in the wanderers' city."

"From Les Rhoderan?"

"Yep."

"He was a shit. I just want to compare, because here we are. Styles?"

"Only if you tell me what you rowdies learnt from Siamis. I hear his name over and over, Siamis this used to teach this, Siamis an expert at that. But all I saw in Mearsies Heili was him in the library, or writing, or listening to Atan and Tahra yapping away in the throne room. But then, his body is really tight —"

"I'm gonna puke." MV moaned. "All right, we'll swap, one for one, if only so I don't have to hear about Siamis's pretty hair, or his pretty face, or his pretty ass."

"It's a great ass, and I don't usually even look at boys," Mildred protested, grinning.

MV rolled his eyes, having so far hidden his own reaction to Mildred — who was exactly the kind of girl he liked most. "What styles?"

Nineteen

Old royal wing – Land of the Venn

CJ SAID TO DETLEV, "She took a whole bottle of kinthus, near as I can tell. It's because of something that she said. Ugh! I'm not making sense!"

And she launched into a rambling, fast-spoken tale of her adventures with Eren, beginning with the girls' arrival in the Land of the Venn and going through most of the experiences they subsequently shared.

It was a relief to talk, to say everything that came into her mind, for Detlev did not get impatient.

"Funny, those towns on the sea. Some of the inland ones, too, but mostly the ones on the sea. They all have those slanted roofs, the short side on the west. I never saw one place with a door on the west wall, or a window. Standing on that side and looking east, you'd think the houses are all windowless boxes. Eren said that's because all their weather comes from the west, and the winds too, and maybe that's why these people are so, so serious. Anyway, you know what it's like, running on walls? Some of the towns we were in, I'd only recognize again from the walls..."

Slowly a picture began to emerge from the torrent of words. CJ never complained about any of the considerable hardships the girls had endured day and night. CJ related the funny exchanges, or moments, or the successful ones, and her own unsuccessful events were outlined with a grimace or a colorful insult or two. It was not, however, difficult to find a pattern among the myriad images and impressions CJ offered.

Erenlara had traveled the length of her country, driving herself to aid the people in as many ways as possible, but always she sought to break the enchantment binding her judicial representatives. (Her army was mostly gone, shifted to reinforce the occupation troops elsewhere in the north. Another cause for sorrow.)

Again and again she asked CJ to tell her about her experiences with making her unity—Dena Yeresbeth—and to relate what she'd heard about those who had it. This was between episodes of fun, danger, and laughter; Eren was a considerate hostess, but she in turn needed the reassurance that a thirteen-year-old could make her unity, that she could live up to a standard that seemed impossible to CJ, but that Eren believed, with all her strength and conviction, that *he* had established.

"*He* was her brother, I guess," CJ said, drawing a shaky breath. "I do know she adored her elder brother. When she was comparing herself to him, she never said his name, just 'he', always, always, when she was hardest on herself, when she couldn't do something impossible, like when she would try and try to contact me mind to mind, until I could tell her head ached. Then she'd say she was weak, and ignorant, that 'he' could do it without even thinking, with no effort. But I can tell she is, like, almost there—her mind is like, oh, Lyren-Sartora, just that one thing is missing. Meanwhile the enchantment over her guardian guys, she calls 'em the Arm of the Crown, and the Eyes of the Crown, it remained unbroken, and they traveled around and enforced the will of the Norsundrians. And nothing that Eren tried ever worked. Does that make sense?"

"It does. Go on."

"Last week was weird. I didn't even think about it being weird at the time because ... oh, the weather was so strange, sometimes almost warm, which meant lots of thunder, and we always seemed to be awake at night, running on fences and spying by the light of streaming torches, but we were acting kind of desperate. We got chased like four times."

She leaned over to drink from her hands, then sat up, and as Detlev waited, with his whole attention, CJ sucked in a short breath and went on.

"Eren did a couple things where the Eye guys could see us. I think she hoped that seeing her, in action, would change 'em.

Yeah. I think so. I mean, she never said. Never complained, just looked more and more tense. Determined. We'd laugh about the mud. Damp beds. Like that. But I knew because on that last one, one of the Eye-guys chasing us was this tall lady with brown hair streaked with gray, and Eren kept looking back at her, like, she didn't want to recognize her but did. I saw when we got near a lit window that Eren was crying. You know, tears, but no sound. Though when we got to the inn those tears were gone."

CJ sighed, shifted position, and rolled an expressive eye toward Detlev. His gaze was on the great tree mosaic, its gold shimmering in the firelight.

CJ straightened her shoulders. "I'm not telling it very well, and don't give me any hogwash about I'm doing fine. I don't know what to say and what to leave out, or where to put my guesses. Um. The worst thing was just the other night. She found another one she knew. A youngish guy. Younger than ol' Rel. She called this one by name, and he didn't react, that is not to his name, just said we were under arrest and were to come away. She said *Can't you remember your vows?* over and over, right in front of his face, looking hard right into his eyes, and then, *I will not go unless you protect me.* Now, *I'd* never say that to any big guy with a sword like that, former good guy or not, but it acted on him just like the jab of an icicle on bare feet. Then he took that sword—they used to not carry them, but they do now—and said, *Come with me,* and she said, *If you strike me you are forever forsworn,* and turkeys! That was just like a mushroom pie in the phizz! Like *that.*"

CJ jerked her face back, as if she'd been slapped by an invisible hand.

"And he said, *If you resist I am to strike to kill,* in this yukky voice. And Eren cried *Do it, Bodvara. If the act breaks the magic then I have done something and if not I cannot live with this blindness anyway,* and I thought, wow, we're in for it now. She's going as loony as them, and no mistake, and she stood right there, in front of him—and, um, well, I sorta tackled her, and when we stopped rolling, I put my mouth next to her ear and yelled *RUN!*"

CJ wiped her brow, her eyes enormous and dark with exhaustion and tension. "She did, but she looked Siamised—ah, hem! I mean enchanted. Weird. When we got to the inn she did that," pointing to half-moon scabs on Erenlara's still, pale flesh, near her hairline. "She covered her face like this, with her hands, dug in her nails, and said, Why am I so blind? and I started blathering at her—then she seemed more normal at once. Said she was sorry, and tried the rest of the evening to laugh, because you know, I'd also gotten some sour letters from Dhana of late, although she says now that Clair's doing all right, and I ought not to worry, Clair says."

CJ sighed.

"So then she said she had to see someone about a thing, and didn't come back, and didn't. I knew she wasn't mad at me—I was worried—so I went to find her. That inn we'd stayed at a bunch of times, the people are really nice. Have kids, but all are away fighting, or running as messengers. Anyway I went there first, thinking I could get word, and found out she was there, and they thought she was sleep. Well, she was on the pallet in the attic, but she had the bottle of that kinthus stuff, and a note."

She shifted, pulled a scrap of paper from her pocket, grimacing as she handed it to Detlev, who unfolded it, saw that it was written in an eye-pleasing hand.

> *CJ. I find I have to try, and alone, so that responsibility*
> *rests solely with me. If I die, I do not appoint an heir, but*
> *I beg you to ask—*

CJ waited until Detlev's hand lowered, then said, "Yecchy, eh? She must've taken the stuff first, and then splatted right before she could write the name. And the worst thing is, I don't know who'd be the person she'd ask. Probably not a relative, if she has any left, because they wouldn't have to be asked—and that 'he' she mentioned, her brother, is already dead."

Detlev said, "Did you save the bottle?"

"No, I didn't think to. I picked it up and sniffed it. No smell, and no color staining the inside, but when I sniffed, there was this funny feeling here." She smacked the heel of her hand against her forehead. "Like fog, or cotton, in my brain. I remembered later she asked a buncha questions about this white kinthus junk, that the Norsundrians use for questioning."

"It has a number of uses," Detlev said, looking down at Eren's still form. "Some are benign, such as the easing of the sick or wounded. But it's dangerous, and for a number of centuries its use was forbidden."

"Cuz of the Norsundrians?"

"No. It was used at one time in rituals that forced a dream state. Madness and death were frequent enough results that it was generally suppressed, especially as its presence in food or drink could not be detected until too late. People with Dena

Yeresbeth can sense it, as you yourself did."

"What's it done to her? Is she, like, permanently dreaming?"

"Close enough."

"Well, to finish, a search was coming so the inn-folk helped me stash her in that chicken coop, and then I wrote you. Can you do anything?" She gasped, and then collapsed in relief when he nodded once. "When? Now? Or do you need anything? Is there anything I can do?"

He smiled a little. "You can. Write to Dhana. Have her transfer in hot food, and request her to send fresh stores, enough for a week."

"Dhana," CJ said. "So—" She asked in a small, uneasy voice, "It's really all right at home? I've been running so hard here, when Dhana says it's all right, and Seshe says that Clair wants me to stay here and help Eren, but she doesn't write me herself— of course I know all those refugees must be keeping her busy —"

"Clair is busy, and she's also in good hands," Detlev said. "Right now, we need to get Eren back on her feet."

"But, if Dhana can transfer things here, maybe she should transfer us home. Wouldn't a nice bed in the white palace be good for Eren?"

"Every transportation must be a necessary one, as it may be our last. And I believe Eren would be better waking in this place, which is an old living space belonging to her family."

"All right," CJ said. "And I'll stay and help her."

Detlev smiled. "Thank you."

CJ turned away, her face burning, and reached for her paper.

Detlev took a deep breath, laid his hands across Erenlara's brow, and shut his eyes.

⁂

Mildred and MV had gradually altered from trading anecdotes about their early martial training to arguing about which styles were better, a vigorous conversation they both thoroughly enjoyed.

Then her exceedingly sharp eyes caught a vague movement in the stippled curtain of falling snow. No more than a slight irregularity, but it came from the place where the road should emerge from round the cliff edge. She stiffened.

MV turned. He stood up slowly, pulling both sword and long knife.

Mildred glanced down in vague surprise: her well-trained hands had already produced two of her own weapons. Her shoulders shrugged her cape off as unnecessary weight.

Weird flickering then resolved into bouncing torches against the gathering gloom. Next, they heard gear clanking and harnesses jingling.

Then they saw two columns of Norsundrians ride into view. Which had never happened before.

Stunned, dismayed, Mildred turned to look at MV, who ripped his muffler free and cast it into the wind.

Ought to world hop. Mildred uttered an ironic laugh.

The column neared their point. Another twenty five paces to their cord...

Ten Norsundrians—six of them Black Knives.

She never would have chosen this world, or this time, for her death—but he would be a fine companion to die with.

MV tipped his head toward the oncoming column. His eyes were wide and gleaming in the reflected orange torchlight, his brows slanting wickedly. He grinned at Mildred in a way that hereto only his own inner circle had seen him grin, and he looked like someone else entirely.

Giving in to impulse, she hooked a wrist around his neck, sword still gripped in her hand, pulled his face to hers, and kissed him soundly. He kissed her back, his warmth shooting heat right through her.

She laughed, the sound ripped away by the wind. "Let's go."

And while in the ancient royal wing of the Land of the Venn, Detlev followed the one connection that tied Erenlara's spirit to her weakened flesh, Mildred and MV raced downhill, sending snow flying before them. The snow they kicked up, plus that falling, plus the glare of the flickering torches effectively hid them from view of the totally unsuspecting Norsundrians until the front two riders were swept clean out of their saddles.

Two figures emerged from the swirling snow to leap onto the backs of the riderless horses. MV and Mildred wheeled the mounts and rode straight at the Black Knives.

An explosion of fire, shouts, red-glowing blades and desperate movement focused all time and meaning to the moment, measured by the thunder of Mildred's heartbeat.

Astonishment at still being alive after the initial charge gave way to a singing exaltation, of fiery exhilaration that was all the fiercer for the knowledge that, any moment, it would surely end.

Wrists, hands, shoulders, knees all responded in a blur of continual motion. She and MV were surrounded, but no one there was as deadly accurate and fast as MV. His being stronger and farther in reach meant that Mildred rode as back-shield. There was no communication between them, nor needed there to be; after months of hard drilling, he knew where she was and what she was doing even as she knew how and where he led.

Fire and steel whirled out of the darkness at them, then they fell away. The parries went uncounted, but some part of Mildred's mind registered the hits she made. Six, seven ... eight ...

Blood singing, laughter on her lips, body responding perfectly to accelerating demands, Mildred glimpsed a profoundly bittersweet insight into the joy of battle —

"Efael! Here!" an enemy shouted, and as both Mildred and MV's heads snapped to look, a load of half-melted sleet was slung at their eyes, and MV, in the front, took it all.

Blinded, MV forced his horse around in a last attempt to cover by Mildred's retreat. She knew that was what he intended, but as his blade smashed blindly through the first attackers despite no vision, two deadly knives flickered at either side of MV, then the Norsundrian horse crashed down into the snow, stabbed by a black-handled Norsundrian knife.

Rage blew away all the joy as MV spun around and fell, too, his weapon flying. Smash, stab, thrust! She vaulted off the horse to land next to him.

Blood splashed everywhere, as the wounded animal kicked wildly to its feet and galloped away. Blood welled in obscene red ribbons from MV, who lay on his back, arms outflung. Standing over him, a foot either side of his head, Mildred swung his heavier blade two-handed. Blood ran in her eyes, but her sword whined and sang with blurring speed that drove the knife-wielding assassins back: their strategy was always to attack joints until the victim was helpless; then came the thousand cuts.

"Come and take me!" she shouted, and as pain exploded one leg in sparkling orange shards, she went down on one knee, still protecting the fallen MV. "Come on, come on!"

⸻

Detlev sat back, and passed a hand over his eyes.

CJ, who'd been hovering nearby during the interminable

ten minutes or so, crouched down. "Is she okay? *You* okay?"

Detlev blinked, looking down at Eren's face, which was still pale. Her breathing had changed, though. "She will waken shortly. I must go. Remember what I said about food and water. She should recover her strength before she leaves."

Eren sighed, her lips moving. Her head turned slowly to one side, then the other.

Detlev swung to his feet.

"Wait! Just a *minute*? She'll want to know—well, everything!" CJ waved her hands.

Detlev said, "Your common sense is the best thing for her right now. You and this place. You will do fine."

He disappeared, and two heartbeats later Eren's eyes opened.

CJ held her breath as her dark blue eyes searched the vaulted chamber as though to find something specific, or someone, and then came at last to CJ.

"Was there ... another?"

"Yup. Old Detsie-poopsie-potsie. Wow, you scared me! Here," CJ said nervously as Eren's eyes narrowed. "You're supposed to eat and drink."

But Eren had turned her head to search again. She looked up at the paintings, glowing silent and golden above.

Then a slow, deep breath. "Very well," she said at last.

With the last of her fading consciousness Mildred watched Detlev appear in the beating torchlight. He only had the one sword, but between one heartbeat and the next his long coat swirled as he leaped, cracked the skull of a Black Knife with a flying back kick, swept the man's weapon from his hand, and landed. Then he charged the remaining Norsundrians, both blades glowing red in vertiginous arcs as blackness enfolded her...

Twenty

Cave outside Efael's lair

MILDRED WOKE TO A world of dark red. Pain. It took an effort to open her eyes, to discover that she was moving—swaying and jolting.

Snowflakes fell on her face.

She tried not to grunt, but the pain brought the noise past her throat. She squinted up at a wad of dark cloth, held by two strong ungloved brown hands. Beyond that, two muscular forearms in a thin coat. Rolfin. From a weird angle, for she was looking up at him. Oh. He was carrying her. On ... a cloak, or something. He and someone a day's ride away across the volcano of pain, down there by her feet. Rolfin saw her open eyes and gave her a quick grin.

Her mouth worked, but sound just wouldn't come. Only those damn grunts.

Rolfin murmured quietly, "Of course I won't drop you—until I find a suitable high cliff. Take it easy."

Her eyes closed gratefully ... and opened, stark, when someone touched the agony in one leg.

"Hang on," someone whispered. Identity slipped away as strong fingers gripped her wrists in such a way that her own fingers could grip their wrists.

"Don't touch. It." That took all the strength she had.

The grip on her wrists loosened as a face hovered near. It

was Yanli. "I just want to check the bandage. May I?"

"Look." Mildred swallowed. "Don't touch."

"All right," Yanli said cheerfully, and Mildred let out the breath she'd been holding, shivering in waves. She watched as Yanli very carefully lifted away Mildred's sliced pant leg. "Hmm," Yanli said. "I just want to peek under the bandage. It'll only take a moment."

"No," Mildred said, gripping her fists again as sweat broke out all over her head. The anguish throbbed harder in her knee, sending bolts of lightning up to her eyeballs. She squinted at Yanli's round face, and her narrow, wide-set eyes. To distract Yanli from trying to torture that leg, Mildred said, "You. Don't. Look like Siamis. At all." Her voice was a thread.

Yanli's cheery smile increased. "That's because we're not related. Oh, he insists we are. But I think—here, may I just quick lift this cloth? See, I'm only touching cloth."

Mildred felt cold air on her knee, not cold enough to numb it. The movement of air hurt. "Isn't Siamis your father?"

Yanli glanced behind Mildred, and as the firm, gripping hands took her wrists again, she went on, "Want to hear it all? I can be fast, as I tell you. Just a tiny bit of cleaning."

"Yes—n—argh," Mildred yelped.

Yanli began talking quickly, as her deft fingers worked. "See, when Siamis was first sent out from the Beyond by Efael, he was not even your age. In physical age. He was very bad and very smart, but he met Isa Cassadas, who was very good, and very much smarter. He was supposed to be hunting and killing, but he liked talking to her better, and then not talking—meaning they got romantic. Teenagers!" She hooted a soft laugh.

The bandage lifted away, and Mildred stiffened all over, but then came a dribble of water so cold it was numbing. "Oh, nice and clean," Yanli crooned. "No, lie back and relax, and I'll tell you the rest of that story. They figured out a way around Efael's orders, and Siamis decided he didn't want to be a Black Knife, and that is when he went back to Detlev, and his real training began..." Yanli spoke softly as her hands worked swiftly. "...Detlev took him back into the Beyond, reporting that Isa Cassadas was dead. But he moved her, and she changed her name. She had a baby. Detlev protected that baby, and that baby's baby, and so on, all the way down to me, in the present day, though it wasn't easy when a lot of years passed between visits, and he had to hide it, even from Siamis, who would not have been able to resist going back. Until Detlev got ready to leave

Norsunder, and out it all came. When Siamis found me, I was an orphan after trouble when Perideth let Norsunder into that kingdom, but Siamis and Detlev say I'm the descendant of Isa Cassadas and Siamis. You know what I think?"

Mildred hung onto every word, as a way not to think about what was happening with her knee. Her utterly ruined knee, and she might not walk again —

"*I* think, I might have one drop of blood from each," Yanli said, wrenching Mildred's attention back. "And maybe a speck of blood from Adamas Dei, who they all say is the father of the Cassadas family. But the rest of it is mine, mine, mine. There!"

The grip on Mildred's wrists loosened.

Yanli sat back. "All done. It really needed the bandage change," she added apologetically. "I did it as fast as I could."

Mildred gritted her teeth as the throbbing panged, and she slid back down into darkness again.

She woke to voices, and a terrifying whining sound. An inhuman, shearing shriek, not human or animal, but larger and far more deadly: the wind. Her eyes opened.

Jilo sat nearby, back to the stone wall, arms crossed on knees, head pillowed on them.

Water, Mildred thought, and tried to get up, to be flattened when instinct tried to bend her knees. Had she made a noise?

Jilo's head jerked up. "Hey. You're awake." He gave her an anxious look, and a flickering smile, then reached behind and grabbed a cup. "Want a drink?"

"Uhn." He took that as a yes, lifted her head, and she sucked down water. When it was done, she assessed herself. From the stinging pulses elsewhere on her body, she understood that she'd taken smaller cuts. She worked her lips, and observed, "I'm alive."

Jilo grinned. That is, his mouth grinned, but his eyes looked pained.

"Plan?" She drew a breath. "MV?"

Jilo's gaze shifted to the cup that he turned around in his fingers. "Plan worked. Turns out Efael didn't bother with more traps, just a few flimsy tracers. Easy as sweeping cobwebs. We got in. Freed Efael's prisoners. Siamis took them away."

"Locks were worthless. Efael's arrogance." Yanli's smooth-cheeked face moved into view, a smile quirking the wide-spaced crescent eyes. "Shontande started an excellent fire in Efael's personal rooms when we found the snow lifting momentarily."

"But?"

"Here's a pastry, cheese and egg and onion. You are to eat it all." Jilo lifted Mildred's head and propped it on his knee, and Yanli held out the bread.

Mildred forced down a few bites, as Yanli went on with running comments, mostly about the ugliness of Efael's castle, and trying to decide which disaster inside was his own taste or leftover from the Sonscarnas.

But Mildred had not forgotten her second question. She turned her head, and saw at last the long shape lying so still in a little alcove by the water. "MV?" she asked, and this time they nodded.

"Not dead. But near." Jilo looked down, his face somber.

Yanli said, "Strike right across the gut. Broken ribs, internal bleeding. Detlev says that kind of thing is beyond him." She sighed. "Way, way beyond me, and I told Siamis I'd come to do any medic needs." She blinked a couple of times, but her eyelashes were wet as she muttered, "Earliest thing I remember about MV is his bragging that he won't wear chain mail. Slows him down."

"We don't have any anyway," Jilo pointed out.

Yanli lifted a shoulder, as if to say that she could have found some. She wiped her eyes, drew in a shaky breath, and said, "We can't transport him, even if Svir wasn't in the fortress right now, nosing around."

"Detlev?"

"Out finding Crow, who slipped off the trail. Shontande and Detlev went back to search. Rolfin is watching the castle."

Mildred sighed, and lay back down flat. "In a blizzard? I can hear it." She tried to make herself comfortable, but her leg hurt too much. "Crow's never been clumsy, and he's been walking pretty straight. What do you mean, slipped?"

"Fainted, possibly," Yanli murmured. "He said nothing to anyone but Rolfin said he niffed pain just before Crow disappeared. Thinks he took a hit in the fight—they caught up at the end, right after Detlev dropped the last Black Knife. Good riddance," she whispered fiercely. "Siamis says they were horrible people before Efael got to them."

"That stubborn twit," Mildred muttered; she didn't hear anything Yanli said about the Black Knives. Her mind was on Crow. "You'd think after all the time I wasted on him, he'd learn." Scalding tears burned in her eyes, and her voice wriggled like a beached fish. She clenched her teeth against sick regret in her chest.

Morning brought Rolfin, stamping the snow caked on his feet. "Storm's breaking up." He stumbled once, not from ice but exhaustion, yet even so his eyes turned Ret's way in question.

Ret shook his head, gaze downward.

Rolfin's eyes closed, keeping pain inside. Then he jerked around, slurped down water, took a bite from some cheese, and rolled up his cloak next to MV's alcove in protective proximity. They heard his breathing go deep almost in moments.

Mildred lay staring upward all day, her eyes dry, her jaw aching from the grit of her teeth. Braced for every breath to be MV's last.

At sunset Shontande and Crow fumbled into the cave, ghost-pale from snow and cold. Crow winced as he looked around, rubbing the bruise on his head. No one said anything as he drained a mug of water, munched a bite of bread, and then rolled up.

Their attention was on Shontande, who removed his coat, and his chain-mail, and quilted padding, with extraordinary — almost blind — care.

"Detlev?" Rolfin snapped.

"Detoured the pursuit. Very close one." Shontande smiled wearily in apology as he blinked the sparkling white snowflakes off his eyelashes. He sank down, put his head on his knees, and went abruptly limp.

Damnation, MV thought with increasing irritation. Still lost.

He looked around again, though the poorly lit halls continued to look vaguely familiar without being recognizable. Have I been this way before? Doesn't matter. It all looks alike. Anyway it was easier to drift along than to stop and try to map some kind of trail. Only why was he so damned tired?

Try one of the shadowed ways? Nah. Detlev said once ... what was it? Ah, never mind. Light makes more sense.

He kept drifting.

Midnight.

Mildred's jaw unclenched when the shadows in the cave

entrance flickered and Detlev appeared. He crossed the cavern, snow on his brows as his eyes the color of the winter-sea took everyone in. He knelt beside MV, brushed questing fingers over MV's bandages, and then his forehead.

All Mildred's nerves strained to see him look up and smile, to hear him say that it would be all right, that of course he could fix everything.

But when he did at last look up, and they were all waiting, he said, just barely audible, "I can't find him."

Orders?
Detlev. Something familiar. Detlev. Yes, look for him, that was it, wasn't it? But where?
Who?

Jilo protested, "What do you mean you can't find him?"

"He's lost the tie between the physical and non-physical."

Jilo saw the stricken faces, and asked what some would not ask, and some could not ask: "I thought you had ways of calling people in that realm."

"One way." Detlev sketched a gesture in the air. "I could find him with the dyr functioning as beacon, except Ilerian would find us first. Only our healers of old could find the severed, but we have none."

He bent his head and tried again.

⸺⸻⸺

MV was mildly glad to note that the halls were melting away, and there, far below, lights moved in patterns. Tiny lights. Interesting. Was he flying, then? Always wanted to give that a try outside of Tsauderei's valley.

He drifted effortlessly now. Yeah, flying. He was almost done, not that he could remember what he was doing, but it no longer mattered, nothing mattered —

Stopped.

Looked, startled, into a face dominated by eyes the color of grass. "Where d'you think you're going?" A familiar voice laughed. A mocking, goading laugh.

Sight sharpened. And hearing.

MV found that he hadn't left the halls after all. Irritation made him stir, but for some reason he couldn't find his voice.

"Twit," his companion said, laughing again. "I heard you whining half the world away, you weak-kneed slacker. I hadn't expected to see you give in so easy when we did meet again. You haven't the balls of a snake."

Found it!

"Soulsucking…" MV began. His throat was strange. Had he been in the snow too long?

"Not I, but *he*'ll be on you fast enough if you don't move your lazy ass. Shit for brains."

MV's annoyance increased. "What's it to you? Who are you, anyway?"

"Shall I claim to be your conscience?" The other laughed, that damn mocking laugh that irritated the crap out of MV. He *knew* that laugh. "You dumped 'em and ran."

"Ran out? Who ran?"

The other moved enticingly across MV's vision again, and paused in one of those glare-bright doorways behind. "You. Ran, like a rabbit. Ran like a mouse. Squeak, squeak!"

A step back.

MV ignored the waves of thick air, the glare, and he stepped after. Another step. Another, keep that turd in sight.

"I know where Detlev is," came the goading voice.

"Detlev?" MV remembered Detlev — wasn't he supposed to be helping — he was! He was! How could he forget?

"Detlev," he said.

"And he doesn't know what I know. What a priceless opportunity for a stab in the back, eh? What a show for the Host! Want to watch, shitbird?"

"Yeah," MV snarled — and lunged.

The other moved effortlessly away.

Frustrated at his slow speed and lack of strength, MV concentrated, and lunged again. He chased the other halfway down a hall before the taunting laugh echoed back.

This time MV recognized the sound. "Imry, you shit!" he yelled, and charged after.

Imry stayed just ahead. MV's speed increased as they ran, but Imry was always that much faster, his mocking voice streaming back, making little sense. "Damn what a mess. Have to admit those blades do cut sharp … there. And there. Looks like your belt buckle kept 'em from gutting you to the spine. What were you doing, sleeping? Just a slice in the top of this intestine … and there! This artery, a nick, but that's all it takes…"

MV didn't listen. Because he sped faster, and remembered

where Detlev was, and what they were doing, and then he remembered the plan, and Mildred standing over him, fighting off four thin-bladed silhouettes.

"There. There. There! Ha ha ha, oh you're going to hate it so much, you'll remember me every damn time you draw a breath…"

Three strikes of white heat hurled MV back into his yammering physical self, and with a gesture of impatience and challenge to the old enemy, he dropped down and took custody.

And slept.

MV had been lying still as death until, abruptly, three tiny bolts of blue-white around his midsection startled them, and MV's entire body jolted. He whooped in a breath, then fainted. But gone was the shallow, slowing breathing; he breathed deeply. Normally.

Detlev looked up. "He's back," he said, and sighed. "When he wakes, he will need water."

He got up, stepped away, and eased around the periphery of the room as everyone began talking at once.

Detlev was the only one, as yet, who knew that Imry was responsible for calling MV back, and sealing whatever it was that he had sensed deep in MV's body; MV was still a mess, but those fuses had turned a mortal wound into a nasty one. And in connecting MV once more to the world, Imry was of course able to identify the time, and the place, where MV's body lay.

Which meant Imry knew exactly where they were.

Detlev withdrew noiselessly into the passage beyond their cavern. He knew that reaction would have struck Imry hard, but once he forced his way out of that, he'd use Detlev as a Destination.

Detlev walked into the farther corridor to meet him, as light flared into being.

Twenty-one

HAVING NO SUN TO guide them in measuring time, CJ and Erenlara slept through a night and day. When they woke, they lay in the fuzzy warm woven rugs that Dhana had sent, and ate, and listened to the water flow.

At last they woke enough to talk, and CJ said, "Let's eat. Detsie said to stay here at least a week."

"Detsie," Eren echoed, with a pensive smile.

"You do know that he was the one who got you out of wherever you were?"

"Did you ask him to come?"

"Yep. Well, who else?"

"What was his judgment?"

CJ wrinkled her nose. "On what?"

"On my action."

"None. What happened after you took the stuff? You started this note — where — oh well, I guess I lost it." CJ hunted fruitlessly for the crumpled paper. "How was I to know what to do about your kingdom? I guess I woulda put it to ol' Atan, even though she's never been there."

"'Twould serve," Eren said slowly. "I am sorry, CJ. Acts of desperation perhaps are better carried out away from helpless bystanders."

CJ hunched her shoulders, looking away from that intent

gaze.

Eren went on, "It was strange. Very frightening, at first. I lay down, and then fell, inside. Through a vast space. Wheeling stars. Darting shadows. Almost at once there was a sense of great danger, very great, but someone came to me, a winged spirit in silver. Someone young, and merry, and a girl. She chided me, but kindly, for what I had done, and she took me to a place of great beauty, where dwell creatures not human, and they kept me safe, and then Detlev found me. He was only there an instant, long enough to bid me to follow the silver spirit back. I obeyed, and the silver spirit showed me how to regain the physical world."

Eren's gaze was at first distant, but then she looked up at the rich gleam of painted patterns running round the high, smooth stone walls. "Yes, it is right to be here. To be reminded of my place in the world, and what must be my work."

"This is an old place, I take it?"

"Very old. My family resided here at one time. It leads to the most ancient part of the city. Shall we wander through it, and I will tell you about the Venn of those days?"

CJ agreed enthusiastically, and so they packed up their things, and began their walk. Eren, whose abilities were now great indeed, bent her new sensitivities toward easing the tension of her companion, though she could not touch the pool of worry that lay just beneath the surface, and beneath that, sorrow for her dead friend, Diana.

Eren felt it, and tried to learn the subtleties of touch, and of shield. At first the rawness of this new sensitivity were all she could bear, but she soon learned to protect herself, and to protect the integrity of CJ, who had served as catalyst, but did not know how great was the effect of her transparency.

⸻ ◈ ⸻

Cave outside Efael's lair

Imry watched Detlev emerge from the confusing shadows that played beyond the reach of the torch. Though Detlev was unarmed, and walked slowly, Imry wanted his hands free.

He thrust the torch into a crack in the granite, while not shifting his gaze from the advancing figure.

Like the last time they met so briefly outside the entrance to a Selenseh Redian, Imry experienced a spurt of amusement to see that Detlev was a palm-width shorter than he. Otherwise (Imry rarely paid any attention to such things as clothing or the length of one's hair) he looked much the same as he ever had.

Except tired. Detlev didn't bother trying to hide it. He spotted and sank down onto a hassock-sized flat stone some three or four paces away, and there he was, forearms on his knees, empty hands dangling weaponless, looking up expectantly.

"I suppose," said Imry, "even now you're weaving a plan against the likelihood that Svir will shortly appear, along with a couple dozen of Efael's finest?"

Detlev smiled wide—almost laughed. "Wouldn't you?"

"What's more, it will be a plan whose basic elements were dinned into my skull before I was seven." A lift of the chin toward the cavern where MV lay. "But you never taught me that."

"No," said Detlev.

Imry's hand had dropped to the hilt of David's black and gold sword, but the movement of his fingers was restless, bare of intent. "You foresaw the possibility."

"Yes."

"What would you have done with me had I stayed?"

"Why do you want to know?"

Irritation tightened Imry's features. "Why else? Curiosity." He took a step toward the cavern, then stopped, as though listening. Turned. "I wasted a great deal of time that would have been better employed elsewhere, this last year, trying to trap you."

Detlev leaned slowly back, and rested his head against an adjacent stone. "True."

"I did my best."

"There were a couple of close ones."

Imry flushed. "Thank you," he said ironically.

Detlev's smile was completely unchallenging.

Imry took another step, this time toward Detlev. "You never failed to send back some sort of stinger."

"I hope you enjoyed them."

Step, turn. "But you never tried to bring me down, did you?"

"No."

"I thought a couple of times you had missed as well. Unaccountably, at first. But then—with Andri. The first time. With the girl."

"The creeping sentiment of old age."

"Is that what you tell the lighters?"

"Few of them have followed my actions that closely."

"David maintains," Imry said shortly, as energy simmered

in the cold air around them, "That you're still in teacher-mode with me. Now. Thirteen years after I left."

Detlev's smile was faint. "Old habit."

"Don't play with me." Imry's face tightened in anger. "Don't you think I couldn't kill you now? Look at you! You're half asleep! Except for Rolfin, they're worthless as aid." He flicked a hand dismissively toward the front cavern. "Well? Couldn't I?"

Detlev's brows lifted consideringly. "I don't know," he admitted.

"Then why are you provoking me?"

"Give you an out. I haven't, lately, and probably should have."

"I don't see how making me lose my temper is being fair," Imry said with mordant humor. He realized that Detlev had defused him yet again, and went on, "Nobody teaches someone whose attention is elsewhere. David maintains we have much the same relationship we did fifteen years ago. Master and apprentice. Do you think, like he does, that my zestfully pursued goal of nailing you down was the attitude of an apprentice?"

"You hinted at that intention when you left. You were very much an apprentice—however rebellious—then."

"I guess assuming that I'm still merely resisting your authority is preferable to admitting that you made an error in judgment at the start, and could never recover it."

"Do you want assurance?" Detlev retorted without heat. "Here's a platitude I gave you boys early on: that parity is achieved less when the student has understood the lessons, than when he understands the teacher."

Anger narrowed Imry's eyes. He began edgily, "And David thinks—"

But then he remembered David's honest assertions to the contrary, and fell silent.

Detlev had known this moment was inevitable, but he'd hoped it would happen much later. He watched without surprise as Imry registered the truth, and began to consider its implications. Torchlight glittered in Imry's angry eyes, and Detlev began to consider how to end the interview with as little damage as possible.

"So, you've played the longest game of all? You and Svir regard us as so many string-pulled puppets?"

"Svirle might trust a puppet, but only to the measure of the string. You notice he never trusted you at all."

"Implication, my game is child's play next to yours, and I could have been part of it if I'd stayed? I may puke again." Imry closed his eyes, miming acute nausea.

As usual, Detlev cut past the posturing. "No, I will not cut your throat if you put a knife in my hand. You've seen that my methods stop short of murder, and you've seen that you don't like them."

"So I'm free," Imry said nastily, "to rip apart the world as long as I consider it a *worthy* goal?"

Detlev said nothing. Someone else might have felt frightened, sitting there before this angry young man who stood fingering the gold-chased hilt of a sword he obviously knew how to use. Detlev was seeing the raw-knuckled boy who had gazed restlessly into a bleak future.

Then Imry's expression altered, and he turned, eyes wide, on the verge of a laugh. "It *was* all a blind, wasn't it? I almost missed the humor. All of it—you as Norsunder's errand boy, Siamis's flounce. Us. Everything you did, from the very beginning, was mere dust thrown in Ilerian's eyes. And Svir's. To hide the one thing Ilerian wanted—still wants—more than land or crowns: the disirad."

Detlev said nothing.

"Did you *know* it would come back?"

"I did not," Detlev said.

Four thousand years of faith—or insanity. Depended on which way you looked at it. And Ilerian had to know it by now.

Imry said abruptly, "You did take out six of Efael's shit stains, four of whom have been diligently trying to stab me in the back as well as sabotage my command. My mood will probably change in a week."

Detlev accepted the warning with a nod. "MV will be out of here before then."

Imry disappeared.

.

PART THREE

NO ONE, HIBERN TOLD herself firmly, goes to the immense trouble of constructing a lattice without a purpose. She was going to find it—though that would be quite a challenge in this place with no graspable physical component.

She paced through the archive, considering what she had determined so far, which was not much: Detlev had worked a lattice within the lattice that formed the Beyond; whether for idle amusement, or at the command of his masters, or some other purpose, he had keyed this lattice through three layers of misdirection, beginning with the lies in the more recent ten-year reports.

She was going to find it because she had to figure out which motive lay behind it, before she carried her investigations further.

The air that was not air charged with what she defined as incipient lightning, and she sidestepped mentally, as Theronezhe's stone spell shot past her. Ah, he suspected something, or was protecting something? Reducing her to the Beyond's equivalent of a stone statue until Ilerian's return was proof he was agitated: it was also proof that, in spite of his vast armies and his weapons (or maybe because of them? Trust did not appear to be much in evidence in this place) he was not privy to everything that happened in the Garden of the Twelve.

She sidestepped again, mentally setting aside the ghost lattice as well as the structural lattice. Now for a search for …

evidence of motivation?

Everything seemed to lead back to Detlev.

She snapped the archive into existence around her. She could see in any direction, and just about in any previous or present time as long as Norsunder had in some way arrived at the given event in order to capture witness by magic. The Host entertained themselves with these captured moments, either events as they had happened — which required strenuous effort to set up beforehand — or the distortions seen reflected through jumps in time. By now she recognized the ice-numbing taint of Ilerian in many of them, who appeared to be able to move to the past. These were the ones she trusted least.

Efael had generated the greatest number of these entertainments. Most appeared to be magical replications of his perversions outside of Sartorias-deles, to be revisited from the safety of the Garden of the Twelve — it was unclear whether these were for the twins to watch themselves, or for Ilerian's entertainment. Perhaps both. After flicking through a number of these, the victims unknown to Hibern, she found them so vile and spirit-dirtying that she snapped them out of existence. Why not? She was already marked for death once the Host caught up with her. Before that happened, she might as well amuse herself with some judicious tidying.

She paused only when she found the captures of Siamis and Detlev.

It was nearly all she could bear, to see Efael toying with Siamis (or "Siamas" — his name was pronounced differently then, a softer, more euphonious sound, *Syah-mas*, rather than the harder *SYE-ah-miss*, like a hissing snake).

She scowled internally, watching his twelve-year-old bravery, all for nothing, his terror, and at last surrender and abasement. Efael had made a lot of memories of that — some real, some fantasy, possibly forced on Siamis to watch as a threat — obviously revisited much over the centuries. She would have wept, had her body been real; so much cruelty would make angels weep: these images she watched until she comprehended that there was nothing here for the lattice search, and so, with a wave of her hand, she unmade the magic forever.

That left the capitulation of Detlev. Again it was a shock how young he was, but at least he had attained adulthood. It was much less terrible to witness than Siamis's, a flurry of fast action and then a standoff as Siamis was brought forth and brandished. His surrender might have been terrible indeed, but Svir, suave in his exulting, made it clear he had plans for a master dyranarya.

After that there were few glimpses of them both. Precisely when Detlev became Svir's servant was either gone or else had not been recorded: he was a passive witness, and then an active agent. If you discounted the record of Detlev's turning of Ilerian, which to Hibern now looked like one of Efael's fantasies, or more specifically, like the Garden of the Twelve: false. The only realistic aspect to it was Detlev himself, still wearing the clothes, the dust, and the blood of his capitulation. Hibern could not guess how Ilerian had found the morvende thousands of years in the future beyond the Fall, but this scene here? She was willing to wager her life it had never happened in the future. It was like a theater setting.

She reached to obliterate it, then hesitated. Anything to do with Efael and Yeres was a waste of time and space, of that she was certain. But matters pertaining to Detlev ought not be so readily extirpated, at least until she figured out this strange pattern she perceived in his reports.

Siamis reappeared again, given to Detlev for training; something had certainly happened between the time he was running vile errands for Efael, and his reassignment. It was harrowing, how much Siamis was like the poopsies, for these were his teen years.

In later records, mostly made by Yeres, Detlev and Siamis bickered over destructive actions long lost in history, the one enforcing his authority, the other fighting for independence. The Host watched, endlessly entertained—

Another magic attack; she whirled it into impotence.

"Oh, Theronezhe, you can do better than that," she said. "Or maybe you can't. They kept you out of the absolute center, didn't they? You with your swords and arrows and knives. You're just an armed door guard."

By turning and looking, then forming and projecting a thought, she sent a sky-high sheet of lightning to rip apart the flat black ceiling above Theronezhe's encamped would-be occupation battalions. Partly in a frustrated urge to see light again, and partly as a warning to Theronezhe, who (she sensed) was planning yet another attack.

Theronezhe then surprised her by vanishing altogether;

good riddance. He could not get to Sartorias-deles any more than she could, but at least (so far) the Host could not seem to get back here. Let Theronezhe busy himself on some other world, hopefully where there were mages aplenty to thwart him.

Meanwhile, she followed his wake in magic, and discovered the way out.

She could leave Norsunder, even if she could not get back home.

One

Cavern outside of Efael's HQ

THEY FIXED UP A splint for Mildred's knee. She couldn't do much except sit, so she volunteered to stay with MV while the others guarded the cavern and watched the castle.

This meant having to change his oozing bandages; Detlev had assured them, after checking, that the most dangerous parts of that slash had been repaired. Mildred was dubious. Why was a gut wound ten times worse to look at than an arm or a leg? Even her own didn't make her feel so queasy, and it still hurt like blazes every time she moved.

She kept her face straight when she saw by the red blotches on the white linen that it was time for a change. Yanli, who had studied with a healer for a year before Erai-Yanya accepted her as a magic student, had showed Mildred how to change bandages.

Mildred worked as fast as she could, hoping to finish before he wakened next, then sat back and wiped her brow on her sleeve. And was glad she'd pulled the blank-face because she discovered MV's eyes open. The rigidity of his jaw and neck muscles, and the tiny beads of sweat on his brow, revealed he'd been awake during the process.

When his gaze met hers, she sent the thought: *Must've felt as good as it looked.*

And saw a responsive twitch in one cheek: *Status?*

She gave it to him as succinctly as possible. Halfway through his eyes closed again but he did not break the contact. At the end, his thought came back: *Imry knows where we are. Got it from me.*

: *Already come and gone. We have a week.*

"Owe you," he whispered.

She grinned, and touched his lips with her forefinger. "I'll collect."

The tense skin around his eyes eased. He did not try to speak again, or contact. His eyes drifted closed and presently his breathing indicated sleep.

Mildred carefully maneuvered her leg out straight and leaned back, sighing without sound. Her entire body ached, and the thin-bladed cuts she'd taken stung, though somewhat less than it all had that morning. At least she healed fast.

A step brought her head up.

Detlev moved across the cavern without disturbing the other sleepers. Mildred glanced his way. Except for a couple slices in his long riding coat—she couldn't remember if they'd been there before—he'd taken no visible marks.

She looked at his face, and made contact: *MV wondered about Llyenthur knowing we're here. Told him you're not worried. But if Llyenthur shows up again?*

: *I do not think he will. I believe he's busying himself elsewhere.*

Mildred scowled in disbelief: *What?*

A trace of humor evidenced in Detlev's thought: *He claimed he wants MV writhing under a sense of obligation. There is also our having taken out certain of the Black Knives, who Efael detailed to sabotage Imry.*

She sighed, muttering, "That was you."

Detlev said aloud, "You and MV between you accounted for two of them, and wounded a third. As well as the escort, all four were well-known for their torture sports in Aldon's dungeons. The order for couriers to transfer in column came straight from Aldon, and Efael is in a rage—Imry cannot be blamed."

Mildred shrugged off Imry Llyenthur, whose life or death meant nothing to her. But MV? Writhing under a sense of obligation? Eh. By now she knew that there were numerous undercurrents within Detlev's circle that made no sense to anyone outside, and Imry Llyenthur, it seemed, was still in their estimation part of the circle.

Detlev sent her one of those interrogative glances, and Mildred grinned: *Why did you send me to Crow anyway? You never did give me a real reason.*

: I thought I had made my reasons sufficiently clear.

: Your reasons why I'd be the best to get through to Marseth Ghandorjien were indeed clear, and what's more, you were right. But there were others who could have done it as well. What you never gave me was what you expected me to get out of that job.

: What did you get out of it?

Mildred sighed inwardly: *Respect. Not just in Crow's island. The way Rolfin looked at me yesterday, though he still teases. Sorting my memories, I can feel that I struck at least four death blows. Torture sport sounds dire, but were they really evil, or just stupidly misguided? I don't even remember their faces. They might not have been there yesterday by choice, only circumstance...*

She had his complete attention, which was intimidating enough. She zapped out a thought: *No response? No sidestepping moral reassurances here, about them not caring if they never remembered me, had I been the one to die?*

He never did the expected, she ought to know that by now. He waited, and she admitted the real truth: *What I've seen in myself was probably there all along. I relished that fight — I understand what bloodlust is now. I don't want to crave it.*

: Then you won't. If it helps, consider this: with every fight, the chance of facing someone faster and stronger increases. Always.

She smiled wanly, and shook her head: *Even you?*

: Even I. Every fight could be my last.

She rubbed her eyes, reliving that vivid memory again, only this time there was no sound, almost no emotion, just the shocking knowledge that she — Mildred — who liked to get along with everyone, and regarded martial skills mostly as sport, had rushed those Black Knives with bloodlust to equal theirs, yelling, *Come on! Come on!*

She considered Detlev's words; she already knew he did not make a life of seeking fights for the sake of fighting. Her guardian, a warrior by choice, had once said, *Only one walks away from a duel. The more your fame spreads, the more the rest of your life will be spent in making sure the one left lying on the ground is not you.*

Retren stirred and sat up, looking around blearily. She said, "Give me a hand, won't you? I think it's time for me to get some shut-eye."

Retren watched in silence as Detlev helped Mildred down from the stone ledge to the pile of blankets that had been sent for her from Mearsies Heili. She grunted and winced until she was flat and straight, then let her breath out with slow relief.

Then she was sleep. So too was Jilo, wrapped like a chrysalis in his cloak and blanket. MV was still as well.

That left Retren actually alone with The Great Man, a thought that congealed his body into ice.

No telling how long he'd have sat there, stiff, hardly daring to breathe. He watched Detlev fill their large water pot and set it with care on the two swords they'd rigged on piled stones around a vagabond fire. Above the fire, the rocky outcroppings were festooned with fabric: bandage strips, and drying socks — which had early on become general property for anyone having to go out — a very fine cambric shirt (Shontande's), a rough-woven lace-up black shirt (Rolfin's), and a small singlet, which had to be Yanli's.

Detlev then sat on the stone ledge and pulled off his shoes and socks. He washed out the socks in the wash bowl set aside for that purpose, and put them on the rack, then selected two of the dry ones, pulled them on, and his shoes. Ret watched this homely task, knowing he was a birdwit for being astonished that Detlev got soggy feet like anyone else.

Detlev tossed the wash water outside, then returned, and when he saw Retren staring, he gave him a faint smile and beckoned.

They went out into the rough-fissured access tunnel, which was lit by a torch someone had turned into vagabond fire. Detlev found a place to sit down, and his smile deepened when Retren stood at attention before him. But the amusement was swiftly hidden, and all Retren saw was the kindness.

"Sit down, Retren," he said. "Aren't you hungry? Or did you want to talk to me?"

Ret's body had moved — at what he'd perceived as a command — but as yet his throat was still a block of fear-ice.

Detlev studied those great gray eyes that had been following his every move, and he tried to ease the boy's terrible inner pressure by approaching obliquely the matter that lay between them.

"You are kin to Senrid?" Detlev asked. "Through your mother to Senrid's mother, is this correct?"

"Yes. Though nobody seems to regard second cousins

from outside the borders of Marloven Hess. Van—Senrid, the king, never referred to it. I myself thought not of it until once when we were in Choreid Dhelerei. Someone showed me a water-color sketch of the little princess Crystal Ingrid, and I saw how much she had resembled my sister Lesra."

"But you kept that to yourself?"

Retren opened his palm. "The king does not talk about the little princess. And ... I did not talk about my family." He glanced up, a fast but searching glance. Detlev didn't seem to have noticed the hatefully weak hesitation.

But he had noticed, Ret was sure of it. All these long months he'd wondered what Detlev looked like, what he sounded like, and why—

And then it came out, just like that. "The king said you helped to save me. Why?"

That a life might be saving merely because everyone deserved to live was a meaningless concept to someone whose first eleven years had not been shaped by any encouragement or conviction of self-worth. A discussion of basic morals, at this moment, would be a betrayal. There had to be a Reason.

Detlev said, "Last week, when you and I caught up with Jilo and Shontande Lirendi. Do you remember what you were trying to tell us?"

"The singing mountain," Ret said, barely audible.

"Who understood that reference?"

"No one. But Jilo allows me to say whatever I—oh." A swift progression of expressions altered Retren's pale face: question, defensive wariness, surprise. Wonder.

"No, it was not your imagination. And yes, there are a very few of us who can 'hear' the resonance deep under that mountain. But it must remain an absolute secret until the Host is expelled from this world."

Those gray eyes, their expression was so very much like Sveneric's. Detlev watched a tentative kindling of hope in the sudden sheen of tears that would never fall. The softly flickering light from Imry's torch in the wall played over the thawing of pain in Retren's young face.

"It's real?"

Detlev opened his hand in the Marlovan gesture of assent, and watched as the narrow-focused, martial reason for living that Retren had striven silently to live up to for eleven years, and then lost one night in the courtyard of his father's castle, was replaced by something new and bright and shining with truth.

"What shall I do?" Retren whispered, every nerve awaiting Lifetime Orders.

"When the world is rid of the enemy, travel. Sail on a ship. Carve wood, or make candles. Try new things. When you are ready—and you'll know it, without a doubt—come to Sartor and seek us on another singing mountain. You'll find us. There your real training will begin." He watched Ret draw a slow, tightly compressed breath, and, aware that Efael's castle was now empty of the Host, said, "Would you fetch Yanli and the rest back?"

Retren's quick smile revealed how much it meant to be entrusted with this errand. He fetched his coat, hat, and gloves, and zipped out into the snow.

A short time later, Shontande stamped in, shaking snow from his legs, just as the sun came up. Jilo woke as he entered the larger cavern. Jilo and Shontande ate together, a quick meal with little talk, and then Shontande withdrew to the far cavern where the hot spring was, to clean up.

MV's eyes opened. His hand drifted to the bandages round his middle, which were spotted with red. Detlev moved to the stream to get a cup of water for him before changing his bandages.

MV's breath hissed between clenched teeth, and Jilo fought a wave of nausea as he looked away, though he couldn't unhear the sounds. Being sensitive to such things seemed worse, not better, since he made coinherence. Figured. Everyone else got stronger, but he got weaker.

Detlev sat down next to him. "Assuming you prevail."

Jilo tensed warily. "Shontande knows all my plans."

But Detlev didn't accept this defensive deflection. "The Chwahir," he said, "must be ruled by Chwahir."

Jilo squeezed his eyes shut again—this time the pain was his. "Yes," he breathed. "Yes. You mean, what after? You're not..."

"Jilo, have you considered what to do first?"

"Every day," Jilo muttered. "Every night. Sometimes the commands are in a different order..." He paused when he saw Detlev's head tip slightly, as if in question. "What?"

"A suggestion only," Detlev said mildly. "Use or discard

as you see fit."

"What?" Jilo asked in a different voice, still not quite believing he wasn't about to have Chwahirsland yanked away.

"One command only, at first. Consider that idea. What ought that to be?"

Jilo struggled against the shock of crumbling fears and expectations. Detlev really wasn't going to enumerate all the logical reasons why some outsider ought to come in and rule the benighted Chwahir?

Still. *One* command? Impossible. Wan-Edhe had perpetrated so very many terrible, insane laws and orders, that Jilo had put a great deal of effort into considering which ones to overturn first. The list kept growing.

Though he was aware that the Chwahir had begun ignoring all that they dared. Which would defang those laws until such time as the laws could be unwritten...

One command?

Was he saying that changing too many might be chaotic? He remembered Senrid talking to him about that once, early in their acquaintance. When he first became king, he'd wanted to get rid of all his uncle's bad decisions, but too many changes got resistance. Senrid had said, "Then your choice is, enforce your will because you can, in which case are you just another tyrant, or compromise."

He'd forgotten that—their situations were so very different then.

They still were different. In a sense. Jilo's theoretical power had changed forever when he gave the military leaders the means of freedom from control. But he knew they would still turn to him, if only out of habit, at least at first. If someone didn't take him out first.

But Detlev wasn't accepting the conditional. And then Jilo thought, as he had so many times: when in doubt, go back to the fundamentals.

"Restore the twi," he said, no louder than a whisper.

Detlev gave a short nod. "That sounds wise."

Rising voices claimed their attention, ending with, Crow's raspy croak, "He *said* they'd be fine."

Shontande's tenor, warm, musical, but with an edge that Jilo recognized, rare as it was—tiredness, and anger. "He said, 'We will do what we can to protect Terry's mountain forces.' He did not seek to burden us with the trivialities of detail."

MV spoke hoarsely, "Shut up, Lirendi."

Jilo saw Shontande ranged before the stone ledge on which MV had somehow managed to sit up. Shontande's heightened color made him look even more princely and splendid as he gazed down into MV's face. But his expression was more troubled than angry as he said softly, "You will permit me no graceless allegations, even?"

MV was clad only in his old, blood-crusted black pants, and he sat with one forearm clenched against his bandaged middle. His complexion was gray clear down to his upper arms, except for two dull red patches on the blade-sharp ridges of his cheekbones. Filthy black hair hung in his eyes as he squinted through it at Shontande Lirendi's smiling but utterly unreadable face.

Jilo lunged up, wondering how to deflect a possible confrontation. He missed seeing the little pile of rubble in his path until his foot caught it, slid, and went flying forward. He would have taken a bad header onto the broken stone had not Rolfin leaped up and caught him under the armpits.

"Argh," Jilo groaned, embarrassed.

Rolfin grinned, then hefted him to his feet with no apparent effort.

"Thanks," Jilo muttered, figuring they could use his burning face for a beacon across mountains.

"Yup." Rolfin crossed over and sat on the stone ledge beside MV. He looked up at Shontande, and grinned again.

Shontande gave a soundless laugh and raised a hand in the fencer's sign for a hit. "Ah-ye, I comprehend." He turned toward the water and cups.

Nobody asked what he comprehended.

Two

MILDRED SMOTHERED A YAWN and said, "I'll take some of that if you're fixing more than just one."

Shontande gave her an absent smile, and went about making up a pot of the summery Sartoran leaf. Mildred sat back, her pupils contracting to vertical slits as her gaze flicked from MV to Shontande and back again.

Nothing whatever could be made from her expression—at least by Jilo—but she was somewhat distractedly thinking that though Shontande was quite probably the most highly finished young man she'd ever laid eyes on, it was MV who kept drawing her covert gaze. Shontande Lirendi was too formidable in his beauty and in his stylized courtly gestures, the more formidable because they were utterly unconscious, trained into habit probably from his very first day. He was like layers and layers of history, all shaped and finished to the perfect work of art, and therefore just as impossible to comprehend.

MV, she understood. Both the bad and the good. Once she would have said there was no good, he was merely a walking, talking weapon. But she'd seen a glimpse of the person behind the martial shield, there in Darchelde, when he worked on helping Crow straighten his twisted body, and in the gruff ways he showed affection to Sveneric, and, oh, up there on the mountain when they kissed, before they ran together down to what they both were convinced was the end of their lives—and almost his last gesture had been a desperate attempt to cover her retreat. Even when he was filthy, lying there in bandages—even when he barked insults with every breath—she found him a complex amalgam of fire and sweetness.

Yanli, who had been vigorously toweling her short, silky hair, ignored them all, except for Jilo. "What we saw, was—"

"Wolves," Crow said with a fierce grin.

Yanli canted a glance of tolerant scorn. "We were busy laying our false trail, in a large and meandering circle. We heard noise in a valley below us. Apparently a search-detail of Norsundrians ordered in by Efael from the far outpost heard as well. We rounded a cliff in time to see some of Terry Larensar's border guard riding at full gallop at a blind cover covered by a heavy snowdrift, chased by a huge pack of wolves. Or we thought they were being chased. The Norsundrians came to the same conclusion, but as they rode in to cut down Terry's people the wolves all turned and swarmed up the mountain and went after *them*."

Silence. She flapped her towel, and folded it. "One Norsundrian got away. Probably was allowed to, though he certainly was not unmarked."

Shontande looked up from his steep. "The Norsundrians' horses?"

"Ran off. Wolves left them alone," Yanli said.

Ret, having shed his wet clothes and put on dry ones, slid up and sat next to Jilo. Everyone else turned soberly to check gear or help pack things up for transfer; only MV sat where he was.

Rolfin yanked a dry shirt off the sword-rack and dropped over it MV's head, then helped him get his hands through. And without bothering to lace the front, he helped ease MV back down into a lying position—MV cursing rudely the while. Everyone there could feel how much he hated being helpless, but still, when MV was successfully shirted and flat, Yanli observed, "Speaking of soul-suckers. And soul-eaters. Do you think invective will change if we do defeat Ilerian? Though we say this or that person is a soul-sucker, he's the only one who actually does it. Yes?""

MV shot her a venomous sneer, which made Mildred hide a snicker, and Yanli stare back, head tipped to one side, arms crossed.

"The image is intense enough to persist," Shontande

murmured in his peacemaking voice. "Though perhaps its immediacy will, ah-ye, lose potency?"

"Not an important curse to the Chwahir," Jilo said. "Right now anything to do with Wan-Edhe is more often used, including the word 'hate,' because he's been The Hate for years. There are many curses in Chwahir that others don't understand, such as tallow-picker. But the very worst is no-family, which isn't even a curse elsewhere. I was so surprised to discover that."

"Whereas 'shit' is universal," Mildred said. "We say it on Geth."

"Erai-Yanya says, that is true anywhere you have the Waste Spell," Yanli put in. "Because you're being deliberately foul to talk about it, much less make it."

MV's *shitbird* was still hanging in the air, an echo. Though Yanli was not baiting him, his eyes narrowed, and Detlev crossed the space to offer MV a cup of water. Then he turned to address them all.

"Dhana of the Mearsieans has created, with artistic and imaginative expertise, a hastily abandoned camp about five days' travel from here. Judging by the search patterns, Efael's people ought to find it day after tomorrow. They will discover an empty cavern roughly five or six times the size of this one, with enough traces of hastily obliterated evidence of recent tenancy to indicate an army of about a thousand strong. Efael will no doubt assume that this army is secreted in the endless maze of subterranean fissures and openings that riddle these mountains. I trust the subsequent search will keep a sizable detachment adequately employed for a while."

Smiles, grins, and snorts of laughter met this news.

"We accomplished our goal: Crimson General Furo is now recovering in a place of safety. Efael is rampaging at various headquarters demanding armies to defend against what he is certain is to be a major attack on his citadel. There is nothing more for us to do here. I suggest you rest until Siamis is able to transfer us to our various destinations."

Jilo was glad to relinquish various worries; he did not, therefore, see Shontande and Detlev disappear through the passage to the outer chamber.

As he walked, Shontande struggled against a lifetime of politesse, though now that he actually had the old enemy right there, he wanted to accuse. To rant.

But Detlev spoke first. "What can you tell me about Curtas's death?" The inscrutable affect was gone—there in his voice and face was unhidden grief.

Shontande let out a breath as if he'd been punched. Then the hard years of training steadied him as he faced the rough wall and repeated their conversation, short as it had been, beginning with the fact that Curtas had pressed the chain mail on Shontande. Even with all those years of control his voice was a thread as he ended, "His last words were that you said to protect the future. He was insistent, and his mind was ..." Shontande's own grief was an invisible hand squeezing his throat. "Open. He believed it. Believed you. There was no conquering in his thoughts, no bloody destruction."

He whirled around to face Detlev. "So *why* did you take my father's mind? Everyone said it was an experiment, a whim, a game played with kings."

"That," Detlev said, "is what Norsunder had to see. To believe."

"Why?"

"Because this war would have happened far too soon. No, Ilerian would not have permitted Svir and Efael and Theronezhe the fun of a war. He would have torched the world to grasp what your father saw."

Shontande had imagined this conversation over the years, always angry, rightness on his side. But never had he imagined the direction it had taken. "I don't understand. First of all, are they not united, Ilerian and Svir?"

"You have to remember that self-interest lies behind every so-called action, every coalition in Norsunder. There is no greater good. There is no doing for the sake of the many. Though Norsunder as a collective prides itself on only the smartest, fastest, and toughest surviving, it is also its own worst enemy in that promotion is attained by treachery and assassination. Which amuses Svir, sitting there in what the Host believe is timelessness. He's not aware that he has gradually— incrementally—stagnated, only that he's bored."

"I don't understand."

"Time has slowed in Norsunder-Beyond. But it has not halted, or its inhabitants would not be able to maneuver at all. Aside from Ilerian, whose true nature is impossible for us to comprehend, human beings learn as they age, or they diminish." Detlev lifted his head, assessing the mental plane, then made a tired gesture. "Enough of the Beyond."

Shontande tried to comprehend, and there came to mind the covert struggles to gain power in his old regency council. The wily old Duchas of Alarcansa, while in no way comparable to Svir otherwise, had amused himself watching the others in their silent, polite duel. The worst of them had been the Count Ariath, whose soft, melodious voice was always full of self-sacrifice and Colend's greater good, but beneath that she wanted to be queen of Colend. She worked specifically to that end, which included undercutting the others whenever possible, even when they were doing something to benefit the kingdom. And they'd hated her for it; the regency council had only united when it came to keeping Shontande from assuming kingship in more than name. "I think I understand that aspect," he said slowly, some of his pent-up resentment returning, "but I do not comprehend why you had to put my father under that enchantment."

"It's dangerous to talk even obliquely, at this moment," Detlev said.

"Retren's singing mountain," Shontande whispered—as if spoken words were the danger. "I thought he was delirious from being half-frozen. You said nothing at the time…"

"Let us continue this conversation if we prevail," Detlev said. And, to the puzzled frustration Shontande Lirendi could not hide, "As for your father, I can say this much now. I was in the Beyond. It was Siamis who discovered your father's—let us call them dreams—almost too late. I had to act fast, and I did not want to kill him. Giving him his dream existence was a compromise that was the best I could do in an emergency. I thought that at least it would preserve his life. It would have sufficed, had not Efael done what he did."

That much, Shontande believed, was true. He turned away. Resentful he still was, but stronger was regret, and grief, and sorrow, and a deepening conviction that he only perceived the reflection of a vast, unseen world.

Protect the future.

Three

Land of the Venn – Hall of Ancestors

UNHAMPERED BY EXTERNAL TIME measurement, CJ and Erenlara wandered through the vast catacombs carved, tiled, and painted by Eren's long-ago ancestors, the family Sofar. They ate when they felt like it, slept when they felt like it, and moved on when they felt like it.

Cheerfully unaware that the clocks in all the surface dwellings said four a.m., they approached the Hall of Ancestors—and an unexpected encounter.

Erenlara, of course, knew her way unerringly. There were four major intersections that were also used as reference points, and the continually running decorative lines at floor or ceiling level had ancient runes worked in that furnished directions—a concept that might have been borrowed from the morvende centuries ago. Erenlara had learned to read runes when she was very small, though the only ones who now used them were archivists and mages at the highest level.

She told stories as they walked, but often the girls stood and looked about them in silence. Glowglobes, perched on slender-legged holders, gave instant and steady soft silver-white light when touched a certain way. The flickerless silvery light imparted an air of mystery to an already awe-inspiring place.

Awe-inspiring to CJ's eyes. She looked around in

amazement at the skillful shaping of rock into vaulting symmetry, and at the blend of painting and natural stone that never hid but always enhanced the already mighty dimensions of the chambers. Once, she jumped when she unexpectedly caught a lifelike glitter of blue up in the staring eyes of a twenty-foot high figure in a long fresco. The ancient sword-wielding queen had sapphire stones in her painted eyes. Elsewhere in the fresco jewels glittered and gold and silver gleamed.

Wow, she thought.

And in return came Eren's contact: *We are very close to the Hall. Should you like to see it?*

: Sure!

At first, though Eren could hear thought-contact, she was unable to return it. She explained her wince and shudder as the reaction of an over-eager and foolish person who, in desiring a fine brown skin, stayed out in the hottest season for two days.

"Supersensitive," CJ had said, abandoning contact.

"Exactly!" Eren said, not indicating that CJ's habitual but superficial shield was in no wise strong enough to mask her thoughts now. Eren knew that her own actions had brought her suddenly to knowledge she ought to have learned gradually, perhaps when she was older — but she must live with the result now, and keep silent about its trials.

In self-defense, she turned her mind to constructing and maintaining a mental shield. Once she could close herself off from CJ's clear and energetic running thoughts, she experimented, tentatively at first, with contact. CJ responded with enthusiastic encouragement.

Now, emboldened by the ease of that brief contact, Eren went on: *The Hall of Ancestors was where my ancient ancestors assembled their people. Now it is only used for state funerals and coronations. Many artifacts remain from that time — some of them we do not really know what was their use. But they are there, along with a hundred different lethal protections, which my brother had to learn when he was very small, and in turn, he taught them to me.*

: That first hall we were in, you said you haven't used it as a residence for years and years?

: Yes. It used to once be a retreat for the mages before they formed the Arm of the Crown. Later, after the treaty forcing us to abandon our use of magic, it was sometimes used as a prison for recalcitrant or restless heirs, or for troublesome relatives.

CJ shivered. She'd felt something, right when Eren

paused. There seemed to be lingering traces of intense emotions, of old triumphs and defeats, somehow pressed into the cold, aged stone.

The two girls walked along in silence, entering the Hall of Ancestors from a side archway. The air smelled like stone, cold and still as if it stirred once in a century. The Hall was lit only by magical torches burning on either side of the main balcony, which they wandered out onto, and found themselves overlooking the mighty space. Opposite them, into a wall like a sheer cliff, had been carved silvery-white trees, ash and elm. These surrounded and intertwined with a greater tree carved a gilt with gold. This tree was huge, reminiscent of the one seen previously, only this one was different, wilder, the roots and branches intertwined with the ash and elm but not confined to neat knotwork, the rays of the sun streaming upward and outward in veins of gold that flashed and glittered in the uneven light.

Uneven light.

Both girls became aware of the torchlight flickering—

Then Eren glanced down, then around, and a heartbeat later she darted soundlessly along the passage some ten fast steps and struck with her palm at one of the stone decorations along the wide balcony. CJ glimpsed a plethora of cables crisscrossing the shadowy vaulting above them, presumably for the hanging of banners; suddenly, silently, the stone urn round which a cable was wound fell and swung down in a silent, deadly arc.

CJ sprang to the balcony in time to catch sight of a pale face far below, before the person was blocked from sight by the swinging stone urn.

Whoever it was must have felt the air stir, and had fast reflexes. A twisting motion, half-seen; Eren and CJ heard the stone crack against a human skull, a nasty but not deadly blow. The heavy stone was not even knocked off course but silently completed its arc, revealing a man sprawled on the marble floor below, something glittering near his fingers, the light coming from the single torch set in a sconce on a column directly below.

The stone began its return swing.

CJ croaked, "What was that?"

"One of the protections. He must have been stealing the Sofar Diamond."

Eren ran noiselessly to a narrow, steep stairway. CJ

followed her down, wincing in readiness of seeing something terrible as they dashed past the still swinging stone and crouched down on either side of the prone man. CJ's fists were clutched tightly between her knees and chest.

"I know this man not," Eren murmured, staring down with no trace of emotion in her face. "But he is as I guessed a thief."

CJ averted her eyes from the gash on the man's temple where the rough stone had scraped open a couple layers of skin. She shifted so she would not have to see drips of blood from the gash, stark against the smooth marble floor, and gazed in wonder at the largest faceted diamond she had ever seen outside of the Selenseh Redian caves. It lay a few inches beyond one of the man's loose hands. Blue, purple, crimson, molten-gold fires glimmered in its center.

"It looks like one of the living stones from the caves," CJ said, pointing.

"That it is," Eren said. "This is a family treasure. It is part of our wards, never spoken of. How could this man know about it?"

CJ pulled her gaze away and peeked again at the man, and this time made a discovery. Her knees klonked onto the marble as she pointed an accusing finger at the unconscious face. "That—that's that puke-face Llyenthur!" A swallow. "Is he dead?"

Eren turned away from the diamond, which still lay on the floor, to the open neck of Llyenthur's shirt. "I think not," she said calmly, pointing to the slight rise and fall of his breast. "He breathes, do you not see? Though slowly. You are certain of his identity?" She looked up, at a terrible gag-face made by CJ.

"Yeah. I only saw this yuck once, but I—and my scalp— won't forget *that* real soon."

Eren made a slight gesture, toward the dull gleam on a polished black hilt visible at the top of one of Llyenthur's boots. "He is the Norsundrian commander, is he not? Should we cut his throat, then?"

CJ shuddered, genuinely sickened. "Not just—like that. Ugh. Like they'd do. Though," she added, her brows thunder-lined, "if it was that that stinking rotten Efael slime-slug—"

"I do not wish to leave him here, to carry on his evil war."

"I forgot to tell you, he's not in charge any more. Maybe we should, like, tie him up or something, and write a note to

Detsie or Rel or Siamis—hey!" Once again CJ's forefinger jabbed outward. "That's David's sword, he's wearing. Or, one just like it. Maybe they all had one, and the others lost theirs."

"Shall we take it?" Eren suggested as she reverently picked up the diamond and cradled it on both palms.

"Sure! *You* do that, and tie him up. Maybe he's got something on him to do that with. I'll write to Detsie on my beige paper..." CJ's brow furrowed in perplexity as she stared down.

"What is it? Another plan?" Eren asked as she stretched out one hand for the hilt of the sword.

"No." CJ flapped a hand at Llyenthur's form stretched out between them. "I mean, I never thought about it before, but what do they *do* when they're not stomping people and things? I mean, do they, like, enjoy the usual stuff? Why grab palaces, and gold, if you don't live in 'em—"

"Ah." Eren sat back on her heels, and laughed softly. "Mean you vices, CJ?"

"Vices? Yeah, vices." CJ wrinkled her nose, reminded of her old battle with grudges. That would be the first vice she could think of. "I guess. I mean, look at this creep. He's not fat, doesn't reek of liquor, no fancy duds—" She waved her hands. "What else is there?"

"Perhaps such an individual would say that only a fool would dilute with gluttony or drunkenness the pleasures of unlimited power," Eren observed, her wide eyes glittering in the reflected light of the torch, a glitter echoed in the diamond on her hand, and in the gold worked into the stone tree far above their heads.

"Unlimited power," CJ muttered. "Well, I bet it's limited some by those Host stinkards, if nothing else."

Eren's eyes narrowed in humor, still reflecting light-shards as did the diamond that she rolled between her fingers. "The Venn learned many years ago that the degree of power one possesses is directly proportional to one's answerability."

CJ snorted, the forefinger offering, with scorn, Llyenthur as prime exhibit. "Answerable. Sure."

"But yes," Eren returned with calm certainty in her soft voice.

Then CJ choked on a retort as, glancing down, she saw that Llyenthur's eyes were open. She began scrambling through the outer layers of her clothing to find her knife.

Imry paid no attention. He blinked once, then sat up, one of his hands going to a pocket, and coming up with—a handkerchief. CJ, having expected a knife, whooshed a breath of surprise and relief.

Mopping gently at the gash on the growing lump on his head, he asked, quite naturally, "What was that?"

"A protection," Eren replied in the same tone, gravely studying the interloper. "I saw someone in the Hall of Ancestors, standing before the place where we keep the family artifacts, and I released it." Her gaze was wary, but steady. "There are many more, some far more dangerous."

CJ had her knife out now, and sat silently, not breathing, awaiting a villainous shout or act of violence.

But Llyenthur blinked, winced, and pressed the cloth to his head.

Eren held the diamond to her chest. "You were in the process of theft. It belongs to the Venn."

"No contest," he replied, and flicked up his free hand. "Carry on."

He startled them both by vanishing by transfer magic.

"Aaargh!" CJ collapsed backward in relief and confusion. Then bolted up again. "What if he comes back with reinforcements?"

"I shall restore the diamond at once." Eren pointed. "And I think I will ignite one of the fire wards. Then we should go."

"But what if he comes back with the Host? Will the fire ward thingie keep *them* out?"

Eren stood up slowly, looking down into the stone in her fingers. "Perhaps not," she said. "I do not know. This, though, for certain. I made a vow to my brother. We cannot remove this stone from here."

They ducked around the great urn, which was still swinging back and forth, soundless except for the deep whoosh of air if one passed near its arc. Eren moved to a wall that CJ had not yet seen, as it was directly below the balcony. Stone and gold were carved into a breathtakingly beautiful tree, a smaller replica of the vast stone tree on the opposite wall. Eren stood on her toes, reached up and touched with explorative fingers the edges of a golden setting at the heart of the sun carving. She rubbed her fingers together, then reached up to place the diamond in its setting; when she set it down a flash of blue-white light coruscated through the chamber, too quick to blind the girls, though they blinked.

When they looked again, the diamond sat in its golden setting, glittering in the reflected torchlight like it was alive.

Eren murmured, "It took no harm of him, at least."

CJ resolutely closed her mouth on the questions piling up, until Eren smiled her way. "I wish I understood, but I do not. It might even be that his intention was not at all what we think."

CJ let out an explosive sigh, peering hunch-shouldered behind her. "Okay if we bucket away from here? I want to write letters home and see how they're doing, but not if that skunk comes tentacling back."

Eren laughed at the image of a skunk with tentacles, but said only, "Let us depart indeed. We have tarried long enough."

When they reached the end of the balcony, she pressed another inlaid tile, and CJ smelled a whiff of metallic singe: the fire ward had been set.

Four

Mearsies Heili

DHANA WAS TELLING CLAIR the latest news: it seemed that Rel and Atan were indeed going to get married at the beginning of New Year's Week, something that for some reason seemed as important to all the adults as the impending attack.

Which she could not talk about.

"So, if this stupid wedding junk means so all-fired much," she complained, "then why haven't we seen any evidence of it? CJ says in her last letter, if this stuff about weddings makes Alsaes offer his ring to his mirror, and the rest of the villains match up with cactus and—Clair, you aren't listening."

Her tone was not even remotely angry under the exasperation, it was anxious.

Clair's eyelids lifted. "Yes I am."

Dhana said grimly, "Then you shoulda been laughing. At least about Alsaes proposing marriage to his mirror."

Clair said with sudden, scarcely suppressed violence, "Did she have a match for Ilerian?"

To hear spoken out loud the name of the person who had been tormenting Clair made Dhana nearly snort smoke. "I'll show them a match for Ilerian." She seethed, breathing hard through her gritted teeth for a few moments. "Has he been getting worse?"

"Not much." Clair shrugged and stretched her fingers

around the gently steaming mug that Janil had brought. Gazing down into the warm brown of her hot chocolate, she said, "And when he does, it's two ways. I don't think he knows that."

"What two ways? You mean you've been in his mind?" Dhana's expression made a radical shift from astonishment to a classic Junky-issue prune-face.

Clair was sitting cross-legged on her bed. Dhana, in passing by after a very long night, had seen her there. Now, looking more closely at her, Dhana wondered if—despite the nightgown and the messy hair—Clair had slept any more than she had. And Clair was human. She did not have recourse to the Lake waters to refresh herself.

"Not mind." Clair gave her head a quick shake. "Not that! I don't think I could b—I don't think I want—oh, never mind. Memories."

"Ugh." Dhana gasped, her fingers going cold and tingly. "But that would be just as bad, wouldn't it?"

Clair thought about those brief glimpses—so brief—of the white-haired boy, her own age, walking in silent enjoyment through a forest. "Not ... um."

"What? What were you going to say?"

"Just, not if you go back far enough. But then you'll say *You shouldn't be in his mind at all* and I'll say *I wouldn't if I had any choice,* and I thought I'd save us both some effort."

What really gave Dhana the creeps was the little smile that accompanied the words.

Swallowing her own hot chocolate in haste, she said, "Ugh. Just so you know what you're doing. *I* don't know what you're doing, and I wish I could help you."

"I don't know what *you're* doing, do I?"

Dhana flushed, shoulders jerking up tightly.

"I'm sorry, Dhana," Clair exclaimed, squeezing her eyes closed. "That was snotty. I know Siamis wants his actions to remain secret when he's not with me, and I know you'd tell me if he hadn't made you promise. The thing is, we are all doing what we can. My own approach—always—has been to stand outside of a situation and try to see it both ways. When action's been required, I've always been too slow. I've always relied on CJ for that. But now, I don't want CJ here. That's because I don't want her to see me until the time for action comes. It will hurt her too much, to see me the way I am now. In the meantime maybe I can determine what is right, and what will just prolong the conflict."

"What? What do you mean?"

"Questions, mostly." Clair shrugged again, her voice hesitating on certain words. "If Detlev shows up again, could you ask him if he has time to talk to me? I have some questions to put to him about aspects of the past."

"Okay," Dhana said cautiously, wondering if she'd do any such thing.

"Thanks!" Clair smiled in a weird, mirthless parody of her old self. "Guess it's time to get dressed."

Dhana watched in consternation as Clair got up with the kind of narrow-eyed, tight-faced wince of someone moving while in the throes of a sick headache.

And then Dhana stiffened with horror when, as Clair passed her bureau—the one that had been there as long as Dhana had been a member of the household—her fingers brushed the edge, then gave it a tiny tap, as though to reassure Clair that it was real.

While waiting for Detlev's transfer signal, Siamis sat his desk scanning once more through scraps of paper mostly detailing requisitions of various kinds, and feeding to the flames each that Dhana had accomplished the night before. Sometimes he paused to appreciate Dhana's pungent comments added underneath the agreed-on code.

He heard Dhana's light step as she ran in, graceful even in panic. "Siamis," she gasped. "Yugh!" She fought for breath, managing only to get a word out between pants and exclamations. "Clair—Delsie—she's in *his* mind—Wants to talk—" While from her came a vivid and emotion-charged jumble of images.

Detlev arrived, looking grimy and tired, smelling of old sweat and mildewing wool. Siamis performed the now familiar cleaning spell for him; if Detlev even noticed, he gave no sign of it. "What's the matter with Clair?"

Silent exchange of Dhana's experience.

Clair was in the library, crouched in her chair before a tray of fresh rolls, butter, and fruit compote, but her attention was on the fire.

Detlev let his step be heard. Clair looked up, relief and apprehension only slightly altering the strain in her face. Detlev did not let show any of his shock at the changes that had occurred in Clair's countenance since they'd seen one another last.

"I'm glad you sent Siamis," Clair said, her breathing shallow and fast. "But Ilerian knows he's here. And he keeps trying to bait Siamis through me. When he can. I, I, I have seen what they did to him. Though he tries hard to prevent me from seeing it. The dreams he sends, that Siamis can ward. But th-the memories, he can't." Clair blinked wide, dry eyes, her pupils huge, the stutter worsening though her speech was slow and painstaking.

"I know. That. Some of the memories are false, that he, he, he is trying to make me think. There's no truth. With all these different truths. I know it's a trick. But. The ones with you. I have to know. He s-s-says—no. He showed me. It was you. Used your dyr. Made *him* evil. Made him go back, and help cause the F-f-fuh." Painful swallow. "The Fall of Sartor." A vein beat in her temple. "He got them all. Your f-f-friends. Your leaders. But first they knew it was you who'd done it."

Detlev reached a decision then, one rarely reached—very rarely indeed.

"It is true that Ilerian was there at the Fall, and killed most of our leaders. And it is also true that he convinced some that I had done it. But the truth is, I did not corrupt the innocent," he said. "How Ilerian found the model for that child, I do not know, because so much is, and was, distortions of truth. You must understand that Ilerian is not human. Never was. I have never been able to comprehend the mystery behind Ilerian."

Clair listened, not even breathing.

"Where Ilerian came from, and when, is impossible to know. I do think that before Ilerian took human form, the entity that adopted that name had no physical presence as we understand it. Ilerian could move through time. I believe it was fascinated by the dichotomies of human nature, how we can be capable of great mercy, joy, and creativity—and also of great cruelty and despair and destruction."

"Yes," Clair whispered.

"I also believe it delighted in how perception of beauty sharpened and heightened our emotions, especially desire. And so chose the most beautiful form to vitiate, then ranged back to the time when we were the most powerful. And used that beauty against us."

"But that memory. It is so real."

"In a sense it was real, but only in a sense. Most of it was a sham, an elaborate setup meant to destroy me, and through me my contemporaries, by implying a future in which I had already succeeded in wrecking the world."

"Then you didn't corrupt a morvende?"

"I did not—but I had to make them believe that I had the capability to do so. Someday I will explain, if you like, what I did to that dyr, but that can wait. It's a matter of magical trickery, like their sham, with a lie at the heart."

Clair closed her eyes. It had shocked her, to see how young Detlev had been when the Host released him, and forced him to enact that sham. So much younger than her physical form now, just short of puberty. Which had long ceased to be the evil she had assumed when young. She saw it now as a part of the human condition.

"Clair."

She looked up: old tension and new relief pulled her face awry, but the release of tears had long since been denied her. He touched her lightly on the forehead, and transferred them to the Selenseh Redian near the disirad. There he left her, and when he returned he held out the fine silver chain he had brought back.

Her thin fingers reached, trembling, and he poured the chain into them. White-silver, glistening, the disirad resonated through physical touch and hearing to the spirit. He sensed her soul hovering there, on the verge of the transfinite, watching.

It is enough to know that I saw the truth of what happened. That pain is not mine.

"… that pain is not mine." Clair whispered the words, making them real. She repudiated cruelty. It was evil and she denied evil. She had seen the truth, and knew she had seen the truth, and though Ilerian could force cruel memories on her, the pain and shame were no longer there..

Ilerian's lies are as nothing.

"His lies are as nothing," she murmured, with the inward gaze of conviction.

When it was done the enormous release, as such things must, translated into physical expression, and she staggered to her own cave overlooking the waterfall, and crumpled, fingers curled protectively around the chain.

Detlev followed, disheartened. There was so little he could do to lessen the torment. A twitch of magic and the chain slid softly from her fingers as easily as water. He had to get it away before Ilerian sensed its presence—because then he would know it existed. The dyr vanished back to the hiding place that had lain undiscovered for nearly five thousand years.

Below and not far away, Siamis's footsteps crunched in the snow. He paused as a bird flapped upward and crashed into some white-laden branches, then flitted toward the heavy gray sky. A delicate white shower drifted down to cool his already cold face. He stared after the bird, recognizing a type that should be wintering far north of here, contently eating weed-seed that now lay unmolested under a blanket of snow and would grow come spring.

Then he walked on, carrying an armload of practice weapons.

The Mearsiean forest below the white castle was utterly silent under its fresh load of snow. He felt no stirring of wind, and the clouds above were uniformly gray from horizon to horizon.

There was beauty to the bare, gray-barked trees and the gently contoured drifts and mounds of blue-white. Siamis's keen aesthetic sense appreciated everything he looked at while the deeper part of his mind increased at every glimpse of faint-gleaming ice and leafless branches the time-distance between this place, and when it had been home.

Siamis closed the old days from his thoughts when he heard Detlev's step. Detlev's eyes, dark gray in this light, hit him with their familiar assessing glance. And as usual, Detlev's face gave no hint of the tally.

Siamis had chosen a clearing the proper size. For a time, as they warmed up, their motions in perfect synchrony, there was silence. Then they began to spar, lightly at first, without weapons.

Presently Detlev said, "Did you know that in his attacks on Clair Ilerian had shifted the burden of memory from your past to mine?"

Siamis made a futile gesture of warding before he blocked a strike. "No. I take it you dealt with that?"

"I gave her the truth. I trust it will help for a time. She must sleep again in the inner cave. I dare not bring out the dyr again, even there."

They switched to swords, though both were tired. But Siamis sensed that Detlev could relax through the familiar rhythms.

Siamis pressed an attack, withdrew, and said, "The assaults have been nearly ceaseless. I do not comprehend how he can compass it, despite the burden of time."

"He's drawing all the life from the land around him," Detlev said, blocking low, then whirling into a back kick that—if it had landed—would have struck the sword from Siamis's hand. A light tap on the hilt, then he said, "I very much fear even if we win, that end of Imar will be lifeless for centuries. And it worsens every day. We bought Clair a little more time, but how much I can't predict. When he discovers that he can no longer reach her through that connection, he'll find another way. Probably your past again."

Another passage, this time each with steel in both hands. Breathing fast, Detlev said, "I asked Yanli to return to the mages. She is willing to fetch and carry. They will need it—Arthur can't do it all."

Siamis easily translated that: Yanli was enjoying her war efforts and saw no need to come to Mearsies Heili.

Siamis's earliest memories of Detlev were dominated by those many assurances that his mother's long absences were necessitated by duty and not inclination. Siamis's mother was selflessly devoted to Reverael. He inherited her sense of place, and lost the place. His daughter was too self-sufficient to need a parent. Ah, the famed Reverael sense of balance!

"When this is over," Detlev said, dropping both points, "my demands on your life shall cease."

For a moment the sense of the words would not come, so fraught with the overlay of memory had been Siamis's thoughts. But as he too lowered his weapons, he considered the work he had been asked to do, and why—always why—and he said, "Even now, with the outcome so uncertain, I do not regret my exertions, only my failures."

"You regret," said Detlev, "that it began. So do I."

Snow squeaked and cracked underfoot as they walked back. The trail broadened, and away to the north a soft haze of white indicated another fall of snow that would soon blanket the mud they had churned up in the clearing.

Siamis thought back and back, recognizing that this was the first such admission he had ever heard out of Detlev, and then he realized that what Detlev was doing was apologizing, in the only way that Siamis would find acceptable.

Yet it was not his fault, had never been his fault. If anyone was at fault, it was Siamis, for getting caught, and for his actions on his release, except who could realistically pin so vast a blame on a boy hunted down by those long experienced in the chase?

As usual, Detlev intuited the direction of his regrets. "There have been compensations."

"Adamas Dei and Isa Cassadas?"

"They are, but never forget, Siamas, that you will always lead the list. Always."

Siamis's throat ached. *When will I ever comprehend his vision of the world?* "Everyone is now gathered in the Ghildraith geliath?" he asked.

"All," said Detlev, "except one."

Five

MV LAY ON A low bed of pillows, recovering after being transferred from the cave outside Efael's HQ. He rose to one elbow when David walked in, then sank back, cursing.

Seeing David's slight grimace, he said unerringly, "Dhana."

"You too? She was muttering about me throwing knives at Clair while she was a prisoner on Five."

"Irenne for me," MV said. "No direct accusations, just comments shot into the air. Dhana ought to be quite fluent with Laban when he does get here, if she wants to rake up the past," MV added with a reminiscent grin. "Pull me up, will you? I can't stand lying flat when I talk to people."

"What's behind it? Just old grudge?" David asked as he helped MV sit up.

"Nah. My guess is, it's the plan. She knows it's us — or nothing."

David's brow cleared. "And so not trusting us is a way to resist that 'or nothing,' eh?"

"Yep." MV's brief grin flared again. "Where's Senrid?"

"He's right behind me, winding up his affairs. Touching, Dhana's faith in us. I wonder if it's generally shared?"

"Let's not put it to the test," MV said derisively, and cursed again.

David studied him. "I suppose the rest of us should be grateful that you are so rarely sick."

"Eat shit and die," MV retorted. "I already heard from Yanli about my cussing. What? I don't cuss. Any worse than anyone else," he added hastily at David's monumental eyeroll.

David noticed the flush along MV's cheeks, reflecting that he had to be in considerable pain, however much he hid it. No fun baiting him now. "What happened?"

MV sketched a slantwise slash across his mid-section. "Black Knives. Six of them. Belt buckle kept me from being completely gutted." Sure enough, his voice weakened. "Imry."

"Healed you?"

"Back of the hand." MV bared his teeth in a grin, which disappeared. "He got everything from me."

"All right, that's … grim. What's Detlev say?"

"About the healing? Said only, Imry'll probably get backlash. Till he gets training. Which we both know he won't. About Imry knowing our plans, says to wait."

"I take it you sprang the Chwahir general?"

"Jilo. Yanli. Shontande Lirendi." MV grimaced. "We ran defense. Two columns appeared. Not the usual three. Four."

"I hear something about that. Sveneric, Dirk, and Darian Selenna have been tearing up Aldon's comms. You sure you should be sitting up?"

"Detlev put the binding spell on my ribs. And on Mildred's knee. Keeps it all in place, but doesn't stop the bones grating."

David saw that the effort of prolonged talk was tiring MV, but he knew better than to comment. "I'm going to see who else turned up." And he left.

His mood changed to one of anticipation as he walked along the stone corridors toward where his inner sense told him most folk were gathered. While he was listening on the mental realm a great silver flash of light arced across his awareness.

He loved the sun and wind and changing light of the surface world, but there was something light and airy-feeling in these ancient stone mazes that had little to do with weather and sunlight. It always seemed one could catch an echo of sweet voices singing in poignant counterpoint, as if the centuries of song had somehow melded with the stone.

He threaded past many white heads and a few dark ones, whose colorful clothes emphasized their sunsider origins. Odd, how he liked seeing bright colors in people's dress on the surface, but down here those same colors somehow brought the walls in closer.

Presently he saw by the narrowing of the tunnels and the gradual diminishing of decorative embellishments that he was nearing an access-way to the outside.

He passed three young morvende, who greeted him courteously. Patrol, eh? Apparently the Norsundrians (Imry, still?) persisted in avian searches for the way in. Patrol, and something — or someone — still outside engaged their interest in a sharp way indeed.

His curiosity intensified as the air changed, and he walked on. It was thinner, and colder, as protective magic diminished. Who was coming? He couldn't sense a specific mind, only an intense presence; a long beam of golden sunlight shot down the tunnel and splashed into glittering shards along the rough contours of the rock.

He rounded the last curve, to find a silhouette limned by the liquid gold of the westering sun. Inwardly he readjusted orientation (late afternoon; that way is west) as outwardly the silhouette resolved into a slim form, short curly hair, feminine curves of shoulder and hip. One not dressed in winter gear, either, despite the season and the height — and the shockingly cold flow of air — he knew that face.

"Marga," he said, on a note of question.

The noon-sky blue eyes were the same. Her smile deepened into mirth as the patrol that had brought her in closed off the entrance, and the light dimmed to the ubiquitous silver of glowglobes.

"Brother David! I've got hair now," she said, fingering the silky curls that ruffled all over her head. "And the scabs — how they itched — went away."

"What have you been doing with yourself since autumn?"

"Flying around, a little." She laughed, and he understood she meant it literally.

"Shape-changing, then?"

"Yes! Mostly bird shapes, because I can get around so much faster. I have discovered in myself a decided inclination for speed—" She broke off, her smile rueful. "Though that does bring its problems. Did try a tree, and found myself wishing to settle in properly, but I forced myself out—and discovered that not an afternoon but a week had passed. I haven't enough control yet for that. But I will be a tree, when the time is right."

"And if you change back, and find that ten years have passed? Or a hundred?"

"Then ten—or a hundred—years shall pass," she said, hands open. "Though I shall be watching."

David considered this concept. Or he tried to consider it, and then had to contemplate the fact that he couldn't compass it. Oh, he knew all about the magic for shape-changing, and the warnings about the resultant twisting of form and sensory awareness and the dangers of changing for too long. He also remembered, as most magic learners did, the story of the king who'd had the brilliant idea of changing his army into a forest in order to draw the enemy in. Only by the time the enemy had come, and were ready to be pounced on and destroyed by the tree-warriors surrounding them, perhaps half altered back to human form, but they had forgotten how to move, or couldn't get their limbs to work; the rest stayed trees. Weird trees.

Marga, it seemed, existed outside of human dangers because she had become something more than human. Perhaps that was why, in so very few months, she had gone from having an empty mind and an identity so open it had made him dizzy to try contact, to having a shield as impervious as Detlev's.

He stared witlessly at her dimpled smile, her wide sky-colored gaze under the mop of shining curls, her slight but definitely female form under the old tunic and baggy riding trousers. Back to the smile. The curve of her lips.

He blinked.

His hands were clammy, his neck hot and his tongue dry, and he needed to be talking. "What are you doing here?"

"First, helping Brother Leander. And Brother Adam, and the Benevolent Elders here, to aid them in understanding … some … of what Benefactor Detlev planned, then and now…" She began walking down the tunnel, David keeping pace.

"Then?" he repeated. "How far back?" Did any of the normal human forms of social interchange hold for her anymore? She had to be taking apart and reweaving her worldview with the same rapidity she turned herself into some kind of bird and went darting cross-country.

As if she heard his thoughts—his shielded thoughts—she admitted with a lilt of mirth, "I have to remember in the eyes of most I am seventeen, and that a few months ago, when you saw me, I was a mindless piebald blob."

David finished for her. "And if I didn't know, there must be a reason?"

She had turned away; when she looked back, her face was crimson.

She did still have human emotions, then, as well as the human form. He thought back to her original comment, which had been offered (he suspected now) not in tolerance, or even reassurance, which would be the same, but in a spirit of amity.

And in the same spirit, he said, "He's never told any of us. Until you, I gather?"

"No, no," Marga said, patting the air between them. "I have not seen him since we were all together with Auntie Liere. But I see the truth between the enemy's lies, you might say."

No honorific, or even a name, for Ilerian, David noted. "From a prudent distance, I trust. But here you are, safe. I'm glad."

Marga gave David a swift, honestly relieved glance that completely disarmed him. Then she said, "I met your brother, you know!"

"I remember."

"No, since. I don't count those first times, before you and Benefactor Detlev and Auntie Liere rescued me. I didn't even remember those until much later. And there had been no real interaction. How could there be? But recently. He was just about to discover Brothers Leander and Adam, and as it happened, I had been spending time with some yeath nearby, after helping Brother Zairna."

"So … you did what? Pursue Imry?"

"More in the nature of a decoy," she said, one eyebrow quirking ruefully. She paused, turned her head from side to side, and then chose a tunnel otherwise unremarkable from all the others. As she passed him, her arm brushed against his and he caught her scent of warm human girl, but with subtle differences that evoked wind and stone and high, soughing firs.

"And?" That sounded normal, didn't it? "What happened with Imry?"

"A little conversation. Not much. He wanted to know who I was."

She cocked her head then, and David became aware of singsong morvende voices echoing up the tunnels. *Marga! Marga! Are you returned?*

She faced him, walking backward, saying, "They do not

know, but I know, how important it is to the world, what you do."

"Marga!"

David said, "Sounds like someone wants you."

She gave him that merry grin again, and he felt it as warmth. Oh not mere warmth. It struck him with all the heat of the summer sun, though his mind was mourning, *No, you idiot, not this one, she will never be for you.*

Six

Wnelder Vee

LYREN-SARTORA WAS IN THE highest of spirits.

She'd discovered (at last) someone who had the same fast-changing moods, the flippant sense of humor that masked the things one takes most seriously. Laban was the big brother she'd never had.

While careening at breakneck speed all through the wintry Wnelder Vee countryside, much of their talk was about shared experience, and about people they both knew. He didn't treat her as a thirteen-year-old brat, though she knew she was one, at times, when her moods got the better of her. He talked to her as if she were one of the gang.

Somehow it was not much of a surprise to Lyren-Sartora, after a few close questions about family background, to hear Laban say, with his watchful blue gaze and his rakish, slightly derisive smile, "I don't know whether the news will delight or enrage you, but it's more than probable that we're related."

"Rage, of course," she said airily, but inside she gloried in the conviction that she was not, in fact, a changeling. All these parts of her nature that she'd been trying to squelch, or alter, or get rid of, seemed to be a big part of the Dei make-up.

Laban laughed. "Well, it's not exactly a recommendation, in many places. With reason. My father was generally hated."

"So was my grandfather," she shot back. "But there are

good ones. Like Merry Dei, and her sister, who is a Knight, and the Commander."

"I know about them. What about on your side?"

"Oh, my great-grandmother was well-liked. And there's my Aunt Marga, I keep forgetting about her, because I haven't met her, but the Fer Eiders say I'm like her. Not always approving. Our liking beautiful things and living above our station—whatever that means when you've lived the way I do, like a street urchin in a palace. But the ones who accepted me also seemed to like Aunt Marga. Anyway, isn't it proof we're not all bad?"

And then she got an idea, which she turned over in her mind until they reached his latest camp, which was up behind an old crossroads inn. She waited until they sat in a warm attic alcove, served by the inn's teenage son, who was a scout for Laban's freedom fighters

"Let's go tell Tahra," she suggested.

Laban had just sipped some hot, spiced pear cider and choked into his cup. When he was done coughing, and had wiped the tears from his face, he gasped, "Kill me now! It'll be faster!"

"Tchah!" She waved an imperious hand. "Does she know what you want to do for this backward, benighted kingdom?"

"I hope not! I did want to lay my hands on proof of my family connections—if any exists—that she'll demand. Before she can seek it out and destroy it," he added with fine irony.

Again an imperious wave. "But the Deis and the Delieths are related over and over. Even I know that much, and she can't deny that. And she likes *us*, meaning Liere and me, so to find out that we might very well all be related—well, wouldn't that go a ways toward making peace?"

He shook his head, his smile grim at the edges. "It will go a ways toward earning you and Liere permanent exile."

Lyren-Sartora's eyes widened. "I'd like to see anyone try to outlaw *me* because of ancestral ties!"

"Remember, O Righteous One, that ancestral ties produce inheritance claims. People like me, for instance, popping out of the dark corners of history and snatching at vacant thrones."

Lyren-Sartora propped a chin on a fist and frowned down at her cider. "Yes, and Merry did say they'd guessed. And Tahra's main objection is that she doubts you're really on our side! She thinks Detlev is on his own side."

"Synonymous with Norsunder." He gave her a twisted smile.

She pounced on that with a crow of triumph. "Regrets!"

"Surprised?"

"But, see! You need only tell her that you regret the Detlev years and his horrors, and she will be sympathetic to that, I'm sure."

Fury flashed like lightning through him. She gave him a puzzled look, one from which malice was entirely absent. He reminded himself of her age, of the fact that her grudge against Detlev had been formed in her babyhood, and was largely habit, rather than conviction. He consciously shed the crackle of anger then said, with considerably diminished irony, "I'd rather take my chances with the noose."

"But—" She flushed with annoyance. "You too? Loyal? Still?"

He laughed. "Jealous?"

She blinked at this unexpected flank attack. "What could I possibly be jealous of?"

"Of Liere's regard for his opinion. Just because you're far more worldly than Liere doesn't mean you are a whit wiser." He grimaced. "I had to learn that one myself."

That sparked a breathless, unwilling laugh from Lyren-Sartora. "Jealous!" But it was half a question, for she remembered certain things Sveneric had said. *Why* did jealousy happen? She had been struggling hard not to be jealous of Liere's being with Andri Elsarion. Maybe there was some jealousy of the boys' respect for Detlev? Whatever caused it, she needed to get rid of the thing that sparked jealousy, so useless an emotion. Useless, joyless.

Laban, never one to belabor, lifted a shoulder. "You're right about Tahra, though. The taint of Detlev for her is the taint of murder."

"You're afraid!" she challenged.

"You bet," he agreed with disappointing alacrity.

"But I'll protect you. See if I don't. I know I can win her over, I'm sure of it. Come with me!"

He could see that the vast, exciting game was still not quite real for her; she was still so young. It was to be expected that there were undercurrents in relationships she had no experience to sound. The remaining scraps of the comforting conviction that life was just a play had burned from his mind when he faced Imry's excoriating tongue again after all those years, and following hard on that, Adam's soul-deep, patient gaze as he pleaded with Laban to remember the firejive.

Still, he was who he was. "All right," he said carelessly.

And within two days, Laban and Lyren-Sartora took one last ride together, south across the border into Everon.

⸻⸻⸙⸻⸻

While Lyren-Sartora dashed, high-hearted and happy, under the snow-laden boughs of the borderland, her cousin Marga Fer Eider ran lightly down to the floor level of the Ghildraith geliath, where everyone was gathering. All around her people smiled, and she smiled back. It had always been that way, her entire life: the closest to an argument she had ever come was before she had set out on the journey that caused her to bond with the world at last, and though she did not know it, she had left an entire harbor town mourning the loss of her presence.

She felt someone looking for her — ahh!

"Benefactor Detlev," she said, coming up to him.

Detlev inclined his head, then said, "To the reason for this gathering. You know what I have to do."

She was surprised how direct he was. So much had changed since they had seen one another last! But she had seen him watching protectively in the dream-realm from time to time, until he understood that she was able to avoid the enemy on her own.

She nodded.

"I know that you cannot fight with us," he went on. "It was the same with Ejhir Sunchild."

"Will you tell me more about him? I see him, mere glimmerings, in the memories of the elder trees, and I detect traces of his presence in the sweet waters below the deepest mountains."

Detlev said, "You are alike and unalike, for at that time the world was in need of healing more than the humanity on it. He was solitary by nature, working to bring into balance the terrible spells ancient mages had wrought in creating mountain borders and the like, for the purposes of kings. You know what happened."

Pain struck, cold and hard, through her awareness. "Yes," she whispered. "I do know what happened to Ejhir."

Detlev said, "Then you are aware of Ilerian's hunt."

"Every moment I am aware, sleeping, awake. I always know where he is, but if I do no magic outside of myself, he cannot find me."

He hesitated. "Stay vigilant," he finally said.

She laughed up at him, a laugh that partook of sadness. "I know how long you mourned Ejhir," she said, and when she heard some dawnsinger girls calling *Marga, Marga! We have to plan the New Year's Firstday dance!* she ran off, leaving him staring after, for once his worry plain to see.

From above, David watched until he became aware of a presence at his side. Adam glanced down into the great cavern where everyone was gathered. "Detlev is here," he observed.

"We're all here," David said.

"Except for Laban." Adam pointed down to the lower cavern, where Detlev had been talking to Marga. "I've never seen him display such overt fatherly pride."

David laughed. It was true—not even with Sveneric, but then they were too close for that, bounded by far too much danger. Given all that he had been learning, for the first time he wondered about the circumstances of Sveneric's birth. As always, nothing had been said: between one visit to the Norsunder outpost on Five and the next, Sveneric had appeared, too much like Detlev even as a baby to be yet another foundling.

The click of toenails presaged the appearance of a long-legged black hound, who sniffed David, then thrust his muzzle under Adam's hand. David was going to ask when Adam had acquired a dog when tall, dark-haired Leander Tlennen-Hess appeared, dressed in a scholar's robe, and joined them, his arm brushing Adam's. David would scarcely have noticed if Leander had then moved apart, ceding the invisible boundary that custom placed around adults; instead, the two stood shoulder to shoulder, and David noticed the subtle signs of ardency in hand and eye, too new for habit.

"Wait. You two?"

Identical smiles—pride and tenderness—in two very different faces.

David grinned stupidly; of all those who had suffered Efael's personal style of violence, Adam had had the worst of it by far. For a time after he had kept a distance from others as if he could not bear the slightest, most indifferent touch; it seemed he had completely recovered.

To bridge any awkwardness, for David didn't know Leander except by sight, he said, "And you've also shaken off heirship, I hear. Good to have things to celebrate."

Leander opened his hand toward David. "I'm told it's you now under that yoke. For which I thank you. You spared me from a tiring, and no doubt fruitless, search for Senrid's cousin Ndand, which I had resolved to make once winter was over, war or no war."

Adam looked down, as David considered the fact that Leander had lived in proximity to Marloven Hess his entire life, he was a well-respected mage as well as a scholar of languages, but he still didn't understand Marlovens.

Leander said soberly, "I could bear the thought of a regency—just—while Crystal Ingrid was alive. Because I knew she would be educated by the Marlovens, and succeed as queen as soon as she was capable. But after she died, the prospect of being king if something happened to Senrid..." He shook his head. "I knew I'd be rotten. I thought the only solution would be to hunt up Ndand, who at least has a blood claim."

"So do several others," Adam murmured.

David hesitated, wondering if he ought to point out that no Marloven would accept Ndand Montredaun-An as queen— not someone who had left the country years before, and whose only skill was music. More telling than that, though, was the fact that her father had been universally hated. And while some Marloven kings had been hated, they had been respected, but not Tdanerend. He had been despised before he went over to Norsunder, which made him the worst kind of traitor. Of course Senrid knew that her claim (assuming she was even willing) would more likely touch off civil war than unite the Marlovens, or he would have exerted himself to find her years ago.

Adam bridged the moment by saying, "Dirk and Crow filled us in on your encounter at Efael's castle. But someone said that you had an encounter with Imry?"

"I did."

They exchanged stories, as below, a crowd gathered, mixing and moving, but always with a small eddy around Detlev, who had yet to advance ten paces. It seemed there were a lot of people waiting for a private moment with Detlev.

Then, through the crowd appeared a slim, straight-shouldered figure in a black and tan uniform, walking alone in the midst of a swarm of linen-draped morvende. Senrid's blond head lifted as he scanned the area, found them, and a short time later he emerged out of a string of chasing children.

Rori trotted up to him to sniff, and when Senrid bent to scruffle the dog's ears, Rori's tail beat the air.

"Senrid?" Leander exclaimed. "I didn't expect to see — why are *you* here?" His brows twitched together. "Bad news?"

"No worse than usual," Senrid said, turning an interrogative eye toward David, who shook his head minutely. He did not have to ask — though Adam might regret it, orders were orders, and keeping the Ilerian-fighting circle a secret was probably the most important order any of them had yet to receive.

Adam turned to Leander. "I did tell you that there will be a coordinated counterattack, spearheaded by Sartor."

Leander's smile diminished. "More war talk, right."

Senrid flicked an assessing glance between Leander and the two of Detlev's boys. "Ferret vanished again. Which is probably something you two would know more about than I." A jerk of his chin at Adam and David. "Before he vanished, he gave Vidanric Renselaeus a map with every Norsundrian outpost in the eastern half of the continent marked. Numbers of warriors. Horses. Weapons storage. Adranis, Chwahir, mercenaries — which companies, as those vary wildly."

If Leander wanted to believe Senrid was here to report that, he was free to.

"Vidanric is recruiting allies for the expected counterattack, but is trying to broker a treaty. Adranis and Chwahir had to obey orders; like it or not, their kings went for Norsunder. Hands off unless they come for the kill. Norsundrian captains, shoot on sight is the compromise."

"Choking off retaliatory slaughters," David said appreciatively — Vidanric, among others, was looking ahead. If the allies lost, the treaty wouldn't matter. But if they won, no one with any wit wanted to see a state of warfare continue as before, the weapons simply switching hands. And there plenty who would try, convinced of the righteousness of their cause.

Senrid said, "Jehan of Khanerenth wrote that his fleet has split and the old ones are coming around south to my end of the continent. Old ones. Didn't really explain. Since I cannot imagine a navy of white-haired grannies and gramps, my guess is he means a fleet of old ships no doubt wrested out of storage, or old traders converted to transport. Norsunder got pretty much everything else."

Adam had been observing Leander, who had nothing to contribute to this talk of counterattack, and Senrid had just ventured—unknowing—onto tricky ground. "It's nearly mealtime, and I'm starved," Adam said. "I smell something savory."

"I'll go with you," Leander said, lifting a hand to Senrid and David, and the pair wandered off, followed by Rori, leaving David wrestling with what to say about Fox's reappearance after eight centuries. It had been easy to avoid the subject when Fox's fleet was on the other side of the world. Apparently that had changed.

Early on, David had asked Detlev what to tell Senrid.

Nothing. Remember, outside of Fox being his ancestor, he knows little about him other than he entertained himself writing about the academy of his day, which he never attended. In Marloven Hess, Inda's legend overshadowed Fox, who was better known in the East. Until Fox returns to Halia, mention will only be a distraction, at a time when Senrid needs no further distractions.

Fox was on the way to Halia—and Senrid was about to sequester himself, a desperately needed part of the circle that would be attacking Ilerian directly. David would not lie to Senrid; better to skip the subject entirely. "Did you write to Rel?"

"I did. Aldon's been futilely chasing phantoms, while Rel's refugees and volunteers pop in and out of places like this morvende cavern as they train for the counterattack."

"Is he going to run Sartor's action?" David asked, relieved that Senrid readily accepted the shift. "He's an experienced tactician, but no background in moving armies. He makes up for it in brutality."

"Atan will command," Senrid predicted. "She's a natural at strategic thinking, I saw that when we had those meetings in Remalna. Did you ever see her situation map in Mearsies Heili? She's continued learning, soaking up some fairly sound stuff from somewhere. Siamis, I expect. Rel says he and Atan are going to marry New Year's Week. Symbolism of union for Sartor, and their allies. I'm glad they like to think so. Might even be true." He shrugged. "What it means in practical terms is, they'll be sharing a royal banner—"

They were interrupted by the call to the meal sounding through the crowd, causing general movement toward one of the enormous caverns.

"Hungry?" David asked.

"Always."

As they ate the thick, savory vegetable soup and crisped oat-and-fruit cakes, Senrid spent a little time calculating what Aldon was likely to send against Rel now that it was his turn to hold Eidervaen, then he stared down at his half-empty bowl, and said, "We've talked about this before—"

"Ivandred," David said. "I haven't forgotten."

"Except I've heard a different answer each time."

"That's because all Siamis, or Detlev, have are guesses. What little they know I've told you. We know Ilerian holds Ivandred in a capture-sphere. We know the First Lancers were deployed once, in Ralanor Veleth, to devastating effect. And not again."

"Because Ivandred tried to make a break for it?"

"Yes. Fighting the magic the entire time he was driving off the Velethi. Detlev thinks Ilerian is reluctant to deploy them again, though Efael has been agitating through Svir for control of them. But Detlev thinks both Ilerian and Svir believe that Ivandred would never attack the Marloven part of Halia."

"Detlev thinks Ivandred has some kind of allegiance to Halia?" Senrid flattened his hand, flicking it away as if dismissing the words.

"He does. He insists that the Sartoran archive, which is all we really have, is … distorted about what actually happened before the ride through the rift."

"But we don't have anything else, other than Vasande Lassiter's memoir," Senrid said. "Which is third-hand. Fourth, really, written after he went back to Colend to be Duchas of Alarcansa." Senrid waved the Colendi off. "It's that assumption, that Ivandred wouldn't attack Halia, that lets me do this." Senrid's voice lowered as his forefinger briefly touched his thumb, meaning his part in the Ilerian-fighting circle. "That and the vital need to cut off the head of the dragon, rather than running around stabbing at its feet. Van Stad and I have talked about this…"

And once again, Senrid launched into an exhaustive account of the patched-together Marloven defenses, should they be attacked from the north, or from the shore, with fresh enemies—and how to handle the occupying forces once they rose.

He and David had been through these conversations, several times. But David understood the urge to be sure, to try to impose this sequence of events over the terrors that came in the night. It was a way to feel in control.

Senrid was still talking when they were interrupted by the sound of a flute.

A circle of dawnsinger girls danced out into the center of the cavern. More instruments joined in, and the dancers formed into a ring, accompanied by sweet music rising, falling, and shifting upward in keys like the changing of seasons.

Senrid paid no attention. He merely raised his voice a little, and went on theorizing about what Stad would do if the Chwahir navy, or the pirate fleet Efael had ravaging the east coast of Toar, brought over Norsundrians from the west.

For a time David watched the dancing and listened to Senrid. At one point, to illustrate a complicated amphibious defense, Senrid shifted around their crockery and utensils; when David looked up, the morvende had been joined by a slim, laughing girl in baggy tunic and trousers, her short, silken curls bouncing.

As Senrid talked, David watched dark-haired Marga weave in and out of the golden-haired dawnsingers. Finally, to test them both, when Senrid paused, David gestured toward the dancers and said, "There's Detlev's summer triumph, the one we searched so hard for."

Senrid glanced up in a perfunctory manner, then away—then back.

Silence.

Then Senrid said in a voice devoid of any emotion, "Relation to the Fer Eiders, I take it?"

"Yes."

Marga danced past, but Senrid's gaze did not follow her.

David fought the impulse to watch her as long as she was in view and leaned forward to grab a hunk of fresh bread from a tray being carried past.

Senrid spotted the black hilt of the dagger David wore in his sleeve. He looked up, this time with interest. "Ildareth dueling dagger," he said unerringly. "Where did you get that?"

"Not long ago," David said. "When I encountered Imry. I am hoping to make an exchange for my sword."

Senrid lifted his brows. "I suggest you return it. Sheathed in stringy brotherly guts."

"That's one solution."

Senrid laughed, and though Marga danced by in another round, he never glanced aside. The shield-wall was up, and to break it would break him.

One thing was clear that hadn't been before. David had thought Detlev had erred in not recruiting Liere Fer Eider into their circle. They desperately needed her strength in Dena Yeresbeth. But they needed the entire group's strength, and although the form her gift took was farsense, that is distance contact — at that she was the best of their entire generation — Detlev far surpassed her in that, and even if he hadn't, he would not have let her spearhead the attack on Ilerian. That he reserved to himself. Her endurance on the mental plane was roughly the same as Andri's, and nowhere near Senrid's. Two out of three was the best Detlev could do; it would have destroyed Senrid if Liere had been among them.

David snagged another freshly-baked bread, tossing it on his palm as he considered the three Fer Eiders he knew. What was it about them? He struggled for perspective, to be objective, if there really was any sort of objectivity in the tangled realm of relationships.

Liere and Marga were the same size and build, yet he was indifferent to the one, and not to the other. Lyren-Sartora, once the world's most famous baby, still was a child in form and outlook. She, like her mother, moved with grace, but it wasn't the trained economy of movement that characterized Liere since her return from Geth, it was something innate.

When Lyren-Sartora wakened to the age of interest, she'd probably detonate half a continent. David made a mental note not to be anywhere near her when it happened. If it happened. If her charm evolved away from the natural self-absorption of thirteen years old, she might handle that, too, with grace; laughing at himself, he watched Marga dancing hand in hand with a pair of morvende girls, and wondered if the Montredaun-Ans had always managed to run into the wall of a first crush in the midst of war.

Seven

Everon – Merry's house

RODERIC DEI HAPPENED TO be there when Lyren-Sartora and Laban walked in.

Lyren-Sartora gave an ecstatic sigh as she flung her frost-stippled cloak across a bench. She and Laban exhibited the high, glowing color of youth — and the vividness of their shared ancestry.

An ancestry also shared with Roderic. Laban's laughing good looks gave Roderic a moment of vertigo. Except for those blue eyes, Laban was a reincarnation of old Grandfather Leskandar, right down to the walk. If Roderic had had a son, he conjectured, that son might have looked just like Laban.

Roderic watched Laban assess the room, and himself, seated peaceably in this corner near the fire, pipe in hand and a tankard before him. Laban's thin, curved brows lifted as he gestured in greeting, but he said nothing.

Lyren-Sartora's curved brows arched as she propped fists on her hips. "What a pleasant surprise?" she addressed Roderic directly.

Roderic ignored the irony. "Bad weather out. I'm grounded — but as New Year's Week is almost on us, what better place to be than with family?" He raised his pipe in a silent greeting to Laban, who flashed him an appreciative smile.

Tahra was on the other side of the room, at the window.

She hadn't looked up from the pile of messages that Roderic had brought.

Lyren-Sartora studied Tahra's bent head as Merry drifted along the perimeter of the room and came to stop at her father's shoulder, her sweet face worried.

Lyren-Sartora's chin lifted as she stalked down the length of the room, heels ringing and her long braids swaying. "Tahra," Lyren-Sartora said with a sigh. "Will you at least listen to a person?"

Tahra's head turned.

Lyren-Sartora knelt on the chair opposite Tahra so they were eye to eye, and she smiled, with the high heart of she who knows that pure motives must carry all before them. "Guess what I've found out! It seems we are related — and if you fling a 'so what' at me I'll be furious!"

Tahra laid her papers down. "Related?"

"To your mother!"

Tahra studied her for a few moments, as the others watched. Tahra did not do well by the comparison; her narrow head and sallow complexion were not enhanced by her habitual expression of closed and tightly controlled anger. Facing her, Lyren-Sartora was the picture of innocent youth, emerging handsomeness — and Dei charisma.

Tahra studied her as if seeing her for the first time. "I suppose it's possible. Likely, even. I take it you've decided this connection bestows on you the right to meddle in my affairs?"

"I'd meddle anyway." Lyren-Sartora admitted with a quick, disarming grin. "Come, Tahra! Listen to me, at least. Only once. Your ruling is your business, I know, but I think everyone has a right to speak up when she sees that one of your judgments is based on false information. Laban's not a Norsundrian. He's fighting 'em, just as we are! You might try to talk to him, just like I—"

Tahra's mouth pressed into a thin white line. Her narrow features seemed carved in volcanic stone, expressing not just anger but cold and depthless hatred.

"Be silent, Lyren-Sartora," she said, softly, but with such venom Lyren-Sartora gasped, her hands going to her chest as if she'd been slugged.

Tahra stood up. She glared at Laban. He returned her regard with interest. Though he wore no visible weapons, and stood in an attitude of ease with hands clasped loosely behind him, Roderic sensed his wariness. "You are the son of Harold Dei?" Tahra said.

"I am."

"He's not the only—" Lyren-Sartora put in, her wide gold gaze going anxiously from one face to the other and back again.

This time Tahra silenced her with a look.

"Understand this," Tahra said. "if I could see you damned for all eternity, I would, for what you've done to me and my family. You and your accursed, blood-smeared gang and that soul-eating Detlev—" She turned her head to spit into the fire. "'Not Norsundrians,'" she repeated with corrosive scorn. "I want first of all an end to war. If you set yourself up as Morgeh Troiad's successor, there is nothing I can do to stop you, but neither shall you have aid from me or mine. As soon as I have word that you have in fact usurped Morgeh's vacant place, then, that day, I shall cease all aid to the people of that kingdom, and there will be no more intercourse at all, in any form, until you leave again. Any attempt made by you from this day forward to ride across the border into Everon will be considered an act of war and will be met with steel. Do you hear me?"

"I do," Laban said.

"Then get you gone! It was not my wish to permit you to live past your crossing the threshold of this house."

Laban bowed. It was a courtly bow, sovereign to sovereign, with his hand over his heart in the time-honored gesture of treaty or good will.

Tahra turned abruptly away, her fingers trembling as she grabbed up her papers. Laban winked at Merry, his expression kindly, then he about-faced and started from the room. Lyren-Sartora hesitated, then hurried after.

At the door, Laban looked round, to find Roderic next to him. "Orders are orders," Roderic said, his tone bland, his expression apologetic. And then that, too, vanished as he added, "We ride when the weather clears."

Laban seemed a little distracted to Lyren-Sartora, but still alert. He smiled quickly. "The preponderance of armed Knights at four upstairs windows, and inside the kitchen, and—no doubt—in the storeroom behind the stable were a result of heavy weather?"

Roderic shrugged philosophically. "We all hate to get our feet wet."

Laban flashed a smile in which only a little strain showed. "And the back window in there and that western dormer take the brunt of the storm?"

"That's right. " Roderic nodded. "Fare well, my boy." He walked back inside the house.

Lyren-Sartora followed Laban out into the cold, sleety air. "I got that!" she whispered, paying no attention to the frigid stinging of face and hands. "You told him that you knew they were all ready for orders to pounce, but there were two escape routes. Am I right? Am I?"

"Mostly."

She sighed. They reached the stable. "Fancy your noticing that. I saw the Knights, of course, and was afraid Tahra had an ambush waiting, but I didn't say because I wasn't sure, we'd just entered, and might be overheard, and anyway you'd notice for certain, I thought—Laban, are you always mind-blocked?"

He led his horse out—noticing with his increasingly fracturing awareness that some unknown hands had thoughtfully curried the beast, cleaned off saddle and gear, and probably fed him too, from the content look in the round brown eyes. He spotted a Knight busy at a rack of harnesses, nodded, and got a nod from her in return.

He didn't mount up at once.

Out in the courtyard, as freezing sleet slashed at them both, he looked down into that face so much like his in so many ways, but so very young. Desperately young. Yet she had to learn sometime, didn't she, if she insisted on messing with the affairs of kings?

"Not here," he said in a low voice, pitched for her ears alone. "He set it up as a message. Concerning the border between Everon and Wnelder Vee, and possible lines of communication. See, I trust you with a secret that can't jeopardize me—that cannot get any worse—but it does jeopardize Roderic."

Her face was utterly serious. "So shall I—"

"Stay here. I know you can help me, but you'd be more help to Tahra. She's going to need it, really need it, because her people are too afraid to talk straight with her. But recover your status first!" He laughed a little, watching his breath vaporize and whip away on the wind. "She's very angry with you."

"But where—"

"Look. I've got something to do right now that doesn't

concern either of these two countries. You work on recovering your status, and also, work on defeating Norsunder. We will be in contact again, but not right away."

"Ugh." She snorted. "I'd love to forget the war. But I won't!"

"Take care, young cousin." He gave one of her braids a flick, and mounted up.

"You too. Cousin!" She smiled, and as he rode away she dashed back inside, her mind working fast on her campaign to soothe Tahra into friendship once again.

In the Ghildraith cavern, the Darchelde circle gathered in MV's chamber to greet Laban, who had just been transferred in. Detlev was still talking to Tarael and the morvende elders.

"What happened with Tahra?" MV half rose, and squinted against the effort it took.

Laban lifted his hands. "Welcomed me like a brother."

MV and Rolfin thought this obvious lie was pretty funny.

Adam waited until the snickers (and coughs, from poor old Andri, who had managed to catch his yearly winter cold right before being transferred in) had abated somewhat, and said, "Wnelder Vee?"

"It's mine. But she did her best to lay the groundwork for a blood feud."

"And let that be a lesson to you," Dirk said with a scowl.

David and Adam both saw in the wide, bright, slightly distracted look in Laban's eyes that he was still too fresh from what must have been quite a scene to treat deftly with anyone else's bitterness about their collective Evil Backgrounds.

David said, "The only thing that's pertinent about Tahra — and Wnelder Vee — is that gossip is bound to get to the Norsundrians, placing Laban firmly there, lurking about in the hills somewhere with Vana."

"As ordered," Laban said. "I even made sure to give 'em a good chase there at the end, though the weather was a trifle brisk. Silvanas will continue to sting them from time to time."

"We're all here now," Adam said in a speculative voice. "This is the end of the diversions for us. What comes next is the real thing."

"Speaking of which." Mildred raised a forefinger.

"Let's hear it." David raised his voice just enough to quell the whispers; he felt the current of reactions.

"That Jilo fellow—a good 'un, I thought—and a couple other people as well, seem to think we're part of 'David's plan.' They think it has something to do with chasing Imry Llyenthur." Mildred paused, and when no one disagreed, "It seems to me—though I admit I left just before I could have heard it first hand—that Detlev stirred hot peppers into the stew at that big meeting last August in Clair's country, by mentioning the fact that David had a plan in mind and wasn't telling him. Detlev, I mean."

"I really was pursuing Imry at that point," David said. "What's your question? Is it 'Do I have a mind?'" David joked.

Naturally that caused a cacophony of catcalls, hoots, and yoks. When the vote of confidence had subsided, Mildred said, "But now all the talk is about Rel's plan. Is it my imagination, or do I detect another hand shaping things here?"

"Surprised?" David snorted.

"Then I was right. So, how about this one. Since this plan didn't just sort of evolve recently, the hand that's been shaping it has shaped more than just this plan, and for longer."

"How long, is your guess?" Roy asked, leaning back against MV's pile of pillows.

Mildred pursed her lips. "Hope I don't tread on any toes, but my guess is, from the time he first started training you dolts. What's more, I've also got the feeling that the inclusion of us—" She jerked a thumb at Andri, Dirk, Zairna, Crow, Senrid and herself. "—makes the plan seem more random. But you know, I had a chance to think things over while we were leaving Marloven Hess, and our rapport pattern didn't develop as we got used to one another. I thought so at the time, but now I know I was just learning something already in existence."

David exchanged a brief glance with Adam, unreadable to those who were covertly watching. "Yes ... and no. How's that?"

"About what I expected." She grinned. "Well, never mind."

"Tell her," said MV.

"One ominous hint too many," she responded. "Let's hear it."

David watched from the ledge on which he'd draped himself, his manner relaxed. Casual. But he could see every single face. He said, "Our suspicion, of late, has been that the guiding hand has been in action since the beginning."

"Since you were born? No." Mildred's eyes slitted. "You mean, since he switched?"

"If he switched." David shrugged.

"I believe he never did," Adam said.

Senrid's eyes narrowed. Andri whistled, slow and soft, under his breath. Zairna looked polite, but he was listening intently. Dirk stared, his amazement obvious.

Sveneric didn't react at all.

"A speculation hitherto kept among ourselves." MV's hoarse voice still managed to convey a very mordant humor.

Mildred nodded slowly, then said, "My guardian once told me there was good, evil, and enlightened self-interest. We know he did terrible things, long ago. Is all that being overlooked?"

"No," Adam said. "But some of us think there's more to them than the records say."

"Like?"

"I'm beginning to believe, especially after some very oblique hints from Siamis, who cannot bring himself to tell a lie, that every wicked deed was calculated for a reversal farther down in time. Every single one. He took the blame for every action, and then he took the blame for the losses. We saw that in our own lives," Adam said.

"Our loyalty was supposedly to Norsunder — or rather to enlightened self- interest," MV said.

"But actually it was to him," Adam said. "So we moved more or less untouched through Norsunder, and when he left, we left with him. At the same time he prepared us to hop the fence, he began to shift himself outside the circle, focusing our loyalty superficially on one another, and then outward to the world, as he tried to cut himself out by distancing from us. All by degrees."

"Too subtle for me." Laban gave a rueful shrug.

"Too slowly for you," Adam corrected calmly. "He went slow because Vana, Curtas, Leef, Noser, and I couldn't accept it any other way, all for differing reasons. Then Efael just had to bustle things along."

Mildred did not understand the brief silence, or the sharp looks, then Andri glanced up, and whistled again.

"What about that Llyenthur twit?" Mildred asked.

"In some ways he's the most loyal of us all," David said. "Whatever he's up to now will probably either prove or disprove that. Here's the thing to remember about my brother: the first thing my shit of a father beat out of him was a sense of empathy."

Mildred waved off the subject of Imry Llyenthur. "Detlev hasn't told you because...?"

"Because the details of his personal life have little relevance or importance to what we're doing now."

"Says he?"

"Says he."

"Do they?" Mildred leaned forward.

MV grunted a laugh.

"Good question," David said. "Sveneric?" David glanced down at Detlev's son, who'd sat silently at the base of the ledge on which David was stretched out.

Sveneric had been staring down at his hands. Now he looked up. "Yes," he said. "But I think the cost is too much for him to talk about. Even with me. It's true for both him and Siamis."

There was a long moment during which the only sound was the cold mountain water tumbling down its stone chute behind MV's pillow-bed.

Then Senrid spoke, in a dry voice: "Don't bore on forever."

Everyone laughed.

Sveneric shrugged sharply. "He's not omniscient, as he would be the first to tell you. He made mistakes. Then there were the, ah, the things that might be mistakes and might not."

"As in?" Andri asked, brows up.

"The Dei family," Sveneric said. "He matched up with Alian Dei, intending to bring Dena Yeresbeth back into the world. He says he was so young at the time—thought he understood its origins, but he didn't."

"But if he hadn't, there would have been no Adamas Dei," David said, his fingers brushing his side where the black sword ought to be—the black sword still in Imry's hands.

"Adamas Dei was Detlev's son?" Senrid asked, looking up sharply. And saw the answer in MV's, David's, Rolfin's, Roy's and Sveneric's eyes.

Sveneric said, "He hid that fact successfully from Norsunder for ages. Siamis says, no doubt aided by the Deis being their own worst enemies." He made a wry face.

David leaned back on his elbows. "Until Yeres sniffed it out a century or two ago, on one of her rare forays into real-time, but she assumed the Deis were merely the result of Detlev getting saddle wood for Alian Dei, back then. Who was said to be so hot she dropped 'em in droves at a hundred paces."

Andri blinked. "I'm … trying to picture him. Flirting?"

"And failing," Laban cracked. "You're not the only one."

Rolfin looked askance. "They did have three children."

MV snickered, a hand pressed to his gut. "You're picturing him cornering her to read a lot of Ancient Sartoran poetry?

"Yep," Andri said. "Until she gives up, gets him drunk and rips his clothes off in order to show him what's what."

Mildred's pupils were vertical slits of mirth. "If she was so hot that everyone in Old Sartor wanted her, but she stayed with him long enough to have three children, that sort of suggests he knew what he was doing, eh? What I have trouble picturing is him having a grand passion in the first place."

"Don't think he ever did," David said. "I think he picked her for brains and looks. He did say he was young. Anyway, after she married Connar Landis and became Queen of Sartor, Adamas Dei left for the west, after which there is no evidence that Detlev ever went back to Sartor, in any guise, from which I take it she was a one-and-done. Curtas made that a project one year, combing the old archive for one of his guises."

"We loved turning them up," Laban admitted. "It was like scavenger hunting."

David went on, "Whereas we are sure he went back to visit Adamas Dei as often as he could. There are turns of phrases in the *Conversations* that remind us of him. Though Adamas Dei only called the other person a master."

Senrid's gaze shifted from one to another, as Sveneric said, "Anyway he began to understand later that it was the world's magic—its natural entities—who very slowly altered humanity again."

"Maybe we were all chosen, and trained, for this particular end," MV said. "But if any of us walked away, right now, he'd do nothing to stop us."

Crow's rasping voice rose. "Then, what you're saying is, it's Detlev's war."

"He will tell you it's Sartorias-deles's war," David said. "Begun four, almost five thousand years ago."

Adam added softly, "He fought to delay it for centuries."

"You're saying he's been, what, working on this for four thousand years?" Crow looked so skeptical that for a moment they actually saw the whites of his eyes.

Another silence.

And David said, "Yes."

Then Sveneric said in an altered voice, "He's coming."

Detlev entered, and looked around at them with mild question. David swung his legs down and sat up straight, freeing up some space, which Detlev then claimed.

"This chamber is warded," he said. "I laid the ward myself some time ago. The morvende call it the Seers Chamber. Here they have traditionally sent those with visions — incipient Dena Yeresbeth. Tarael and their council of elders believe you are sequestered here, in this quiet space, to use Dena Yeresbeth in aid of the mages."

"Dena Yeresbeth has been around for longer the recent generation?" Mildred asked.

"Only in nascent form," Detlev said. "And in rare individuals. It showed up as a sensitivity to changing seasons, to animals, to the presence of other people, seen and unseen. There are records you can read at your leisure. Right now, I suggest you sit in a circle, as beginning dyranarya did when I was young. I will help orient you on the mental plane, as you concentrate on two things: concealing your identity and sharing your strength with Adam..."

Eight

Enaeren – Elsarion ancestral castle

THIS TIME, LIERE TIMED it right.

Last time, she had prevailed upon Andri to come with her to meet the third shipment of weapons and arrows, so they could thank Trevor Macael Elsarion in person. "I don't think it's a good idea," Andri had said after Liere had unsuccessfully tried to meet Macael following the second shipment. "He's staying shy for a reason. Makes sense. If the Norsundrians sniff out a visit between the two of us, he's going to lose his freedom of movement."

"But he brought us *boxes and boxes* of arrows, as well as all those swords."

Andri shrugged. "If he wanted to meet us, he'd send a message," was all he said, but after he saw the splendid array of steel that Macael Elsarion had contrived to get for them—smoothly and quietly transferred—he changed his mind.

To no avail. They arrived at the old Elsarion castle to discover that their benefactor was nowhere to be found. Andri decided Cousin Macael staying at a distance was prudent.

Shortly after that, the word came from Detlev that it was time for him to go, and Dhana appeared to take Andri away.

Liere was one of the very few who knew about the true purpose of the Ilerian-fighting circle—her farsense being so advanced, there was a real danger of her checking on Andri at the worst time. A lightning-fast exchange in the world of dreams between Liere, Siamis, and Detlev had straightened that out. She did not want to know who else was in that circle, and she assiduously kept her mind from reaching for Andri. That was easier now than it might have been, as she had for the past year been suppressing the instinct to reach for Senrid, which her dream-brain stubbornly persisted in trying now and then, usually late at night.

Oh, habits, she thought in disgust as she rode alone toward Elsarion. It was better to keep that door closed — Senrid had more than enough to do in Marloven Hess.

She turned her thoughts firmly to considering Macael, still very much an enigma. He was self-effacing but she had discovered that he was thorough. Perhaps, as Andri surmised, he oversaw the delivery from afar, but she was convinced that he would check on his ancestral home himself, after the departure of Andri's party.

That is, she was convinced on the long, cold ride north. When she got there and oversaw the transfer, as usual with no Macael in sight, she wondered if she was wrong. She felt foolish giving her excuse to stay behind and inspect, but she did it.

When the last of the laden horses plodded up the snowy trail at an orderly and unmolested gait, she wheeled her own mount, and by the light of a drifting half-moon rode back past Ovaish. Presently her horse picked its way down the icy valley, and up the trail to Elsarion, long-time home of Andri's and Macael's forebears.

She studied the moon-washed castle as she rode. When she emerged from an avenue of ancient trees, she was rewarded by the dim yellowish glow of a lamp behind a high window. Of course it could be just a caretaker, but what would a caretaker be doing up in the residence portion of the castle during a frigid night, an hour before the dawn watch? She sent out a tendril of farsense — and met the expected block.

She rode into the nearly empty stable, and noticed a single mount there, a young, high-bred black beast. A solitary stable hand slumbered in a room above the stable. Since she usually rode with a mere saddle pad and halter (except when she needed to use saddlebags as transport) it took her only moments to tend her still-fresh gray. Leaving the horse with food, she made her way softly into the dark interior of the castle.

The lower levels were equally deserted. Macael had indeed been thorough, sending his servants elsewhere and making the castle appear to be deserted. It was chill with the peculiar coldness of stone buildings in winter.

Soundlessly she made her way up into the smallish but well-designed rooms of the family's residence wing. Shafts of pale bluish light flowed in curtainless windows and touched the ghostly shapes of sheet-draped furniture.

Yellow light slanted from a door opened a hand's breadth, and she slowed her steps. She meant to glimpse the occupant of the room, and if she found Macael she'd retreat and make a noise to announce her presence, but almost the same moment her gaze fell on Macael's black hair and familiar Elsarion build he looked up sharply. There was no spontaneous expression past that single surprised lift of his head. Andri would have either grinned or let out some sort of exclamation suitable to the moment (if not to most drawing rooms) but Macael's face shuttered with inscrutable courtesy. "Liere, this is a surprise. What can I do for you?"

His glance was brief and entirely polite, but once again she became acutely aware of her appearance. At least it was nothing out of the ordinary: sturdy gray riding clothes under a heavy gray wool cloak. Her braids were only two days old, and reasonably clean.

Her mind, working rapidly, decided it must be the contrast between the cousins that caused this reaction, for Andri's attitude toward appearance was exactly the same as hers: clothing was supposed to be functional, clean when you can get near cleaning frames, comfortable at all times, which allows for a random delight in a fine shirt or well-made cloak. If one happens upon such.

Macael was dressed in black outer garments, which might be expected of one doing a lot of night-sneaking. But the cloak thrown back over one shoulder was luxurious merino, lined with black silk, and there wasn't a gapping seam or frayed corner anywhere on it. She suspected from the muted sheen that his black tunic was an expensive blend of wool, linen, and silk, exquisitely tailored. Even the glimpse of the linen shirt at the high neck of his tunic exhibited no trace of clumsy stitchery or worn edges.

Well, she thought, at least this time I'm not sporting half the road between here and Shiovhan.

"Do I make an adequate conspirator?" Macael asked.

It was his second question; she realized she had been staring far too long.

"Except for the lamp," she said, her breath freezing and falling. "It's how I knew someone was here. Also, there's the jewel." She pointed to his sapphire ring glittering with flashes of cobalt intensity that brought Marga's eyes unexpectedly to mind. "And that no doubt expensive and certainly discreet silver belt buckle that would make a good target for an assassin with a good longbow."

Macael smiled ruefully. "Outside I wear these." He touched a pair of beautifully woven black gloves folded neatly over his blackweave belt at one side. "But the others are yet new lessons."

"Ah, there aren't any Norsundrians around for a night's ride," Liere said, now wondering if she'd sounded like a pompous know-it-all.

"I saw no one," he said. "But then I thought I was the last of our two parties."

"So you do oversee the transfers." At his nod, she said, "That's what we do, too. Mind-checking as well as watching. For both parties, as much as we can." And waited for a similar assurance — thus letting her know whether or not he had Dena Yeresbeth.

"I feel responsible for those laborers," Macael said — a sidestep. As usual. "Most of them are ill-spared from various friends, should the need for a defense arise."

"Adranis? What, retainers from big holdings? We noticed that they seemed well provided with animals and equipment."

Macael shrugged slightly. "I know so few in Enaeran, whereas I have family connections in Sles Adran, as well as old friends from my frequent boyhood visits. I do not know any of Andri's new landholders. Speaking of Andri, where is he?"

"Up in the western hills, giving a hand to the organizing there." As she spoke the half-truth agreed on between them — to be given to everyone from Gared outward — she was aware of a pang of regret for the lie.

Still, she stuck to the agreement. After all, it also protected Macael, who was riding around using lamps and wearing a gleaming silver belt-buckle. "We were here together last time, hoping to meet up with you. He wanted so much to thank you in person for the unsurpassed quality of your aid. Four times, now! And horses, that second time! Andri also wanted to compliment you on the excellence of those blades, obviously all from a first-rate forge."

"I'm afraid I invoked blood rights that time." Macael opened his hand, a wry gesture. "I won't be able to make a nuisance of myself in that way with any frequency."

Liere shook her head. "Please. Don't get yourself into trouble with your Adrani connections. You've done so much. More than we had allowed ourselves to hope, and in so short a time. We need more—always—but not if you put yourself into a difficult position. Somehow, we shall manage."

"Have you brought Andri extensive foreign aid?"

Liere laughed. "I wish!"

"Extensive foreign contacts, then?" Macael smiled in response.

"Some—well, some. Though he's done at least as well on his own," she added, thinking of the winter before, and how he'd made friends with MV and the poopsies. But she didn't want to bring Detlev's name into any conversation.

"Do you have some notion of how affairs are progressing outside our borders?"

"A little."

"Outside news is something to which my access is severely limited."

"But—well." She glanced around, distracted by too many things to think of at once. "Um. Are you rushing right off when you're done doing whatever it was that I interrupted? Because otherwise I could give you a rundown on what I know. My news, as it happens, is fairly fresh." No need to tell him that she'd gotten it via beige paper from Andri just that afternoon.

Macael turned to the handsomely bound pile of books that he had laid down on her entrance, and finished packing them into a saddlebag. "Access to reading material is also quite limited in our isolated valley," he said. "I am here to raid my own library."

"Ah, this is your study." Liere twirled around. "Yep. There's the portrait of Uncle Thunder. Andri didn't tell me he looks more like a rogue, or a pirate chief at the very least, than the respected head of the family."

Macael gave a soft laugh. "He was a singular individual."

"This is a very pretty room." She looked more closely at the two splendid wall-hangings, and the bindings of the books in the large bookcase.

"It is comfortable enough when the air is not freezing," Macael said. "Would you care for a glass of cognac?"

"No thanks," she said, shuddering. "Especially not just before dawn. But don't let my squeamishness stop you." She dropped into one of the large armchairs and curled her legs beneath her. "Feel free."

"Thank you." He reached into a cabinet, pulled out a decanter, and a heavy cut crystal glass, then poured out a goodly slug. Andri hadn't mentioned Macael having a penchant for liquor during their travels last winter.

Well, neither had he known about the music.

Liere said, as he carried his glass to the other chair and sat down, "Where shall I begin?"

"With the rumors about the Queen of Sartor assembling an army for a counterattack." He had not brought the lamp, and his chair sat outside the circle of light, so she could not make out any more of his face than a pale blob. "Also, rumors about a king."

"All true. Good old Rel! He looks like a King of Sartor ought to look. No doubt the spectacle of him wearing Landis violet and gold and wielding a two-handed broadsword as long as he is tall will figure greatly in rumors to come, and I hope it has a suitably bracing effect for our side."

"That will depend, will it not, on whether he is successful?"

"Not as much as you'd think. Remember the harvest fires? A fine example of how much stronger symbols can be than deeds."

"I take it you know this Rel?"

"Yes," Liere said, smiling. "We've been friends for a long time, as it happens."

"What is his background?"

"Suitably exalted for any sniff-noses who demand royal blood, though that turned out to be a surprise to—"

"Not Rel the Wanderer? From, ah, Tser Mearsies?"

"Yes. You have heard of him, then?"

"Who has not?" Macael retorted with amusement. "Always in context with war and your childhood conflict with the Unspeakable Siamis?" Liere heard his smile in his voice, as his expression had not changed.

"Um," she said, "that story has gotten twisted a lot since

it happened. A lot."

"I'm aware that rumor can seldom be trusted, old or new. As for recent rumors, apparently Rel was involved with an alleged attack on Efael of the Host?"

Liere repeated what Andri had passed along, "He organized it—"

"Though it was Detlev's mysterious assassins who carried it out?"

"That's what I've heard," she said. "Efael's castle was fired, and the prisoners released. Apparently Efael was quite angry, and I've been waiting to hear what has happened since."

"The former commander-in-chief. Ah, Llyenthur. He is dead, then?"

"The rumors I've heard insist he's acting on his own."

"On command of the Host, no doubt," Macael said. "What can you tell me of them?"

Liere's back chilled at this mention of the true enemy— nothing to do with the icy air in this decorative room. "Nobody is certain what Ilerian is doing, besides trying to create a magical powerbase in Imar. Svir's actions seem somewhat random, but that probably just means no one knows the extent of them, much less the reason."

"He attacks individuals, then?"

"Mostly. Not always. A couple weeks ago he walked in on some of our allies in Flendere. A very small group, in no way remarkable, or so it would seem. Spent a couple of days getting acquainted, for of course they did not know at first who he was. Left, came back, took just two of their leaders, and turned them over to Efael. And with the resultant knowledge extracted from them, returned and took out a smallish geliath in the southern hills. Then left again."

"Took out?"

She told him.

He sat back in his chair, uttering something in a soft undervoice. Then he set his empty glass on a side table. It rang with a clear sound. "That's mindless savagery," he said at last, his voice showing more emotion than she'd ever heard him use, even when he'd spoken about Chantala's mother's death by slow poison. "Now I wish I hadn't asked. I guess we here ought to consider ourselves privileged we have only Adon Marsael in this kingdom, and Kinarde in Sles Adran, with which to deal." He shook his head. "No one seems to be concerned with our side's communication systems?"

"Llyenthur had been very much concerned with them. Squelching forming lines, or else using our relays for his own purposes, in a few places, and monitoring the results. But Svir and Ilerian are unlikely to bother with that, any more than they bother with the grunt and sweat of military actions. Oh! I see why you asked—"

"Implies a remarkable setup, you getting recent news of Flendere, which is located on another continent, if I recall my long-ago map-studying days. Either that or you have better connections than I guessed."

She bit her lip, wondering if she'd made a mistake. If so, what kind? Macael, after all, was an ally. "We do have a good setup, via magic," she said at last.

"And you can communicate with Andri via it, even when you are not together?"

"If the need arose. Why?"

He rose, and picked up his heavy satchel of books, displaying no more effort than Andri would have. "Because I would wish you to convey to him a cordial invitation to Chantala's and my wedding, which is to take place after New Year's Week, on the first day of the new year, at Halli Elardian's summer home near the river. You remember her? She mentioned having met you last year."

Surprise blanked Liere's mind. Surprise so strong it was almost shock, as she considered the implications—the *obvious* implications. Macael would become Chantala's consort, and she was the royal heir! Would he be expected to become an Adrani?

"Of course you have my best wishes for happiness," she said. Remembering Chantala's delight in his company, she smiled. "I do remember Halli."

"You are, it does not need saying, invited as well," he added. Gesturing toward the window, "It is dawn. We ought to be on our respective ways."

And so they were, after adjuring one another to convey greetings to Andri and Chantala respectively. Liere soon rode alone up the path as the blue light of dawn lit the pristine snow, as she compounded with tiredness and the amazing news.

A royal consort—for the Adrani kingdom?

Bartal na Shagal would likely lose his throne if Norsunder was defeated. The Shagal line reached back centuries, so it was equally likely Chantala would be crowned queen, as she was the only Shagal left. But would she be able to handle the postwar mess? For there was the matter of Adrani purple occupying a good part of the eastern half of the continent. Ah, there surely were relations to the Shagals readying to step up to that empty throne. Would they expect Macael's allegiance?

She considered the idea of quiet, musical, bookish Macael finding himself embroiled in Adrani politics. What had Macael said to her once? "I am by nature more of a seneschal than a war chieftain." Maybe he would be in a position to petition for peace between the Adranis and the Enaeraneth at last!

"Yes," she said aloud, as her horse's ears twitched. The cousins got along well. Chantala liked both her and Andri. Having an ally in Sles Adran, even if Macael and Chantala divided their time between Denwy and Elsarion, would be one bit of light in the gloom of the immediate future.

She absolutely had to be at that wedding to show her firm support.

Nine

EFAEL LOATHED THE BRAIN-SCRAPING suddenness of a summons by Svir, but it seemed especially threatening when he found himself not far from his own HQ.

He looked around. Some sort of cave. A cave? He peered out the narrow fissure, recognizing the shape of the closest peak: indignantly, he realized he stood within a short walk from a vantage from which someone with a good glass could observe the Sonscarna fortress he'd taken over. In other words, someone had been spying on *him*.

His first reaction was rage, and he vowed that whatever happened now, his next move would be to flay the perimeter guard captains before their assembled incompetents.

Hells. Bloodlust had to be stayed. If he culled his forces again he wouldn't get any more of Bostian's best, for which that shit Aldon could not be blamed. Oh, Aldon was going to get his, and that one would last weeks. *Months.* Long hours of exquisite pleasure for Efael, and for Aldon every breath unending pain and mouse-squeaks for mercy.

But not until Aldon obliterated this rumored rabble the Sartorans had raised. Anyway, Efael had to admit as he turned around and walked back toward Svir, this cave was located perfectly. The route he himself had laid out for his outer perimeter to patrol would never have turned it up. A subtlety he put beyond the ability of those fools in Danara —

"Detlev was here." Svir stood with one kidskin-clad foot propped on a stone ledge stained rust-colored with old blood, and shot an appraising smile at Efael. "Imry was as well. But it appears he was too late to do anything."

"If he didn't betray us," Efael retorted. Svir could smile, but Efael longed to get his fingers round that throat —

"To what end? He never does anything without purpose," Svir drawled, studying those bloodstains.

Rage seared Efael's nerves. Svir still found Imry's damned, fatuous utterances amusing, whether truth or lies.

Not strangling, Efael thought, closing his eyes. First a fight. Beat him almost senseless. Then let him waken, bound to a chair, to contemplate the balance of power. And, what, a thumb in one of those green eyes, all the way up into the skull ... and then the other eye ... and then a time to anticipate what was to come next, unseen, but oh, not unfelt. Not unfelt.

Svir's smile turned his way, and Efael gasped from the knife-strike of mind-invasion, then the wrench of his bloodlust sucked away, and sent to bolster Ilerian; it was merely a spurt, a sip when a cataract was needed, but Ilerian relished the piquancy of Efael's bloodlust, and it was always good to remind minions where the power lies, for ever and ever.

Drained, Efael muttered, "Detlev really was here?"

Svir shifted his stance, wove his fingers together, and turned them palms down toward the ground. "The evidence, outside of the blood — that must have been one of his boys, I forget which one — is subtle."

MV. The description from the single survivor of the attack on the south road (who ran early to summon reinforcements) had been clear enough. Efael once had wanted MV for his Black Knives, his own personal guard. They held the highest place in Norsunder — everyone was afraid of them, and with reason. Yet MV had had the gall to refuse, after Efael put his own mark on him, and relished the doing. How he'd struggled!

Svir continued, in a contemplative drawl, "I believe Imry tracked him here. The question is, when?"

"Convenient." Efael sneered. "And convenient that he missed."

"It is. Isn't it?" Svir laughed without sound, a chilling sight. "Ah, I never expected this much diversion." He looked around once more, slowly. As though imagining who was where, doing what. "You have forgotten Kessler? That would be an oversight."

Kessler? How had *he* gotten into this conversation? Efael sorted the dulcet words for threat. Decided there was none, for Svir and Ilerian too had failed to find any trace. But the reminder of the world still warded from Norsunder-Beyond might be a threat…

Svir snapped his fingers, wrenching Efael's focus back. "Your sister may continue her pursuit of Imry. But if she does contrive to trap him, remember he is mine. Play all you like, but do not kill him…" Svir smiled. "Perhaps it might be enlightening to see what he has to say, since we are here."

Imry had perhaps one heartbeat's warning before the summons came, and with it a transfer Destination.

He appeared in the cave where Detlev and MV had hid. Svir was there — and there was Efael, lurking malevolently in the background.

Svir's gaze went to the bloodstained rag Imry had tied around his bruised head before saying, "It appears you are organizing some of our restless and disaffected troops."

Nothing about the cave, then — except as context. But contexts could be very dangerous indeed. Imry dropped down onto the shelf where MV had lain, the blood dried to rust stains. "You object?" he countered, knowing that he might be rude, but he must never be predictable.

"On the contrary. I shall be watching with interest. Tell me. Will this coincide with Aldon's little revolt, or follow?"

So he knew about Aldon's conspiracy against Efael. Figured.

"I'd replace Aldon anyway." Imry leaned one arm against the rough wall, the point of the black sword scraping the stone.

Svir laughed — that flash of teeth, no sound. Very bad sign, for someone. Imry swung his leg, back and forth, but Svir's attention had gone to the black sword in its shoulder harness.

"Ah," Svir said. "You still carry Detlev's weapon."

Imry shrugged. "I thought it was my brother's. The idea was to lure David with it. I'd hate to miss an opportunity, so I bring it with me when I hop about."

Svir smiled as he took a step, then another, approaching Imry on that stone bench. "They will be in Imar very soon."

Svir was now within arm's reach, but Imry knew better

than to betray any reaction.

Svir bent. A finger touched the pattern of leaves engraved round the guard. Feint, beat, lunge.

"Take it." Imry opened his hands. "Spoil my fun." He looked straight across the cave at Efael. "I want my command back, and I intend to have it."

"Excellent! Strive, my boys, strive. That can only redound to our benefit," Svir said, his finger still tracing the circular leaf pattern on the hilt-guard, round and round, a hand's breadth from Imry's head, as Imry's mind moved fast: their relative positions, his own hidden weapons. He *might* be able to take Svir, assuming he actually got beyond whatever formidable magic protections Svir had loaded on himself—but not both of them.

Svir lifted his hand away from the sword. "When Detlev attacks, I want you in attendance." He vanished, leaving the two facing one another.

Imry was still too concussed from that swinging ball in Venn to be sure he'd win a fight—and he didn't have anyone in place in Sartor even if he did. He gave Efael an ironic salute before the other could cross the cave, and also vanished.

Efael transferred to the relative safety of his castle, and threw himself into a chair, furious with everyone. Svir—Imry— most of all the press of time malaise. *Do not kill him.* Meaning that Imry was eventually Ilerian's—and Svir was onto some new hunt. Had it to do with Kessler's ward?

Efael kicked at the table leg in utter disgust, and when Yeres turned up, he poured his version of the interview into her ear. The two then embarked on one of their endless debates about why Svir and Ilerian permitted Imry to run free.

Efael said bitterly, "I know it wasn't Rel's people who took out my best three trackers in those stinking Sartoran mountains, riddled with morvende shit-holes. I think it was Imry."

"In retaliation?" Yeres said. "Or was it dear Siamis?"

Efael waved a hand. "They're all the same, when you come to it. Detlev's menials…"

Which gave him an idea, and he grinned.

Ah. Until they caught up with Imry, there were always Imry's own menials. Maybe it was time to find out what was in their minds.

Ten

FROM THE OUTSIDE IT appeared to be the unlikeliest of friendships, one no one who knew either Jilo or Shontande would ever have predicted.

Neither Shontande nor Jilo bonded easily with others, for drastically differing reasons. We have seen much of Jilo's experiences and reasoning, but little of Shontande Lirendi's.

Raised in a formidably sophisticated court, and aware from childhood of the dangers facing Colend, Shontande had been predisposed to favor Jilo from the very start, because Jilo was everything that the loathed King of the Chwahir was not — and he was also everything the Colendi courtiers despised. A weak, inexperienced king in Chwahirsland would suit Colend very well.

Shontande found, when they got to know each other, a very bright, refreshingly plain-spoken, quick-learning and scrupulously honest fellow who somehow — raised in a barren culture and surrounded by soul-killing ugliness — had managed to become deeply responsive to beauty.

Two days after Dhana transferred Shontande, Jilo, and Retren Ndarga back to the girls' school on Colend's northern border, Shontande looked across the pretty bedroom chamber that had become his headquarters, a room decorated in a soft salmon shade, trimmed with spring green, as would please a young girl of taste. Jilo sat on the narrow bed with its lace and flounces, surrounded by papers. On tiny chairs, or on the floor, sat some of Shontande's conspirators, along with two of Jilo's—a third cousin, a patrol captain in Wan-Edhe's army, and Erol, one of Detlev's boys.

In the room, thanks to Jilo, a vagabond fire burned brightly in the fireplace; they could all get their papers into it in moments, if Kendra on guard outside began to sing. It had happened four times last fall, and once this winter.

"... and Shontande has all my own stuff," Jilo was saying, looking up right then. His pale brown eyes glowed amber in this mellow light, his brow furrowed slightly in question.

"Yes," Shontande said, turning to Erol, Detlev's mole in Narad, and Jilo's contact within Chwahirsland.

"I've got the signal," Erol said. "Will get word to Crimson General Furo."

The former general of the Crimson Army—still given his title by the Chwahir, another small sign that they were mentally separating from their horrible king—was now secreted in Chwahirsland, setting up, person by person, an inside line of communication: though he had been rescued, Wan-Edhe had tried to recall him, of course to have him killed. In Wan-Edhe's views, a Chwahir once a prisoner had been tainted by the enemy.

But to the Chwahir, Furo had become a hero.

The meeting was over. Erol got to his feet, nodded to them both, and then left, marching out with that flatfooted heavy tread characteristic of Chwahir. Terry of Erdrael Danara had joked once, early after Shontande met them both, that Jilo's countrymen walked as if they'd be shot if they entered a room silently—something considered good manners in Alsais' court circles—and to his surprise, Jilo had nodded, no hint of humor, and said, "Yes. In Wan-Edhe's circles, entering a room without your step being heard can cost you your life."

Shontande's own cousin Nashande—good-natured, capable, steady, brave, loyal, and blessedly uncomplicated—grinned from the floor, where he sat cross-legged. "Right enough, Shon. I'm off soon's the surprise inspection's over."

He and the others got up and filed out, except for Talian Ariath, who lingered, intending to be alone with Shontande. He busied himself with his papers so he wouldn't see her predatory gaze. And Jilo sat where he was without moving.

Already irritated because the Colendi ought to respect the distinctions of rank—the commoners ought to confine themselves to the floor, leaving the chair and the bed to the nobles—Talian shot a glare Jilo's way, then exited. There was always next time.

The door closed softly behind her, and Shontande let his breath out in a silent sigh. Talian was brave, and capable, but she was not uncomplicated, and despite her formidable arsenal of pleasing manners, she was not in the least good-natured. But she, like Nash, would be—if peace were ever obtained—part of the orderly dance of Colendi government. If Colend was to obtain peace, it would be his job to maintain that order, which required good relations with his court, whether he liked them as persons or not.

"I'd better change into an outside gown," Shontande said. "Want me to leave?"

"Not unless you find the spectacle offensive."

Jilo blushed and mumbled something disjointed. There was another thing that Shontande appreciated about him. Jilo's admiration was refreshingly free of the least hint of desire, or possession, a quality treasured by someone who had been told all his life how beautiful, how gorgeous, how handsome, how...

The repellent superlatives streamed through Shontande's mind as he selected a sturdy gown that deemphasized male contours, enhancing female contours that didn't exist, as did all his robes and gowns. Thinking of the smothering compliments about his beauty that from his earliest memory people had used preparatory to using him (or attempting to use him) left that tinge of nausea—which was why this room had no mirror.

One of the human traits he'd identified very young, and had come to hate, was this notion that beauty must be possessed, whether it was the beauty of a work of art, or a stretch of land—or a person. Was that why he loved music so much, because it must be shared? Because you could not grasp it from the air and imprison it, or stake it with a fence and fight off trespassers? You could not rifle it with soft fingers, or the insinuating voice of masked desire.

He shifted his attention from the endless internal dialogue to externals as he partly laced up the rose-colored winter gown, stuffed a couple of fresh sock-balls in his chest, and finished lacing. "Ah-ye, we're as ready as we can be. Is my bosom even?"

Jilo glanced up, blushed again at the word 'bosom', but said only, "Right side high."

Shontande shrugged and punched his socks into alignment, and said, "Shall we depart, each to our tasks, then?" He opened the door, his steps automatically mincing, his posture taking on the rounded movements that had become second nature as soon as he felt the weight of a gown on him.

Music greeted them, the far-off rise and fall of young girls' voices, busy with practice scales. Kendra, one of his personal stewards, waited at the bottom of the stairs. "Bee passed the word that they are on the east road, two columns," she murmured.

Bee Keperi, Shontande's chief scribe, was blind, but his hearing was more practiced than anyone's. If he heard two columns, then two columns would be expected. They dispersed, Jilo to slip into Alsais in order to inform trusted individuals about Crimson General Furo's rescue, and to discuss what options the Chwahir had for the counterattack.

Shontande watched him slouch away, once again aware that there was no knowing what the Chwahir would do if Norsunder was defeated. Jilo would order a retreat — he had promised to. But no one knew whether or not the Chwahir would follow Jilo or not; there were matters Jilo and his Chwahir kept to themselves.

Which was fine, because Shontande had his own difficulties to contend with, strictly Colendi affairs.

The patrol rode in. The Norsundrian leader looked past a scrawny fellow hauling compost out to the heap beside the kitchen garden that would get spread out come spring. Wait. An able-bodied man? He reined up. "Hai! You."

"Uh?"

The compost hauler stopped, and blinked his way, mouth open.

"Come here!"

"Uhn?"

"Come here."

"Uhn?"

The patrol leader looked down into a mouth-open face, vacant eyes, and a line of green snot running from one nostril to the edge of the idiot's mouth.

"Leave him," someone said, "We've got soulbound for slop work. And with the orders for 5th to head south first of the new year, outpost'll be half empty anyway."

The patrol captain grunted (sounding, if he only knew it, no different than Snot Nose there), and they rode on, bored with the routine.

Ferret—born Alaki, one of Detlev's boys—waited until they were gone, then carefully peeled his snot wax from his lip and tucked it into his pocket, pleased that his risk of being seen had paid off with that tidbit about orders. Then Erol's mental call came, and he began loping toward the classroom square.

The young singers had finished their scale warm-ups at last. Their voices were louder now, coming from the open windows, for though snow lay on the ground, it was mushy, and the air under the clear sunlight warm. The entire school had been thrown open to air out during this brief thaw, for though it was regularly cleaned by both real inhabitants and those who led double lives, it was inevitable that the long wintry sieges made the air musty and close.

Erol intercepted Shontande, who halted, surprised—and wary.

"There's something you need to know," Erol said, without any honorifics, his verb endings strictly neutral—which Colendi commoners took as polite in trade dealings, and nobles tended to regard as disrespectfully encroaching. Especially from Chwahir.

"Please enlighten me," Shontande replied, still wary, though his palms met in the peace. "You chose not to speak while Jilo was present?"

Erol turned his head, and to Shontande's surprise, a second person emerged from beyond a classroom. Shontande's instinctive response was to dismiss the skinny, dough-faced young man whose age could have been anywhere from sixteen to forty. He was dressed in a dull servant's smock and trousers, and carried a slop bucket.

Erol said, "This is Ferret."

Ferret's voice was as undistinguished as his appearance. "This is a Colendi matter. Not Chwahir. There is a trap set for some of your people. Tonight."

Shontande's first instinct was to walk away, ignoring them, for he'd comprehended by now that Erol's very short chain of command had Detlev at the top. Not Jilo, or maybe also Jilo—when Detlev permitted. Introducing this Ferret out of nowhere could only mean another Detlev spy.

But that also meant that both of them had been Curtas's brethren. Shontande had promised himself to at least listen to Curtas's brethren and so to Detlev, and he had already made enough errors that could not be blamed on Detlev or his boys. Then there were the decisions that might be errors — or not. No one yet knew.

One of the tension points in occupied Colend was the cooperation between the pleasure house people with the Norsundrians. Early on after the invasion, Shontande had thought himself so clever in passing the word that the crown would recompense pleasure houses for food eaten and drinks consumed as well as musicians and the upstairs workers, his thinking being that if the enemy was stuffed and drunk and relaxed, they'd be less likely to go on killing sprees. Also, they might blab information.

Alas, a lot of the strike troops had eaten till they puked, drank till they were wall-eyed, rutted themselves comatose — and afterward, smashed up places just because they could. Meanwhile, it became evident that information could go both ways. Shontande was fairly certain he had discovered all the collaborators, at least in Alsais, two among the nobles. If the war ended with Norsunder defeated, he knew it would be his job — no matter how distasteful — to get to them before the lynch mobs did.

"Speak," he said.

"There is a group of resistors following the lead of Mathias-Caid Lassiter, now Duchas of Alarcansa," Ferret said, reeling the name out easily. He hadn't at first, until Siamis repeated it two or three times.

Shontande stilled. Oh yes, here was one of the matters that he did not share with Jilo — how there were fractures among the Colendi. A sizable group, mostly bitter northeasterners, seemed to feel that the Lirendis had ruled too long, had gone soft, had become stupid, largely because the only military resistance to invasion had been hard, bloody fighting at the eastern pass, through Alarcansa.

The Alarcansa defense had lost, but at least (so, many felt) they had tried. The rest of Colend had surrendered without so much as lifting a weapon — a decision Shontande had come to after painful consideration. Mathias-Caid was at large, and so far had not responded to any of Shontande's attempts to communicate. There was no knowing if these had actually reached him.

All this ran through his mind in disjointed fashion, memory images and recollected bits of conversation, as Erol and Ferret waited.

Becoming aware of a pause lengthening into a silence, Shontande blinked himself to the present. Shouldn't he at least get what information he could, and decide what to do about it later?

Ferret saw awareness return to his gaze, and said, "Tonight being the last night of the year, you probably know that all the garrisons are celebrating. The Alarcansa duchas plans to raid Venias's outpost for weapons, while they are whooping it up. But it's a trap. The captain there, a mercenary from up north, laid it—he wants promotion once the last Norsunder Base company transfers to Khanerenth coming after the first of the year."

Venias—a crossroads town roughly halfway between here and Alarcansa. If Shontande rode now, he could easily get there before midnight.

But not with Detlev spies tagging along, for whatever reason.

"Thank you," he said, and waited for them to leave.

Eleven

A SHORT TIME LATER, Siamis rapidly read through succinct reports from both; Ferret and Erol knew that Detlev and Siamis liked their different views on the same events. Ferret wrote his from the rooftop of the school's library — his habit was to go up to where he could see and not be seen — and Erol from Narad, once he'd been transferred back by Dhana.

Siamis retreated to the inner chamber of the Selenseh Redian, where Detlev was in the process of shaking out bedding to be spread on the uneven ground. When Detlev looked up with a *What now?* expression on his tired face, Siamis quoted the two reports.

Before Siamis finished, Detlev had refolded the bedding, and reached for the weapons on a folding rack.

"I'll go," Siamis said.

Detlev's hand checked, but then picked up the wrist knife. "Siamis, if this offer is prompted by more guilt over Curtas —"

"Of course it is," Siamis interrupted, a little too forcefully, especially in that small, quiet space. They both turned their heads, but there was no sound from the other end of the curved tunnel, except the soothing rise and fall of Seshe's voice as she read to Clair — who remained asleep.

Siamis lowered his voice. "I know I cannot be faulted for suggesting Curtas be sent to befriend Shontande, the perfect inside eyes. None of us could predict what happened. Maybe the logic of that will matter one day, but right now it doesn't.

My mind returns to the familiar road: we *ought* to have known it, and that our interference resulted in the deaths of two innocents."

Detlev opened his hand. Carlael Lirendi had been difficult, and his talent absolutely had to be hidden, but the fact remained he was helpless against Efael's attack because of the enchantment laid over him. An innocent. As for Curtas, strictly speaking, his death was not innocent in that he had not told them when he went to rescue Shontande — which meant there was no chance of sending Adam, or Ferret, as backup. Curtas had known the risks. None of that lessened the grief — or the awareness of the effect of their interference in the Lirendis' lives.

What to say? Memory: a year or two after Detlev had begun what the two of them had termed in their private code *rat-catching*, the gathering of his group. Siamis had been proud to be brought into it; he'd been equally proud when he contacted Detlev with what he thought of as his first find.

They had transferred to Alsais's royal palace, and stood on the edge of the famed rose garden, looking at the two-year-old Shontande. In a very short time they watched this small child dance around the edge of a pond with far more physical control than a child three times his age, and then respond, despite the lisp of the two-year-old soft palate, in a perfect regional accent to his governess — and then in pure court Kifelian to a passing lady.

Take this one, Siamis had said, mind to mind: *Carlael can get another heir when you let him out of the enchantment; he'll never notice this one missing. You'll never find a better prospect*, Siamis had added, only to see Detlev shaking his head, though his gaze stayed on the child: *Not this one. Look at that face.*

Siamis regarded the cherubic child-face; at that time, to him, most two-year-old faces were fairly interchangeable.

But Detlev transferred the two of them elsewhere, where they could not be overheard, and he'd said, "That boy is a throwback to Mathias Lirendi. He is sure to catch Efael's eye."

To prevent that, they had contrived Shontande's isolation from a distance, prisoned in silks and marble and secluded gardens, except for occasional strictly controlled visits to court. But the price was loneliness. Which resulted in Siamis suggesting they send Curtas —

Siamis watched Detlev frowning in reverie. That was not

a good sign. But pointing out that Detlev was dangerously exhausted was a waste of breath. They both knew it — as well as they both knew that Detlev was facing the worst challenge of his life. "Detlev, Clair has slept the last two nights. She walks the Purrad every night, and Seshe reads her to sleep."

"You have that list of transfers you promised Atan to make," Detlev said.

"New Year's Firstday is still half a day off," Siamis said. "And Dhana has charge of the list. As for me," he admitted, "I could use a little action. The way you could use some uninterrupted sleep."

Detlev picked up the bedding again in surrender.

Siamis made sure all was peaceful in Mearsies Heili, then braced for a dreary, altogether virulent duty: whatever you called it in military terms, it was no less than a mind-raid. Though Yeres was the target, Siamis knew quite well that delving into her memory without her knowledge was yet another action that put him on their level. Detlev hated it as much as Siamis did, but Siamis knew them better after having been their prisoner and pet for that protracted time. Too much was at stake to be high-minded: at least he could spare Detlev this one filthy necessity.

A quick, superficial scan: she was in Imar, which was far too dangerous for him to risk. Svir was often in both the twins' minds, bored as he was.

Relieved at being able to postpone that for later, he went to find Dhana. She transferred him to the quiet town of Venias, where the sun had recently set. Too early for the Norsundrian trap — the target hadn't appeared yet. Siamis used the intervening time in reconnaissance.

And here they came.

Three cats trotted along fences surrounding the former Guildhall of Venias, tails high, their chatoyant-green eyes glowing as they gazed down into the courtyard, then they crouched low, alert. But it wasn't the clink of glass and raucous laughter and yells rising from behind the lit windows of the guildhall that made them wary.

"What's that?" a sentry said. Flat voice. Soulbound. Siamis knew that empty tone, an abiding threat from his days in Norsunder.

"Cats, you soul-rotted ass. Now shut up," said his irritated partner.

The cats leaped out of sight.

Siamis knew what was coming next, and was already running lightly along the wall when his ears caught the end of a whispered order, "... stay alert!"

He eased up to one of the jasmine shrubs bordering this guildhall-turned-outpost, and glimpsed Shontande Lirendi's profile, muffled in scarf and dark clothing, in the dim glow of the roof torches. Good, he had not discounted Ferret's report merely because he was one of Detlev's. Bad: Shontande, inexperienced, had brought only three of his most trusted friends. *And that is what I'm here for.*

Siamis scanned for clear lines of advance and retreat before Mathias-Caid Lassiter of Alarcansa gestured for his party to advance. Siamis was already moving in unseen parallel.

Shontande converged with the Alarcansa party as they sneaked up. "It's a trap," Shontande said in an urgent undervoice. "Retreat."

"Whose trap," Alarcansa began, with a revealing glance back—he had been completely taken by surprise, and was trying to hide it from his followers.

His and Shontande's heads turned sharply when a Norsundrian strolled into the courtyard below. "Let's get this party started!"

And the trap began to close when twenty figures rose from behind barrels and sheds and on the rooftops.

Siamis had both his sword Emeth and his long knife out, his eyes taking in everyone's position, attack and defense. Denied the release of action for endless weeks of patience and slow mental torture, Siamis lived in the now, blades whooshing in his hands as he charged the Norsundrians, who until this moment had been anticipating a recreational slaughter.

Mathias-Caid and Shontande stilled as a tall blond man appeared out of the shadows, the center of a whirr of steel, to scythe his way through the Norsundrians.

Mathias-Caid stared in dismay, the action far too fast to follow. He'd been trained! He had to show that Lirendi sot what leadership truly was! But this was his first battle, after months of well-meant though humiliating imprisonment by his family, who had been shaken badly by the carnage at Alarcansa Pass a year ago.

He tried to get ahead of the Lirendi prince he had been raised to replace, his courage high, but his defense was a heartbeat or two late, until a sharp pain behind his head dropped him abruptly.

Caid woke, looking up into a face he remembered from his childhood. Only the deposed king was dressed as a girl.

Caid's mouth worked. Memory came crashing back, along with the vilest headache he'd ever had, not even as bad as his first drunk.

"Prince. Sh—Sho..."

"Don't talk, Mathias-Caid. It'll hurt worse," came a soothing whisper. "Your people are fine. Cut up a bit—as are mine—but they're fine."

"Caid," the Alarcansa duchas mumbled as he tried to struggle up. "You were right. About the trap." Humiliation—that familiar shadow—forced him up onto his elbows, but then his guts revolted. He had just enough presence of mind to manage the Waste Spell; the nausea vanished along with the contents of his churning insides, leaving him sweating and breathing in shaky gasps.

That man who'd saved them—he was no Colendi. And that fighting style was nothing he'd ever seen. What's more, Shontande Lirendi had turned up, too, only *he'd* known it was all a trap. Caid's bitter conclusion was that he had been set up to fail.

Shontande could see the trend of his thoughts as Caid's expression tightened from pain to anger.

"We must unite, Caid," Shontande murmured, using the verb endings and tones of intimacy, usually shared among siblings or those acknowledged as brethren, instead of parent-to-child, the only mode of intimacy expected of kings. "Or we will never recover even if we win."

Caid's eyes were nearly all pupil as he gazed at Shontande. "You didn't even try to fight last year," he said hoarsely.

How to answer that? The older generation was largely gone, at least those who'd held any power. The regency council had vacillated for the last four years of their ten-year rule, finding this and that excuse to prevent their handing over the crown to Shontande—strictly limiting his contact with his peers. Many of whom had assumed his mind was shaped by the regents, and that he agreed with them. Until he escaped them entirely, going to Sartor and forcing the issue in what was now known as the Battle of Lilies and Roses.

That had been a Colendi battle, that is, entirely metaphorical—without any hint of steel. Shontande's first requirement was that no one be hurt. The city of Alsais had known that, to some degree. But up there in Alarcansa, how had his actions been perceived? There had been no time to get to know the younger generation of courtiers before actual steel entered Colend, brought by the invading Chwahir, Adranis, and Norsundrians. By Shontande's decree, king for barely two weeks, no one was to fight—but Alarcansa, guarding the eastern pass for centuries, had fought, hard, to defend that pass. And lost.

"Other than the mountains between us and the Chwahir, Colend has no defensible border," Shontande said. "And the heralds are not an army."

He paused, and saw in Caid's blinking gaze that both those points had registered as true.

"I didn't want Alarcansa to fight. I wanted your people to withdraw up into the mountains, where they hid centuries ago. I didn't send reinforcements because I had none. The heralds had been marked early on by the enemy, and most were rounded up and either killed or marched away in the first days of the invasion, while Alarcansa was still fighting."

"We didn't hear that."

"Because the scribe desks were destroyed, remember? Communication had to be mouth to ear. It broke down when our messengers, no matter what age, were shot as soon as they were spotted."

Caid's gaze shifted.

"My first concern was to preserve as many lives as I could. Because war is not a duel between two matched contestants, buffered by rules of civility—it's what you saw in Alarcansa, harmless people smashed down as well as warriors, to make way for the invaders."

Caid's head pounded. When it was clear that Alarcansa could not hold the pass against the Chwahir, his elders had forced him to hide, the heir too precious to expose to that steel, but he had seen the carnage. Much as his head hurt, he still heard those words, *war is not a duel between matched contestants*, which echoed the scorn he'd overheard from Norsundrian mercenaries who led the Chwahir, as they tramped around looting, afterward.

Shontande, listening intently on the mental plane, had to filter out Caid's pain and nausea, to catch the confusion of memories and tangled thoughts. He said, "To preserve lives, we've bowed our heads. And lives have been preserved, though it has not been bloodless."

Caid swallowed. "I'd rather die than spend my life as a slave to them."

"I know," Shontande said. "We all feel that way. Not only Colendi, but all over the world. Here's what is important. We are going to rise together. Soon. Not Colend on its own, for we still face the same limits — worse, because of the loss of so many of our heralds. But Sartor and Sarendan and Khanerenth and little Gyrn and all the small river kingdoms, and the big ones out west."

Caid's lips parted. "No one told us."

"Because you have been hiding, quite rightly. But you know now. Our part here in Colendi is to take out the central command in Alsais, and at two other key garrisons. I need your help for that, you and your trained followers from up north."

Now Caid was listening.

"Ah-ye! Your head must feel like splitting," Shontande said, betraying no sign of relief. "We've some healer steep, and then I suspect we'd all do better to be long gone before the inevitable search. But I will show you the map first. Will you join us?"

Caid stared, trying to find the coward prince in these words. And failing, requiring a new way of thinking. "A counterattack? Yes."

He was gone before the rising sun touched the snow on the rooftops to the color of cream.

Neither Siamis nor Detlev expected anything but increased suspicion. After that rarity, six uninterrupted hours of rest, Detlev volunteered to deal with the inevitable detritus following Siamis's timely appearance.

When Shontande turned away after seeing Caid ride off in company with his followers who had been housed nearby, he was startled but not all that surprised to discover Detlev waiting next to a wagon with a broken axel.

"Thank you," Detlev said, in hopes of deflecting some of the suspicion, "for heeding Erol and Ferret."

Shontande studied him silently, then ventured a remark, "You are expecting me to cavil?"

"The thought did occur. Ferret's been crossing Colend in order to assess, as well as he can, the Chwahir position. When he sniffed out this local plot for some New Year's Week fun, he reported to us—and we reached Erol, who was already here. It was mere hours before Erol first spoke to you."

Shontande bowed in the peace, accepting that conditionally: Curtas's brethren, he reminded himself. And Siamis had not remained behind to use moral superiority after his sanguinary routing of the would-be attackers, to establish ascendancy. He had appeared, warded what would have been a slaughter, and vanished again.

Detlev went on, "I don't think it is overstating things to say that everyone at least in this half of the continent is wondering what will happen if Norsunder is defeated. If Wan-Edhe goes down with them. Which is not at all certain. Though there are those who are used to dismissing the Chwahir as negligible. "

"I take the Chwahir seriously," Shontande said—as before, finding this not-quite-attack unexpected. "I take very seriously a huge kingdom full of warriors, even badly supplied ones, whose insane king spends most of his time either creating more rings of defense around himself, or plotting ways to conquer his neighbors. I feel that in some sense, the tragedy that is Chwahirsland now is my tragedy, too."

Detlev gave him an inquiring glance, and Shontande found himself on uncertain ground, wondering if he had sounded pompous. His hands swooped in the gesture for *rue*. "I realize about all I can do is help Jilo in whatever way he asks, though I see quite well that the contempt goes both ways. The Chwahir seem to see us as a flock of brightly-colored birds, and hear our most serious words as the utterances of parrots."

Now that Detlev had shifted him off the pinnacle of Mount Moral Superiority, he said, "I am here in the guise of usher for Atan, but if you still have questions for me, there is time. I might not be able to say that after the next few days."

Shontande clasped his hands tightly behind his back. "Atan," he said—remembering the prospective wedding. Right now, tired as he was, that seemed as relevant as the most distant stars. Unlike the thoughts that occupied his restless nights. Words rushed out of him: "You did not tell me exactly why you saw it necessary to enchant my father. Other than dropping hints about protecting something that cannot be named. I struggle against not finding that a convenience," he added, which was rudely direct for a Colendi.

Detlev inclined his head, as if this response had been expected. "Then let us leave that question for one we can discuss, in a general sense. Dena Yeresbeth has been re-emerging rapidly. Your father was one of the earliest. It could have been hidden, but the direction of his talent, and his habit of using the Lirendi Diamond, enabled him to sense the unnamed. Until we can be rid of Norsunder, I did what I could to deflect, even to halt, certainly to hide, it."

"Halt?" Shontande repeated. "Then you *were* killing people."

Detlev sighed. "More than a century ago, at Norsunder Base there was an ambitious mage named Jeniad, ejected from the Sartoran Magic Guild. On the pretext of gaining access to better soil for Norsunder Base, Jeniad proposed invading Sartor. Svir of the Host gave him the Base and its force, as he wanted to witness a battle. Jeniad attacked Eidervaen, his true desire to make himself king. I'm sure you are aware of this general history."

"That is the battle that made Atan an orphan, am I correct? And you contrived a spell to remove Sartor from the rest of the world for a century?"

"I saw certain signs that Dena Yeresbeth was reemerging in Sartor, and Jeniad was going to have his war anyway, backed by Svir. I used that war to halt Dena Yeresbeth's reappearance too soon by removing Sartor for a time. Though Jeniad's war claimed far too many lives, no one died in that enchantment."

Shontande remembered reading accounts of that war, by people still alive. One of the witness reports was that when the enchantment receded, the invaders had vanished. Not the Sartorans. The attackers had vanished—some surmised in the way that a person using a faulty or warded transfer spell vanishes between Destinations—forever.

Shock chilled Shontande's nerves. He sensed once again that he was only seeing one tree in a forest, and of course he could not prove any of it one way or another. "That does not explain my father, and your cruel enchantment."

"Cruel from the outside, I will concede. It was not within his own mind. He lived an imaginary life of endless rounds of entertainment, culture, and pleasure. I laid the enchantment, but within it, he fashioned the dream world into what he wanted most."

Shontande looked up, then down, a line of question between his winged brows, and Detlev sustained a palimpsest, that same exact look of puzzlement in a face long ago. But he was used to these, and blinked it away. He stood up from the wagon, and dusted his clothes off. "Did you remember the wedding? It's nearly time."

Shontande frowned, then realization cleared his brow. "You mean, right now?"

Detlev lifted his hands. "Behold me, the usher."

Shontande remembered then the world-wide concerns, and enemy or not, here the man was, answering his questions. His accusations. "Where is the gathering? I have not yet changed. This is my everyday guise, not appropriate clothing for a royal wedding."

"This wedding is taking place in Shendoral Wood," Detlev said. "The clothing matters little — some might be in night-gear. It is still night in Sartor; no one will see what anyone wears."

Shontande bowed in the peace, and Detlev gave Dhana the signal.

Shontande transferred.

Zaplights glowed and faded, slow magical fireflies, as people appeared. The somnolent air of Shendoral charged with magic, making the skin tingle and the edges of vision glimmer.

Twelve

SHIOVHAN, ENAERAN'S MUCH-BATTERED CAPITAL city, endured the terrific snowstorm that had lumbered in from the icy Ghildraith peaks the day before. Liere sat waiting in a cellar hideout, a heavy hooded cloak over one arm ready to be put on. She had bathed, rebraided her hair, and put on her fresh riding outfit.

She had said nothing to the other Enaeraneth but, "I might disappear for a time. Do not be alarmed, for it is only an errand." She had been warned that the transfer could occur at any time, and so she had sat up most of the night, dozing off and on, sometimes listening to others in the low-ceilinged, stuffy and dim-lit shelter.

The transfer did indeed come without warning. She had been so sure that Siamis was doing the magic that she looked for him to ask for a status report, but the words never formed; she got only the vaguest impression of a cave, and Dhana's face, and then she transferred again.

When she had blinked away the transfer reaction, she stood in the misty, peaceful silence of ancient Shendoral wood, scarcely discernable figures in the silvery mist between the great trees. The cold night air smelled wonderfully of duff, of bark, of pine and fallen leaves.

A zaplight flared, cold-blue. Here was Detlev, wearing a

hooded cloak. With a smile of amusement he took the cloak from her arm and dropped it around her shoulders. She blushed, but he was already passing on, the gray of his cloak blending into the vapors drifting in slow dream-wreaths around him.

Liere followed, the distant figures resolving into knots of people. Some she recognized, but most she did not. Sartorans? This was a place of peace, yet the exigencies of impending conflict kept peace from soothing hearts and minds; status reports passed from whispering lips into head-bent ears around the tight little groups.

Then faces turned eastward, and Liere turned, too, recognizing the pale blue light of impending dawn painting the woodland in silhouettes.

Without being asked, the company fell silent, gathering in a semi-circle before the two figures dressed alike in white and green, who appeared on a little rise under a canopy of silvery argan-branches. The white and green of light, of spring, of promise and renewal — wedding colors.

The light strengthened, warming with tinges of rose, as the rim of the sun crowned the far-off peaks bordering Sarendan, the mist dissolving. Without fanfare of any kind Atan and Rel spoke their vows, their voices rising and falling; Liere, deferring to the Sartorans, remained at the back, from which she could not clearly hear the words, but she didn't have to. It was enough to see their hands, each with the new rings of silver-chased gold, laid palm to palm, the sun rising behind them, flooding the forest with shafts of slanting gold.

Liere clasped her own hands together and wrung them, breathing in sweet, piercing anguish at the beauty of the morning, and the voices she knew so well speaking with unhidden depths of emotion.

As chance would have it, Shontande Lirendi stood nearby, though neither had ever met the other. Liere's distracted glance took in a very tall, blonde young woman with a striking profile, her chin well defined. Shontande saw only a hooded figure of slight build and tightly gripped hands.

He did not really know Rel. His friend was Atan. He had learned from Atan, whom he had gone to meet with the intention of seducing into relinquishing Sartor's claim on the Music Festival. But he'd found honesty, forthrightness, and clear vision, and though she had found him attractive, she had turned him down, teaching him that honor was real, that respect was necessary as breathing, that friendship was possible, and so was love. Not with him. That lesson had changed his life.

He and Liere stood in silence, needing the time of peace, and of isolation, in the surrounding woodland glory.

When at last the final vow was spoken in unison, the tingle of magic stirred the assembled guests, and people began to vanish, one by one.

In Enaeran, the atmosphere had altered so materially that when Liere arrived back in the cellar hideout, and had had a chance to shake free of emotional reaction, she blinked around at the silent faces in bemusement.

Dawn was still far off here. Alarm suffused her. Emergency?

"Here is something hot to drink," Marten said, appearing at her side.

She took the whisky-laced coffee, something she really disliked, but it was a customary drink among the Enaeraneth, so she forced herself to sip. And the heat, the bracing taste of coffee and liquor did revive her a little.

While she sipped came Marten's carefully framed thought, carrying apology (and humor): *Rumor was ahead of you — they knew where you were.*

Liere glanced at him in mute surprise.

Marten smiled, then said in a somewhat leading tone, "And so the Queen of Sartor is well and truly married?"

"Yes," Liere said.

"And is the rumor true that Rel the Traveler is actually of royal blood?"

Anyone who read a history of Sartor knew that the ruling Landis family, while reaching back to the beginning, had actually branched many times, mostly by adoption. No one would quibble at that. Whereas the Chwahir connection — with the Chwahir aligned with Norsunder — was to be hidden. Atan had told Liere herself that Rel was quite proud of his mother, and wanted it known that he was Gwasan Sonscarna's son, but he'd agreed to wait until Jilo could bring that benighted kingdom out of darkness.

Mindful of what had been agreed-on, Liere said, "It is. His parentage was hidden because of war, but it will come out once the war is over. The important thing is that he is now the king of Sartor, sharing Atan's throne. He is adopting into the Landises."

Liere smiled around—to find exchanges of glances, and bowed heads. She sensed powerful ambivalence, and braced herself before lowering her mind-shield for a few heartbeats.

Sure enough, emotion-driven thoughts battered her. Of course the world famous Sartora would be required to be there, but why did not Sartora trust them enough to mention something of such vast import?

Sartora. It seemed she was *never* going to escape that silliness, so long regretted. But she knew the power of old stories, especially in grim times. Andri had said not long before he left, "My prestige at having managed to marry the world-saving Sartora and bring her to Enaeran is probably why I'm able to hold my throne despite my rotten rep, uninspiring manner of dress, uncouth manners—not to mention the disastrous beginning to my reign."

She'd dismissed this as joking, as one of his easy-going efforts to alleviate her worries that the Enaeraneth wouldn't accept a foreigner, but here, now, she could see that underneath the teasing, he'd spoken no more than the truth.

Even worse, she saw signs of hurt—that she hadn't trusted them enough to tell them where she was going?

She said, "I didn't dare speak of it, lest Norsunder find out about the magic transfers."

"Oh-h-h-h-h!"

She felt that collective oh, the relief and nods of understanding. Of course. What could be more natural? Sartora was under orders from Sartor, for security reasons—now *that* made *perfect* sense.

And so, as elsewhere the rest of their resistance camp celebrated the new year with an abandon fired by a year of living on the run, in that cellar, she described the royal Sartoran wedding, including what she'd seen of Atan's gown. Her auditors, mostly women, listened so closely that Liere realized they, in turn, were going to partake of that ephemeral prestige by spreading the story out into ever widening circles.

Then the street-orphan Althora, accompanied by two local women, approached her. They exchanged encouraging glances before tough Althora said diffidently, "Is it right to ask what you'll be wearing to the Other Wedding?"

The Other Wedding meant, of course, Chantala's—until today known just as The Wedding. Of deep local interest, of course, for Sles Adran and Enaeran had once been a single kingdom, and even though they'd been nominally at war for some generations, there were still kinship bonds both sides of the border.

Liere hesitated. Her first instinct had been to say, "What I have on will suffice." But because she was listening, she caught the anxiety behind the question. She said slowly, "I hadn't really thought. You know how short we are on supplies. Have you a suggestion?"

And watched, amazed, as Althora's face reddened as she exchanged more covert glances with the other two.

Liere had learned very early in life how to shut out the emotion-charged noise of people's thoughts. She knew they were unaware of how loud they were on the mental plane. But this matter seemed important enough to warrant another lowering of her mind-shield, for none of them even thought of shielding, though they'd all been taught.

And she was astonished to discover that they, and their friends waiting above, were afraid that Sartora—otherwise so good and kind and brave and superlative with a blade—would disgrace them before those snobby Sles Adrani nobles.

Liere stared at Althora's plain, square face, paralyzed by the conflicting images. Althora stared back, sick with apprehension: had she mortally offended the Great Sartora, Andri's chosen bride?

That shocked Liere out of her own resistance to drawing attention to herself in any way. Dressing plainly was not just practical, it had always been safer—in spite of five years of training in Geth, deep down, ten years of her father's corrosive *Who do you think you are?* still shaped her self-perception.

Always, the need of others brought her out of her own inner conflicts, enabling her to act.

"I don't know what to do to get a proper gown," she said. "I have to leave no later than mid-week if I am to get to the wedding in time. May I turn to you for advice?"

"I think," Althora said, beaming, "we can fix that."

Thirteen

AS THE YEAR ENDED and winter deepened, Fox and his fleet ran before the scouring winter winds, rarely seeing the sun except in fleeting glimpses, a pale disc hanging low in the northern sky. Life was lived in a ship at a permanent slant as the *Treason* and its consorts raced southward. The beautiful dragon prow had been struck down into the hold at the outset, and the heavy winter sails raised. Timbers clattered, hummed, creaked, and groaned as wild winds rose to a roar, waters frothing to the rail as the deck slanted steeply.

Fox felt at times that navigation was more by instinct than by landmarks, but at least the enemy would be as visually hindered as they.

The mouth of the Sartoran Sea slipped by, along with the last of the old year, before they were aware. By the beginning of New Year's Week, they had nearly reached what once was Pirate Island when the lookout peered westward, wiped her eyes, and peered again, leaning out from the parabolic swing of the topgallant mast at a dangerous angle, as if that hand-span would bring those distant juts of rock nearer.

The clouds had parted briefly — enough for not only the drakan's lookout but those on a couple of the other ships to recognize the distinctive shape of the Pirate Island heights. If they proceeded much farther, they would be visible to any lookouts on the island.

"Signal to the fleet," Fox called, "haul wind."

His first mate repeated the order in a voice devoid of emotion—thus registering strong disapproval—but the second and third mates were not nearly so reticent.

"Aw, really? We don't get to take a whack at Pirate Island?" asked the third mate, a middle-aged woman whose taste for rousting pirates hadn't lessened a whit since she was sixteen and fresh at sea. Substitute Norsunder for pirates, and she was ready to board and carry.

The second mate poked his bony chin in a nod, saying, "We could even use our old ruses, back when we were the *Death*. Nobody here's gonna remember that!"

Fox eyed his crew, trying to hide his own annoyance. "What happens if we take it?"

"Loot," the third mate stated, as others exchanged expressive glances. "What's wrong with that? Enemy holds it, right?"

"Right. Enemy, with magic signals, or whatever they call it. Which means we've given away our position, all for a barrel or two of gold."

Right, right, right. Just because they had been isolated for all these weeks, the enemy wasn't, especially in these modern times, with magic being thrown about on all sides.

As everyone turned back to their tasks in disappointment, weather-reddened noses sunk into scarves and collars, Fox called down to the tender riding in their lee, "Cut straight north. We should be near The Narrows. Scout for enemies and for ice."

Fox returned to his cabin, and dropped into his chair to scowl at the chart that he had made when Inda decided to leave the Fox Banner fleet—his enormously successful, wealthy fleet—and return home to possible execution. That was Inda, lost in his head half the time, and stubborn exactly when he shouldn't be.

Fox peered out at the dark green sea. Until now, this return to the world had seemed a separate existence—not that he'd forgotten, but it felt like eight centuries had passed. He'd avoided using the magic door that had been built into the back of the cabin, which gave access to his tower at Darchelde. He'd hated using that magic. It always felt as if an invisible hand had pushed him through, and it took a while to recover.

After hearing what David had told him weeks ago, it had been an easy decision to ignore that door, believing it was better to let the past lie in the past. He'd had their ruses to plan, and then their wild race south of the Sartoran continent through successive gales.

But now the water was as quiet as it ever got so far south in winter, and the past had somehow become immediate again. Making him curious about the homeland lying on the other side of the land bridge.

He opened a trunk and removed a stick—very like a firestick, except with a different feel, as if covered with invisible fuzz—to outline the door. It still worked: the wooden bulkhead vanished, leaving a door into darkness. He moved toward the door then sniffed—and sneezed, hard. It seemed that all the world's dust lay in there.

He plucked a gold-edged lamp off its chain and held it up to the darkness. Multiple tiny glitters packed together in a vaguely round shape reflected the flame back, and Fox found himself face to face with a huge spider. It sat in the middle of a web bigger than he was, its thick, sticky cables limned in his cabin's reflected light.

Hastily he sketched the stick the other way, closing that door, then ran his hands over the bulkhead to make sure that spider was behind wood again; normally he and spiders lived indifferent to one another, but that thing had been *huge*.

He sneezed again, and sat down. Had he just looked at eight hundred years of ruin? Eight centuries ago, he'd sailed through that rift believing that his sensible son ruled over peaceful Darchelde. His nerves tightened and he lifted his head. A new note in the song of the timbers presaged a sense of the wind shifting, and he bolted out the cabin and to the foredeck as a white line across the eastern horizon rushed toward them. "Brail up! Brail up!"

The sailors were already hauling clew and buntlines, others aloft desperately reefing as the gale struck, nearly throwing the ship on its beam ends. That put the wind broadside to. The masts groaned as the crew fought the icy sails into gaskets, leaving only a scrap; four burly sailors held the helm. With the press of sail eased, the ship wallowed less and recovered, slowly gaining northing.

Steady, steady—the entire crew fought to keep the ship on course as the long wintry night gave way to bleak, dim day. Fox peered grimly into the world of bleak, icy white—would they be swept entirely past The Narrows—no.

They surged past the sentinel stones into the passage. Quite suddenly the gale dropped to shrill whining from the peaks as the towering rocks took the brunt of it, and the fleet raced into what felt in comparison like peaceful waters, though the green-gray breakers still reached the topsails before smashing the rocks at either side.

They scarcely needed the scout now, but back it came to report no enemy in sight, and the only ice was on either side. By this time, eight centuries ago, this passage was often full of dangerous icebergs—or worse. Had winters warmed? Impossible. Winter was winter, and all those gales were nothing like summer.

They sailed northward into fast-moving waters, at least somewhat protected from the howling winds by the snow-topped, sky-scraping cliffs at either side. Fox found himself recognizing much of the bizarre rocky formations. It was unnerving, as if time had somehow slid backward, and if he shut his eyes, he would find himself not on the deck of this ancient Venn ship, but once again on the narrow, rake-masted *Death*, Barend at the wheel, Gillor in the foretop. That strange Chwahir Thog down in the waist, and Tau lounging aft, irritating as ever. And in the cabin, bending over the chart—

Now he was just getting maudlin.

He returned to the cabin to scowl down at his own chart depicting the familiar shoreline of Halia, as if he couldn't draw it out in his sleep.

Unnoticed, the new year began. Firstday, second. Late the next night they eased single-file through the narrowest point, everyone on watch-and-watch, bouncing and shivering within arm's reach of sheet and sail. Memory was both unsettling and steadying—the latter because of the familiarity of the dangers. Weather and rocks you could fight against; magic, you were helpless before. The only thing they dreaded besides ice was a north wind, but neither threat materialized, and once the entire fleet was past the tightest point, they returned to regular watches so that the exhausted mariners might catch up on sleep.

Fox couldn't sleep. He walked the deck instead, gaze moving from palisades to sails and down to the inky waters, as the inexorable tide of memory flooded.

Midnight arrived, and with it memory of Inda's voice as they gathered around the chart to discuss the disposition for battle against Marshig of the Brotherhood of Blood; Inda's voice was so clear, *There are two things that could destroy our plans at the outset. The first is the Venn. The second … is Captain Ramis of the Knife.*

Fox shut his eyes—and dove for his weapons when another well-remembered voice commented, "Reminiscing?"

Fox uttered a forced laugh as he shoved his wrist knives back into their sheaths. "What brings you here? Bad news, of course."

The man he thought of as Ramis was thinner than Fox remembered, but not weaker. There was an intensity to his gaze, to the line of his mouth, even in the set of his shoulders that threw Fox back again to Inda, only this time the Inda ten years older, in the days before the battle in the strait.

He shook that away, wishing he'd been able to sleep, as Detlev glanced upward. "The fox banner was sufficiently obscure on the other side of the world to pass unnoticed, but that will not be true here. You will have to haul it down, unless you want to be associated with Norsunder."

"What?"

Detlev tapped the chart. "In your day," he remarked, "the Venn were the great power on the sea. It was not only the excellence of their ships and their sailing, but they had the advantage of navigation beyond line-of-sight, and instant communication, through their sea dags."

"I have not forgotten," Fox said dryly. "Why would my personal banner be associated with Norsunder?"

Detlev ignored the question, which startled Fox a little, since the first thing out of his mouth had been the order to take the banner down. "Before the Venn rose to power, the key to strategic importance as well as trade and communication in the seas west of Sartor were the Delfin Islands."

Again Fox was surprised enough to cause him to mentally set aside the fox banner question: this conversation was so disjointed, for the first time since he met this man. "Are you about to tell me the Delfs are gone? I haven't seen any turn up so far."

"What I'm telling you is that with the destruction of the communication system in the present day, which happened at the outset of the attack, the Delfin Islands potentially regained that importance. It's not completely the same. Our side has limited communications, and while Norsunder has the advantages the Venn once had, Efael has done his best to completely cut Imry Llyenthur out, lest he gain more maritime control."

"And the Delfin Islands?"

"If Efael knew anything about the sea, or Sartorias-deles's maritime history, he would be holding those islands — though it would take an effort to get control of them. But he's completely ignored them, thinking that he has the entire world to serve as supply outposts. He believes his fleet will be faster without troubling with stops along the way."

"Are we to secure the Delfin Islands, then?"

Detlev waved a hand. "I've sent *Lheit* in case the Delfs need aid." And, without explaining who *Lheit* was, "I'm giving you a superficial background, before getting to two outstanding matters to consider. One. Holding the Halian coast when Efael sends reinforcements. We have to expect that he will; I suspect his obsessions will cause him to begin another invasion here."

"And the other matter?"

"What the Chwahir, who are the most numerous and disciplined fleet out there, will choose to do. Especially if Efael bypasses their king, giving orders directly."

Fox tapped the chart. "Tell me about this Efael."

"He's an assassin and a dungeon-master, not an effective commander on land or sea, though he believes differently."

"So far, he sounds like a typical princeling."

"He's becoming more obsessed with his rival commander, Imry Llyenthur, whose origin is here in Halia. If the possible outcome were not so tragic, it would be ironic, how he mistakes another Norsundrian named Aldon's obsession with ruling your Marloven descendants for Imry Llyenthur's. But he sees what he wants to see."

"That definitely sounds like a spoiled prince."

"Efael's origin is actually quite different, but irrelevant now. He is suffering from time malaise, and is slowly disintegrating, resorting more often to torturing various targets, including on his own side, on the pretext of garnering information. It's the surest way for him to reinforce his sense of control, as well as to satiate his bloodlust."

"Now he sounds like Marshig."

"Not dissimilar. Though he had Marshig put to death almost the moment his flagship emerged from the Beyond. The rest of Marshig's pirates have been marauding up and down the coast of Toar, which Efael sees as an extension of his power, without recognizing that the pirates are doing what they do anyway; there is a possibility they will ignore Efael if he orders them to become transports, without clear loot promised at the other end. Which brings us to the Chwahir."

"I remember: mad king."

"More importantly, like the pirates, we do not know what this king will do if Efael tries to command their entire fleet."

Fox sighed. "I suspect you're about to tell me we're alone, is that so? Jehan of Khanerenth has to remain in the east against attack by the Chwahir?"

"Correct. At the worst, the Chwahir, and the various pirate fleets, will obey Efael and bring enchanted Venn and Fhlerians as well as northern mercenaries south."

Fox began assembling the pieces. "Let me guess. My part is to hold Halia's west coast, so whatever they send cannot land?"

"Yes."

Fox fell silent. The entire ship was silent, the only sound the ticking of his heart. Though the wind still blew, the air was thick with tension.

From their first meeting, Fox had always had the sense that, however powerful Ramis of the *Knife* was, he lived on the run. Fox remembered the chilling references to the mysterious Garden of the Twelve. Whose inhabitants now were somewhere to the north, fighting to hold the world.

"A question before you vanish again," he said. "I told David I wasn't interested in the Darchelde of today, but that's no longer true. I did attempt the door you gave me, and found myself eyeball to eyeball with a spider the size of my head. That argues ruin for a very long time. Did you destroy Darchelde behind my disappearance into your Rift? Is that why my banner is associated with the enemy we are fighting?"

"The ruin happened several generations later—which, yes, is related to why you cannot fly the fox banner on this side of the continent—but your record is still there, safe. The spiders and mice cannot get to that chamber, which is sealed. Assuming any of us get past the present threat, there will be leisure to explain more fully. And, I hope, for you to introduce your record to the present-day Marloven king, who is, incidentally, your descendant—"

Detlev's head turned sharply, and another man walked in with soft step, this one tall and slim, with fair hair. For a heartbeat it was as if Taumad Dei had entered—but Fox saw immediately that this man was no older than thirty, if that. Further, though he shared a similar hair color and build to Tau, their features were as different as their manner. Tau had lounged through the world. This young man moved like one trained in martial skills.

Siamis murmured for Detlev's ear only, "Svir summoned Imry."

"When?"

"It's already been a few days. I got it from Yeres. But she's back in Imar. I dare not press further."

Detlev frowned at the deck of the ship he had taken from an especially bloody Venn king so long ago, then said, "It's time for us to withdraw." He lifted his head to address Fox. "This is Siamis. He will be coordinating the land defense."

And before Fox could say anything, Ramis of the *Knife* was gone.

Fox eyed the newcomer. "What was that?"

Siamis uttered a sound that might have been a laugh, and shook his head. "I found out," he said, "that Svir forced an interview on … someone who knows all of our plans. All. But we do not know what was said." He passed a hand over his face, then added, "I'll need to go. But I can answer a few questions, if you have them."

Fox wanted to say, *That man does not expect to survive what's coming,* But he didn't know this Siamis. "The fox banner. Why can't I fly it?"

"That … is a long story, and involves another of your descendants. Who might turn up." Siamis looked away, regret obvious, then turned back. "Do you still have the magic-paper?"

Fox went to the desk. "Here it is. But no one has written on it, and I did not remember how it worked—it was handled by one of Jehan's people. I wasn't sure if the magic was gone."

"We were waiting until you reached these waters. I'm the person at the other end of the paper, in case some of those questions occur to you: think of me, write my name, Siamis, then your message. I will share whatever reports I receive."

Fox asked doubtfully, "Can you read script from my day?"

Siamis's eyes crinkled. "I can."

Fox turned up his palm in assent, and Siamis vanished.

Fox sighed, and waved to the signals sailor hovering outside the door with half the rest of the crew. "Haul down the fox banner. Then signal for *All captains*," he said.

And, as the northern sun rose over the part of the world into which Fox had been born, he gathered the somber Prince Yviski and the phlegmatic Captain Ghaer around, and traced his finger down the coast of Halia. "I want the scouts to set sail as soon as you can provision; we need to know exactly how the coast has changed. Ghaer, send your river boat captains along, because we're going to need to evaluate estuaries, marshes, and basic soundings. In my day, Halia offered two great harbors, Parayid in the extreme south, and Lindeth at the north end, below the peninsula…"

Fourteen

Near the border of Sles Adran

THAT SAME DAY, AT the same time, in Sles Adran, Liere Fer
Eider was writing a letter to Andri from a barn she had sneaked
into, when the snow she had been riding through turned into a
blizzard.

> *I left the style of a gown to them, saying that all I
> required was something simple. I did not want them
> handing over their hoarded treasures to waste on
> something so impractical! It just needed to show
> Chantala respect, and to be a credit to Enaeran, and
> they assured me it would be done. They then went into
> unintelligible detail about hang, and bias, which I
> believe has to do with drape.*
>
> *I can confess to you that I was less interested in a new
> gown than in the hands making it. Willing hands, from
> such different women — with such different hands. Long
> palms and fingers, short, deft fingers attached to palms
> broad at the base. Thick fingers, thin, gnarled knuckles,
> young untried hands. They are so expressive! Slow and
> assured, slow and uncertain, quick, darting, clever
> fingers, impatient hands, careful ones. Young, old.*

*They finished within two days, in spite of all the
fittings, and such tiny stitches in the cold air, and I had
to leave straight away, which is why I did not write to
you. Everything conspired to slow me, with my mare
sometimes up to her chest in powder. Then there was a
patrol that spotted me at the river, and it meant losing
more time to make a false trail.*

*I'm sorry to say that I got there a day late — the day of
the wedding. I really wanted to get there in advance,
which would be more proper — and also give me some
time with Chantala. I know that it's none of my
business, but I felt an urgency to make certain that
Chantala was happy.*

Liere sat back, still feeling guilty, and vaguely anxious.
She wrote on:

*When I arrived, I saw from the stable full of horses and
the side-yard crowded with carriages that I was indeed
late. I slipped into the horse stall next to the one where
the stable hands saw to my mare and washed up in a
bucket of icy water in hopes of killing any horse smell,
then I flung off my riding clothes, shivered my way into
my new clothes, put on the slippers that I bought the
summer I met you, ran a comb through my hair, and
asked servants to point the way.*

*Do you want a description of the Elardian summer
estate? The place was built for summer use, rooms
opening into rooms to make most of the breezes off the
water. The great hall was carved from 'moon' marble,
the white sort with veins of silver. It could have been
dead in winter, but this time it was careful, clever
Adrani hands that made it come alive with flowering
plants and fine-leafed shrubs in beautiful pots of
midnight blue. A lot of the plants were golden starliss
as well as white lilies, I suspect from neighbors'
conservatories. The effect I found prettier than a lot of
expensive decoration.*

I was inexcusably late, so I thought the only possible

*thing to do was to slip into the back. Only which door
gave onto the back? I peeked in, and discovered to my
relief that I was at the back. The only people who saw
me were Macael and Chantala, just finishing their
vows! I was poised to run — it was so embarrassing —
but then good, kind, sweet Chantala smiled at me,
finished her words, and came my way, so I had to grit
my teeth and do my best to recover whatever prestige
I'd managed to destroy with my late appearance…*

Liere always told the truth as she saw it, but at the same time, in spite of her talents and recent training, she was the least likely of all her generation to see herself as others saw her.

What did the wedding couple and their guests see?

The wedding couple stood midway down the ballroom under a bower made by two tall flowering shrubs whose tops had been tied by blue and gold and white ribbons to form an arch. Macael and Chantala faced the company gathered inside the grand door, at which stood a second bower of emerald leaves starred by five-pointed lilies with palest blue interiors.

Liere paused in the center of this bower, illuminated in golden light from crystal chandeliers, which cast a shimmer over her beautifully draped robe of pale blue silk edged with midnight-blue braided trim, slashed up the sides, worn over a perfectly fitted underdress of white brocade. Her only ornaments were her long stream of golden hair and her wide eyes, which shone golden in candlelight.

Only the wedding pair saw her. Chantala stuttered inaudibly through the last few words of her vow, then suddenly smiled when she recognized Liere. Macael stilled.

Liere had just noted all the backs — relief! — when everyone turned to stare. A whisper serried through the gathered crowd when they saw Liere standing alone, framed in the bower of lilies; Halli Elardian reached Liere first, ahead of her husband, who'd been lamed in last year's fighting with Enaeran.

Chantala then crossed the room, everyone bowing and giving way before her. Her thin face flushed with happiness as she stretched out her hands in welcome.

Liere smiled at the sight of the new ring gleaming on Chantala's heart-finger. "I apologize for my lateness — I meant to slip in without drawing notice," she whispered.

"I am so glad you are here," Chantala said, her soft voice

almost lost in the well-bred clamor of welcome from all sides. "Come in, come in!"

"Welcome," said Macael, joining them.

...I blundered and stuttered a morass of unintelligible words as I tried to apologize, remembered in time not to upset Chantala, so I bit off mentioning that chase over the frozen river, until I saw that I was confusing her even more. But it didn't matter. She seemed so happy to see me. As for Macael, he said nothing beyond that one word, welcome. I couldn't tell whether or not he was annoyed at my rude, awkward interruption, but Halli and Chantala both insisted I sit with Chantala, which I took to mean they were seeing me not just as me, but as Enaeran's representative! At least Bartal was not there, and no one declared war on Enaeran because of my blunder!

At least I had interrupted the very end of the vows, and they then carried on with the schedule. It turned out that the Adranis had not brought gifts, but either a poem or a song, whether theirs or someone else's. Halli whispered to me that it had been Macael's idea, and very well received it was. I think the nobles over there in Sles Adran have been taxed to the toenails, as my parents' generation used to say in Imar, on top of so many young people being conscripted and sent over the border into other countries. But what I noticed was how this was the best possible sort of setting for Chantala. She listened closely to every offering, even the ones that were so conventional you knew what five words would follow the one being spoken, and she replied with verses — all well-chosen. Certainly better chosen than half those poems.

There was occasional music, but Macael did not take part, even when some of the guests were inspired to join the musicians in a familiar tune. Then the wedding supper, and Chantala insisted I sit with them.

Liere paused. The words vanished.

Andri's handwriting appeared, dashing across the page:

*You say the decorations were wedding white and green
mixed with blue and white and gold? Elsarion colors, in
Sles Adran? Is either of them adopting into the other's
family? That wouldn't matter in the ordinary way, but
when there's a throne that might be empty soon,
especially given that Bartal was not present, that seems
significant. Did you talk to either of 'em about that?*

She wrote back:

*I could not think of a diplomatic way of asking about
her uncle, but Chantala whispered to me that she
wished to renounce her hated name, and adopt into the
Elsarion family, however Macael said it was better to
wait until there was peace. Then right after supper was
dancing, so I hadn't any chance to talk to Macael, even
when Chantala insisted he dance with me after she did,
in addition to their duty with all the rest of the Adrani
court. There was no chance to chat — he was watching
Chantala, as well as the rest of the room, and I
wondered if he and Halli shared host duties, for
Chantala's benefit.*

Liere paused, rubbing her tired eyes as she reflected back.
Their dance had been a partners dance, and he very properly
had offered her the top of his hand, which was the custom for
married people in love-matches. The palm was the sign of
gallantry, of courtship, of expectation.

She'd smiled at his ring with real pleasure, with trust, at
last, in his regard for the gentle Chantala. That smile had come
from a heart that truly wished for happiness of not only
Chantala, but for Macael and for Halli and everyone else in
sight, a smile that illumined her face as she and Macael whirled
about the middle of the floor as the word "Sartora" whispered
after them like a comet tail.

Liere still felt that she had missed an opportunity to say
something diplomatic about peace between the lands, and good
will, but what could she say that wouldn't sound fatuous in the
middle of a war?

She frowned at her empty magic-paper as she sat there on
her hassock, rubbing her pilly mittens together for warmth.
Then she realized that the words had faded from the paper.

That meant it had been some time since Andri had answered.

She dashed off a query:

Anything wrong?

The answer came back fairly quickly:

Two things going on at once — both of 'em damned important — one of them is trying to figure out if Macael has a political sense that should put him up there playing toss-the-crown with Detlev and his like, leaving fools like me gaping at the gate —

She blinked.

What?

What do you mean, what? Didn't you see it? From everything you report, he walked in and set up his fiddle in that kingdom, and got 'em all dancing to his tune — Chantala taking our name? Using OUR House colors, in Sles Adran —

Shitfire! I have to go. Detlev's snapping his fingers. I'll be back soon's I find out what's steaming under his hat — if you can, I want you to find out from Macael, when you see him next, who is giving the orders to the army —

She waited a little, then longer, and the sun had risen completely when she realized she was half frozen, staring down at a blank piece of paper. She pocketed it safely, and curled up in a pile of hay.

Two days later, when she reached Shiovhan, she wrote again, and this time got no answer.

Fifteen

DETLEV REAPPEARED, SAYING, "I need everyone's attention."

"What happened?" Dirk burst out.

"Is this the attack?" Mildred asked

"No," Laban said, "if it was the attack, he'd shut us up. That's the *here comes a talk* tone."

The rest talking at once—except for Andri, scribbling to Liere.

MV lay on cushions behind Andri, who sat on the floor, writing on a stool. Looking over Andri's shoulder, MV said reasonably, "If Macael can hold 'em, why shouldn't he be king? Bartal was a shit, and you yourself said the niece is fog-headed."

"Right, right." Andri threw the quill down and scrubbed his hands up his face. "It's just that it took me by surprise— wedding—our House colors—Adrani court setting. I would've thought he'd do the deed in Elsarion, if Chantala is going to adopt in and become Enaeraneth. But what Liere describes, it sounds like Macael is going to walk right in and take Bartal's throne, which comes with that vast army."

"Who says he'll take over the army? He hasn't any training, you said. I'm sure they expect him to sit with Fog-Head on the throne and be decorative, while some other relation does the actual work. Including bringing that army home without causing another war," MV said. "I would not want that job to be mine. There's no faster way to lose respect—and your life—than commanding a retreat after losing a war."

David turned a serious gaze to Andri. "Do you want to rule Sles Adran?"

"No! Got enough trouble with Enaeran. But. Last I heard, I was supposed to be rescuing the Adranis from the evil Bartal, and they're right there on my eastern border, so it's more that I have to take an interest. And that I didn't *know*—"

"I remember that Andri-the-rescuer talk," David said. "Could be, to them one Elsarion hero is as good as another. Is Macael Elsarion interested in allying with Norsunder?"

"No." Andri flipped up the back of his hand. "That I can attest to. He hates them all."

"Then what are you worried about? You don't want Sles Adran. You and Macael get along."

"Then why didn't he tell me?"

"Do you tell him everything?"

"I would—I might—if he asked." Andri shrugged. "But I can see that. He's used to being solitary. And I looked so bad from a distance, for so long. Except he knows that was all Marsael's slander. Eh, most of it." He grinned. "Some of it's true. I am a street rat. But whose fault was that?"

David said, "It sounds to me as if Liere's got the right idea. You're all friends, including with the fog-minded heir. Everyone wants peace, am I right?"

"Yes—" Andri dipped the quill and began scribbling again, but halfway through a sentence a hand reached over his shoulder and nipped it away.

Andri twisted around to see Detlev behind him.

Detlev reached down and drew a line right to left—and Andri's magic-paper vanished.

"Ho," Andri protested, but Detlev ignored him, going from one to the next demanding magic-papers. Surprised and troubled, everyone who had one surrendered it, whereupon Detlev ripped them apart, made a pass of his hand, and the pieces flared briefly, then fell in ash.

Then, an unsettling sensation briefly gripped them all, and released them in a new cavern, very different from the previous.

They stared. The transfer had not only been painless, but for the first time ever, they had transferred in a group. Yet there was no smell of hot metal, no transfer malaise.

"I don't understand," Senrid said. "What just happened?"

"That was a very old transfer token. Nearly five thousand years old," Detlev said, and then paused to let them take in their surroundings.

The caverns curving around them were formed of a glistening white stone, aglow with its own light. Streamers of ferny leaves hung in a living green drapery over a wall, beyond which they saw the reflection of light on water flowing over stone.

Plants underground? Mildred was continually amazed; this world, she knew, had in ancient times been rent by quakes and volcanoes, which had not happened on Geth, at least to so great a degree. There were so many mountains, and they all appeared to be honeycombed with caverns, water, gems. Hot water from deep, deep down, cold melting from the heights.

She stepped back and gazed up at the delicate ferns that had never been damaged by any winds or weather-changes. Water, like sky captured in crystal, fell just beyond the hanging ferns, flowed into a wide pool, and disappeared somewhere between cracks visible on the lower level.

"You needn't remain crowded in the transfer area," Detlev said, leaping lightly down what they saw now was a broad, shallow curved stair, into the larger area below.

Andri scanned his surroundings as he joined the others following Detlev to the lower level. This was not a natural cavern. Someone had put those stairs in, and had created a low, round table of the white stuff off to one side. Adjacent to it, near the pool, was a low shelf. On it rested a neat stack of scrolled rice paper, pens, and carved glass bottles of what had to be ink. At the other end of the shelf sat a wide, shallow bowl made of burnished silver. In it something frosty-silver glistened.

MV had followed more slowly, one hand pressed to his bandaged middle. He leaned against a wall, an action that pulled slightly less painfully on his slashed stomach muscles than sitting down and having to get up again. "Svir niffed us, is that it? There's no escaping the fact that Imry got the whole plan from my skull."

"Until recently, for whatever reason, Imry appears to have kept it to himself," Detlev said. "But Siamis found out that Svir summoned Imry a few days ago." He waited for the curses and exclamations to die down, then said, "We are here because Svir might now know about this circle. Who you are. It is also possible that he will track down and try to elicit—as publicly as possible—your whereabouts from your connections. But you will not know. No one except Siamis knows where this place is, and you will not be permitted to return to fight for the safety of allies and dependents when the counterattack commences; once again I remind you that the land and sea battles are merely the deflection. The real battle is ours, against the entity called Ilerian."

"Who wants to devour all life," Mildred said, her statement halfway to question.

"Correct."

"I'm not arguing, but what about the other one, Svir? I've heard his name a lot, but it's always sounded like all he does is sit around scaring people."

"Active support of Ilerian. His role is much the same as yours, supplying strength, and he handles a lot of the magical tasks. The two of them don't need a circle, even if they would trust one. Svir's been at it for millennia, and he wants to live forever. He might seem lazy, but he will fight as hard and as viciously as he can to back Ilerian. But you need not concern yourselves with him; the mages will be making him their specific focus, and of course Efael and Yeres will be kept busy by the coordinated counterattack."

"Got it," Mildred said. "Then the counterattack is happening *now*? This moment?"

"Not this moment. The Host has not acted yet. As near as we can tell, they are still making an immense effort to break Kessler's ward binding the world. Which suggests that they are close. After which, of course, they will have all the power of the Beyond, against which we will not prevail."

"I'm sorry I asked," Mildred muttered under her breath.

Detlev made no sign of hearing it. "This is the only respite we will have, because you are not ready. Siamis will give me the sign when he thinks they are about to make their move."

Looks semaphored; others shuffled, or ran clammy hands down their thighs.

"We are going to stay here and train, hard, until then. You have worked with Adam until now, to make it easier for you. That ends today. I am going to attempt to cram years of training into you in days. Maybe hours. Therefore, I want your minds off that counterattack. If the Host is not defeated, we merely prolong the world's suffering, because Ilerian will *never* yield. And I repeat, we are not ready."

Silence met these words—appalled, angry, stunned, grieving.

"The Seer chamber is empty, with a mirror ward to diffuse attempts to penetrate it by magic, but the morvende do not know that," Detlev said. "It provides another layer of security for us, and for them. I will not release you until I defeat Ilerian, or die in the attempt. The choice is no longer yours, it is mine." He picked up the shallow silver bowl and carried it toward the lower caverns. "As soon as you are ready, join me." He vanished inside the first chamber on the left.

Laban raised his hands in invitation. "You are now free to revile."

"I had as little choice as you," Sveneric said, rising. "But since it is done..." He abandoned speech and followed Detlev into the chamber he'd chosen.

Adam's gaze was on the table, his mouth somber.

David said to him, "I think—I believe—he warned them. Tarael and the geliath council. It's part of a plan. That's probably been in place since we were cutting teeth, if not before." And he recounted his conversation with Marga.

Adam's eyes looked somewhat less stricken when he finished. "Yes," he said, thinking hard. "She was indeed telling you. Both things. But how did she know?"

"I can't even begin to answer that. She didn't get it from Detlev, for they've seen one another only twice, and I was there both times." David paused, remembering that far-off conversation, seen from the cavern bridge. Except that was after Marga had dropped her hints. He shrugged, making an effort to push her out of his mind, where she'd showed a tendency to stay, shining there in memory, like a morning star. Think. Geliath. "But if he did warn them, they made their choice."

"Everybody did." Crow's hoarse voice intruded, in a harsh tone. "All of us had our chance to leave, anytime these past few months. We didn't. We're fighting a war. If we win here and I go home to find my gang dead, I can rebuild in peace. And if it's me who dies, they know what to do." There was a tremor in the last word, but no one reacted. He scrambled to his feet.

"Wait up, wart," MV said lazily, wincing as he moved again, more slowly. Pounding a fist lightly on Crow's nearly straight shoulder, MV said with a grin, "Where's the fire?"

Andri thumped his elbows on the table and dug the heels of his hands into his eyes. The timing couldn't be worse. He'd been right in the middle of an important, a vital, communication with Liere!

He fought against rage, against impending loss, because they weren't going to net him anything. He considered that interrupted exchange with Liere via magic-paper. At least she knew about the circle. And, yeah, he'd cut her off abruptly, but wasn't it better that way? It would have been more painful had they both known it was coming. The parting had been quick, she happy for Chantala, and confident that their friendship with Macael would bring peace between the two countries. Hope.

It meant he wouldn't be there for the counterattack. But he'd never run a major battle. Though she hated the Sartora myth, the truth was, Liere had a world of experience he didn't have. She would probably do a better job running a battle than he would; she had yet to fail in any task he had seen her take on. That especially included anything to do with magic, about which he was even more ignorant. That left him here, where supposedly he could do some good.

All right, he'd fight the fight from here, and if fury helped him fight better mentally as it did with sword and knife in his hands, ah, he was ready, more than ready to go.

He sat back and looked at the others still at the table, faces closed, except for David, who was watching. Across from him was Senrid, who was always blank, void of emotion around Andri—and Andri knew why. He'd never say anything directly. But maybe he could let Senrid know, obliquely, that Liere was safe.

Andri turned to David. "At least I happened to be writing home when Detlev pinched us, eh?"

David, as he'd figured, wasn't slow. "Liere had things well in hand, I trust?"

"What else?" And without looking at Senrid (who wouldn't react outwardly anyway) Andri got to his feet and sauntered after MV and Crow, his long yellow hair swinging as David watched him go.

In spite of the situation, he laughed inwardly: Andri had pretty much the same insouciant saunter as MV, though the two had never known of the other until the previous summer.

David had been wishing that Mac had turned up before Kessler closed the world; he doubted the circle was strong enough to take down Ilerian. Everyone had drawbacks. Senrid would continue to shield himself in order to blend mentally with forbearing Andri; he was capable of it, as were few, but it would cost. As for Andri, his Dena Yeresbeth was powerful indeed, but still so untrained. Could he catch up fast enough? Would Dirk be able to sustain the shield? He was so young. Or Crow, there, who had been raised to distrust everyone but himself. Would he adjust to the level of trust the blending would require? Could Zairna, from a far different culture, give himself to the cause?

David smothered his doubts and looked around at the remaining people. "I have to say, I heard more promising speculation about Detlev's origins, tastes, and probable future back in our barracks at Norsunder Base. Anyone want to elaborate?"

Mildred flashed a semblance of her usual grin. "Wish I coulda heard those! I think curse words in other languages are so funny. Look. The choice would've been a killer. I'm for his way. I just want to hear what everyone else thinks."

David sat back. "If we get out, and what we find is bad, then you can blame him, and not yourselves, for the rest of your lives. Your very short lives. And I'm here, ready and willing to argue until you understand why it has to be this way."

Silence.

David looked from face to face. "Dirk. Anything to say?"

Dirk snapped, "Why? I already know what you'd say in return."

"Try me." David smiled.

Dirk shook his head—and then paused with the intent face of one who listened inward. A long pause stretched into another silence, and then Dirk's face relaxed a little; that had to be Sveneric reassuring him.

David smiled. "Anyone wish to speak? How about you, Senrid?"

Senrid's gaze was cool and expressive as glass. "No," he said, his voice flat.

The new chamber was circular, built around a low table carved from stone.

"Someone live here?" Mildred asked when everyone was

gathered. She ran her fingers over the smooth, light stone of the walls.

Holding the silver bowl in one hand, Detlev laid his free palm on a section of wall and a silent cupboard opened, revealing a neat arrangement of big, embroidered cushions and pillows in soft and soothing colors; another cupboard revealed more in jewel-toned silk. He gestured at the pillows and said, "We do, now. And will, until I, or Siamis, releases us. We are in the catacombs under the Ghost Lakes. There is no physical access to this place for any save the water folk. Norsunder will not find this particular chamber because it was sealed, for precisely this purpose, four thousand years ago. Here we will remain until the attack."

As he spoke, David and Mildred both pulled armloads of pillows and cushions out, strewing them around the low platform. Mildred made a nest of them near MV, then she and Rolfin each took one of his arms and helped lower him down to the pillows.

MV heaved a sigh, wiped his sweaty forehead, then said, "Our part of which will be carried out from here?"

"Correct."

"I don't remember hearing anything about this place." Laban tossed down two pillows and collapsed onto them.

"No one alive knew of its existence outside of Siamis, and that relatively recently. It was made by the dyranarya when we understood that we would not win that war. Our purpose was to preserve knowledge. Every book I burned for Svir and Ilerian has a copy here."

Laban whistled.

Mildred asked. "Did you stay here back then?" She poked cautiously at another section of the walls, and discovered that on the touch of a human hand the subtly delineated alcoves opened, revealing more stores.

"No," Detlev said. "It was finished after I was taken."

A covert exchange of glances: proof, if anyone still needed it, that he had surrendered only in outward form.

"It was not until much later that I dared return, to find it like this. I knew that none of my circle had survived, but on my return I discovered that they had all kept the secret until the end." The silence was so complete they heard the murmur of water from the higher chamber. "The time has come to use it."

Mildred poked at a cupboard full of folded clothes. The

style was a type of draped and tied robe, which looked like something in one of Bereth Ferian's most ancient tapestries — the ones that had gone old and fragile after having been repaired and repaired again over the centuries, until all the original threads had been replaced several times over.

She saw Zairna unrolling one of the scrolls with careful, patient fingers. "Whee! Are those the missing records, Zairna?"

He looked up. "They are blank, at least the ones I have examined so far."

"These waiting scrolls are for records to be put into them," Detlev said.

Mildred grinned. "And you forgot to tell the Host about it during the interim?"

"I didn't forget," he replied, smiling.

Yep, there was her proof — as if she'd doubted. "Then you weren't a very good ally, were you?" She chuckled, pulling out another robe, this one deep violet, and shook it to see it shimmer.

"I was not an ally. I was a prisoner, and then a servant," he said, still holding the silver bowl in both hands. "Beyond that wall is an archive, everything we could preserve."

Adam glanced across the wide chamber at David, who was gazing raptly at Detlev.

Mildred breathed in deeply, then let out an explosive laugh. "The air is so pure here! Makes me feel a little drunk!"

"Get used to it as quickly as you can. We will begin practicing once you all get something to eat."

"But there is something else here," Adam murmured.

"True." Detlev smiled.

"That Norsunder would want. Desperately." Adam turned this way and that, gaze roaming the white walls, the water, plants, alcoves. He looked up, his eyes round with wonder.

"You are right."

"Disirad," Adam said under his breath, his eyes now shut, his face lifted, as if to the warm sun after an eternity of winter.

Detlev set the silver bowl down in the center of the round table. "Apparently Nevraeth had enough forewarning to get her dyr here before Sfenaraec trapped her, possibly through one of the other members of our circle. They all bespelled their dyra to transfer here once they had reached the point of no escape, and the plan was for them to be carrying false dyra, to fool the enemy. When I became aware that our circle was being systematically hunted down and that I had been set up as a target, I severed all communication with the others, so all I know of the end of their stories lies here: their dyra." He touched the rim of the bowl.

Everyone stared at that silver bowl.

Adam said, "You couldn't use this place until the disirad was back in the world, yes?"

"Yes."

Sveneric said, "And that's why you went through the world, destroying knowledge?"

Detlev said, "My reasons were twofold. I had to prove to Svir that I was his creature, and the best way to do that was to add to the destruction, by destroying the testaments to civilization. By then I had begun to understand the nature of Norsunder-Beyond, and the inherent weakness of those who would hide beyond the reach of time. Destroying knowledge was in fact meant to remove all mention of disirad. Yes, the people of Sartorias-deles forgot it, and after enough centuries had passed it was as if it had never been. Which was exactly what Svir wanted. It was also what I wanted, for a completely different reason: I believed it would return. He wanted to make certain it was gone."

"But Ilerian thought it might return?" Andri asked.

"He wanted it to return, and he needed to catch it in the early stage, when his strength would prevail."

"Which is why you had to hide its reemergence as long as you could, right?" Senrid spoke for the first time. "Was that what Peitar Selenna sensed?"

"Yes, and yes."

Senrid fell silent then, but those who knew Peitar Selenna of Sarendan were thinking, *And you killed him for it.* Rolfin looked down at his hands, his profile grim.

Adam was also thinking it, but he had been monitoring Peitar Selenna in the realm of the spirit, and knew that Peitar had died in the Selenseh Redian, his spirit fled into the very mystery he sought so hard to find, in spite of duty, even family. But that secret Adam had kept so long that he looked past it, his attention on the bowl. "If I'm understanding right, disirad and Selenseh Redian ... go together? And Dena Yeresbeth is also a part?"

"In a sense. Suffice it to say that I had to deflect

Norsunder's attention away from certain kinds of coinherence, as well as the reappearance of the disirad." Detlev bent, reached into the bowl, and pulled up a fine braid-linked chain made of the glistening material that wasn't quite stone or yet quite metal, called disirad. "This is Nevraeth's dyr. Adam! Hands out."

With a quick gesture, he tossed the chain to Adam. There was a sweet, soft musical *ching!* as it landed on his palm.

"Put it on, Adam. Wear it sleeping and waking. You are going to act as our link."

As Adam stood still, gazing down at the chain in his hands, questions on myriad related subjects lanced at Detlev from all around him.

"I thought dyra were like coins!"

"No, though many preferred that shape. Others shaped theirs into jewelry, and still others did not alter the shape at all. Or changed it from time to time."

"I thought dyra were bound somehow to the holder."

"In a sense, but that could be changed as well."

"Four thousand years! But it's so clean and fresh in here!"

"It was bound in time, as I said, until one of us should enter it again."

"So ... if you didn't know what happened after you were pitched out of the action, then conceivably you could have walked in here and found Ilerian waiting with a ready lunch!"

"Which is why, the first time, I came alone."

Adam finally spoke, still looking down at the chain resting on his fingers. "But what Ilerian wanted to prevent is not just the room, or this chain. It's the room, and the chain, *and* Dena Yeresbeth." He looked up at Detlev. "Isn't it?"

Not many heard him, and out of half of them, two paid his words any attention, for they sounded so obvious as to be stupid; the sound of flowing water masked his tone, and the normal perspectives of youth—focused on the immediate—his context.

"It is."

David, who did comprehend, sat down abruptly on one of the stairs. Sveneric suddenly smiled, though he said nothing. "So that's what Marga meant," David began, and Sveneric turned his way, lips parted.

Andri was one of those who had heard Adam, and to him the conversation was so superficial it was a waste of time. It was obvious that they were all here, wasn't it? In a room kept hidden for ages? And that Detlev would gather as many with Dena Yeresbeth as he could get his hands on? The only question was, why weren't there more? "We're here," he said. "And it seems to me since we are here, we should do what we're supposed to be doing so we can get out again and go home."

Detlev turned to him. "Then why don't you set out a meal? Perhaps we can resolve the last of the questions while we eat something. Then we will begin the next level of training while — if — we still have time."

Andri had just bent down to inspect one of the storage alcoves. Taking out and thrusting a stack of shallow ceramic bowls onto the table, he said, "I can't read any of the writings on these jars and things."

Detlev helped him sort through the cupboards, translating the Ancient Sartoran script. Rolfin and Zairna came to help; they discovered not only sacks of flour, rice, nuts, dried fish and fowl, but jars and jars of herbs, spices, and various dried ingredients like mushrooms, onions, garlic, and peppers. There was even dried egg, in a manner that no one there understood: when it was mixed with hot water, it turned into fluffy shirred eggs, as if freshly cooked. For cooking there was a hole in a stone slab, with a shallow cooking bowl fitted into it, just as many used today. They started a vagabond fire below it.

As they rapidly designed and set out a substantial feast, Sveneric's thoughts broke reluctantly from the bright, interlocked threads of a very intricate pattern, woven through time and across uncounted distances, that he had just perceived, one that had to have been made in utter isolation and maintained through faith alone.

Dirk glanced at the other side of the room, to where Detlev, Andri, and Zairna were busy with the food, and muttered, "I don't like being cut off this way."

Dirk's voice brought Sveneric back to the immediate. His eyes focused on the glimmering chain still swinging from Adam's fingers.

David said, "Our biggest loss is Siamis, but he has to guard Clair. As well as coordinate the military side, because neither Rel nor Atan has Dena Yeresbeth. As for Detlev, he is who he is. How much do you think he gave up to preserve Siamis's life? The fact that you don't know — nobody does — should suggest just how bad it was."

Enlightenment made Dirk shudder. "Oh."

Sveneric's face was wry. "We're here, and Svir can do what he likes to try to flush us out, but we won't know it. Only Detlev will. He will bear the burden of knowledge, as he always has, and the responsibility for shielding us from unbearable choices."

Including himself, Dirk saw. He had known ever since he became aware of the past, and how it affected the present, that Kessler was in some way aware that he was incapable of many emotions. Love wasn't in Kessler's vocabulary. And yet he felt it, or some semblance of it, Sveneric had convinced him when they were little. He never expressed it in words, but in actions, like permitting Dirk to spend so much time with Sveneric and Darian, and the others; even if the principal intent was to have ears and eyes within Detlev's inner circle, surely he could have found another way.

David clapped Dirk on the shoulder. "Rest easy," he said, with a sardonic smile. "This way we can either all win, or else all snuff it together."

Dirk snorted a laugh, wondering where Kessler was, and then — because there was no answer — dismissed the subject, as Mildred sang out, "Bor-ring!"

Detlev said, "Problem?"

"Why am I the only girl?"

"The others I wanted are all too crucial for other concerns. We shall do our best to entertain you."

Mildred scanned the huge chamber, and her features altered mirthfully when she spotted Rolfin, who had gone over to stand with Roy and Senrid in low-voiced conversation. "Entertainment? Let us begin with him!"

Her voice carried. Rolfin looked up, making a gesture of fear and warding.

Adam stood alone, thoughts remote in time and space.

MV wondered how Adam was going to bind this bunch together. *Better him than me.* "All right, shitbirds," he said, jerking his thumb at the table, where Zairna was setting out shallow dishes, while behind him, Andri toasted various ingredients in the oiled pan. "Stop the yap and fall in."

Sixteen

WHILE THEY GATHERED AROUND the table for their first meal in the dyranarya sanctuary, far to the south in Mearsies Heili, Dhana crouched over a rumpled beige paper, and with pauses for occasional sneaky looks over her shoulder, she scribbled as fast as she could.

> *...and oh, CJ, the WORST thing is something weird Clair's been doing so much that it's become a habit. She doesn't even know she keeps touching furniture she's known ever since we girls first came, touching it or patting it or rubbing it, like she has to make sure it's real!*

CJ wrote back: *Double-skunks! How is Aurora dealing with all this?*

Dhana's impatient scrawl came back with startling rapidity:

> *She's getting tutoring lessons from Siamis, and regular lessons with Madelon Delieth and the twins, and they spend a lot of time in the Junkyard, since we are all up here on guard over Clair.*

Dhana looked around guiltily, in an agony of ambivalence. She knew where Detlev had taken his group, using a transfer token so old that its origins lay back when the oldest of her kind were young; the peoples of all the lakes moved back and forth between those lakes as they willed. She could hop into the cascade below Clair's chamber right now, and pop up above where Detlev was if she wanted to. But she wouldn't.

She didn't dare.

Oh, CJ, to not be able to tell Clair things, and even worse, to have to lie!

CJ wrote with many underlinings:

<u>I know</u>. Believe me I know. Remember last summer? What about June and the cup, and Clair's plan about faking them out with it?

Dhana wrote in a nearly illegible scrawl:

I don't know. That is, she still has the plan, but I don't know when she wants to use it, or even how. It sounded so good at the start, but what worries us is, if the idea is a stone spell on the fake one, so when it gets handed off to Ilerian, he turns into stone long enough for Siumis or Detlev or Frai-Yanyu, or someone, to get there and make it permanent, then how does the cup get there in the first place? I WON'T SEND CLAIR TO IMAR.

CJ wrote firmly:

GOOD. If she even makes a squeak about going, I don't care how worried she is about me seeing her like she is now. I WILL COME HOME AT ONCE.

How about this. If it seems she's going to do ANYTHING weird, then you get me. Fast. Don't even waste time writing to me. Then get Aurora <u>away</u>. The important thing is, if anything is going to happen to Clair, that we all be together to face it, but keep Aurora safe so she can't be used against Clair. Are you still wearing your medallion?

Dhana: *Of course!*

CJ: *Is Clair?*

Dhana frowned, thinking, then wrote: *I'm not sure.*

CJ: *If you can, make sure she is. Ask her 'Why not?'*

*and remind her that NO stinky-feet Norsundrian is
going to break up the gang! We all wear these
medallions around our necks for a reason!*

Dhana: *Okay.*

Unaware that Siamis was aware of this comforting exchange, Dhana and CJ ended the correspondence.

Siamis was grateful the girls had forgotten their mindshields. They had bolstered one another's spirits enough to carry on, which was what he needed to help protect Clair. Sherry and Gwen sat with Clair now, over the breakfast he hoped she was eating; Seshe, after reading patiently over Clair's slumbering form all night, had gone to bed.

Siamis swept his eyes over his situation map. Rel and Atan had pulled a force together in catacombs behind Eidervaen. Over in Sarendan, Derek Diamagan's rebel rabble had reformed again after all these years, older and grimmer. Some of them had gotten military training elsewhere. Unlike their first essay into war, they would not be taken by surprise again.

Colend poised—no one could expect a battle front from them; Ferret had worked hard to give the Colendi the information for a precision attack, which would bypass the Chwahir and target the Norsundrian leadership. Khanerenth was poised to take action, either land or sea. As was Geranda.

Silvanas had made covert contact with old Roderic Dei in Everon; north and west of Everon and Wnelder Vee, the polities were so small, or so sparsely populated, that there was little but token Norsundrian presence.

Goerael's north, same, where the enchanted Venn guardians did not roam. In the south, Markham Glenereth and his contacts were waiting. South of there, Toar, had the largest infestation of mercenaries, in aid of the governments that had allied with Norsunder, like Bartal of Sles Adran. Siamis had eyes there, from his wandering scribe days.

Siamis considered the latest reports pinned on the map, and then studied the seas. Fox Montredavan-An's fleet was deploying up the coast—Siamis was going to have to find time now to introduce Fox to Van Stad, the area of most concern. The Marlovens, and the coastal Iascans, would not trust anyone they didn't know, especially someone who appeared in a drakan with black sails, looking very like the pirate ships that Efael had loosed on the shores of Toar.

He wondered if Fox and Senrid would meet.

He wondered where, and how, Ivandred and his First Lancers would be used.

Then he turned away: such speculation was so far ahead that it was next to useless.

Of all the responsibilities weighing on Siamis's mind right now, this one right here irked the most steadily. *Don't try to make Dhana understand why you are doing what you do*, Detlev had said before he'd returned to Ghildraith. *Even if you convince her rational awareness, you will only increase her considerable emotional turmoil. Instead, give orders in a take-no-prisoners voice. Make yourself into the annoying adult villain if you have to. She will then spend the major portion of what is going to be a bleak, increasingly tense interval safely reviling against you and the conspiracy of adulthood. And when this is over, there will have been no doubts about Clair to undermine their relationship. Instead, the conspiracy will bring them closer, which Clair is going to need.*

Good advice. Play the villain. That role wasn't new. But in those days he hadn't really known any of the lighters.

He entered the kitchen. Janil was putting together a breakfast to send to the children down in the Junky. She looked up, and smiled a welcome as he reached for one of Janil's homely steep cups, and poured out the steep, the browny-green stream steaming gently, giving off summery vapors. It seemed as if someone else's hands curled around the bark-brown liquid in which light ringed because he could not, after all, hold it steady.

He sipped steep, which scalded his tongue. He coughed, and blinked away pain tears.

Janil clucked in sympathy, dusting her floury hands. "Now, I don't have to tell you to pay attention to what you're doing, hmmm?"

Siamis drew his wrist across his eyes. "I'll try not to make a mess, Janil," he said, smiling.

She gave him a glance of the same sort of tolerant exasperation she turned on Puddlenose and Christoph when they used to blitz through on kitchen raids in easier days. As Siamis walked out onto the chilly balcony, he reflected with some chagrin, *I feel like I'm fifteen years old.*

Detlev had been full of logical, unassailable reasons why it must be Siamis holding the chariot-reins at the end. Each reason had a valid explanation. There had been no glimpses of any underlying cause, but Siamis knew Detlev too well to think that it was not there.

Siamis suspected his role had been designed to afford him the wherewithal to make whatever sort of life he might choose—assuming they survived. Most people would hear about, and celebrate, the King and Queen of Sartor leading the alliance of lighters into battle; the savvy heads of state, and the world of mages, would hear about Siamis coordinating the magical and the military counterattack.

Siamis felt sick when he thought of Detlev deliberately setting out to put together this last gift. Fox had no mind-shield, so Siamis had caught that thought: even Fox, who barely knew Detlev and that only in one of his many guises, saw that Detlev didn't expect to live.

But that was a misstatement. Siamis understood that it wasn't so much expectation as the drive to complete everything, to finish behind him, so to speak, in case. This was no recent preparation. Detlev had begun cutting himself off from the boys in the past few years in order to (he thought) lessen the pain of his passing, should that come to be. Though Detlev had made plans for the future—starting the dyranarya academy again being his most ardent wish—he had designed those plans so that others could carry on. He never permitted himself any thought of reward, much less a life of his own, but he was human. Siamis knew he wanted to live. One had only to see him with Sveneric to appreciate that.

And it would be too much to say that Detlev had never had a life of his own. He had, once. Siamis's earliest memory of him was the huge clan Attainment Celebration, Detlev still squeak-voiced, proud of being the youngest dyranarya in generations. Then he'd gone away to study the arts of order, as security and protection was known then, and returned as a young man: popular, relishing sports, fond of music and art, close to both his parents and to his tightly bonded dyranarya circle. All of that ripped away, because Detlev had been the best of the best—

"Siamis?"

Clair appeared in the doorway, shrouded in a nightgown from chin to feet, so that no one could see how thin she had become. She'd apparently tried to eat, but he understood that wretched grinding churn inside that made the most delicious foods look inedible.

Neither spoke as he rose, and accompanied her away from the kitchen and dining wing. Half-forgotten childhood habit prompted him to glance at the windows, in order to choose the correct spire to match the time, and they began the climb upward, stair after stair.

Clair's breathing slowed as they began to ascend the Purrad.

It always got easier, somehow, above the first level, a little as if she floated. It wasn't flying, like in Tsauderei's Valley, but it was easier to walk. The magic was stronger. She had begun to suspect that sometime in its past, this castle might have been some sort of healing center, and if you found the right rhythm for the climb, it became easier to move, until your toes barely touched each step.

They walked in silence, Siamis quiet because she was quiet. If she spoke, he would answer, but he never said anything first. She had begun to rely on that.

At the very end, when they reached the sunrise tower, she turned in a circle, face raised to the new sun. She felt ... not whole—never that—but as if she could get through another day.

Another night.

Shying away from that thought, she turned to face him, saying, "Thank you for tutoring Aurora." She said it often, but probably not often enough.

"She's a good student. And I enjoy teaching." He looked a question, then said, "Would it help you to summon CJ back? She says Erenlara is doing well, or as well as can be expected with her kingdom guardians still under enchantment, but at least the enchanted guardians do no harm, just roam about. I think CJ might be a bit bored, if I understand Dhana's mutterings."

Clair's mouth twitched, a wan smile, at the mention of Dhana's mutterings, but she shook her head decisively, tangled white hair swinging.

"Not until I have the words to explain my betrayal."

Siamis sighed. "Clair. It is not a betrayal to loosen the Child Spell."

She raised haunted eyes. "I didn't loosen it. It dissolved. And I promised." Her voice trembled on the last word.

He raised both hands. "I apologize. I ought not to have said anything, but since I've come this far, I'll say only this:

though CJ will inevitably be loud, I believe she will come to understand. But I won't interfere again."

"Thank you. Sherry and Gwen are probably done with breakfast by now. I had better get ready for morning court." A flick of white hair and flannel, and she was gone.

Siamis transferred to the Selenseh Redian, and braced himself for what he thought of as muck duty. Both the twins were disintegrating to the extent that Svir, concentrating on Kessler's ward, had gradually loosened his hold on their minds. Siamis could, and did, raid Efael's, but found Yeres slightly less disgusting, especially when he came face to face with himself in the gutter of their memories.

Ghost Lakes Sanctuary

: We're not strong enough.

: Yeah. Got that.

: Is it Senrid?

: He's actually the best at shielding identity. Remember, Laban, we are not the ones attacking Ilerian. We're here to send strength.

: Why do I not find that comforting?

: We'll pause briefly. That was Detlev, breaking into the narrow-focus rapport between MV, Laban, and Rolfin consequent to the first big practice session.

They all looked up, or down, depending on their favorite posture while in focus, stretching, breathing, rubbing eyes or foreheads, or moving aimlessly about the chamber. A couple people went out, in search of water or food or just to be moving.

"Question," Senrid spoke.

Detlev looked up from his contemplation of the chain in Adam's hands.

"Clair, you said before. She's getting hammered, I know, because the Host want to break Mearsieanne's enchantment. Were you implying that there's a connection to what we're doing here?"

"Yes."

Senrid frowned. "Are they assuming you planted some kind of compulsion in her, or secretly recruited her, when you took her to your retreat on the fifth world in '48?"

"Perhaps." Detlev added, "You have probably surmised

that she must have morvende in her background, which lends itself to her considerable abilities with Dena Yeresbeth. But it also increases the link with Ilerian, in ways none of the rest of us can truly comprehend."

"Ugh," Mildred said.

"The Alshi cup," Roy said. "That's there, too. It does look like a conspiracy, in a strange way. Was the Guardian of the cup one of those people you mentioned that had been connected to you in the past? Your dyranarya?"

"No. And yes. I met the Guardian twice, both times in connection with this desperate, hasty plan put together as the world was disintegrating. I had no idea what had happened to her or the magical object she'd guarded until June told me how she'd recovered it."

"Thrust into the future," David mused. "I can't imagine the magic that does that, except that it probably has to do with parallel world-gates, which might partly explain the necessity for an off-worlder, from the right world."

"I think so," Detlev said. "Pending further information."

"Further information? So the cup's useless to us now?" Mildred plopped down, chin on hands.

"On the contrary. Ilerian is trying very hard to get at the cup through Clair. June knows, of course, but is cooperating with Clair's plans to deceive Ilerian. She will respond to Siamis's signal."

Senrid's brow creased. "Clair can't fake Ilerian out. Can she?"

"Not really."

"Then why—"

"If," Detlev said with deceptive gentleness, "you'd spared your old friend Clair a quarter-hour in these past long months, you would've seen that any interference from any adults at all—on either side—would send her at once across the border to hide."

"Then smash," Mildred said, smacking her hands together.

"Right."

"I had no idea it was that bad," Roy said, with quiet distress. "I wish I had thought to visit her as long as she wanted. Needed."

"You had your orders. She has been laboring to prevent anyone from knowing, as much as she can: CJ is still in the Land of the Venn."

The statements to Roy did nothing to mitigate the rebuke to Senrid. Adam, still abnormally sensitive in the aftermath of rapport, had to get physical distance between himself and discord. He moved to the wider chamber, toward the pure, clear, sky-colored water.

The urge to immerse himself seized him, to be free from sight and sound. Dropping the dyr-chain on a flat rock, he dove into the water.

Shocking cold. But a cold, clear cold. Not bitter, not winter.

He kicked off his mocs and swam the length of the pool, then suspended himself about an arm's length below the surface and blew huge, crystalline bubbles. He watched the perfect spheres glitter, rise, and vanish.

Then he broke the surface, and wished he'd shucked his clothes.

: Adam?

: Detlev, I can't act as a link, I'm not strong enough.

: Don't try yet. Rapport with each one separately. Non-interference, just listening, and learning their fears and vulnerabilities.

: Senrid is doing his best —

: Within self-imposed limitations. We cannot allow for that luxury.

: But he can't bear to lift the barrier between himself and the group.

: He can through you, but it must be effected through the form of a challenge. Leave him to me for a time. Remember, you will be the conduit between them and me. Do your best to shield them, but if you need to, leave that to Dirk and concentrate on sending strength to me. I need you to act if I falter. I am trusting you to cut me off if I am wrong, and Ilerian prevails.

Adam understood how it worked. The circle was akin to the physical act of reinforcement, like a pair of strong hands coming to help pull a bow when one was first learning to shoot. Each person contributed strength; alone, Detlev could not challenge Ilerian, who had consumed vast numbers, and expect to survive.

No one, including Detlev, understood Ilerian's true nature; he suspected that even Svir was included in that number. Perhaps the human mind was unable to fully comprehend this entity. But Detlev, after observation all this while, had formed certain ideas, and on these he had based his strategy. Because he was uncertain, he had declared that the attack—the risk—must belong solely to him.

Adam knew that the true reason Siamis was outside of the circle, much as he was needed, was to spare him the choice that he himself might face: if Detlev was wrong, or not strong enough—if Ilerian prevailed—it was Adam who would have to jettison Detlev, so that he could not be permitted to endanger the others, or the world.

In other words, Detlev's life lay in Adam's hands.

They *had* to be strong enough to back him.

Adam climbed out, shivering as Zairna silently handed him a voluminous towel, and a mug of hot steep. Then it was Adam, and not Detlev, who went around from person to person, and in a steely voice quite unlike his usual, said, "Back to work."

Seventeen

Efael's HQ

It was getting hard to breathe in Imar, but of course one would never dare say so. Why couldn't there be timelessness without that discomfort?

Yeres had transferred to her brother's citadel, which he'd finished warding again. She'd curled up in the wingback chair near the great fire in the otherwise dark, mostly empty main hall of her brother's cold, damp stone citadel with its three rings of vigilant guards.

Once upon a time she would have gone down to the dungeons herself to see what he was doing, and maybe even join in, if she saw someone fun. Of course, her idea of a fun victim differed from Efael's. He liked them strong first of all, and though he'd torment the old, civilian women, or brats if he had a need for whatever it was they knew, he considered them boring. Yeres thought the ones who hid their emotions dull. She adored pleading, weeping, and groveling. There was nothing in the universe funnier, and sometimes she laughed until she was giddy. Another delicious pleasure was witnessing beautiful women lose their beauty forever under knife or brand or rack. Their reactions were priceless — but only to her. Efael did not like to mar beauty, especially in boys. There were so many other ways to elicit pain.

Oh, how she looked forward to getting hold of Imry! How

funny that they were both obsessed with him. That had happened only rarely — the best one of course had been Siamis.

Siamis. She sighed over old memories, old pleasures, like 'rescuing' him from Efael, when she was in a languorous mood.

She was too damn cold for any of her old fun. Well, that, and the truth was, the smell of blood made her mouth go dry and her stomach lurch. It was already difficult to eat. Disgusting, to have to wear oneself out enduring night and day, eating, and while the Waste Spell made the stenches and messes of the lower body minimal, that was a convenience doing little to mitigate the maddening awareness that one still *aged*. She loathed it. As for sleep, that was impossible!

She hated being stuck in time, with no access to the easement of Norsunder-Beyond. Only fun could make it bearable, and there had been scant fun since Connanre was shredded by Ilerian. Now she wished she hadn't turned him down so casually: while she very much liked sex, unless she knew the man, there was enough of her childhood left in her to make it impossible unless she was the one in control.

After prowling back and forth in front of the fire, thinking these dreary thoughts, she summoned one of the guards and sent him down to fetch Efael, saying that she was too busy to seek him herself. Then she snapped up some candlelight and leaned toward the fire, until she heard his heels ring on the stone floor.

She assumed a languid pose. "I hope you were enjoying yourself," she drawled, eyeing her brother as he entered.

His hair hung down on his brow, and his hands were nasty to look at. "I was! Just finished with Imry's spy."

She waved a hand. "Phew. Obviously! You reek of sweat and blood." She spoke carelessly, feigning fastidious airiness, but she was glad that he wore black, so nothing could be seen on his clothes.

She did not like how old and familiar sights and smells made her so sick. Oh, how she'd love to get that Kessler and flens him, and take weeks to do it. No, let Efael do it, and this one she would watch.

She swallowed, and said with a careless tone, "Who? Find anything?"

Efael shrugged, pulled his knife, and sat down opposite her. "First one. Kentiur from up north, knew nothing. Interesting. Second one — Bergan —"

"Oh yes. Dear Bergan. So very obsequious."

"Yapped lots. Also interesting."

"What'd he say?"

Efael turned his blade, scraping dried blood off the backs of his fingers as he thought this over. Then he pointed the knife at Yeres. "Why aren't you out chasing Imry?"

"I'm *cold*," Yeres said in their home language, irritated at the spasm of annoyance that creased Efael's brows. Maybe it was time to remind him that she was not his slave. Better than looking at that disgusting brownish crud he kept flicking off his fingers with that knife. Her stomach heaved and she turned to face the fire.

"You should've had Imry by now. You had better stop drinking that poppy tincture."

Fury burned away her other emotions when she saw the accusation in Efael's face. Of all the things she loathed, detested, and despised, hearing *You should have by now* topped the list, exceeded only by *You had better*. "You should've as well," she snapped. "You've been boring on forever about how stupid and sloppy and obvious Imry is? The way I see it, he still would be mucking about in noisy, impossible Larkadhe if *I* hadn't taken action."

Efael merely continued to shave the blade over the backs of his hands, *whish, whish*, quick motions borne of experience.

When she realized he was silent not because he was thinking over her challenge but because he had dismissed it, she added snidely, "You couldn't even win a fair fight."

"So we won't have any more fair fights," he retorted. "I've been waiting for you to bring him to me." And when she muttered that nothing mattered until Ilerian got the Beyond back, he snapped, "Nothing will matter if we don't use what we've got. Imry wants Halia back, and Aldon means to get it first, if we don't act."

Yeres sighed and sat up as Efael went on, "I've sent the two Chwahir armies to Halia to reinforce what's left of Bostian's rabble, and the mercenaries from up north, now that Ralanor Veleth is quiet—the Fhlerians can hold them. But Chwahir are stupid, and slow, and that shit Wan-Edhe won't tolerate their speaking any language but their own. And I'm out of captains who speak Chwahir. I need more. I need a demonstration of *real* power…"

Yeres had heard that rant so many times that she began to

slip into poppy reverie. Efael's voice flowed over her like water as he described killing four successive pirate captains in a row on their own decks. He distracted himself by going into detail about which tendons he cut, when he noticed she was not listening. "If you're cold, then go back to Imar, and wheedle Svir. I said, none of these are enough. Halia needs putting down *hard*. I know they're sneaking around like rats, breeding trouble. I want the Ivandred capture-sphere."

Yeres jerked her shoulder up impatiently. "I tried. I tried and tried! But Svir says the First Lancers are too unruly, and he thinks Ilerian should reserve them to kill for power. As for Imar, it's so *suffocating*. If we can *just* get off this accursed cesspit of a world, and back to the Beyond until Ilerian can win against time, I'll be *perfectly fine*."

Efael's lips curled in scorn, his steady dark gaze reflecting twin leaping fires from the grate behind her. "You're weak. If you won't go to Imar, then at least go find Imry."

"First you tell me what was so interesting about what his men said, or didn't say."

"That fool Kentiur was—you said—one of his trusted lieutenants."

"He was! I told you why Imry put Elzhier the spy with him up north, and that—"

Efael gestured lazily with the knife to shut her up. Leaping firelight on the blade flickered dark orange, and as he turned it, the edge glowed a deep, angry red. She looked away. "I remember your report," he said, in the dialect of Sartoran that Svir had taught them. "And it seemed reasonable enough. Thing is, if Imry is rallying his old staff, why did this fool know nothing?"

Yeres began to say *You just found out nothing*, but shrugged off what would surely be a boring argument about it. "What about Bergan? I overheard him bragging to Asiarch. He knew Aldon's plans to take Halia."

Efael shrugged. "You'd think he knew something," he said sardonically. "But it was all Aldon, Aldon, Aldon, shit we know already. Nothing about Imry, except fart noise about him transferring here and there and everywhere, Bergan thinks he's looking for something."

"Such as?"

Efael scowled. "It's all lies. Even Larkadhe was a lie—right there in the north of Halia. Imry jaws on about how he doesn't care about Marloven Hess, but he squatted directly north of it.

At one time, Larkadhe was part of the Marloven empire." He pointed his knife at Yeres. "That's why I want a slash-and-burn. Torch Halia, and the entire world will behave—and *both* Imry and Aldon will come to heel. Bring me one of them, preferably Imry."

Yeres bridled. "I've tried! He's playing hard to get." Her mind slid sideways, unmoored by poppies. Oh, to dally somewhere in the sunlight, and run her toes through his hair—she paused to contemplate that, and to decide which would be more exciting, whether he hated it or liked it. Either way, he'd be tied up first, but then, eh, he had boring hair. Running her toes over—

"Ereis!" Efael snapped, "You're not listening!"

Her pleasing picture shattered. "*You* listen," she said. "I *have* been trying. Why don't you send your pais after him? They don't have anything to do, it seems to me."

"No. You can thank Dena Yeresbeth for that. My Black Knives are better employed chasing Rel, who would keep us both entertained for quite a while, without our crossing Svir."

Yeres considered Rel—tall, strong, and quite, quite handsome. Maybe he'd be more fun to seduce than Imry. Except he was so boringly stolid, and Imry was delightfully elusive.

She frowned. "So what you're saying is, Imry really might be running renegade?"

"He's got the old magic."

"But he must know he can't stand against Ilerian. Or Svir. But especially Ilerian—they are so close to breaking Kessler's ward."

"He 'mustn't' know anything. Find him!" Efael tapped the knife hilt on the arm of his chair. "Have your fun, but bring him to me when you're done. I'll find out what he knows." And, suddenly, he threw the knife across the space between them.

Yeres saw the brief golden flicker of fire on metal, then the thud vibrated the chair back a finger's breadth from her ear.

"Temper, temper," she chided. "It's not me you should be scolding, it's Ilerian. And Svir! I was just there, and all they seem to be doing is sitting around and jawing about Mearsies Heili, and that white-haired Clair. Why don't *they* go out and do something about her?"

It was a rhetorical question—Yeres knew very well the type of enchantment that protected Mearsies Heili. She had even wasted precious time trying to break it, to no avail. But she also knew that no enchantment was thoroughly comprehensive, and there were always ways around them.

What she did not know was how many tries in various ways both Ilerian and Svir had made to get around it. Ilerian was human enough not to discuss his failures, and as for Svir, he was never wrong, ever. If he was thwarted, someone else was to blame, and they seldom survived it.

Those failures were also known to Siamis and Clair, who also did not speak of them, for different reasons.

Clair knew that every sign of those attacks on her hurt her friends. It took all her strength to hide them from her daughter.

"Of course she shuts me out," Aurora was heard by Siamis to say to Carl Delieth. "We're 'posed to be learning mind-shields as well as how to manage Dena Yeresbeth. Also, she gets those headaches. And doesn't want me getting 'em, too. Let's get our maths slog out of the way, and go make snow forts. It's perfect powder today!"

Siamis and the other adult caretakers encouraged the children to spend New Year's Week playing outside as much as possible, and camping in the underground Junky, which the under-twelves had taken over. Aurora found the Junky comforting, a place designed by Clair, her presence in every direction you looked. The furnishings were kid-sized, and so battered you could play with them as much as you wanted, and no one worried about scratches or dings. Clair had even said they could draw on the murals, or make new ones — CJ and the other girls had made new ones whenever they got tired of the old.

For Clair, each night was a silent battle, while Aurora lay asleep underground. Seshe had begun reading to Clair, which worked for a time. When she ran out of comfort books — or rather Clair restlessly waved off those she had heard too many times — Seshe began quoting poetry. She had never talked about her life before she joined the gang, but at some time, she had learned pages and pages of poetry. Mostly ballads, and most of those with girls at the center. Every ballad featured animals, and magic, beauty, and peace — at the end, at least, if they were adventuresome. Clair liked the quiet, contemplative ones the most, even in her sleep.

Her broken sleep.

She began waking suddenly, often with a gasp, and a wild, blind look about. When this happened, she would rise, and tired as she was—even if she'd only slept an hour—she would mumble that she needed to walk the Purrad. This began to happen twice a night, then three times. If Siamis was not there—he could not be all the time, though he tried to be—she walked alone, for the pattern had worn itself into her bones. She invariably said some version of, "I could walk it in my sleep. If I could sleep. No, don't go. Get some rest. Nothing happens to me in the spires."

Seshe tried to stay awake, but when Clair would start on a second round, she sometimes slipped into slumber while sitting on the bottom step, her shoulder leaning against the wall, chin on her chest, until Falinneh, or Gwen, or Sherry would insist on her going to bed, and they would take her place.

But afterward Clair could be coaxed, tired and stumbling, to bed. Seshe, or whoever had the duty that night, would pick up where they left off. Gwen told stories, using her talent for voices. Falinneh would reminisce, trying to be as funny as possible. Sherry also reminisced, about their earliest days, when Puddlenose was a boy, and Clair and Sherry had a Chwahir friend named Jennet.

The second night of the new year, Falinneh was describing her first play, when Clair silently rose, eyes still closed, and began walking, straight toward the opening to the falls.

"Clair? Should I stop—Clair? Do you want a different play—Clair!"

But Clair didn't hear her. Falinneh darted after her; Siamis appeared in the archway as Falinneh grabbed Clair's hand.

Clair halted.

"What do I do now?" Falinneh whispered, staring down at Clair's pale fingers gripping her own freckled one.

Some of the girls had been huggers, others (like Diana) had been skittish about being touched. Sherry had always been a hand-holder, but it wasn't in Falinneh's wary, troubled, shape-changer background.

Siamis murmured, "Try leading her back to her bed."

Falinneh tugged gently, and Clair obediently shuffled back to her nest of cushions and pillows and quilts and lay back down. Still holding her hand, Falinneh went on talking.

The next night, it was Seshe's turn, and the same thing happened. Siamis said, "Just keep holding her hand, if she sleepwalks. It seems to help." He transferred out on his endless rounds.

Eighteen

BEING MARRIED, REL THOUGHT, felt like a natural state. In a way, they'd been married for years, all but the public vows. Now those were done, and the nobles who once had banded together in disapproval at the sight of him now bowed every time they saw him. Even to his back.

That was the problem. He relished being a married man, but thought the kingship that went with it a fraud. Even more painful—or more laughable—was his promotion to Commander of the Allied Counterattack.

A week after their wedding, a few days into the new year, he still felt that way as he roamed the vast caverns of the abandoned geliath that the morvende had left for the resistance. He made no complaints to anyone, even to his old friend Hinder, who had taken charge of organizing the swarm of refugees and resistors—except Rel did complain to Atan, once.

She shrugged and said with rather more pleasure than was seemly, under the circumstances, "Ah, who else could it be? I do not speak for the rest of the world, but Detlev could never command our Sartorans. They wouldn't follow him down a garden path."

Rel said, "Detlev told me much the same thing when he asked if I objected to being made a figurehead."

"When?" Atan stared in surprise. "Not last summer, when

they first proposed we begin planning the counterattack?" And on Rel's nod, "Fancy his being so straightforward about it!"

The outcome of the battle was going to be the same whether Rel kept his tongue between his teeth beforehand, or grabbed everyone by the shirt-laces and blathered out his worries about his suitability as a Heroic King.

Nah, that wasn't what griped his guts. He could stride around looking competent and brave, because the bolstering effect was clearly visible. Every time he won a match in drill the others looked on it as a battle won. Symbolic, all of it. So if it turned out he got killed, well, then he'd be dead, and the war would be someone else's problem.

What he couldn't stick was taking credit for a truly astounding amount of unceasing labor that he was only beginning to comprehend. He knew that everyone being exactly in the place he or she was best suited for was no set of unrealted coincidences. Right down to Julian, still grieving over Dtheldevor's gang, now employed as their unofficial chief of communications with the Sarendan allies over the eastern border. *Take her with you,* Siamis had said, with that easy smile of his. As if it was the thought of the moment, a mere suggestion. *She might enjoy running messages — you know how much she relishes travel, and she has friends everywhere. It would give her something to do.*

Rel and Atan had very soon seen the new appointment give Julian purpose.

Unaware of the trend of Rel's thoughts, Atan Landis walked through one of the rougher and seldom used tunnels away from the higher levels where the hill folk had taken refuge, and down toward the vast cavern containing the encampment, on the edge of a great underground lake. Winter's bite had reached this far down at last, making the smell of moss and cold stone feel oppressive. Harsh as it was, they knew that it was even colder in Eidervaen, not very far away.

It was those hill-folk drums. She winced against a corresponding panging in her temples. They never stopped. She'd thought they did that sort of thing to unnerve the enemy! Was their plan for the counterattack to go out foggy from tension while Aldon's forces were fresh from quiet sleep?

She increased her speed and presently the steady, menacing *bom! bom! bom!* began to fade behind her, though unexpected air currents or variations in the water-carved structure of the rock brought echoes to her, and she found herself stepping in time with that beat.

Entering the big cavern, she discovered the other difficulty. Everywhere—on all sides—as soon as she was seen, all conversation and activity ceased, everything except the constant martial drills. The people became an audience in an eyeblink, and bowed low—which forced her into assuming the posture and demeanor of Queen Yustnesveas V.

People also moved aside, creating a path, and as she passed, all those eyes studied her expectantly, but if she met any of those gazes the people self-consciously looked down or returned self-consciously to their tasks. And when the crowd shifted from the direction of the drills and Rel appeared on his own path, striding toward her, the same attitude surrounded him, burdening him with a long, invisible kingly mantle of expectation. Even those fierce bands of nomads from the plains of Jaro, men and women, looked to them with an intensity of anticipation that Atan felt as heavy as the crown she had only worn once.

"Any news from Siamis?" Rel asked as people edged away, giving them space. He spoke low, in Mearsiean; physical space they had, but not auditory.

He took her arm and they began to stroll, maintaining calm demeanors. They knew others took cues from their behavior. Stroll. Smile. It wasn't time, then. But still the eyes watched their progress. Ears, she knew, strained to listen, to catch a word, and pass it on—along with commentary.

"Only that he got your reports, and that Detlev and his band have gone into hiding. It seems that Svir confronted Llyenthur, and they are waiting for some sign. If Detlev knows what that is, as usual, he's not sharing."

"Might not know either," Rel said. "All he can do is watch from afar. You know that the biggest traps of all are laid for him."

"Yes." She felt a sharper pang, and whispered, "Those drums. They are making me crazy."

"Ah, the Lamancans." Rel smiled as he glanced up the tunnel toward their cavern. "They know the end is close, and that appears to be their way of getting into the proper frame of mind for leading the attack."

"They know? Have you told—"

"I've said nothing. But just because they haven't access to

our communication doesn't mean they don't have their own."

"You mean spying on us? No." She tried to think the way a war leader would think. "Ah. I guess it makes sense. If you guessed right, and Detlev is the one behind all our efforts, he'd insure that the message got around in various ways. I really hate the idea that he's moving us around like tokens in a game of Cards'n'Shards."

"Then think it a fancy borne of little sleep." Rel squeezed her arm against him. "Since I suspect we'll never find out the whole truth of it, no matter what happens."

She remained silent for ten or twelve steps, then said in a low voice, "You know I won't just think it. It'll bother me and worry me until I find out. Even if it takes me years."

"Good. Because then I'll know if I guessed right."

She lifted her arm and walked away. Rel's smile deepened, then he moved off through an adjacent cavern to return to the drills.

Atan kept going as though nothing had happened. Her reaction to his teasing had to remain private, or the whispers that soughed through all the people would come out at the other end as a bloody battle between them. Fear-propelled, of course. She clutched her elbows close. *How* she wished it would end.

Except she didn't want the end to start.

Invariably this sort of thinking reminded her of the Sartorans living under the Norsundrian thumb in Eidervaen, as well as the rest of the kingdom, and guilt would prod her. Sometimes she wished she had Dena Yeresbeth only so she could know what was happening to Eidervaen. Other times she suspected it was better not to know until she could do something about it.

The only people she spared little thought to were her enemies. To be fair, they spared her little thought as well—except for the ones who longed for captures, prizes, promotion.

Duin, Imry Llyenthur's former aide-de-camp, mainly thought about survival. If only someone would have jumped back half a year, when they were complaining about how annoying Imry Llyenthur was, to tell them that life under Aldon would be so very much worse.

At first, each day was seen as another opportunity to do something—however small—in reprisal. Now he simply wanted to survive. A week into the new year, the ground outside iron hard, the air bitter, and he wondered if he was going to see the next day.

"Duin!" someone bellowed up the stairs, then a mocking, gloating voice, "Fassler Duin, you are summoned to the Presence!"

Always a bad sign.

Aldon demanded instant obedience, so Duin ran up the stairs, but still, as he reached the handsome carpeted hallway on which Aldon had set up his office, Duin paused in view of the two sentries before the door to straighten his uniform and tuck the logbook more securely under his arm. He needed the time to concentrate on an expression of question, mentally holding a blank wall to hide his inner thoughts, a trick he'd learned in Llyenthur's command center...

Aldon was waiting, a big, scarred brute whose lust for cruelty had been carved into his face. He was grinning. Very bad sign.

Behind him stood the duty officer. Nothing to be seen in his face, of course. He'd kept his job—and his life—by being as wooden as a post. And there in the corner—damn. Duin burned with hatred. Kielig, Aldon's pet mind reader.

Relax. The blank must be easy. Not obvious. Remember what Llyenthur said: *Kielig's one of those weasels whose ambition far exceeds his talent. Suitable for Aldon.* "Sir!"

"Why was Bergan taken by Efael?" Aldon began bluntly.

Duin felt Kielig invading his thoughts. He forced himself to not react, to think about the desk, the chair. Past orders. "I don't know. Rumor said something about a plot Llyenthur was hatching. Bergan was Efael's eyes in Llyenthur's HQ."

"You were also one of Llyenthur's staff aides."

"Yes."

"When did you see him last?"

Duin answered truthfully (and let them feel *that*), "Day he was ousted."

"Not since?"

"Not since."

But he'd found out through another Chwahir that Llyenthur was the one who'd slipped in to pass on the salve. To save a life. There couldn't be any other motive because there'd been no communication since. No requests, no reminders, questions, even. Nothing. He'd saved Duin, which Duin believed because Colleron insisted that Llyenthur had saved him, too, though no one else believed it.

"What do you know about this plot of Llyenthur's, to retake control. Supposedly his old staff is all in on it."

"Rumors," Duin said truthfully. Sensed two minds weighing his complete conviction.

"Bergan discuss it with you?"

"Just the rumors, and he always asked questions of me. Reported everything to Efael. We all knew it, when we were at Larkadhe."

Little reference there to Bergan's being Aldon's spy. Bergan never saw that no one ever believed anything he said, or told him the truth, after that got around.

"So no one has approached you or communicated with you in any way."

"No."

"Do you believe that these rumors are true?"

Odd question—and trust Aldon to trash someone for a mere belief. Tchah, answer to protect us both. My life is my life, and Llyenthur saved it.

"No."

"When you worked for Llyenthur, did he ever use Theronezhe's command codes?"

"Never." Feel that one! Truth.

"No one before, or since, gave you the magic keys to those codes?"

"No." *He said when we first set up our command center, 'The first thing I did when I left Detlev was crack Theronezhe's absurd codes. Never let me catch you using 'em, Duin! This is how we'll set up...'*

"Give me your log book."

"Sir!" Duin handed it over, knowing it was a match for the one in Aldon's office. He'd been very careful about that. He glanced down in apparent unconcern, to watch Aldon looking from one to the other...

And noticed, just before Kielig smirked and pointed, saying, "There's one, sir," that this was yet a third log. One he'd never known existed. Kept (from the knowing, smug grin) by Kielig himself.

"There's another, the 32nd." Aldon looked up, fury pinching his long features. "You put me to a great deal of trouble, Duin. Who generated these secret messages? You or Llyenthur?"

You don't earn promotions, you take them, Llyenthur once said. But he never slanged loyalty, not really.

The nascent moral discoveries were not permitted to continue. "Thinking it over, Duin?" Aldon inquired corrosively. And, to the duty officer, "See to it he lasts long enough for the shift change. I want them all to share in the inspiring example."

The guards from outside the door closed in on either side, and yanked him out. The last sound in that office was the glutinous whoop of Kielig's gloating laughter.

"Plotting, eh?" One of the guards prodded him in the ribs.

"I didn't know you desk rabbits had it in ya," the other commented. "Or was it just orders from outside? Rel, maybe?"

They laughed at this essay in wit, but Duin scarcely heard them. His mind was paralyzed. He didn't hear the subsequent drollery on the part of the two guards, nor — at first — did he hear the sudden violent commotion in the outer courtyard where the floggings always took place.

<hr>

Yeres arrived in time to see blood everywhere in Aldon's parade ground. The smell hit her as the transfer malaise was fading, causing acrid nastiness to burn her throat. Dashing tears from her eyes, she stumbled forward, rapidly scanning past a wounded man lying on the bloody ground to the fight still going on.

There was Imry — white shirt in the midst of all that gray and black. Just a shirt and trousers, no mail, no padding, what arrogance! She stared, watching his lethal speed. At the very same moment Imry looked over his shoulder, straight into her eyes, his hair flying, arms in constant motion.

He ducked a humming blade, swooped down, grabbed up a crossbow from one of the fallen, and for a heartbeat stood there, long legs braced, arm muscles straining against his sleeves, head cocked, eyes narrowed to take aim. He loosed a bolt directly into the knee of the foremost attacker, and smashed the crossbow into the face of the second one. Then looked around for another bolt to shoot Aldon — but the commander had ducked behind two of his biggest guards, bellowing, "Grab him, grab him!"

Imry shouted, "Now!" And his two helpers sprang to cut

Duin free of the post, then caught him before he could fall. Imry smacked all four in succession, and they vanished in a series of transfers that sent hot, burnt-metal air whooshing through the smelly, echoing court.

Aldon shrieked, "Impossible! This court was warded! Who failed to keep the ward—"

Yeres lifted her fingers and wiggled them coyly.

"Shit." Aldon got control of himself. It would never do to attack her directly. Even if she didn't throw spells at him, the brother would be sure to, and Aldon was not ready to take Efael on. He swallowed his rage, saying in a less surly tone, "How many with him?"

"Two," Yeres said, inwardly reviewing the vivid image of that slim figure in the very middle of the battle, the straight shoulders shaping the old shirt, the laughing glance from those green eyes. War and sex, there just was nothing better. Sex, pain, death. Desire gripped her viscerally; *he's waiting for me.* She shivered at the delicious thought. Otherwise, why that look? Of course he was. No man turned her down.

"Who were those two with him," Aldon insisted. "One had a blue headband, yellow hair. The other was dark."

Yeres knew what was coming next: questions about what wards she might have put here in order to be alerted, and whether or not she or Efael had tampered with Aldon's own wards. But she was *not* his lackey. She twiddled a couple of fingers at him, and did the transport spell.

Imry was not, of course, in Imar. He seemed to be avoiding it even more than she and Efael. Nor was he in the two lairs she'd discovered since the last close call.

As soon as she recovered from the three transfers, she remembered Elzhier, queening it up there in Yaldar, and braced herself for the long transfer. Pleasant summery air and the strong northern sun bathed her senses. When she opened her eyes, she found herself on the terrace that Elzhier had designated her transfer destination. The woman herself was sitting at a table with a decanter and glass before her. Heavy liquor. Yeres looked at it then convulsively swallowed. Liquor was a problem on both sides, these days, but much worse in the south, caught in the grip of winter. And not just the troops, spinning away days and nights in inaction. Efael had been drinking heavily.

Did it really mask the inexorable weight of time? If only it didn't make her puke! "Imry," Yeres said.

"Just here," Elzhier replied, opening her hands. Her bland face was only mildly sardonic, but Yeres, studying her, decided it was her usual affect, and not a goad. "Left a message for you."

"Of course." If Elzhier didn't know it was a spent chase, no use in making it clear. Yeres sat down, affecting unconcern, but in reality she was glad to be sitting. Her joints ached, after traversing the world—something that had been easy enough a year ago.

Elzhier closed her eyes. "'Find me when the time is propitious.'" She opened her eyes. "Did I get the tone? Propitious. What a snot that boy is! He assured me you'd be along momentarily, and I left nothing out. Is there a problem?"

Yeres veered between rage and intrigue. She smiled, knowing those blank eyes were trying to bore into her skull. At least Elzhier did not have Dena Yeresbeth. But she—one of the best spies Connanre had ever put in the field—was adept at reading the subtlest clues.

"I do so hate to duplicate efforts," Yeres said, glad that drawls masked so very many emotions. "What orders did he give?"

"None." Elzhier shrugged. "Asked the usual questions. Oh. Wanted to know when Efael would send Kentiur back. I'd like to know that myself. Kentiur handled all the dreary tasks that I hate doing, and he did it well."

"You'll have to ask Efael directly," Yeres said, sidestepping Kentiur's lingering death—and all for nothing. She dismissed the flunky from her mind, considering her own situation. Wouldn't do to have everyone aware that she'd been singularly unsuccessful in her pursuit. But then Yeres had seen to it that Elzhier kept her command here after Imry's departure from Larkadhe, and had seen to it that the woman knew it. Add to that Elzhier's healthy dislike of Imry... Yes. As far as Yeres could trust anyone, she could trust Elzhier. At least in this instance.

Besides, though she very much wanted to see Imry, she wanted to pick the time and place. "Better yet, send Imry. In fact..." She let her voice draw the word out, as though she were considering a new plan. "In fact, you might just see to it. Efael feels that Imry is overdue for a lesson in manners."

"Decades overdue!" There was no mistaking the genuine hatred in Elzhier's face. "Am I to understand you want a disarm-and-secure awaiting Imry's next visit?"

"He's so flighty," Yeres replied.

Elzhier laughed, and drank off her whiskey. "By his own lackeys! I adore it!"

"It will be fun," Yeres said, simpering. "But let me know, not my brother."

Maybe she'd even let Elzhier play with him when she was done with him.

And Efael could wait his turn.

Nineteen

HIBERN CONTEMPLATED THAT METAPHORICAL open doorway, gazing at the glowing marks that were the equivalent of a Destination: she could transfer to Geth. And leave the lattice mystery unsolved? Outside, clean light and real air, growth and good life. Behind her, vileness to every degree, testament to the worst in human nature.

She hesitated, longing for freedom.

But she never left a task undone. Lilith had said, before recommending Hibern to Erai-Yanya, *A mage accepts responsibility. If you are capable of doing a needed task, you roll up your sleeves and do it. Whether it's restoring an important ward, or weeding the vegetable garden.*

"Time to weed that Garden," she muttered.

She turned her back on the way to light and life, took a single mental step, and here she was in the Garden of the Twelve again, and its mockery of light, of life.

She was done reviewing the reports: she had the lattice. But what was its purpose? It was time to return to those memories centering around Detlev. Once more she watched his capture, freezing the images to examine from all sides. No sense of magic hidden anywhere, no tracers, wards, or signs. Dreading the catalogue that surely existed of all his evil deeds, she moved on to the one instinct clamored was faked up, the corruption of Ilerian by dyr.

Once again she froze the image, examining it from all sides —

And there it was, without fanfare. Almost missed, near — very near — a ward bound to Detlev's fingers as he touched Ilerian's smooth forehead. The ward itself was a gloat, so sinister and obvious it had to be a mask.

Such wards were like glosses in written records; in these magical captures of moments, they were usually commentary appended later, by mages to mages farther down in time. She did not intend to view what was in the ward — she sensed the gloating in the magic forming the ward, which indicated she found find more cruel blather. Why his finger?

She remembered that one of the patterns in the report lies had centered around "hands." She had been taught to move with precision and care; what she did not stop to consider was how drastically her perceptions had altered in this place. Believing she was too old for Dena Yeresbeth, she had made coinherence within this place, without being at all aware of it.

Moving cautiously, she avoided the ward altogether as she stepped into the image behind it, until her feet replaced Ilerian's, and the ghostly fingers hovered a hair's breadth from her metaphorical forehead.

There.

Careless, triumphant, exulting, the Host had obviously never considered a ward within a ward, one hidden as a shadow — either that or this shadow was relatively new.

Startled, she moved — and it was gone. Though she had no physical presence, this was a matter of precise concentration. Like looking into a prism, in which the slightest movement shifted the refractions.

Once again she took Ilerian's place. And there it was again. Right there, in that simulacrum of Detlev's first action — Ilerian's first action — in the heart of the Garden of the Twelve.

She teased open the shadow ward, to discover an armature of light, a ghostly globe of the world superimposed over the lattice that formed the structure of the vast mirror ward of the Beyond. And everywhere the lattice touched the misty globe, a pinpoint of light gleamed.

But what was the correct sequence for disassembling it? She knew without even trying that random attempts would ignite horrible traps.

She looked again at the specific points, each corresponding to locations within the sequences of the reports.

Eidervaen ... Bereth Ferian ... If you knew how far apart in time each city was from the preceding, then you could see the pattern: adding the hours of difference in time, each was the sum of the two preceding numbers. Choreid-Dhelerei ... Thand-Ator, way up north. Back south again to Ferdrian, capital of Everon.

Once the lower number pattern was established in the number of hours between cities, the larger numbers were the same pattern. 34, 55, 89, 144, 233, 377, 610 — and higher.

She tried the first numbers, holding her illusory breath, and the lights winked out. She sensed the inner snapping of a spell. This was it.

Everywhere that the ghost lattice touched the true structure, she loosened the bindings, until she sensed a powerful shifting. The ghost lattice supports slipped into place of Ilerian's, which dissolved. In her mind, the structure reassembled as a geometric figure made up of ladders — lattices — the old the red of danger, until dissolved and replaced by blue. She liked blue. It was a humble color, the first and easiest of dyes, history maintained. Blue was the color of scholars' robes, and mages' robes.

She worked until the entire mirror was framed altogether in blue, taut and thrumming with power. Her body thrummed as well, and making yet a greater effort, she altered the image again. Gone was the ladder structure: she had framed a huge house with countless rooms, from which she had systematically removed all the locks.

She no longer doubted Detlev's motivation: this entire ghost lattice had been fashioned to a single purpose, to destroy Norsunder-Beyond from within.

What to do now? Ilerian could return at any moment, and he would know what she had done. She would not be able to prevail against him, not with him reinforced by the thousands and thousands of life-spirits he had constrained to feed that reservoir of power. She had only herself.

He *would* return.

But until then, why not ... go on?

Her first discovery — shocking her deeply — was the presence of other prisoners. How could she have missed that? By avoiding the presence of humans, of course — that is,

Theronezhe's vast, waiting army, collected over centuries. Her first duty must be to free the prisoners, that was plain.

As had become habit, awareness brought proximity. She concentrated, hearing the whispered murmur of thousands of voices. Some were prisoned alone by insubstantial barriers; others sat, blank-minded and silent, in shadow-shrouded groups. She began to speak to them one by one, and at first, she feasted her spirit on the hope in their eyes when they comprehended "Would you like to leave? I can set you free." She reveled in their gratitude as she touched each one and waved them toward that Destination she had discovered, the one that opened to light and air. Where that led, she did not know, yet. Except it was not home, to Sartorias-deles. She knew that by instinct.

She turned back to freeing them, one after another, then room after room.

After a time the smiles, the tears, the fervent whispered words, became numbing. There were so many, and they were so patient. But those were the easy ones; those who had lost their humanity, or who had been there so long that time and place had lost all meaning, they fled back into the dark places, minds howling in terror.

Detlev's intent might have been to take the place for himself, but surely if he had wanted it, would he not replace said walls and floors and windows with his own design? Think how splendid, how powerful!

The pleasing little notion almost flickered away unnoticed, because her mind had been working fast for so very long, and she was tired, and because she was fighting evil and doing good. But she had learned in watching those horrible collections of past actions how the smallest self-deceptions set one on a path leading to this place. She retreated to the Garden of the Twelve, the only locus of beauty in Norsunder, to pace the grass and to think. Was she posing herself as spiritual judge? Was she, now, on the path to self-aggrandizement through power?

Yes, and yes.

She looked around slowly. Someone had once gone to a dell, and found it exquisite, but no plant will grow without sun. They had sucked up every vestige of life from blade of grass to tall tree, then froze the dell at the point of death, transferring it here. The beauty was still there, but it was lifeless.

Sick to the heart of the ubiquitous malice of this place, Hibern waved a hand.

At once, bright with streaming light, the portal appeared.

This time, Hibern stepped through, and as if a hitherto unperceived vice suddenly released her spirit, she felt giddy, almost delirious, as she drew in pure, sweet, healing air.

Then, once more she turned back, for she never left a task undone. With a wave of her hand, she brought that fresh air and sunlight into the Garden of the Twelve; At soon as the sunbeams bathed those dead trees and flowers and grasses, they turned the white of ash.

Hibern concentrated, and they flamed bright, then vanished. Dusting her hands, she closed the portal again, looking around. She had removed the locks; now to remove the doors. Then the walls. And finally the floors. Leaving only that army, boxed inside the empty house.

Twenty

"IT'S ONE OF THE tenders," the lookout roared down to Fox standing aft by the wheel. "Press of sail. Rigging looks like *Aka's Kiss*."

Aka's Kiss. Fox had to think a moment, before recollecting that this tender belonged to a pair of Prince Yviski's youngsters who had been born and raised on the sea. Tension beat against Fox's ribs: those two had been assigned to scout the southernmost curve of Land's End, west of The Narrows. Marshig of the Brotherhood of Blood's old cruising grounds.

The tender slanted over the whitecaps, then spilled its wind expertly, rounding to in the lee of the *Treason*.

"Pirate fleet coming, full sail!" The boy's voice cracked.

"Tacking south!" the girl shrilled.

The boy was barely old enough for the hypothetical beard spell—since Fox's fleet had no mages, those who had not already had a healer perform the spell for them before they had been taken into the Beyond were going to have to wait.

Fox took in those words, and his amusement at the boy fingering the fuzz on his upper lip vanished. "How many?"

"We counted nineteen hull down. Orders were, don't let them see us, so we ran downwind before they could spot us," was the prompt reply, ending on a note of question: did we do right?

Those waters off the Land Bridge had been pirate paradise for centuries before Marshig. After the Fox Banner fleet had defeated the Brotherhood, that area had stayed clear, but every time Fox came through in the decades after, he'd always sent someone to scout it.

He turned toward the sailor on signals watch, then froze: there was no summoning All Captains. The prince ought to be most of the way to Lindeth by now, and Ghaer would be at Halia's middle harbor, whatever they'd decided to call Tarual after Fox left.

He was about to dispatch *Aka's Kiss* up the coast, then remembered that magic paper, and the young man named Siamis who could read Ancient Sartoran. Fox wrote a three-line report, then added, *I'm on my way toward Parayid. Surely someone will understand my Marlovan!*

In Mearsies Heili, Siamis read the note, read it again, and understood with increasingly sickening certainty that he had been outmaneuvered. He should have known about so large a fleet launching. It could only mean that his eyes in eastern Toar had been silenced.

And Efael had even made reference to this fleet, he understood now. The four captains Efael had bragged about torturing to death on their own decks — that had not been one of Efael's random descents on his own people. That had been his way of forcing his marauding pirates to serve as transports, though there was no chance of loot in war-torn Halia.

This, here, was the worst aspect of mucking around in the twins' minds. Yeres had heard what Efael said, and assumed that Efael's broken sentence implied that the mercenaries were still holding Ralanor Veleth. She had missed the context, thinking that the torture of the four captains was Efael having fun because he was angry at Aldon and Imry, so Siamis had also, busy as he was filtering out the noxious emotion-charged images that jumbled her mind. Any mind, really, but he had to concentrate hard on filtering the twins — like squinting one's eye nearly closed when peering at something very near the eye-searing sun.

Siamis gazed around the chamber, struggling with the inescapable conviction that he'd made a lethal error. There were still mercenaries holding Ralanor Veleth. But clearly sometime in the last couple of months, while Siamis was everywhere else in the world, Efael had reassigned the rest of those mercenaries, forcing the pirates to act as transports *for the mercenary army coming to attack Halia right now.*

There was no calling Detlev to fix his blunder.

He shut his eyes. The time was three or so in the morning. Clair slept in the far chamber. Siamis heard the rise and fall of Seshe's voice. Seshe was the most responsible of the Mearsieans, who all had magic papers; they were constantly writing back and forth to CJ. Seshe would write to him if anything looked amiss. Keritar from up north, acting as minder and tutor, would scoop Aurora into lessons with the Delieth children if he had to miss their early rising.

He shoved his paper in his pocket and transferred to the deck of Fox's drakan, startling them all. "You can't go to Parayid," he said as soon as the transfer malaise faded enough to let him speak.

He took in the blank faces, and sustained a sharp insight into Detlev's recent habit of leaping abruptly from possible error to nascent disaster when he spoke to anyone.

Siamis said to Fox's wary expression, "I'll restate that. You could go to Parayid, but Perideth—what used to be Fera-Vayir—is now hostile to Marlovens. There is a semblance of an alliance, but it does not relate to the sea, and there is no time for negotiation. We need to talk to Stad, an introduction I ought to have made days ago…"

Siamis raised his hand in a gesture Fox recognized from Ramis all those years ago. He barely had time to draw a breath to brace for magic before he found himself hurled out of the world and back in again. It always felt like an invisible boot the size of a draft horse punting him, with prejudice.

Fox and Siamis appeared on a palisade above the small inlet known as Tarual Harbor, which was not even wide enough to let in a single capital ship, only small boats. While the two blinked away transfer malaise, Commander Stad broke off the tense conversation he was holding with two middle-aged women who were struggling to find a common language, as Marloven warriors ranged behind them, and below, faces looked up from Captain Ghaer's newly-arrived fleet of mostly river boats, that had hugged the coast on coming north.

With a strong sense of relief, Stad recognized Siamis, whom the king had brought to him right before the end of the previous year. Stad had no idea who he was, but in spite of his foreign-sounding name, he looked like a Marloven, and bore himself like a man with military training.

Siamis thumbed his eyes, blinked, then said to Fox, "This is Indevan Stad, commander of the counterattack for the Marloven king. Stad, it seems you've already met Captain Ghaer, part of your naval relief. Here's another one. Permit me to introduce Commander Savarend Montredavan-An."

Fox waved a hand. "Fox will do," he said. "I never sailed under that name."

He looked appraisingly at tough, black-haired Van Stad, who stared at the tall old man with the silver-touched horsetail, like Marlovens straight out of a tapestry. The cut of Fox's black coat also evoked those old heroic poses, but his language was peculiar. At first it sounded garbled, except the man's consonants were so precise. And hadn't he heard that name before? So much like the king's—

Siamis said, more sharply than he intended, "This is not the time to establish family backgrounds. The enemy is on the way with a sizable fleet. I'm fairly certain that this is the promised retaliatory strike that Efael has been planning."

"I'm Van Stad," Stad then said to Fox and Ghaer. "I welcome naval relief, but what can boats do, unless you are bringing us another army?"

"Have you explained the situation?" Fox asked Ghaer.

"We did not get that far," Ghaer said to Fox, with some asperity. "How was I to prove we are not the enemy?"

Stad had learned Sartoran. Everyone at the academy command class had done so, but her Sartoran was even more difficult to make out than this Fox's Marloven. This Fox wearing ruby pirate earrings swinging at his ears, Stad saw belatedly, and flattened his hand. "We don't trust anyone but ourselves," he said heavily.

Siamis snapped his fingers. "There is no time for—" He halted as his magic-paper prodded him with that inward tick that meant a message—two—three. Now four, piling up. Fighting the urge to look at it at once, he said, "Commander Stad. Fox, Ghaer, and one more captain have combined their fleets to aid you—all of Halia—in dealing with the enemy. Please listen to their report. I can stay long enough to help translate if you cannot follow their speech."

A frigid wind scraped their ears and noses as Stad said bleakly, "I only ask, what can boats do? If you've brought us military reinforcements, good. Add them to my command. We know what to do once they land."

Fox had not been surprised to hear that Indevan was still a common name, but hearing it shortened to "Van"—not even "Vana"—sounded wrong. He said to Stad, "I understand you have become accustomed to facing several times your number, but why not avoid that? We don't want them to land at all."

Stad's brows shot upward, then furrowed, as if he wasn't certain he'd heard that right. Fox forced himself to slow down. "There are three likely entry points for an invasion: Parayid, Tarual, and Lindeth, or whatever they are called now. The coast of Olavayir is impossible. The danger is all south of Tarual—"

Stad's brow wrinkled further. "Olavayir?"

"Ianavair, and southern Visegn," Siamis cut in as another letter ticked at his hand.

"—where the five rivers empty to the sea. Those rivers in my day always froze in winter."

"In my day?" A few decades ago? Why would a matter of a few years make that much difference? But Stad accepted with an opening of his palm, because the king had been very succinct in his orders: *While I am gone, you command our army. Siamis will coordinate with the general counterattack, but if he offers advice, at least listen.*

Stad was listening as Fox said slowly and distinctly, "It was Inda before the Andahi passage battle who said that Marlovans had always regarded the waters as a barrier. That's a mistake. To those who attack from the sea, water is a conduit. That must be broken *before* they land."

"I can agree with that much," Stad said cautiously. "How?"

"Captain Ghaer is the expert at estuaries and rivers." Fox opened his hand toward Ghaer, then out over the marshy tidepools below, winter-stubborn cattails as well as waxy leddas sticking up through patches of dirty snow.

Ghaer said, "There is a lot of castle defense that you can adapt for the sea. You have two very high tides each turn of the sun, here, yes?"

"That is true."

"At low tide, they will not want to slog through the icy bog. High tide is when to expect them, the one before dawn being the most dangerous. Flood time is when they will try to come up to your door in flat boats. The water is on their side. There are ways to see that the water is on our side. The first thing to do is to get boat-piercing weapons beneath the surface of the water."

"Boat piercing weapons?" Stad repeated.

"Don't your castles have red-gates?" Ghaer gestured, indicating a row of iron spears welded together. These were often buried under a finger's breadth of dirt or sand or gravel in a castle forecourt. Once the enemy broke down the gate and rode in, the spear gate would be winched up at an angle, spearheads piercing the rushing mass.

Here, the second older woman stepped up next to Van Stad.

"This is Captain Dannor Keriam," Stad said. "Leading the defense along this coast. She and her daughter have been working with the Iascans." And to her in a low voice, "Do you follow him? What accent is that?"

Dannor Keriam, niece of the Commander Keriam who had served as academy headmaster for longer than most of the Marlovens present there had been alive, gave a short nod. "Archivist. Before." The shortness of that "before" made it clear that she was a replacement for one of the many dead army captains. And, to Stad, "I can follow the old Sartoran." She raised her voice, addressing Siamis, Fox, and Ghaer. "We have red-gates. What else?"

Ghaer, looking relieved, crossed over to speak to her directly, and as the two women began talking defense technicalities, Fox gestured to Stad. "Will the coastal Iascans fight?"

The makeup of the Halian population in Fox's time had been Iascans and Marlovans, four or five generations after the Marolo-Venn had ridden in and claimed the vast Halian plains, and moved into the Iascan castles, pushing the Iascans toward the unwanted coast and the forests. It seemed that since that time, Iascan and Marlovan had mixed, becoming Marloven — except for the language of the coastal Iascans, stubbornly sticking to its old ways.

"Some," Stad said. "Most will take to their boats with their families and what they can carry, and go out to sea."

Fox grunted an assent. Jeje sa Jeje had been a typical Iascan of Fox's day. They were tough, after contending with the sea and the weather and the meager coastal soil for generation after generation, but as for war: life was already a challenge, why look for more trouble?

"The Rualese Council of Elders met with our king," Stad

said. "Many civs have already gone into hiding. The rest are with us. Though they have their own ways and weapons, mostly slings of various sorts that toss boulders off the palisades onto anyone coming to the shore."

Fox said, "Good. That's a start. Ghaer will take the rest of the estuary defense from here." And to Siamis, "We have to get a message to Prince Yviski, and then I must get back to the *Treason*."

Siamis had sneaked out his magic-paper while the two men spoke: Leefan, reporting Asiarch's movements; Arthur, reporting that Mondros and Tsauderei had planted another ward on Wan-Edhe; Seshe saying Clair had sleepwalked, but went right back to bed when she tugged her hand.

Siamis forced his mind back. He had to get away as soon as possible, but he'd already blundered badly. No leaving until he was certain he'd done what he could here. "Remember what I said at the outset. Parayid — Perideth — the Fera-Vayir of your day — is hostile to Marloven Hess now."

Stad's brain froze. The horsetail — the old-time accent and names of places — above all, the casual mention of Inda, as if a legend had stepped down from one of the tapestries in the throne room at Choreid Dhelerei, and begun to speak. They had said that Detlev and this Siamis here came from thousands of years ago, though Siamis looked like he could have gone through the academy a few years after Stad. Was it possible that miracles also brought the Marloven heroes out of ancient days?

Fox's lip curled. "No help from Parayid, eh? Ah, no different from when we took on the Brotherhood of Blood." Then he was gone, followed by Siamis, leaving Stad staring at the air where Fox had been.

His aide came forward a tentative step. "Is that … who I think it is?"

Stad turned his head, and caught the whisper rustling through his waiting company: *Elgar the Fox … Inda … the ghost of Inda, riding to our aid.* The wide-eyed wonder, the excitement in the angles of hands, of heads caused Stad to shrug away doubts about whether this Fox — whose name was closer to the king's than to Algara-Vayir, Inda's name — was or wasn't a miracle out of time. He was going to let that rumor fly free. From the effect he was seeing here, the boost to morale would be worth the extra two or three wings of aid that they were not going to get.

Twenty-one

AND THAT, SIAMIS WAS thinking as he recovered from the transfer, is why Detlev never told the Marlovens that Fox was coming. Its happening now was an unlooked-for boost, the "miracle" they desperately needed. He shrugged off the battering of Stad's thoughts as a lookout hailed, "Deck! Scout, west by south!"

Fox leaned on the rail, hiding how much the two transfers had wrenched his old bones.

The new scout raced up on the strengthening wind. "They're right behind us," she screamed. "Sixty-eight warships, but half hauled wind north by east."

Fox jerked his chin down. "Heading up the coast," he murmured. "That still gives me thirty-four, against my four here, and my tenders."

"We counted ten enemy scouts, acting as a vanguard." The tender's chief reminded Fox of Eflis, less in looks than in manner. She called up, "We got close to a brigantine and a brig during a squall, close enough to get a squint inside. Holds full of warriors."

"Sailing in column?" Fox called.

Her arm swooped around, expressive of righteous disgust. "No order."

"Pirates," Fox said, speaking rapidly now. "Ten scouts right in front of them … The entire world is their enemy, and they are predators, not prey. They never used to scout long-range, unless they are being hunted by a navy. Pirate strategy is nearly always board-and-carry rather than maneuvering." He turned his head. "Signal in line!"

"What does that mean?" Siamis asked.

"You have military experience?"

"Yes. Land, not sea."

"Line is the same as riding single file," Fox said. "Hide our number until the signal to disperse and cut them up as best we can. It's how Inda put us when we faced that soul-sucker Marshig, right here. It'll do again."

Fox lifted his glass to study the enemy. His crew was in motion, everyone to their task. Siamis pushed away from the rail, uncertain what he ought to do next. It seemed Fox was leading his small party straight toward death.

And it was his error killing them.

He checked when his magic-paper ticked. He pulled it out: Clair was at breakfast; Erol reporting that Wan-Edhe was in full rant mode over some new magic attack; wards tripped in Roth Drael, but the mages hid in time; Chwahir seen in line approaching The Fangs, Jehan Merindar's fleet standing off.

Fox used those moments to scan details of the oncoming attack: captured traders, patched for piracy, topgallants and studdingsails added to a squat trysail that strained at the press of sail; extra preventer stays on a raffee, oh, that one, handled well, would be fast; the trysail with the huge ram bolted onto the prow, causing its forefoot to sag...

Fox's teeth showed. "Ahhhh," a guttural sound. "That big brigantine hanging back in the second row? Gold fire on the red foresail? That was Marshig's flagship. Let's see who is running it now..." He turned his head sharply. "What can magic do?"

"Only illusion, of minimal use," Siamis said, and then understood what Fox wanted. What he needed.

Sure enough. "Can you make my scouts hard to see?"

"I can," Siamis said. The transfers to accomplish it were going to hurt—he didn't dare risk drawing Svir with that many slide-transfers, using the old magic—but who else was there to do it?

He began a fast, wrenching series of transfers, during which he threw illusion over each of the cluster of single-masted tenders and scout ships following the drakan, ducklings after a swan. When the building headache became a nosebleed, Siamis transferred back, holding onto the rail, where

Fox had not moved as he studied the enemy: rigging, sails, above all, speed as the fleets drew inexorably together.

Hiss, zip, arced the first arrows, landing in the water well short.

"Bad discipline," Fox said, and that was the last time they spoke.

Siamis backed out of the way as Fox and his four capital ships sailed straight at the enemy in a line. The Norsunder ships clumped and crowded together in a half-circle, plainly eager to make the kill. As the drakan—wearing its magnificent dragon prow again—surged toward their center, the outer edges of the enemy fleet began tacking in to envelope Fox's fleet.

On a signal that Siamis missed, the blurred small craft peeled off, like branches from a tree, and suddenly fires erupted on the sails of all those outer ships, and boarders crowding the rails began falling into the sea, each pierced by an arrow.

Cra-a-a-k! Graunch!

Two pirates rammed together in their eagerness to get away from the invisible source of fire; the enemy was by now shooting their own fire arrows, but their archers could easily be seen.

Siamis dodged arrows, ducking behind the tightly packed hammocks along the rail, then used his magic to douse the tiny flames of arrows that pierced the upper sails, though those had been well-wetted down. The ship abruptly heeled, and Siamis turned in time to see the drakan scrape alongside the first pirate, the air thick with arrows going both ways.

The warriors crowding the pirate ship readied to board, then their ship gave a huge lurch, sending most of them flying back to land on their fellows on the deck. More fell from the tops, as Fox's underwater ram gouged a huge hole below the pirate's waterline.

On the other side, the cut-boom scraped with devastating effect along one of the patched traders; The crash and creak of wood, shouts and screams, and the whoosh of expertly tended sails made the action difficult to keep up with. Siamis listened on the mental plane: the word "Ghosts!" howled skyward here and there, and fear spiked among those who saw the dragon prow bearing down on them.

Siamis turned to the rail. At least illusion was easy, if flimsy: using quick motions, he created vaporous shapes flying through the air, steel in hand, toward the pirates.

The illusions dissolved, of course, before they reached the deck, but the arrows from the invisible scouts found their marks as pirates and mercenaries stared in horror, the last sight they ever saw.

Siamis didn't need to follow Fox's strategy. He now had his own. He threw some more images—skulls with fire in the eye sockets, blood falling out of the sky—and gouts of sky-reaching flame, which threw a good part of the mercenaries into a panic. Some began fighting each other; everyone was an enemy now.

Efael's fleet master, a survivor, recognized stage illusions at once, but the rest of the fleet—most of whom had spent a year terrorizing a civilian population, without any discipline whatsoever—paid scant attention to the signals, which caused them to run into the few who heeded the signal to wear.

Fox's drakan surged straight for the flagship. The *Treason* lurched as it rammed the big brigantine broadside, and the helm team threw the ship hard over, so that the ram tore out the brigantine's side clear to the stern-quarter. Fox hefted his cutlass and roared, "Boarders away!"

Siamis lost sight of him. There was nothing more he could do here. The enemy was slipping downwind and away in ones, twos, and then five. No doubt that was the start of a general flight.

Siamis transferred back to Tarual. He found Stad, and said abruptly, "I know what to do."

Van Stad could see the battle-fatigue in Siamis's remote gaze, but that was an old companion. "Wait," he said. "Is that man you called Fox, is that really Inda, *our* Inda, who saved us at Andahi, come alive again?"

"No," Siamis said. "But Fox sailed with Inda. He's actually the real Elgar the Fox, and he's never been dead. Just stashed outside of time, against this day."

Stad pinched his brows. "I'm confused."

Siamis said, "I need to be several places at once. Let me say this: if we survive, I can promise you will be hearing a lot more about the Fox Banner fleet. But if it helps to believe that Inda is among you again, let it happen." He left Stad to supervise his drill, and ran down to the bluff overlooking the water.

Outside the small inlet great boulders thrust up from the seabed. Siamis mirrored the sea and sky around them with illusion, and then went about creating a semblance of the harbor that would lead the enemy straight onto the rocks. If the sun was bright enough when Efael's fleet arrived, a wary lookout would spot the blurring and blink it away, especially if warned. Someone in that fleet back at Parayid no doubt was communicating with at least one of the other mercenary ships right now—probably bypassing Efael, at a guess. But the mercenaries might come in under cover of weather, or at night, and miss the blur.

Siamis then went about Tarual, creating illusions. He reinforced them with repeated spells that ought to linger for a couple of weeks—unless, he said over and over, they were dispersed. Easily done. Whereas Ghaer and her river boats were down there laboring hard to create lethal obstacles for attack boats.

The shadows had lengthened and blended when he transferred to Prince Yviski, explained what was coming and what he had done, and then began with more illusions at Lindeth Harbor. He had moved from ships to boats when the hoarse cry of a lookout caused everyone to stop working and face the sea.

There, out on the horizon as the small red ball sank into the sea, the tiny silhouettes of columns of Chwahir capital ships lined the entire horizon.

Efael had prevailed over Wan-Edhe, and had ordered the two strongest fleets of the Chwahir navy south. The holds filled with Gold and Silver armies?

The rising wind had numbed Siamis's lips and ears. The tick of his paper jerked his mind back to the rest of his worries. In the fading light, he squinted down at the nearly illegible scrawl, and shock burned his nerves:

Clair is gone.

Twenty-two

SIAMIS SHOT A THOUGHT to Detlev: *Svir has Clair. Begin the attack.*

And in the sanctuary beneath the Ghost Lakes, Detlev stilled. "Circle!"

After nearly two weeks of constant work between quick meals and brief rests in turn, the snap in his tone caused his group to drop eating utensils, to waken, to abandon exercise, and scramble to the far chamber to form their circle, knee to knee.

Detlev looked into faces. Adam, to Detlev's right, already breathing in the mode for inward focus; Senrid, white-lipped from his inescapable headaches; David, who smiled expectantly. Sveneric, whose intent and unwavering gaze was as clear as a forest pool. Rolfin, Laban, and Andri grinning with reckless challenge; MV derisive. Crow and Dirk watchful, Mildred smiling, chin up, Zairna alert. Roy, at Detlev's left, pensive.

"It is I," Detlev said, "who must shape the attack. If you lose me, you are to withdraw as rapidly as you can, and get Siamis to shift you to other places where your various other talents can best be applied."

And to them all: *Begin!*

—as Siamis risked a slide-transfer to Mearsies Heili, with the Selenseh Redian as Destination: by now, if Svir detected a transfer using the old magic, it wouldn't tell him anything he didn't already know.

Siamis leaned down, hands on his knees, permitting himself three long, slow breaths before he slid again to the white palace, an eyeblink of a shift that Ilerian and Svir could detect all they wanted — they could not get access —

Clair.

He bolted for the kitchen, which was where Clair's girl gang tended to gather whenever there was trouble. Above the pounding of his head in rhythm with his steps, he heard high voices. Surrounded by Falinneh, tear-streaked Seshe, and short, wary Gwen was a familiar face: stark, staring blue eyes framed by long, straight black hair, and a diminutive form in white and green with a black vest: "CJ," he said, carefully neutral. "I see you're back."

"You've got blood leaking out of your nose," CJ said to Siamis.

"Too many dark magic transfers." He thumbed away the blood, then dunked his hand in the cleaning bucket. "What happened?"

"We don't know," CJ said, as Dhana looked wildly from one to the other. "Dhana says Sherry was with Clair, as Seshe hadn't had any sleep, and Falinneh and Gwen were down in the Junky playing with Aurora and the Delieth kids. They both disappeared."

"I'm sorry, I'm sorry," Seshe whispered, silently weeping.

"Don't blame yourself," Siamis said to her. "My guess is, whatever happened was a long-laid plan." As he spoke, he began to assemble possible elements of the pattern: the sleepwalking? Probably. What else? Could be through the physical contact between Clair and the others when they led her back, so innocent. Oh, yes, that had Svir's psychic taint all over it. The girls' strong bond, their loyalty and affection for one another, had been used against them. Specifically Sherry, as harmless as a bunny, and not much smarter, though she was such a genuinely sweet girl they all adored her. All the other girls might feel uneasy, or even suspicious, and question, but Sherry would never detect the insidious worm of Ilerian's compulsion reaching through physical contact.

Ilerian had assuredly found her the weak link, and just as assuredly, Siamis wasn't going to tell them. "Very long-laid," he said. "Listen. I have to send the signal for the counterattack right now, then we can discuss what to do. All right?" Did that sound sufficiently unthreatening — unlike their loathed Adult Authority?

He took their silence for consent, and slipped back to his space in the Selenseh Redian, where he dropped down, put his head in his hands, and reached for Clair, who as much as she was able during the merciless, nearly continuous mental onslaught, had come to trust him.

Her mind-shield was tightly shut, but he detected enough of a whiff of the Imaran semblance of the Beyond to know she was there, a prisoner in the Dei manor. They had her, but she had withdrawn utterly. It would suffice for as long as she could stay awake to hold that mind-shield — and if Ilerian and Svir were sufficiently distracted to leave a concentrated attack for later. He had to act fast.

Siamis grabbed the paper he had bespelled with all the names of the counterattack leaders, the mages, and the scouts and observers, such as Ferret, Leefan, and Silvanas, and wrote: *Begin the counterattack.*

It was evening in Sartor, and Atan and Rel had just retired when they both felt their respective magic-papers tick.

"I'll read it. I've still got light on my side," she murmured, holding her magic-paper up to the light of the single candle.

Rel was just as happy not to have to pull that benighted paper from beneath the pillow. It always seemed to be either bad, or alarming, news. Sometimes both. But then Atan put hers down and Rel knew from the shock in her eyes that the time they had braced for was not spring, or next month, or next week, it was now.

She flung aside the quilt and ran to the door fitted into the chamber's round archway. "Gehlei," she told her steward, whose room was across the uneven stone ground. "It's now."

She slammed the door, whirled, and in two steps reached Rel's arms. One last, lingering kiss, sweet, trembling, mixed with the salt of tears, led to a desperate, wordless congress as much to take and to give comfort as to momentarily forget themselves in the all too brief flame of desire. Atan broke away first, fighting against the sob that lodged in her chest.

They shared the wash basin, and in tight voices repeated back and forth the series of orders they had argued over for weeks out as they pulled on their war gear. Rel was fast out of long habit; when her shaking fingers began to fumble with her bodice laces, he was already shrugging into his heavy mail shirt.

Leaving her laces dangling, she sprang to him, helped pull the quilted tunic straight beneath the mail, then to align the heavy linked seams, though it took both hands. They got his battle-tunic over his head, and then he held his arms out as she wrapped his long, heavy, steel-link reinforced blackweave belt twice around his waist, pausing only to attach the two long knife sheaths. Then it was her turn.

Last, their weapons. She, a pair of knives that she only marginally knew how to use. He strapped knife sheaths against every long bone within reach, and last, pulled on his shoulder harness, sliding home the big two-handed sword and positioning it behind his shoulder.

She wore chain mail at his behest, and the knives, but the only object that meant anything to her was the ancient Landis scepter, supposedly brought from another world when humans first came to this one. It was no weapon, only a powerful symbol, one Sartorans only saw at the most serious court events. It might serve, she thought grimly, to whack an attacker alongside the head.

She kept blinking back tears, but she tried to smile, for she did not want Rel's last sight of her to be a face distorted by fear or grief. She could see the anticipation of battle in the corners of his mouth and in his black eyes, but she rejoiced, for anything that would help him to lead she wished him to have.

Together they stepped out of the cave that had been their first home as a married couple, to find their people lined and ready, just as they had drilled so many times during the days that had fled so rapidly away.

Atan clutched the scepter against her. "Our first task is to free Eidervaen. You all have your targets," she cried, her voice pitched to be heard against the far walls of the great cavern, and peal after peal of trumpet-charges rang, reverberating, through the stone citadel.

Before they faded, the weird ululations of the hill warriors' death-charge shrilled, splintering into crazy echoes.

Rel was already gone, swallowed into the readying formation that was busy mounting up on tail-switching, sidling horses. Atan turned to the left, and pointed her scepter. She glimpsed Hinder's white hair, his peace headband tied around his head, and stone knife at hand.

She turned to the right. Young, old, hefting a variety of weapons. Many grinned, but here and there she saw furtive glances, and the stiff shoulders of fear.

She hesitated. *I swore to protect them, to give them a kingdom in which they could find love and laughter, pleasure and warmth, old age amongst their children, and after I raise my arm I will see some of them lying like crumpled dolls, red-splashed and lifeless.* Tears coursed down her face.

"For Sartor and freedom!" Julian called out, her voice young and high, as she scribbled furiously on a beige magic-paper to Darian Selenna in Sarendan.

"SARTOR AND FREEDOM!" came a roar, loud and prompt.

"Sarendan and freedom!" someone in the back called—a reminder of their alliance.

"SARENDAN AND FREEDOM!"

"Mardgar and freedom!"

"MARDGAR AND FREEDOM!"

By now it had become a chant.

"Eth Endra and freedom!"

On the refrain, Atan lifted the scepter one last time, and they poured out of the hideouts and streamed toward the city below; unlike the hapless defense when they were first invaded, this time everyone knew where to go and what to do.

It was midway through the night in Everon. Tahra Delieth strode without ceremony into Roderic Dei's tent, where he sat with a book on his lap. He dropped his pipe in well-mimed surprise as she said curtly, "We ride to the attack now."

He bowed, and she walked out again. Roderic Dei set aside the book he'd just opened; Silvanas had already sent word, Laban having seen to it that Roderic Dei had a magic-paper. Commander Dei was glad to see that Tahra had cooperated this far. He hoped—if they prevailed—this would be the first step toward true peace.

He turned to the night-duty herald. "Ban, sound the summons to battle."

In Colend, Jilo packed his book on top of his one change of

clothes, aware of his fingers trembling. His stomach was in knots, but he knew that everyone else probably felt the same. His inner voice kept gibbering *This is it, this is it,* though strictly speaking it wasn't, for him. He still had to get into Narad, capital of Chwahirsland, and he could not transfer. It was dangerous enough to walk in, for there had to be wards waiting. He had to be alert enough to detect and dismantle them—and hope that the latest antidotes to the wards, fashioned by Mondros and Tsauderei, would still be good. Wan-Edhe did absolutely nothing else but sit in his lair thinking of new ways to protect himself and ward off absolutely everyone else. Including his own guards.

Jilo left the stable, not surprised to see golden lamplight in the row of dormitories and cottages of the school. He walked into Shontande Lirendi's room to find Shontande dressed like a man. He was in the act of carefully packing the long blond wig he'd worn since autumn.

The hair had been donated by one of Shontande's aunts-by-marriage; if he'd asked the young courtiers, he would have had an entirely shorn court as a result, and any one of them would have seen his gesture as one of intimacy. Which was why he did not ask anyone but those older, well established with families.

Until he'd agreed to join the counterattack, Shontande had startled Jilo by changing his hair color every season or so—an easy way of disguising himself, he'd said. Blonde was the color he'd used most because his cousin Nash had observed that he somehow looked shorter when he was a blonde. But it took several hours for hair colorists to do their magic, and Erol had pressed upon them the need for speed: "When it happens, it's got to be simultaneous, or as near as we can get," Erol had said. "Divide Norsunder in a thousand ways." Shontande turned to wigs.

He smiled at Jilo, then said, "Even if I don't live past tomorrow, when the survivors look at my corpse, I want them to see *me.*"

Whom else would they see, Jilo wondered, but he didn't say it. This surely was another of those Colendi things he couldn't hope to understand.

Then Shontande crossed the room, and set both hands on Jilo's shoulders—another surprise, they seemed to have somehow become eye to eye. When did that happen? No wonder Shontande really did seem shorter in the blonde wig; Jilo had grown, unnoticed, these past few months.

"Let us meet again," Shontande murmured, "in victory and in joy."

Jilo jerked his head in a nod, his tongue too dry for response. Then, to his utter astonishment, Shontande pulled him in for a short, fervent hug. Jilo's arms flapped like overcooked noodles as, so briefly, Jilo felt Shontande's warmth, the rapid tattoo of his heart against his ribs, quite as fast as Jilo's own. Then he let go. In a few quick steps he vanished out the door, and the last Jilo heard was his ringing tenor as he issued instructions to his followers.

Jilo used the latest Norsunder transfer spell that Erol had given him, and shifted to the border of Erdrael Danara and Chwahirsland. Then he hitched his worn knapsack over his shoulder and started down the steep goat trail toward Narad.

As he toiled along the trail, his steps squeaking on fresh snow, he tried not to think about Wan-Edhe, the army, or the war, for what would happen would happen. Instead, he thought about that hug. His first hug—in memory, anyway. His skin still felt the totally unfamiliar impact of person to person without violent intent, and he wondered what it would feel like to hug … a girl?

In Enaeran, Licre's camp was settling down to evening activities; they had moved again. The night watch had already taken off for perimeter patrol, and Liere looked from her bedding to the ever-growing pile of requests and promises. If Enaeran recovered its sovereignty, it was going to take considerable time to disentangle all these, and honor them—

The tick of her paper was a relief.

Then it wasn't.

"Gared?"

There was a note to Sartora's voice that caused not only Gared but several others to put down what they were doing and rush to Liere's tent. She stood there, her golden hair limned in the lamplight as she said, "It's begun: tomorrow, we unseat Adon Marsael."

"First, Wilsar," Gared growled.

A roar rose, spreading through the camp, which was very

soon deserted.

Ralanor Veleth. Damondaen. Hael Morvendrion. Fhleria. Geranda. Toar, Venn, Khanerenth. All the kingdoms whose cultures had fostered standing armies or organized militia turned with pent-up ferocity on Norsundrian garrisons, and bloody battle ensued.

The signal spread from there, an echo of the speed of Imry Llyenthur's autumn fires.

Predictably, Efael was already in Imar, ranting about the useless mercenaries in the process of being decimated by a navy that seemed to have sprung out of the ocean.

"No navy has sprung out of the ocean," Svir said, amused. "I expect it was another of Detlev's lies, this one about the capture-spheres. He clearly had some left. Go take them out! You have the power."

"I don't," Efael retorted. "The Chwahir are so damned slow. And that stupid old man refuses to let us put the Universal Language spell on any of them, so not a one understands an order. We're forced to go through interpreters. Who keep vanishing! I want the First Lancers."

"You wanted to be commander," Svir said softly. "Command."

"I want the First Lancers," Efael repeated. "If they burn down Halia, then everyone will understand I mean what I say."

Both turned to Ilerian, but he sat in his chair, his gaze on the fire.

"It's an attack," Svir said. "He should be able to deal with it presently. But if he needs me, he will not like my being distracted by minutiae that our military commander, who has all our forces at hand, ought to be dealing with."

This threat sent Efael in retreat to his lair to brood, as, far north of Imar, Erai-Yanya, Arthur, and Kessler Sonscarna watched the conversation.

"And there is our cue," Erai-Yanya murmured.

Kessler had, as promised, set up this window. Erai-Yanya had no idea how these things worked, only that they burned up enormous magical potential—she could smell that nasty hot-metal singe. It harrowed her soul to see so much magic squandered, except that they needed to watch the enemy, and to the amazement of all the mages, Kessler had accepted a truce. They had no idea why, but it was time to keep up their end of the bargain.

"Let's begin," she said to Arthur. She would not dare to say anything that might sound like orders to Kessler.

Arthur nodded. "We and the student mages will get started on the tree protections. That ought to annoy Svir."

Erai-Yanya, experienced mage that she was, sensed the Sartoran Mage Council far away in Shendoral joining the magic attack on Imar's enchantment, which wrung the life force out of everything in its reach.

Trees, grass, dormant seeds, animals—the mages had been hoarding spells for months for just this attack. Alone, their efforts would do nothing but annoy the Host, and perhaps cause terrible retribution, but in conjunction with all the other efforts, well, she hoped it worked.

She pulled her book over, took a deep breath, and began the spells that would free the winter birds that the spreading of Imar's evil enchantment had mired.

Efael scowled at the array of dispatch trays, wanting to see only reports of success. But there were none. Aldon in retreat back to Norsunder Base ... Ellir in the hands of that floating rabble that no one in the east seemed to be able to find. Same on the far west, at Halia. Even Alsais, a country full of rabbits and peacocks, had successfully overcome the Norsundrian command—though the latest report said that they were in a stand-off with the Chwahir, who were far more numerous. They would all have to be beaten back into submission, and he intended to see it done, personally, as soon as Svir broke through. He said it was imminent.

At least Efael had been able to force Wan-Edhe to extend a part of his time-distortion over this castle, relatively close to Narad. Neither Efael nor Wan-Edhe cared how many extra lives the magic squeezed to stabilize the spell.

His eyes stung. He knew it was very late, but unless he drank poppy tincture, he would not be able to sleep until dawn. He sat in the dark, listening to the rush of blood through the heart in his chest, and hating it, hating the weight of the world, hating time.

If only sleep brought the dreams you wanted, the things you do when awake. The pleasures of violence—when you, only you, are in control, and your enemy utterly at your mercy. But too often dreams stirred up old memories, when he was the one forced to beg and plead for the invasive pain he didn't want, enduring the poking, prodding, sweaty paws, to the sound of drunken laughter—

He shook his head, violently, and was about to reach for the poppy-infused wine when a familiar sense, almost a scent, caused every nerve to snap alert.

His head jerked up, one hand extended to gesture a zaplight into existence as the other reached for his knife. But his wrist was caught in a grip of steel.

Imry whispered in his ear, his warm breath stirring Efael's hair, "If you want to live, stay in the south with Aldon's scuttling band. Don't go near Imar."

The grip eased.

Efael lunged out of his chair, knife in hand. Light!—

No one in the room.

He roused the frozen guards, and watched, white with fury, as they were flogged senseless.

Twenty-three

IN MEARSIES HEILI'S SPIRED castle, CJ knocked on June's door.

"CJ," June said. "You're back." *Finally*, she wanted to add, but she swallowed it. She had always hated girl gangs—probably because she'd never been invited into one—and she had taken an instant dislike to this one. They were so silly, with their middle school giggling and private jokes that they all thought so hilarious, never noticing that absolutely no one else agreed.

But as Clair got worse and worse, June found herself sympathizing, and from there her tolerance gradually widened: Diana had been awesome; Seshe never giggled, ever, but more important she was kind to the heart. You could see it in her eyes when she was tired, there was no fake goodie-two-shoes here. Gwen, the one with the Australian accent, was scrappy, and just liked to play. June could accept that. Girls just wanna have fun. Falinneh was loud and wild, but once in a while she did manage to be actually funny, moreover, June had noticed that she clowned when things were tense. It wasn't all a bid for attention, the way that Kyale had been. Coping mechanism, that was something June could understand.

Dhana was really strange. *Really* strange. Kind of like all the anime tropes of a girl slapped together, with glimpses of someone, some*thing*, way different leaking out. Shining out? Because it wasn't scary, just different. But the others accepted her the way they pretty much accepted everyone. Including

June herself. She knew she was difficult to get along with. As for Sherry, she was definitely the giggliest of them all, and the silliest, but she was also genuinely sweet. Not once had June heard her say anything mean or snide. If anything, her big eyes would get bigger and her smile would vanish if conversation took a right turn at Backbiting Blvd.

Moreover, this gang stuck together even when the sky was issuing a metaphorical rain of crap. Not once had any of them failed 24/7 duty babysitting Clair. Except, of course, CJ. Which made June want to demand why Clair's so-called bestie kept hanging out a zillion miles away with some other girl. Except that she herself had heard Clair, repeatedly, say, "No! I can't bear for her to see me like this," when anyone suggested bringing CJ back. And once or twice, "I know she'll want to do something about it, and get herself killed. No, no, it's better with her far away."

So when CJ knocked at June's door, she didn't slam it in her face. "CJ, you're back," she said. There, that was neutral enough, wasn't it?

CJ crossed her arms. "We're going to go rescue Clair and Sherry," she stated. "No one else will."

Aaaaand this right here was reason number two why Clair didn't want CJ finding out, June thought. She stated, in English, "No one else will because *everybody* says the Host are toxic dumpster fires. That usually means it takes another toxic dumpster fire to mess with them. Anyone else is smoking stupid-juice."

"I can't not try," CJ retorted. "Just because everyone says they are scary." She actually made air quotes around *everyone says*, which pissed June to the max. And there went the neutrality.

"CJ, in case you haven't heard, one of them is a 100% psychopath, and the other is an actual black hole that borrowed the form of a guy. They won't listen to a middle school-aged kid, they'll take one look and cut you up for lunch."

CJ's intense blue gaze shifted, her jaw jutted, then she said, "The fake cup. I want to trade it for Clair and Sherry. I was very careful when I put the stone spell on it. All Ilerian, or Svir, has to do is touch it. Instant statue. Then nobody will be cutting anybody up."

June shook her head. "I don't think they're stupid enough to fall for that."

"That's for me to decide. And it's better than taking the real one, which they would surely turkey up in some horrible way."

June snorted. "If I thought for half a second that they would actually do the trade, I'd *give* them the real one. There's no contest between a living person and some doohickey, magical or not. But I don't believe they'll trade. They sound exactly like the sort of assholes who *always* cheat."

To June's horror, CJ's eyelids gleamed with water as she said fiercely, "Then I'll go alone."

"Fucking *hell*, you are so *stupid*," June snapped, hissing a sigh. "Why not leave it to Detlev and Siamis, and the rest of the mages?"

"I'm sure they're doing what they are supposed to do," CJ stated. "I'm sure of it. Siamis has already gone off somewhere, Dhana says. But what they need to do is fight, I dunno, grand battles, and things, and they'll all say that the needs of the many are more important than one girl. But Clair is *my best friend*, and Sherry is *her* oldest friend, and they *need* me."

June gave up. "Then I'd better go with you."

CJ said, "This is not your world."

June jerked a shoulder. "Nowhere is my world. But this seems to be my job; I guess I took it when I went and got that damn cup down, though nobody ever thought to mention anything unimportant like, you know, actual wages. But I will do it."

"Then we'll all go," CJ said—in Mearsiean. "And stop speaking English. It makes me feel like I've got cigarette ashes in my mouth."

"How do we even get there—" June started, then her shoulders sagged as the girls crowded around the doorway turned expectantly toward Dhana.

"Fine. We'll take both cups," June said.

CJ grabbed the false one from her hand, knowing it well from when she'd loaded spells onto it. It was ceramic, but painted silver in such a way that it did resemble the other one remarkably closely.

June went to her trunk, and dug down to where she kept the real one, wrapped in her old Earth jeans, where it had lived since Siamis had given it back to her after Jilo left. "It cannot help Clair right now," he'd said. "It might even hurt in the sense of drawing Ilerian to it through her. I have put a spell on it to transfer her to the Selenseh Redian if she touches it."

But she never had. Nor had she gone near June's room, with the false cup sitting right out on the dresser. June unwrapped the real one, scowling at it. Maybe it would be useful after all. All June had to do would be to touch Clair with the cup, and straight to the Selenseh Redian she'd go. Dhana could get the rest of them out. Maybe. "All right, let's do this," she muttered.

Dhana's face was mutinous as she transferred the entire group together. The magic didn't hurt, but appearing in Imar did. They stumbled, shuddering and gasping, onto a wide, beautiful terrace that June had seen before. The sight hadn't improved. The darkness around them was unnatural and unending. They faced the bank of gleaming window-squares in the center of which, just beyond the doors of glass, they could make out two tall figures seated in great chairs before a leaping fire, the white-haired one plainly dressed, the dark-haired man in a richly gleaming robe with voluminous sleeves. Over at the side, two smaller figures sat on a couch, hip and shoulder pressed together, Clair's white hair curiously lifeless in the weird air, and Sherry's round, tear-stained face drawn with misery.

CJ gulped, gathered her courage, and stopped just outside the doors open to the outside.

The tall man with the mustache turned his head. That one had to be Svir; the white-haired one's light gaze was diffuse in a creepy way, and he didn't seem to see them. That was A-okay with CJ.

"I'll take that cup," Svir said.

"Only if you let them go," CJ stated, as firmly as she could, but her voice shook. Make him think she was reluctant, she thought. If she gave in too easily, he might suspect something.

Svir stroked his mustache, a sign to those who had spent much time in his presence that he was irritated. Ilerian was playing chase in the mental realm with Detlev, who was proving to be maddeningly elusive. Which intrigued Ilerian the more. Not a good sign; intrigue very often turned to fury in an instant.

Svir waved a hand, gathering and releasing magic in a cruel twist that sent a gnarl of fire into the cup CJ held. It super-heated. She tried to toss it at him, but not before the ceramic exploded, cutting her with little shards.

June thought, so Detlev had been right that they'd know in an instant. She kept the silver cup behind her back, sick with apprehension. Now was the time to get this cup to touch Clair, and get her out of this hell-mouth. Only that man sat right there, between June and the couch where Clair sat with Sherry. And what was wrong with Clair? June tried to covertly catch her eye, but Clair just sat there with a zombie stare.

Svir said to June, "You went to some trouble to deceive your friend." A nod at Clair, who didn't react. "Why?"

"Gee. I wonder," June said, with all the caustic insolence of an Earth adolescent who loathes and despises every semblance of adult coercion.

"You had better give me the real one, hadn't you?" he asked.

June's mouth soured, though her heart slammed hard in her chest. Here it was, then, what she'd dreaded, and she could see in that remorseless gaze that it would be every bit as bad as she'd feared. Probably worse.

But then Svir blinked, as though bringing some distant speck into focus, and shot a coldly amused glace June's way. "You will pardon me for a moment." With a mocking inclination of his head, he seemed to dissolve into shadow, making it difficult to look in that direction.

June let out her breath in a whoosh. Was that Detlev? The mages? Somewhere, somehow, *some*one had gone on the attack. June looked around the library. Both wingback chairs held shadows that strobed in the creepiest way, no-light flickering in the distorted light. It hurt her eyes to look. The two head snakes seemed to be there, but not there, and June saw no guards. No servants, even.

She tried to dart toward the couch, but horror flashed her nerves: her foot barely lifted from the ground. Her free hand moved with infinite slowness, as if she was stuck in a gigantic pot of invisible glue. No matter how hard she struggled, her body felt like it was sinking in quicksand.

Falinneh and Gwen also tried to run in, but they looked like cartoon characters in total slo-mo. June turned back to Clair, who still on the couch with Sherry. Clair looked, in fact, much as Tarael had, last spring. "Clair," June said. "We've got to get outside. See? Dhana is out there on the terrace."

Clair didn't move, even when Sherry tugged at her.

"It's okay. Part of a plan," June said slowly and distinctly.

"Let's go outside."

CJ lumbered in slo-mo behind Falinneh and Seshe, a knife in her hand, the cuts on her face and hands sluggishly bleeding. Her long skirt rippled so slowly it looked like a giant worm under there.

CJ gritted her teeth, striving to get moving. They had to get Clair and escape! The air was so thick. It was like the kind of dreams she hated most, when she tried to run, but stumbled stooping to the ground, as if her body weighed a thousand tons.

Gwen gave up trying to get inside and stood sentinel at the door, looking out into the darkness at where Dhana prowled back and forth—for her, approaching the open doors was akin to walking into fire. She could not do it. But she could wait for the others to leave, so she could get them away.

Then CJ, Falinneh, and Seshe stopped as Imry Llyenthur appeared before them.

Sherry scrunched down, but Clair did not react. She did not even seem to see Llyenthur, whom she had never met.

Abruptly the weird light around them, already so false, began to fade, as though it were being somehow stretched. June glanced from side to side; Llyenthur frowned, glancing from the cup to June's face. "Ilerian and Svir are separately occupied, so it appears our various moments of retribution have been postponed." He dropped his hand on the black and gold sword hilt at his side. "Can you tell me where Detlev is?"

"No," said June.

"Then perhaps it's time for some diversion." He broke off and glanced upward, in the same direction Clair was gazing, his eyes narrowed, then he exited through the shadowy door next to the couch where Clair and Sherry sat.

CJ didn't waste time trying to figure him out. She scowled, bent her head, and strove to close the distance to Clair and Sherry, one sloggy step at a time. She made it halfway across the room when the terrace doors slammed shut.

The white-haired man had reemerged in his chair by the fire. CJ looked away, longing for some way to escape, to discover a new figure had appeared. He was tall, with a sharply boned face. He wore all black under a black-dyed leather duster. He began talking, no, arguing with Ilerian. And though she hated to admit it to anyone, CJ understood the Norsundrian language.

"...and they skyved off from Lindeth altogether. I've sent

a team to take ship and find them and set them all on fire, but I *need* the First Lancers. Everything is falling apart. Aldon has actually dared to scuttle back to Norsunder Base! I know he's plotting to stab me in the back. I need to make a strong demonstration—"

"The First Lancers are unruly," Ilerian said, mildly enough. "You cannot trust them."

Efael's mouth twisted in a cruel semblance of a smile. "I thought of that. I got the blood poison spell from Wan-Edhe. I'll douse them before I even let them out of the capture-sphere, and then warn them that they won't get the antidote unless they obey my orders."

Ilerian said, "That was well-thought," in the manner of a being that only occasionally had to trouble with the weaknesses of a physical body. "Yes, you may have them." He made a gesture of dismissal, and returned to the duel in the realm of the spirit, paying no attention to the girls. Detlev was out there at last, truly revealed. He would make a feast, oh, such a feast! Ilerian had found that the piquancy of human anguish, desire, longing, rage, and utter despair heightened the intensity of their souls' dissolution. To whelm Detlev would be akin to ingesting a star.

But first to capture him.

For Detlev's group the battle on the mental plane was like diving through air, bracing for contact with cold water, and slamming instead into deadly black ice.

But Adam found his way very swiftly. Rejecting the encountered images, he used their energy to fashion another image altogether. *We are a ring*, he sent to them all: *We are this chain of braided silver*.

He moved, around and around, suppressing individual identities and melding them into a true circle. It protected them, and strengthened them.

And, strengthened, they found their way past the ice. But movement was slow in the lifeless vortex of force that Svir and Ilerian had created in the realm of the spirit. And when Svir turned his attention to them, movement stopped.

Twenty-four

HIBERN HAD MADE A portal twice, now. She could do it again. To be safe, she concentrated, and formed a shield of air between the Beyond and whatever lay behind the world-gates, and then reached.

A portal glowed into being, humming with power. She looked out at glowing red, oozing slowly in fascinating patterns against a black sky. Heat blasted through the portal, vibrating the air shield, and she quickly dismissed that portal.

It cost a tremendous surge of magic, but she had it to spend. She made another, and another. An ice world. Another ice world. One as dead as ash. Another full of weird plants, but the heat blasted nearly as hot as the one with the liquid fire, with a billowing stench of rot.

She waved that portal away. Another five, then six, and she comprehended that sorting randomly through worlds might take longer than she was alive. She concentrated on specific requirements. Air, life. The next portal showed her a green sky at twilight with three moons, one full and two at other stages. These moons shone between tall buildings that looked as if they had been grown from fungus, right to the massive caps at the top. Devices flew between the caps, their lines too straight to be living creatures. On the ground walked shiny-skinned blue spider-like beings, only with four legs, their underslung bodies swinging as they moved about in singles and groups, antennae canted alertly on bulbous heads; they looked to Hibern like people attending to everyday matters.

This world was closer to what she sought — the air coming through her shield smelled dusty and strange, a bit like peanuts and old oranges, but breathable. Except … she remembered the nature of those she was sending out: warriors. The blue inhabitants did not need human warriors dumped on them.

Another twenty tries, and she found at last what she wanted: a world with no ambulatory or winged beings of human, avian, or animal variety. This world had air, water, a variety of green growing plants, low and lush, and the largest live things in sight were insects. A thousand types of insect she had never seen before, which meant life could sustain itself there.

Now, how to get those armies there? Early on, Theronezhe had attempted to intimidate her by showing her a shadow of Ivandred-Harvald of old Marloven Hesea. She had figured very quickly that this was a mere shadow.

She could create shadows, too.

She envisioned a semblance of Theronezhe, and then used it to open the last door, to the box that held the vast military camps. She projected summons trumpets sounding. She used the Marloven fanfares of early childhood, and imagined her ghostly Theronezhe riding through the portal … and yes, the warriors followed, marching in column after column.

She obscured herself from their notice with a wave of her hand, observing different types of armor, and helms, a variety of uniforms and weapons, as these fighters collected over centuries followed their "leader" out into this new world. She did not know if these warriors had volunteered or had been volunteered. She was not a killer. Her intent was to leave these men and women on a world where they could find themselves a life, if they so wished, without making war on others. From the looks of this one, they'd be too busy learning how to plant and plow, grow and harvest, to be attacking each other, but that was now up to them.

When the last of them marched through, she sensed the emptiness left behind, and further, the last vestiges of the power eddying around the world-gate portal she had created. In haste, she concentrated on Geth, since Sartorias-deles was still warded.

This time, she stepped through, and waved the portal shut behind her.

Efael's lair

"Unruly." Yeres found that hilarious.

Efael shrugged it off. "Ilerian isn't human," he reminded her annoyingly as they pored over the map of Halia, comparing it to the reports of uprisings all over. "*I* know human weakness. That's what matters."

Yeres snickered in agreement, in charity with him because she was full of poppy. "Who wants to die slowly over days by blood poison? They'll obey you once they understand who's master. Besides, why wouldn't they? Before Detlev pulled them through the rift, weren't they fighting the rest of the kingdom?"

"I made sure of that," Efael said. "Those reports were accurate. I still don't understand what Svir is going on about, with Detlev and the Beyond."

"Some Dena Yeresbeth thing," Yeres said dismissively. Both twins believed in what was concrete, as long as no one was actually invading their minds. "Even I've heard of Bloody Ivandred and the First Lancers, lords of the wind. Riding straight into Norsunder. Even though it turns out we lost the rift that year, they still make us sound so wicked," she gloated. "Are you going to kill one or two to remind them who is in command?"

"Shouldn't have to." Efael stared down at the carefully drawn borders of Marloven Hess. "Ivandred slaughtered some of his own jarls, and they were chasing him to overthrow him. 'Won't fight Marlovens!' Ilerian really doesn't understand humans. Now, where to put them?" He tapped the map. "How about right here, along the northern border of Marloven Hess? They can scorch a path all the way to the Sartoran Sea. Burn every house. Kill every man over fifteen."

"Over ten," Yeres said. "It's going to take time to get them really obedient, especially if you want me to come up with spells once we get *real* control. A fifteen-year-old turns twenty in five years—oh." She blinked, whispered, and patted Efael's cheek. "One of my wards! It was so toilsome laying those down, but you were right to insist I ward that Chwahir border. I caught us a good one."

"Imry?"

"No, but perhaps as good. It's that Jilo. Wan-Edhe will give us anything for him. Anything! How about those stone spell bindings?"

"Go get him. Stash him here until we decide what we want from Wan-Edhe, then I want you tracking Aldon. I know he's plotting something, probably in Marloven Hess. He hasn't given up wanting to make himself king."

Yeres disappeared.

Efael had to work fast, because he knew Imry was plotting as much as Aldon. That sudden appearance, "warning" Efael away from Imar, could only mean one thing: Imry was trying to get a wedge between the Host and Efael himself. He had to block Imry from access to Imar in addition to all these other fronts.

He set out the pearlescent capture-sphere and hastened through the blood poison spell, altering it to focus specifically on humans, avoiding the horses. Those horses the Marlovens rode needed to carry their warriors all the way to the southern coast without falling down the second day: the poison spell, he reflected with pleasure, if released, would really hurt. He needed that extra control, since (at least so far) Ilerian had not given him the wherewithal to recapture them in another sphere if they did prove to be "unruly."

Then he transferred to the Marloven border, which he'd reinforced with pretty much everyone left at Larkadhe, in addition to the toughest survivors Bostian had left behind. The outer perimeter sentries spotted them. Efael turned his back on them, knowing he would be recognized, and an aide should be along before he actually needed one.

He peered to the north, and here was the broad, snowy field he remembered. He did the magic to release the capture-sphere. *VOOM*—a ring of air punched outward. He braced against the buffet and its accompanying reek of hot metal, and waited impatiently as the Marlovens got control of their animals and reined into formation.

There, where the banners on spears clustered. That tall blond man had to be Ivandred. Efael strode among them and snapped his fingers to get the man's attention. "You feel a little queasy?" he said in Norsundrian. "It's a blood poison spell, a warning. You should be able to fight just fine. Aren't you the best in the world?"

Ivandred sat there on his horse, unmoving.

Did he hear? Efael lifted his voice. "As long as you obey my commands, you will experience nothing worse. My command is simple: you ride straight south, burning every house in your way, and killing every male over ten. I want a swathe of destruction down the center of Marloven Hess, to teach them obedience. When you reach the southern border, I'll give you the antidote, and further orders. If you have done well, it will probably be to occupy your former homeland. Or you'll go to Sartor, and retake that, if you like. Please me—become my right arm—and you can have anything you want. Understood?"

The Marloven king hesitated, then said, "Understood." His breath froze in the air, and fell.

Efael pointed to tents on the horizon. "There is my local army. They are holding the border. Show them a real Marloven charge!"

The First Lancers listened in silence, their attention on their king.

Efael sighed, wondering how long it would take to get them all into position. Assassination was so much faster.

Ivandred gazed at Efael as Efael waited for words of obedience.

Not long after Ivandred of Marloven Hesea had ridden into the land of twilight, the treacherous Herskalt had come to him, but he wore not the garb of the Marloven warrior. He had arrayed himself in a short coat of gray, made high on the neck, over black trousers and riding boots, and Ivandred understood then that he was a creature of the Norsundrians.

The Herskalt had said, "You may blame me for betrayal, and I will not gainsay, but it is the excellence of your skills of war that brought you under the eye of those who would make war a way of life."

As a very young man, Ivandred might have argued with that, but his trip across the continent had shown him other ways of living. Those ways had brought him Lasva.

Ivandred had raised a hand, signifying he comprehended so far. Indeed, he comprehended more, in that he understood this language the Herskalt spoke in, which was Sartoran and yet not Sartoran.

"It is the Norsundrian tongue," the Herskalt said—his thoughts following Ivandred's own, as had happened so many times. Ivandred had believed once that their thoughts paralleled one another's in the way of two warriors. Now, it seemed, there was another cause, probably related to the dark magic the Herskalt had taught him.

"You betrayed me," he said.

"I did," the Herskalt replied. "I brought you here before those deemed more dangerous could. They still believe that you cleave to their purpose, which is to fight to be fighting. They will use you to destroy the world for their pleasure. What I have striven to do is to give you a choice, when it comes to pass. You will not get even that, if you choose to follow them." And with these words, the Herskalt raised his hand, and the twilight world of gray opened onto a garden under a garish light, wherein sat a man with long white hair. At his feet, a young man with a sharply boned face and curling black hair shorn at the neck. He was dressed in black.

"The one on the throne is the eater of souls, who commands this place," the Herskalt said. "The one at his feet deems himself a commander, though he is merely an assassin. There are others," and the Herskalt had shown them to Ivandred, but in the two instances he had been brought out of the twilight, he had seen these others not.

The Herskalt had said at the end of the parley, "Though it may feel as if you left Darchelde last night, four centuries have passed, and the world is very different. These two will destroy it if they can."

"Lasva?" Ivandred said, intending to neither believe nor disbelieve.

"Four hundred years brings the changes you would expect," the Herskalt said. "Your descendant through Lasva's son sits upon the Marloven throne. Lasva finished out her life not in Choreid Dhelerei, but near Sindan-An, in a house where she made a garden. It stands to this day."

Then he was gone, and though Ivandred had hardened his heart against the man who had seemed a tutor and a guide, when he and the First Lancers were brought out into the world again, it was the white-haired man who brought them, and ordered them to fight, and if they fought well, they would be free.

Ivandred and the First Lancers fought, but Ivandred had

seen in his opponents' eyes that these were no enemy. The First Lancers smashed through these opponents. Then Ivandred signaled to disengage rather than chase and slaughter the shattered remains of that army, and to ride downwind from battle to freedom. But though they had devastated this enemy who was no enemy at the first charge, they were not permitted to ride. It was all as the Herskalt had said. The man with white hair lied, forcing them back into the magical prison; before they vanished entirely he said that the First Lancers would fight or die at his pleasure.

Now, here they were again in the world. The one with the sharp face, and an aura of death, had smirked as he described the poison in their blood, and then ordered them to kill Marlovens. Not warriors, but men and boys, and burn their houses to the ground.

Ivandred raised his hand, signifying understanding. "We will seek the right ground," he said. "This place, it is too near water. Our horses will swiftly mire, and be blown before they reach the enemy lines."

Efael shrugged. He knew nothing of charges, other than rare splinters of childhood memory: a tumbled chariot, a wheel spinning slowly in a hot wind, and beyond, where the brothel had lain, the burnt ruins of buildings, and a field of bones on which carrion crows hopped, and picked, cawing and cawing.

He turned to the expected Black Knife, who always carried transfer tokens. "Report as soon as they begin. I want to watch. I'll be at Imar."

The Black Knife saluted crisply, and Efael transferred back to Imar, as much to leave such memories as to get back to the seat of power. He had to be there at Svir's right hand if anything changed; he would use that to gain ascendance over Aldon at last, and over Imry as well, still maddeningly at large.

Chwahir border- above Narad

It was so very cold, dangerously so. Jilo was glad that David had taught him how to raise his inner fire, but he longed for a real fire. For moments. Just to warm this frozen bread.

He searched around, found a twig, and snapped a vagabond fire into existence. Surely that was safe—it was so easy—practically illusion, not like regular spells at all, which were too dangerous to use. Oh, it felt so good to warm his hands through his gloves. He fished for his bread, held it out…

Transfer magic sparkled. Jilo recoiled, then gazed into the sharp-cut face of a girl of eighteen or twenty. She had the black hair common to Chwahir, but not their pale skin. Jilo tried to swallow in a throat tight with new fear: she'd used dark magic. Who would fearlessly use dark magic so close to Chwahirsland? This had to be Yeres, sister to the horrible Efael.

Yeres of the Host.

"Wan-Edhe wants you—" she began.

Another flicker, and here was a tall young man. His lip curled when he saw Yeres. He glanced at Jilo briefly, then away, as if he was not worth noticing.

"Imry! You came," Yeres cooed.

"Didn't I say I would?" he replied, and forcefully thrust Jilo away. "Yeres is mine."

Poor Jilo hadn't a hope of regaining his balance. He heard Yeres laughing as he slid in the icy slush and hit the ground with a splat. Imry stepped in his place, one hand reaching up to catch the long ribbon fluttering in the wind from her hair.

Yeres uttered a delighted trill, for of course that shove was jealous spite. "You really think I'd take an interest in a Chwahir? Wan-Edhe wants this idiot. We're going to use him to trade for bindings."

"Bindings?" Imry Llyenthur said.

"Stone spell bindings. Wan-Edhe went to all the trouble to do the work, so why should I have to toil? Did you know that Aldon is slipping his followers into Marloven Hess? We think he's posing as reinforcements to the troublemakers, so he can take them from within. Efael wants me to go in there and drop stone spells on them all, but he also wants *you*. And here you are! But I want you first."

"And here I am," Imry said, running his hand up the ribbon toward her hair.

She stood poised to use any of the instant and lethal magics she always had ready. This had been such a long chase, and as he said, here he was at last. She blinked, the poppies blending real with dream.

"I thought it time to let you catch me," he said, and she tittered with anticipation. Oh, it was real.

On the word *catch*, he reached a finger toward her chin,

and she laughed again, taking a step toward him, the poppies enhancing the dream-quality of the moment. His hand curved toward her cheek as if to caress it as the other hand followed the ribbon to the knot of curls at the back of her head. Then, still smiling, he closed his hands at either side of her skull, and twisted. Hard.

Jilo recoiled at the loud snap! Yeres's triumphant gaze blanked, staring in disbelief at the sky. Imry lifted his hands, stepped away, and she flopped on the ground, dead.

Then he reached down to haul Jilo to his feet. Jilo tried to scramble back, forgetting everything David had drilled into him as he waited for his own neck to be snapped. But Imry brushed a clump of snow off Jilo's ear, then spoke, quite naturally—as if he hadn't just killed someone—"I wanted to ask you. Would you consider taking on a very skilled communications desk ... scribe, I guess you'd call him?"

Jilo stared at Imry Llyenthur, who was in the process of wiping his hands on the edge of the dead woman's cloak. He straightened up, his mouth crimped in disgust, then he turned his back on the corpse as Jilo croaked, "What?"

"Duin. Fassler is his first name, and I think his actual family name was Bi or Di or Do. Something like that, but he goes as Fassler Duin. I have no idea what, if anything, these various names mean in Chwahir. I'm trying to find a place for him."

Jilo's mouth opened. *But isn't he your follower?* he wanted to ask. Of course he was. Why would Jilo want a Norsunder spy planted on him?

Llyenthur waited as Jilo stared at him. They'd said this Imry Llyenthur had been kicked out of his command. Had he left Norsunder? He'd just killed one of the Host. Still didn't make him an ally.

Jilo shook his head; "left Norsunder" implied questions that many were going to find nearly impossible to answer. Including the Chwahir, who were put under Norsundrian command by their king. Who had, early on, fought and killed for Norsunder.

He focused on what mattered. "Do you want to take over Chwahirsland?"

"No," Llyenthur said, hands raised as if pushing something away. "No, no, no. Madness. For what it's worth, I don't intend to ever see Duin again. But he was loyal—Aldon tried to kill him for it. And he works hard."

"Bo? Or Bi?" Jilo repeated, his mind still swimming around and around, then grabbing at another floating twig.

"All I know is, he was a cull at a very young age, and his birth name is something short. Bi, or Da, or Bo, something similar. He really hates Wan-Edhe," Llyenthur added.

Jilo understood immediately: the army culls from commoners were clumped together, given the name Bo if there were enough of them to put into a twi (in the days when twis were permitted) and the leftovers, at the very bottom of the ranks, were Bi. If Duin was a Bi, joining Norsunder would probably have seemed a step up.

"If he comes back, and works, he will not be turned away," Jilo said, aware that this was his first difficult decision. But not his last.

Llyenthur gave Jilo a whack on the shoulder. "Carry on. But. If you want to get wherever it is you're going, no more magic. Certainly not the old magic."

Jilo's lips moved, "...vagabond."

"Jilo, that *is* old magic. Yeres laid a ward with your name on it, and spread it all through these mountains. Gnaw your bread cold! The closer you get to Narad, the more wards will be lurking. You ought to know that."

"I thought that would be within Narad," Jilo began to mumble. "That I'd be safe out here as long as I didn't do any regular spells, and walked—"

But Imry Llyenthur had already vanished, leaving Jilo staring down at Yeres's corpse. He was aware of a sense of sorrow for a life so suddenly ended, for in death her face was so young and peaceful.

She had also been a killer. He turned away. The Words of Disappearance were there in mind, one of the mysteries. Would using them set off one of those wards? If it did, it did. He would not leave anyone, even an enemy, to rot in the open air.

He said the words, and when she vanished, leaving barely a print in the wind-stirred snow, he continued on down the trail, gnawing his frozen bread.

Twenty-five

THE PROBLEM WITH USING light magic in a duel was its inherent weakness. Svir found it more distracting than challenging to keep dispersing the mages' attempts to weaken the Imar enchantment by targeting the life forms within it. This mage freed the birds — or tried to. That one, the hedgerows. A third, the oaks. The more specific the spell, the more effort it took to dissolve the attempts. That was not saying much.

Unexpectedly, Ilerian had not yet defeated Detlev, who hid behind a thick shield. Svir sensed a number of minds behind that shield, pooling their strength. No one had tried such a thing since the old days, at the end of the previous defeat. By then, they had learned that Ilerian's power was greater than any one of them on their own, and the hapless fools had to invent the concept of banding together behind shields for defense, when they hadn't had the slightest notion about how to make war in the mental realm. Too little, too late. *How* he had utterly loathed the dyranarya, and their maudlin there-is-no-civilization-without-peace chatter. Human beings are predators, he liked to remind his minions in the Garden. King of the predators, the world their prey.

Given that, there was an order of magnitude above human, and Ilerian was right here, still striving. Svir was aware that he was at fault for believing that Detlev had been utterly defeated back when they had begun their magnificent undertaking. But he *was!* His abasement had been quite thorough—Svir had seen to that. To make certain of him, they'd made him carry out the bloodiest retributions personally, as Svir watched and Ilerian savored.

Svir waved off another set of spells, spending immense power to make it easier. One comfort: Detlev couldn't win. He was human, and even the most disciplined human still tired if you waited long enough, whereas Ilerian could jettison his human form if he so desired—*it* so desired. Except then he'd lose the savor of his enemies' despair, humiliation, and sorrow in defeat. Ilerian was addicted to the zest of personal loss, but he had to be in human form to get the most pleasure out of it.

Alas, he tended to display a human's impatience when thwarted. It was perhaps better to deflect that before he emerged from the mental realm to indulge his temper.

Svir leaned forward, addressing the air. "Kessler Sonscarna, did you really think I would not recognize a window? I know you are listening. You care as little about the expenditure of magic as I do." Now came the guesswork. Kessler would not watch unless his boy was part of that shield; from all reports, Kessler cared nothing for anyone else. "If you lift your ward from the world—it's going to be broken imminently anyway—then I will exempt your boy from annihilation when Ilerian brings Detlev to heel once again."

In Roth Drael, the watchers reacted with surprise and consternation. And amusement—that was Kessler. He leaned forward, still and intent.

"What was that?" Erai-Yanya had jerked upright, her eyes round in horror.

Yanli exclaimed, "It's a trap."

"Of course it is," Kessler stated flatly, without turning from the window. "But I have plans of my own."

He did, too. The Host had always been very careful never to let anyone see them make a portal between the Beyond and the world. It had been the same with Detlev and Siamis, when they were in Norsunder. Kessler did not care whether their shift from Norsunder to the lighters was real or not. He had one desire: to take the Beyond for his own, for he could use that power for a righteous cause. He had never abandoned his plan to systematize ruling, permitting power only to those with equivalent merit. If he straightened out the world's governments, there would never be another Wan-Edhe.

It had taken him years to prepare for this day. Not even Dirk knew the extent of his plans, for he, too, must earn merit before being brought in.

Quick Svir and Ilerian might be, but now Kessler had only a single word and gesture left to perform, which would be quicker. He began to finish the spells he'd prepared as secondary measures, as back in Imar, Svir looked around, deciding that a demonstration might be in order. He remembered the brats, still caught in the partial stone spell, and said to June, "The cup." He held out his hand in an indolent gesture that still managed to be peremptory.

June's mouth tightened. Before she could refuse, Svir made a gesture of casual cruelty, tugging at the cup so hard that it broke her fingers. She gasped in shock and pain; she would have fallen to her knees if the partial stone spell had not forced her to stand where she was, the cup still gripped in her other hand. She thought bleakly, *so that's how it's going to be. No matter what world you go to, if there are humans, there will be thugs like this guy.*

But then Svir saw Kessler appear at the terrace door.

Kessler didn't bother talking to Svir, who he didn't believe anyway. He remained on the terrace, out of the reach of the partial stone spell that he could feel, and with care and deliberation, he reversed his great world-binding ward.

Every mage who understood world transfer felt the snap: Sartorias-deles was now free to transfer to and from.

And so was Norsunder-Beyond.

"Ah," Svir said, and brought his hand down sharply in summons.

Kessler readied his word—a single word—and the Beyond would be his.

Then he, Ilerian, and Svir stared at the portal that opened with sunlight shining through.

Sunlight? They gazed in shock at the utterly empty shell of the Beyond.

"What have you done?" The voice, unrecognizable with anguish, belonged to Kessler.

And so he was unaware as Efael's thin-bladed dueling

dagger attacked from behind, slicing from ear to ear. Kessler's spirit fled—snatched at too late by Ilerian, whose towering anger struck even faster than Efael: denied Kessler, he ignored the gnats in the room, and blue lightning writhed from chair to chair.

Svir screamed, and screamed again, until his voice ranged high and inhuman. Then his desiccated corpse sagged sideways as Ilerian's form glowed with renewed power.

And returned to the attack.

Marloven Hess – northern border

The triumph that Van Stad, now commander of what was left of the Marloven army, experienced at the sight of pirate ships crashing on the rocks off Tarual in the middle of a blizzard did not last.

When the snows cleared away, leaving a sky the color of watery milk, the winter sun barely clearing the distant blue peaks in the north, it was to discover that the Norsundrian patrol along the border had thickened considerably.

He stood with Jan Senelac. Both peered northward, one with his hands tucked in his armpits, the other blowing on much-darned mittens. Supplies were even shorter than the numbers who could fight, Stad thought grimly.

Van Marlovair rode up and dismounted. "Looks like their orders have changed," he remarked.

No one argued. The Norsundrians had patrolled in line-of-sight to keep the Marlovens from slipping over the border and away; now, all the signs were there of an impending action.

Stad issued orders to be ready for defense, which would begin with adapting some of Ghaer's water tricks to keep the enemy from an easy crossing of the ice-slick river.

But nothing happened that day, or the next.

Morning of the third, he was just drinking down the wash-water dregs of much-used scalded coffee beans when one of Jan's runners burst into the tent, and gabbled as she saluted, "Did you hear that, Commander?"

"I thought I heard thunder boom," he remarked. "It's not impossible in winter, though rare."

"No, it was only one thunderbolt, only it wasn't thunder. Short Lnand saw it. She said a big wind happened, and knocked some of them down. We felt it, too, like a—a sudden gust of wind, but *whew* did it stink, like a forge at the end of a workday. Only, um, you better come look for yourself, she says. The banner—ah, Braids Lnand said to report to you that we don't like to say." These last few words were a mumble.

Stad flung aside his cup and hauled his cloak over his coat as he strode out of the tent. He stared through the field glass. And though the air was so clear you could count the feathers on an eagle half a day away, as they say, he breathed on the glass, wiped it on his coat, and looked again.

Still there: banners, black and gold. Not the plain rectangles of today, but longer, with streamers hanging down. Black, and in the center, not the screaming eagle, but a golden, raptorish fox face.

Stad peered at those banners, which were forbidden, and yet everybody over the age of twelve or so recognized them. Irresistible to thirteen-year-old boys, to draw the Fox Banner that had first been Inda's, then centuries later belonged to the Bloody First Lancers, led by Ivandred-Harvaldar. A name stricken from the records, and only spoken of as a cautionary tale. But everybody knew that tale as well as they knew the banner.

Stad swept the glass from the banners to the warriors astride the horses. They wore their braided hair high, and their coats were long, brushing the tops of their boots.

Stad's heart drummed.

"I can't believe it," Van Marlovair whispered, stepping beside him. "I wouldn't believe it, except for all those rumors about Inda coming back again."

"One for us, one against us?" Dannor Keriam asked, shouldering aside Van Marlovair in the easy way of someone known since childhood and related by marriage.

"Signal, shield line," Stad said bleakly. "All the stories say they would attack with a charge." He turned his head. "Captain Keriam, what can you do about that ice?"

"Captain Ghaer is preparing something now," Dannor said. "Beginning with spear catapults."

Clouds had begun to streak the sky, gradually blocking the sunlight, which rendered the world in shades of gray and brown by the time the Norsundrians had formed up behind the First Lancers, making it plain that the legendary wing of the best and fasted cavalry warriors in the world were expected to take the brunt of Stad's defense.

Ghaer's people huddled off to one side, behind a row of wagons, waiting for a signal to deploy. They had prepared a variety of defensive measures, from spear catapults to bags of carefully rounded pebbles that, when strewn across ice, would trip up horses, threatening broken legs. Stad watched the silent line on the other side of the river, motionless except for the rising wind toying with hair, manes, and the skirts of those long sashed coats.

The First Lancers began to move forward at a slow walk. Stad raised his hand in signal, and horns blasted the alert. Gear jingled and bows creaked as the skirmishers on the outside, and the longbow archers behind them, nocked arrows in readiness for the signal to shoot.

The First Lancers' horses walked toward the river, a perfect line, the riders' lances held upright. How could something so beautiful be so deadly, Stad thought as he watched the walk gradually become a trot, every horse precisely on a beat, though he could not see the drummer. How could something so deadly be so beautiful?

The trot quickened. The distance between the First Lancers and the Norsundrians widened as it shortened to the riverside. Were the First Lancers to fight alone? No, the Norsundrians began to form up in ragged clumps, a contrast to the First Lancers' unnerving discipline. The Norsundrians' distant voices rose like the caws of crows as they called insults to be carried over the river. Laughter.

The central figure of that perfect line raised a fist, and the entire line turned, each horse at precisely the same moment: twenty-seven of them to the right, twenty-seven to the left, and the twenty-seven in the middle, including the pale-haired king.

The lances came down, level to the ground, and the horses sprang into a gallop. And charged the Norsundrians.

The First Lancers hit the enemy straight on, with a crashing impact that carried over the cold air, to devastating effect. A few moments' total shock on both sides, and then Stad recovered, signaling his own charge. To Dannor's surprised face, he bellowed, "They're *for* us!"

She flung up a hand, acknowledging the need for a change in tactics.

Unseen by Stad, the astonished, then furious Black Knife transferred away; ten, fifteen heartbeats later, when Stad and his force was halfway to the battle to reinforce Ivandred's wing, he saw the First Lancers jerk in their saddles, as if an invisible wind had struck them all, but they recovered and fought on.

And in Imar, Efael having awakened the dormant poison spell, cursed at his inability to drag them back into the capture-sphere. But after what had just happened to Svir, he must be very careful not to interrupt Ilerian. He exclaimed in a murderous undervoice, "Go back. New orders: kill them all!"

The Black Knife transferred away. Then, looking for someone to vent his temper on, Efael noticed the gaggle of girls still littering the library, red-faced in their slow struggle against the partial stone spell, and pulled a knife in each hand.

For Detlev and the circle, there was no knowing how long they had been striving against Ilerian. It could have been six hours, or six months, in the world's time. The distinction was almost meaningless anyway, for while they contested with Ilerian, they were partly pulled into timelessness, their bodies suspended by the magic over the sanctuary.

The only sure thing was this dangerous exhaustion. When Ilerian so suddenly shifted his attention otherwhere, they gasped as if they'd been running in full armor. It *felt* like it had been six months.

Detlev was aware of enervation, but hid it. "Get some water. Food. Sleep, even if it's for less than a sandglass of time. Be ready for the call. He's not done with us."

It was difficult to move, but they stirred and separated. And when Ilerian attacked again, this time with such power they all felt the increase as an internal blow, there was no forming a circle again. They dropped where they were, reaching for one another by instinct.

It had been difficult before, but this time was so very much worse.

Dismay ringed the circle: Ilerian had found access to more force. Where had he taken it from? Whom had he killed? Had he regained access to the Beyond? To Mearsies Heili and Clair, perhaps Siamis? There was no knowing, only that they were being pressed with inexorable power, as if squeezed into a container the size of a cup.

This, Detlev knew, was failure.

He had nearly broken past the defenses to discover what Ilerian hid, but almost was not enough. It was time, while he was conscious, to preserve the others as long as he could, and cut free—killing himself in the process, to deny Ilerian the use of his own dwindling strength.

He readied. Then he faltered, his last lingering thought on Sveneric, to whom he dared not reach.

And in that hesitation, that pressure abruptly lifted.

Adam, the most perceptive outside of Detlev himself, was the first to sense the warmth, the brightness that he did not recognize, but then Detlev did, too.

"Marga?" he said aloud, as in that desecrated manor house in ruined Imar, a new figured appeared on the terrace, and threw open the doors with a gesture.

Marga had given up wearing shoes, as it felt so much more natural to go barefoot. In this way, she could feel the living world and its magic beneath her feet. The cold of winter had ceased to trouble her; it was a small matter of will to ward the effects of ice.

But the moment she stepped into that library, she staggered, bewildered by the dead affect beneath her feet. For the first time in half a year she was utterly cut off from the world. Nothing lived around her, above her, beneath her, aside from the cluster of people in the library.

But she was not alone.

Ilerian had returned from the successful attack in an eyeblink, for he, too sensed that advent of a new star, and looked with interest as Marga crossed the library, the stone spell melting around her.

For the first time in uncounted centuries, the stirrings of physical interest caused Ilerian to raise a hand, and shift the both of them to another room, where a couch sat facing a broad window that had once overlooked a lake. Marga regarded him with curiosity. His smile was mild, his amber eyes curiously lightless to her perception. Behind him the fire leaping on the grate seemed somehow weak and counterfeit.

No whisper of the world in this tower room. Ilerian watched her patiently as her solemn gaze took in the plain room, the fine rug on the floor, the carved wooden couch with its satin cushions. The wide windows no longer overlooked the lake because the strength of the wards here had so warped the light that it conveyed no image. Just eternal shadow, for this room had become the center of Ilerian's domain, and he did not need to see with his eyes when he could see so much sharper and so much farther with his mind.

Marga had no access to the world's magic through air, or ground. Her puny physical strength would be no match for his. But she had all the qualities she'd ever had, long before she bonded with the world: joy, curiosity, love, hope, and above all faith in everyone who manifested even the tiniest semblance of faith in return, whether it was in the trusting gaze of a puppy, or in the hard-won compassion of the aged, or in the confidence of the farm folk that the world would bloom again in spring.

"Sit down," Ilerian said.

Marga sat, fists on her knees.

He sat down next to her, stretching his arm along the back of the couch, so that his fingertips lightly touched her forehead; when she moved her head aside, he laughed. His mind was completely open to her. To perceive it was like looking across an endless pool of ice, frozen and opaque, lightless white. His thought moved over it like slow lightning: *Have you seen the other one, Ejhir? He was dark, like you.*

"I have seen them all, in world memory," she replied aloud, and the lightning struck.

The last sirei-atanrial—perhaps because then the world had required such—had been a loner, more in harmony with the non-living portions of the world than with the walkers on its face. Closed away in Norsunder for seemingly limitless time, he had at last surrendered in despair.

But Marga had absolute faith in the world and its life, and though she could not draw magic from beneath her feet, she had not come unprepared.

Ilerian was wide open to her because sirei-atanrial do not—cannot—attack. They are unable to destroy. Nor did she try. Sunlight she carried in her right hand and in her left: she opened her palms, both in the real world and in the realm of the mind, and as Ilerian laughed at this puny gesture, her faith requited: Detlev was waiting.

His focus, thin as a needle, threaded through the center of that sunlight…

And was at last inside.

In that instant, Detlev saw in Marga's light that he had been right about Ilerian's true nature: the predator could prison, and feed off of, souls, but it could not actually absorb that which sparked life any more than it could create life. There before Detlev extended rank on rank of tightly cocooned souls, stripped of all sensation, memory, and identity. Rank on rank of naked life force, absorbed with excruciating slowness through the filaments of the cocoons. Those were the conduit of Ilerian's power.

Detlev's needle of focus had pulled Marga's effulgence within, and he scattered it wide. The moment the light touched those cocoons, they burned to ash, freeing the prisoned life essences, pinpoints of starry radiance.

Ilerian howled.

Winds of darkness hurled across the immensity, but wind cannot touch sunlight: though these were not true winds, nor true sunlight, the effect was the same, and what had once been a devouring manifestation dissolved into fragments that spun away into nothing as, in the mental realm, a vast bridge of brilliant stars arced across the entire horizon, witnessed in wonder by all the worlds who had the wherewithal to perceive. Then they were gone. Sped into the infinite, leaving Detlev alone, a mote yearning for the bliss of inenarrable freedom.

Twenty-six

DETLEV SLAMMED BACK INTO the physical world.

He drew a shuddering breath in a chest that ached, then another, as memory prisoned him again within his identity. *Siamis?*

Images flowed between them, too fast for words: Svir dead, Ilerian's latest victim—Ilerian utterly destroyed—Clair still in the Dei mansion, surrounded by her protective girls, all targets themselves—Kessler dead by Efael's hand—Marga there, with Efael at large.

Detlev opened his eyes as the others in the sanctuary stirred. Sveneric turned his way, question in his gaze. The need of the dyranarya to reassure transcended the clamor of sensations, bringing the strangeness of the unexpected resolution: *Ilerian's gone. I am here.*

Sveneric said nothing, but his eyes gathered light, which spilled over into tears. And there was the absolution of that ineffable bond, son for father, and father for son.

"We won, yes? No?" Laban said, going to the cascade of fresh water. He drank, gasped, drank again, then ducked his head in it and shook like a dog, spraying droplets all over Mildred and Andri, who were right behind him.

Andri scooped water into his hands, slurped it, then, with his chin dripping, gasped, "Ilerian … fainted? Called for a cup of wine? I can't believe he's gone."

"*It's* gone," Detlev said. And then forced himself to rise.

"But not the dangers. Marga was there, in Imar. She provided the distraction that enabled our final attack. I don't yet know the circumstances of her appearance there, or how much danger she might still be in."

David and Adam looked up from the pool. "I'll go," they said, their voices clashing.

Everyone was either drinking thirstily or had fallen into the pool outright. They were still integrated mentally with one another, painfully so, the effect in the physical world a little like someone shouting in one's ear.

"Leave Imar to me," Detlev said.

"Still protecting us?" David said, laughing. "Detlev, Ilerian is gone."

Detlev smiled back, and released the ancient spell that had formed a shell around them.

Senrid was the first to transfer out, and David the second.

In the Dei manor library, June gripped the cup in her one functioning hand, fighting the sluggishness of the partial stone spell as Efael advanced, dissolving the partial stone spell around himself, so that the others were still ensnared. The First Lancers were surely feeling the penalty of their stupidity now. He could have his fun here, cutting up these brats, and still get back there in time to watch them die.

With a grin of anticipation, Kessler's blood still wet on that thin blade, Efael advanced on June.

Who strained to get the cup past her hip to where she could see it. But she didn't need to see it, did she? She remembered what she had done there, out in the desert, and shut her eyes against the advancing menace. She couldn't do anything about him anyway. She concentrated on sucking the sluggish evil spell into the cup. Had her arm moved a tiny bit faster?

And wham! Out of nowhere bombed a small figure as Dhana rammed straight into Efael's side. Then she flickered out of reach and back to the terrace, gasping, as CJ yelled, "Good one, Dhana!"

Denied the one, Efael turned his cruel gaze to CJ. He backhanded her across the face, laughing at her slow fall in the grip of the partial stone spell. He'd cut her to ribbons slowly, one tendon at a time—

Imry Llyenthur walked in and looked around with an air of a bumpkin just arrived at a market on festival day. Except he was fully armed, the black sword at his back, knife hilts in his boot tops, sleeves, and at one hip.

"What's happening?" he asked. To Efael's annoyance, Imry had already dissolved the partial stone spell around himself. "You." Imry addressed CJ on the floor, his back to June. "What are you brats doing here? Want some help finding the way out?" He kicked the air, miming a boot in the butt.

"Is that supposed to be help, or just bullying?" CJ demanded, recognizing him without any enthusiasm.

"Oh, help, help," Imry replied, palms up.

CJ scowled. "Who are you helping?" she asked.

"Good question," said Efael, smiling with vicious intent. "Answer it."

"Myself," Imry said, clearly surprised it wasn't obvious.

"*You*," CJ uttered, glaring at Efael as she struggled to rise. "I know who you are. You're the one that tortured Diana. I'm gonna make sure you never do that again!"

Efael laughed, and brought his knife around—

That was when David arrived. He muttered a counter to the partial stone spell, ending it. Then he spotted Svir's corpse in the wingback chair, and hid his exultation. No time for that. "You really are a turd, Efael," he said, drawing from his belt the Ildareth dagger that Imry had carried so briefly weeks before.

Efael's sharp face turned, as Imry faded into the shadows of the archway opposite the terrace door. Efael pulled a second blade, and altered his stance, awaiting a much more promising fight.

Behind them, June's cup began—very faintly—to glow; released from the stone spell, she held the cup between one hand and the wrist of the other, wincing at the painful throb of her fingers.

David and Efael circled and from time to time feinted or lunged, hands blurring fast, Efael with a knife held along each forearm, blade out. David smiled, but he was tired from the circle. He knew he could not win this one, even if he had two blades. He hoped he'd come out of it alive.

CJ picked herself up from the floor, and shakily wiped

back her hair. Her face around the cuts and the forming bruise from Efael's blow was the color of paper, her eyes blue and intense. "No," she gasped. "Not until I know he'll never do it again."

And—desperate, hopeless, but determined to the last—she tucked her head down and charged once more, causing a desperate flurry of action, and a crack of laughter from Efael, who stepped aside, shifting so that the angry girl would run straight onto his blade and impale herself. A tangle of metal, limbs, and hair, then CJ was propelled by David to safety, but in his half-turn Efael struck hard and fast. David whirled away, but not before the blade ripped through his shoulder and across his back.

CJ fell to her knees and choked on a sob. She hurt all over, but the horror of memory of similar abuse when she was small, the intensity of her vow over Diana's dead body, forced her to her feet.

Then gentle hands caught her arms and steadied her as she tried to rise. Soothing mind-touch briefly eased some of the pain-haze and awakened grief, and she looked up through tear-blurry eyes into Detlev's face. "Will you permit me to resolve this matter for you?" he asked.

Sick with pain, heart-wrung, she gulped. "Do it."

"David."

Detlev took a step toward the two. David had shifted the blade to his left hand, his right hanging useless as blood dripped down onto the white tiles. He tossed the knife, spinning, and Detlev plucked it out of the air.

Clutching his shoulder, David backed up, keeping himself between Efael and June, who alone did not watch the two on the terrace, but stood with the gleaming cup still outstretched, the glittering air above it swirling with dreamlike slowness.

Efael stared into Detlev's face, seeing the marks of exhaustion there, and laughed. Svir was dead, which put Efael on top at last. All he had to do was prolong this duel, until Detlev fell flat. Then what, hamstring him? Cut him to ribbons while he flopped around? What sweetness, to be known forever as the one who took Detlev down.

He muttered his transfer spell: Yeres would thoroughly enjoy watching, and maybe even give him a cut or two, once Detlev was at their feet. Only she did not come. Odd.

Siamis arrived then, whispering to Dhana to collect the girls and get them out of there. He eased past Falinneh and got his first look at Detlev's set face, and the lines of tension from what had to be a ferocious headache. Dread tightened his chest; he spotted Imry, who spotted him. Impasse, Siamis thought. Make a move on Detlev and it will be your last.

Imry raised a hand in ironic salute.

Detlev paid no heed to either of them. He was tired, desperately so, but he had stayed alive this long by being able to gauge precisely how far he could go — and when to focus the last of his strength; Efael, who already had the advantage with two blades, was obviously planning to make the fight last.

Efael shouted, "Yeres! Are you upstairs? Where is Ilerian? Tell him to come down and play."

"Oh, she's dead," Imry said from the archway. "And … I'm not sure about Ilerian."

Efael's head snapped toward Imry, faster than a striking snake.

Imry dusted his hands. "But Yeres? Quite dead. Deader than dead."

In a venomous undervoice, Efael muttered vile taunts, all references to the past, so vile that CJ, hearing some of it, did not comprehend. Nor did she want to, for his tone was enough to make her flinch.

But Detlev did not hear. The voice spewing sordid imputations was distant noise. This time, unlike four thousand years ago, there was no sister to cheat, and no helpless prisoner to protect. He knew he had the wherewithal to strike once, fast, and so he watched for his moment.

David observed with clinical appreciation, and CJ in apprehensive wonder, the rare sight of Detlev moving in for the kill as Efael flung himself to the attack. Detlev seemed to flow straight through the middle of that fury of blows, shifting just enough to block or deflect, until the black-handled knife slid straight between Efael's ribs and into his heart.

Efael gasped, fingers scrabbling at the hilt, his vision fading. He looked for his twin, for reprieve, for the mercy he had never granted, or been granted, and found nothing.

He fell to the floor near Svir's feet as CJ sobbed quietly, "He's gone, Diana."

Siamis turned away to hide the visceral pleasure that

gripped him, for there was no room in his heart for compassion, not for these two who had utterly destroyed his family, and his world, and who had exulted for centuries over the doing.

Detlev leaned against the wall, hair in his eyes, looking down. Unlike Siamis, he found little to rejoice in. Efael and Yeres had been unceasing enemies, their careers characterized by vicious horrors, but he had seen in the siblings' bond, twisted as it was, what the two might have been before they were perverted beyond redemption, and Svirle had set them loose on the world.

"Here you all are. I got lost in the other wing." Marga ran past Imry with a slight smile over her shoulder. Both brothers watched her as she gestured, and Efael's, Svir's, and Kessler's bodies vanished.

June paid no heed to any of them. The cup in her hands began to glow and then to coruscate brilliant enough to cause the eyes to tear. A flash and quiet snap at June's broken fingers. She gasped, shook her hand, then used her palm to help hold the cup as in the air above it appeared a faint twisting line of black, like a funnel of air and darkness.

The glow expanded to a globe of pearlescent light. June's thick mat of hair began to lift, silver sparks leaping from one strand to another. Her rumpled, prosaic clothes ruffled slightly in a breeze not of air stirring but of building power. The cup was now too bright to look at directly: the center incandesced blue, like a newborn star.

The blackness thickened, twisting and writhing as the cup lost form altogether, a sphere of radiance, and June slowly drew apart her hands. The light remained where it was, casting its glow over the entire terrace. True light, after more than a year.

Imry's hand swept to his side, not to draw the gold-hilted sword, but to remove it and its sheath from the belt-link. As Siamis and Detlev began to cross the terrace toward him, he ignored them both and called to his brother: "David, catch!"

The sword—still sheathed—arced through the air, and David caught it one-handed, gazing in blank amazement.

"Have fun," Imry added, laughing, and then, with a jaunty wave at Detlev and Siamis, he vanished.

—and the brilliance that had been the Alshi cup, fifth protection, exploded in white light.

Dazed, those still standing recoiled, blinking. CJ

scrambled to her feet and stumbled to Clair, whose gaze found her, and Sherry, and lifted wearily. "He was hurting Sherry," she whispered. "From the inside."

"I'm sorry, I'm sorry," Sherry sobbed. "I don't know what I did *wroooong*."

"Not your fault. It was that stench-worm tricking you," CJ said to Sherry. "Let's get Clair home."

"Your face," Clair murmured as CJ and Sherry each held one of Clair's arms.

"No worse than when I got kicked around back on Earth," CJ said with typical, and unconvincing, bravado. "Let's scram."

They stumbled out the open terrace doors onto the hill beyond, that had once led into a garden, and took in the vast stretch of land still lifeless and gray in the pure light of a new day.

Winter air soughed over the landscape in slow drafts as David said, "It'll be years before life returns here. Centuries."

"What now?" June asked, blinking. As yet she had not noticed that her hair, though no longer sparking, had remained a pure silver, as if spun from very fine and supple wire. No one had ever called her frizzled brown mat pretty, and it was still frizzled, but it was no longer brown. Even her eyebrows and eyelashes had turned silver.

The Mearsieans completely ignored their surroundings. All their attention was on Clair as Falinneh said with an attempt at cheer, "You'll feel a lot better at home."

"I don't think so," Clair said wearily. "It will remind me of *him*. Everything will remind me of him."

Siamis exchanged a look with Detlev, then said to her, "We have another suggestion. It's one of the things we were striving to protect. A long story—which you can hear one day if you like. Right now, it might be the best place for you, though it will mean sleeping on a plateau that as yet has no buildings. We do have tents."

Clair lifted her gaze to his face. "I need fresh air. Lots of fresh air."

"You will get the freshest."

"I like sleeping in a tent," Clair said, with the tiniest return of her old self.

CJ turned to Detlev. "I don't know if you know. I mean, you always seem to know everything. But I understand

Norsundrian, and I heard that creep say that he did that blood poison spell on some people. Lancers, I think he called them?"

Siamis's head turned sharply. "What?"

CJ repeated herself.

Siamis turned stricken eyes to Detlev. "I was with Efael all the time—almost all—I even caught Svir, when he was being complacent—except a few times when I had to—"

"Go," Detlev said. "I will take Clair to the disirad."

And all three were gone.

Twenty-seven

THE WINTRY WINDS BLEW Fox and his fleet straight up the coast, as they bent to the work of repair—replacing several spars, reinforcing the starboard cut-boom, and above all, yanking the bristle of arrows out of hull and masts, then sanding and refletching them to Fox's exacting standards. The youngest sailors, mostly children of Ghaer's followers who had been on the tenders, had circled about pulling arrows out of the water once the surviving pirates limped away. That bolstered their supply.

Spirits were reasonably good as the current carried them northward: they had driven off the enemy; though the pirates might all be clumped, lying in wait up north, they'd have Ghaer, at least, and maybe more. That was all another day, another sea. Today, they had won.

They did not know that fishers off Parayid had carried back the astonishing news about something that looked like a Venn ship of old emerging from The Narrows as if from lost times, which attacked and drove off a fleet no one had known was coming on the attack. Astonishment, and then equivalent anger, muttered like distant thunder through the coastal lands especially, for the people of Perideth had been forced by their king to house Norsunder "allies" for some time now, and no one saw any benefit, except not being outright killed. And even that was not guaranteed, as there were too many stories about drunken Norsundrians getting into fights with each other, and laying waste all around, or attacking people for no reason. Now everyone was talking of the sea battle led by a dragon ship of old—following which the rescue fleet did not try landing, but sailed north to the Marlovens. Were they Marlovens?

Unaware that he had left behind another eddy of rumor, Fox decided to find Commander Stad again. He'd written to Siamis, but as yet had received only the most cryptic reply yet: *Protect the coast.*

As they sailed, they watched the lines of Chwahir warships, each perfectly on station, tacking and wearing far to the west: Fox was thrown back in memory to the way the Venn had observed the Brotherhood of Blood battle from a distance, then sailed away.

Fox turned his back on them as the lookout hailed the deck, "Tarual in sight."

"We'll offer our aid," Fox said to his first mate. "And it's probably time to find out what's going on in the world. That young Vana, Van Stad ought to know."

The first mate shrugged, still elated from the victory. All the same to him.

The wooden world of a ship is isolated, an island, so it's easy to assume the rest of the world will largely be where they'd been when seen last. The first sign that things had changed more than Fox expected was the sight of timbers still washing up along the shoreline, carried by the current northwards along the shore. Looked like Ghaer had either had a very tough fight, or they had had some superlative ruses deflecting the enemy onto those rocks. Only where were her ships? He swept the seas fast, then more slowly—and caught vague blurs the color of sea and sky. Was that what his own fleet had looked like to the pirates?

Fox signaled for the boat to be lowered, and before he and a party headed for shore, he issued orders for the drakan to stand off the harbor, ready to fight or flee.

By the time they dragged their boat up onto the beach, the hidden watchers had alerted the local defenders, and Fox was relieved to see Ghaer's lugubrious countenance stumping down a steep path cut into the side of the palisade to meet them.

"I'm here, with my people, guarding this inlet, as I said I'd do," she said abruptly. "The prince is north at Lindeth, doing the same. But truth is, I don't know what we can do if those

Chwahir warships decide to land. There has to be two hundred of them. More, like as not."

"I saw them," Fox said. "I also saw fishers, and nobody bothering them. The Chwahir seem to be a vanguard, anyone's guess for whom. Anything else?"

"Not maritime," she said. "But on land, ayah, I don't know what to make of it. I don't think anyone does."

"Which means?"

"It's more people like us." She thumped the front of her shapeless woolen coat. "Famous, infamous. Warriors. But something is wrong with them." She shivered in the cold wind. "Their wounds don't heal. Even so, they fight better than anyone, and they've been leading the locals in clearing out Norsunder. Stad and his people are now following them, though they thought to be against them. But something's wrong when they puke blood after battle." She shook her head. "I don't really understand these people."

"I'm tempted to say that I do, but I'm not sure that's true. Here's what I know. The Chwahir out there have removed the need for us to guard the coast: if they attack Halia, we won't be able to stop them. I'm going to take the Marlovans among my crew—assuming any want to go—and follow the action. If it leads all the way to the royal city, eh, I did always want to see it once before I die."

The action did take Fox and his party—half mariners who had been with him since the days when they first put rubies in their ears on the bloody deck of a pirate trysail, and half his own people from Darchelde—all the way to Choreid Dhelerei. They followed the ruins of Norsundrian garrisons, over which the Marlovens had been flying the black and gold eagle banner, in the teeth of Norsunder's command. That almost began to look like … could the war be over, and Fox had missed the end? Wild rumors were flying—Norsunder retreated but would come again—Sartor was still fighting—the Marlovens were being defended by ghost riders galloping straight out of the days of ballads.

Fox became convinced that the war was over when two captains (one older than Fox, and another not much over sixteen) took one glance at his banner, stared, then offered horses. Inda had once said that you can always tell wartime on land: there's not a horse to be had in any direction for days.

When they sighted the towers of the royal city on the three hills, Fox reflected that he hadn't walked out of the past so much as into the future. Except it did not feel like the future. The snowy plains, the sky, the appearance of a castle on the horizon were a perpetual now.

Outer perimeter scouts encountered them first. Their eyes went to Fox's banner, then to him. The chief scout tapped two fingers to her chest, saying, "Commander Stad's orders are to send you through if you turned up."

Dannor Keriam, or maybe that Senelac scamp, had sent messengers ahead. Fox should have expected that. "What can you tell me about the state of things? Are we needed as reinforcement?"

The scout's eyes flicked from the fox banner back to Fox's face. "Keep your weapons loose. Still rousting out the last of 'em."

Fox and his party formed up for defense and approached what once had been the city gates. Fox assessed in a sweeping gaze. Only one gate remained, partially demolished. Other signs of detritus littered the road as well as the broad street inside the gates. A group of buildings on the west side of the castle looked very much like someone had been using them as target practice for mangonel catapults.

Fox halted when a familiar figure emerged from a crowd of armed civilians roaming about in the dirty slush, their voices angry. "Siamis," Fox exclaimed, and when the blond young man reached them, "I tried writing to you. Did the magic on the paper run out?"

Siamis was far too wretched and angry with himself to explain that he'd sensed Fox coming. "You're here because?"

"Before we brushed against some pirates off Parayid, your Van Stad made it clear he was short-handed. From what I've seen, we were a day or two behind some fairly brisk action. Successful, I should say."

"Led by the First Lancers," Siamis said, and breathed out hard. "I suspect you don't know who they are?"

"You are correct. Am I to congratulate you?"

"Not I," Siamis said, his mouth thin. "Not I. One of my many failures was listening at the wrong time, and missing a crucial order. I just now got done performing the antidote to a blood poison spell I hope will be lost forever. But those things always seem to reappear," he added in an under-breath.

"Blood spells? I remember talk of that about Dag Erkric of the Venn." Fox flipped up the back of his hand. "Wasn't he mixed up in similar pursuits in my day?"

"And we saw the end-result today," Siamis said. "Almost half the First Lancers survived. If you can call it that. I am very much afraid not for long—"

"Here's another of these soul-suckers," someone shouted, not ten paces away, as Marloven guards muscled a crimson-faced man out from an alley, and threw him to the ground.

The man leaped to his feet, bellowing threats, until three arrows zipped from three locations—the city wall behind Fox, a rooftop, and a castle tower to the left—and the man dropped dead.

From another direction an even bigger crowd emerged, at the center a tall, muscular man whose face scars writhed white against his flushed skin, his dark hair hanging in his eyes. He struggled violently between four guards trying to hold him, two of those teenagers, and one gray-haired man.

"We have their leader! He was hiding in Papermakers' Lane!"

A woman shrilled, "They took us hostage! Killed my nephew, and my daughter!"

The square filled fast, and Fox found himself at the front of a sizable crowd, the Marloven tongue spoken quick and fast, but at least he could follow it now.

The prisoner between the guards threw his head back. "Siamis the traitor. Going about free, I see. How did you lie your way into that?"

A new voice: "What did you find?"

Siamis turned his head, and Fox gazed in interest at a straight-backed, wire-thin young man, as blond as Siamis, who appeared from the direction of the royal castle. He wore an old riding coat that reminded Fox of those in his day; everyone saluted, fist to heart, and backed to give him space. "I take it this shit is Aldon?" the newcomer addressed Siamis, pointing to the prisoner.

"Yes," Siamis said.

"So he turned up after all." And to Aldon, "I've been hearing about you wanting my throne ever since you shits invaded. What's your dispute with us?"

"I can tell you this much," Siamis said, as Aldon stood there between the guards, head cocked, his mouth derisive. "He was born near Eveneth, named Aldred, five generations back, then joined Norsunder. Seven or eight name changes later, he became Aldon when he posed as a Fhlerian in order to build a personal army. Wasn't that to make Fhleria as great as the Venn, I think was the claim?"

Aldon hawked and spat. "I could make the Marlovens mighty again. You just need to get rid of the Iascan weaklings, and go back to the days of the renowned Kethadrend, son of Senrid—we could win back all of Halia!"

Fox, Siamis, and Senrid were watching the gathering crowd more than Aldon. Most people exclaimed in protest— disgust—anger. There were a few—predominantly men, one or two older, a small cluster younger, who shifted, exchanged glances, and muttered a cautious agreement.

Senrid raised his voice. "You mean the Kethadrend who beggared the kingdom so badly that it took two generations to recover? And all we had to show for it were the treaties binding us to the middle plains, and a list of dead that took half a watch to read every New Year's Firstday?"

One of the women who had followed the guards holding Aldon pointed a finger up into his face and shouted in a quivering voice, "You killed my uncle, and my daughter! You knifed her in the back!"

"…with my own eyes!"

"He took us hostage, and my daughter went through the drying room window for help, and he threw a knife—"

Senrid raised his hand, and the crowd fell silent. "We all know he's got a murder list as long as his arm. Aldon, if you really are Marloven, then you'll understand Marloven justice. Either you get put up against the wall or you can fight for your life. Either way, you won't see the sun set today."

Senrid looked around as if for a sword. Fox was going to protest, as the young man looked as if a gust of wind would blow him away, but Siamis strolled forward, his hands empty. "Aldon and I know one another of old. And you've got more important matters to see to, Senrid-Harvaldar—"

With a roar and a lunge, Aldon used his enormous strength and ripped the sword from the guard at his left. He charged Siamis, who was not armed. The guards dashed after, and Fox leaped forward, wrist knives in his hands.

Aldon swung the sword in a swathe, and the mostly-unarmed crowd scrambled back, except for Siamis, standing between Senrid and Aldon. As the guards grimly charged Aldon again, Fox took hold of Siamis's shoulder and jerked him around to face him. Yes, there was that look that Inda had had at the end—one step away from death.

"I'm good," Fox said. "But I'm not the best anymore. Protect them."

At that moment, Aldon cut the old guard down, leaped over his slumping form, and charged the crowd, who scattered.

Fox pressed his knives into Siamis's hands. "Protect them," Fox repeated.

Siamis blinked, and his expression altered as he advanced on Aldon. The two young guards, both with bleeding cuts, helped the old one to his feet, and away; the circle fell silent.

Protect them. Siamis had nearly lost sight of that; what had Detlev said, when Siamis was young, and had first blundered? *Guilt is one of the hiltless knives. Don't cut yourself with it. Train yourself to be better.*

Siamis advanced. He knew Aldon's style. Stronger and faster than most, Aldon had always favored the brute smash. Siamis scarcely had to listen on the mental plane to predict Aldon's next move as he turned his head, shifted his stance, and avoided two swinging blows.

Fox perceived the alteration in intent by Siamis's stance, his hawk-still profile, watching, watching. As Siamis flowed into action, always a hair's breadth out of reach, Fox was thrown back in memory to Inda, who had also fought this way, as if he knew every move before his opponent made it. Ah, he had. Did Siamis carry a ghost, too?

Siamis smiled, obliquely watching the same two young men Senrid watched. Then he struck the knife hilt to Aldon's elbow, precisely hitting the nerve cluster that caused the sword to drop with a clatter.

"Pick it up. Try again," Siamis said, and Fox appreciated a masterly demonstration proving which of the two had the better martial skills, without offering a word of argument to those inclined to believe Aldon's claims. Sadly, in eight hundred years, it seemed, certain types of people still admired the loudest bull in the barn.

Siamis once again dodged, sidestepped, dodged, then made two fast strikes, mid-chest and gut. A feint, he kicked the blade from Aldon's hand, swung in a perfect arc, cutting his throat. Aldon was dead before he hit the ground.

"Disappear him," Senrid said to the guards who had pounded up. "He was a liar and a murderer. No need for any ceremonial. Finish flushing the rest of them out."

The guards saluted crisply, and Senrid, who had heard Fox's thought about Inda, turned to him. "You are...?"

"I believe," Fox said in his old manner—minus the insolence—"I'm your grandfather, many times over."

Senrid stared. "You..."

"Savarend was my name. Gone out of style, eh? What peeves me is that I put a great deal of effort into writing my record, as true as I could make it, and nobody seems to have seen it."

Senrid's intense gray-blue gaze widened. "What record?" he husked.

"I left it in Darchelde. Which I'm told is a ruin," Fox said, as snow began falling in earnest, and the crowd hastily broke up, encouraged by a gust of icy, sleeting wind.

"I don't understand," Senrid said, pressing the heels of his hands into his eyes. "We know Ivandred rode into Norsunder. He seems to have had a change of heart—either that or the records are completely wrong. But you..."

"Oh, I sailed my ship through the Black Gate to damnation," Fox said. "My choice. Though if you ask why I did it, I'm not sure I can tell you even now. The fact is, I'm still alive."

Senrid said, "I'm still trying to get my mind around Ivandred not just coming back again, but to our rescue. But that's another ... situation. Ah, perhaps I ought to restore Darchelde? I'm sorry to report it's quite overgrown. There was a significant magical blast there. As it happens, at the time Ivandred left."

Fox waved a lazy hand. "Don't trouble yourself. I'll never return. No one who mattered to me is there anymore. I live on my ship. Sufficient for my needs, and if I get tired of the scenery, I can change it by morning."

Senrid gazed back at him, and for a heartbeat, as Fox had

said the words *no one who matters*, he saw Inda in Senrid's gaze. Then it was gone. There was utterly no other resemblance, aside from that same expression of yearning without hope, in Inda's case when someone talked about families, during those early days on the *Death*.

Siamis said, "Senrid, are you going to meet Ivandred?"

"Before I meet him, how bad is it?"

"It's a miracle he's alive," Siamis said, his mouth pained. "Or, less trite, perhaps, I'd attribute it to strength of will. I heard some of his thought when I performed Jilo's antidote. It was important to him to free the capital. If he could. He did not expect to live beyond that."

Fox was still trying to get a sense of who had done what. He addressed Senrid, "I take it you were elsewhere when Ivandred rode south?"

Senrid turned his way. "I just got back not four hours ago, and it's been all reports, except for the hunt for Aldon. I was..." He blinked. "It's beginning to sink in that they are really gone. That I can say it, I was fighting the Host, for..." Another press of his palms against his eye-sockets. "I have no idea how long. It feels like hours, but we went into hiding right after the turn of the year."

"Almost a month," Siamis said.

Senrid didn't hear him. He was studying Fox. "Eight hundred years," he murmured. "What was it like? No, what was *he* like?"

Again Fox saw Inda in that wide gaze — this time, the suppressed grief. "I wrote it all out," he said, a lot more mildly than he might have to someone else. "That record I mentioned. It's all there. Probably more than anyone wants to know."

"And it's safe," Siamis said. "This, for once, is very simple to amend. I can be back in moments."

"But I won't be able to read it in moments," Senrid commented wryly. "I suspect there is a line leading all the way to the stable, waiting in whatever's left of my study. I never made it that far."

"But when you're ready, it'll be there waiting," Siamis said, and vanished.

Senrid said to Fox, "I've had Ivandred and his lancers put in the guest wing, as the lazarette is full. And though it seems the Norsundrians used this castle partly as HQ, partly as a stable, and the academy end as target practice, some rooms are usable." Then, under his breath, "I wish I'd seen that first charge."

"Me, too," Fox admitted.

In the guest wing, both Senrid and Fox were equally shocked at the gaunt, hollow-eyed figure on the bed. His skin was bleached of color, almost translucent. This man had fought and won battles? It didn't look as if he'd survive walking downstairs.

Senrid sat beside him. "I'm Senrid Montredaun-An," he said. "I want to express gratitude on the part of everyone in this kingdom, to you, and to your lancers. We will do everything we can to find the best healers."

"I expected to die," Ivandred said quietly.

Here was yet another reminder of Inda in the bad days after the battle at the strait. Was it always like this after people were slaughtering each other, and Fox hadn't noticed? Only the good ones, Fox thought wryly. I was never that.

He pushed past Senrid, and patted Ivandred's shoulder in a grandfatherly manner. "What's the hurry?" he said with brisk cheer. "We have the rest of all time to be dead. Ah, I probably ought to tell you that I'm Savarend Montredavan-An. Likely your ancestor, strange as that may sound—I'm assuming my boy either got himself a son by some means or other, or else the name persisted through my sister's children. I was never a king, due to some dirty-work on the part of the apparently long-gone Montreivayirs. For which I have learned to be very grateful. I had a far better life sailing with Inda under my fox banner than I probably would ever have had stuck here in this city, waiting for the Venn to attack."

"Inda…" Ivandred's expression eased incrementally during these words. At the end, he murmured on a note of wonder, "Fox banner fleet. You sailed with *that* Inda?"

"The only one I knew—ah, except for my boy. But we never called him Inda. I sailed with Inda Algara-Vayir, the one they renamed the strait after. I remember him laughing about that, saying it wouldn't stick ten years. I can tell you as many stories about him as you like, but you'll have to survive to hear them…"

South in Darchelde, Siamis transferred to the sealed room,

where, as expected, Fox's record lay beside Emras the Scribe's true testament, both yellowing but otherwise unharmed. Siamis leaned his knuckles against the table, his head bowed, and reached for Detlev, at first guardedly, then he remembered there was no need. No predatory mind lay in wait: *Detlev, I don't think I can face Ivandred again. As far as I can ascertain, the blood poison spell destroyed their bone marrow; the antidote was meant for the dormant phase, and though it halted the spell, it does not cure it. We need magic.*

: I regret to say that no magic can restore something destroyed, any more than it can regrow a limb.

: I wish we'd saved the Alshi cup. Or we could find Autumn. Or even Imry! I remember how Autumn cured Jilo, years ago.

: The end result would be the same, except that Imry would die trying — assuming we could get him to try — because he is untrained. The Alshi cup was merely Autumn's people's magic caught in an object. She, and it, could cure general malaise, but Wan-Edhe's spell was cast to that specific purpose. Jilo knew not to awaken the dormant phase when he tested the blood poison spell on himself in creating the antidote, or he would not be among the living now.

: Detlev, I should have heard Efael, how could I have missed that?

: We can go over everything if you must; you still have his memories, and you can plunge into the muck in self-abnegation, but I suspect that the lives of Ivandred and his wing meant so little to Efael that he never thought consciously of the matter after he first bespelled them, or after he released the lethal phase. And you were skimming his immediate thoughts, not his memories. You had not enough time for sorting memories; remember that you were responsible for all else, and that you succeeded in all else.

: All I can think is that I failed Ivandred and his people. It is costing their lives.

: Will it make you feel better if I enumerate all my similar blunders? Beginning with Kessler Sonscarna? I will never cease regretting that; his list of murders in the name of his righteous world could all have been prevented.

: I share that one, too. Siamis uttered a ragged laugh.

: No: you were on the fifth world at that time. You could not possibly have known of his birth. All I can say now is, regret will be our companion for the remainder of our lives, but let us not permit it to be our only companion. Reading Fox's memoir will be good for

Senrid. It's time for him to see it.

: Clair? David?

: David is still there in Imar. I expect the time distortion is persisting, in which case he probably thinks we just left.

: And Clair?

: Clair sleeps here, on the plateau. Adam and I set up our old tents. It's true sleep. I think a week with the dyr will enable her to go home again. She has a loving family she made herself, and before I release her, I will get her to promise to ask for help if she needs it. This will be Adam's first actual observation of dyr work; let us learn from our errors, use the skills we have, and go on.

Twenty-eight

TIME INDEED STILL STOOD suspended, there on the gentle hill surrounded by a broad circle of lifelessness. David was tired, and in pain, but he lingered, his gaze on slight, merry Marga, the wind ruffling through her short curls.

David remembered the friendliness of their last meeting. Once Siamis had talked to David and the boys about the endless varieties of subtle communication possible when eyes met eyes. There was no speculation in her glance, none of the warmth of attraction, much less invitation. Whatever might lie in her future, right now she was familial with the entire world. He bowed his head, one hand clutching his shoulder, and willed himself to accept and move on.

Then Marga walked to the edge of the terrace, chin lifted, her gaze reaching to the rim of the world. She held out her hands, palms up, and from all around rose a cool, delicious breeze. Balmy, full of the promise of spring, even though this was still Firstmonth, and deep in winter.

From all horizons winds and water spiraled skyward, forming first in clouds, towering ever higher. The haze of dawn limned the billowing, tumbling clouds as they sailed overhead.

Marga turned her palms down, and it began to rain.

All across the lifeless expanse silver sheets of water fell from the sky. Rain washed the faces of the silent, exhausted company. They never noticed their hair streaming, or the soaking of their clothes, for the air and showers both were sweet and warm. Water gathered in spreading pools, then in splashing rivers, flowing at last into a swirling lake. Time was still suspended; only when the water lapped at the crest of their hill did Marga stir, and with a wave of her hand, she used the tremendous strength of the ambient magic to transfer them to Mearsies Heili's terrace outside the kitchen, where the girls always instinctively gathered. David was with them; only Marga was not.

CJ knuckled her eyes, wishing the beauty of Marga's magic would never end. It left her with a curious longing inside, but it wasn't sadness, not any more, for the rain seemed to have washed away all the agony. She still remembered — would always remember — but at least now the memories did not hurt.

A moment later a shriek sounded from inside and Aurora banged through the door, barefoot of course, yelling in happy welcome. She bounded around in a circle, her voice high and shrill as she greeted everyone; CJ was trying to figure out how to say that Detlev had taken Clair away, but Aurora stated triumphantly, "I can hear Clair." She tapped her head. "She's having *good* dreams!"

"Let's go inside. I'm cold," Falinneh suggested, bouncing up and down. "Aurora, you're going to freeze your toes!"

"I'm tough," Aurora of course replied, but she was hopping from foot to foot.

The girls crowded inside, June stumbling after, her mind still caught in that radiance. Unconsciously she flexed her hand gently; the magic had aligned her broken finger bones, but had not suddenly healed them. Her fingers were still very tender. "I have to wrap my hand," she muttered, to no one in particular.

"Right here," Seshe said, for she'd been already spoken to Janil, who'd sent her staff running for bandages.

A spasm of pain jabbed from David's shoulder blade through his body, and he winced, his hand shifting grip on his sword. His sword.

He looked down. He'd almost forgotten it. What was Imry about, tossing him the sword like that? David's shoulder pulled as his other hand slid up toward the hilt, then he paused, feeling the inward cottony sensation of intense magic. Very intense magic. Lethal?

He closed his eyes. With the Host gone, gone too was the ancient truce forbidding anyone from using the old magic. If they could master it. He still felt like a child trying to shape water into discreet forms, but he did know a little. He mentally pulled some of the ambient magic and shaped it around the hilt, testing...

There was no threat here. Something else. Something quite different.

He slid his fingers around the grip, familiar for most of his life, and felt the internal *snap!* of a released spell. Something powerful indeed.

His vision smeared into dazzle, then a complicated image flitted across his inner eye, and he gasped, sending a thought: *Detlev, Imry seems to have keyed all his enchantments onto this sword, and the first level of release was me touching the sword again.*

Silence for a moment, then Detlev's thought was clear: *Ward or tracer?*

: Nothing. Or if there is, it's beyond my skills.

: I don't think his skills are beyond yours.

: Then … does he want me to go through the world trumpeting his regrets as I wave the sword and take away the enchantments the mages are sweating over now?

David felt Detlev's laughter, which was reassuring. It had been far too long since there had been any laughter: *Does that sound at all like Imry?*

: No, it doesn't. I can't imagine what his motive is.

: You don't need to. My suggestion is, get that shoulder of yours wrapped up, eat a meal, get some sleep, then go unobtrusively to each enchantment site, remove its enchantment, and move on.

: Hand through the water. Right.

: I do encourage you to go to the Land of the Venn first. That one is the cruelest, being tied to the guardians' own oath spells bound into their tattoos. Just as well Imry seems to have lost interest in that method of magic once he accomplished it — probably to infuriate the twins, who never had Dena Yeresbeth.

Then Detlev was gone, and David swayed, and jolted himself upright. Then he looked down, appalled to see that he'd splattered the clean snow with blood drips. He kicked the snow over them, then slunk into the kitchen, where an older woman said, "There you are! We're ready for you, now that CJ and June are wrapped up. I have an expert with the needle right here."

David shook his head. "No stitching. I don't care about scars."

"I see that," Janil said, in mild disapproval as she eased the ruined shirt away from David's back.

"Just wrap it up tight, thanks." His mind moved outward. He had his orders. What about the rest of the circle?

What about Dirk?

Adam's voice was there, as if he stood at David's side: *Sveneric and Darian Selenna are trying to get Dirk to sleep. Detlev says he will listen for him. Mildred, MV, and Zairna are at Detlev's house. Rolfin and Leef have gone to hunt down the rest of the Black Knives. I think Ferret is sniffing them out first. Everyone else has gone home.*

David covered his eyes with his left hand as the bandage wound steadily around his shoulder and chest. His awareness reached farther outward, dismaying him as he considered the wreckage yet to be dealt with. He knew he would probably never have quite this effortless reach again. None of them would. But while he had it, he ranged the world, reveling in the utter absence of those prowling minds.

The Chwahir appeared to be poised, listening.

Chwahir. *Adam? Where is Erol?*

: Exactly where you would expect, waiting for Jilo. Who is crossing into Chwahirsland right now, half a day perhaps from Narad. And we are all warded. We cannot help.

Midway through the night in Sarendan, Dirk Sonscarna had been asleep for perhaps three hours when he woke from a sobbing nightmare. He gasped for breath, his body cold and gritty with sweat.

He flung off the damp, clinging coverlet, scrambled out of bed, and moved to the window. He staggered once, vertigo making his vision swim, and gazed out over the snow-blanketed rooftops of Miraleste, blue-white in quiet moonlight. He regained his sense of balance by controlled breathing, and then forced himself to turn around and look at the tumbled bed. Memory of the nightmare struck, and he fiercely wiped his eyes.

I have to know.

He raised his hand to transfer, but then a faint sound made him stay his hand: music, softly played.

Dirk sent a mental probe. No identity.

He stepped through the cleaning frame—for he always slept in his clothes, in case of attack, just like—

Anguish. Barefoot, he ran downstairs, following the sound to its source. He passed by Darian's suite, and felt him on the mental realm, deep in slumber.

The music came from the royal palace's smaller parlor, where the family had often gathered. A single, rare instrument, silver hammers on glass, pouring a long, complicated melody through the quiet night air, a riverflow of major chord, step, minor chord. Dirk knew little of music; his father had been unable to hear it except as noise. This music was beautifully executed. Its expertise, and the contemplative harmonics, plucked at tight strings inside him, making his head hum.

At once the magic stopped. It had been magic. He even knew how that worked, for Clair of the Mearsieans had learned the spell for capturing sound within a spell, so one could release it again and again. The Mearsieans never had enough music.

Dirk opened the door, and saw a lone figure there on the couch.

"A pleasant way of passing the time," Detlev murmured, and then he raised a hand as if to clap the glowglobes on.

"Don't," Dirk said, and regretted it. He braced to be truculent if Detlev asked why.

"You were going to seek me?" Detlev asked.

Dirk was glad of the truculence now, for it got the question out in one try. "Did Ilerian get him?"

"No. It was Efael, a knife. It was so sudden he cannot have suffered but an instant."

Deep breath. Another. Another. Ah, how breathing hurt, no, the anguish was inside, much further inside.

"In the dream." Dirk couldn't talk, only whisper. "In the dream ... he did. Kessler always said, when he died, his mind and spirit would be rendered as nothing."

"So he said. It's a reasonable assumption, but that does not make it true."

"Do you know what ... where ...?"

"No. I can only tell you that he escaped Ilerian. So have

the rest of Ilerian's former prey from this world, even Sfenaraec, worst of them all, and the oldest victim. The center of Norsunder exists no longer, except in memory."

Dirk choked off a ragged breath. "But ... he's not ..." He shut his teeth. Fought for control. Tried again. "But you don't know for certain."

"I am finite, like you. Accepting that, doesn't it seem a trifle short-sighted to deny all the possibilities of the infinite?"

Dirk sagged onto the other end of the couch. "He said ghosts are mirage. But Darian has seen one."

"If I were your father, and I found myself watching, I would want to see an end to old battles."

Dirk gulped. What old battles? He sucked in a breath. "Wan-Edhe," he whispered.

"Jilo is entering Narad now. I hope he can catch all the wards against his name," Detlev said. "I would go, except there are even more wards lying in wait for me. The only person Wan-Edhe hasn't warded, because he knows nothing of your existence, is you."

"I know how to break wards," Dirk said, knuckling his eyes. He no longer cared if Detlev saw he'd been weeping. "Kessler taught me to break my first ward as soon as I learned to read." He vanished.

<hr>

Intent. To kill?

The thought threw Jilo back in memory to autumn, when Retren had suffered the nightmares that made his moods so wild. It had worried Jilo enough that he'd wanted to take Retren back to Marloven Hess and tell Senrid that he could do nothing for the boy. But in Mearsies Heili, Siamis had been able to help a little, and after the attack on Efael's castle, Retren's nightmares had ended, and he had accepted eagerly when Mondros had offered to teach him magic while he and Tsauderei tried to aid Jilo by fighting Wan-Edhe's spells from a distance. As far as Jilo knew, Retren was right now happily curled up in that cottage studying, or learning how to cook delicious things.

He trudged down the main road, and joined in the slow, sober market-traffic. He bent his head, walking with all the other dark-clad people with sallow or blanched skin like his, the matte black hair, the shuffling walk.

Did the city gate guards recognize Jilo? He tried never to force them into an untenable choice. What dismal streets! What a smell! Why should Wan-Edhe want the gutters to run with clogged mud and stable refuse? Perhaps seeing others forced to live in dirt reinforced his sense of power.

Every time Jilo was away, the deliberate—unnecessary— ugliness struck him anew. Windows small, ostensibly to withstand attack, except that Chwahirsland hadn't been attacked for hundreds of years. All their problems were internal—and the windows remained small because there was nothing to look out at, except trouble. Wan-Edhe had had people executed for the way they stared down from windows. Especially women.

Jilo lifted his head to glance into faces. Closed faces, furtive glances, angry and sullen foreheads and mouths. Here and there some lighter emotions leaked through, but those were secret thoughts, and the faces gave no clues. They believed their lives would shuffle on, their pleasures small and secret, or perhaps some waited for a promise to be kept.

Jilo intended to keep his appointment with death, and he thought again about Yeres, and Imry Llyenthur's quick twist that had abruptly ended her life. How could Jilo judge? He intended to see Wan-Edhe die.

As he walked, the old fears crowded back, prominent the fear that when he came face to face with Wan-Edhe, he would not be able to perform the magic that he knew would kill him. Even in the name of justice. That was how Wan-Edhe had begun his career as king, when he was Shnit Sonscarna of the long, proud line of Sonscarna kings.

What is justice? Moral equity? Shontande said justice was the right to be heard, to be judged either by peers or by one you have accepted as authority in a social contract extending both ways. The right to the assumption that no one is regarded as the moral superior until the facts are understood, regardless of social or economic rank, age, or gender. That sounded so fine, except what if the facts are ambiguous? The closest humans could get to justice, the Chwahir of old had believed, was reached through consensus. Not crowd mood—the very opposite of consensus.

The fundamental premise of the twi was consensus. Jilo wanted a consensus government, though how to make it happen had kept him awake at night for years. When he wasn't imagining exactly what it would feel like to be struck down, at just such a moment as now.

Murder was not moral equity. A man comes at him with sword upraised. He raises his own blade in defense. The man presses to the attack, Jilo defends himself. Then he see an opening in the attacker's guard. Is it defense to strike home through his heart and kill him?

What if what you defend is your home? And your opponent will always consider his borders extending past yours?

The castle lay ahead.

Jilo's focus reached unconsciously: *Detlev, what would you say?* He nearly stumbled when an answer came: *I cannot tell you what to do tomorrow. That is your choice — yours and your people. Today? Exactly as you planned.*

Then he was gone.

The smell of iron, and steel, and the tinge of fear sweat lay over the eternal dust-and-mold ambience. Sweat. Jilo wiped his damp palms and began the slow-breathing that David had taught him as he registered furtive whispers, and then the rapid tattoo of retreating feet.

Jilo slipped inside the castle. No wards on his name, though wards there were in plenty, That meant Wan-Edhe expected him to come. Wanted him to come. Had planned for him to come. That didn't mean Jilo had to blunder witlessly into the waiting trap.

He chose the old passages he'd discovered on his own. What long-forgotten Sonscarna, or enemy of same, had put those passages in? He'd never been able to find any references in one of those moldering records upstairs. How odd it was that a family like the Sonscarnas, prone to killing one another off in its later generations, exhibited such a penchant for records. They could not have peace with their peers, so did they look for approval from their successors?

All these things streamed through Jilo's mind as he trod up the stone steps, one, then the next, then the next, his sharpened senses detecting wards with his name, all intended to bind him. By now it was a matter of a heartbeat's concentration with what he privately thought of as vagabond magic to break the wards. No awkward spells. No tracers left over.

Familiar smell of mossy stone.

The sound of his shoes grating on the granite.

The chill of winter still in the air.

Puddlenose's voice, echoing down the years from when they were boys, both prisoners: "Ever noticed how Wan-Edhe's castle's secret passages are a great gauge of the weather half a year ago?"

Jilo stopped, braced his forehead against the cool stone, and sent his awareness outward, then stood before the door, guts cramping, a chill tightening across his shoulders. His old flogging scars itched.

He opened the door to the magic chamber.

It was empty.

All right. Act fast. He crossed to the shelves, then heard voices in the alcove. "... walked straight into my trap." That wavering voice, thready with anger and spite. That voice meant fear, and pain. Low, raspy, edged with permanent bad temper.

Wan-Edhe shuffled in, bearing a very old book, the glow globe high up shedding light on the wool of his robe and the tangled white hair and beard.

"Wan-Edhe," Jilo said. He heard his own voice. It sounded high, weak, and nasal in the still, stale air of that alcove.

Wan-Edge glared, sneer-lines in his gaunt face deepening, his frog-eyes narrowed unpleasantly. Those eyes, the Landis shape distorted by decades of anger. "Well, if it isn't my brother's most laughable mistake," he snarled. "I never thought you'd actually be stupid enough to walk back in here."

"I am here to offer you a choice," Jilo said, his voice breaking. "To return to the way Chwahir governed themselves before the nanijos —"

Wan-Edhe stared — pop-eyed — then laughed. Any humor in that laugh had leached away years ago. Decades ago. It was just a sound, a loud, harsh sound. Then he made a sign to close his trap.

"—made themselves kings. We governed ourselves with faith and trust by reaching consensus —"

Warning hummed in Jilo's bones and teeth. The singe of fire burned in the air, but he held his ground and spoke the antidote to the one spell Wan-Edhe had been repeating for ages, repeating so often that he had forgotten that there even was an antidote: the dark magic spell to halt aging. That, Jilo had decided after agonizing alone for months, might be considered murder by some, by others merely a return to what nature had intended. The question that galled Jilo most was whether it would be mercy to kill him right off, or to keep his hands relatively clean by shoving the frail old wreck into a warded room to die by degrees of the ravages of age. Surely he wouldn't last but a day or two. But that would be a day or two of torture.

Wan-Edhe staggered, utterly taken by surprise. He'd prepared for so many other types of magic attack, the sort of attack he had used against others for all his long life. Rage flushed through him as he withered to a nightmare figure before Jilo's eyes, but he still forced his hand up as greenish fire glowed around claw-like hands. His only thought was to kill. But before Jilo could use the ward he'd prepared to sequester Wan-Edhe, the old mage-king's eyes widened, and Jilo blinked, aware of the afterimage of a silver glint.

Motion stopped. Time seemed to halt as Jilo and Wan-Edhe gazed down at the knife hilt protruding from the brittle bones of the king's chest. Shock blanched his withered face when he looked past Jilo to Dirk, so very much like Kessler, the last time grandfather had seen grandson. Then Wan-Edhe collapsed, brittle bones crackling, sending up a sour stink like unwashed laundry.

Dirk kicked him. "He's dead." His chest heaved. "My very first lesson was with a knife, and my second to dispell the ward against steel. *He* said, I should know how to escape. If that man..." He kicked Wan-Edhe again. "...ever got me. Then I would not endure. What he did. Before he escaped. Do you think he knows?"

Dazed, Jilo barely had time to grasp that the 'he' meant Kessler, when Dirk turned away, choking on a sob, made a sign, and vanished.

And Detlev's contact came: *Sveneric and Darian will find him. Carry on.*

Numb with shock, Jilo stumbled out. He reached Wan-Edhe's old viewing balcony, where Wan-Edhe had leaned for so many years, watching parades, and tortures, and executions.

Jilo yelled, "Wan-Edhe is dead. Everyone here is to lay

down his weapons."

Confusion broke out, for many recognized Jilo, and remembered the promise of promotion—prizes—on his capture or death.

"Now," he cried, though his voice was nearly lost in the echoing voices just below.

An arrow flew from above into the crowd. The would-be shooter fell, bow and arrow clattering.

Somehow that stopped them all.

These were Chwahir. Following orders had been hammered into them by one sure emotion: fear. But whose orders to follow? The one who'd shot at him had probably been following an order from Wan-Edhe. Jilo had to keep Chwahir from turning on Chwahir, everyone angry and fearful. Chaos would unleash a civil war that no one would win.

"Lay down your arms," Jilo shouted. "Return to your barracks until further orders are issued." Then, softer, "Erol?"

Erol emerged from the shadows, there in plain sight of two hundred armed men, and threw his bow off the balcony. Everyone watched it crash on the stones, then *clang! thunk!* they all shed their weaponry, and with it responsibility.

Jilo's joints turned to water as he watched them form ranks, leading off to the right, and file back inside.

Jilo could imagine them sitting in rows, cold with sweat, no one wanting to stand out and draw the eye. Wan-Edhe's former toadies, bought with fear or false promises, would be afraid of exposure. Everyone else just afraid, because Wan-Edhe had wanted them that way. Jilo could bind them into order by strict laws and patrols. It would be easy, because it would be expected. But that was the path that Wan-Edhe had walked. It was a predictable path, worn with the footsteps of human habit.

Or, he could follow his own plan, knowing that he might not live past an hour.

He walked back downstairs, dismantling wards as soon as he encountered them. One thing that steadied him: his concentrated magic studies of these past few years made it so very easy. Was it slightly easier to breathe when he reached the ground level? Or was that the knowledge finally beginning to sink in that Wan-Edhe was gone forever?

Didn't matter. He continued walking until he reached the

main court, and crossed it, still openly destroying wards. Ah, here at last was the main one, like a great twisted chain with so many names bound into it, keeping Detlev and Mondros and so very many others out. Jilo uttered the words to snap it. Green flashed, limning his silhouette—Jilo had no idea how eerie he looked, walking alone as he flung magic in flares and flashes of spring-green lightning. That one at the outside gate lit up the entire city for less than a heartbeat.

Under the eyes of the guards still on the walls, some with weapons hidden at their feet, he walked into the main street. The empty street. He sensed eyes without number peering from behind curtains and shades and shutters and cracks, oh, so many cracks, as behind him one then two furtive figures crept along that upper hall, and found the corpse.

It was true.

The Hate was dead.

Dead! They spat on that withered figure, then spat again, and it did not move. Then they slipped away, and word spread faster, and more skulked up there, to spit upon the loathed king and then to carry away the joyful news: the rescuer of the Sunrise Generation had truly prevailed, and The Hate was dead at last.

Jilo kept walking alone. Unnoticed, Erol slipped along behind him, though his guardianship was not needed: human nature being what it is, disaffection was bound to arise, but for now the entire city was rapt with wonder.

Jilo walked until he reached a grimy, gray-walled house midway down the street, where he had obtained a meal so many times, because the women inside shared what little they had with those who were hungrier than they.

He stood outside the door, and called, "May this one be invited within?"

A long pause. Had he miscalculated? A painful blush worked up from his chest, and he laughed inwardly. Surely, of all emotions, humiliation ought to be the most familiar?

But then the door opened, and there were all three women, old, middle-aged, and one perhaps sixteen. "Please, come within," said the old one.

Jilo walked inside, and sat. They brought him watery rice soup, and he drank it down, and thanked them. They brought him a heel of stale bread, made from scrapings, and he worked it past his teeth, though it took some swallowing. He thanked them.

Then he stood, and looked at the blank wall—the clean, blank wall, for at least people were permitted to clean inside their homes. He looked long enough for the older woman to come forward, and to say tremulously, "Would … the guest honor the house with a word or two?"

Jilo smiled. "This one has the worst handwriting in the world, and naught of worth to say."

"Please."

All three bowed low, the elder weeping silently, and Jilo went to the wall, and dipped his forefinger in the black grime around the torch, as women had been forbidden the means to write.

He might never restore power, but until he died, he would strive to restore meaning. And one of the oldest Chwahir customs, so old it stretched back to the time of dragons, it was said, was the custom of travelers sharing a picture, a poem, a thought, with the house that shared food and shelter.

Awkwardly, he wrote on the wall the ditty his nurse had sung over him when he was in his cradle:

> *My mother made the silken quilt — eight*
> *patches each lapping eight patches.*

A sob escaped someone crowding into the back of the room, as the word "twi" serried in whispers through the watching multitude, along with the word "mother."

Jilo's ungainly scrawl continued:

> *My sister stitched the crimson robes upon the*
> *rack — red for wedding lapping red for our*
> *shared blood.*

> *My nanijo's banner hangs bravely in the empty*
> *courtyard — filling ever filling.*

> *We walk the road as sunlight blesses mountains*
> *lapping mountains.*

Twenty-nine

HIBERN TOOK IN HER surroundings. Not just the trees, and the quality of light, which was different than that of Sartorias-deles. Subtly bluer, somehow. She studied the grasses, and the weeds, and the insects. The fresh water running over rocks that gleamed, wet and cool, in the afternoon light. Silver flickers of fish. Chattering, scolding birds overhead. All both familiar and unfamiliar in color and shape.

She felt the life-potential in all these things. The magic. Sensed stronger magic under her feet, like a humming harp string.

She closed her eyes, simply breathing. When she opened her eyes again, the shadows had moved. The sky above was a darker blue, the air cooler. Time. She'd forgotten time. While she sat there thinking, unnoticed, time had moved steadily forward.

She looked down at her gray-dusted feet and hem, then bent to lave her fingers in the cold water. She touched one of the stones on the stream bank, still warm from the sun, and physical impressions began to clamor, one by one. The staleness of her clothing. Dry eyes. Dust-caked hair. Hunger, for the first time since the evening she found herself face-to-face with Ilerian.

She flung off her mage scholar's robe and the clothes beneath, and bathed in the stream, gasping when the water first sluiced like ice over her skin. But it soon felt good. And when she stepped out, she applied the knowledge that seemed a part of her now, and used sunlight and water magic to dash the grime from her clothes before she dressed again. Then she lay down on the soft grass under a tree, and the rushing sound of the water sang her into a deep sleep.

She opened her eyes to sunshine, and gently ruffling leaves overhead — and awareness that she was no longer alone. She sat up, and found a blue-gowned older woman seated comfortably a little distance away, tossing crumbs to hopping birds.

"Lilith!" Hibern cried.

The birds twittered in protest and flapped away with a whirr of wings. Lilith dusted her fingers and said, "A very pleasant spot here."

"How long have you been there?"

"Oh, not long. Would you care for some home steep?"

On a folded blanket near her knee lay not only a gently steaming pot, but fresh bread, cheese, fruit. Clean dishes waited to be used.

Hibern looked from this simple meal to the comfortable face under the shapeless blue hat, and sensed Lilith's strength, and her very real affection, boundless as the seas at home.

"You still cannot get to Sartorias deles?" Hibern asked, pouring out steep. She gloried in the sound, so homey, and the sight of steam, and the summery aroma.

"The ward is broken. I believe it broke shortly after you abandoned the empty Norsunder-Beyond. Before I ask about that, I will quickly deal with I imagine is your first question: I was mostly on Songre Silde seeking aid, until Theronezhe turned up on Geth, trying to find the remainder of the old Norsunder site. The Geth mages sent a message, saying that they had seized him. He was on trial, and I was invited as witness to his transgressions. Then I left, for he was caught by them on their world, and I cannot interfere with their judgment. And to your second question: the Host have been defeated, utterly. You can get the details from those who accomplished it. I could not, having been warded until after it was over. Now, to you?"

"What happened to me..." Hibern thought, and thought some more, but the words would not come, or else would take a lifetime to speak. Finally she said, "I'm minded to try an experiment." She looked around with a distracted air, then gestured, and a column of lightning shot into the sky.

When it faded, their clothes puffed and crackled and their

hair lifted and stirred. Hibern didn't really notice; Lilith made a gesture and dispersed the static.

"Light and dark magic. They're the same," Hibern said.

"The difference is magnitude," Lilith said. "Think."

Hibern looked away over the valley. Beside her, Lilith was still and silent. Question, apprehension, wonder were all locked away inside her breast with the patient determination that she had practiced over the centuries.

Hibern found it easier to show Lilith her memories of her experiences in Norsunder, than to fumble with tongue and teeth, breath, and words.

Around them, unnoticed by Hibern, time passed, marked by the sun's journey, until they stood in long shadows and slanting light, and then the shadows deepened and melded as Erhal touched the rim of the far mountain and its fire dimmed to ruddy spark, and extinguished.

Stars glimmered when Hibern said at last, "When I used Ilerian's power, it dispersed. When I use that around me, because I alter nothing and destroy nothing, it returns to its source, with only a fragmentary diminishment. But already it is restoring itself." She looked around, then blinked, and rubbed her hands up her arms. "I'm cold," she observed, in vague surprise.

"May I suggest we return to a place of more comfort?"

Hibern nodded, and Lilith transferred them to a room, with pillows on the floor, and a low table. Outside the window was darkness. Hibern did not know where she was — even what sort of building the room was in — or the date. Yet none of those things mattered; she still had not truly yet rejoined herself to time and place.

Hibern ran her finger back and forth along the edge of the table. "I see my error. I took magic without understanding what is free and what is not." She glanced up. "It is easy, is it not?"

"A few would think so." Lilith smiled. "Very few. Not many master the old magic. You, it seems, have."

Hibern said, quickly, "Shall I not do that again?"

"You will have to decide," Lilith said.

"If I resist, it will be inevitable, will it not, that I'll come to face the choice again?"

"For times beyond count."

Hibern said, "So it's not a question of ease."

"Svir and Ilerian would certainly have thought it was."

Hibern's gaze diffused. "When I arrived there, almost the first thing that Theronezhe did was to show me a record of Detlev suborning Ilerian. I did not believe it, of course."

"We believed it," Lilith said. "The real circumstances still are hidden, though I now — after all these centuries — know them to be false."

"Yes," Hibern said, frowning. "Well, I didn't believe it because the morvende appear in records on Sartorias-deles *after* the Fall. How could he travel to the future?"

"He couldn't. But Ilerian could, as an unbodied entity."

"And there they were, Detlev and Svir, and Detlev used his dyr against Ilerian, who was ... a boy."

"A beautiful boy, unlike anyone at that time. But still from our world, so living proof he was from the future. I think that that was what we found most terrifying, and thereby convincing, that the clever, gifted Detlev had found a way to the future to master unknown powers, thence to return to change the course of the world toward that ruined future."

Hibern sighed. "I do not understand how the Ancient Sartorans could not see that Ilerian was altogether a different thing."

"Yet it happened. I was there, and I was fooled, wanting to believe the best, which I do not regret. But seeing what I wanted to see — he was so very beautiful — which I do regret, deeply." Lilith pressed her lips together, then said, "Ilerian at first destroyed our leaders one by one, always gaining access with his beauty, his grace, his fine voice and mild manner. He seduced, and when each victim had reached, ah, call it the fullness of heart, he destroyed them. And as he left behind a lengthening trail of death, he made it known that the clever Lef Hindraeldrei, promoted earlier than anyone else, master of not one but two callings before the age of twenty, had in his pride suborned this innocent beauty. For there had been some hidden envy over Detlev's attainments so early in life. And so, at the end, everyone turned against Detlev, and he was isolated, fighting alone. And then, as a last gesture, he burned all our archives, except for a few minor records here and there, and then he vanished."

"He truly did destroy knowledge?"

"Everything," Lilith whispered. "That was when I knew he

had turned his mind to evil. Or, I thought I did."

"You thought?"

"There was a time, not long ago, when we met on the fifth world. This was when I was still protecting the people in their mountain cave, as in turn they protected all that world's life, though by then they had long forgotten what it was they protected. I thought it better that way. Less likelihood of Norsunder discovering. Anyway, Yeres and Connanre were there, having recently emerged from the Beyond after much time had passed. They were furious about the discovery of those people who had survived in secret deep under the mountains for millennia. Wanting to lay blame. Detlev was there, and he confronted me." Lilith looked away, sighing. "So few words to make such a profound difference."

"Few words?"

"His manner was threatening, for Connanre and Yeres were watching. But what he said was more of a warning, and oblique. Very oblique."

"What did he say?"

"He said, for my ear only, *I destroyed every reference to the disirad. It's back.* And of course, the implication was that Connanre and Yeres did not know. And if they did not know, the Host did not know. It meant that he'd had a goal from the beginning. And that he was trusting me with this knowledge, which, if I only uttered a few words, would get him destroyed. Along with the world," Lilith added dryly.

Hibern frowned. "I don't understand. I have no quarrel with the Detlev of now. But it seems to me ... uncharacteristic for him to destroy the records of civilization. I suggests a terrible rage, doesn't it?"

Lilith said, "It does indeed. That, more than acts of killing, would convince Svir, and Ilerian, that they had successfully turned him."

"I tried to go back in time to witness the process of Norsunder's creation. Yet it had no true record."

"Because that creation took place outside Norsunder as well as within."

"You saw?"

"I have a memory," Lilith murmured. "I have never shared it, but I think, perhaps, the time has come. It was mere chance that I was there to witness it, for I had been Sfenaraec's prisoner, and was in the process of escaping. I was able to shield myself from sight, using the magic that had kept me warded."

And there, between their two minds, once again lived Lilith's old enemy, his thin-lipped mouth, long red-burnished hair, small, cruel hands—and then came his betrayal, and the agony that resulted as Ilerian founded the Beyond using Sfenaraec's life.

"Sfenar-ray-ec," Hibern whispered.

"One of the first acts of the Fall was him choking Deteri Reverael, Detlev's mother, to death. But the evil must have lain in us, or how could he and Svir and Ilerian—and of course Detlev—have brought it into existence so rapidly?"

Hibern spoke quickly. "I saw that there were no records of that man. When the archives related to the Host themselves, they beckoned the watcher to follow, yet those were lies. Distortions, attempts to create the truth they wanted others to see."

She stopped, and clasped her hands.

"But those are now gone, and I don't regret destroying them. What I have learned is this. I have the strength now to take what magic I need. Not just that which lies around us, but that which lies in every living thing. This, then, is the old magic of Sartor, is it not? It is how Ilerian amassed his power, he drained living things of life."

"Yes," Lilith said. "But you must also remember that sometimes living things give freely of themselves, when the cause is great."

"What is good, then, and what is not, when one uses such destructive power?"

"A question you must always ask, again and again, for the rest of your existence."

"I must now live always facing so terrible a choice?"

"You can choose never to use your knowledge."

Hibern looked beyond the walls and windows. "That would be like stopping up my ears and eyes. And cutting off my hands," she whispered.

Lilith took a long, slow breath. "I cannot tell you what to do." She smiled. "Though I am perfectly free to give you advice."

"Then?" Hibern asked, opening her hands.

"First, you must eat and drink. Then you must rest. I do not mean for a night. I mean for a time, for you do not yet comprehend all your changes."

"Changes? I haven't changed! I merely figured out a puzzle. I've done puzzles all my life."

Lilith's smile was tender. "My dear, you have made your unity at last."

"Made my—you mean, Dena Yeresbeth? No. I mean, I'm too old for that. surely?"

"Coinherence—unity, 'got' Dena Yeresbeth—though I like that one least, as you do not get it, like a new robe. Look past the various labels. You work as easily in the realm of the mind as you do speaking, do you not?"

"But I—" Hibern halted, reflecting on her actions, and tried to remember when she had ceased the one and took up the other. She licked dry lips. "And then?"

Lilith dusted some drifting dandelion fuzz from her robe. "If you wish to join the ranks of world guardians, then you must have some knowledge of the creatures whose lives you will be guarding. Not just creatures of the air and water and ground, for they have their guardians. You are going to have to gain some knowledge of your fellow humans. It is a part of human nature, in love and in hate, to seek leaders or to lead, for human survival in the very beginning depended on groups acting together. You need to understand when to act, and when to wait. When to teach, and when to allow discovery. You will make mistakes, because you are human, but that too is a part of learning."

Hibern smiled. "I'm not tired. And I spent long enough in an evil place, watching evil people, that I think I will always be able to spy it out quickly enough."

Lilith leaned over to touch her hand. The physical contact, brief and warm, was the first physical contact Hibern had experienced since Ilerian grasped her shoulder so long ago. "There are other aspects to life besides the existence of evil, and the determination to fight it."

Hibern observed sadness in Lilith's face.

"You require an example?"

"Please."

"You have yet no notion, despite all you've learned, and done, how you failed a friend, there, almost the first day of this terrible war. You were present, but watching uncomprehending, when a friend crossed the threshold into loneliness and despair. Support, friendship, perhaps some words of comfort, could have averted much resultant pain, but you did not see, and it will probably be years before it is resolved."

Hibern was silent, amazed and aghast.

"My last advice, therefore, is: once you have reunited with Erai-Yanya, and each of you has taught the other, go to Songre Silde, and the norss. Walk the paths on that world. Listen to their long wisdom, and get reacquainted with your own heart. Then return."

"My heart?"

"A symbolic but neutral term. It was both a strength and a weakness, your habit of avoiding the person in the mirror."

Hibern made a low bow, student to teacher. Lilith returned it, but with the bow of peer to peer, implying all its attendant responsibility.

Hibern then shifted back to her beloved Roth Drael, where Erai-Yanya, Arthur, and Yanli exclaimed joyfully, welcoming her, and there was much talk far into the night.

Thirty

MELIARA, QUEEN, STUDENT MAGE, and mother of three, sprinted like a girl half her age when she was excited. She was excited now. She burst into the storeroom off the kiln at the pottery serving as their latest hideout, and heaved a sigh of relief. "Danric! You're alone. I'm so glad."

"It's not quite dawn," Vidanric Renselaeus, king of Remalna, said, amused.

"We've been keeping such odd hours I was afraid that I'd burst in on a court ball," she retorted, ignoring the dimensions of the room, which might have admitted four more people at most. "I finally got Oria to sleep, and then I found out that my letter to Atan in Sartor worked! Her notecase worked! She wrote me back, and I wrote back, and *she* wrote back, and oh, Danric, I have so much juicy gossip."

Vidanric set aside the duty roster and looked at her expectantly. Ferret had vanished, ending the old communication relay. Remalna had been isolated since. "Might you dignify that a bit?" Vidanric inquired, to tease her.

"Oh, if we were back in the throne room — and I really wish we were, only so that Flauvic would hear *this* news," she amended, thinking of the great goldenwood tree growing inside that space, "I would be as dignified as the stuffiest envoy, and speak of tidings, and intelligence, and reports, but really what are all those but gossip?"

"Very true," he conceded solemnly as she sat on the cushion beside him, tucking herself under his arm.

"Atan's note says that the Destination won't be restored for some time yet — Norsunder damaged it terribly — but the mages have begun on the scribe desks. She dug up her old golden notecase, and there was the note I'd written before the troubles. She wanted to let me know that the magic works now."

"That is excellent. But is that the gossip?"

"Of course that isn't the gossip. That's *news*. The *gossip* is that the horrible Bartal na Shagal of Sles Adran turned out to be dead for weeks, and that Norsundrian they put in his place, you know, that slimy snake from Sarendan —"

"Arandos Kinarde," he murmured.

" — the one who wanted to harvest the goldenwoods to sell, which is exactly as bad as that dreadful Mandracar who wanted them chopped down in case we were hiding there — which we were — oh, I lost myself. No. I remember. Kinarde killed Bartal, without telling anyone, and was speaking for him, but right after the counterattack some Adranis sneaked in during the night and were going to free the king, and half the court wanted to dethrone him, and the other half wanted him dead, when they discovered that Kinarde had done the job for them. By morning, Kinarde was dead, too, and all his Norsunder minions. Minions! Minions. How I adore that word. I want to have minions."

"You have minions, Mel."

"No, I don't! I've never heard of minions who scold you for your own good, and take away your magic books if you study too late, and caution you that it is beneath your dignity to teach your children the insults you thought up with your brother when you were small." Meliara thumbed the end of her long braid, which had fallen over one ear, back into its coronet, and scowled. "I lost myself again. Where was I?"

"I believe you got to Kinarde's death."

She said, "I'd complained in my first note that we'd heard the Chwahir are leaving up north, but the Adranis are still here, and though Frente isn't horrible, we want her and her regiment out of here. Atan said that yes, what we heard is true. Right now, as we are talking, the Chwahir are marching out of Colend, back through the mountains, in the snow! But here *we* still are, occupied by the Adranis." She paused for breath.

"And?"

"*And,* the rest of the treaty-allies have *also* been sending messengers and notes to Atan, as fast as they can find their old notecases, asking her advice on what to do! We don't want to be part of an Adrani empire, nor do we want to start another war."

"Thank you, Mel," Vidanric said, and kissed her. "May I borrow that notecase of yours? Or can you examine mine for leftover Norsunder wards and traps?"

"Does that mean there's going to be more fighting?" she asked anxiously.

"I'd rather not, but what if it's the only choice: fight off the Adranis, or become part of their empire permanently?"

Meliara chewed her underlip. "I *hate* the thought of more fighting. But I also hate the thought of having the Adranis ruling us."

No one in Remalna liked Frente, or her Adranis, but most agreed that the Adrani occupation could have been worse. A company of Frente's regiment had even soundly thrashed a ship of deserters from Aldon's Sartoran force who had taken a ship from Mardgar, and tried to turn pirate, their first attack being on Remalna, half a day's journey away. There wasn't a second.

But the Adranis also had, everyone claimed bitterly, taken more than their share of the autumn harvest, and they strictly enforced the curfew. Even now, when all the rumors insisted that the mysterious and sinister lords of Norsunder were all gone, anyone caught with a weapon was sent to Chovilun, which the Norsundrians had converted back to a prison. No one knew if they were dead or alive.

"I agree completely," Vidanric said. "Because Frente is reasonable, I do not want to escalate all the way. I'll try to find a middle ground."

Two days later, after the last of a howling blizzard left the world pillowed in white, Commander Nila Frente emerged from the palace Athanarel to find that the stalemate that was not quite a truce had ended with warriors in blue quietly and efficiently taking all the outposts. She considered the underlying messages in this action: No one was dead—the night watch was tied up, and stashed elsewhere—and one of the younger runners had been turned loose to say that the Renselaeus Blues were ready at the main garrisons, prepared to attack, and would she parley.

Vidanric Renselaeus, it seemed, knew exactly what he was doing.

Norsunder had not permitted parleys, or truces. Neither had Bartal. But both were now gone. The only orders from the capital since the fall of Norsunder had been a general order to hold in place, and defend only if attacked. That order had been issued under the crown seal, the last item received by the Norsundrian communication relay, right after the news that Bartal was dead, which argued that someone had control there in Nente. But silence since.

She sent the runner back under truce-flag to agree to the meeting.

Vidanric and Frente met outside the royal city, at a crossroads from which they could see in all directions. Parties from both sides had burrowed into the snow, weapons at hand, as the two rode together, and stopped.

Vidanric bowed politely over his horse's withers, then held up a rolled paper. "I have here, signed by the governing bodies of five kingdoms, plus the Queen of Sartor, a demand for the withdrawal of the Adrani forces from our border."

Frente blew out a clouding breath. "Our king is dead," she began.

"I heard."

"With that and Norsunder's defeat, communications channels have been disrupted," she said. "If you release my people, I will regard that as an exercise in … earnest wishes, and communicate such."

"How long will your new channels take?" Vidanric asked, politely.

"It used to be instant, via dispatch desk. But that magic seems to have vanished with our former allies in Norsunder," she said flatly. "Unless someone restores transfers, it'll be a week to send a courier by boat. Two to three weeks to ride over the passes."

"I can hold my people—and yours—for a week. At that time, at least an explanation would be welcome," he said, still polite, but the sight of those blue-uniformed warriors—that the most assiduous search had never found—and their quiet efficiency was all the threat she needed.

Before dawn the next morning, Commander Frente issued some orders, laid aside her purple uniform, and dressed soberly in commoners' brown over undyed linen. She rode with only one guard to the Denlieff garrison on the border, where she met with Hani Dosanian, a man her own age, who had risen through the ranks at roughly the same time as she. They each had two children in the service as well—she two in the army, he one in the navy and one serving under him as a patrol captain.

They met over lunch, and once the dishes had been taken away and they were alone, she said, "What have you heard? Remalna is so far from anything, what we get is always third-hand."

"We aren't any better as far as official dispatches are concerned," Dosanian replied. "What I can tell you is rumor, through my family: the heir will be crowned, but there'll be two thrones. Her new husband will be king, not merely consort."

"No! Not Navor Mandracar!"

Dosanian laughed shortly. "You *are* behind the times, Nila. The heir divorced Mandracar last year. Besides, he is dead. And good riddance."

She nodded fervently. Everyone knew he'd sell his own mother for promotion, and he was far too fond of floggings for entertainment. Not always prisoners, either. "Three times over the past year I heard he was dead, and each time it turned out to be a rumor. I didn't believe this latest one."

"Rumor has it the new king was behind it. But that's rumor—no facts have emerged that my grandfather believes. Though he's gone pretty deaf, he's still the best at sifting intelligence."

She signified agreement. Ran Dosanian had been Commander in Chief of the army in the old days, but he had retired when Bartal came to the throne. "Who is the new king?"

Dosanian reflected that Nila was the daughter of a quartermaster, unacquainted with the nobility. He was not a noble himself, but his cousin had married a baras, and between his grandfather and this baras, government gossip flowed to the rest of the family, especially now that the old personal notecases seemed to be working again. "He's an Elsarion, cousin to the Enaeraneth king."

"*Enaeraneth?* And no one objected? Are you sure you have the right one? I remember hearing all those rumors of the common folk threatening uprisings, early on, and wanting the Elsarion king to rescue us from Bartal and Norsunder."

"No, it's his cousin, two or three times removed. He's got Adrani relations. Connected through Denwy, somehow, and has lands of his own on our side of the border."

"Denwy!" She whistled. "But … does he know what he's doing?"

"It's said," Dosanian stated after a quick look around, "that he was behind the general order to hold without attacking, only defending, and that the reason we haven't had further orders yet is that he did not want the army coming home until court was stable."

"Stable?" she repeated. His tone had been too flat for an otherwise positive word. "What does that mean in court parlance?"

"My grandfather says that it means until he got control of the court, one by one. In a very civilized way. Then he can bring the army home."

"In other words, he's—very politely—holding court as hostage against our good behavior?"

"The army has twice before swapped kings," he reminded her, his thick red brows bristling. "Though they were always Shagals, one of those was a terrible choice, and the other wasn't much better."

She laughed.

"What do you find funny?" He refilled both their dishes with hot spiced wine.

"I just find it ironic we've suddenly got an Elsarion on the throne, when everyone in upper command was so furious last winter over the rumors about the Enaeraneth king coming to save us from Norsunder. Which I always figured was my fellow commoners giving the army the back of the hand for following Norsunder's orders—as if we had any choice."

"Bad times." Dosanian's brows drew together. "But few of them knew of the purges and assassinations. Never mind that. We did what we had to, we held to our oaths as we could, we survived and the gray-coats didn't. My grandfather thinks the Andri Elsarion rumors were also to remind us that we were once all one kingdom. Perhaps a reminder to Bartal, though he never took heed."

Frente sobered. "Does this new Elsarion have army experience?"

"It's said not, but it's also said he knows which end of a

sword to hold. Which was more than Bartal ever did. More to the point, perhaps, if this is true about securing the court, it argues that he knows what he's doing."

Knows what he's doing—just like Vidanric Renselaeus.

It was a sober regimental commander who rode back to her posting in Remalna that night, a mood not entirely due to the wine fumes. Dosanian had promised to use his notecase to convey her situation up the ladder; "Maybe that'll get them to hasten fresh orders," he'd said on a note of hope. Tiny Remalna was not the only still-occupied territory rumbling with complaint.

Two days before the promised week was up, Vidanric and Meliara woke to the sound of an aide banging on the lintel outside the curtained door, shouting, "They're gone! They're gone!"

The Adranis were indeed gone. Vidanric threw on some clothes, and he and a party of Blues followed the mass of footprints to the shoreline, where they were in time to see their former Adrani prisoners, just released, running down to join the last of the boats loading purple-clad warriors onto three big transports.

The rest of the day, reports flooded in: the Adranis had taken their supplies—including the comestibles they had demanded from the Remalnans—but Captain Nessaren's company discovered in Chovilun, not only those who had been locked up for curfew violation—including two of the Blues' own runners, and a dozen or so ex-Norsundrian vagrants caught looting or stealing food—but also the art and fine furnishings taken from Athanarel and some of the other palaces soon after the invasion. It had been stored neatly, with papers listing each item with a precise description, and where it had been taken from.

"This," Meliara said, when she and Vidanric had ridden there to inspect, "was on Bartal's command, Atan said. He wanted to be able to pick and choose, but mostly what he'd wanted was from Colend. She says that Shontande Lirendi reported flatboats full of Colendi loot left at the border river. Itemized, just like this. A lot missing, of course."

Vidanric turned to his captains. "No letters—nothing from Commander Frente?"

They shook their heads, and Meliara held out a much-folded piece of paper. "Atan said it was the same all over."

Vidanric was thinking past the massive, orderly withdrawal to the unknown king who had commanded it. "It's going to be interesting when he does decide to speak to the world," he said.

> *… and Vidanric said* [Meliara wrote to Atan] *it'll be interesting when the new Adrani king decides to speak to the world, but as far as I'm concerned, we've heard more than enough from the Adranis, and I hope they stay inside their borders and talk to themselves from now on. Savona — you remember him, our former ambassador to the Adranis? — commented that, no doubt they'll have plenty to say, as their treasury must be a wreck, especially as Bartal had expanded their army to three or four times its former size. Wars, said Tamara, are only worth it for the winners. And they didn't win.*
>
> *Enough about them! I know I've written a lot over the past couple of days, and you have plenty of people clamoring for your attention, so this will be my last until we start sending ambassadors back and forth again. I just want to add that, with the Adranis marching out, we decided it was safe for the refugees to leave the Colorwoods. They are all on their way home.*
>
> *That includes the centaurs, Sharly and Sedris. I don't know if you ever met them, but they both asked me to beg the favor of a message to your cousin Julian, who they know from their privateer days, and to say that they are now going north. I hope you and Rel are happy!*

Atan and Rel were happy, even though they were not always certain where they would sleep from one night to the next.

They had decided that more tasks would be seen to the quicker if they each acted separately. Rel's first night as a king in his capital was spent camping out, along with a number of homeless people of high rank and low, in borrowed bedrolls on the stable floor. Atan stayed with elders, wounded, and those with very small children in the housekeeper's rooms, among the crockery and linens—no one wanted to touch the rooms where the enemy had been living, until everything was scoured out, and all traces of them gone. The kitchen wing was at least clean; unlike the terrible days under Bostian and Aldon, Asiarch's brief reign had seen a little order restored as he couldn't abide dirty rooms or dishes.

Pockets of fighting went on intermittently in Sartor, after the initial counterattack. Rel and Atan permitted some of the more enthusiastic warriors to pursue fleeing Norsundrians, especially the remains of Bostian's and Aldon's savage followers. A month of hue and cry seemed to go a long way in recovering a sense of self-respect, after more than a year of enduring a particularly barbarous occupation.

But the time came when the Queen and King together sent out the word that Sartorans should lay down their weapons and take up tools for rebuilding. The Norsundrians were not all gone, it was true, but their threat certainly was. A little vigilance would suffice; armed bands riding about looking for heads to club were definitely last year's fashion.

Atan took the lead, just as she had when she first came to her throne as an inexperienced fifteen-year-old, in carrying out the cleaning and renewing. Though the season was still winter, and the labor was arduous, every day that saw improvement lifted spirits.

Rebuilding the scribe desk was a priority. Scribes and mages and heralds connected to the multi-tiered complexity that had been the scribe desk at first were overwhelmed at the immensity of the task. But, as the Chief Scribe said to Atan one morning, "We all had to study how it evolved. We do not need to invent it. All we need to do is reproduce it."

"Let me, us, know what you need," Atan said—smiling at the stumble. Oh, it was so good to halve the unending tasks. She still never caught up. At least she did not feel at the end of each day that she was farther behind than when she'd begun it.

But always in mind was her worry about Tsauderei. The first note she'd sent when she resurrected her notecase was to him, stating that they'd won. He'd written back only a single line, in a shaky scrawl: *Well done!*

Nothing more. And that shakiness concerned her.

As the days went by and she heard nothing further, she

decided to visit him, to discover that the Destination outside his cottage was either blocked or destroyed. She wrote immediately to Mondros, who wrote back from Narad in Chwahirsland.

> *Atan: I won't lie to you. He suffered a stroke. He can't talk anymore, and no, don't try to go. He doesn't want anyone to see him like that. I'm warded, too, or I'd have gone to fetch him at the outset. I think he intends to die alone in that cottage, the stubborn old goat — but at least he got his wish, he lived to see Norsunder's defeat.*

Atan showed that to Rel that night, when they bedded down among the dishes; Gehlei, Atan's aged steward, and her servants, wouldn't let them near the residence wing yet. "What do you make of that? I can't figure out his tone."

"Mondros is trying to be cheering."

"Well, it's not working."

Rel grinned ruefully. "I see that."

"I don't want Tsauderei, who raised me, to die alone."

"He seems to want to. As is his right. He's lived well over a century. He ought to get what he wants at the end."

But Atan could not believe that anyone would choose to die alone, perhaps in pain, or thirst, or want. After a few more days, and a lot of internal muttering, she wrote to Detlev, half-expecting to get the same response from him, only more cryptic. If at all.

But what she got back was: *I'll go see.*

That was fine, but wasn't he warded?

He was not.

Detlev used the slide. It was a little victory every time he used it. He glanced through the window, to find Tsauderei sagging in his chair. He was clean — magic could accomplish that — but his once-tidy hair and beard were uncombed, and he was mere skin and bones under that fine robe. His eyes were the only lively thing about him as Detlev entered, bringing in fresh air, if bitingly cold.

Tsauderei stirred and grunted, but Detlev waved him off. "I can hear you if you lift your mind-shield."

Tsauderei wasn't shielded, but it was a courtesy to pretend he was: his pain and discomfort, bordering on despair, was shocking.

Tsauderei's white brows twitched and he carefully framed

words: *Stubborn body won't die. Even though I keep telling it, you're done now. You outlasted them.*

"I wanted to thank you on Jilo's behalf," said Detlev. "You and Mondros were of great benefit to him."

: Doing well?

"He's proceeding very cautiously. His vast army is on its way home, and he is making ready for them by removing as many of Wan-Edhe's poisonous wards as he can. Mondros, as I'm sure you're aware, is helping him, especially now that he can enter Narad."

Tsauderei grunted, and his face furrowed with a spasm of pain. Then he looked up at his old enemy with a plea in his black eyes, and framed the words: *No ward against you. Hoped you might show up, and put a knife between these damn ribs. Every day I wake up is...*

Tsauderei stopped there, because he loathed whining. Detlev said, "Tsauderei, if you are truly ready, you do not need violence. The Selenseh Redian is there. That was where we went in my day, when we were ready."

Tsauderei struggled in his chair in his effort to say, *Take me now.* But the thought was clear, and so Detlev touched him on the forehead, shifting them both to the heart of the Selenseh Redian.

Detlev gently lowered the frail old mage onto the smooth ground. He slipped off his cloak, rolled it up, and slid it under Tsauderei's head. The old mage let out a long sigh: *Already I feel better. It reminds me of floating in a pool at the height of summer, far in the north, under the dancing lights.*

"Yes," said Detlev.

Tsauderei closed his eyes, smiling a little. Another thought came, as if from a distance: *When did you change from enemy to friend?*

: I was never your enemy.

A tremor of laughter met this, and a mildly triumphant: *It took me a while. But I finally figured that out...*

And that was all. But Detlev sensed that the wily old mage liked having another person there, and so, because it was quiet, and because he in his exhaustion fugue was poised between worlds, he closed his eyes as well, accepting whatever was to come.

When he rose again through layer after layer of memory-laced dream, he found himself alone. For the first time since he opened his eyes back in the sanctuary under the lake, he was aware of anticipation: he was ready to get back to work.

He transferred to his house, where he wrote to Atan: *He's gone. It was a peaceful end.*

He walked downstairs, to where MV was lying on a couch, looking disgruntled as he watched the snow falling. MV gave Detlev a narrow glance, then said, "The geez?"

"Selenseh Redian. He was grateful to go."

MV nicked his chin down in a minute nod. "Wanted to last it out. He got that. Guess it's for the best."

"Did you have an arrangement with him?"

"Of sorts," MV said. "Gave me the spell to the cottage. Said I could read whatever I chose. Which is good—I will want to get back to magic studies. But I don't want to live there, and he never tried to make me promise to hold to it. Far as I'm concerned, you can add that place to your academy. It used to be for mages. Why not dyranarya?"

"There is time enough to discuss that in future." Detlev moved on, to where he found Adam and David with plans spread out on one of the big tables. They looked up. "Curtas's designs for the dyranarya academy, already?"

"Examining the layout," Adam said. "Leander asked if there was going to be a library. I was sure there was, but wanted to check."

Detlev laughed at that. "If there hadn't been, he could always add his own. David, I know the last of the enchantment bindings have been broken."

David grinned. The mage world was full of speculation about how that had come to pass, most of it wrong. David had enjoying transferring from one place to another by the old magic slide-transfer, and releasing each enchantment that was keyed onto his sword. He still did not know why Imry had used his sword for the enchantments any more than he could guess why Imry had then given it back to David; if Imry had wanted his name coupled with gratitude, he was going to have to emerge from wherever he was and claim it himself.

Then Detlev wiped away David's smile by asking, "Have you been back to Marloven Hess?"

David shook his head. "Senrid has Fox and Ivandred. I backed off."

"Don't. Ivandred might last out the year. If that. Fox will get restless before then, if he's not already gone. Besides, Senrid needs a peer."

David moaned. "He's going to start up his academy again! Those wild-eyed Marlovens under eighteen are already out in that west yard heaving the stones into piles to rebuild it. He's going to make me teach at it if I turn up, I know he will."

"See the tears?" Detlev asked, without a vestige of sympathy.

David moaned again, but he'd been feeling the inner prompt ever since he'd finished the last of the disenchantments. His shoulder was scarcely an ache now; he'd begun warmups again, but he was still restless.

He calculated the time difference, and transferred when the sun rose over Marloven Hess the next morning. He found what looked like the entire city of Choreid Dhelerei busy, the sound of hammers and chisels tapping and clattering everywhere.

Senrid was in his study, which willing hands had managed to restore almost exactly the way it was. The noise of rebuilding drifted through the open windows overlooking the academy, carried on frigid air.

Senrid sat at the desk, surrounded by piles of paper. He looked up, and addressed David as if they had seen one another at breakfast, rather than not for nearly three weeks. "Fox said to tell you, you know where to find him."

"He left already?"

"Something or other about currents. He took it into his head to see the Land of the Venn, and I guess at this time of year the storms that place is famous for are mostly down here."

"Have you read his record yet? Siamis said he brought it out of Darchelde for you."

Senrid tapped one of the piles, which David saw now was a different color than the others, and very carefully stacked. "I suspect why he really left was, he couldn't stomach the thought of someone actually looking at it right in front of him. I've promised myself to save it until certain things were accomplished, one of which was to get Ivandred settled at Tannentaun."

"That was my next question," David said.

"He insists he's fine, but you've only to look at him to know that he isn't," Senrid said, leaning back in the chair, fingers of one hand drumming on the desk. "But he seems to like that house. Leander made it over to him."

"What will he do there?" David asked.

"He said he wants to tend Lasva's garden," Senrid said. "His ambitions extend no farther than that."

"He saw his name restored?"

"Oh, that he did. He didn't say anything, and I made no commands, but I let Forth—" Senrid winced, and corrected himself, "Stad know that Ivandred was going to Crestel for recovery. The castle here is overflowing with wounded, and I don't think his memories of this castle were doing him any good."

How about yours, David wondered.

"… and when we got him downstairs into the covered cart, the entire city had turned out. Fox banners everywhere. The city guard and those from the army who could hobble out of their beds, all lined up and gave him the salute for a king, to the royal drumroll. Nine drums. He'd given me his banner, and I made sure it's up there in the throne room. Even though the rest of that room is still empty."

"Good. I'd say he earned that."

"Fox was cackling like a madman. That was the day before he took off for the coast. I suspect the name Ivandred will come back into use by this time next year."

David smiled. "Ivandred. Van, Vana. You'll have to shift the nickname for Indevan back to Inda."

Senrid looked up through the window. "It's so very strange, that Fox knew Inda as a boy. We had a regular gathering over in that wing, after the night watch drum. I wish you could have been there. It's your ancestry, too. Fox came into the long room where the Lancers were, and told stories. Not just the battles. In truth, I strongly suspect those stories about how happy Inda was after he retired from academy teaching, and spent his days riding his land, gave Ivandred the idea of retiring to that house in Tannentaun."

"Did Fox intend to do that?"

"Who knows. He learned mind-shields very fast, not that I'd trespass. He's an irascible old scrapper. But those stories … one reason I haven't read that pile of papers yet is because I feel I know most of it, listening to those nighttime stories. I thought half of those invalids would wheeze themselves to death at Fox's account of Inda's first encounter with sex."

"Sex? I can't reconcile Inda with any kind of sex."

"Apparently neither could he. Sounds a bit like Jilo, I mean the fact that he apparently mooned around after some shopkeeper, while he was *living in* a pleasure house. For free."

David snorted. "That does sound like Jilo. Who is apparently still alive."

Senrid smiled pensively. "He has a grand plan to gradually get the swords out of Chwahir hands. And here I am, with every fiery-eyed youth in my kingdom clamoring for the academy to start again. The most fiery of them is Hatch Senelac, Ret Forthan's oldest boy. He's got his father's speed and skill, and the Senelac looks. He'll be academy leader within the first week. And their passion is to become as good as the First Lancers."

Senrid made a flat-handed gesture, pushing the subject away. "I ought to have asked what you've been doing."

David hesitated, then approached his true question obliquely. "Detlev has kept us on the hop. We'll commence building the dyranarya academy as soon as the ground up there thaws. Have you had a chance to keep up with the rest of the circle?"

"Siamis has been by now and again, bringing famed healers from various places, for Ivandred and the rest. I wish I could say that they have had great success, but there is no cure. We've lost three so far, all who took wounds that just would not heal. One of the three was Haldren Marlovair, who'd been Ivandred's right hand."

"I'm very sorry to hear that. Did Captain Marlovair get to meet his ancestor, at least?"

"Oh, yes. I gave Van leave to remain here. It seemed to help Haldren a lot to have Van around, chattering his ear off. He seemed quite content, but one morning he just … didn't wake up. Right after we gave Haldren the full memorial—and the entire city has turned out for them all, so far—that was when Ivandred decided to go to Crestel. Anyway. Circle. Siamis said that Zairna Raadi walked through a world-gate a week or so ago, dressed like a prince in a tapestry. I suspect he's going to confront the evil queen-mother at last. Crow returned to Ama Hazanth. You'd know better than I about the rest, though I'm not sure about Mildred."

"Oh, she's been at Detlev's house, then off to Geth to see Dak, then back again, where she and MV agreed that as soon as they both can get through the warmup without fainting, they're going to sail MV's boat from where I left it to Jaro, and spend the summer flirting with all the sailor girls. I think that promise is the only thing keeping MV sane. He's the worst patient I've ever seen, ever. Roy went to Bereth Ferian to help Arthur start cleaning up that mess. And Laban, of course, is trying to wrest Wnelder Vee from the wreckage there."

David hesitated before bringing up Andri, which would inevitably lead to Liere. He took in Senrid's calm face, and the desk full of urgent demands, and resolved to let things lie. "So," he said. "I'm here. What can I do? Put me to work."

The subject that would not be brought up between them was, just then, sitting in a cozy den in Brydon, Enaeran's huge barracks of a palace, with her husband.

Liere and Andri had spent days alternately catching up with one another's news and dealing with innumerable small crises. Most of these were solved by assigning people to wait, or camp out, or take up temporary quarters, in Brydon. Like Marloven Hess's center of government, it had been originally built to house (or guard) not just numerous royal kin but all their retainers, which amounted sometimes to private armies. It had been held by a former family member who had declared himself king, and even after Adon Marsael was assassinated by a mob of angry dockside workers, it had sustained relatively little damage.

Just as well. Enaeran had suffered years of civil war, and was a dismal mess. It seemed as if half the kingdom was housed with them, until burned homes could be rebuilt as soon as the weather eased.

This was the first time that Liere and Andri had been able to retreat and be alone. He was afflicted with his yearly winter cold; the bad eating and sleeping habits he'd adopted while living on the streets as a disinherited prince, plus scarring from rough treatment, had weakened his constitution, though typically he shrugged that off.

"If we had something to toast with, I'd offer one to the New Year. If a month late," he said, stretched out his legs toward the fire, and sneezed. "I still wake up wondering where we ought to move the camp."

"We don't need a glass to salute the New Year," Liere replied. Was she happy? Of course she was very happy, who wouldn't be? Here she was, warm and cozy, with the man she had chosen. It's true that everything was so new—she still felt like she was a pretend queen—and her daughter, visited by magic earlier, had flatly refused to live with her, claiming that Enaeran was very nice, but not a home. "There's no place for me here," Lyren-Sartora had said, and plowed on before Liere could disclaim. "But there is in Everon. Tahra wants me to be a companion to Carl, and when I need to get away, Laban said I could help in Wnelder Vee. Silvanas is going to teach me to train horses!"

Liere had forced herself to smile, and nod, and agree. After all, Lyren-Sartora sounded happy and at last she had found useful work, of a sort. That was all one could ask, wasn't it?

There was one old friend she hadn't seen, and it was surprisingly difficult to bring up his name. As a snowstorm drummed at the windows, she said, "Are you still bound to your circle?"

"At first," Andri said, yawning. "I had to shut them out, they were so loud. I never really understood your farsense until then. But it's been fading. Adam said it would if I didn't use it."

"I trust that everyone was all right before you lost contact?"

"Some I heard from. Still do. MV, who hates being tied to a bed, and sometimes pops up in my dreams. I never really knew Sveneric or Dirk. They have their own circle, with the Selenna boy."

Liere said lightly, "And Senrid?"

"Not a word."

"Oh."

She thought that pretty neutral, but Andri gave her a mildly questioning look, then ventured a reminder, "Went home to face that empty room."

Liere winced. She had only met Senrid's little daughter once. But she ought to remember the weight of grief he had to be feeling, all the more because Senrid would typically keep it to himself. "Everything's changed," she said, hardly aware she had spoken, and then she looked up, startled, apprehensive of being misunderstood.

But Andri did not look as though anything were amiss. He

chuckled, turning toward the door. A heartbeat later it banged open and Gared shouldered his way in, bearing a loaded tray, Marten behind him, the first of a string of friends. "Cook is back! And even better, some of her people discovered Wilsar's stash. It's loaded with stores — we could feel half the city."

"That's good, because half the city is living with us," Andri said, rubbing his hands. "Ah, hot pear cider. Exactly what I'd been wishing for." He passed a glass to Liere, smiling at her over the brim. "Here's our toast!"

"Toast!" Gared shouted. "To Adon Marsael gone for good!"

"Toast!"

"Toast!"

"Seems so strange," Marten murmured, "not to be looking over our shoulders constantly."

"Changes for everyone," Andri agreed, and he leaned over to take Liere's hand. "Which means a new life."

She smiled, her own sweet smile, and raised her glass to him, and to her fellow Enaeraneth. "Here's to new life," she vowed.

About the Author

Sherwood Smith writes fantasy, science fiction, and historical fiction. Her full bibliography can be found on her website at https://www.sherwoodsmith.net.

About Book View Cafe

Book View Café is an author-owned cooperative of professional writers, publishing in a variety of genres including fantasy, science fiction, romance, mystery, and more.

Its authors include New York Times and USA Today best-sellers as well as winners and nominees of many prestigious awards such as the Agatha Award, Hugo Award, Lambda Literary Award, Locus Award, Nebula Award, RITA Award, Philip K. Dick Award, World Fantasy Award, and many others.

Since its debut in 2008, Book View Café has gained a reputation for producing high quality books in both print and electronic form. BVC's e-books are DRM-free and distributed around the world.

Book View Café's monthly newsletter includes new releases, specials, author news, and event announcements. To sign up, visit https://www.bookviewcafe.com/bookstore/newsletter/

9 781636 321219